NOBEL PRIZE LIBRARY

HEMINGWAY

HAMSUN

HESSE

Nobel Prize Library

PUBLISHED UNDER THE SPONSORSHIP OF THE
NOBEL FOUNDATION & THE SWEDISH ACADEMY

Ernest Hemingway

Knut Hamsun

Hermann Hesse

ALEXIS GREGORY, *New York*, AND
CRM PUBLISHING, *Del Mar, California*

CONTENTS

Ernest Hemingway

1954

"For his powerful mastery of

the art of storytelling,

most recently displayed in

The Old Man and the Sea,

and for his influence on

contemporary style"

Illustrated by ROBERT SHORE
(for *The Old Man and the Sea* & *A Farewell to Arms*)
and *JOHN GROTH* (for *The Sun Also Rises*)

PRESENTATION ADDRESS

By ANDERS ÖSTERLING

PERMANENT SECRETARY
OF THE SWEDISH ACADEMY

In our modern age, American authors have set their stamp more and more strongly on the general physiognomy of literature. During the last few decades, our generation in particular has seen a reorientation of literary interest which implies not only a temporary change in the market but, indeed, a shifting of the mental horizon, with far-reaching consequences. All these swiftly rising new authors from the United States, whose names we now recognize as stimulating signals, had one thing in common: they took full advantage of the Americanism to which they were born. And the European public greeted them with enthusiasm; it was the general wish that Americans should write as Americans, thereby making their own contribution to the contest in the international arena.

One of these pioneers is the author who is now the focus of attention. It is hardly an exaggeration to say that Ernest Hemingway, more than any of his American colleagues, makes us feel we are confronted by a still young nation which seeks and finds its exact form of expression. A dramatic tempo and sharp curves have also characterized Hemingway's own existence, in many ways so unlike that of the average literary man. With him, this vital energy goes its own way, independent of the pessimism and the disillusionment so typical of the age. Hemingway evolved his style in the hard school of journalistic reporting. In the editorial office of the Kansas City newspaper where he served his apprenticeship, there was a kind of pressman's catechism, the first dictum of which was: "Use short sentences. Use short paragraphs." Hemingway's purely technical training clearly led to an artistic self-discipline of uncommon strength. Rhetoric, he has said, is merely the blue sparks from the dynamo. His master in older American literature was Mark Twain in *Huckleberry Finn,* with its rhythmical stream of direct and unconventional narrative prose.

The young journalist from Illinois was flung headlong into World War I, when he volunteered to serve as an ambulance driver in Italy, where he received his baptism of fire at the Piave front and was severely wounded by shell splinters. The nineteen-year-old's first violent experience of war is an essential factor in Hemingway's biography. Not that he was daunted by it; on the contrary, he found that it was a priceless asset for a writer to see war at first hand—like Tolstoy at Sevastopol—and to be able to depict it truthfully. Several years were to elapse, however, before he could bring himself to give an artistically complete account of his painfully confused impressions from the Piave front in 1918: the result was the novel *A Farewell to Arms* in 1929, with which he really made his name, even if two very talented books with a European post-war setting, *In Our Time* (1942) and *The Sun Also Rises* (1926), had already given proof of his individuality as a storyteller. In the following years, his instinctive predilection for harrowing scenes of action and grim spectacle drew him to Africa with its big-game hunting and to Spain with its bullfighting. When the latter country was transformed into a theater of war, he found inspiration there for his second significant novel, *For Whom the Bell Tolls* (1940), in which an American champion of liberty fights for "man's dignity"—a book in which the writer's personal feelings seem more deeply involved than anywhere else.

When mentioning these principal elements in his production, one should not forget that his narrative skill often attains its highest point when cast in a smaller mold, in the laconic, drastically pruned short story, which, with a unique combination of simplicity and precision, nails its theme into our consciousness so that every blow tells. Such a masterpiece, more than any other, is *The Old Man and the Sea* (1952), the unforgettable story of an old Cuban fisherman's duel with a huge swordfish in the Atlantic. Within the frame of a sporting tale, a moving perspective of man's destiny is opened up; the story is a tribute to the fighting spirit, which does not give in even if the material gain is nil, a tribute to the moral victory in the midst of defeat. The drama is enacted before our eyes, hour by hour, allowing the robust details to accumulate and take on momentous significance. "But man is not made for defeat," the book says. "A man can be destroyed but not defeated."

It may be true that Hemingway's earlier writings display brutal, cynical, and callous sides which may be considered at variance with the Nobel Prize's requirement for a work of an ideal tendency. But on the other hand, he also possesses a heroic pathos which forms the basic element in his awareness of life, a manly love of danger and adventure with a natural admiration for every individual who fights the good fight in a world of reality overshadowed by violence and death. In any event, this is the positive side of his cult of manliness, which otherwise is apt to become demonstrative, thereby defeating its own ends. It should be remembered, however, that courage is Hemingway's central theme—the bearing of one who is put to the test and who steels himself to meet the cold cruelty of existence, without, by so doing, repudiating the great and generous moments.

On the other hand, Hemingway is not one of those authors who write to illustrate theses and principles of one kind or another. A descriptive writer must be objective and not try to play God the Father—this he learned while still in the editorial office in Kansas City. That is why he can conceive of war as a tragic fate having a decisive effect on the whole of his generation; but he views it with a calm realism, void of illusion, which disdains all emotional comment, a disciplined objectivity, stronger because it is hard-won.

Hemingway's significance as one of this epoch's great molders of style is apparent in both American and European narrative art over the past twenty-five years, chiefly in the vivid dialogue and the verbal thrust and parry, in which he has set a standard as easy to imitate as it is difficult to attain. With masterly skill he reproduces all the nuances of the spoken word, as well as those pauses in which thought stands still and the nervous mechanism is thrown out of gear. It may sometimes sound like small talk, but it is not trivial when one gets to know his method. He prefers to leave the work of psychological reflection to his readers, and this freedom is of great benefit to him in spontaneous observation.

When one surveys Hemingway's production, definite scenes flare up in the memory—Henry's flight in the rain and mud after the panic at Caporetto, the desperate blowing up of the bridge in the Spanish mountains when Jordan sacrifices his life, or the old fisherman's solitary fight with the sharks in the nocturnal glow of lights from Havana.

Moreover, one may trace a distinctive linking thread—let us say a symbolic warp reaching back a hundred years in the loom of time—between Hemingway's latest work, *The Old Man and the Sea,* and one of the classic creations of American literature, Herman Melville's novel *Moby Dick,* the white whale which is pursued in blind rage by his enemy, the monomaniacal sea captain. Neither Melville nor Hemingway wanted to create an allegory; the salt ocean depths with all their monsters are sufficiently rewarding as a poetic element. But with different means, those of romanticism and of realism, they both attain the same theme—a man's capacity of endurance and, if need be, of at least daring the impossible. "A man can be destroyed but not defeated."

This year's Nobel Prize for Literature has therefore been awarded to one of the great authors of our time, one of those who, honestly and undauntedly, reproduces genuine features in the hard countenance of the age. Hemingway, now fifty-six years old, is the fifth American author so far to be honored in this way. As the Prizewinner himself is unfortunately unable to be present for reasons of health, the Prize will now be handed to the United States Ambassador.

ACCEPTANCE SPEECH

By ERNEST HEMINGWAY

HAVING NO FACILITY for speech-making and no command of oratory or any domination of rhetoric, I wish to thank the administrators of the generosity of Alfred Nobel for this Prize.

No writer who knows the great writers who did not receive the prize can accept it other than with humility. There is no need to list these writers. Everyone here may make his own list according to his knowledge and his conscience.

It would be impossible for me to ask the Ambassador of my country to read a speech in which a writer said all of the things which are in his heart. Things may not be immediately discernible in what a man writes, and in this sometimes he is fortunate; but eventually they are quite clear and by these and the degree of alchemy that he possesses he will endure or be forgotten.

Writing, at its best, is a lonely life. Organizations for writers palliate the writer's loneliness but I doubt if they improve his writing. He grows in public stature as he sheds his loneliness and often his work deteriorates. For he does his work alone and if he is a good enough writer he must face eternity, or the lack of it, each day.

For a true writer each book should be a new beginning where he tries again for something that is beyond attainment. He should always try for something that has never been done or that others have tried and failed. Then sometimes, with great luck, he will succeed.

How simple the writing of literature would be if it were only necessary to write in another way what has been well written. It is because we have had such great writers in the past that a writer is driven far out past where he can go, out to where no one can help him.

I have spoken too long for a writer. A writer should write what he has to say and not speak it. Again I thank you.

A CLEAN, WELL-LIGHTED PLACE

By ERNEST HEMINGWAY

It was late and every one had left the café except an old man who sat in the shadow the leaves of the tree made against the electric light. In the daytime the street was dusty, but at night the dew settled the dust and the old man liked to sit late because he was deaf and now at night it was quiet and he felt the difference. The two waiters inside the café knew that the old man was a little drunk, and while he was a good client they knew that if he became too drunk he would leave without paying, so they kept watch on him.

"Last week he tried to commit suicide," one waiter said.

"Why?"

"He was in despair."

"What about?"

"Nothing."

"How do you know it was nothing?"

"He has plenty of money."

They sat together at a table that was close against the wall near the door of the café and looked at the terrace where the tables were all empty except where the old man sat in the shadow of the leaves of the tree that moved slightly in the wind. A girl and a soldier went by in the street. The street light shone on the brass number on his collar. The girl wore no head covering and hurried beside him.

"The guard will pick him up," one waiter said.

"What does it matter if he gets what he's after?"

"He had better get off the street now. The guard will get him. They went by five minutes ago."

The old man sitting in the shadow rapped on his saucer with his glass. The younger waiter went over to him.

"What do you want?"

The old man looked at him. "Another brandy," he said.

"You'll be drunk," the waiter said. The old man looked at him. The waiter went away.

"He'll stay all night," he said to his colleague. "I'm sleepy now. I never get into bed before three o'clock. He should have killed himself last week."

The waiter took the brandy bottle and another saucer from the counter inside the café and marched out to the old man's table. He put down the saucer and poured the glass full of brandy.

"You should have killed yourself last week," he said to the deaf man. The old man motioned with his finger. "A little more," he said. The waiter poured on into the glass so that the brandy slopped over and ran down the stem into the top saucer of the pile. "Thank you," the old man said. The waiter took the bottle back inside the café. He sat down at the table with his colleague again.

"He's drunk now," he said.

"He's drunk every night."

"What did he want to kill himself for?"

"How should I know."

"How did he do it?"

"He hung himself with a rope."

"Who cut him down?"

"His niece."

"Why did they do it?"

"Fear for his soul."

"How much money has he got?"

"He's got plenty."

"He must be eighty years old."

"Anyway I should say he was eighty."

"I wish he would go home. I never get to bed before three o'clock. What kind of hour is that to go to bed?"

"He stays up because he likes it."

"He's lonely. I'm not lonely. I have a wife waiting in bed for me."

"He had a wife once too."

"A wife would be no good to him now."

"You can't tell. He might be better with a wife."

"His niece looks after him. You said she cut him down."

"I know."

"I wouldn't want to be that old. An old man is a nasty thing."

"Not always. This old man is clean. He drinks without spilling. Even now, drunk. Look at him."

"I don't want to look at him. I wish he would go home. He has no regard for those who must work."

The old man looked from his glass across the square, then over at the waiters.

"Another brandy," he said, pointing to his glass. The waiter who was in a hurry came over.

"Finished," he said, speaking with that omission of syntax stupid people employ when talking to drunken people or foreigners. "No more tonight. Close now."

"Another," said the old man.

"No. Finished." The waiter wiped the edge of the table with a towel and shook his head.

The old man stood up, slowly counted the saucers, took a leather coin purse from his pocket and paid for the drinks, leaving half a peseta tip.

The waiter watched him go down the street, a very old man walking unsteadily but with dignity.

"Why didn't you let him stay and drink?" the unhurried waiter asked. They were putting up the shutters. "It is not half-past two."

"I want to go home to bed."

"What is an hour?"

"More to me than to him."

"An hour is the same."

"You talk like an old man yourself. He can buy a bottle and drink at home."

"It's not the same."

"No, it is not," agreed the waiter with a wife. He did not wish to be unjust. He was only in a hurry.

"And you? You have no fear of going home before your usual hour?"

"Are you trying to insult me?"

"No, hombre, only to make a joke."

"No," the waiter who was in a hurry said, rising from pulling down the metal shutters. "I have confidence. I am all confidence."

"You have youth, confidence, and a job," the older waiter said. "You have everything."

"And what do you lack?"

"Everything but work."

"You have everything I have."

"No. I have never had confidence and I am not young."

"Come on. Stop talking nonsense and lock up."

"I am of those who like to stay late at the café," the older waiter said. "With all those who do not want to go to bed. With all those who need a light for the night."

"I want to go home and into bed."

"We are of two different kinds," the older waiter said. He was now dressed to go home. "It is not only a question of youth and confidence although those things are very beautiful. Each night I am reluctant to close up because there may be some one who needs the café."

"Hombre, there are bodegas open all night long."

"You do not understand. This is a clean and pleasant café. It is well lighted. The light is very good and also, now, there are shadows of the leaves."

"Good night," said the younger waiter.

"Good night," the other said. Turning off the electric light he continued the conversation with himself. It is the light of course but it is necessary that the place be clean and pleasant. You do not want music. Certainly you do not want music. Nor can you stand before a bar with dignity although that is all that is provided for these hours. What did he fear? It was not fear or dread. It was a nothing that he knew too well. It was all a nothing and a man was nothing too. It was only that and light was all it needed and a certain cleanness and order. Some lived in it and never felt it but he knew it all was nada y pues nada y nada y pues nada. Our nada who art in nada, nada be thy name thy kingdom nada thy will be nada in nada as it is in nada. Give us this nada our daily nada and nada us our nada as we nada our nadas and nada us not into nada but deliver us from nada; pues nada. Hail nothing full of nothing, nothing is with thee. He smiled and stood before a bar with a shining steam pressure coffee machine.

"What's yours?" asked the barman.

"Nada."

"Otro loco más," said the barman and turned away.

"A little cup," said the waiter.

The barman poured it for him.

"The light is very bright and pleasant but the bar is unpolished," the waiter said.

The barman looked at him but did not answer. It was too late at night for conversation.

"You want another copita?" the barman asked.

"No, thank you," said the waiter and went out. He disliked bars and bodegas. A clean, well-lighted café was a very different thing. Now, without thinking further, he would go home to his room. He would lie in the bed and finally, with daylight, he would go to sleep. After all, he said to himself, it is probably only insomnia. Many must have it.

THE OLD MAN AND THE SEA

By ERNEST HEMINGWAY

[Excerpt]

The tuna, the fishermen called all the fish of that species tuna and only distinguished among them by their proper names when they came to sell them or to trade them for baits, were down again. The sun was hot now and the old man felt it on the back of his neck and felt the sweat trickle down his back as he rowed.

I could just drift, he thought, and sleep and put a bight of line around my toe to wake me. But today is eighty-five days and I should fish the day well.

Just then, watching his lines, he saw one of the projecting green sticks dip sharply.

"Yes," he said. "Yes," and shipped his oars without bumping the boat. He reached out for the line and held it softly between the thumb and forefinger of his right hand. He felt no strain nor weight and he held the line lightly. Then it came again. This time it was a tentative pull, not solid nor heavy, and he knew exactly what it was. One hundred fathoms down a marlin was eating the sardines that covered the point and the shank of the hook where the hand-forged hook projected from the head of the small tuna.

The old man held the line delicately, and softly, with his left hand, unleashed it from the stick. Now he could let it run through his fingers without the fish feeling any tension.

This far out, he must be huge in this month, he thought. Eat them, fish. Eat them. Please eat them. How fresh they are and you down there six hundred feet in that cold water in the dark. Make another turn in the dark and come back and eat them.

He felt the light delicate pulling and then a harder pull when a sardine's head must have been more difficult to break from the hook. Then there was nothing.

"Come on," the old man said aloud. "Make another turn. Just smell them. Aren't they lovely? Eat them good now and then there is the tuna. Hard and cold and lovely. Don't be shy, fish. Eat them."

He waited with the line between his thumb and his finger, watching it and the other lines at the same time for the fish might have swum up or down. Then came the same delicate pulling touch again.

"He'll take it," the old man said aloud. "God help him to take it."

He did not take it though. He was gone and the old man felt nothing.

"He can't have gone," he said. "Christ knows he can't have gone. He's making a turn. Maybe he has been hooked before and he remembers something of it."

Then he felt the gentle touch on the line and he was happy.

"It was only his turn," he said. "He'll take it."

He was happy feeling the gentle pulling and then he felt something hard and unbelievably heavy. It was the weight of the fish and he let the line slip down, down, down, unrolling off the first of the two reserve coils. As it went down, slipping lightly through the old man's fingers, he still could feel the great weight, though the pressure of his thumb and finger were almost imperceptible.

"What a fish," he said. "He has it sideways in his mouth now and he is moving off with it."

Then he will turn and swallow it, he thought. He did not say that because he knew that if you said a good thing it might not happen. He knew what a huge fish this was and he thought of him moving away in the darkness with the tuna held crosswise in his mouth. At that moment he felt him stop moving but the weight was still there. Then the weight increased and he gave more line. He tightened the pressure of his thumb and finger for a moment and the weight increased and was going straight down.

"He's taken it," he said. "Now I'll let him eat it well."

He let the line slip through his fingers while he reached down with his left hand and made fast the free end of the two reserve coils to the loop of the two reserve coils of the next line. Now he was ready. He had three forty-fathom coils of line in reserve now, as well as the coil he was using.

"Eat it a little more," he said. "Eat it well."

Eat it so that the point of the hook goes into your heart and kills you, he thought. Come up easy and let me put the harpoon into you. All right. Are you ready? Have you been long enough at table?

"Now!" he said aloud and struck hard with both hands, gained a yard of line and then struck again and again, swinging with each arm alternately on the cord

with all the strength of his arms and the pivoted weight of his body.

Nothing happened. The fish just moved away slowly and the old man could not raise him an inch. His line was strong and made for heavy fish and he held it against his back until it was so taut that beads of water were jumping from it. Then it began to make a slow hissing sound in the water and he still held it, bracing himself against the thwart and leaning back against the pull. The boat began to move slowly off toward the north-west.

The fish moved steadily and they travelled slowly on the calm water. The other baits were still in the water but there was nothing to be done.

"I wish I had the boy," the old man said aloud. "I'm being towed by a fish and I'm the towing bitt. I could make the line fast. But then he could break it. I must hold him all I can and give him line when he must have it. Thank God he is travelling and not going down."

What I will do if he decides to go down, I don't know. What I'll do if he sounds and dies I don't know. But I'll do something. There are plenty of things I can do.

He held the line against his back and watched its slant in the water and the skiff moving steadily to the north-west.

This will kill him, the old man thought. He can't do this forever. But four hours later the fish was still swimming steadily out to sea, towing the skiff, and the old man was still braced solidly with the line across his back.

"It was noon when I hooked him," he said. "And I have never seen him."

He had pushed his straw hat hard down on his head before he hooked the fish and it was cutting his forehead. He was thirsty too and he got down on his knees and, being careful not to jerk on the line, moved as far into the bow as he could get and reached the water bottle with one hand. He opened it and drank a little. Then he rested against the bow. He rested sitting on the un-stepped mast and sail and tried not to think but only to endure.

Then he looked behind him and saw that no land was visible. That makes no difference, he thought. I can always come in on the glow from Havana. There are two more hours before the sun sets and maybe he will come up before that. If he doesn't maybe he will come up with the moon. If he does not do that maybe he will come up with the sunrise. I have no cramps and I feel strong. It is he that has the hook in his mouth. But what a fish to pull like that. He must have his mouth shut tight on the wire. I wish I could see him. I wish I could see him only once to know what I have against me.

The fish never changed his course nor his direction all that night as far as the man could tell from watching the stars. It was cold after the sun went down and the old man's sweat dried cold on his back and his arms and his old legs. During the day he had taken the sack that covered the bait box and spread it in the sun to dry. After the sun went down he tied it around his neck so that it hung down over his back and he cautiously worked it down under the line that was across his shoulders now. The sack cushioned the line and he had found a way of leaning forward against the bow so that he was almost comfortable. The position actually was only somewhat less intolerable; but he thought of it as almost comfortable.

I can do nothing with him and he can do nothing with me, he thought. Not as long as he keeps this up.

Once he stood up and urinated over the side of the skiff and looked at the stars and checked his course. The line showed like a phosphorescent streak in the water straight out from his shoulders. They were moving more slowly now and the glow of Havana was not so strong, so that he knew the current must be carrying them to the eastward. If I lose the glare of Havana we must be going more to the eastward, he thought. For if the fish's course held true I must see it for many more hours. I wonder how the baseball came out in the grand leagues today, he thought. It would be wonderful to do this with a radio. Then he thought, think of it always. Think of what you are doing. You must do nothing stupid.

Then he said aloud, "I wish I had the boy. To help me and to see this."

No one should be alone in their old age, he thought. But it is unavoidable. I must remember to eat the tuna before he spoils in order to keep strong. Remember, no matter how little you want to, that you must eat him in the morning. Remember, he said to himself.

During the night two porpoises came around the boat and he could hear them rolling and blowing. He could tell the difference between the blowing noise the male made and the sighing blow of the female.

"They are good," he said. "They play and make jokes and love one another. They are our brothers like the flying fish."

Then he began to pity the great fish that he had hooked. He is wonderful and strange and who knows how old he is, he thought. Never have I had such a strong fish nor one who acted so strangely. Perhaps he is too wise to jump. He could ruin me by jumping or by a wild rush. But perhaps he has been hooked many times before and he knows that this is how he should make his fight. He cannot know that it is only one man against him, nor that it is an old man. But what a great fish he is and what will he bring in the market if the flesh is good. He took the bait like a male and he pulls like a male and his fight has no panic in it. I wonder if he has any plans or if he is just as desperate as I am?

He remembered the time he had hooked one of a pair of marlin. The male fish always let the female fish feed first and the hooked fish, the female, made a wild, panic-stricken, despairing fight that soon exhausted her, and all the time the male had stayed with her, crossing the line and circling with her on the surface. He had stayed so close that the old man was afraid he would cut the line with his tail which was sharp as a scythe and almost of that size and shape. When the old man had gaffed her and clubbed her, holding the rapier bill with its sandpaper edge and clubbing her across the top of her head until her colour turned to a colour almost like the backing of mirrors, and then, with the boy's aid, hoisted her aboard, the male fish had stayed by the side of the boat. Then, while the old man was clearing the lines and preparing the harpoon, the male fish jumped high into the air beside the boat to see where the female was and then went down deep, his lavender wings, that were his pectoral fins, spread wide and all his wide lavender stripes showing. He was beautiful, the old man remembered, and he had stayed.

That was the saddest thing I ever saw with them, the old man thought. The boy was sad too and we begged her pardon and butchered her promptly.

"I wish the boy was here," he said aloud and settled himself against the rounded planks of the bow and felt the strength of the great fish through the line he held across his shoulders moving steadily toward whatever he had chosen.

When once, through my treachery, it had been necessary to him to make a choice, the old man thought.

His choice had been to stay in the deep dark water far out beyond all snares and traps and treacheries. My choice was to go there to find him beyond all people. Beyond all people in the world. Now we are joined together and have been since noon. And no one to help either one of us.

Perhaps I should not have been a fisherman, he thought. But that was the thing that I was born for. I must surely remember to eat the tuna after it gets light.

Some time before daylight something took one of the baits that were behind him. He heard the stick break and the line begin to rush out over the gunwale of the skiff. In the darkness he loosened his sheath knife and taking all the strain of the fish on his left shoulder he leaned back and cut the line against the wood of the gunwale. Then he cut the other line closest to him and in the dark made the loose ends of the reserve coils fast. He worked skillfully with the one hand and put his foot on the coils to hold them as he drew his knots tight. Now he had six reserve coils of line. There were two from each bait he had severed and the two from the bait the fish had taken and they were all connected.

After it is light, he thought, I will work back to the forty-fathom bait and cut it away too and link up the reserve coils. I will have lost two hundred fathoms of good Catalan *cardel* and the hooks and leaders. That can be replaced. But who replaces this fish if I hook some fish and it cuts him off? I don't know what that fish was that took the bait just now. It could have been a marlin or a broadbill or a shark. I never felt him. I had to get rid of him too fast.

Aloud he said, "I wish I had the boy."

But you haven't got the boy, he thought. You have only yourself and you had better work back to the last line now, in the dark or not in the dark, and cut it away and hook up the two reserve coils.

So he did it. It was difficult in the dark and once the fish made a surge that pulled him down on his face and made a cut below his eye. The blood ran down his cheek a little way. But it coagulated and dried before it reached his chin and he worked his way back to the bow and rested against the wood. He adjusted the sack and carefully worked the line so that it came across a new part of his shoulders and, holding it anchored with his shoulders, he carefully felt the pull of the fish and then felt with his hand the progress of the skiff through the water.

I wonder what he made that lurch for, he thought. The wire must have slipped on the great hill of his back. Certainly his back cannot feel as badly as mine does. But he cannot pull this skiff forever, no matter how great he is. Now everything is cleared away that might make trouble and I have a big reserve of line; all that a man can ask.

"Fish," he said softly, aloud, "I'll stay with you until I am dead."

He'll stay with me too, I suppose, the old man thought and he waited for it to be light. It was cold now in the time before daylight and he pushed against the wood to be warm. I can do it as long as he can, he thought. And in the first light the line extended out and down into the water. The boat moved steadily and when the first edge of the sun rose it was on the old man's right shoulder.

"He's headed north," the old man said. The current will have set us far to the eastward, he thought. I wish he would turn with the current. That would show that he was tiring.

When the sun had risen further the old man realized that the fish was not tiring. There was only one favorable sign. The slant of the line showed he was swimming at a lesser depth. That did not necessarily mean that he would jump. But he might.

"God let him jump," the old man said. "I have enough line to handle him."

Maybe if I can increase the tension just a little it will hurt him and he will jump, he thought. Now that it is daylight let him jump so that he'll fill the sacks along his backbone with air and then he cannot go deep to die.

He tried to increase the tension, but the line had been taut up to the very edge of the breaking point since he had hooked the fish and he felt the harshness as he leaned back to pull and knew he could put no more strain on it. I must not jerk it ever, he thought. Each jerk widens the cut the hook makes and then when he does jump he might throw it. Anyway I feel better with the sun and for once I do not have to look into it.

There was yellow weed on the line but the old man knew that only made an added drag and he was pleased. It was the yellow Gulf weed that had made so much phosphorescence in the night.

"Fish," he said, "I love you and respect you very much. But I will kill you dead before this day ends."

Let us hope so, he thought.

A small bird came toward the skiff from the north. He was a warbler and flying very low over the water. The old man could see that he was very tired.

The bird made the stern of the boat and rested there. Then he flew around the old man's head and rested on the line where he was more comfortable.

"How old are you?" the old man asked the bird. "Is this your first trip?"

The bird looked at him when he spoke. He was too tired even to examine the line and he teetered on it as his delicate feet gripped it fast.

"It's steady," the old man told him. "It's too steady. You shouldn't be that tired after a windless night. What are birds coming to?"

The hawks, he thought, that come out

to sea to meet them. But he said nothing of this to the bird who could not understand him anyway and who would learn about the hawks soon enough.

"Take a good rest, small bird," he said. "Then go in and take your chance like any man or bird or fish."

It encouraged him to talk because his back had stiffened in the night and it hurt truly now.

"Stay at my house if you like, bird," he said. "I am sorry I cannot hoist the sail and take you in with the small breeze that is rising. But I am with a friend."

Just then the fish gave a sudden lurch that pulled the old man down onto the bow and would have pulled him overboard if he had not braced himself and given some line.

The bird had flown up when the line jerked and the old man had not even seen him go. He felt the line carefully with his right hand and noticed his hand was bleeding.

"Something hurt him then," he said aloud and pulled back on the line to see if he could turn the fish. But when he was touching the breaking point he held steady and settled back against the strain of the line.

"You're feeling it now, fish," he said. "And so, God knows, am I."

He looked around for the bird now because he would have liked him for company. The bird was gone.

You did not stay long, the man thought. But it is rougher where you are going until you make the shore. How did I let the fish cut me with that one quick pull he made? I must be getting very stupid. Or perhaps I was looking at the small bird and thinking of him. Now I will pay attention to my work and then I must eat the tuna so that I will not have a failure of strength.

"I wish the boy were here and that I had some salt," he said aloud.

Shifting the weight of the line to his left shoulder and kneeling carefully he washed his hand in the ocean and held it there, submerged, for more than a minute watching the blood trail away and the steady movement of the water against his hand as the boat moved.

"He has slowed much," he said.

The old man would have liked to keep his hand in the salt water longer but he was afraid of another sudden lurch by the fish and he stood up and braced himself and held his hand up against the sun. It was only a line burn that had cut his flesh. But it was in the working part of his hand. He knew he would need his hands before this was over and he did not like to be cut before it started.

"Now," he said, when his hand had dried, "I must eat the small tuna. I can reach him with the gaff and eat him here in comfort."

He knelt down and found the tuna under the stern with the gaff and drew it toward him keeping it clear of the coiled lines. Holding the line with his left shoulder again, and bracing on his left hand and arm, he took the tuna off the gaff hook and put the gaff back in place. He put one knee on the fish and cut strips of dark red meat longitudinally from the back of the head to the tail. They were wedge-shaped strips and he cut them from next to the back bone down to the edge of the belly. When he had cut six strips he spread them out on the wood of the bow, wiped his knife on his trousers, and lifted the carcass of the bonito by the tail and dropped it overboard.

"I don't think I can eat an entire one," he said and drew his knife across one of the strips. He could feel the steady hard pull of the line and his left hand was cramped. It drew up tight on the heavy cord and he looked at it in disgust.

"What kind of a hand is that," he said. "Cramp then if you want. Make yourself into a claw. It will do you no good."

Come on, he thought and looked down

into the dark water at the slant of the line. Eat it now and it will strengthen the hand. It is not the hand's fault and you have been many hours with the fish. But you can stay with him forever. Eat the bonito now.

He picked up a piece and put it in his mouth and chewed it slowly. It was not unpleasant.

Chew it well, he thought, and get all the juices. It would not be bad to eat with a little lime or with lemon or with salt.

"How do you feel, hand?" he asked the cramped hand that was almost as stiff as rigor mortis. "I'll eat some more for you."

He ate the other part of the piece that he had cut in two. He chewed it carefully and then spat out the skin.

"How does it go, hand? Or is it too early to know?"

He took another full piece and chewed it.

"It is a strong full-blooded fish," he thought. "I was lucky to get him instead of dolphin. Dolphin is too sweet. This is hardly sweet at all and all the strength is still in it."

There is no sense in being anything but practical though, he thought. I wish I had some salt. And I do not know whether the sun will rot or dry what is left, so I had better eat it all although I am not hungry. The fish is calm and steady. I will eat it all and then I will be ready.

"Be patient, hand," he said. "I do this for you."

I wish I could feed the fish, he thought. He is my brother. But I must kill him and keep strong to do it. Slowly and conscientiously he ate all of the wedge-shaped strips of fish.

He straightened up, wiping his hand on his trousers.

"Now," he said. "You can let the cord go, hand, and I will handle him with the right arm alone until you stop that nonsense." He put his left foot on the heavy line that the left hand had held and lay back against the pull against his back.

"God help me to have the cramp go," he said. "Because I do not know what the fish is going to do."

But he seems calm, he thought, and following his plan. But what is his plan, he thought. And what is mine? Mine I must improvise to his because of his great size. If he will jump I can kill him. But he stays down forever. Then I will stay down with him forever.

He rubbed the cramped hand against his trousers and tried to gentle the fingers. But it would not open. Maybe it will open with the sun, he thought. Maybe it will open when the strong raw tuna is digested. If I have to have it, I will open it, cost whatever it costs. But I do not want to open it now by force. Let it open by itself and come back of its own accord. After all I abused it much in the night when it was necessary to free and untie the various lines.

He looked across the sea and knew how alone he was now. But he could see the prisms in the deep dark water and the line stretching ahead and the strange undulation of the calm. The clouds were building up now for the trade wind and he looked ahead and saw a flight of wild ducks etching themselves against the sky over the water, then blurring, then etching again and he knew no man was ever alone on the sea.

He thought of how some men feared being out of sight of land in a small boat and knew they were right in the months of sudden bad weather. But now they were in hurricane months and, when there are no hurricanes, the weather of hurricane months is the best of all the year.

If there is a hurricane you always see the signs of it in the sky for days ahead, if you are at sea. They do not see it ashore because they do not know what to look for, he thought. The land must make a difference too, in the shape of the clouds. But we have no hurricane coming now.

He looked at the sky and saw the white cumulus built like friendly piles of ice cream and high above were the thin feathers of the cirrus against the high September sky.

"Light *brisa*," he said. "Better weather for me than for you, fish."

His left hand was still cramped, but he was unknotting it slowly.

I hate a cramp, he thought. It is a treachery of one's own body. It is humiliating before others to have a diarrhoea from ptomaine poisoning or to vomit from it. But a cramp, he thought of it as a *calambre*, humiliates oneself especially when one is alone.

If the boy were here he could rub it for me and loosen it down from the forearm, he thought. But it will loosen up.

Then, with his right hand he felt the difference in the pull of the line before he saw the slant change in the water. Then, as he leaned against the line and slapped his left hand hard and fast against his thigh he saw the line slanting slowly upward.

"He's coming up," he said. "Come on hand. Please come on."

The line rose slowly and steadily and then the surface of the ocean bulged ahead of the boat and the fish came out. He came out unendingly and water poured from his sides. He was bright in the sun and his head and back were dark purple and in the sun the stripes on his sides showed wide and a light lavender. His sword was as long as a baseball bat and tapered like a rapier and he rose his full length from the water and then reentered it, smoothly, like a diver and the old man saw the great scythe-blade of his tail go under and the line commenced to race out.

"He is two feet longer than the skiff," the old man said. The line was going out fast but steadily and the fish was not panicked. The old man was trying with both hands to keep the line just inside of breaking strength. He knew that if he could not slow the fish with a steady pressure the fish could take out all the line and break it.

He is a great fish and I must convince him, he thought. I must never let him learn his strength nor what he could do if he made his run. If I were him I would put in everything now and go until something broke. But, thank God, they are not as intelligent as we who kill them; although they are more noble and more able.

The old man had seen many great fish. He had seen many that weighed more than a thousand pounds and he had caught two of that size in his life, but never alone. Now alone, and out of sight of land, he was fast to the biggest fish that he had ever seen and bigger than he had ever heard of, and his left hand was still as tight as the gripped claws of an eagle.

It will uncramp though, he thought. Surely it will uncramp to help my right hand. There are three things that are brothers: the fish and my two hands. It must uncramp. It is unworthy of it to be cramped. The fish had slowed again and was going at his usual pace.

I wonder why he jumped, the old man thought. He jumped almost as though to show me how big he was. I know now, anyway, he thought. I wish I could show him what sort of man I am. But then he would see the cramped hand. Let him think I am more man than I am and I will be so. I wish I was the fish, he thought, with everything he has against only my will and my intelligence.

He settled comfortably against the wood and took his suffering as it came and the fish swam steadily and the boat moved slowly through the dark water. There was a small sea rising with the wind coming up from the east and at noon the old man's left hand was uncramped.

"Bad news for you, fish," he said and shifted the line over the sacks that covered his shoulders.

He was comfortable but suffering, although he did not admit the suffering at all.

"I am not religious," he said. "But I will say ten Our Fathers and ten Hail Marys that I should catch this fish, and I promise to make a pilgrimage to the Virgin of Cobre if I catch him. That is a promise."

He commenced to say his prayers mechanically. Sometimes he would be so tired that he could not remember the prayers and then he would say them fast so that they would come automatically. Hail Marys are easier to say than Our Fathers, he thought.

"Hail Mary full of Grace the Lord is with thee. Blessed art thou among women and blessed is the fruit of thy womb, Jesus. Holy Mary, Mother of God, pray for us sinners now and at the hour of our death. Amen." Then he added, "Blessed Virgin, pray for the death of this fish. Wonderful though he is."

With his prayers said, and feeling much better, but suffering exactly as much, and perhaps a little more, he leaned against the wood of the bow and began, mechanically, to work the fingers of his left hand.

The sun was hot now although the breeze was rising gently.

"I had better re-bait that little line out over the stern," he said. "If the fish decides to stay another night I will need to eat again and the water is low in the bottle. I don't think I can get anything but a dolphin here. But if I eat him fresh enough he won't be bad. I wish a flying fish would come on board tonight. But I have no light to attract them. A flying fish is excellent to eat raw and I would not have to cut him up. I must save all my strength now. Christ, I did not know he was so big."

"I'll kill him though," he said. "In all his greatness and his glory."

Although it is unjust, he thought. But I will show him what a man can do and what a man endures.

"I told the boy I was a strange old man," he said. "Now is when I must prove it."

The thousand times that he had proved it meant nothing. Now he was proving it again. Each time was a new time and he never thought about the past when he was doing it.

I wish he'd sleep and I could sleep and dream about the lions, he thought. Why are the lions the main thing that is left? Don't think, old man, he said to himself. Rest gently now against the wood and think of nothing. He is working. Work as little as you can.

It was getting into the afternoon and the boat still moved slowly and steadily. But there was an added drag now from the easterly breeze and the old man rode gently with the small sea and the hurt of the cord across his back came to him easily and smoothly.

Once in the afternoon the line started to rise again. But the fish only continued to swim at a slightly higher level. The sun was on the old man's left arm and shoulder and on his back. So he knew the fish had turned east of north.

Now that he had seen him once, he could picture the fish swimming in the water with his purple pectoral fins set wide as wings and the great erect tail slicing through the dark. I wonder how much he sees at that depth, the old man thought. His eye is huge and a horse, with much less eye, can see in the dark. Once I could see quite well in the dark.

Not in the absolute dark. But almost as a cat sees.

The sun and his steady movement of his fingers had uncramped his left hand now completely and he began to shift more of the strain to it and he shrugged the muscles of his back to shift the hurt of the cord a little.

"If you're not tired, fish," he said aloud, "you must be very strange."

He felt very tired now and he knew the night would come soon and he tried to think of other things. He thought of the Big Leagues, to him they were the *Gran Ligas,* and he knew that the Yankees of New York were playing the *Tigres* of Detroit.

This is the second day now that I do not know the result of the *juegos,* he thought. But I must have confidence and I must be worthy of the great DiMaggio who does all things perfectly even with the pain of the bone spur in his heel. What is a bone spur? he asked himself. *Una espuela de hueso.* We do not have them. Can it be as painful as the spur of a fighting cock in one's heel? I do not think I could endure that or the loss of the eye and of both eyes and continue to fight as the fighting cocks do. Man is not much beside the great birds and beasts. Still I would rather be that beast down there in the darkness of the sea.

"Unless sharks come," he said aloud. "If sharks come, God pity him and me."

Do you believe the great DiMaggio would stay with a fish as long as I will stay with this one? he thought. I am sure he would and more since he is young and strong. Also his father was a fisherman. But would the bone spur hurt him too much?

"I do not know," he said aloud. "I never had a bone spur."

As the sun set he remembered, to give himself more confidence, the time in the tavern at Casablanca when he had played the hand game with the great Negro from Cienfuegos who was the strongest man on the docks. They had gone one day and one night with their elbows on a chalk line on the table and their forearms straight up and their hands gripped tight. Each one was trying to force the other's hand down onto the table. There was much betting and people went in and out of the room under the kerosene lights and he had looked at the arm and hand of the Negro and at the Negro's face. They changed the referees every four hours after the first eight so that the referees could sleep. Blood came out from under the fingernails of both his and the Negro's hands and they looked each other in the eye and at their hands and forearms and the bettors went in and out of the room and sat on high chairs against the wall and watched. The walls were painted bright blue and were of wood and the lamps threw their shadows against them. The Negro's shadow was huge and it moved on the wall as the breeze moved the lamps.

The odds would change back and forth all night and they fed the Negro rum and lighted cigarettes for him. Then the Negro, after the rum, would try for a tremendous effort and once he had the old man, who was not an old man then but was Santiago *El Campeón,* nearly three inches off balance. But the old man had raised his hand up to dead even again. He was sure then that he had the Negro, who was a fine man and a great athlete, beaten. And at daylight when the bettors were asking that it be called a draw and the referee was shaking his head, he had unleashed his effort and forced the hand of the Negro down and down until it rested on the wood. The match had started on a Sunday morning and ended on a Monday morning. Many of the bettors had asked for a draw because they had to go to work on the docks loading sacks of sugar or at the Havana Coal Company. Otherwise everyone would have wanted it to go to a finish. But he had finished it anyway and before anyone had to go to work.

For a long time after that everyone had called him The Champion and there had been a return match in the spring. But not much money was bet and he had won it quite easily since he had broken the confidence of the Negro from Cienfuegos in the first match. After that he had a few matches and then no more. He decided that he could beat anyone if he wanted to badly enough and he decided that it was bad for his right hand for fishing. He had tried a few practice matches with his left hand. But his left hand had always been a traitor and would not do what he called on it to do and he did not trust it.

The sun will bake it out well now, he thought. It should not cramp on me again unless it gets too cold in the night. I wonder what this night will bring.

An airplane passed overhead on its course to Miami and he watched its shadow scaring up the schools of flying fish.

"With so much flying fish there should be dolphin," he said, and leaned back on the line to see if it was possible to gain any on his fish. But he could not and it stayed at the hardness and water-drop shivering that preceded breaking. The boat moved ahead slowly and he watched the airplane until he could no longer see it.

It must be very strange in an airplane, he thought. I wonder what the sea looks like from that height? They should be able to see the fish well if they do not fly too high. I would like to fly very slowly at two hundred fathoms high and see the fish from above. In the turtle boats I was in the cross-trees of the mast-head and even at that height I saw much. The dolphin look greener from there and you can see their stripes and their purple spots and you can see all of the school as

they swim. Why is it that all the fast-moving fish of the dark current have purple backs and usually purple stripes or spots? The dolphin looks green of course because he is really golden. But when he comes to feed, truly hungry, purple stripes show on his sides as on a marlin. Can it be anger, or the greater speed he makes that brings them out?

Just before it was dark, as they passed a great island of Sargasso weed that heaved and swung in the light sea as though the ocean were making love with something under a yellow blanket, his small line was taken by a dolphin. He saw it first when it jumped in the air, true gold in the last of the sun and bending and flapping wildly in the air. It jumped again and again in the acrobatics of its fear and he worked his way back to the stern and crouching and holding the big line with his right hand and arm, he pulled the dolphin in with his left hand, stepping on the gained line each time with his bare left foot. When the fish was at the stern, plunging and cutting from side to side in desperation, the old man leaned over the stern and lifted the burnished gold fish with its purple spots over the stern. Its jaws were working convulsively in quick bites against the hook and it pounded the bottom of the skiff with its long flat body, its tail and its head until he clubbed it across the shining golden head until it shivered and was still.

The old man unhooked the fish, rebaited the line with another sardine and tossed it over. Then he worked his way slowly back to the bow. He washed his left hand and wiped it on his trousers. Then he shifted the heavy line from his right hand to his left and washed his right hand in the sea while he watched the sun go into the ocean and the slant of the big cord.

"He hasn't changed at all," he said. But watching the movement of the water against his hand he noted that it was perceptibly slower.

"I'll lash the two oars together across the stern and that will slow him in the night," he said. "He's good for the night and so am I."

It would be better to gut the dolphin a little later to save the blood in the meat, he thought. I can do that a little later and lash the oars to make a drag at the same time. I had better keep the fish quiet now and not disturb him too much at sunset. The setting of the sun is a difficult time for all fish.

He let his hand dry in the air then grasped the line with it and eased himself as much as he could and allowed himself to be pulled forward against the wood so that the boat took the strain as much, or more, than he did.

I'm learning how to do it, he thought. This part of it anyway. Then too, remember he hasn't eaten since he took the bait and he is huge and needs much food. I have eaten the whole bonito. Tomorrow I will eat the dolphin. He called it *dorado*. Perhaps I should eat some of it when I clean it. It will be harder to eat than the bonito. But, then, nothing is easy.

"How do you feel, fish?" he asked aloud. "I feel good and my left hand is better and I have food for a night and a day. Pull the boat, fish."

He did not truly feel good because the pain from the cord across his back had almost passed pain and gone into a dullness that he mistrusted. But I have had worse things than that, he thought. My hand is only cut a little and the cramp is gone from the other. My legs are all right. Also now I have gained on him in the question of sustenance.

It was dark now as it becomes dark quickly after the sun sets in September. He lay against the worn wood of the bow and rested all that he could. The first stars were out. He did not know the name of Rigel but he saw it and knew soon they would all be out and he would have all his distant friends.

"The fish is my friend too," he said aloud. "I have never seen or heard of such a fish. But I must kill him. I am glad we do not have to try to kill the stars."

Imagine if each day a man must try to kill the moon, he thought. The moon runs away. But imagine if a man each day should have to try to kill the sun? We were born lucky, he thought.

Then he was sorry for the great fish that had nothing to eat and his determination to kill him never relaxed in his sorrow for him. How many people will he feed, he thought. But are they worthy to eat him? No, of course not. There is no one worthy of eating him from the manner of his behaviour and his great dignity.

I do not understand these things, he thought. But it is good that we do not have to try to kill the sun or the moon or the stars. It is enough to live on the sea and kill our true brothers.

Now, he thought, I must think about the drag. It has its perils and its merits. I may lose so much line that I will lose him, if he makes his effort and the drag made by the oars is in place and the boat loses all her lightness. Her lightness prolongs both our suffering but it is my safety since he has great speed that he has never yet employed. No matter what passes I must gut the dolphin so he does not spoil and eat some of him to be strong.

Now I will rest an hour more and feel that he is solid and steady before I move back to the stern to do the work and make the decision. In the meantime I can see how he acts and if he shows any changes. The oars are a good trick; but it has reached the time to play for safety. He is much fish still and I saw that the hook was in the corner of his mouth and he has kept his mouth tight shut. The punishment of the hook is nothing. The punishment of hunger, and that he is against something that he does not comprehend, is everything. Rest now, old man, and let him work until your next duty comes.

He rested for what he believed to be two hours. The moon did not rise now until late and he had no way of judging the time. Nor was he really resting except comparatively. He was still bearing the pull of the fish across his shoulders but he placed his left hand on the gunwale of the bow and confided more and more of the resistance to the fish to the skiff itself.

How simple it would be if I could make the line fast, he thought. But with one small lurch he could break it. I must cushion the pull of the line with my body and at all times be ready to give line with both hands.

"But you have not slept yet, old man," he said aloud. "It is half a day and a night and now another day and you have not slept. You must devise a way so that you sleep a little if he is quiet and steady. If you do not sleep you might become unclear in the head."

I'm clear enough in the head, he thought. Too clear. I am as clear as the stars that are my brothers. Still I must sleep. They sleep and the moon and the sun sleep and even the ocean sleeps sometimes on certain days when there is no current and a flat calm.

But remember to sleep, he thought. Make yourself do it and devise some simple and sure way about the lines. Now go back and prepare the dolphin. It is too dangerous to rig the oars as a drag if you must sleep.

I could go without sleeping, he told himself. But it would be too dangerous.

He started to work his way back to the stern on his hands and knees, being careful not to jerk against the fish. He may be half asleep himself, he thought. But I do not want him to rest. He must pull until he dies.

Back in the stern he turned so that his left hand held the strain of the line across his shoulders and drew his knife from its sheath with his right hand. The stars were bright now and he saw the dolphin clearly and he pushed the blade of his knife into his head and drew him out from under the stern. He put one of his feet on the fish and slit him quickly from the vent up to the tip of his lower jaw. Then he put his knife down and gutted him with his right hand, scooping him clean and pulling the gills clear. He felt the maw heavy and slippery in his hands and he slit it open. There were two flying fish inside. They were fresh and hard and he laid them side by side and dropped the guts and the gills over the stern. They sank leaving a trail of phosphorescence in the water. The dolphin was cold and a leprous gray-white now in the starlight and the old man skinned one side of him while he held his right foot on the fish's head. Then he turned him over and skinned the other side and cut each side off from the head down to the tail.

He slid the carcass overboard and looked to see if there was any swirl in the water. But there was only the light of its slow descent. He turned then and placed the two flying fish inside the two fillets of fish and putting his knife back in its sheath, he worked his way slowly back to the bow. His back was bent with the weight of the line across it and he carried the fish in his right hand.

Back in the bow he laid the two fillets of fish out on the wood with the flying fish beside them. After that he settled the line across his shoulders in a new place and held it again with his left hand resting on the gunwale. Then he leaned over the side and washed the flying fish in the water, noting the speed of the water against his hand. His hand was phosphorescent from skinning the fish and he watched the flow of the water against it. The flow was less strong and as he rubbed the side of his hand against the planking of the skiff, particles of phosphorus floated off and drifted slowly astern.

"He is tiring or he is resting," the old man said. "Now let me get through the eating of this dolphin and get some rest and a little sleep."

Under the stars and with the night colder all the time he ate half of one of the dolphin fillets and one of the flying fish, gutted and with its head cut off.

"What an excellent fish dolphin is to eat cooked," he said. "And what a miserable fish raw. I will never go in a boat again without salt or limes."

If I had brains I would have splashed water on the bow all day and drying, it would have made salt, he thought. But then I did not hook the dolphin until almost sunset. Still it was a lack of preparation. But I have chewed it all well and I am not nauseated.

The sky was clouding over to the east and one after another the stars he knew were gone. It looked now as though he were moving into a great canyon of clouds and the wind had dropped.

"There will be bad weather in three or four days," he said. "But not tonight and not tomorrow. Rig now to get some sleep, old man, while the fish is calm and steady."

He held the line tight in his right hand and then pushed his thigh against his right hand as he leaned all his weight against the wood of the bow. Then he passed the line a little lower on his shoulders and braced his left hand on it.

My right hand can hold it as long as it is braced, he thought. If it relaxes in sleep my left hand will wake me as the line goes out. It is hard on the right hand. But he is used to punishment. Even if I sleep twenty minutes or half an hour it is good. He lay forward cramping himself against the line with all of his body, putting all his weight onto his right hand, and he was asleep.

He did not dream of the lions but instead of a vast school of porpoises that stretched for eight or ten miles and it was in the time of their mating and they would leap high into the air and return into the same hole they had made in the water when they leaped.

Then he dreamed that he was in the village on his bed and there was a norther and he was very cold and his right arm was asleep because his head had rested on it instead of a pillow.

After that he began to dream of the long yellow beach and he saw the first of the lions come down onto it in the early dark and then the other lions came and he rested his chin on the wood of the bow where the ship lay anchored with the evening off-shore breeze and he waited to see if there would be more lions and he was happy.

The moon had been up for a long time but he slept on and the fish pulled on steadily and the boat moved into the tunnel of clouds.

He woke with the jerk of his right fist coming up against his face and the line burning out through his right hand. He had no feeling of his left hand but he braked all he could with his right and the line rushed out. Finally his left hand found the line and he leaned back against the line and now it burned his back and his left hand, and his left hand was taking all the strain and cutting badly. He looked back at the coils of line and they were feeding smoothly. Just then the fish jumped making a great bursting of the ocean and then a heavy fall. Then he jumped again and again and the boat was going fast although line was still racing out and the old man was raising the strain to breaking point and raising it to

breaking point again and again. He had been pulled down tight onto the bow and his face was in the cut slice of dolphin and he could not move.

This is what we waited for, he thought. So now let us take it.

Make him pay for the line, he thought. Make him pay for it.

He could not see the fish's jumps but only heard the breaking of the ocean and the heavy splash as he fell. The speed of the line was cutting his hands badly but he had always known this would happen and he tried to keep the cutting across the calloused parts and not let the line slip into the palm nor cut the fingers.

If the boy was here he would wet the coils of line, he thought. Yes. If the boy were here. If the boy were here.

The line went out and out and out but it was slowing now and he was making the fish earn each inch of it. Now he got his head up from the wood and out of the slice of fish that his cheek had crushed. Then he was on his knees and then he rose slowly to his feet. He was ceding line but more slowly all the time. He worked back to where he could feel with his foot the coils of line that he could not see. There was plenty of line still and now the fish had to pull the friction of all that new line through the water.

Yes, he thought. And now he has jumped more than a dozen times and filled the sacks along his back with air and he cannot go down deep to die where I cannot bring him up. He will start circling soon and then I must work on him. I wonder what started him so suddenly? Could it have been hunger that made him desperate, or was he frightened by something in the night? Maybe he suddenly felt fear. But he was such a calm, strong fish and he seemed so fearless and so confident. It is strange.

"You better be fearless and confident yourself, old man," he said. "You're holding him again but you cannot get line. But soon he has to circle."

The old man held him with his left hand and his shoulders now and stooped down and scooped up water in his right hand to get the crushed dolphin flesh off of his face. He was afraid that it might nauseate him and he would vomit and lose his strength. When his face was cleaned he washed his right hand in the water over the side and then let it stay in the salt water while he watched the first light come before the sunrise. He's headed almost east, he thought. That means he is tired and going with the current. Soon he will have to circle. Then our true work begins.

After he judged that his right hand had been in the water long enough he took it out and looked at it.

"It is not bad," he said. "And pain does not matter to a man."

He took hold of the line carefully so that it did not fit into any of the fresh line cuts and shifted his weight so that he could put his left hand into the sea on the other side of the skiff.

"You did not do so badly for something worthless," he said to his left hand. "But there was a moment when I could not find you."

Why was I not born with two good hands? he thought. Perhaps it was my fault in not training that one properly. But God knows he has had enough chances to learn. He did not do so badly in the night, though, and he has only cramped once. If he cramps again let the line cut him off.

When he thought that he knew that he was not being clear-headed and he thought he should chew some more of the dolphin. But I can't, he told himself. It is better to be light-headed than to lose your strength from nausea. And I know I cannot keep it if I eat it since my face was in it. I will keep it for an emergency until it goes bad. But it is too late to try for strength now through nourishment. You're stupid, he told himself. Eat the other flying fish.

It was there, cleaned and ready, and he picked it up with his left hand and ate it chewing the bones carefully and eating all of it down to the tail.

It has more nourishment than almost any fish, he thought. At least the kind of strength that I need. Now I have done what I can, he thought. Let him begin to circle and let the fight come.

The sun was rising for the third time since he had put to sea when the fish started to circle.

He could not see by the slant of the line that the fish was circling. It was too early for that. He just felt a faint slackening of the pressure of the line and he commenced to pull on it gently with his right hand. It tightened, as always, but just when he reached the point where it would break, line began to come in. He slipped his shoulders and head from under the line and began to pull in line steadily and gently. He used both of his hands in a swinging motion and tried to do the pulling as much as he could with his body and his legs. His old legs and shoulders pivoted with the swinging of the pulling.

"It is a very big circle," he said. "But he is circling."

Then the line would not come in any more and he held it until he saw the drops jumping from it in the sun. Then it started out and the old man knelt down and let it go grudgingly back into the dark water.

"He is making the far part of his circle now," he said. I must hold all I can, he thought. The strain will shorten his circle each time. Perhaps in an hour I will see him. Now I must convince him and then I must kill him.

But the fish kept on circling slowly and the old man was wet with sweat and tired deep into his bones two hours later. But the circles were much shorter now and from the way the line slanted he could tell the fish had risen steadily while he swam.

For an hour the old man had been seeing black spots before his eyes and the sweat salted his eyes and salted the cut over his eye and on his forehead. He was not afraid of the black spots. They were normal at the tension that he was pulling on the line. Twice, though, he had felt faint and dizzy and that had worried him.

"I could not fail myself and die on a fish like this," he said. "Now that I have him coming so beautifully, God help me endure. I'll say a hundred Our Fathers and a hundred Hail Marys. But I cannot say them now."

Consider them said, he thought. I'll say them later.

Just then he felt a sudden banging and jerking on the line he held with his two hands. It was sharp and hard-feeling and heavy.

He is hitting the wire leader with his spear, he thought. That was bound to come. He had to do that. It may make him jump though and I would rather he stayed circling now. The jumps were necessary for him to take air. But after that each one can widen the opening of the hook wound and he can throw the hook.

"Don't jump, fish," he said. "Don't jump."

The fish hit the wire several times more and each time he shook his head the old man gave up a little line.

I must hold his pain where it is, he thought. Mine does not matter. I can control mine. But his pain could drive him mad.

After a while the fish stopped beating at the wire and started circling slowly again. The old man was gaining line steadily now. But he felt faint again. He lifted some sea water with his left hand and put it on his head. Then he put more on and rubbed the back of his neck.

"I have no cramps," he said. "He'll be up soon and I can last. You have to last. Don't even speak of it."

He kneeled against the bow and, for a moment, slipped the line over his back again. I'll rest now while he goes out on the circle and then stand up and work on him when he comes in, he decided.

It was a great temptation to rest in the bow and let the fish make one circle by himself without recovering any line. But when the strain showed the fish had turned to come toward the boat, the old man rose to his feet and started the pivoting and the weaving pulling that brought in all the line he gained.

I'm tireder than I have ever been, he thought, and now the trade wind is rising. But that will be good to take him in with. I need that badly.

"I'll rest on the next turn as he goes out," he said. "I feel much better. Then in two or three turns more I will have him."

His straw hat was far on the back of his head and he sank down into the bow with the pull of the line as he felt the fish turn.

You work now, fish, he thought. I'll take you at the turn.

The sea had risen considerably. But it was a fair-weather breeze and he had to have it to get home.

"I'll just steer south and west," he said. "A man is never lost at sea and it is a long island."

It was on the third turn that he saw the fish first.

He saw him first as a dark shadow that took so long to pass under the boat that he could not believe its length.

"No," he said. "He can't be that big."

But he was that big and at the end of this circle he came to the surface only thirty yards away and the man saw his tail out of water. It was higher than a big scythe blade and a very pale lavender above the dark blue water. It raked back and as the fish swam just below the surface the old man could see his huge bulk and the purple stripes that banded him. His dorsal fin was down and his huge pectorals were spread wide.

On this circle the old man could see the fish's eye and the two gray sucking fish that swam around him. Sometimes they attached themselves to him. Sometimes they darted off. Sometimes they would swim easily in his shadow. They were each over three feet long and when they swam fast they lashed their whole bodies like eels.

The old man was sweating now but from something else besides the sun. On each calm placid turn the fish made he was gaining line and he was sure that in two turns more he would have a chance to get the harpoon in.

But I must get him close, close, close, he thought. I mustn't try for the head. I must get the heart.

"Be calm and strong, old man," he said. On the next circle the fish's back was out but he was a little too far from the boat. On the next circle he was still too far away but he was higher out of water and the old man was sure that by gaining some more line he could have him alongside.

He had rigged his harpoon long before and its coil of light rope was in a round basket and the end was made fast to the bitt in the bow.

The fish was coming in on his circle now calm and beautiful looking and only his great tail moving. The old man pulled on him all that he could to bring him closer. For just a moment the fish turned a little on his side. Then he straightened himself and began another circle.

"I moved him," the old man said. "I moved him then."

He felt faint again now but he held on

the great fish all the strain that he could. I moved him, he thought. Maybe this time I can get him over. Pull, hands, he thought. Hold up, legs. Last for me, head. Last for me. You never went. This time I'll pull him over.

But when he put all of his effort on, starting it well out before the fish came alongside and pulling with all his strength, the fish pulled part way over and then righted himself and swam away.

"Fish," the old man said. "Fish, you are going to have to die anyway. Do you have to kill me too?"

That way nothing is accomplished, he thought. His mouth was too dry to speak but he could not reach for the water now. I must get him alongside this time, he thought. I am not good for many more turns. Yes you are, he told himself. You're good for ever.

On the next turn, he nearly had him. But again the fish righted himself and swam slowly away.

You are killing me, fish, the old man thought. But you have a right to. Never have I seen a greater, or more beautiful, or a calmer or more noble thing than you, brother. Come on and kill me. I do not care who kills who.

Now you are getting confused in the head, he thought. You must keep your head clear. Keep your head clear and know how to suffer like a man. Or a fish, he thought.

"Clear up, head," he said in a voice he could hardly hear. "Clear up."

Twice more it was the same on the turns. I do not know, the old man thought. He had been on the point of feeling himself go each time. I do not know. But I will try it once more.

He tried it once more and he felt himself going when he turned the fish. The fish righted himself and swam off again slowly with the great tail weaving in the air.

I'll try it again, the old man promised, although his hands were mushy now and he could only see well in flashes.

He tried it again and it was the same. So he thought, and he felt himself going before he started; I will try it once again.

He took all his pain and what was left of his strength and his long gone pride and he put it against the fish's agony and the fish came over onto his side and swam gently on his side, his bill almost touching the planking of the skiff and started to pass the boat, long, deep, wide, silver and barred with purple and interminable in the water.

The old man dropped the line and put his foot on it and lifted the harpoon as high as he could and drove it down with all his strength, and more strength he had just summoned, into the fish's side just behind the great chest fin that rose high in the air to the altitude of the man's chest. He felt the iron go in and he leaned on it and drove it further and then pushed all his weight after it.

Then the fish came alive, with his death in him, and rose high out of the water showing all his great length and width and all his power and his beauty. He seemed to hang in the air above the old man in the skiff. Then he fell into the water with a crash that sent spray over the old man and over all of the skiff.

The old man felt faint and sick and he could not see well. But he cleared the harpoon line and let it run slowly through his raw hands and, when he could see, he saw the fish was on his back with his silver belly up. The shaft of the harpoon was projecting at an angle from the fish's shoulder and the sea was discolouring with the red of the blood from his heart. First it was dark as a shoal in the blue water that was more than a mile deep. Then it spread like a cloud. The fish was silvery and still and floated with the waves.

THE SUN ALSO RISES

By ERNEST HEMINGWAY

[Excerpt]

CHAPTER XV

At noon of Sunday, the 6th of July, the fiesta exploded. There is no other way to describe it. People had been coming in all day from the country, but they were assimilated in the town and you did not notice them. The square was as quiet in the hot sun as on any other day. The peasants were in the outlying wine-shops. There they were drinking, getting ready for the fiesta. They had come in so recently from the plains and the hills that it was necessary that they make their shifting in values gradually. They could not start in paying café prices. They got their money's worth in the wine-shops. Money still had a definite value in hours worked and bushels of grain sold. Late in the fiesta it would not matter what they paid, nor where they bought.

Now on the day of the starting of the fiesta of San Fermin they had been in the wine-shops of the narrow streets of the town since early morning. Going down the streets in the morning on the way to mass in the cathedral, I heard them singing through the open doors of the shops. They were warming up. There were many people at the eleven o'clock mass. San Fermin is also a religious festival.

I walked down the hill from the cathedral and up the street to the café on the square. It was a little before noon.

Robert Cohn and Bill were sitting at one of the tables. The marble-topped tables and the white wicker chairs were gone. They were replaced by cast-iron tables and severe folding chairs. The café was like a battleship stripped for action. To-day the waiters did not leave you alone all morning to read without asking if you wanted to order something. A waiter came up as soon as I sat down.

"What are you drinking?" I asked Bill and Robert.

"Sherry," Cohn said.

"Jerez," I said to the waiter.

Before the waiter brought the sherry the rocket that announced the fiesta went up in the square. It burst and there was a gray ball of smoke high up above the Theatre Gayarre, across on the other side of the plaza. The ball of smoke hung in the sky like a shrapnel burst, and as I watched, another rocket came up to it, trickling smoke in the bright sunlight. I saw the bright flash as it burst and another little cloud of smoke appeared. By the time the second rocket had burst there were so many people in the arcade, that had been empty a minute before, that the waiter, holding the bottle high up over his head, could hardly get through the crowd to our table. People were coming into the square from all sides, and down the street we heard the pipes and the fifes and the drums com-

[31]

ing. They were playing the *riau-riau* music, the pipes shrill and the drums pounding, and behind them came the men and boys dancing. When the fifers stopped they all crouched down in the street, and when the reed-pipes and the fifes shrilled, and the flat, dry, hollow drums tapped it out again, they all went up in the air dancing. In the crowd you saw only the heads and shoulders of the dancers going up and down.

In the square a man, bent over, was playing on a reed-pipe, and a crowd of children were following him shouting, and pulling at his clothes. He came out of the square, the children following him, and piped them past the café and down a side street. We saw his blank pockmarked face as he went by, piping, the children close behind him shouting and pulling at him.

"He must be the village idiot," Bill said. "My God! look at that!"

Down the street came dancers. The street was solid with dancers, all men. They were all dancing in time behind their own fifers and drummers. They were a club of some sort, and all wore workmen's blue smocks, and red handkerchiefs around their necks, and carried a great banner on two poles. The banner danced up and down with them as they came down surrounded by the crowd.

"Hurray for Wine! Hurray for the Foreigners!" was painted on the banner.

"Where are the foreigners?" Robert Cohn asked.

"We're the foreigners," Bill said.

All the time rockets were going up. The café tables were all full now. The square was emptying of people and the crowd was filling the cafés.

"Where's Brett and Mike?" Bill asked.

"I'll go and get them," Cohn said.

"Bring them here."

The fiesta was really started. It kept up day and night for seven days. The dancing kept up, the drinking kept up, the noise went on. The things that happened could only have happened during a fiesta. Everything became quite unreal finally and it seemed as though nothing could have any consequences. It seemed out of place to think of consequences during the fiesta. All during the fiesta you had the feeling, even when it was quiet, that you had to shout any remark to make it heard. It was the same feeling about any action. It was a fiesta and it went on for seven days.

That afternoon was the big religious procession. San Fermin was translated from one church to another. In the procession were all the dignitaries, civil and religious. We could not see them because the crowd was too great. Ahead of the formal procession and behind it danced the *riau-riau* dancers. There was one mass of yellow shirts dancing up and down in the crowd. All we could see of the procession through the closely pressed people that crowded all the side streets and curbs were the great giants, cigar-store Indians, thirty feet high, Moors, a King and Queen, whirling and waltzing solemnly to the *riau-riau*.

They were all standing outside the chapel where San Fermin and the dignitaries had passed in, leaving a guard of soldiers, the giants, with the men who danced in them standing beside their resting frames, and the dwarfs moving with their whacking bladders through the crowd. We started inside and there was a smell of incense and people filing back into the church, but Brett was stopped just inside the door because she had no hat, so we went out again and along the street that ran back from the chapel into town. The street was lined on both sides with people keeping their place at the curb for the return of the procession. Some dancers formed a circle around Brett and started to dance. They wore big wreaths of white garlics around their necks. They took Bill and me by the arms and put us in the circle. Bill started to dance, too. They were all chanting. Brett wanted to dance but they did not want her to. They wanted her as an image to dance around. When the song ended with the sharp *riau-riau!* they rushed us into a wine-shop.

We stood at the counter. They had Brett seated on a wine-cask. It was dark in the wine-shop and full of men singing, hard-voiced singing. Back of the counter they drew the wine from casks. I put down money for the wine, but one of the men picked it up and put it back in my pocket.

"I want a leather wine-bottle," Bill said.

"There's a place down the street," I said. "I'll go get a couple."

The dancers did not want me to go out. Three of them were sitting on the high wine-cask beside Brett, teaching her to drink out of the wine-skins. They had hung a wreath of garlics around her neck. Some one insisted on giving her a glass. Somebody was teaching Bill a song. Singing it into his ear. Beating time on Bill's back.

I explained to them that I would be back. Outside in the street I went down the street looking for the shop that made leather wine-bottles. The crowd was packed on the sidewalks and many of the shops were shuttered, and I could not find it. I walked as far as the church, looking on both sides of the street. Then I asked a man and he took me by the arm and led me to it. The shutters were up but the door was open.

Inside it smelled of fresh tanned leather and hot tar. A man was stencilling completed wine-skins. They hung from the roof in bunches. He took one down, blew it up, screwed the nozzle tight, and then jumped on it.

"See! It doesn't leak."

"I want another one, too. A big one."

He took down a big one that would hold a gallon or more, from the roof. He blew it up, his cheeks puffing ahead of the wine-skin, and stood on the bota holding on to a chair.

"What are you going to do? Sell them in Bayonne?"

"No. Drink out of them."

He slapped me on the back.

"Good man. Eight pesetas for the two. The lowest price."

The man who was stencilling the new ones and tossing them into a pile stopped.

"It's true," he said. "Eight pesetas is cheap."

I paid and went out and along the street back to the wine-shop. It was darker than ever inside and very crowded. I did not see Brett and Bill, and some one said they were in the back room. At the counter the girl filled the two wine-skins for me. One held two litres. The other held five litres. Filling them both cost three pesetas sixty centimos. Some one at the counter, that I had never seen before, tried to pay for the wine, but I finally paid for it myself. The man who had wanted to pay then bought me a drink. He would not let me buy one in return, but said he would take a rinse of the mouth from the new wine-bag. He tipped the big five-litre bag up and squeezed it so the wine hissed against the back of his throat.

"All right," he said, and handed back the bag.

In the back room Brett and Bill were sitting on barrels surrounded by the dancers. Everybody had his arms on everybody else's shoulders, and they were all singing. Mike was sitting at a table with several men in their shirt-sleeves, eating from a bowl of tuna fish, chopped onions and vinegar. They were all drinking wine and mopping up the oil and vinegar with pieces of bread.

"Hello, Jake. Hello!" Mike called. "Come here. I want you to meet my

friends. We're all having an hors-
d'oeuvre."

I was introduced to the people at the
table. They supplied their names to Mike
and sent for a fork for me.

"Stop eating their dinner, Michael,"
Brett shouted from the wine-barrels.

"I don't want to eat up your meal," I
said when some one handed me a fork.

"Eat," he said. "What do you think it's
here for?"

I unscrewed the nozzle of the big wine-
bottle and handed it around. Every one
took a drink, tipping the wine-skin at
arm's length.

Outside, above the singing, we could
hear the music of the procession going by.

"Isn't that the procession?" Mike
asked.

"Nada," some one said. "It's nothing.
Drink up. Lift the bottle."

"Where did they find you?" I asked
Mike.

"Some one brought me here," Mike
said. "They said you were here."

"Where's Cohn?"

"He's passed out," Brett called.
"They've put him away somewhere."

"Where is he?"

"I don't know."

"How should we know," Bill said. "I
think he's dead."

"He's not dead," Mike said. "I know
he's not dead. He's just passed out on
Anís del Mono."

As he said Anís del Mono one of the
men at the table looked up, brought out a
bottle from inside his smock, and handed
it to me.

"No," I said. "No, thanks!"

"Yes. Yes. Arriba! Up with the
bottle!"

I took a drink. It tasted of licorice and
warmed all the way. I could feel it warming in my stomach.

"Where the hell is Cohn?"

"I don't know," Mike said. "I'll ask.

Where is the drunken comrade?" he
asked in Spanish.

"You want to see him?"

"Yes," I said.

"Not me," said Mike. "This gent."

The Anís del Mono man wiped his
mouth and stood up.

"Come on."

In a back room Robert Cohn was
sleeping quietly on some wine-casks. It
was almost too dark to see his face. They
had covered him with a coat and another
coat was folded under his head. Around
his neck and on his chest was a big
wreath of twisted garlics.

"Let him sleep," the man whispered.
"He's all right."

Two hours later Cohn appeared. He
came into the front room still with the
wreath of garlics around his neck. The
Spaniards shouted when he came in.
Cohn wiped his eyes and grinned.

"I must have been sleeping," he said.

"Oh, not at all," Brett said.

"You were only dead," Bill said.

"Aren't we going to go and have some
supper?" Cohn asked.

"Do you want to eat?"

"Yes. Why not? I'm hungry."

"Eat those garlics, Robert," Mike said.
"I say. Do eat those garlics."

Cohn stood there. His sleep had made
him quite all right.

"Do let's go and eat," Brett said. "I
must get a bath."

"Come on," Bill said. "Let's translate
Brett to the hotel."

We said good-bye to many people and
shook hands with many people and went
out. Outside it was dark.

"What time is it do you suppose?"
Cohn asked.

"It's to-morrow," Mike said. "You've
been asleep two days."

"No," said Cohn, "what time is it?"

"It's ten o'clock."

"What a lot we've drunk."

"You mean what a lot *we've* drunk. You went to sleep."

Going down the dark streets to the hotel we saw the skyrockets going up in the square. Down the side streets that led to the square we saw the square solid with people, those in the centre all dancing.

It was a big meal at the hotel. It was the first meal of the prices being doubled for the fiesta, and there were several new courses. After the dinner we were out in the town. I remember resolving that I would stay up all night to watch the bulls go through the streets at six o'clock in the morning, and being so sleepy that I went to bed around four o'clock. The others stayed up.

My own room was locked and I could not find the key, so I went up-stairs and slept on one of the beds in Cohn's room. The fiesta was going on outside in the night, but I was too sleepy for it to keep me awake. When I woke it was the sound of the rocket exploding that announced the release of the bulls from the corrals at the edge of town. They would race through the streets and out to the bull-ring. I had been sleeping heavily and I woke feeling I was too late. I put on a coat of Cohn's and went out on the balcony. Down below the narrow street was empty. All the balconies were crowded with people. Suddenly a crowd came down the street. They were all running, packed close together. They passed along and up the street toward the bull-ring and behind them came more men running faster, and then some stragglers who were really running. Behind them was a little bare space, and then the bulls galloping, tossing their heads up and down. It all went out of sight around the corner. One man fell, rolled to the gutter, and lay quiet. But the bulls went right on and did not notice him. They were all running together.

After they went out of sight a great roar came from the bull-ring. It kept on. Then finally the pop of the rocket that meant the bulls had gotten through the people in the ring and into the corrals. I went back in the room and got into bed. I had been standing on the stone balcony in bare feet. I knew our crowd must have all been out at the bull-ring. Back in bed, I went to sleep.

Cohn woke me when he came in. He started to undress and went over and closed the window because the people on the balcony of the house just across the street were looking in.

"Did you see the show?" I asked.

"Yes. We were all there."

"Anybody get hurt?"

"One of the bulls got into the crowd in the ring and tossed six or eight people."

"How did Brett like it?"

"It was all so sudden there wasn't any time for it to bother anybody."

"I wish I'd been up."

"We didn't know where you were. We went to your room but it was locked."

"Where did you stay up?"

"We danced at some club."

"I got sleepy," I said.

"My gosh! I'm sleepy now," Cohn said. "Doesn't this thing ever stop?"

"Not for a week."

Bill opened the door and put his head in.

"Where were you, Jake?"

"I saw them go through from the balcony. How was it?"

"Grand."

"Where you going?"

"To sleep."

No one was up before noon. We ate at tables set out under the arcade. The town was full of people. We had to wait for a table. After lunch we went over to the Iruña. It had filled up, and as the time for the bull-fight came it got fuller, and the tables were crowded closer. There was a close, crowded hum that came every day before the bull-fight. The café did not make this same noise at any other time, no matter how crowded it was. This hum went on, and we were in it and a part of it.

I had taken six seats for all the fights. Three of them were barreras, the first row at the ring-side, and three were sobrepuertos, seats with wooden backs, half-way up the amphitheatre. Mike thought Brett had best sit high up for her first time, and Cohn wanted to sit with them. Bill and I were going to sit in the barreras, and I gave the extra ticket to a waiter to sell. Bill said something to Cohn about what to do and how to look so he would not mind the horses. Bill had seen one season of bull-fights.

"I'm not worried about how I'll stand it. I'm only afraid I may be bored," Cohn said.

"You think so?"

"Don't look at the horses, after the bull hits them," I said to Brett. "Watch the charge and see the picador try and keep the bull off, but then don't look again until the horse is dead if it's been hit."

"I'm a little nervy about it," Brett said. "I'm worried whether I'll be able to go through with it all right."

"You'll be all right. There's nothing but that horse part that will bother you, and they're only in for a few minutes with each bull. Just don't watch when it's bad."

"She'll be all right," Mike said. "I'll look after her."

"I don't think you'll be bored," Bill said.

"I'm going over to the hotel to get the glasses and the wine-skin," I said. "See you back here. Don't get cock-eyed."

"I'll come along," Bill said. Brett smiled at us.

We walked around through the arcade to avoid the heat of the square.

"That Cohn gets me," Bill said. "He's got this Jewish superiority so strong that he thinks the only emotion he'll get out of the fight will be being bored."

"We'll watch him with the glasses," I said.

"Oh, to hell with him!"

"He spends a lot of time there."

"I want him to stay there."

In the hotel on the stairs we met Montoya.

"Come on," said Montoya. "Do you want to meet Pedro Romero?"

"Fine," said Bill. "Let's go see him."

We followed Montoya up a flight and down the corridor.

"He's in room number eight," Montoya explained. "He's getting dressed for the bull-fight."

Montoya knocked on the door and opened it. It was a gloomy room with a little light coming in from the window on the narrow street. There were two beds separated by a monastic partition. The electric light was on. The boy stood very straight and unsmiling in his bull-fighting clothes. His jacket hung over the back of a chair. They were just finishing winding his sash. His black hair shone under the electric light. He wore a white linen shirt and the sword-handler finished his sash and stood up and stepped back. Pedro Romero nodded, seeming very far away and dignified when we shook hands. Montoya said something about what great aficionados we were, and that we wanted to wish him luck. Romero listened very seriously. Then he turned to me. He was the best-looking boy I have ever seen.

"You go to the bull-fight," he said in English.

"You know English," I said, feeling like an idiot.

"No," he answered, and smiled.

One of three men who had been sitting on the beds came up and asked us if we spoke French. "Would you like me to interpret for you? Is there anything you would like to ask Pedro Romero?"

We thanked him. What was there that you would like to ask? The boy was nineteen years old, alone except for his sword-handler, and the three hangers-on, and the bull-fight was to commence in twenty minutes. We wished him "Mucha suerte," shook hands, and went out. He was standing, straight and handsome and altogether by himself, alone in the room with the hangers-on as we shut the door.

"He's a fine boy, don't you think so?" Montoya asked.

"He's a good-looking kid," I said.

"He looks like a torero," Montoya said. "He has the type."

"He's a fine boy."

"We'll see how he is in the ring," Montoya said.

We found the big leather wine-bottle leaning against the wall in my room, took it and the field-glasses, locked the door, and went down-stairs.

It was a good bull-fight. Bill and I were very excited about Pedro Romero. Montoya was sitting about ten places away. After Romero had killed his first bull Montoya caught my eye and nodded his head. This was a real one. There had not been a real one for a long time. Of the other two matadors, one was very fair and the other was passable. But there was no comparison with Romero, although neither of his bulls was much.

Several times during the bull-fight I looked up at Mike and Brett and Cohn, with the glasses. They seemed to be all right. Brett did not look upset. All three were leaning forward on the concrete railing in front of them.

"Let me take the glasses," Bill said.

"Does Cohn look bored?" I asked.

"That kike!"

Outside the ring, after the bull-fight was over, you could not move in the crowd. We could not make our way through but had to be moved with the whole thing, slowly, as a glacier, back to town. We had that disturbed emotional feeling that always comes after a bull-fight, and the feeling of elation that comes after a good bull-fight. The fiesta was going on. The drums pounded and the pipe music was shrill, and everywhere the flow of the crowd was broken by patches of dancers. The dancers were in a crowd, so you did not see the intricate play of the feet. All you saw was the heads and shoulders going up and down, up and down. Finally, we got out of the crowd and made for the café. The waiter saved chairs for the others, and we each ordered an absinthe and watched the crowd in the square and the dancers.

"What do you suppose that dance is?" Bill asked.

"It's a sort of jota."

"They're not all the same," Bill said. "They dance differently to all the different tunes."

"It's swell dancing."

In front of us on a clear part of the street a company of boys were dancing. The steps were very intricate and their faces were intent and concentrated. They all looked down while they danced. Their rope-soled shoes tapped and spatted on the pavement. The toes touched. The heels touched. The balls of the feet touched. Then the music broke wildly and the step was finished and they were all dancing on up the street.

"Here come the gentry," Bill said.

They were crossing the street.

"Hello, men," I said.

"Hello, gents!" said Brett. "You saved us seats? How nice."

"I say," Mike said, "that Romero what's his name is somebody. Am I wrong?"

"Oh, isn't he lovely," Brett said. "And those green trousers."

"Brett never took her eyes off them."

"I say, I must borrow your glasses to-morrow."

"How did it go?"

"Wonderfully! Simply perfect. I say, it is a spectacle!"

"How about the horses?"

"I couldn't help looking at them."

"She couldn't take her eyes off them," Mike said. "She's an extraordinary wench."

"They do have some rather awful things happen to them," Brett said. "I couldn't look away, though."

"Did you feel all right?"

"I didn't feel badly at all."

"Robert Cohn did," Mike put in. "You were quite green, Robert."

"The first horse did bother me," Cohn said.

"You weren't bored, were you?" asked Bill.

Cohn laughed.

"No. I wasn't bored. I wish you'd forgive me that."

"It's all right," Bill said, "so long as you weren't bored."

"He didn't look bored," Mike said. "I thought he was going to be sick."

"I never felt that bad. It was just for a minute."

"I thought he was going to be sick. You weren't bored, were you, Robert?"

"Let up on that, Mike. I said I was sorry I said it."

"He was, you know. He was positively green."

"Oh, shove it along, Michael."

"You mustn't ever get bored at your first bull-fight, Robert," Mike said. "It might make such a mess."

"Oh, shove it along, Michael," Brett said.

"He said Brett was a sadist," Mike said. "Brett's not a sadist. She's just a lovely, healthy wench."

"Are you a sadist, Brett?" I asked.

"Hope not."

"He said Brett was a sadist just because she has a good, healthy stomach."

"Won't be healthy long."

Bill got Mike started on something else than Cohn. The waiter brought the absinthe glasses.

"Did you really like it?" Bill asked Cohn.

"No, I can't say I liked it. I think it's a wonderful show."

"Gad, yes! What a spectacle!" Brett said.

"I wish they didn't have the horse part," Cohn said.

"They're not important," Bill said. "After a while you never notice anything disgusting."

"It is a bit strong just at the start," Brett said. "There's a dreadful moment for me just when the bull starts for the horse."

"The bulls were fine," Cohn said.

"They were very good," Mike said.

"I want to sit down below, next time." Brett drank from her glass of absinthe.

"She wants to see the bull-fighters close by," Mike said.

"They are something," Brett said. "That Romero lad is just a child."

"He's a damned good-looking boy," I said. "When we were up in his room I never saw a better-looking kid."

"How old do you suppose he is?"

"Nineteen or twenty."

"Just imagine it."

The bull-fight on the second day was much better than on the first. Brett sat between Mike and me at the barrera, and Bill and Cohn went up above. Romero was the whole show. I do not think Brett saw any other bull-fighter. No one else did either, except the hard-shelled technicians. It was all Romero. There were two other matadors, but they did not count. I sat beside Brett and explained to Brett what it was all about. I told her about watching the bull, not the horse, when the bulls charged the picadors, and got her to watching the picador place the point of his pic so that she saw what it was all about, so that it became more something that was going on with a definite end, and less of a spectacle with unexplained horrors. I had her watch how Romero took the bull away from a fallen horse with his cape, and how he held him with the cape and turned him, smoothly and suavely, never wasting the bull. She saw how Romero avoided every brusque movement and saved his bulls for the last when he wanted them, not winded and discomposed but smoothly worn down. She saw how close Romero always worked to the bull, and I pointed out to her the tricks the other bull-fighters used to make it look as though they were working closely. She saw why she liked Romero's cape-work and why she did not like the others.

Romero never made any contortions, always it was straight and pure and natural in line. The others twisted themselves like cork-screws, their elbows raised, and leaned against the flanks of the bull after his horns had passed, to give a faked look of danger. Afterward, all that was faked turned bad and gave an unpleasant feeling. Romero's bull-fighting gave real emotion, because he kept the absolute purity of line in his movements and always quietly and calmly let the horns pass him close each time. He did not have to emphasize their closeness. Brett saw how something that was beautiful done close to the bull was ridiculous if it were done a little way off. I told her how since the death of Joselito all the bull-fighters had been developing a technic that simulated this appearance of danger in order to give a fake emotional feeling, while the bull-fighter was really safe. Romero had the old thing, the holding of his purity of line through the maximum of exposure, while he dominated the bull by making him realize he was unattainable, while he prepared him for the killing.

"I've never seen him do an awkward thing," Brett said.

"You won't until he gets frightened," I said.

"He'll never be frightened," Mike said. "He knows too damned much."

"He knew everything when he started. The others can't ever learn what he was born with."

"And God, what looks," Brett said.

"I believe, you know, that she's falling in love with this bull-fighter chap," Mike said.

"I wouldn't be surprised."

"Be a good chap, Jake. Don't tell her anything more about him. Tell her how they beat their old mothers."

"Tell me what drunks they are."

"Oh, frightful," Mike said. "Drunk all day and spend all their time beating their poor old mothers."

"He looks that way," Brett said.

"Doesn't he?" I said.

They had hitched the mules to the dead bull and then the whips cracked, the men ran, and the mules, straining forward, their legs pushing, broke into a gallop, and the bull, one horn up, his head on its side, swept a swath smoothly across the sand and out the red gate.

"This next is the last one."

"Not really," Brett said. She leaned forward on the barrera. Romero waved his picadors to their places, then stood, his cape against his chest, looking across the ring to where the bull would come out.

After it was over we went out and were pressed tight in the crowd.

"These bull-fights are hell on one," Brett said. "I'm limp as a rag."

"Oh, you'll get a drink," Mike said.

The next day Pedro Romero did not fight. It was Miura bulls, and a very bad bull-fight. The next day there was no bull-fight scheduled. But all day and all night the fiesta kept on.

[39]

CHAPTER XVI

In the morning it was raining. A fog had come over the mountains from the sea. You could not see the tops of the mountains. The plateau was dull and gloomy, and the shapes of the trees and the houses were changed. I walked out beyond the town to look at the weather. The bad weather was coming over the mountains from the sea.

The flags in the square hung wet from the white poles and the banners were wet and hung damp against the front of the houses, and in between the steady drizzle the rain came down and drove every one under the arcades and made pools of water in the square, and the streets wet and dark and deserted; yet the fiesta kept up without any pause. It was only driven under cover.

The covered seats of the bull-ring had been crowded with people sitting out of the rain watching the concourse of Basque and Navarrais dancers and singers, and afterward the Val Carlos dancers in their costumes danced down the street in the rain, the drums sounding hollow and damp, and the chiefs of the bands riding ahead on their big, heavy-footed horses, their costumes wet, the horses' coats wet in the rain. The crowd was in the cafés and the dancers came in, too, and sat, their tight-wound white legs under the tables, shaking the water from their belled caps, and spreading their red and purple jackets over the chairs to dry. It was raining hard outside.

I left the crowd in the café and went over to the hotel to get shaved for dinner. I was shaving in my room when there was a knock on the door.

"Come in," I called. Montoya walked in.

"How are you?" he said.

"Fine," I said.

"No bulls to-day."

"No," I said, "nothing but rain."

"Where are your friends?"

"Over at the Iruña."

Montoya smiled his embarrassed smile.

"Look," he said. "Do you know the American ambassador?"

"Yes," I said. "Everybody knows the American ambassador."

"He's here in town, now."

"Yes," I said. "Everybody's seen them."

"I've seen them, too," Montoya said. He didn't say anything. I went on shaving.

"Sit down," I said. "Let me send for a drink."

"No, I have to go."

I finished shaving and put my face down into the bowl and washed it with cold water. Montoya was standing there looking more embarrassed.

"Look," he said. "I've just had a message from them at the Grand Hotel that they want Pedro Romero and Marcial Lalanda to come over for coffee to-night after dinner."

"Well," I said, "it can't hurt Marcial any."

"Marcial has been in San Sebastian all day. He drove over in a car this morning with Marquez. I don't think they'll be back to-night."

Montoya stood embarrassed. He wanted me to say something.

"Don't give Romero the message," I said.

"You think so?"

"Absolutely."

Montoya was very pleased.

"I wanted to ask you because you were an American," he said.

"That's what I'd do."

"Look," said Montoya. "People take a boy like that. They don't know what he's worth. They don't know what he means. Any foreigner can flatter him. They start this Grand Hotel business, and in one year they're through."

"Like Algabeno," I said.

"Yes, like Algabeno."

"They're a fine lot," I said. "There's one American woman down here now that collects bull-fighters."

"I know. They only want the young ones."

"Yes," I said. "The old ones get fat."

"Or crazy like Gallo."

"Well," I said, "it's easy. All you have to do is not give him the message."

"He's such a fine boy," said Montoya. "He ought to stay with his own people. He shouldn't mix in that stuff."

"Won't you have a drink?" I asked.

"No," said Montoya, "I have to go." He went out.

I went down-stairs and out the door and took a walk around through the arcades around the square. It was still raining. I looked in at the Iruña for the gang and they were not there, so I walked on around the square and back to the hotel. They were eating dinner in the down-stairs dining-room.

They were well ahead of me and it was no use trying to catch them. Bill was buying shoe-shines for Mike. Bootblacks opened the street door and each one Bill called over and started to work on Mike.

"This is the eleventh time my boots have been polished," Mike said. "I say, Bill is an ass."

The bootblacks had evidently spread the report. Another came in.

"Limpia botas?" he said to Bill.

"No," said Bill. "For this Señor."

The bootblack knelt down beside the one at work and started on Mike's free shoe that shone already in the electric light.

"Bill's a yell of laughter," Mike said.

I was drinking red wine, and so far behind them that I felt a little uncomfortable about all this shoe-shining. I looked around the room. At the next table was Pedro Romero. He stood up when I nodded, and asked me to come over and meet a friend. His table was beside ours, almost touching. I met the friend, a Madrid bull-fight critic, a little man with a drawn face. I told Romero how much I liked his work, and he was very pleased. We talked Spanish and the critic knew a little French. I reached to our table for my wine-bottle, but the critic took my arm. Romero laughed.

"Drink here," he said in English.

He was very bashful about his English, but he was really very pleased with it, and as we went on talking he brought out words he was not sure of, and asked me about them. He was anxious to know the English for *Corrida de toros,* the exact translation. Bull-fight he was suspicious of. I explained that bull-fight in Spanish was the *lidia* of a *toro.* The Spanish word *corrida* means in English the running of bulls—the French translation is *Course de taureaux.* The critic put that in. There is no Spanish word for bull-fight.

Pedro Romero said he had learned a little English in Gibraltar. He was born in Ronda. That is not far above Gibraltar. He started bull-fighting in Malaga in the bull-fighting school there. He had only been at it three years. The bull-fight critic joked him about the number of *Malagueño* expressions he used. He was nineteen years old, he said. His older brother was with him as a banderillero, but he did not live in this hotel. He lived in a smaller hotel with the other people who worked for Romero. He asked me how many times I had seen him in the ring. I told him only three. It was really only two, but I did not want to explain after I had made the mistake.

"Where did you see me the other time? In Madrid?"

"Yes," I lied. I had read the accounts of his two appearances in Madrid in the bull-fight papers, so I was all right.

"The first or the second time?"

"The first."

"I was very bad," he said. "The second time I was better. You remember?" He turned to the critic.

He was not at all embarrassed. He talked of his work as something altogether apart from himself. There was nothing conceited or braggartly about him.

"I like it very much that you like my work," he said. "But you haven't seen it yet. To-morrow, if I get a good bull, I will try and show it to you."

When he said this he smiled, anxious that neither the bull-fight critic nor I would think he was boasting.

"I am anxious to see it," the critic said. "I would like to be convinced."

"He doesn't like my work much." Romero turned to me. He was serious.

The critic explained that he liked it very much, but that so far it had been incomplete.

"Wait till to-morrow, if a good one comes out."

"Have you seen the bulls for to-morrow?" the critic asked me.

"Yes. I saw them unloaded."

Pedro Romero leaned forward.

"What did you think of them?"

"Very nice," I said. "About twenty-six arrobas. Very short horns. Haven't you seen them?"

"Oh, yes," said Romero.

"They won't weigh twenty-six arrobas," said the critic.

"No," said Romero.

"They've got bananas for horns," the critic said.

"You call them bananas?" asked Romero. He turned to me and smiled. "*You* wouldn't call them bananas?"

"No," I said. "They're horns all right."

"They're very short," said Pedro Romero. "Very, very short. Still, they aren't bananas."

"I say, Jake," Brett called from the next table, "you *have* deserted us."

"Just temporarily," I said. "We're talking bulls."

"You *are* superior."

"Tell him that bulls have no balls," Mike shouted. He was drunk.

Romero looked at me inquiringly.

"Drunk," I said. "Borracho! Muy borracho!"

"You might introduce your friends," Brett said. She had not stopped looking at Pedro Romero. I asked them if they would like to have coffee with us. They both stood up. Romero's face was very brown. He had very nice manners.

I introduced them all around and they started to sit down, but there was not enough room, so we all moved over to the big table by the wall to have coffee. Mike ordered a bottle of Fundador and glasses for everybody. There was a lot of drunken talking.

"Tell him I think writing is lousy," Bill said. "Go on, tell him. Tell him I'm ashamed of being a writer."

Pedro Romero was sitting beside Brett and listening to her.

"Go on. Tell him!" Bill said.

Romero looked up smiling.

"This gentleman," I said, "is a writer."

Romero was impressed. "This other one, too," I said, pointing at Cohn.

"He looks like Villalta," Romero said, looking at Bill. "Rafael, doesn't he look like Villalta?"

"I can't see it," the critic said.

"Really," Romero said in Spanish. "He looks a lot like Villalta. What does the drunken one do?"

"Nothing."

"Is that why he drinks?"

"No. He's waiting to marry this lady."

"Tell him bulls have no balls!" Mike shouted, very drunk, from the other end of the table.

"What does he say?"

"He's drunk."

"Jake," Mike called. "Tell him bulls have no balls!"

"You understand?" I said.

"Yes."

I was sure he didn't, so it was all right.

"Tell him Brett wants to see him put on those green pants."

"Pipe down, Mike."

"Tell him Brett is dying to know how he can get into those pants."

"Pipe down."

During this Romero was fingering his glass and talking with Brett. Brett was talking French and he was talking Spanish and a little English, and laughing.

Bill was filling the glasses.

"Tell him Brett wants to come into—"

"Oh, pipe down, Mike, for Christ's sake!"

Romero looked up smiling. "Pipe down! I know that," he said.

Just then Montoya came into the room. He started to smile at me, then he saw Pedro Romero with a big glass of cognac in his hand, sitting laughing between me and a woman with bare shoulders, at a table full of drunks. He did not even nod.

Montoya went out of the room. Mike was on his feet proposing a toast. "Let's all drink to—" he began. "Pedro Romero," I said. Everybody stood up. Romero took it very seriously, and we touched glasses and drank it down, I rushing it a little because Mike was trying to make it clear that that was not at all what he was going to drink to. But it went off all right, and Pedro Romero shook hands with every one and he and the critic went out together.

"My God! he's a lovely boy," Brett said. "And how I would love to see him get into those clothes. He must use a shoe-horn."

"I started to tell him," Mike began.

"And Jake kept interrupting me. Why do you interrupt me? Do you think you talk Spanish better than I do?"

"Oh, shut up, Mike! Nobody interrupted you."

"No, I'd like to get this settled." He turned away from me. "Do you think you amount to something, Cohn? Do you think you belong here among us? People who are out to have a good time? For God's sake don't be so noisy, Cohn!"

"Oh, cut it out, Mike," Cohn said.

"Do you think Brett wants you here? Do you think you add to the party? Why don't you say something?"

"I said all I had to say the other night, Mike."

"I'm not one of your literary chaps." Mike stood shakily and leaned against the table. "I'm not clever. But I do know when I'm not wanted. Why don't you see when you're not wanted, Cohn? Go away. Go away, for God's sake. Take that sad Jewish face away. Don't you think I'm right?"

He looked at us.

"Sure," I said. "Let's all go over to the Iruña."

"No. Don't you think I'm right? I love that woman."

"Oh, don't start that again. Do shove it along, Michael," Brett said.

"Don't you think I'm right, Jake?"

Cohn still sat at the table. His face had the sallow, yellow look it got when he was insulted, but somehow he seemed to be enjoying it. The childish, drunken heroics of it. It was his affair with a lady of title.

"Jake," Mike said. He was almost crying. "You know I'm right. Listen, you!" He turned to Cohn: "Go away! Go away now!"

"But I won't go, Mike," said Cohn.

"Then I'll make you!" Mike started toward him around the table. Cohn stood up and took off his glasses. He stood

[43]

waiting, his face sallow, his hands fairly low, proudly and firmly waiting for the assault, ready to do battle for his lady love.

I grabbed Mike. "Come on to the café," I said. "You can't hit him here in the hotel."

"Good!" said Mike. "Good idea!"

We started off. I looked back as Mike stumbled up the stairs and saw Cohn putting his glasses on again. Bill was sitting at the table pouring another glass of Fundador. Brett was sitting looking straight ahead at nothing.

Outside on the square it had stopped raining and the moon was trying to get through the clouds. There was a wind blowing. The military band was playing and the crowd was massed on the far side of the square where the fireworks specialist and his son were trying to send up fire balloons. A balloon would start up jerkily, on a great bias, and be torn by the wind or blown against the houses of the square. Some fell into the crowd. The magnesium flared and the fireworks exploded and chased about in the crowd. There was no one dancing in the square. The gravel was too wet.

Brett came out with Bill and joined us. We stood in the crowd and watched Don Manuel Orquito, the fireworks king, standing on a little platform, carefully starting the balloons with sticks, standing above the heads of the crowd to launch the balloons off into the wind. The wind brought them all down, and Don Manuel Orquito's face was sweaty in the light of his complicated fireworks that fell into the crowd and charged and chased, sputtering and cracking, between the legs of the people. The people shouted as each new luminous paper bubble careened, caught fire, and fell.

"They're razzing Don Manuel," Bill said.

"How do you know he's Don Manuel?" Brett said.

"His name's on the programme. Don Manuel Orquito, the pirotécnico of esta ciudad."

"Globos illuminados," Mike said. "A collection of globos illuminados. That's what the paper said."

The wind blew the band music away.

"I say, I wish one would go up," Brett said. "That Don Manuel chap is furious."

"He's probably worked for weeks fixing them to go off, spelling out 'Hail to San Fermin,' " Bill said.

"Globos illuminados," Mike said. "A bunch of bloody globos illuminados."

"Come on," said Brett. "We can't stand here."

"Her ladyship wants a drink," Mike said.

"How you know things," Brett said.

Inside, the café was crowded and very noisy. No one noticed us come in. We could not find a table. There was a great noise going on.

"Come on, let's get out of here," Bill said.

Outside the paseo was going in under the arcade. There were some English and Americans from Biarritz in sport clothes scattered at the tables. Some of the women stared at the people going by with lorgnons. We had acquired, at some time, a friend of Bill's from Biarritz. She was staying with another girl at the Grand Hotel. The other girl had a headache and had gone to bed.

"Here's the pub," Mike said. It was the Bar Milano, a small, tough bar where you could get food and where they danced in the back room. We all sat down at a table and ordered a bottle of Fundador. The bar was not full. There was nothing going on.

"This is a hell of a place," Bill said.

"It's too early."

"Let's take the bottle and come back later," Bill said. "I don't want to sit here on a night like this."

"Let's go and look at the English," Mike said. "I love to look at the English."

"They're awful," Bill said. "Where did they all come from?"

"They come from Biarritz," Mike said. "They come to see the last day of the quaint little Spanish fiesta."

"I'll festa them," Bill said.

"You're an extraordinarily beautiful girl." Mike turned to Bill's friend. "When did you come here?"

"Come off it, Michael."

"I say, she *is* a lovely girl. Where have I been? Where have I been looking all this while? You're a lovely thing. *Have* we met? Come along with me and Bill. We're going to festa the English."

"I'll festa them," Bill said. "What the hell are they doing at this fiesta?"

"Come on," Mike said. "Just us three. We're going to festa the bloody English. I hope you're not English? I'm Scotch. I hate the English. I'm going to festa them. Come on, Bill."

Through the window we saw them, all three arm in arm, going toward the café. Rockets were going up in the square.

"I'm going to sit here," Brett said.

"I'll stay with you," Cohn said.

"Oh, don't!" Brett said. "For God's sake, go off somewhere. Can't you see Jake and I want to talk?"

"I didn't," Cohn said. "I thought I'd sit here because I felt a little tight."

"What a hell of a reason for sitting with any one. If you're tight, go to bed. Go on to bed."

"Was I rude enough to him?" Brett asked. Cohn was gone. "My God! I'm so sick of him!"

"He doesn't add much to the gayety."

"He depresses me so."

"He's behaved very badly."

"Damned badly. He had a chance to behave so well."

"He's probably waiting just outside the door now."

"Yes. He would. You know I do know how he feels. He can't believe it didn't mean anything."

"I know."

"Nobody else would behave as badly. Oh, I'm so sick of the whole thing. And Michael. Michael's been lovely, too."

"It's been damned hard on Mike."

"Yes. But he didn't need to be a swine."

"Everybody behaves badly," I said. "Give them the proper chance."

"You wouldn't behave badly." Brett looked at me.

"I'd be as big an ass as Cohn," I said.

"Darling, don't let's talk a lot of rot."

"All right. Talk about anything you like."

"Don't be difficult. You're the only person I've got, and I feel rather awful to-night."

"You've got Mike."

"Yes, Mike. Hasn't he been pretty?"

"Well," I said, "it's been damned hard on Mike, having Cohn around and seeing him with you."

"Don't I know it, darling? Please don't make me feel any worse than I do."

Brett was nervous as I had never seen her before. She kept looking away from me and looking ahead at the wall.

"Want to go for a walk?"

"Yes. Come on."

I corked up the Fundador bottle and gave it to the bartender.

"Let's have one more drink of that," Brett said. "My nerves are rotten."

We each drank a glass of the smooth amontillado brandy.

"Come on," said Brett.

As we came out the door I saw Cohn walk out from under the arcade.

"He *was* there," Brett said.

"He can't be away from you."

"Poor devil!"

"I'm not sorry for him. I hate him, myself."

"I hate him, too," she shivered. "I hate his damned suffering."

We walked arm in arm down the side street away from the crowd and the lights of the square. The street was dark and wet, and we walked along it to the fortifications at the edge of town. We passed wine-shops with light coming out from their doors onto the black, wet street, and sudden bursts of music.

"Want to go in?"

"No."

We walked out across the wet grass and onto the stone wall of the fortifications. I spread a newspaper on the stone and Brett sat down. Across the plain it was dark, and we could see the mountains. The wind was high up and took the clouds across the moon. Below us were the dark pits of the fortifications. Behind were the trees and the shadow of the cathedral, and the town silhouetted against the moon.

"Don't feel bad," I said.

"I feel like hell," Brett said. "Don't let's talk."

We looked out at the plain. The long lines of trees were dark in the moonlight. There were the lights of a car on the road climbing the mountain. Up on the top of the mountain we saw the lights of the fort. Below to the left was the river. It was high from the rain, and black and smooth. Trees were dark along the banks. We sat and looked out. Brett stared straight ahead. Suddenly she shivered.

"It's cold."

"Want to walk back?"

"Through the park."

We climbed down. It was clouding over again. In the park it was dark under the trees.

"Do you still love me, Jake?"

"Yes," I said.

"Because I'm a goner," Brett said.

"How?"

"I'm a goner. I'm mad about the Romero boy. I'm in love with him, I think."

"I wouldn't be if I were you."

"I can't help it. I'm a goner. It's tearing me all up inside."

"Don't do it."

"I can't help it. I've never been able to help anything."

"You ought to stop it."

"How can I stop it? I can't stop things. Feel that?"

Her hand was trembling.

"I'm like that all through."

"You oughtn't to do it."

"I can't help it. I'm a goner now, anyway. Don't you see the difference?"

"No."

"I've got to do something. I've got to do something I really want to do. I've lost my self-respect."

"You don't have to do that."

"Oh, darling, don't be difficult. What do you think it's meant to have that damned Jew about, and Mike the way he's acted?"

"Sure."

"I can't just stay tight all the time."

"No."

"Oh, darling, please stay by me. Please stay by me and see me through this."

"Sure."

"I don't say it's right. It is right though for me. God knows, I've never felt such a bitch."

"What do you want me to do?"

"Come on," Brett said. "Let's go and find him."

Together we walked down the gravel path in the park in the dark, under the trees and then out from under the trees and past the gate into the street that led into town.

Pedro Romero was in the café. He was

at a table with other bull-fighters and bull-fight critics. They were smoking cigars. When we came in they looked up. Romero smiled and bowed. We sat down at a table half-way down the room.

"Ask him to come over and have a drink."

"Not yet. He'll come over."

"I can't look at him."

"He's nice to look at," I said.

"I've always done just what I wanted."

"I know."

"I do feel such a bitch."

"Well," I said.

"My God!" said Brett, "the things a woman goes through."

"Yes?"

"Oh, I do feel such a bitch."

I looked across at the table. Pedro Romero smiled. He said something to the other people at his table, and stood up. He came over to our table. I stood up and we shook hands.

"Won't you have a drink?"

"You must have a drink with me," he said. He seated himself, asking Brett's permission without saying anything. He had very nice manners. But he kept on smoking his cigar. It went well with his face.

"You like cigars?" I asked.

"Oh, yes. I always smoke cigars."

It was part of his system of authority. It made him seem older. I noticed his skin. It was clear and smooth and very brown. There was a triangular scar on his cheek-bone. I saw he was watching Brett. He felt there was something between them. He must have felt it when Brett gave him her hand. He was being very careful. I think he was sure, but he did not want to make any mistake.

"You fight to-morrow?" I said.

"Yes," he said. "Algabeno was hurt to-day in Madrid. Did you hear?"

"No," I said. "Badly?"

He shook his head.

"Nothing. Here," he showed his hand.

Brett reached out and spread the fingers apart.

"Oh!" he said in English, "you tell fortunes?"

"Sometimes. Do you mind?"

"No. I like it." He spread his hand flat on the table. "Tell me I live for always, and be a millionaire."

He was still very polite, but he was surer of himself. "Look," he said, "do you see any bulls in my hand?"

He laughed. His hand was very fine and the wrist was small.

"There are thousands of bulls," Brett said. She was not at all nervous now. She looked lovely.

"Good," Romero laughed. "At a thousand duros apiece," he said to me in Spanish. "Tell me some more."

"It's a good hand," Brett said. "I think he'll live a long time."

"Say it to me. Not to your friend."

"I said you'd live a long time."

"I know it," Romero said. "I'm never going to die."

I tapped with my finger-tips on the table. Romero saw it. He shook his head.

"No. Don't do that. The bulls are my best friends."

I translated to Brett.

"You kill your friends?" she asked.

"Always," he said in English, and laughed. "So they don't kill me." He looked at her across the table.

"You know English well."

"Yes," he said. "Pretty well, sometimes. But I must not let anybody know. It would be very bad, a torero who speaks English."

"Why?" asked Brett.

"It would be bad. The people would not like it. Not yet."

"Why not?"

"They would not like it. Bull-fighters are not like that."

"What are bull-fighters like?"

He laughed and tipped his hat down over his eyes and changed the angle of

[47]

his cigar and the expression of his face.

"Like at the table," he said. I glanced over. He had mimicked exactly the expression of Nacional. He smiled, his face natural again. "No. I must forget English."

"Don't forget it, yet," Brett said.

"No?"

"No."

"All right."

He laughed again.

"I would like a hat like that," Brett said.

"Good. I'll get you one."

"Right. See that you do."

"I will. I'll get you one to-night."

I stood up. Romero rose, too.

"Sit down," I said. "I must go and find our friends and bring them here."

He looked at me. It was a final look to ask if it were understood. It was understood all right.

"Sit down," Brett said to him. "You must teach me Spanish."

He sat down and looked at her across the table. I went out. The hard-eyed people at the bull-fighter table watched me go. It was not pleasant. When I came back and looked in the café, twenty minutes later, Brett and Pedro Romero were gone. The coffee-glasses and our three empty cognac-glasses were on the table. A waiter came with a cloth and picked up the glasses and mopped off the table.

CHAPTER XVII

Outside the Bar Milano I found Bill and Mike and Edna. Edna was the girl's name.

"We've been thrown out," Edna said.

"By the police," said Mike. "There's some people in there that don't like me."

"I've kept them out of four fights," Edna said. "You've got to help me."

Bill's face was red.

"Come back in, Edna," he said. "Go on in there and dance with Mike."

"It's silly," Edna said. "There'll just be another row."

"Damned Biarritz swine," Bill said.

"Come on," Mike said. "After all, it's a pub. They can't occupy a whole pub."

"Good old Mike," Bill said. "Damned English swine come here and insult Mike and try and spoil the fiesta."

"They're so bloody," Mike said. "I hate the English."

"They can't insult Mike," Bill said. "Mike is a swell fellow. They can't insult Mike. I won't stand it. Who cares if he is a damn bankrupt?" His voice broke.

"Who cares?" Mike said. "I don't care. Jake doesn't care. Do *you* care?"

"No," Edna said. "Are you a bankrupt?"

"Of course I am. You don't care, do you, Bill?"

Bill put his arm around Mike's shoulder.

"I wish to hell I was a bankrupt. I'd show those bastards."

"They're just English," Mike said. "It never makes any difference what the English say."

"The dirty swine," Bill said. "I'm going to clean them out."

"Bill," Edna looked at me. "Please don't go in again, Bill. They're so stupid."

"That's it," said Mike. "They're stupid. I knew that was what it was."

"They can't say things like that about Mike," Bill said.

"Do you know them?" I asked Mike.

"No. I never saw them. They say they know me."

"I won't stand it," Bill said.

"Come on. Let's go over to the Suizo," I said.

"They're a bunch of Edna's friends from Biarritz," Bill said.

"They're simply stupid," Edna said.

"One of them's Charley Blackman, from Chicago," Bill said.

"I was never in Chicago," Mike said. Edna started to laugh and could not stop.

"Take me away from here," she said, "you bankrupts."

"What kind of a row was it?" I asked Edna. We were walking across the square to the Suizo. Bill was gone.

"I don't know what happened, but some one had the police called to keep Mike out of the back room. There were some people that had known Mike at Cannes. What's the matter with Mike?"

"Probably he owes them money," I said. "That's what people usually get bitter about."

In front of the ticket-booths out in the square there were two lines of people waiting. They were sitting on chairs or crouched on the ground with blankets and newspapers around them. They were waiting for the wickets to open in the morning to buy tickets for the bull-fight. The night was clearing and the moon was out. Some of the people in the line were sleeping.

At the Café Suizo we had just sat down and ordered Fundador when Robert Cohn came up.

"Where's Brett?" he asked.

"I don't know."

"She was with you."

"She must have gone to bed."

"She's not."

"I don't know where she is."

His face was sallow under the light. He was standing up.

"Tell me where she is."

"Sit down," I said. "I don't know where she is."

"The hell you don't!"

"You can shut your face."

"Tell me where Brett is."

"I'll not tell you a damn thing."

"You know where she is."

"If I did I wouldn't tell you."

"Oh, go to hell, Cohn," Mike called from the table. "Brett's gone off with the bull-fighter chap. They're on their honeymoon."

"You shut up."

"Oh, go to hell!" Mike said languidly.

"Is that where she is?" Cohn turned to me.

"Go to hell!"

"She was with you. Is that where she is?"

"Go to hell!"

"I'll make you tell me"—he stepped forward—"you damned pimp."

I swung at him and he ducked. I saw his face duck sideways in the light. He hit me and I sat down on the pavement. As I started to get on my feet he hit me twice. I went down backward under a table. I tried to get up and felt I did not have any legs. I felt I must get on my feet and try and hit him. Mike helped me up. Some one poured a carafe of water on my head. Mike had an arm around me, and I found I was sitting on a chair. Mike was pulling at my ears.

"I say, you were cold," Mike said.

"Where the hell were you?"

"Oh, I was around."

"You didn't want to mix in it?"

"He knocked Mike down, too," Edna said.

"He didn't knock me out," Mike said. "I just lay there."

"Does this happen every night at your fiestas?" Edna asked. "Wasn't that Mr. Cohn?"

"I'm all right," I said. "My head's a little wobbly."

There were several waiters and a crowd of people standing around.

"Vaya!" said Mike. "Get away. Go on."

The waiters moved the people away.

"It was quite a thing to watch," Edna said. "He must be a boxer."

"He is."

"I wish Bill had been here," Edna said.

"I'd like to have seen Bill knocked down, too. I've always wanted to see Bill knocked down. He's so big."

"I was hoping he would knock down a waiter," Mike said, "and get arrested. I'd like to see Mr. Robert Cohn in jail."

"No," I said.

"Oh, no," said Edna. "You don't mean that."

"I do, though," Mike said. "I'm not one of these chaps likes being knocked about. I never play games, even."

Mike took a drink.

"I never liked to hunt, you know. There was always the danger of having a horse fall on you. How do you feel, Jake?"

"All right."

"You're nice," Edna said to Mike. "Are you really a bankrupt?"

"I'm a tremendous bankrupt," Mike said. "I owe money to everybody. Don't you owe any money?"

"Tons."

"I owe everybody money," Mike said. "I borrowed a hundred pesetas from Montoya to-night."

"The hell you did," I said.

"I'll pay it back," Mike said. "I always pay everything back."

"That's why you're a bankrupt, isn't it?" Edna said.

I stood up. I had heard them talking from a long way away. It all seemed like some bad play.

"I'm going over to the hotel," I said. Then I heard them talking about me.

"Is he all right?" Edna asked.

"We'd better walk with him."

"I'm all right," I said. "Don't come. I'll see you all later."

I walked away from the café. They were sitting at the table. I looked back at them and at the empty tables. There was a waiter sitting at one of the tables with his head in his hands.

Walking across the square to the hotel everything looked new and changed. I

had never seen the trees before. I had never seen the flagpoles before, nor the front of the theatre. It was all different. I felt as I felt once coming home from an out-of-town football game. I was carrying a suitcase with my football things in it, and I walked up the street from the station in the town I had lived in all my life and it was all new. They were raking the lawns and burning leaves in the road, and I stopped for a long time and watched. It was all strange. Then I went on, and my feet seemed to be a long way off, and everything seemed to come from a long way off, and I could hear my feet walking a great distance away. I had been kicked in the head early in the game. It was like that crossing the square. It was like that going up the stairs in the hotel. Going up the stairs took a long time, and I had the feeling that I was carrying my suitcase. There was a light in the room. Bill came out and met me in the hall.

"Say," he said, "go up and see Cohn. He's been in a jam, and he's asking for you."

"The hell with him."

"Go on. Go on up and see him."

I did not want to climb another flight of stairs.

"What are you looking at me that way for?"

"I'm not looking at you. Go on up and see Cohn. He's in bad shape."

"You were drunk a little while ago," I said.

"I'm drunk now," Bill said. "But you go up and see Cohn. He wants to see you."

"All right," I said. It was just a matter of climbing more stairs. I went on up the stairs carrying my phantom suitcase. I walked down the hall to Cohn's room. The door was shut and I knocked.

"Who is it?"

"Barnes."

"Come in, Jake."

I opened the door and went in, and set

down my suitcase. There was no light in the room. Cohn was lying, face down, on the bed in the dark.

"Hello, Jake."

"Don't call me Jake."

I stood by the door. It was just like this that I had come home. Now it was a hot bath that I needed. A deep, hot bath, to lie back in.

"Where's the bathroom?" I asked.

Cohn was crying. There he was, face down on the bed, crying. He had on a white polo shirt, the kind he'd worn at Princeton.

"I'm sorry, Jake. Please forgive me."

"Forgive you, hell."

"Please forgive me, Jake."

I did not say anything. I stood there by the door.

"I was crazy. You must see how it was."

"Oh, that's all right."

"I couldn't stand it about Brett."

"You called me a pimp."

I did not care. I wanted a hot bath. I wanted a hot bath in deep water.

"I know. Please don't remember it. I was crazy."

"That's all right."

He was crying. His voice was funny. He lay there in his white shirt on the bed in the dark. His polo shirt.

"I'm going away in the morning."

He was crying without making any noise.

"I just couldn't stand it about Brett. I've been through hell, Jake. It's been simply hell. When I met her down here Brett treated me as though I were a perfect stranger. I just couldn't stand it. We lived together at San Sebastian. I suppose you know it. I can't stand it any more."

He lay there on the bed.

"Well," I said, "I'm going to take a bath."

"You were the only friend I had, and I loved Brett so."

"Well," I said, "so long."

"I guess it isn't any use," he said. "I guess it isn't any damn use."

"What?"

"Everything. Please say you forgive me, Jake."

"Sure," I said. "It's all right."

"I felt so terribly. I've been through such hell, Jake. Now everything's gone. Everything."

"Well," I said, "so long. I've got to go."

He rolled over, sat on the edge of the bed, and then stood up.

"So long, Jake," he said. "You'll shake hands, won't you?"

"Sure. Why not?"

We shook hands. In the dark I could not see his face very well.

"Well," I said, "see you in the morning."

"I'm going away in the morning."

"Oh, yes," I said.

I went out. Cohn was standing in the door of the room.

"Are you all right, Jake?" he asked.

"Oh, yes," I said. "I'm all right."

I could not find the bathroom. After a while I found it. There was a deep stone tub. I turned on the taps and the water would not run. I sat down on the edge of the bath-tub. When I got up to go I found I had taken off my shoes. I hunted for them and found them and carried them down-stairs. I found my room and went inside and undressed and got into bed.

I woke with a headache and the noise of the bands going by in the street. I remembered I had promised to take Bill's friend Edna to see the bulls go through the street and into the ring. I dressed and went down-stairs and out into the cold early morning. People were crossing the square, hurrying toward the bull-ring. Across the square were the two lines of men in front of the ticket-booths. They were still waiting for the tickets to go on sale at seven o'clock. I hurried across the street to the café. The waiter told me that my friends had been there and gone.

"How many were they?"

"Two gentlemen and a lady."

That was all right. Bill and Mike were with Edna. She had been afraid last night they would pass out. That was why I was to be sure to take her. I drank the coffee and hurried with the other people toward the bull-ring. I was not groggy now. There was only a bad headache. Everything looked sharp and clear, and the town smelt of the early morning.

The stretch of ground from the edge of the town to the bull-ring was muddy. There was a crowd all along the fence that led to the ring, and the outside balconies and the top of the bull-ring were solid with people. I heard the rocket and I knew I could not get into the ring in time to see the bulls come in, so I shoved through the crowd to the fence. I was pushed close against the planks of the fence. Between the two fences of the runway the police were clearing the crowd along. They walked or trotted on into the bull-ring. Then people commenced to come running. A drunk slipped and fell. Two policemen grabbed him and rushed him over to the fence. The crowd were running fast now. There was a great shout from the crowd, and putting my head through between the boards I saw the bulls just coming out of the street into the long running pen. They were going fast and gaining on the crowd. Just then another drunk started out from the fence with a blouse in his hands. He wanted to do capework with the bulls. The two policemen tore out, collared him, one hit him with a club, and they dragged him against the fence and stood flattened out against the fence as the last of the crowd and the bulls went by. There were so many people running ahead of the bulls that the mass thickened and slowed up going through the gate into the ring, and as the bulls passed, galloping together, heavy, muddy-sided, horns swinging, one shot ahead, caught a man in the running crowd in the back and lifted him in the air. Both the man's arms were by his sides, his head went back as the horn went in, and the bull lifted him and then dropped him. The bull picked another man running in front, but the man disappeared into the crowd, and the crowd was through the gate and into the ring with the bulls behind them. The red door of the ring went shut, the crowd on the outside balconies of the bull-ring were pressing through to the inside, there was a shout, then another shout.

The man who had been gored lay face down in the trampled mud. People climbed over the fence, and I could not see the man because the crowd was so thick around him. From inside the ring came the shouts. Each shout meant a charge by some bull into the crowd. You could tell by the degree of intensity in the shout how bad a thing it was that was happening. Then the rocket went up that meant the steers had gotten the bulls out of the ring and into the corrals. I left the fence and started back toward the town.

Back in the town I went to the café to have a second coffee and some buttered toast. The waiters were sweeping out the café and mopping off the tables. One came over and took my order.

"Anything happen at the encierro?"

"I didn't see it all. One man was badly cogido."

"Where?"

"Here." I put one hand on the small of my back and the other on my chest, where it looked as though the horn must have come through. The waiter nodded his head and swept the crumbs from the table with his cloth.

"Badly cogido," he said. "All for sport. All for pleasure."

He went away and came back with the

long-handled coffee and milk pots. He poured the milk and coffee. It came out of the long spouts in two streams into the big cup. The waiter nodded his head.

"Badly cogido through the back," he said. He put the pots down on the table and sat down in the chair at the table. "A big horn wound. All for fun. Just for fun. What do you think of that?"

"I don't know."

"That's it. All for fun. Fun, you understand."

"You're not an aficionado?"

"Me? What are bulls? Animals. Brute animals." He stood up and put his hand on the small of his back. "Right through the back. A cornada right through the back. For fun—you understand."

He shook his head and walked away, carrying the coffee-pots. Two men were going by in the street. The waiter shouted to them. They were grave-looking. One shook his head. "Muerto!" he called.

The waiter nodded his head. The two men went on. They were on some errand. The waiter came over to my table.

"You hear? Muerto. Dead. He's dead. With a horn through him. All for morning fun. Es muy flamenco."

"It's bad."

"Not for me," the waiter said. "No fun in that for me."

Later in the day we learned that the man who was killed was named Vicente Girones, and came from near Tafalla. The next day in the paper we read that he was twenty-eight years old, and had a farm, a wife, and two children. He had continued to come to the fiesta each year after he was married. The next day his wife came in from Tafalla to be with the body, and the day after there was a service in the chapel of San Fermin, and the coffin was carried to the railway-station by members of the dancing and drinking society of Tafalla. The drums marched ahead, and there was music on the fifes, and behind the men who carried the coffin walked the wife and two children. . . . Behind them marched all the members of the dancing and drinking societies of Pamplona, Estella, Tafalla, and Sanguesa who could stay over for the funeral. The coffin was loaded into the baggage-car of the train, and the widow and the two children rode, sitting, all three together, in an open third-class railway-carriage. The train started with a jerk, and then ran smoothly, going down grade around the edge of the plateau and out into the fields of grain that blew in the wind on the plain on the way to Tafalla.

The bull who killed Vicente Girones was named Bocanegra, was Number 118 of the bull-breeding establishment of Sanchez Taberno, and was killed by Pedro Romero as the third bull of that same afternoon. His ear was cut by popular acclamation and given to Pedro Romero, who, in turn, gave it to Brett, who wrapped it in a handkerchief belonging to myself, and left both ear and handkerchief, along with a number of Muratti cigarette-stubs, shoved far back in the drawer of the bed-table that stood beside her bed in the Hotel Montoya, in Pamplona.

Back in the hotel, the night watchman was sitting on a bench inside the door. He had been there all night and was very sleepy. He stood up as I came in. Three of the waitresses came in at the same time. They had been to the morning show at the bull-ring. They went upstairs laughing. I followed them up-stairs and went into my room. I took off my shoes and lay down on the bed. The window was open onto the balcony and the sunlight was bright in the room. I did not feel sleepy. It must have been half past three o'clock when I had gone to bed and the bands had waked me at six. My jaw was sore on both sides. I felt it with my thumb and fingers. That damn

Cohn. He should have hit somebody the first time he was insulted, and then gone away. He was so sure that Brett loved him. He was going to stay, and true love would conquer all. Some one knocked on the door.

"Come in."

It was Bill and Mike. They sat down on the bed.

"Some encierro," Bill said. "Some encierro."

"I say, weren't you there?" Mike asked. "Ring for some beer, Bill."

"What a morning!" Bill said. He mopped off his face. "My God! what a morning! And here's old Jake. Old Jake, the human punching-bag."

"What happened inside?"

"Good God!" Bill said, "what happened, Mike?"

"There were these bulls coming in," Mike said. "Just ahead of them was the crowd, and some chap tripped and brought the whole lot of them down."

"And the bulls all came in right over them," Bill said.

"I heard them yell."

"That was Edna," Bill said.

"Chaps kept coming out and waving their shirts."

"One bull went along the barrera and hooked everybody over."

"They took about twenty chaps to the infirmary," Mike said.

"What a morning!" Bill said. "The damn police kept arresting chaps that wanted to go and commit suicide with the bulls."

"The steers took them in, in the end," Mike said.

"It took about an hour."

"It was really about a quarter of an hour," Mike objected.

"Oh, go to hell," Bill said. "You've been in the war. It was two hours and a half for me."

"Where's that beer?" Mike asked.

"What did you do with the lovely Edna?"

"We took her home just now. She's gone to bed."

"How did she like it?"

"Fine. We told her it was just like that every morning."

"She was impressed," Mike said.

"She wanted us to go down in the ring, too," Bill said. "She likes action."

"I said it wouldn't be fair to my creditors," Mike said.

"What a morning," Bill said. "And what a night!"

"How's your jaw, Jake?" Mike asked.

"Sore," I said.

Bill laughed.

"Why didn't you hit him with a chair?"

"You can talk," Mike said. "He'd have knocked you out, too. I never saw him hit me. I rather think I saw him just before, and then quite suddenly I was sitting down in the street, and Jake was lying under a table."

"Where did he go afterward?" I asked.

"Here she is," Mike said. "Here's the beautiful lady with the beer."

The chambermaid put the tray with the beer-bottles and glasses down on the table.

"Now bring up three more bottles," Mike said.

"Where did Cohn go after he hit me?" I asked Bill.

"Don't you know about that?" Mike was opening a beer-bottle. He poured the beer into one of the glasses, holding the glass close to the bottle.

"Really?" Bill asked.

"Why he went in and found Brett and the bull-fighter chap in the bull-fighter's room, and then he massacred the poor, bloody bull-fighter."

"No."

"Yes."

"What a night!" Bill said.

"He nearly killed the poor, bloody bull-fighter. Then Cohn wanted to take Brett away. Wanted to make an honest woman of her, I imagine. Damned touching scene."

He took a long drink of the beer.

"He is an ass."

"What happened?"

"Brett gave him what for. She told him off. I think she was rather good."

"I'll bet she was," Bill said.

"Then Cohn broke down and cried, and wanted to shake hands with the bull-fighter fellow. He wanted to shake hands with Brett, too."

"I know. He shook hands with me."

"Did he? Well, they weren't having any of it. The bull-fighter fellow was rather good. He didn't say much, but he kept getting up and getting knocked down again. Cohn couldn't knock him out. It must have been damned funny."

"Where did you hear all this?"

"Brett. I saw her this morning."

"What happened finally?"

"It seems the bull-fighter fellow was sitting on the bed. He'd been knocked down about fifteen times, and he wanted to fight some more. Brett held him and wouldn't let him get up. He was weak, but Brett couldn't hold him, and he got up. Then Cohn said he wouldn't hit him again. Said he couldn't do it. Said it would be wicked. So the bull-fighter chap sort of rather staggered over to him. Cohn went back against the wall.

" 'So you won't hit me?'

" 'No,' said Cohn. 'I'd be ashamed to.'

"So the bull-fighter fellow hit him just as hard as he could in the face, and then sat down on the floor. He couldn't get up, Brett said. Cohn wanted to pick him up and carry him to the bed. He said if Cohn helped him he'd kill him, and he'd kill him anyway this morning if Cohn wasn't out of town. Cohn was crying, and Brett had told him off, and he

wanted to shake hands. I've told you that before."

"Tell the rest," Bill said.

"It seems the bull-fighter chap was sitting on the floor. He was waiting to get strength enough to get up and hit Cohn again. Brett wasn't having any shaking hands, and Cohn was crying and telling her how much he loved her, and she was telling him not to be a ruddy ass. Then Cohn leaned down to shake hands with the bull-fighter fellow. No hard feelings, you know. All for forgiveness. And the bull-fighter chap hit him in the face again."

"That's quite a kid," Bill said.

"He ruined Cohn," Mike said. "You know I don't think Cohn will ever want to knock people about again."

"When did you see Brett?"

"This morning. She came in to get some things. She's looking after this Romero lad."

He poured out another bottle of beer.

"Brett's rather cut up. But she loves looking after people. That's how we came to go off together. She was looking after me."

"I know," I said.

"I'm rather drunk," Mike said. "I think I'll *stay* rather drunk. This is all awfully amusing, but it's not too pleasant. It's not too pleasant for me."

He drank off the beer.

"I gave Brett what for, you know. I said if she would go about with Jews and bull-fighters and such people, she must expect trouble." He leaned forward. "I say, Jake, do you mind if I drink that bottle of yours? She'll bring you another one."

"Please," I said. "I wasn't drinking it, anyway."

Mike started to open the bottle. "Would you mind opening it?" I pressed up the wire fastener and poured it for him.

[55]

"You know," Mike went on, "Brett was rather good. She's always rather good. I gave her a fearful hiding about Jews and bull-fighters, and all those sort of people, and do you know what she said: 'Yes. I've had such a hell of a happy life with the British aristocracy!'"

He took a drink.

"That was rather good. Ashley, chap she got the title from, was a sailor, you know. Ninth baronet. When he came home he wouldn't sleep in a bed. Always made Brett sleep on the floor. Finally, when he got really bad, he used to tell her he'd kill her. Always slept with a loaded service revolver. Brett used to take the shells out when he'd gone to sleep. She hasn't had an absolutely happy life, Brett. Damned shame, too. She enjoys things so."

He stood up. His hand was shaky.

"I'm going in the room. Try and get a little sleep."

He smiled.

"We go too long without sleep in these fiestas. I'm going to start now and get plenty of sleep. Damn bad thing not to get sleep. Makes you frightfully nervy."

"We'll see you at noon at the Iruña," Bill said.

Mike went out the door. We heard him in the next room.

He rang the bell and the chambermaid came and knocked at the door.

"Bring up half a dozen bottles of beer and a bottle of Fundador," Mike told her.

"Si, Señorito."

"I'm going to bed," Bill said. "Poor old Mike. I had a hell of a row about him last night."

"Where? At that Milano place?"

"Yes. There was a fellow there that had helped pay Brett and Mike out of Cannes, once. He was damned nasty."

"I know the story."

"I didn't. Nobody ought to have a right to say things about Mike."

"That's what makes it bad."

"They oughtn't to have any right. I wish to hell they didn't have any right. I'm going to bed."

"Was anybody killed in the ring?"

"I don't think so. Just badly hurt."

"A man was killed outside in the runway."

"Was there?" said Bill.

CHAPTER XVIII

At noon we were all at the café. It was crowded. We were eating shrimps and drinking beer. The town was crowded. Every street was full. Big motor-cars from Biarritz and San Sebastian kept driving up and parking around the square. They brought people for the bull-fight. Sight-seeing cars came up, too. There was one with twenty-five English-women in it. They sat in the big, white car and looked through their glasses at the fiesta. The dancers were all quite drunk. It was the last day of the fiesta.

The fiesta was solid and unbroken, but the motor-cars and tourist-cars made little islands of onlookers. When the cars emptied, the onlookers were absorbed into the crowd. You did not see them again except as sports clothes, odd-looking at a table among the closely packed peasants in black smocks. The fiesta absorbed even the Biarritz English so that you did not see them unless you passed close to a table. All the time there was music in the street. The drums kept on pounding and the pipes were going. Inside the cafés men with their hands gripping the table, or on each other's shoulders, were singing the hard-voiced singing.

"Here comes Brett," Bill said.

I looked and saw her coming through the crowd in the square, walking, her head up, as though the fiesta were being staged in her honor, and she found it pleasant and amusing.

"Hello, you chaps!" she said. "I say, I *have* a thirst."

"Get another big beer," Bill said to the waiter.

"Shrimps?"

"Is Cohn gone?" Brett asked.

"Yes," Bill said. "He hired a car."

The beer came. Brett started to lift the glass mug and her hand shook. She saw it and smiled, and leaned forward and took a long sip.

"Good beer."

"Very good," I said. I was nervous about Mike. I did not think he had slept. He must have been drinking all the time, but he seemed to be under control.

"I heard Cohn had hurt you, Jake," Brett said.

"No. Knocked me out. That was all."

"I say, he did hurt Pedro Romero," Brett said. "He hurt him most badly."

"How is he?"

"He'll be all right. He won't go out of the room."

"Does he look badly?"

"Very. He was really hurt. I told him I wanted to pop out and see you chaps for a minute."

"Is he going to fight?"

"Rather. I'm going with you, if you don't mind."

"How's your boy friend?" Mike asked. He had not listened to anything that Brett had said.

"Brett's got a bull-fighter," he said. "She had a Jew named Cohn, but he turned out badly."

Brett stood up.

"I am not going to listen to that sort of rot from you, Michael."

"How's your boy friend?"

"Damned well," Brett said. "Watch him this afternoon."

"Brett's got a bull-fighter," Mike said. "A beautiful, bloody bull-fighter."

"Would you mind walking over with me? I want to talk to you, Jake."

"Tell him all about your bull-fighter," Mike said. "Oh, to hell with your bull-fighter!" He tipped the table so that all the beers and the dish of shrimps went over in a crash.

"Come on," Brett said. "Let's get out of this."

In the crowd crossing the square I said: "How is it?"

"I'm not going to see him after lunch until the fight. His people come in and dress him. They're very angry about me, he says."

Brett was radiant. She was happy. The sun was out and the day was bright.

"I feel altogether changed," Brett said. "You've no idea, Jake."

"Anything you want me to do?"

"No, just go to the fight with me."

"We'll see you at lunch?"

"No. I'm eating with him."

We were standing under the arcade at the door of the hotel. They were carrying tables out and setting them up under the arcade.

"Want to take a turn out to the park?" Brett asked. "I don't want to go up yet. I fancy he's sleeping."

We walked along past the theatre and out of the square and along through the barracks of the fair, moving with the crowd between the lines of booths. We came out on a cross-street that led to the Paseo de Sarasate. We could see the crowd walking there, all the fashionably dressed people. They were making the turn at the upper end of the park.

"Don't let's go there," Brett said. "I don't want staring at just now."

We stood in the sunlight. It was hot and good after the rain and the clouds from the sea.

"I hope the wind goes down," Brett said. "It's very bad for him."

"So do I."

"He says the bulls are all right."

"They're good."

"Is that San Fermin's?"

Brett looked at the yellow wall of the chapel.

"Yes. Where the show started on Sunday."

"Let's go in. Do you mind? I'd rather like to pray a little for him or something."

We went in through the heavy leather door that moved very lightly. It was dark inside. Many people were praying. You saw them as your eyes adjusted themselves to the half-light. We knelt at one of the long wooden benches. After a little I felt Brett stiffen beside me, and saw she was looking straight ahead.

"Come on," she whispered throatily. "Let's get out of here. Makes me damned nervous."

Outside in the hot brightness of the street Brett looked up at the tree-tops in the wind. The praying had not been much of a success.

"Don't know why I get so nervy in church," Brett said. "Never does me any good."

We walked along.

"I'm damned bad for a religious atmosphere," Brett said. "I've the wrong type of face.

"You know," Brett said, "I'm not worried about him at all. I just feel happy about him."

"Good."

"I wish the wind would drop, though."

"It's liable to go down by five o'clock."

"Let's hope."

"You might pray," I laughed.

"Never does me any good. I've never gotten anything I prayed for. Have you?"

"Oh, yes."

"Oh, rot," said Brett. "Maybe it works for some people, though. You don't look very religious, Jake."

"I'm pretty religious."

"Oh, rot," said Brett. "Don't start

proselyting to-day. To-day's going to be bad enough as it is."

It was the first time I had seen her in the old happy, careless way since before she went off with Cohn. We were back again in front of the hotel. All the tables were set now, and already several were filled with people eating.

"Do look after Mike," Brett said. "Don't let him get too bad."

"Your frients haff gone up-stairs," the German maitre d'hôtel said in English. He was a continual eavesdropper. Brett turned to him:

"Thank you, so much. Have you anything else to say?"

"No, ma'am."

"Good," said Brett.

"Save us a table for three," I said to the German. He smiled his dirty little pink-and-white smile.

"Iss madam eating here?"

"No," Brett said.

"Den I think a tabul for two will be enuff."

"Don't talk to him," Brett said. "Mike must have been in bad shape," she said on the stairs. We passed Montoya on the stairs. He bowed and did not smile.

"I'll see you at the café," Brett said. "Thank you, so much, Jake."

We had stopped at the floor our rooms were on. She went straight down the hall and into Romero's room. She did not knock. She simply opened the door, went in, and closed it behind her.

I stood in front of the door of Mike's room and knocked. There was no answer. I tried the knob and it opened. Inside the room was in great disorder. All the bags were opened and clothing was strewn around. There were empty bottles beside the bed. Mike lay on the bed looking like a death mask of himself. He opened his eyes and looked at me.

"Hello, Jake," he said very slowly. "I'm getting a lit tle sleep. I've want ed a lit tle sleep for a long time."

"Let me cover you over."

"No. I'm quite warm."

"Don't go. I have n't got ten to sleep yet."

"You'll sleep, Mike. Don't worry, boy."

"Brett's got a bull-fighter," Mike said. "But her Jew has gone away."

He turned his head and looked at me. "Damned good thing, what?"

"Yes. Now go to sleep, Mike. You ought to get some sleep."

"I'm just start ing. I'm go ing to get a lit tle sleep."

He shut his eyes. I went out of the room and turned the door to quietly. Bill was in my room reading the paper.

"See Mike?"

"Yes."

"Let's go and eat."

"I won't eat down-stairs with that German head waiter. He was damned snotty when I was getting Mike up-stairs."

"He was snotty to us, too."

"Let's go out and eat in the town."

We went down the stairs. On the stairs we passed a girl coming up with a covered tray.

"There goes Brett's lunch," Bill said.

"And the kid's," I said.

Outside on the terrace under the arcade the German head waiter came up. His red cheeks were shiny. He was being polite.

"I haff a tabul for two for you gentle-men," he said.

"Go sit at it," Bill said. We went on out across the street.

We ate at a restaurant in a side street off the square. They were all men eating in the restaurant. It was full of smoke and drinking and singing. The food was good and so was the wine. We did not talk much. Afterward we went to the café and watched the fiesta come to the boiling-point. Brett came over soon after lunch. She said she had looked in the room and that Mike was asleep.

When the fiesta boiled over and to-ward the bull-ring we went with the crowd. Brett sat at the ringside between Bill and me. Directly below us was the callejón, the passageway between the stands and the red fence of the barrera. Behind us the concrete stands filled solidly. Out in front, beyond the red fence, the sand of the ring was smooth-rolled and yellow. It looked a little heavy from the rain, but it was dry in the sun and firm and smooth. The sword-handlers and bull-ring servants came down the callejón carrying on their shoulders the wicker baskets of fighting capes and muletas. They were blood-stained and compactly folded and packed in the baskets. The sword-handlers opened the heavy leather sword-cases so the red wrapped hilts of the sheaf of swords showed as the leather case leaned against the fence. They unfolded the dark-stained red flannel of the muletas and fixed batons in them to spread the stuff and give the matador something to hold. Brett watched it all. She was absorbed in the professional details.

"He's his name stencilled on all the capes and muletas," she said. "Why do they call them muletas?"

"I don't know."

"I wonder if they ever launder them."

"I don't think so. It might spoil the color."

"The blood must stiffen them," Bill said.

"Funny," Brett said. "How one doesn't mind the blood."

Below in the narrow passage of the callejón the sword-handlers arranged everything. All the seats were full. Above, all the boxes were full. There was not an empty seat except in the Presi-dent's box. When he came in the fight would start. Across the smooth sand, in the high doorway that led into the cor-rals, the bull-fighters were standing, their arms furled in their capes, talking, waiting for the signal to march in across the arena. Brett was watching them with the glasses.

"Here, would you like to look?"

I looked through the glasses and saw the three matadors. Romero was in the centre, Belmonte on his left, Marcial on his right. Back of them were their people, and behind the banderilleros, back in the passageway and in the open space of the corral, I saw the picadors. Romero was wearing a black suit. His tricornered hat was low down over his eyes. I could not see his face clearly under the hat, but it looked badly marked. He was looking straight ahead. Marcial was smoking a cigarette guardedly, holding it in his hand. Belmonte looked ahead, his face wan and yellow, his long wolf jaw out. He was looking at nothing. Neither he nor Romero seemed to have anything in common with the others. They were all alone. The President came in; there was handclapping above us in the grand stand, and I handed the glasses to Brett. There was applause. The music started. Brett looked through the glasses.

"Here, take them," she said.

Through the glasses I saw Belmonte speak to Romero. Marcial straightened up and dropped his cigarette, and, looking straight ahead, their heads back, their free arms swinging, the three matadors walked out. Behind them came all the procession, opening out, all striding in step, all the capes furled, everybody with free arms swinging, and behind rode the picadors, their pics rising like lances. Behind all came the two trains of mules and the bull-ring servants. The matadors bowed, holding their hats on, before the President's box, and then came over to the barrera below us. Pedro Romero took off his heavy gold-brocaded cape and handed it over the fence to his sword-handler. He said something to the sword-handler. Close below us we saw Romero's lips were puffed, both eyes

were discolored. His face was discolored and swollen. The sword-handler took the cape, looked up at Brett, and came over to us and handed up the cape.

"Spread it out in front of you," I said.

Brett leaned forward. The cape was heavy and smoothly stiff with gold. The sword-handler looked back, shook his head, and said something. A man beside me leaned over toward Brett.

"He doesn't want you to spread it," he said. "You should fold it and keep it in your lap."

Brett folded the heavy cape.

Romero did not look up at us. He was speaking to Belmonte. Belmonte had sent his formal cape over to some friends. He looked across at them and smiled, his wolf smile that was only with the mouth. Romero learned over the barrera and asked for the water-jug. The sword-handler brought it and Romero poured water over the percale of his fighting-cape, and then scuffed the lower folds in the sand with his slippered foot.

"What's that for?" Brett asked.

"To give it weight in the wind."

"His face looks bad," Bill said.

"He feels very badly," Brett said. "He should be in bed."

The first bull was Belmonte's. Belmonte was very good. But because he got thirty thousand pesetas and people had stayed in line all night to buy tickets to see him, the crowd demanded that he should be more than very good. Belmonte's great attraction is working close to the bull. In bull-fighting they speak of the terrain of the bull and the terrain of the bull-fighter. As long as a bull-fighter stays in his own terrain he is comparatively safe. Each time he enters into the terrain of the bull he is in great danger. Belmonte, in his best days, worked always in the terrain of the bull. This way he gave the sensation of coming tragedy. People went to the corrida to see Belmonte, to be given tragic sensations, and perhaps to see the death of Belmonte. Fifteen years ago they said if you wanted to see Belmonte you should go quickly, while he was still alive. Since then he has killed more than a thousand bulls. When he retired the legend grew up about how his bull-fighting had been, and when he came out of retirement the public were disappointed because no real man could work as close to the bulls as Belmonte was supposed to have done, not, of course, even Belmonte.

Also Belmonte imposed conditions and insisted that his bulls should not be too large, nor too dangerously armed with horns, and so the element that was necessary to give the sensation of tragedy was not there, and the public, who wanted three times as much from Belmonte, who was sick with a fistula, as Belmonte had ever been able to give, felt defrauded and cheated, and Belmonte's jaw came further out in contempt, and his face turned yellower, and he moved with greater difficulty as his pain increased, and finally the crowd were actively against him, and he was utterly contemptuous and indifferent. He had meant to have a great afternoon, and instead it was an afternoon of sneers, shouted insults, and finally a volley of cushions and pieces of bread and vegetables, thrown down at him in the plaza where he had had his greatest triumphs. His jaw only went further out. Sometimes he turned to smile that toothed, long-jawed, lipless smile when he was called something particularly insulting, and always the pain that any movement produced grew stronger and stronger, until finally his yellow face was parchment color, and after his second bull was dead and the throwing of bread and cushions was over, after he had saluted the President with the same wolf-jawed smile and contemptuous eyes, and handed his sword over the barrera to be wiped, and put back in its case, he passed through into the callejón and leaned on the barrera below us, his head on his arms, not seeing, not hearing anything, only going through his pain. When he looked up, finally, he asked for a drink of water. He swallowed a little, rinsed his mouth, spat the water, took his cape, and went back into the ring.

Because they were against Belmonte the public were for Romero. From the moment he left the barrera and went toward the bull they applauded him. Belmonte watched Romero, too, watched him always without seeming to. He paid no attention to Marcial. Marcial was the sort of thing he knew all about. He had come out of retirement to compete with Marcial, knowing it was a competition gained in advance. He had expected to compete with Marcial and the other stars of the decadence of bull-fighting, and he knew that the sincerity of his own bull-fighting would be so set off by the false æsthetics of the bull-fighters of the decadent period that he would only have to be in the ring. His return from retirement had been spoiled by Romero. Romero did always, smoothly, calmly, and beautifully, what he, Belmonte, could only bring himself to do now sometimes. The crowd felt it, even the people from Biarritz, even the American ambassador saw it, finally. It was a competition that Belmonte would not enter because it would lead only to a bad horn wound or death. Belmonte was no longer well enough. He no longer had his greatest moments in the bull-ring. He was not sure that there were any great moments. Things were not the same and now life only came in flashes. He had flashes of the old greatness with his bulls, but they were not of value because he had discounted them in advance when he had picked the bulls out for their safety, getting out of a motor and leaning on a fence, looking over at the herd on the ranch of his friend the bull-breeder. So he had two small, manageable bulls without much horns, and when he felt the greatness again coming, just a little of it through the pain that was always with him, it had been discounted and sold in advance, and it did not give him a good feeling. It was the greatness, but it did not make bull-fighting wonderful to him any more.

Pedro Romero had the greatness. He loved bull-fighting, and I think he loved the bulls, and I think he loved Brett. Everything of which he could control the locality he did in front of her all that afternoon. Never once did he look up. He made it stronger that way, and did it for himself, too, as well as for her. Because he did not look up to ask if it pleased he did it all for himself inside, and it strengthened him, and yet he did it for her, too. But he did not do it for her at any loss to himself. He gained by it all through the afternoon.

His first "quite" was directly below us. The three matadors take the bull in turn after each charge he makes at a picador. Belmonte was the first. Marcial was the second. Then came Romero. The three of them were standing at the left of the horse. The picador, his hat down over his eyes, the shaft of his pic angling sharply toward the bull, kicked in the spurs and held them and with the reins in his left hand walked the horse forward toward the bull. The bull was watching. Seemingly he watched the white horse, but really he watched the triangular steel point of the pic. Romero, watching, saw the bull start to turn his head. He did not want to charge. Romero flicked his cape so the color caught the bull's eye. The bull charged with the reflex, charged, and found not the flash of color but a white horse, and a man leaned far over the horse, shot the steel point of the long hickory shaft into the hump of muscle on the bull's shoulder, and pulled his horse sideways as he pivoted on the pic, mak-

ing a wound, enforcing the iron into the bull's shoulder, making him bleed for Belmonte.

The bull did not insist under the iron. He did not really want to get at the horse. He turned and the group broke apart and Romero was taking him out with his cape. He took him out softly and smoothly, and then stopped and, standing squarely in front of the bull, offered him the cape. The bull's tail went up and he charged, and Romero moved his arms ahead of the bull, wheeling, his feet firmed. The dampened, mud-weighted cape swung open and full as a sail fills, and Romero pivoted with it just ahead of the bull. At the end of the pass they were facing each other again. Romero smiled. The bull wanted it again, and Romero's cape filled again, this time on the other side. Each time he let the bull pass so close that the man and the bull and the cape that filled and pivoted ahead of the bull were all one sharply etched mass. It was all so slow and so controlled. It was as though he were rocking the bull to sleep. He made four veronicas like that, and finished with a half-veronica that turned his back on the bull and came away toward the applause, his hand on his hip, his cape on his arm, and the bull watching his back going away.

In his own bulls he was perfect. His first bull did not see well. After the first two passes with the cape Romero knew exactly how bad the vision was impaired. He worked accordingly. It was not brilliant bull-fighting. It was only perfect bull-fighting. The crowd wanted the bull changed. They made a great row. Nothing very fine could happen with a bull that could not see the lures, but the President would not order him replaced.

"Why don't they change him?" Brett asked.

"They've paid for him. They don't want to lose their money."

"It's hardly fair to Romero."

"Watch how he handles a bull that can't see the color."

"It's the sort of thing I don't like to see."

It was not nice to watch if you cared anything about the person who was doing it. With the bull who could not see the colors of the capes, or the scarlet flannel of the muleta, Romero had to make the bull consent with his body. He had to get so close that the bull saw his body, and would start for it, and then shift the bull's charge to the flannel and finish out the pass in the classic manner. The Biarritz crowd did not like it. They thought Romero was afraid, and that was why he gave that little sidestep each time as he transferred the bull's charge from his own body to the flannel. They preferred Belmonte's imitation of himself or Marcial's imitation of Belmonte. There were three of them in the row behind us.

"What's he afraid of the bull for? The bull's so dumb he only goes after the cloth."

"He's just a young bull-fighter. He hasn't learned it yet."

"But I thought he was fine with the cape before."

"Probably he's nervous now."

Out in the centre of the ring, all alone, Romero was going on with the same thing, getting so close that the bull could see him plainly, offering the body, offering it again a little closer, the bull watching dully, then so close that the bull thought he had him, offering again and finally drawing the charge and then, just before the horns came, giving the bull the red cloth to follow with that little, almost imperceptible, jerk that so offended the critical judgment of the Biarritz bull-fight experts.

"He's going to kill now," I said to Brett. "The bull's still strong. He wouldn't wear himself out."

Out in the centre of the ring Romero profiled in front of the bull, drew the sword out from the folds of the muleta, rose on his toes, and sighted along the blade. The bull charged as Romero charged. Romero's left hand dropped the muleta over the bull's muzzle to blind him, his left shoulder went forward between the horns as the sword went in, and for just an instant he and the bull were one, Romero way out over the bull, the right arm extended high up to where the hilt of the sword had gone in between the bull's shoulders. Then the figure was broken. There was a little jolt as Romero came clear, and then he was standing, one hand up, facing the bull, his shirt ripped out from under his sleeve, the white blowing in the wind, and the bull, the red sword hilt tight between his shoulders, his head going down and his legs settling.

"There he goes," Bill said.

Romero was close enough so the bull could see him. His hand still up, he spoke to the bull. The bull gathered himself, then his head went forward and he went over slowly, then all over, suddenly, four feet in the air.

They handed the sword to Romero, and carrying it blade down, the muleta in his other hand, he walked over to in front of the President's box, bowed, straightened, and came over to the barrera and handed over the sword and muleta.

"Bad one," said the sword-handler.

"He made me sweat," said Romero. He wiped off his face. The sword-handler handed him the water-jug. Romero wiped his lips. It hurt him to drink out of the jug. He did not look up at us.

Marcial had a big day. They were still applauding him when Romero's last bull came in. It was the bull that had sprinted out and killed the man in the morning running.

During Romero's first bull his hurt

face had been very noticeable. Everything he did showed it. All the concentration of the awkwardly delicate working with the bull that could not see well brought it out. The fight with Cohn had not touched his spirit but his face had been smashed and his body hurt. He was wiping all that out now. Each thing that he did with this bull wiped that out a little cleaner. It was a good bull, a big bull, and with horns, and it turned and recharged easily and surely. He was what Romero wanted in bulls.

When he had finished his work with the muleta and was ready to kill, the crowd made him go on. They did not want the bull killed yet, they did not want it to be over. Romero went on. It was like a course in bull-fighting. All the passes he linked up, all completed, all slow, templed and smooth. There were no tricks and no mystifications. There was no brusqueness. And each pass as it reached the summit gave you a sudden ache inside. The crowd did not want it ever to be finished.

The bull was squared on all four feet to be killed, and Romero killed directly below us. He killed not as he had been forced to by the last bull, but as he wanted to. He profiled directly in front of the bull, drew the sword out of the folds of the muleta and sighted along the blade. The bull watched him. Romero spoke to the bull and tapped one of his feet. The bull charged and Romero waited for the charge, the muleta held low, sighting along the blade, his feet firm.

Then without taking a step forward, he became one with the bull, the sword was in high between the shoulders, the bull had followed the low-swung flannel, that disappeared as Romero lurched clear to the left, and it was over. The bull tried to go forward, his legs commenced to settle, he swung from side to side, hesitated, then went down on his knees, and

Romero's older brother leaned forward behind him and drove a short knife into the bull's neck at the base of the horns. The first time he missed. He drove the knife in again, and the bull went over, twitching and rigid. Romero's brother, holding the bull's horn in one hand, the knife in the other, looked up at the President's box. Handkerchiefs were waving all over the bull-ring. The President looked down from the box and waved his handkerchief. The brother cut the notched black ear from the dead bull and trotted over with it to Romero. The bull lay heavy and black on the sand, his tongue out. Boys were running toward him from all parts of the arena, making a little circle around him. They were starting to dance around the bull.

Romero took the ear from his brother and held it up toward the President. The President bowed and Romero, running to get ahead of the crowd, came toward us. He leaned up against the barrera and gave the ear to Brett. He nodded his head and smiled. The crowd were all about him. Brett held down the cape.

"You liked it?" Romero called.

Brett did not say anything. They looked at each other and smiled. Brett had the ear in her hand.

"Don't get bloody," Romero said, and grinned. The crowd wanted him. Several boys shouted at Brett. The crowd was the boys, the dancers, and the drunks. Romero turned and tried to get through the crowd. They were all around him trying to lift him and put him on their shoulders. He fought and twisted away, and started running, in the midst of them, toward the exit. He did not want to be carried on people's shoulders. But they held him and lifted him. It was uncomfortable and his legs were spraddled and his body was very sore. They were lifting him and all running toward the gate. He had his hand on somebody's shoulder. He looked around at us apologetically. The crowd, running, went out the gate with him.

We all three went back to the hotel. Brett went upstairs. Bill and I sat in the down-stairs dining-room and ate some hard-boiled eggs and drank several bottles of beer. Belmonte came down in his street clothes with his manager and two other men. They sat at the next table and ate. Belmonte ate very little. They were leaving on the seven o'clock train for Barcelona. Belmonte wore a blue-striped shirt and a dark suit, and ate soft-boiled eggs. The others ate a big meal. Belmonte did not talk. He only answered questions.

Bill was tired after the bull-fight. So was I. We both took a bull-fight very hard. We sat and ate the eggs and I watched Belmonte and the people at his table. The men with him were tough-looking and businesslike.

"Come on over to the café," Bill said. "I want an absinthe."

It was the last day of the fiesta. Outside it was beginning to be cloudy again. The square was full of people and the fireworks experts were making up their set pieces for the night and covering them over with beech branches. Boys were watching. We passed stands of rockets with long bamboo stems. Outside the café there was a great crowd. The music and the dancing were going on. The giants and the dwarfs were passing.

"Where's Edna?" I asked Bill.

"I don't know."

We watched the beginning of the evening of the last night of the fiesta. The absinthe made everything seem better. I drank it without sugar in the dripping glass, and it was pleasantly bitter.

"I feel sorry about Cohn," Bill said. "He had an awful time."

"Oh, to hell with Cohn," I said.

"Where do you suppose he went?"

"Up to Paris."

"What do you suppose he'll do?"

"Oh, to hell with him."

"What do you suppose he'll do?"

"Pick up with his old girl, probably."

"Who was his old girl?"

"Somebody named Frances."

We had another absinthe.

"When do you go back?" I asked.

"To-morrow."

After a little while Bill said: "Well, it was a swell fiesta."

"Yes," I said; "something doing all the time."

"You wouldn't believe it. It's like a wonderful nightmare."

"Sure," I said. "I'd believe anything. Including nightmares."

"What's the matter? Feel low?"

"Low as hell."

"Have another absinthe. Here, waiter! Another absinthe for this señor."

"I feel like hell," I said.

"Drink that," said Bill. "Drink it slow."

It was beginning to get dark. The fiesta was going on.

I began to feel drunk but I did not feel any better.

"How do you feel?"

"I feel like hell."

"Have another?"

"It won't do any good."

"Try it. You can't tell; maybe this is the one that gets it. Hey, waiter! Another absinthe for this señor!"

I poured the water directly into it and stirred it instead of letting it drip. Bill put in a lump of ice. I stirred the ice around with a spoon in the brownish, cloudy mixture.

"How is it?"

"Fine."

"Don't drink it fast that way. It will make you sick."

I set down the glass. I had not meant to drink it fast.

"I feel tight."

"You ought to."

"That's what you wanted, wasn't it?"

"Sure. Get tight. Get over your damn depression."

"Well, I'm tight. Is that what you want?"

"Sit down."

"I won't sit down," I said. "I'm going over to the hotel."

I was very drunk. I was drunker than I ever remembered having been. At the hotel I went up-stairs. Brett's door was open. I put my head in the room. Mike was sitting on the bed. He waved a bottle.

"Jake," he said. "Come in, Jake."

I went in and sat down. The room was unstable unless I looked at some fixed point.

"Brett, you know. She's gone off with the bull-fighter chap."

"No."

"Yes. She looked for you to say good-bye. They went on the seven o'clock train."

"Did they?"

"Bad thing to do," Mike said. "She shouldn't have done it."

"No."

"Have a drink? Wait while I ring for some beer."

"I'm drunk," I said. "I'm going in and lie down."

"Are you blind? I was blind myself."

"Yes," I said, "I'm blind."

"Well, bung-o," Mike said. "Get some sleep, old Jake."

I went out the door and into my own room and lay on the bed. The bed went sailing off and I sat up in bed and looked at the wall to make it stop. Outside in the square the fiesta was going on. It did not mean anything. Later Bill and Mike came in to get me to go down and eat with them. I pretended to be asleep.

"He's asleep. Better let him alone."

"He's blind as a tick," Mike said. They went out.

I got up and went to the balcony and looked out at the dancing in the square. The world was not wheeling any more. It was just very clear and bright, and inclined to blur at the edges. I washed, brushed my hair. I looked strange to myself in the glass, and went down-stairs to the dining-room.

"Here he is!" said Bill. "Good old Jake! I knew you wouldn't pass out."

"Hello, you old drunk," Mike said.

"I got hungry and woke up."

"Eat some soup," Bill said.

The three of us sat at the table, and it seemed as though about six people were missing.

A FAREWELL TO ARMS

By ERNEST HEMINGWAY

[Excerpt]

CHAPTER I

In the late summer of that year we lived in a house in a village that looked across the river and the plain to the mountains. In the bed of the river there were pebbles and boulders, dry and white in the sun, and the water was clear and swiftly moving and blue in the channels. Troops went by the house and down the road and the dust they raised powdered the leaves of the trees. The trunks of the trees too were dusty and the leaves fell early that year and we saw the troops marching along the road and the dust rising and leaves, stirred by the breeze, falling and the soldiers marching and afterward the road bare and white except for the leaves.

The plain was rich with crops; there were many orchards of fruit trees and beyond the plain the mountains were brown and bare. There was fighting in the mountains and at night we could see the flashes from the artillery. In the dark it was like summer lightning, but the nights were cool and there was not the feeling of a storm coming.

Sometimes in the dark we heard the troops marching under the window and guns going past pulled by motor-tractors. There was much traffic at night and many mules on the roads with boxes of ammunition on each side of their pack-saddles and gray motor trucks that carried men, and other trucks with loads covered with canvas that moved slower in the traffic. There were big guns too that passed in the day drawn by tractors, the long barrels of the guns covered with green branches and green leafy branches and vines laid over the tractors. To the north we could look across a valley and see a forest of chestnut trees and behind it another mountain on this side of the river. There was fighting for that mountain too, but it was not successful, and in the fall when the rains came the leaves all fell from the chestnut trees and the branches were bare and the trunks black with rain. The vineyards were thin and bare-branched too and all the country wet and brown and dead with the autumn. There were mists over the river and clouds on the mountain and the trucks splashed mud on the road and the troops were muddy and wet in their capes; their rifles were wet and under their capes the two leather cartridge-boxes on the front of the belts, gray leather boxes heavy with the packs of clips of thin, long 6.5 mm. cartridges, bulged forward under the capes so that the men, passing on the road, marched as though they were six months gone with child.

There were small gray motor cars that passed going very fast; usually there was an officer on the seat with the driver and more officers in the back seat. They splashed more mud than the camions even and if one of the officers in the back was very small and sitting between two generals, he himself so small that you could not see his face but only the top of his cap and his narrow back, and if the car went especially fast it was probably the King. He lived in Udine and came out in this way nearly every day to see how things were going, and things went very badly.

At the start of the winter came the permanent rain and with the rain came the cholera. But it was checked and in the end only seven thousand died of it in the army.

CHAPTER II

The next year there were many victories. The mountain that was beyond the valley and the hillside where the chestnut forest grew was captured and there were victories beyond the plain on the plateau to the south and we crossed the river in August and lived in a house in Gorizia that had a fountain and many thick shady trees in a walled garden and a wistaria vine purple on the side of the house. Now the fighting was in the next mountains beyond and was not a mile away. The town was very nice and our house was very fine. The river ran behind us and the town had been captured very handsomely but the mountains beyond it could not be taken and I was very glad the Austrians seemed to want to come back to the town some time, if the war should end, because they did not bombard it to destroy it but only a little in a military way. People lived on in it and there were hospitals and cafés and artillery up side streets and two bawdy houses, one for troops and one for

officers, and with the end of the summer, the cool nights, the fighting in the mountains beyond the town, the shell-marked iron of the railway bridge, the smashed tunnel by the river where the fighting had been, the trees around the square and the long avenue of trees that led to the square; these with there being girls in the town, the King passing in his motor car, sometimes now seeing his face and little long necked body and gray beard like a goat's chin tuft; all these with the sudden interiors of houses that had lost a wall through shelling, with plaster and rubble in their gardens and sometimes in the street, and the whole thing going well on the Carso made the fall very different from the last fall when we had been in the country. The war was changed too.

The forest of oak trees on the mountain beyond the town was gone. The forest had been green in the summer when we had come into the town but now there were the stumps and the broken trunks and the ground torn up, and one day at the end of the fall when I was out where the oak forest had been I saw a cloud coming over the mountain. It came very fast and the sun went a dull yellow and then everything was gray and the sky was covered and the cloud came on down the mountain and suddenly we were in it and it was snow. The snow slanted across the wind, the bare ground was covered, the stumps of trees projected, there was snow on the guns and there were paths in the snow going back to the latrines behind trenches.

Later, below in the town, I watched the snow falling, looking out of the window of the bawdy house, the house for officers, where I sat with a friend and two glasses drinking a bottle of Asti, and, looking out at the snow falling slowly and heavily, we knew it was all over for that year. Up the river the mountains had not been taken; none of the mountains beyond the river had been taken. That was all left for next year. My friend saw the priest from our mess going by in the street, walking carefully in the slush, and pounded on the window to attract his attention. The priest looked up. He saw us and smiled. My friend motioned for him to come in. The priest shook his head and went on. That night in the mess after the spaghetti course, which every one ate very quickly and seriously, lifting the spaghetti on the fork until the loose strands hung clear then lowering it into the mouth, or else using a continuous lift and sucking into the mouth, helping ourselves to wine from the grass-covered gallon flask; it swung in a metal cradle and you pulled the neck of the flask down with the forefinger and the wine, clear red, tannic and lovely, poured out into the glass held with the same hand; after this course, the captain commenced picking on the priest.

The priest was young and blushed easily and wore a uniform like the rest of us but with a cross in dark red velvet above the left breast pocket of his gray tunic. The captain spoke pidgin Italian for my doubtful benefit, in order that I might understand perfectly, that nothing should be lost.

"Priest to-day with girls," the captain said looking at the priest and at me. The priest smiled and blushed and shook his head. This captain baited him often.

"Not true?" asked the captain. "To-day I see priest with girls."

"No," said the priest. The other officers were amused at the baiting.

"Priest not with girls," went on the captain. "Priest never with girls," he explained to me. He took my glass and filled it, looking at my eyes all the time, but not losing sight of the priest.

"Priest every night five against one." Every one at the table laughed. "You understand? Priest every night five

against one." He made a gesture and laughed loudly. The priest accepted it as a joke.

"The Pope wants the Austrians to win the war," the major said. "He loves Franz Joseph. That's where the money comes from. I am an atheist."

"Did you ever read the 'Black Pig'?" asked the lieutenant. "I will get you a copy. It was that which shook my faith."

"It is a filthy and vile book," said the priest. "You do not really like it."

"It is very valuable," said the lieutenant. "It tells you about those priests. You will like it," he said to me. I smiled at the priest and he smiled back across the candle-light. "Don't you read it," he said.

"I will get it for you," said the lieutenant.

"All thinking men are atheists," the major said. "I do not believe in the Free Masons however."

"I believe in the Free Masons," the lieutenant said. "It is a noble organization." Some one came in and as the door opened I could see the snow falling.

"There will be no more offensive now that the snow has come," I said.

"Certainly not," said the major. "You should go on leave. You should go to Rome, Naples, Sicily——"

"He should visit Amalfi," said the lieutenant. "I will write you cards to my family in Amalfi. They will love you like a son."

"He should go to Palermo."

"He ought to go to Capri."

"I would like you to see Abruzzi and visit my family at Capracotta," said the priest.

"Listen to him talk about the Abruzzi. There's more snow there than here. He doesn't want to see peasants. Let him go to centres of culture and civilization."

"He should have fine girls. I will give you the addresses of places in Naples.

Beautiful young girls—accompanied by their mothers. Ha! Ha! Ha!" the captain spread his hand open, the thumb up and fingers outspread as when you make shadow pictures. There was a shadow from his hand on the wall. He spoke again in pidgin Italian. "You go away like this," he pointed to the thumb, "and come back like this," he touched the little finger. Every one laughed.

"Look," said the captain. He spread the hand again. Again the candle-light made its shadows on the wall. He started with the upright thumb and named in their order the thumb and four fingers, "soto-tenente (the thumb), tenente (first finger), capitano (next finger), maggiore (next to the little finger), and tenente-colonello (the little finger). You go away soto-tenente! You come back soto-colonello!" They all laughed. The captain was having a great success with finger games. He looked at the priest and shouted, "Every night priest five against one!" They all laughed again.

"You must go on leave at once," the major said.

"I would like to go with you and show you things," the lieutenant said.

"When you come back bring a phonograph."

"Bring good opera disks."

"Bring Caruso."

"Don't bring Caruso. He bellows."

"Don't you wish you could bellow like him?"

"He bellows. I say he bellows!"

"I would like you to go to Abruzzi," the priest said. The others were shouting. "There is good hunting. You would like the people and though it is cold it is clear and dry. You could stay with my family. My father is a famous hunter."

"Come on," said the captain. "We go whorehouse before it shuts."

"Good-night," I said to the priest.

"Good-night," he said.

CHAPTER III

When I came back to the front we still lived in that town. There were many more guns in the country around and the spring had come. The fields were green and there were small green shoots on the vines, the trees along the road had small leaves and a breeze came from the sea. I saw the town with the hill and the old castle above it in a cup in the hills with the mountains beyond, brown mountains with a little green on their slopes. In the town there were more guns, there were some new hospitals, you met British men and sometimes women, on the street, and a few more houses had been hit by shell fire. It was warm and like the spring and I walked down the alleyway of trees, warmed from the sun on the wall, and found we still lived in the same house and that it all looked the same as when I had left it. The door was open, there was a soldier sitting on a bench outside in the sun, an ambulance was waiting by the side door and inside the door, as I went in, there was the smell of marble floors and hospital. It was all as I had left it except that now it was spring. I looked in the door of the big room and saw the major sitting at his desk, the window open and the sunlight coming into the room. He did not see me and I did not know whether to go in and report or go upstairs first and clean up. I decided to go on upstairs.

The room I shared with the lieutenant Rinaldi looked out on the courtyard. The window was open, my bed was made up with blankets and my things hung on the wall, the gas mask in an oblong tin can, the steel helmet on the same peg. At the foot of the bed was my flat trunk, and my winter boots, the leather shiny with oil, were on the trunk. My Austrian sniper's rifle with its blued octagon barrel and the lovely dark walnut, cheek-fitted, *schutzen* stock, hung over the two beds. The telescope that fitted it was, I remembered, locked in the trunk. The lieutenant, Rinaldi, lay asleep on the other bed. He woke when he heard me in the room and sat up.

"Ciaou!" he said. "What kind of time did you have?"

"Magnificent."

We shook hands and he put his arm around my neck and kissed me.

"Oughf," I said.

"You're dirty," he said. "You ought to wash. Where did you go and what did you do? Tell me everything at once."

"I went everywhere. Milan, Florence, Rome, Naples, Villa San Giovanni, Messina, Taormina——"

"You talk like a time-table. Did you have any beautiful adventures?"

"Yes."

"Where?"

"Milano, Firenze, Roma, Napoli——"

"That's enough. Tell me really what was the best."

"In Milano."

"That was because it was first. Where did you meet her? In the Cova? Where did you go? How did you feel? Tell me everything at once. Did you stay all night?"

"Yes."

"That's nothing. Here now we have beautiful girls. New girls never been to the front before."

"Wonderful."

"You don't believe me? We will go now this afternoon and see. And in the town we have beautiful English girls. I am now in love with Miss Barkley. I will take you to call. I will probably marry Miss Barkley."

"I have to get washed and report. Doesn't anybody work now?"

"Since you are gone we have nothing but frostbites, chilblains, jaundice, gonorrhea, self-inflicted wounds, pneumonia and hard and soft chancres. Every week some one gets wounded by rock fragments. There are a few real wounded. Next week the war starts again. Perhaps it starts again. They say so. Do you think I would do right to marry Miss Barkley —after the war of course?"

"Absolutely," I said and poured the basin full of water.

"To-night you will tell me everything," said Rinaldi. "Now I must go back to sleep to be fresh and beautiful for Miss Barkley."

I took off my tunic and shirt and washed in the cold water in the basin. While I rubbed myself with a towel I looked around the room and out of the window and at Rinaldi lying with his eyes closed on the bed. He was good-looking, was my age, and he came from Amalfi. He loved being a surgeon and we were great friends. While I was looking at him he opened his eyes.

"Have you any money?"

"Yes."

"Loan me fifty lire."

I dried my hands and took out my pocket-book from the inside of my tunic hanging on the wall. Rinaldi took the note, folded it without rising from the bed and slid it in his breeches pocket. He smiled, "I must make on Miss Barkley the impression of a man of sufficient wealth. You are my great and good friend and financial protector."

"Go to hell," I said.

That night at the mess I sat next to the priest and he was disappointed and suddenly hurt that I had not gone to the Abruzzi. He had written to his father that I was coming and they had made preparations. I myself felt as badly as he did and could not understand why I had not gone. It was what I had wanted to do and I tried to explain how one thing had led to another and finally he saw it and understood that I had really wanted to go and it was almost all right. I had drunk much wine and afterward coffee and Strega and I explained, winefully, how we did not do the things we wanted to do; we never did such things.

We two were talking while the others argued. I had wanted to go to Abruzzi. I had gone to no place where the roads were frozen and hard as iron, where it was clear cold and dry and the snow was dry and powdery and hare-tracks in the snow and the peasants took off their hats and called you Lord and there was good hunting. I had gone to no such place but to the smoke of cafés and nights when the room whirled and you needed to look at the wall to make it stop, nights in bed, drunk, when you knew that that was all there was, and the strange excitement of waking and not knowing who it was with you, and the world all unreal in the dark and so exciting that you must resume again unknowing and not caring in the night, sure that this was all and all and all and not caring. Suddenly to care very much and to sleep to wake with it sometimes morning and all that had been there gone and everything sharp and hard and clear and sometimes a dispute about the cost. Sometimes still pleasant and fond and warm and breakfast and lunch. Sometimes all niceness gone and glad to get out on the street but always another day starting and then another night. I tried to tell about the night and the difference between the night and the day and how the night was better unless the day was very clean and cold and I could not tell it; as I cannot tell it now. But if you have had it you know. He had not had it but he understood that I had really wanted to go to the Abruzzi but had not gone and we were still friends, with many tastes alike, but with the difference between us. He had always known what I did not know and what, when I learned it, I was always able to forget. But I did not know that then, although I learned it

later. In the meantime we were all at the mess, the meal was finished, and the argument went on. We two stopped talking and the captain shouted, "Priest not happy. Priest not happy without girls."

"I am happy," said the priest.

"Priest not happy. Priest wants Austrians to win the war," the captain said. The others listened. The priest shook his head.

"No," he said.

"Priest wants us never to attack. Don't you want us never to attack?"

"No. If there is a war I suppose we must attack."

"Must attack. Shall attack!"

The priest nodded.

"Leave him alone," the major said. "He's all right."

"He can't do anything about it anyway," the captain said. We all got up and left the table.

CHAPTER IV

The battery in the next garden woke me in the morning and I saw the sun coming through the window and got out of the bed. I went to the window and looked out. The gravel paths were moist and the grass was wet with dew. The battery fired twice and the air came each time like a blow and shook the window and made the front of my pajamas flap. I could not see the guns but they were evidently firing directly over us. It was a nuisance to have them there but it was a comfort that they were no bigger. As I looked out at the garden I heard a motor truck starting on the road. I dressed, went downstairs, had some coffee in the kitchen and went out to the garage.

Ten cars were lined up side by side under the long shed. They were topheavy, blunt-nosed ambulances, painted gray and built like moving-vans. The mechanics were working on one out in the yard. Three others were up in the mountains at dressing stations.

"Do they ever shell that battery?" I asked one of the mechanics.

"No, Signor Tenente. It is protected by the little hill."

"How's everything?"

"Not so bad. This machine is no good but the others march." He stopped working and smiled. "Were you on permission?"

"Yes."

He wiped his hands on his jumper and grinned. "You have a good time?" The others all grinned too.

"Fine," I said. "What's the matter with this machine?"

"It's no good. One thing after another."

"What's the matter now?"

"New rings."

I left them working, the car looking disgraced and empty with the engine open and parts spread on the work bench, and went in under the shed and looked at each of the cars. They were moderately clean, a few freshly washed, the others dusty. I looked at the tires carefully, looking for cuts or stone bruises. Everything seemed in good condition. It evidently made no difference whether I was there to look after things or not. I had imagined that the condition of the cars, whether or not things were obtainable, the smooth functioning of the business of removing wounded and sick from the dressing stations, hauling them back from the mountains to the clearing station and then distributing them to the hospitals named on their papers, depended to a considerable extent on myself. Evidently it did not matter whether I was there or not.

"Has there been any trouble getting parts?" I asked the sergeant mechanic.

"No, Signor Tenente."

"Where is the gasoline park now?"

"At the same place."

"Good," I said and went back to the house and drank another bowl of coffee at the mess table. The coffee was a pale gray and sweet with condensed milk. Outside the window it was a lovely spring morning. There was that beginning of a feeling of dryness in the nose that meant the day would be hot later on. That day I visited the posts in the mountains and was back in town late in the afternoon.

The whole thing seemed to run better while I was away. The offensive was going to start again I heard. The division for which we worked were to attack at a place up the river and the major told me that I would see about the posts for during the attack. The attack would cross the river up above the narrow gorge and spread up the hillside. The posts for the cars would have to be as near the river as they could get and keep covered. They would, of course, be selected by the infantry but we were supposed to work it out. It was one of those things that gave you a false feeling of soldiering.

I was very dusty and dirty and went up to my room to wash. Rinaldi was sitting on the bed with a copy of Hugo's English grammar. He was dressed, wore his black boots, and his hair shone.

"Splendid," he said when he saw me. "You will come with me to see Miss Barkley."

"No."

"Yes. You will please come and make me a good impression on her."

"All right. Wait till I get cleaned up."

"Wash up and come as you are."

I washed, brushed my hair and we started.

"Wait a minute," Rinaldi said. "Perhaps we should have a drink." He opened his trunk and took out a bottle.

"Not Strega," I said.

"No. Grappa."

"All right."

He poured two glasses and we touched

them, first fingers extended. The grappa was very strong.

"Another?"

"All right," I said. We drank the second grappa, Rinaldi put away the bottle and we went down the stairs. It was hot walking through the town but the sun was starting to go down and it was very pleasant. The British hospital was a big villa built by Germans before the war. Miss Barkley was in the garden. Another nurse was with her. We saw their white uniforms through the trees and walked toward them. Rinaldi saluted. I saluted too but more moderately.

"How do you do?" Miss Barkley said. "You're not an Italian, are you?"

"Oh, no."

Rinaldi was talking with the other nurse. They were laughing.

"What an odd thing—to be in the Italian army."

"It's not really the army. It's only the ambulance."

"It's very odd though. Why did you do it?"

"I don't know," I said. "There isn't always an explanation for everything."

"Oh, isn't there? I was brought up to think there was."

"That's awfully nice."

"*Do* we have to go on and talk this way?"

"No," I said.

"That's a relief. Isn't it?"

"What is the stick?" I asked. Miss Barkley was quite tall. She wore what seemed to me to be a nurse's uniform, was blonde and had a tawny skin and gray eyes. I thought she was very beautiful. She was carrying a thin rattan stick like a toy riding-crop, bound in leather.

"It belonged to a boy who was killed last year."

"I'm awfully sorry."

"He was a very nice boy. He was going to marry me and he was killed in the Somme."

"It was a ghastly show."

"Were you there?"

"No."

"I've heard about it," she said. "There's not really any war of that sort down here. They sent me the little stick. His mother sent it to me. They returned it with his things."

"Had you been engaged long?"

"Eight years. We grew up together."

"And why didn't you marry?"

"I don't know," she said. "I was a fool not to. I could have given him that anyway. But I thought it would be bad for him."

"I see."

"Have you ever loved any one?"

"No," I said.

We sat down on a bench and I looked at her.

"You have beautiful hair," I said.

"Do you like it?"

"Very much."

"I was going to cut it all off when he died."

"No."

"I wanted to do something for him. You see I didn't care about the other thing and he could have had it all. He could have had anything he wanted if I would have known. I would have married him or anything. I know all about it now. But then he wanted to go to war and I didn't know."

I did not say anything.

"I didn't know about anything then. I thought it would be worse for him. I thought perhaps he couldn't stand it and then of course he was killed and that was the end of it."

"I don't know."

"Oh, yes," she said. "That's the end of it."

We looked at Rinaldi talking with the other nurse.

"What is her name?"

"Ferguson. Helen Ferguson. Your friend is a doctor, isn't he?"

"Yes. He's very good."

"That's splendid. You rarely find any one any good this close to the front. This is close to the front, isn't it?"

"Quite."

"It's a silly front," she said. "But it's very beautiful. Are they going to have an offensive?"

"Yes."

"Then we'll have to work. There's no work now."

"Have you done nursing long?"

"Since the end of 'fifteen. I started when he did. I remember having a silly idea he might come to the hospital where I was. With a sabre cut, I suppose, and a bandage around his head. Or shot through the shoulder. Something picturesque."

"This is the picturesque front," I said.

"Yes," she said. "People can't realize what France is like. If they did, it couldn't all go on. He didn't have a sabre cut. They blew him all to bits."

I didn't say anything.

"Do you suppose it will always go on?"

"No."

"What's to stop it?"

"It will crack somewhere."

"We'll crack. We'll crack in France. They can't go on doing things like the Somme and not crack."

"They won't crack here," I said.

"You think not?"

"No. They did very well last summer."

"They may crack," she said. "Anybody may crack."

"The Germans too."

"No," she said. "I think not."

We went over toward Rinaldi and Miss Ferguson.

"You love Italy?" Rinaldi asked Miss Ferguson in English.

"Quite well."

"No understand," Rinaldi shook his head.

"Abbastanza bene," I translated. He shook his head.

"That is not good. You love England?"

"Not too well. I'm Scotch, you see."

Rinaldi looked at me blankly.

"She's Scotch, so she loves Scotland better than England," I said in Italian.

"But Scotland is England."

I translated this for Miss Ferguson.

"Pas encore," said Miss Ferguson.

"Not really?"

"Never. We do not like the English."

"Not like the English? Not like Miss Barkley?"

"Oh, that's different. You mustn't take everything so literally."

After a while we said good-night and left. Walking home Rinaldi said, "Miss Barkley prefers you to me. That is very clear. But the little Scotch one is very nice."

"Very," I said. I had not noticed her. "You like her?"

"No," said Rinaldi.

CHAPTER V

The next afternoon I went to call on Miss Barkley again. She was not in the garden and I went to the side door of the villa where the ambulances drove up. Inside I saw the head nurse, who said Miss Barkley was on duty—"there's a war on, you know."

I said I knew.

"You're the American in the Italian army?" she asked.

"Yes, ma'am."

"How did you happen to do that? Why didn't you join up with us?"

"I don't know," I said. "Could I join now?"

"I'm afraid not now. Tell me. Why did you join up with the Italians?"

"I was in Italy," I said, "and I spoke Italian."

"Oh," she said. "I'm learning it. It's beautiful language."

"Somebody said you should be able to learn it in two weeks."

"Oh, I'll not learn it in two weeks. I've studied it for months now. You may come and see her after seven o'clock if you wish. She'll be off then. But don't bring a lot of Italians."

"Not even for the beautiful language?"

"No. Nor for the beautiful uniforms."

"Good evening," I said.

"A rivederci, Tenente."

"A rivederla." I saluted and went out. It was impossible to salute foreigners as an Italian, without embarrassment. The Italian salute never seemed made for export.

The day had been hot. I had been up the river to the bridgehead at Plava. It was there that the offensive was to begin. It had been impossible to advance on the far side the year before because there was only one road leading down from the pass to the pontoon bridge and it was under machine-gun and shell fire for nearly a mile. It was not wide enough either to carry all the transport for an offensive and the Austrians could make a shambles out of it. But the Italians had crossed and spread out a little way on the far side to hold about a mile and a half on the Austrian side of the river. It was a nasty place and the Austrians should not have let them hold it. I suppose it was mutual tolerance because the Austrians still kept a bridgehead further down the river. The Austrian trenches were above on the hillside only a few yards from the Italian lines. There had been a little town but it was all rubble. There was what was left of a railway station and a smashed permanent bridge that could not be repaired and used because it was in plain sight.

I went along the narrow road down toward the river, left the car at the dressing station under the hill, crossed the pontoon bridge, which was protected by a shoulder of the mountain, and went through the trenches in the smashed-down town and along the edge of the slope. Everybody was in the dugouts. There were racks of rockets standing to be touched off to call for help from the artillery or to signal with if the telephone wires were cut. It was quiet, hot and dirty. I looked across the wire at the Austrian lines. Nobody was in sight. I had a drink with a captain that I knew in one of the dugouts and went back across the bridge.

A new wide road was being finished that would go over the mountain and zig-zag down to the bridge. When this road was finished the offensive would start. It came down through the forest in sharp turns. The system was to bring everything down the new road and take the empty trucks, carts and loaded ambulances and all returning traffic up the old narrow road. The dressing station was on the Austrian side of the river under the edge of the hill and stretcher-bearers would bring the wounded back across the pontoon bridge. It would be the same when the offensive started. As far as I could make out the last mile or so of the new road where it started to level out would be able to be shelled steadily by the Austrians. It looked as though it might be a mess. But I found a place where the cars would be sheltered after they passed that last bad-looking bit and could wait for the wounded to be brought across the pontoon bridge. I would have liked to drive over the new road but it was not yet finished. It looked wide and well made with a good grade and the turns looked very impressive where you could see them through openings in the forest on the mountain side. The cars would be all right with their good metal-to-metal brakes and anyway, coming down, they would not be loaded. I drove back up the narrow road.

Two carabinieri held the car up. A shell had fallen and while we waited three others fell up the road. They were seventy-sevens and came with a whishing rush of air, a hard bright burst and flash and then gray smoke that blew across the road. The carabinieri waved us to go on. Passing where the shells had landed I avoided the small broken places and smelled the high explosive and the smell of blasted clay and stone and freshly shattered flint. I drove back to Gorizia and our villa and, as I said, went to call on Miss Barkley, who was on duty.

At dinner I ate very quickly and left for the villa where the British had their hospital. It was really very large and beautiful and there were fine trees in the grounds. Miss Barkley was sitting on a bench in the garden. Miss Ferguson was with her. They seemed glad to see me and in a little while Miss Ferguson excused herself and went away.

"I'll leave you two," she said. "You get along very well without me."

"Don't go, Helen," Miss Barkley said.

"I'd really rather. I must write some letters."

"Good-night," I said.

"Good-night, Mr. Henry."

"Don't write anything that will bother the censor."

"Don't worry. I only write about what a beautiful place we live in and how brave the Italians are."

"That way you'll be decorated."

"That will be nice. Good-night, Catherine."

"I'll see you in a little while," Miss Barkley said. Miss Ferguson walked away in the dark.

"She's nice," I said.

"Oh, yes, she's very nice. She's a nurse."

"Aren't you a nurse?"

"Oh, no. I'm something called a V. A. D. We work very hard but no one trusts us."

"Why not?"

"They don't trust us when there's nothing going on. When there is really work they trust us."

"What is the difference?"

"A nurse is like a doctor. It takes a long time to be. A V. A. D. is a short cut."

"I see."

"The Italians didn't want women so near the front. So we're all on very special behavior. We don't go out."

"I can come here though."

"Oh, yes. We're not cloistered."

"Let's drop the war."

"It's very hard. There's no place to drop it."

"Let's drop it anyway."

"All right."

We looked at each other in the dark. I thought she was very beautiful and I took her hand. She let me take it and I held it and put my arm around under her arm.

"No," she said. I kept my arm where it was.

"Why not?"

"No."

"Yes," I said. "Please." I leaned forward in the dark to kiss her and there was a sharp stinging flash. She had slapped my face hard. Her hand had hit my nose and eyes, and tears came in my eyes from the reflex.

"I'm so sorry," she said. I felt I had a certain advantage.

"You were quite right."

"I'm dreadfully sorry," she said. "I just couldn't stand the nurse's-evening-off aspect of it. I didn't mean to hurt you. I did hurt you, didn't I?"

She was looking at me in the dark. I was angry and yet certain, seeing it all ahead like the moves in a chess game.

"You did exactly right," I said. "I don't mind at all."

"Poor man."

"You see I've been leading a sort of a

funny life. And I never even talk English. And then you are so very beautiful." I looked at her.

"You don't need to say a lot of nonsense. I said I was sorry. We do get along."

"Yes," I said. "And we have gotten away from the war."

She laughed. It was the first time I had ever heard her laugh. I watched her face.

"You are sweet," she said.

"No, I'm not."

"Yes. You are a dear. I'd be glad to kiss you if you don't mind."

I looked in her eyes and put my arm around her as I had before and kissed her. I kissed her hard and held her tight and tried to open her lips; they were closed tight. I was still angry and as I held her suddenly she shivered. I held her close against me and could feel her heart beating and her lips opened and her head went back against my hand and then she was crying on my shoulder.

"Oh, darling," she said. "You will be good to me, won't you?"

What the hell, I thought. I stroked her hair and patted her shoulder. She was crying.

"You will, won't you?" She looked up at me. "Because we're going to have a strange life."

After a while I walked with her to the door of the villa and she went in and I walked home. Back at the villa I went upstairs to the room. Rinaldi was lying on his bed. He looked at me.

"So you make progress with Miss Barkley?"

"We are friends."

"You have that pleasant air of a dog in heat."

I did not understand the word.

"Of a what?"

He explained.

"You," I said, "have that pleasant air of a dog who——"

"Stop it," he said. "In a little while we would say insulting things." He laughed.

"Good-night," I said.

"Good-night, little puppy."

I knocked over his candle with the pillow and got into bed in the dark.

Rinaldi picked up the candle, lit it and went on reading.

CHAPTER VI

I was away for two days at the posts. When I got home it was too late and I did not see Miss Barkley until the next evening. She was not in the garden and I had to wait in the office of the hospital until she came down. There were many marble busts on painted wooden pillars along the walls of the room they used for an office. The hall too, that the office opened on, was lined with them. They had the complete marble quality of all looking alike. Sculpture had always seemed a dull business—still, bronzes looked like something. But marble busts all looked like a cemetery. There was one fine cemetery though—the one at Pisa. Genoa was the place to see the bad marbles. This had been the villa of a very wealthy German and the busts must have cost him plenty. I wondered who had done them and how much he got. I tried to make out whether they were members of the family or what; but they were all uniformly classical. You could not tell anything about them.

I sat on a chair and held my cap. We were supposed to wear steel helmets even in Gorizia but they were uncomfortable and too bloody theatrical in a town where the civilian inhabitants had not been evacuated. I wore one when we went up to the posts and carried an English gas mask. We were just beginning to get some of them. They were a real mask. Also we were required to wear an automatic pistol; even doctors and sanitary officers. I felt it against the back of the chair. You were liable to arrest if you did not have one worn in plain sight. Rinaldi carried a holster stuffed with toilet paper. I wore a real one and felt like a gunman until I practised firing it. It was an Astra 7.65 caliber with a short barrel and it jumped so sharply when you let it off that there was no question of hitting anything. I practised with it, holding below the target and trying to master the jerk of the ridiculous short barrel until I could hit within a yard of where I aimed at twenty paces and then the ridiculousness of carrying a pistol at all came over me and I soon forgot it and carried it flopping against the small of my back with no feeling at all except a vague sort of shame when I met English-speaking people. I sat now in the chair and an orderly of some sort looked at me disapprovingly from behind a desk while I looked at the marble floor, the pillars with the marble busts, and the frescoes on the wall and waited for Miss Barkley. The frescoes were not bad. Any frescoes were good when they started to peel and flake off.

I saw Catherine Barkley coming down the hall, and stood up. She did not seem tall walking toward me but she looked very lovely.

"Good-evening, Mr. Henry," she said.

"How do you do?" I said. The orderly was listening behind the desk.

"Shall we sit here or go out in the garden?"

"Let's go out. It's much cooler."

I walked behind her out into the garden, the orderly looking after us. When we were out on the gravel drive she said, "Where have you been?"

"I've been out on post."

"You couldn't have sent me a note?"

"No," I said. "Not very well. I thought I was coming back."

"You ought to have let me know, darling."

We were off the driveway, walking under the trees. I took her hands, then stopped and kissed her.

"Isn't there anywhere we can go?"

"No," she said. "We have to just walk here. You've been away a long time."

"This is the third day. But I'm back now."

She looked at me, "And you do love me?"

"Yes."

"You did say you loved me, didn't you?"

"Yes," I lied. "I love you." I had not said it before.

"And you call me Catherine?"

"Catherine." We walked on a way and were stopped under a tree.

"Say, 'I've come back to Catherine in the night.' "

"I've come back to Catherine in the night."

"Oh, darling, you have come back, haven't you?"

"Yes."

"I love you so and it's been awful. You won't go away?"

"No. I'll always come back."

"Oh, I love you so. Please put your hand there again."

"It's not been away." I turned her so I could see her face when I kissed her and I saw that her eyes were shut. I kissed both her shut eyes. I thought she was probably a little crazy. It was all right if she was. I did not care what I was getting into. This was better than going every evening to the house for officers where the girls climbed all over you and put your cap on backward as a sign of affection between their trips upstairs with brother officers. I knew I did not love Catherine Barkley nor had any idea of loving her. This was a game, like bridge, in which you said things instead of playing cards. Like bridge you had to pretend you were playing for money or playing for some stakes. Nobody had mentioned what the stakes were. It was all right with me.

"I wish there was some place we could go," I said. I was experiencing the masculine difficulty of making love very long standing up.

"There isn't any place," she said. She came back from wherever she had been.

"We might sit there just for a little while."

We sat on the flat stone bench and I held Catherine Barkley's hand. She would not let me put my arm around her.

"Are you very tired?" she asked.

"No."

She looked down at the grass.

"This is a rotten game we play, isn't it?"

"What game?"

"Don't be dull."

"I'm not, on purpose."

"You're a nice boy," she said. "And you play it as well as you know how. But it's a rotten game."

"Do you always know what people think?"

"Not always. But I do with you. You don't have to pretend you love me. That's over for the evening. Is there anything you'd like to talk about?"

"But I do love you."

"Please let's not lie when we don't have to. I had a very fine little show and I'm all right now. You see I'm not mad and I'm not gone off. It's only a little sometimes."

I pressed her hand, "Dear Catherine."

"It sounds very funny now—Catherine. You don't pronounce it very much alike. But you're very nice. You're a very good boy."

"That's what the priest said."

"Yes, you're very good. And you will come and see me?"

"Of course."

"And you don't have to say you love me. That's all over for a while." She stood up and put out her hand. "Goodnight."

I wanted to kiss her.

"No," she said. "I'm awfully tired."

"Kiss me, though," I said.

"I'm awfully tired, darling."

"Kiss me."

"Do you want to very much?"

"Yes."

We kissed and she broke away suddenly. "No. Good-night, please, darling." We walked to the door and I saw her go in and down the hall. I liked to watch her move. She went on down the hall. I went on home. It was a hot night and there was a good deal going on up in the mountains. I watched the flashes on San Gabriele.

I stopped in front of the Villa Rossa. The shutters were up but it was still going on inside. Somebody was singing. I went on home. Rinaldi came in while I was undressing.

"Ah, ha!" he said. "It does not go so well. Baby is puzzled."

"Where have you been?"

"At the Villa Rossa. It was very edifying, baby. We all sang. Where have you been?"

"Calling on the British."

"Thank God I did not become involved with the British."

CHAPTER VII

I came back the next afternoon from our first mountain post and stopped the car at the *smistamento* where the wounded and sick were sorted by their papers and the papers marked for the different hospitals. I had been driving and I sat in the car and the driver took the papers in. It was a hot day and the sky was very bright and blue and the road was white and dusty. I sat in the high seat of the

Fiat and thought about nothing. A regiment went by in the road and I watched them pass. The men were hot and sweating. Some wore their steel helmets but most of them carried them slung from their packs. Most of the helmets were too big and came down almost over the ears of the men who wore them. The officers all wore helmets; better-fitting helmets. It was half of the brigata Basilicata. I identified them by their red and white striped collar mark. There were stragglers going by long after the regiment had passed—men who could not keep up with their platoons. They were sweaty, dusty and tired. Some looked pretty bad. A soldier came along after the last of the stragglers. He was walking with a limp. He stopped and sat down beside the road. I got down and went over.

"What's the matter?"

He looked at me, then stood up.

"I'm going on."

"What's the trouble?"

"—— the war."

"What's wrong with your leg?"

"It's not my leg. I got a rupture."

"Why don't you ride with the transport?" I asked. "Why don't you go to the hospital?"

"They won't let me. The lieutenant said I slipped the truss on purpose."

"Let me feel it."

"It's way out."

"Which side is it on?"

"Here."

I felt it.

"Cough," I said.

"I'm afraid it will make it bigger. It's twice as big as it was this morning."

"Sit down," I said. "As soon as I get the papers on these wounded I'll take you along the road and drop you with your medical officers."

"He'll say I did it on purpose."

"They can't do anything," I said. "It's not a wound. You've had it before, haven't you?"

"But I lost the truss."

"They'll send you to a hospital."

"Can't I stay here, Tenente?"

"No, I haven't any papers for you."

The driver came out of the door with the papers for the wounded in the car.

"Four for 105. Two for 132," he said. They were hospitals beyond the river.

"You drive," I said. I helped the soldier with the rupture up on the seat with us.

"You speak English?" he asked.

"Sure."

"How you like this goddam war?"

"Rotten."

"I say it's rotten. Jesus Christ, I say it's rotten."

"Were you in the States?"

"Sure. In Pittsburgh. I knew you was an American."

"Don't I talk Italian good enough?"

"I knew you was an American all right."

"Another American," said the driver in Italian looking at the hernia man.

"Listen, lootenant. Do you have to take me to that regiment?"

"Yes."

"Because the captain doctor knew I had this rupture. I threw away the goddam truss so it would get bad and I wouldn't have to go to the line again."

"I see."

"Couldn't you take me no place else?"

"If it was closer to the front I could take you to a first medical post. But back here you've got to have papers."

"If I go back they'll make me get operated on and then they'll put me in the line all the time."

I thought it over.

"You wouldn't want to go in the line all the time, would you?" he asked.

"No."

"Jesus Christ, ain't this a goddam war?"

"Listen," I said. "You get out and fall down by the road and get a bump on

[81]

your head and I'll pick you up on our way back and take you to a hospital. We'll stop by the road here, Aldo." We stopped at the side of the road. I helped him down.

"I'll be right here, lieutenant," he said.

"So long," I said. We went on and passed the regiment about a mile ahead, then crossed the river, cloudy with snow-water and running fast through the spiles of the bridge, to ride along the road across the plain and deliver the wounded at the two hospitals. I drove coming back and went fast with the empty car to find the man from Pittsburgh. First we passed the regiment, hotter and slower than ever: then the stragglers. Then we saw a horse ambulance stopped by the road. Two men were lifting the hernia man to put him in. They had come back for him. He shook his head at me. His helmet was off and his forehead was bleeding below the hair line. His nose was skinned and there was dust on the bloody patch and dust in his hair.

"Look at the bump, lieutenant!" he shouted. "Nothing to do. They come back for me."

When I got back to the villa it was five o'clock and I went out where we washed the cars, to take a shower. Then I made out my report in my room, sitting in my trousers and an undershirt in front of the open window. In two days the offensive was to start and I would go with the cars to Plava. It was a long time since I had written to the States and I knew I should write but I had let it go so long that it was almost impossible to write now. There was nothing to write about. I sent a couple of army Zona di Guerra post-cards, crossing out everything except, I am well. That should handle them. Those post-cards would be very fine in America; strange and mysterious. This was a strange and mysterious war zone but I supposed it was quite well run and

grim compared to other wars with the Austrians. The Austrian army was created to give Napoleon victories; any Napoleon. I wished we had a Napoleon, but instead we had Il Generale Cadorna, fat and prosperous, and Vittorio Emmanuele, the tiny man with the long thin neck and the goat beard. Over on the right they had the Duke of Aosta. Maybe he was too good-looking to be a great general but he looked like a man. Lots of them would have liked him to be king. He looked like a king. He was the King's uncle and commanded the third army. We were in the second army. There were some British batteries up with the third army. I had met two gunners from that lot, in Milan. They were very nice and we had a big evening. They were big and shy and embarrassed and very appreciative together of anything that happened. I wish that I was with the British. It would have been much simpler. Still I would probably have been killed. Not in this ambulance business. Yes, even in the ambulance business. British ambulance drivers were killed sometimes. Well, I knew I would not be killed. Not in this war. It did not have anything to do with me. It seemed no more dangerous to me myself than war in the movies. I wished to God it was over though. Maybe it would finish this summer. Maybe the Austrians would crack. They had always cracked in other wars. What was the matter with this war? Everybody said the French were through. Rinaldi said that the French had mutinied and troops marched on Paris. I asked him what happened and he said, "Oh, they stopped them." I wanted to go to Austria without war. I wanted to go to the Black Forest. I wanted to go to the Hartz Mountains. Where were the Hartz Mountains anyway? They were fighting in the Carpathians. I did not want to go there anyway. It might be good though. I could go to Spain if there was no war. The sun was going down and the day was cooling off. After supper I would go and see Catherine Barkley. I wish she were here now. I wished I were in Milan with her. I would like to eat at the Cova and then walk down the Via Manzoni in the hot evening and cross over and turn off along the canal and go to the hotel with Catherine Barkley. Maybe she would. Maybe she would pretend that I was her boy that was killed and we would go in the front door and the porter would take off his cap and I would stop at the concierge's desk and ask for the key and she would stand by the elevator and then we would get in the elevator and it would go up very slowly clicking at all the floors and then our floor and the boy would open the door and stand there and she would step out and I would step out and we would walk down the hall and I would put the key in the door and open it and go in and then take down the telephone and ask them to send a bottle of capri bianca in a silver bucket full of ice and you would hear the ice against the pail coming down the corridor and the boy would knock and I would say leave it outside the door please. Because we would not wear any clothes because it was so hot and the window open and the swallows flying over the roofs of the houses and when it was dark afterward and you went to the window very small bats hunting over the houses and close down over the trees and we would drink the capri and the door locked and it hot and only a sheet and the whole night and we would both love each other all night in the hot night in Milan. That was how it ought to be. I would eat quickly and go and see Catherine Barkley.

They talked too much at the mess and I drank wine because to-night we were not all brothers unless I drank a little and talked with the priest about Archbishop Ireland who was, it seemed, a noble man and with whose injustice, the injustices he had received and in which I participated as an American, and of which I had never heard, I feigned acquaintance. It would have been impolite not to have known something of them when I had listened to such a splendid explanation of their causes which were, after all, it seemed, misunderstandings. I thought he had a fine name and he came from Minnesota which made a lovely name: Ireland of Minnesota, Ireland of Wisconsin, Ireland of Michigan. What made it pretty was that it sounded like Island. No that wasn't it. There was more to it than that. Yes, father. That is true, father. Perhaps, father. No, father. Well, maybe yes, father. You know more about it than I do, father. The priest was good but dull. The officers were not good but dull. The King was good but dull. The wine was bad but not dull. It took the enamel off your teeth and left it on the roof of your mouth.

"And the priest was locked up," Rocca said, "because they found the three per cent bonds on his person. It was in France of course. Here they would never have arrested him. He denied all knowledge of the five per cent bonds. This took place at Béziers. I was there and reading of it in the paper, went to the jail and asked to see the priest. It was quite evident he had stolen the bonds."

"I don't believe a word of this," Rinaldi said.

"Just as you like," Rocca said. "But I am telling it for our priest here. It is very informative. He is a priest; he will appreciate it."

The priest smiled. "Go on," he said. "I am listening."

"Of course some of the bonds were not accounted for but the priest had all of the three per cent bonds and several local obligations, I forget exactly what they were. So I went to the jail, now this is the point of the story, and I stood outside his cell and I said as though I were going to confession, 'Bless me, father, for you have sinned.' "

There was great laughter from everybody.

"And what did he say?" asked the priest. Rocca ignored this and went on to explain the joke to me. "You see the point, don't you?" It seemed it was a very funny joke if you understood it properly. They poured me more wine and I told the story about the English private soldier who was placed under the shower bath. Then the major told the story of the eleven Czecho-slovaks and the Hungarian corporal. After some more wine I told the story of the jockey who found the penny. The major said there was an Italian story something like that about the duchess who could not sleep at night. At this point the priest left and I told the story about the travelling salesman who arrived at five o'clock in the morning at Marseilles when the mistral was blowing. The major said he had heard a report that I could drink. I denied this. He said it was true and by the corpse of Bacchus we would test whether it was true or not. Not Bacchus, I said. Not Bacchus. Yes, Bacchus, he said. I should drink cup for cup and glass for glass with Bassi, Fillipo Vincenza. Bassi said no that was no test because he had already drunk twice as much as I. I said that was a foul lie and, Bacchus or no Bacchus, Fillipo Vincenza Bassi or Bassi Fillippo Vicenza had never touched a drop all evening and what was his name anyway? He said was my name Frederico Enrico or Enrico Federico? I said let the best man win, Bacchus barred, and the major started us with red wine in mugs. Half-way through the wine I did not want any more. I remembered where I was going.

"Bassi wins," I said. "He's a better man than I am. I have to go."

"He does really," said Rinaldi. "He has a rendezvous. I know all about it."

"I have to go."

"Another night," said Bassi. "Another night when you feel stronger." He slapped me on the shoulder. There were lighted candles on the table. All the officers were very happy. "Good-night, gentlemen," I said.

Rinaldi went out with me. We stood outside the door on the patch and he said, "You better not go up there drunk."

"I'm not drunk, Rinin. Really."

"You'd better chew some coffee."

"Nonsense."

"I'll get some, baby. You walk up and down." He came back with a handful of roasted coffee beans. "Chew those, baby, and God be with you."

"Bacchus," I said.

"I'll walk down with you."

"I'm perfectly all right."

We walked along together through the town and I chewed the coffee. At the gate of the driveway that led up to the British villa, Rinaldi said good-night.

"Good-night," I said. "Why don't you come in?"

He shook his head. "No," he said. "I like the simpler pleasures."

"Thank you for the coffee beans."

"Nothing, baby. Nothing."

I started down the driveway. The outlines of the cypresses that lined it were sharp and clear. I looked back and saw Rinaldi standing watching me and waved to him.

I sat in the reception hall of the villa, waiting for Catherine Barkley to come down. Some one was coming down the hallway. I stood up, but it was not Catherine. It was Miss Ferguson.

"Hello," she said. "Catherine asked me to tell you she was sorry she couldn't see you this evening."

"I'm so sorry. I hope she's not ill."

"She's not awfully well."

"Will you tell her how sorry I am?"

"Yes, I will."

"Do you think it would be any good to try and see her to-morrow?"

"Yes, I do."

"Thank you very much," I said. "Good-night."

I went out the door and suddenly I felt lonely and empty. I had treated seeing Catherine very lightly, I had gotten somewhat drunk and had nearly forgotten to come but when I could not see her there I was feeling lonely and hollow.

CHAPTER VIII

The next afternoon we heard there was to be an attack up the river that night and that we were to take four cars there. Nobody knew anything about it although they all spoke with great positiveness and strategical knowledge. I was riding in the first car and as we passed the entry to the British hospital I told the driver to stop. The other cars pulled up. I got out and told the driver to go on and that if we had not caught up to them at the junction of the road to Cormons to wait there. I hurried up the driveway and inside the reception hall I asked for Miss Barkley.

"She's on duty."

"Could I see her just for a moment?"

They sent an orderly to see and she came back with him.

"I stopped to ask if you were better. They told me you were on duty, so I asked to see you."

"I'm quite well," she said, "I think the heat knocked me over yesterday."

"I have to go."

"I'll just step out the door a minute."

"And you're all right?" I asked outside.

"Yes, darling. Are you coming to-night?"

"No. I'm leaving now for a show up above Plava."

"A show?"

"I don't think it's anything."

"And you'll be back?"

"To-morrow."

She was unclasping something from her neck. She put it in my hand. "It's a Saint Anthony," she said. "And come to-morrow night."

"You're not a Catholic, are you?"

"No. But they say a Saint Anthony's very useful."

"I'll take care of him for you. Good-by."

"No," she said, "not good-by."

"All right."

"Be a good boy and be careful. No, you can't kiss me here. You can't."

"All right."

I looked back and saw her standing on the steps. She waved and I kissed my hand and held it out. She waved again and then I was out of the driveway and climbing up into the seat of the ambulance and we started. The Saint Anthony was in a little white metal capsule. I opened the capsule and spilled him out into my hand.

"Saint Anthony?" asked the driver.

"Yes."

"I have one." His right hand left the wheel and opened a button on his tunic and pulled it out from under his shirt.

"See?"

I put my Saint Anthony back in the capsule, spilled the thin gold chain together and put it all in my breast pocket.

"You don't wear him?"

"No."

"It's better to wear him. That's what it's for."

"All right," I said. I undid the clasp of the gold chain and put it around my neck and clasped it. The saint hung down on the outside of my uniform and I undid the throat of my tunic, unbuttoned the shirt collar and dropped him in under the shirt. I felt him in his metal box against my chest while we drove. Then I forgot about him. After I was wounded I never found him. Some one probably got it at one of the dressing stations.

We drove fast when we were over the bridge and soon we saw the dust of the other cars ahead down the road. The road curved and we saw the three cars looking quite small, the dust rising from the wheels and going off through the trees. We caught them and passed them and turned off on a road that climbed up into the hills. Driving in convoy is not unpleasant if you are the first car and I settled back in the seat and watched the country. We were in the foot-hills on the near side of the river and as the road mounted there were the high mountains off to the north with snow still on the tops. I looked back and saw the three cars all climbing, spaced by the interval of their dust. We passed a long column of loaded mules, the drivers walking along beside the mules wearing red fezzes. They were bersaglieri.

Beyond the mule train the road was empty and we climbed through the hills and then went down over the shoulder of a long hill into a river-valley. There were trees along both sides of the road and through the right line of trees I saw the river, the water clear, fast and shallow. The river was low and there were stretches of sand and pebbles with a narrow channel of water and sometimes the water spread like a sheen over the pebbly bed. Close to the bank I saw deep pools, the water blue like the sky. I saw arched stone bridges over the river where tracks turned off from the road and we passed stone farmhouses with pear trees candelabraed against their south walls and low stone walls in the fields. The road went up the valley a long way and then we turned off and commenced to climb into the hills again. The road climbed steeply going up and back and forth through chestnut woods to level finally along a ridge. I could look down through the woods and see, far below, with the sun on it, the line of the river that separated the two armies. We went along the rough

new military road that followed the crest of the ridge and I looked to the north at the two ranges of mountains, green and dark to the snow-line and then white and lovely in the sun. Then, as the road mounted along the ridge, I saw a third range of mountains, higher snow mountains, that looked chalky white and furrowed, with strange planes, and then there were mountains far off beyond all these that you could hardly tell if you really saw. Those were all the Austrians' mountains and we had nothing like them. Ahead there was a rounded turn-off in the road to the right and looking down I could see the road dropping through the trees. There were troops on this road and motor trucks and mules with mountain guns and as we went down, keeping to the side, I could see the river far down below, the line of ties and rails running along it, the old bridge where the railway crossed to the other side and across, under a hill beyond the river, the broken houses of the little town that was to be taken.

It was nearly dark when we came down and turned onto the main road that ran beside the river.

CHAPTER IX

The road was crowded and there were screens of corn-stalk and straw matting on both sides and matting over the top so that it was like the entrance at a circus or a native village. We drove slowly in this matting-covered tunnel and came out onto a bare cleared space where the railway station had been. The road here was below the level of the river bank and all along the side of the sunken road there were holes dug in the bank with infantry in them. The sun was going down and looking up along the bank as we drove I saw the Austrian observation balloons above the hills on the other side dark against the sunset. We parked the cars beyond a brickyard. The ovens and some deep holes had been equipped as dressing stations. There were three doctors that I knew. I talked with the major and learned that when it should start and our cars should be loaded we would drive them back along the screened road and up to the main road along the ridge where there would be a post and other cars to clear them. He hoped the road would not jam. It was a one-road show. The road was screened because it was in sight of the Austrians across the river. Here at the brickyard we were sheltered from rifle or machine-gun fire by the river bank. There was one smashed bridge across the river. They were going to put over another bridge when the bombardment started and some troops were to cross at the shallows up above at the bend of the river. The major was a little man with upturned mustaches. He had been in the war in Libya and wore two wound-stripes. He said that if the thing went well he would see that I was decorated. I said I hoped it would go well but that he was too kind. I asked him if there was a big dugout where the drivers could stay and he sent a soldier to show me. I went with him and found the dugout, which was very good. The drivers were pleased with it and I left them there. The major asked me to have a drink with him and two other officers. We drank rum and it was very friendly. Outside it was getting dark. I asked what time the attack was to be and they said as soon as it was dark. I went back to the drivers. They were sitting in the dugout talking and when I came in they stopped. I gave them each a package of cigarettes, Macedonias, loosely packed cigarettes that spilled tobacco and needed to have the ends twisted before you smoked them. Manera lit his lighter and passed it around. The lighter was shaped like a

Fiat radiator. I told them what I had heard.

"Why didn't we see the post when we came down?" Passini asked.

"It was just beyond where we turned off."

"That road will be a dirty mess," Manera said.

"They'll shell the —— out of us."

"Probably."

"What about eating, lieutenant? We won't get a chance to eat after this thing starts."

"I'll go and see now," I said.

"You want us to stay here or can we look around?"

"Better stay here."

I went back to the major's dugout and he said the field kitchen would be along and the drivers could come and get their stew. He would loan them mess tins if they did not have them. I said I thought they had them. I went back and told the drivers I would get them as soon as the food came. Manera said he hoped it would come before the bombardment started. They were silent until I went out. They were all mechanics and hated the war.

I went out to look at the cars and see what was going on and then came back and sat down in the dugout with the four drivers. We sat on the ground with our backs against the wall and smoked. Outside it was nearly dark. The earth of the dugout was warm and dry and I let my shoulders back against the wall, sitting on the small of my back, and relaxed.

"Who goes to the attack?" asked Gavuzzi.

"Bersaglieri."

"All bersaglieri?"

"I think so."

"There aren't enough troops here for a real attack."

"It is probably to draw attention from where the real attack will be."

"Do the men know that who attack?"

"I don't think so."

"Of course they don't," Manera said. "They wouldn't attack if they did."

"Yes, they would," Passini said. "Bersaglieri are fools."

"They are brave and have good discipline," I said.

"They are big through the chest by measurement, and healthy. But they are still fools."

"The granatieri are tall," Manera said. This was a joke. They all laughed.

"Were you there, Tenente, when they wouldn't attack and they shot every tenth man?"

"No."

"It is true. They lined them up afterward and took every tenth man. Carabinieri shot them."

"Carabinieri," said Passini and spat on the floor. "But those grenadiers; all over six feet. They wouldn't attack."

"If everybody would not attack the war would be over," Manera said.

"It wasn't that way with the granatieri. They were afraid. The officers all came from such good families."

"Some of the officers went alone."

"A sergeant shot two officers who would not get out."

"Some troops went out."

"Those that went out were not lined up when they took the tenth man."

"One of those shot by the carabinieri is from my town," Passini said. "He was a big smart tall boy to be in the granatieri. Always in Rome. Always with the girls. Always with the carabinieri." He laughed. "Now they have a guard outside his house with a bayonet and nobody can come to see his mother and father and sisters and his father loses his civil rights and cannot even vote. They are all without law to protect them. Anybody can take their property."

"If it wasn't that that happens to their families nobody would go to the attack."

"Yes. Alpini would. These V. E. soldiers would. Some bersaglieri."

"Bersaglieri have run too. Now they try to forget it."

"You should not let us talk this way, Tenente. Evviva l'esercito," Passini said sarcastically.

"I know how you talk," I said. "But as long as you drive the cars and behave——"

"——and don't talk so other officers can hear," Manera finished.

"I believe we should get the war over," I said. "It would not finish it if one side stopped fighting. It would only be worse if we stopped fighting."

"It could not be worse," Passini said respectfully. "There is nothing worse than war."

"Defeat is worse."

"I do not believe it," Passini said still respectfully. "What is defeat? You go home."

"They come after you. They take your home. They take your sisters."

"I don't believe it," Passini said. "They can't do that to everybody. Let everybody defend his home. Let them keep their sisters in the house."

"They hang you. They come and make you be a soldier again. Not in the auto-ambulance, in the infantry."

"They can't hang every one."

"An outside nation can't make you be a soldier," Manera said. "At the first battle you all run."

"Like the Tchecos."

"I think you do not know anything about being conquered and so you think it is not bad."

"Tenente," Passini said. "We understand you let us talk. Listen. There is nothing as bad as war. We in the auto-ambulance cannot even realize at all how bad it is. When people realize how bad it is they cannot do anything to stop it because they go crazy. There are some people who never realize. There are people who are afraid of their officers. It is with them the war is made."

"I know it is bad but we must finish it."

"It doesn't finish. There is no finish to a war."

"Yes there is."

Passini shook his head.

"War is not won by victory. What if we take San Gabriele? What if we take the Carso and Monfalcone and Trieste? Where are we then? Did you see all the far mountains to-day? Do you think we could take all them too? Only if the Austrians stop fighting. One side must stop fighting. Why don't we stop fighting? If they come down into Italy they will get tired and go away. They have their own country. But no, instead there is a war."

"You're an orator."

"We think. We read. We are not peasants. We are mechanics. But even the peasants know better than to believe in a war. Everybody hates this war."

"There is a class that controls a country that is stupid and does not realize anything and never can. That is why we have this war."

"Also they make money out of it."

"Most of them don't," said Passini. "They are too stupid. They do it for nothing. For stupidity."

"We must shut up," said Manera. "We talk too much even for the Tenente."

"He likes it," said Passini. "We will convert him."

"But now we will shut up," Manera said.

"Do we eat yet, Tenente?" Gavuzzi asked.

"I will go and see," I said. Gordini stood up and went outside with me.

"Is there anything I can do, Tenente? Can I help in any way?" He was the quietest one of the four. "Come with me if you want," I said, "and we'll see."

It was dark outside and the long light from the search-lights was moving over the mountains. There were big search-lights on that front mounted on camions that you passed sometimes on the roads at night, close behind the lines, the camion stopped a little off the road, an officer directing the light and the crew scared. We crossed the brickyard, and stopped at the main dressing station. There was a little shelter of green branches outside over the entrance and in the dark the night wind rustled the leaves dried by the sun. Inside there was a light. The major was at the telephone sitting on a box. One of the medical captains said the attack had been put forward an hour. He offered me a glass of cognac. I looked at the board tables, the instruments shining in the light, the basins and the stoppered bottles. Gordini stood behind me. The major got up from the telephone.

"It starts now," he said. "It has been put back again."

I looked outside, it was dark and the Austrian search-lights were moving on the mountains behind us. It was quiet for a moment still, then from all the guns behind us the bombardment started.

"Savoia," said the major.

"About the soup, major," I said. He did not hear me. I repeated it.

"It hasn't come up."

A big shell came in and burst outside in the brickyard. Another burst and in the noise you could hear the smaller noise of the brick and dirt raining down.

"What is there to eat?"

"We have a little pasta asciutta," the major said.

"I'll take what you can give me."

The major spoke to an orderly who went out of sight in the back and came back with a metal basin of cold cooked macaroni. I handed it to Gordini.

"Have you any cheese?"

The major spoke grudgingly to the orderly who ducked back into the hole again and came out with a quarter of a white cheese.

"Thank you very much," I said.

"You'd better not go out."

Outside something was set down beside the entrance. One of the two men who had carried it looked in.

"Bring him in," said the major. "What's the matter with you? Do you want us to come outside and get him?"

The two stretcher-bearers picked up the man under the arms and by the legs and brought him in.

"Slit the tunic," the major said.

He held a forceps with some gauze in the end. The two captains took off their coats. "Get out of here," the major said to the two stretcher-bearers.

"Come on," I said to Gordini.

"You better wait until the shelling is over," the major said over his shoulder.

"They want to eat," I said.

"As you wish."

Outside we ran across the brickyard. A shell burst short near the river bank. Then there was one that we did not hear coming until the sudden rush. We both went flat and with the flash and bump of the burst and the smell heard the singing off of the fragments and the rattle of falling brick. Gordini got up and ran for the dugout. I was after him, holding the cheese, its smooth surface covered with brick dust. Inside the dugout were the three drivers sitting against the wall, smoking.

"Here, you patriots," I said.

"How are the cars?" Manera asked.

"All right."

"Did they scare you, Tenente?"

"You're damned right," I said.

I took out my knife, opened it, wiped off the blade and pared off the dirty outside surface of the cheese. Gavuzzi handed me the basin of macaroni.

"Start in to eat, Tenente."

"No," I said. "Put it on the floor. We'll all eat."

"There are no forks."

"What the hell," I said in English.

I cut the cheese into pieces and laid them on the macaroni.

"Sit down to it," I said. They sat down and waited. I put thumb and fingers into the macaroni and lifted. A mass loosened.

"Lift it high, Tenente."

I lifted it to arm's length and the strands cleared. I lowered it into the mouth, sucked and snapped in the ends, and chewed, then took a bite of cheese, chewed, and then a drink of the wine. It tasted of rusty metal. I handed the canteen back to Passini.

"It's rotten," he said. "It's been in there too long. I had it in the car."

They were all eating, holding their chins close over the basin, tipping their heads back, sucking in the ends. I took another mouthful and some cheese and a rinse of wine. Something landed outside that shook the earth.

"Four hundred twenty or minnenwerfer," Gavuzzi said.

"There aren't any four hundred twenties in the mountains," I said.

"They have big Skoda guns. I've seen the holes."

"Three hundred fives."

We went on eating. There was a cough, a noise like a railway engine starting and then an explosion that shook the earth again.

"This isn't a deep dugout," Passini said.

"That was a big trench mortar."

"Yes, sir."

I ate the end of my piece of cheese and took a swallow of wine. Through the other noise I heard a cough, then came the chuh-chuh-chuh-chuh—then there was a flash, as when a blast-furnace door is swung open, and a roar that started white and went red and on and on in a

rushing wind. I tried to breathe but my breath would not come and I felt myself rush bodily out of myself and out and out and out and all the time bodily in the wind. I went out swiftly, all of myself, and I knew I was dead and that it had all been a mistake to think you just died. Then I floated, and instead of going on I felt myself slide back. I breathed and I was back. The ground was torn up and in front of my head there was a splintered beam of wood. In the jolt of my head I heard somebody crying. I thought some-body was screaming. I tried to move but I could not move. I heard the machine-guns and rifles firing across the river and all along the river. There was a great splashing and I saw the star-shells go up and burst and float whitely and rockets going up and heard the bombs, all this in a moment, and then I heard close to me some one saying "Mama Mia! Oh, mama Mia!" I pulled and twisted and got my legs loose finally and turned around and touched him. It was Passini and when I touched him he screamed. His legs were toward me and I saw in the dark and the light that they were both smashed above the knee. One leg was gone and the other was held by tendons and part of the trouser and the stump twitched and jerked as though it were not connected. He bit his arm and moaned, "Oh mama mia, mama Mia," then, "Dio te salve, Maria. Dio te salve, Maria. Oh Jesus shoot me Christ shoot me mama mia mama Mia oh purest lovely Mary shoot me. Stop it. Stop it. Stop it. Oh Jesus lovely Mary stop it. Oh oh oh oh," then choking, "Mama mama mia." Then he was quiet, biting his arm, the stump of his leg twitching.

"Porta feriti!" I shouted holding my hands cupped. "Porta feriti!" I tried to get closer to Passini to try to put a tourniquet on the legs but I could not move. I tried again and my legs moved a little. I could pull backward along with my arms and elbows. Passini was quiet now. I sat beside him, undid my tunic and tried to rip the tail of my shirt. It would not rip and I bit the edge of the cloth to start it. Then I thought of his puttees. I had on wool stockings but Passini wore puttees. All the drivers wore puttees but Passini had only one leg. I unwound the puttee and while I was doing it I saw there was no need to try and make a tourniquet because he was dead already. I made sure he was dead. There were three others to locate. I sat up straight and as I did so something inside my head moved like the weights on a doll's eyes and it hit me inside in back of my eyeballs. My legs felt warm and wet and my shoes were wet and warm inside. I knew that I was hit and leaned over and put my hand on my knee. My knee wasn't there. My hand went in and my knee was down on my shin. I wiped my hand on my shirt and another float-ing light came very slowly down and I looked at my leg and was very afraid. Oh, God, I said, get me out of here. I knew, however, that there had been three others. There were four drivers. Passini was dead. That left three. Some one took hold of me under the arms and some-body else lifted my legs.

"There are three others," I said. "One is dead."

"It's Manera. We went for a stretcher but there wasn't any. How are you, Tenente?"

"Where is Gordini and Gavuzzi?"

"Gordini's at the post getting ban-daged. Gavuzzi has your legs. Hold on to my neck, Tenente. Are you badly hit?"

"In the leg. How is Gordini?"

"He's all right. It was a big trench mortar shell."

"Passini's dead."

"Yes. He's dead."

A shell fell close and they both

dropped to the ground and dropped me. "I'm sorry, Tenente," said Manera. "Hang onto my neck."

"If you drop me again."

"It was because we were scared."

"Are you unwounded?"

"We are both wounded a little."

"Can Gordini drive?"

"I don't think so."

They dropped me once more before we reached the post.

"You sons of bitches," I said.

"I am sorry, Tenente," Manera said. "We won't drop you again."

Outside the post a great many of us lay on the ground in the dark. They carried wounded in and brought them out. I could see the light come out from the dressing station when the curtain opened and they brought some one in or out. The dead were off to one side. The doctors were working with their sleeves up to their shoulders and were red as butchers. There were not enough stretchers. Some of the wounded were noisy but most were quiet. The wind blew the leaves in the bower over the door of the dressing station and the night was getting cold. Stretcher-bearers came in all the time, put their stretchers down, unloaded them and went away. As soon as I got to the dressing station Manera brought a medical sergeant out and he put bandages on both my legs. He said there was so much dirt blown into the wound that there had not been much hemorrhage. They would take me as soon as possible. He went back inside. Gordini could not drive, Manera said. His shoulder was smashed and his head was hurt. He had not felt bad but now the shoulder had stiffened. He was sitting up beside one of the brick walls. Manera and Gavuzzi each went off with a load of wounded. They could drive all right. The British had come with three ambulances and they had two men on each ambulance. One of their drivers came over to me, brought by Gordini who looked very white and sick. The Britisher leaned over.

"Are you hit badly?" he asked. He was a tall man and wore steel-rimmed spectacles.

"In the legs."

"It's not serious I hope. Will you have a cigarette?"

"Thanks."

"They tell me you've lost two drivers."

"Yes. One killed and the fellow that brought you."

"What rotten luck. Would you like us to take the cars?"

"That's what I wanted to ask you."

"We'd take quite good care of them and return them to the villa. 206 aren't you?"

"Yes."

"It's a charming place. I've seen you about. They tell me you're an American."

"Yes."

"I'm English."

"No!"

"Yes, English. Did you think I was Italian? There were some Italians with one of our units."

"It would be fine if you would take the cars," I said.

"We'll be most careful of them," he straightened up. "This chap of yours was very anxious for me to see you." He patted Gordini on the shoulder. Gordini winced and smiled. The Englishman broke into voluble and perfect Italian. "Now everything is arranged. I've seen your Tenente. We will take over the two cars. You won't worry now." He broke off, "I must do something about getting you out of here. I'll see the medical wallahs. We'll take you back with us."

He walked across to the dressing station, stepping carefully among the wounded. I saw the blanket open, the light came out and he went in.

"He will look after you, Tenente," Gordini said.

"How are you, Franco?"

"I am all right." He sat down beside me. In a moment the blanket in front of the dressing station opened and two stretcher-bearers came out followed by the tall Englishman. He brought them over to me.

"Here is the American Tenente," he said in Italian.

"I'd rather wait," I said. "There are much worse wounded than me. I'm all right."

"Come, come," he said. "Don't be a bloody hero." Then in Italian: "Lift him very carefully about the legs. His legs are very painful. He is the legitimate son of President Wilson." They picked me up and took me into the dressing room. Inside they were operating on all the tables. The little major looked at us furious. He recognized me and waved a forceps.

"Ça va bien?"

"Ça va."

"I have brought him in," the tall Englishman said in Italian. "The only son of the American Ambassador. He can be here until you are ready to take him. Then I will take him with my first load." He bent over me. "I'll look up their adjutant to do your papers and it will all go much faster." He stooped to go under the doorway and went out. The major was unhooking the forceps now, dropping them in a basin. I followed his hands with my eyes. Now he was bandaging. Then the stretcher-bearers took the man off the table.

"I'll take the American Tenente," one of the captains said. They lifted me onto the table. It was hard and slippery. There were many strong smells, chemical smells and the sweet smell of blood. They took off my trousers and the medical captain commenced dictating to the sergeant-adjutant while he worked, "Multiple superficial wounds of the left and right thigh and left and right knee and right foot. Profound wounds of right knee and

foot. Lacerations of the scalp (he probed—Does that hurt?—Christ, yes!) with possible fracture of the skull. Incurred in the line of duty. That's what keeps you from being court-martialled for self-inflicted wounds," he said. "Would you like a drink of brandy? How did you run into this thing anyway? What were you trying to do? Commit suicide? Antitetanus please, and mark a cross on both legs. Thank you. I'll clean this up a little, wash it out, and put on a dressing. Your blood coagulates beautifully."

The adjutant, looking up from the paper, "What inflicted the wounds?"

The medical captain, "What hit you?"

Me, with the eyes shut, "A trench mortar shell."

The captain, doing things that hurt sharply and severing tissue—"Are you sure?"

Me—trying to lie still and feeling my stomach flutter when the flesh was cut, "I think so."

Captain doctor—(interested in something he was finding), "Fragments of enemy trench mortar shell. Now I'll probe for some of this if you like but it's not necessary. I'll paint all this and— Does that sting? Good, that's nothing to how it will feel later. The pain hasn't started yet. Bring him a glass of brandy. The shock dulls the pain; but this is all right, you have nothing to worry about if it doesn't infect and it rarely does now. How is your head?"

"Good Christ!" I said.

"Better not drink too much brandy then. If you've got a fracture you don't want inflammation. How does that feel?"

Sweat ran all over me.

"Good Christ!" I said.

"I guess you've got a fracture all right. I'll wrap you up and don't bounce your head around." He bandaged, his hands moving very fast and the bandage coming taut and sure. "All right, good luck and Vive la France."

"He's an American," one of the other captains said.

"I thought you said he was a Frenchman. He talks French," the captain said. "I've known him before. I always thought he was French." He drank a half tumbler of cognac. "Bring on something serious. Get some more of that Anti-tetanus." The captain waved to me. They lifted me and the blanket-flap went across my face as we went out. Outside the sergeant-adjutant knelt down beside me where I lay, "Name?" he asked softly. "Middle name? First name? Rank? Where born? What class? What corps?" and so on. "I'm sorry for your head, Tenente. I hope you feel better. I'm sending you now with the English ambulance."

"I'm all right," I said. "Thank you very much." The pain that the major had spoken about had started and all that was happening was without interest or relation. After a while the English ambulance came up and they put me onto a stretcher and lifted the stretcher up to the ambulance level and shoved it in. There was another stretcher by the side with a man on it whose nose I could see, waxy-looking, out of the bandages. He breathed very heavily. There were stretchers lifted and slid into the slings above. The tall English driver came around and looked in, "I'll take it very easily," he said. "I hope you'll be comfy." I felt the engine start, felt him climb up into the front seat, felt the brake come off and the clutch go in, then we started. I lay still and let the pain ride.

As the ambulance climbed along the road, it was slow in the traffic, sometimes it stopped, sometimes it backed on a turn, then finally it climbed quite fast. I felt something dripping. At first it dropped slowly and regularly, then it pattered into a stream. I shouted to the driver. He stopped the car and looked in through the hole behind his seat.

"What is it?"

"The man on the stretcher over me has a hemorrhage."

"We're not far from the top. I wouldn't be able to get the stretcher out alone." He started the car. The stream kept on. In the dark I could not see where it came from the canvas overhead. I tried to move sideways so that it did not fall on me. Where it had run down under my shirt it was warm and sticky. I was cold and my leg hurt so that it made me sick. After a while the stream from the stretcher above lessened and started to drip again and I heard and felt the canvas above move as the man on the stretcher settled more comfortably.

"How is he?" the Englishman called back. "We're almost up."

"He's dead I think," I said.

The drops fell very slowly, as they fall from an icicle after the sun has gone. It was cold in the car in the night as the road climbed. At the post on the top they took the stretcher out and put another in and we went on.

CHAPTER X

In the ward at the field hospital they told me a visitor was coming to see me in the afternoon. It was a hot day and there were many flies in the room. My orderly had cut paper into strips and tied the strips to a stick to make a brush that swished the flies away. I watched them settle on the ceiling. When he stopped swishing and fell asleep they came down and I blew them away and finally covered my face with my hands and slept too. It was very hot and when I woke my legs itched. I waked the orderly and he poured mineral water on the dressings.

That made the bed damp and cool. Those of us that were awake talked across the ward. The afternoon was a quiet time. In the morning they came to each bed in turn, three men nurses and a doctor and picked you up out of bed and carried you into the dressing room so that the beds could be made while we were having our wounds dressed. It was not a pleasant trip to the dressing room and I did not know until later that beds could be made with men in them. My orderly had finished pouring water and the bed felt cool and lovely and I was telling him where to scratch on the soles of my feet against the itching when one of the doctors brought in Rinaldi. He came in very fast and bent down over the bed and kissed me. I saw he wore gloves.

"How are you, baby? How do you feel? I bring you this—" It was a bottle of cognac. The orderly brought a chair and he sat down, "and good news. You will be decorated. They want to get you the medaglia d'argento but perhaps they can get only the bronze."

"What for?"

"Because you are gravely wounded. They say if you can prove you did any heroic act you can get the silver. Otherwise it will be the bronze. Tell me exactly what happened. Did you do any heroic act?"

"No," I said. "I was blown up while we were eating cheese."

"Be serious. You must have done something heroic either before or after. Remember carefully."

"I did not."

"Didn't you carry anybody on your back? Gordini says you carried several people on your back but the medical major at the first post declares it is impossible. He had to sign the proposition for the citation."

"I didn't carry anybody. I couldn't move."

"That doesn't matter," said Rinaldi.

He took off his gloves.

"I think we can get you the silver. Didn't you refuse to be medically aided before the others?"

"Not very firmly."

"That doesn't matter. Look how you are wounded. Look at your valorous conduct in asking to go always to the first line. Besides, the operation was successful."

"Did they cross the river all right?"

"Enormously. They take nearly a thousand prisoners. It's in the bulletin. Didn't you see it?"

"No."

"I'll bring it to you. It is a successful coup de main."

"How is everything?"

"Splendid. We are all splendid. Everybody is proud of you. Tell me just exactly how it happened. I am positive you will get the silver. Go on tell me. Tell me all about it." He paused and thought. "Maybe you will get an English medal too. There was an English there. I'll go and see him and ask if he will recommend you. He ought to be able to do something. Do you suffer much? Have a drink. Orderly, go get a corkscrew. Oh you should see what I did in the removal of three metres of small intestine and better now than ever. It is one for *The Lancet*. You do me a translation and I will send it to *The Lancet*. Every day I am better. Poor dear baby, how do you feel? Where is that damn corkscrew? You are so brave and quiet I forget you are suffering." He slapped his gloves on the edge of the bed.

"Here is the corkscrew, Signor Tenente," the orderly said.

"Open the bottle. Bring a glass. Drink that, baby. How is your poor head? I looked at your papers. You haven't any fracture. That major at the first post was a hog-butcher. I would take you and never hurt you. I never hurt anybody. I learn how to do it. Every day I learn to do things smoother and better. You must forgive me for talking so much, baby. I am very moved to see you badly wounded. There, drink that. It's good. It cost fifteen lire. It ought to be good. Five stars. After I leave here I'll go see that English and he'll get you an English medal."

"They don't give them like that."

"You are so modest. I will send the liaison officer. He can handle the English."

"Have you seen Miss Barkley?"

"I will bring her here. I will go now and bring her here."

"Don't go," I said. "Tell me about Gorizia. How are the girls?"

"There are no girls. For two weeks now they haven't changed them. I don't go there any more. It is disgraceful. They aren't girls; they are old war comrades."

"You don't go at all?"

"I just go to see if there is anything new. I stop by. They all ask for you. It is a disgrace that they should stay so long that they become friends."

"Maybe girls don't want to go to the front any more."

"Of course they do. They have plenty of girls. It is just bad administration. They are keeping them for the pleasure of dugout hiders in the rear."

"Poor Rinaldi," I said. "All alone at the war with no new girls."

Rinaldi poured himself another glass of the cognac.

"I don't think it will hurt you, baby. You take it."

I drank the cognac and felt it warm all the way down. Rinaldi poured another glass. He was quieter now. He held up the glass. "To your valorous wounds. To the silver medal. Tell me, baby, when you lie here all the time in the hot weather don't you get excited?"

"Sometimes."

"I can't imagine lying like that. I would go crazy."

"You are crazy."

"I wish you were back. No one to come in at night from adventures. No one to make fun of. No one to lend me money. No blood brother and roommate. Why do you get yourself wounded?"

"You can make fun of the priest."

"That priest. It isn't me that makes fun of him. It is the captain. I like him. If you must have a priest have that priest. He's coming to see you. He makes big preparations."

"I like him."

"Oh, I knew it. Sometimes I think you and he are a little that way. You know."

"No, you don't."

"Yes, I do sometimes. A little that way like the number of the first regiment of the Brigata Ancona."

"Oh, go to hell."

He stood up and put on his gloves.

"Oh I love to tease you, baby. With your priest and your English girl, and really you are just like me underneath."

"No, I'm not."

"Yes, we are. You are really an Italian. All fire and smoke and nothing inside. You only pretend to be American. We are brothers and we love each other."

"Be good while I'm gone," I said.

"I will send Miss Barkley. You are better with her without me. You are purer and sweeter."

"Oh, go to hell."

"I will send her. Your lovely cool goddess. English goddess. My God what would a man do with a woman like that except worship her? What else is an Englishwoman good for?"

"You are an ignorant foul-mouthed dago."

"A what?"

"An ignorant wop."

"Wop. You are a frozen-faced . . . wop."

"You are ignorant. Stupid." I saw that

word pricked him and kept on. "Uninformed. Inexperienced, stupid from inexperience."

"Truly? I tell you something about your good women. Your goddesses. There is only one difference between taking a girl who has always been good and a woman. With a girl it is painful. That's all I know." He slapped the bed with his glove. "And you never know if the girl will really like it."

"Don't get angry."

"I'm not angry. I just tell you, baby, for your own good. To save you trouble."

"That's the only difference?"

"Yes. But millions of fools like you don't know it."

"You were sweet to tell me."

"We won't quarrel, baby. I love you too much. But don't be a fool."

"No. I'll be wise like you."

"Don't be angry, baby. Laugh. Take a drink. I must go, really."

"You're a good old boy."

"Now you see. Underneath we are the same. We are war brothers. Kiss me good-by."

"You're sloppy."

"No. I am just more affectionate."

I felt his breath come toward me. "Good-by. I come to see you again soon." His breath went away. "I won't kiss you if you don't want. I'll send your English girl. Good-by, baby. The cognac is under the bed. Get well soon."

He was gone.

CHAPTER XI

It was dusk when the priest came. They had brought the soup and afterwards taken away the bowls and I was lying looking at the rows of beds and out the window at the tree-top that moved a little in the evening breeze. The breeze came in through the window and it was cooler with the evening. The flies were on the ceiling now and on the electric light bulbs that hung on wires. The lights were only turned on when some one was brought in at night or when something was being done. It made me feel very young to have the dark come after the dusk and then remain. It was like being put to bed after early supper. The orderly came down between the beds and stopped. Some one was with him. It was the priest. He stood there small, brown-faced, and embarrassed.

"How do you do?" he asked. He put some packages down by the bed, on the floor.

"All right, father."

He sat down in the chair that had been brought for Rinaldi and looked out of the window embarrassedly. I noticed his face looked very tired.

"I can only stay a minute," he said. "It is late."

"It's not late. How is the mess?"

He smiled. "I am still a great joke," he sounded tired too. "Thank God they are all well."

"I am so glad you are all right," he said. "I hope you don't suffer." He seemed very tired and I was not used to seeing him tired.

"Not any more."

"I miss you at the mess."

"I wish I were there. I always enjoyed our talking."

"I brought you a few little things," he said. He picked up the packages. "This is mosquito netting. This is a bottle of vermouth. You like vermouth? These are English papers."

"Please open them."

He was pleased and undid them. I held the mosquito netting in my hands. The vermouth he held up for me to see and then put it on the floor beside the bed. I held up one of the sheaf of English papers. I could read the headlines by turning it so the half-light from the window was on it. It was *The News of the World*.

"The others are illustrated," he said.

"It will be a great happiness to read them. Where did you get them?"

"I sent for them to Mestre. I will have more."

"You were very good to come, father. Will you drink a glass of vermouth?"

"Thank you. You keep it. It's for you."

"No, drink a glass."

"All right. I will bring you more then."

The orderly brought the glasses and opened the bottle. He broke off the cork and the end had to be shoved down into the bottle. I could see the priest was disappointed but he said, "That's all right. It's no matter."

"Here's to your health, father."

"To your better health."

Afterward he held the glass in his hand and we looked at one another. Sometimes we talked and were good friends but tonight it was difficult.

"What's the matter, father? You seem very tired."

"I am tired but I have no right to be."

"It's the heat."

"No. This is only the spring. I feel very low."

"You have the war disgust."

"No. But I hate the war."

"I don't enjoy it," I said. He shook his head and looked out of the window.

"You do not mind it. You do not see it. You must forgive me. I know you are wounded."

"That is an accident."

"Still even wounded you do not see it. I can tell. I do not see it myself but I feel it a little."

"When I was wounded we were talking about it. Passini was talking."

The priest put down the glass. He was thinking about something else.

"I know them because I am like they are," he said.

"You are different though."

"But really I am like they are."

"The officers don't see anything."

"Some of them do. Some are very delicate and feel worse than any of us."

"They are mostly different."

"It is not education or money. It is something else. Even if they had education or money men like Passini would not wish to be officers. I would not be an officer."

"You rank as an officer. I am an officer."

"I am not really. You are not even an Italian. You are a foreigner. But you are nearer the officers than you are to the men."

"What is the difference?"

"I cannot say it easily. There are people who would make war. In this country there are many like that. There are other people who would not make war."

"But the first ones make them do it."

"Yes."

"And I help them."

"You are a foreigner. You are a patriot."

"And the ones who would not make war? Can they stop it?"

"I do not know."

He looked out of the window again. I watched his face.

"Have they ever been able to stop it?"

"They are not organized to stop things and when they get organized their leaders sell them out."

"Then it's hopeless?"

"It is never hopeless. But sometimes I cannot hope. I try always to hope but sometimes I cannot."

"Maybe the war will be over."

"I hope so."

"What will you do then?"

"If it is possible I will return to the Abruzzi."

His brown face was suddenly very happy.

"You love the Abruzzi?"

"Yes, I love it very much."

"You ought to go there then."

"I would be too happy. If I could live there and love God and serve Him."

"And be respected," I said.

"Yes and be respected. Why not?"

"No reason not. You should be respected."

"It does not matter. But there in my country it is understood that a man may love God. It is not a dirty joke."

"I understand."

He looked at me and smiled.

"You understand but you do not love God."

"No."

"You do not love Him at all?" he asked.

"I am afraid of Him in the night sometimes."

"You should love Him."

"I don't love much."

"Yes," he said. "You do. What you tell me about in the nights. That is not love. That is only passion and lust. When you love you wish to do things for. You wish to sacrifice for. You wish to serve."

"I don't love."

"You will. I know you will. Then you will be happy."

"I'm happy. I've always been happy."

"It is another thing. You cannot know about it unless you have it."

"Well," I said. "If I ever get it I will tell you."

"I stay too long and talk too much." He was worried that he really did.

"No. Don't go. How about loving women? If I really loved some woman would it be like that?"

"I don't know about that. I never loved any woman."

"What about your mother?"

"Yes, I must have loved my mother."

"Did you always love God?"

"Ever since I was a little boy."

"Well," I said. I did not know what to say. "You are a fine boy," I said.

"I am a boy," he said. "But you call me father."

"That's politeness."

He smiled.

"I must go, really," he said. "You do not want me for anything?" he asked hopefully.

"No. Just to talk."

"I will take your greetings to the mess."

"Thank you for the many fine presents."

"Nothing."

"Come and see me again."

"Yes. Good-by," he patted my hand.

"So long," I said in dialect.

"Ciaou," he repeated.

It was dark in the room and the orderly, who had sat by the foot of the bed, got up and went out with him. I liked him very much and I hoped he would get back to the Abruzzi some time. He had a rotten life in the mess and he was fine about it but I thought how he would be in his own country. At Capracotta, he had told me, there were trout in the stream below the town. It was forbidden to play the flute at night. When the young men serenaded only the flute was forbidden. Why, I had asked. Because it was bad for the girls to hear the flute at night. The peasants all called you "Don" and when you met them they took off their hats. His father hunted every day and stopped to eat at the houses of peasants. They were always honored. For a foreigner to hunt he must present a certificate that he had never been arrested. There were bears on the Gran Sasso D'Italia but it was a long way. Aquila was a fine town. It was cool in the summer at night and the spring in Abruzzi was the most beautiful in Italy. But what was lovely was the fall to go hunting through the chestnut woods. The birds were all good because they fed on grapes and you never took a lunch because the peasants were always honored if you would eat with them at their houses. After a while I went to sleep.

CHAPTER XII

The room was long with windows on the right-hand side and a door at the far end that went into the dressing room. The row of beds that mine was in faced the windows and another row, under the windows, faced the wall. If you lay on your left side you could see the dressing-room door. There was another door at the far end that people sometimes came in by. If any one were going to die they put a screen around the bed so you could not see them die, but only the shoes and puttees of doctors and men nurses showed under the bottom of the screen and sometimes at the end there would be whispering. Then the priest would come out from behind the screen and afterward the men nurses would go back behind the screen to come out again carrying the one who was dead with a blanket over him down the corridor between the beds and some one folded the screen and took it away.

That morning the major in charge of the ward asked me if I felt that I could travel the next day. I said I could. He said then they would ship me out early in the morning. He said I would be better off making the trip now before it got too hot.

When they lifted you up out of bed to carry you into the dressing room you could look out of the window and see the new graves in the garden. A soldier sat outside the door that opened onto the garden making crosses and painting on them the names, rank, and regiment of the men who were buried in the garden.

He also ran errands for the ward and in his spare time made me a cigarette lighter out of an empty Austrian rifle cartridge. The doctors were very nice and seemed very capable. They were anxious to ship me to Milan where there were better X-ray facilities and where, after the operation, I could take mechano-therapy. I wanted to go to Milan too. They wanted to get us all out and back as far as possible because all the beds were needed for the offensive, when it should start.

The night before I left the field hospital Rinaldi came in to see me with the major from our mess. They said that I would go to an American hospital in Milan that had just been installed. Some American ambulance units were to be sent down and this hospital would look after them and any other Americans on service in Italy. There were many in the Red Cross. The States had declared war on Germany but not on Austria.

The Italians were sure America would declare war on Austria too and they were very excited about any Americans coming down, even the Red Cross. They asked me if I thought President Wilson would declare war on Austria and I said it was only a matter of days. I did not know what we had against Austria but it seemed logical that they should declare war on her if they did on Germany. They asked me if we would declare war on Turkey. I said that was doubtful. Turkey, I said, was our national bird but the joke translated so badly and they were so puzzled and suspicious that I said yes, we would probably declare war on Turkey. And on Bulgaria? We had drunk several glasses of brandy and I said yes by God on Bulgaria too and on Japan. But, they said, Japan is an ally of England. You can't trust the bloody English. The Japanese want Hawaii, I said. Where is Hawaii? It is in the Pacific Ocean. Why do the Japanese want it? They don't really want it, I said. That is all talk. The

Japanese are a wonderful little people fond of dancing and light wines. Like the French, said the major. We will get Nice and Savoia from the French. We will get Corsica and all the Adriatic coast-line, Rinaldi said. Italy will return to the splendors of Rome, said the major. I don't like Rome, I said. It is hot and full of fleas. You don't like Rome? Yes, I love Rome. Rome is the mother of nations. I will never forget Romulus suckling the Tiber. What? Nothing. Let's all go to Rome. Let's go to Rome to-night and never come back. Rome is a beautiful city, said the major. The mother and father of nations, I said. Roma is feminine, said Rinaldi. It cannot be the father. Who is the father, then, the Holy Ghost? Don't blaspheme. I wasn't blaspheming, I was asking for information. You are drunk, baby. Who made me drunk? I made you drunk, said the major. I made you drunk because I love you and because America is in the war. Up to the hilt, I said. You go away in the morning, baby, Rinaldi said. To Rome, I said. No, to Milan. To Milan, said the major, to the Crystal Palace, to the Cova, to Campari's, to Biffi's, to the galleria. You lucky boy. To the Gran Italia I said, where I will borrow money from George. To the Scala, said Rinaldi. You will go to the Scala. Every night, I said. You won't be able to afford it every night, said the major.

The tickets are very expensive. I will draw a sight draft on my grandfather, I said. A what? A sight draft. He has to pay or I go to jail. Mr. Cunningham at the bank does it. I live by sight drafts. Can a grandfather jail a patriotic grandson who is dying that Italy may live? Live the American Garibaldi, said Rinaldi. Viva the sight drafts, I said. We must be quiet, said the major. Already we have been asked many times to be quiet. Do you go to-morrow really, Federico? He goes to the American hos-

pital I tell you, Rinaldi said. To the beautiful nurses. Not the nurses with beards of the field hospital. Yes, yes, said the major, I know he goes to the American hospital. I don't mind their beards, I said. If any man wants to raise a beard let him. Why don't you raise a beard, Signor Maggiore? It could not go in a gas mask. Yes it could. Anything can go in a gas mask. I've vomited into a gas mask. Don't be so loud, baby, Rinaldi said. We all know you have been at the front. Oh, you fine baby, what will I do while you are gone? We must go, said the major. This becomes sentimental. Listen, I have a surprise for you. Your English. You know? The English you go to see every night at their hospital? She is going to Milan too. She goes with another to be at the American hospital. They had not got nurses yet from America. I talked to-day with the head of their riparto. They have too many women here at the front. They send some back. How do you like that, baby? All right. Yes? You go to live in a big city and have your English there to cuddle you. Why don't I get wounded? Maybe you will, I said. We must go, said the major. We drink and make noise and disturb Federico. Don't go. Yes, we must go. Good-by. Good luck. Many things. Ciaou. Ciaou. Ciaou. Come back quickly, baby. Rinaldi kissed me. You smell of lysol. Good-by, baby. Good-by. Many things. The major patted my shoulder. They tiptoed out. I found I was quite drunk but went to sleep.

The next day in the morning we left for Milan and arrived forty-eight hours later. It was a bad trip. We were side-tracked for a long time this side of Mestre and children came and peeked in. I got a little boy to go for a bottle of cognac but he came back and said he could only get grappa. I told him to get it and when it came I gave him the change and the man beside me and I got drunk and slept until past Vicenza where I woke up and was very sick on the floor. It did not matter because the man on that side had been very sick on the floor several times before. Afterward I thought I could not stand the thirst and in the yards outside of Verona I called to a soldier who was walking up and down beside the train and he got me a drink of water.

I woke Georgetti, the other boy who was drunk, and offered him some water. He said to pour it on his shoulder and went back to sleep. The soldier would not take the penny I offered him and brought me a pulpy orange. I sucked on that and spit out the pith and watched the soldier pass up and down past a freight-car outside and after a while the train gave a jerk and started.

THE LIFE AND WORKS OF

ERNEST HEMINGWAY

By JOHN BROWN

It is now more than ten years since Ernest Hemingway's tragic death at the age of sixty-two. The image of "the public figure," of the swashbuckling Byronic hero of our time has begun to fade and the work itself, long obscured by the myths surrounding its creator, stands forth more clearly. During his agitated life, Hemingway played so many roles— "hardboiled" newspaper man, fearless hunter and fisherman, aficionado, boxer, literary Tarzan, epic drinker, hairy-chested he-man—that it was sometimes forgotten that he was above all a writer and that his work, in the end, was the only thing which counted for him. And in the end, when he felt that along with his physical strength his creative powers were somehow failing him too, he simply could see no reason for going on at all. For his work had always been the only defense against the sense of *nada*, of nothingness, of the absurd that had pursued him over the years. Now that all the masks are down, we see that they concealed the sensitive, even morbidly sensitive, visage of a scrupulous and dedicated artist.

Hemingway was not a prolific writer. He had none of the torrential abundance of that fellow giant of contemporary American letters, William Faulkner. He revised endlessly to achieve his effects of artless simplicity. Some of the passages of *A Farewell to Arms* were rewritten twenty times and more. In spite of the care and the labor he lavished on his books, some of them already bear the marks of time. But others, notably the short stories, and his first two novels, *The Sun Also Rises* and *A Farewell to Arms,* have left their mark on the way people speak and even how they feel, have exercised their influence on novelists in Europe as well as in America, and will probably last as long as anything in twentieth-century American literature.

Hemingway always insisted that a writer must write about what he knows. And naturally the basis of his knowledge is always a knowledge of himself and of his own experience. Hemingway's work, in the broadest sense, is autobiographical and his life provided the materials from which he fashioned his books. The two exist in a synergetic relationship, one reinforcing and fulfilling the other. In the best of his writing, he transformed his personal experience into the archetypal experience of the entire generation that came to maturity during World War I, and the behavior of his characters indicated a new kind of moral code for the time. Sometimes he achieves a universality that embraces not only his own generation and his own culture, but men everywhere, as in the noble simplicity of *The Old Man and the Sea.*

He was born on July 21, 1899, in Oak Park, a comfortable, middle-class suburb of Chicago. He had a younger brother and four sisters, several of whom have now written unconsciously revealing memoirs about life at the Hemingways'. The mother dominated the family group. She was a monumental, Wagnerian figure, who sang and painted and loved "refinement." She participated in women's clubs and in community affairs and had firmly decided that all her children should be "successful" and "successful" according to her standards. She wanted her elder son to be a musician and arranged for him to take cello lessons. But his father, a doctor, gave him a rifle and took him hunting in the forests "up in Michigan."

Dr. Hemingway was a complex figure, prudish, secretive, outwardly deferential toward his wife. He committed suicide in 1928. Mrs. Hemingway subsequently sent her son the pistol with which his father had killed himself; "an omen or a prophecy" Hemingway later remarked about this in a letter to his publisher. He speaks of his father on many occasions, particularly in the early Nick Adams stories, where he describes his boyhood. In "Fathers and Sons" he writes: "Like all men with a faculty that surpasses human requirements, his father was very nervous. Then, too, he was sentimental, and, like most sentimental people, he was both cruel and absurd. . . . Nick . . . was very grateful to him for two things; fishing and shooting. His father was as sound on those two things as he was unsound on sex, for instance. . . ."

And Robert Jordan, the hero of *For Whom the Bell Tolls,* recalling his father's suicide, says: "I'll never forget how sick it made me the first time I knew he was a coward . . . If he wasn't a coward, he would have stood up to that woman [his mother] and wouldn't have let her bully him. I wonder what I would have been like if he had married a different woman?"

Hemingway's family was shocked and outraged when they received copies of *In Our Time,* his first collection of short stories. His sister, in her book *At the Hemingways,* notes that her father "was so incensed that a son of his would so far forget his Christian training that he could use the subject matter and the vulgar expressions this book contained, that he returned all six copies to the Three Mountains Press in Paris. He wrote to Ernest and told him that no gentleman spoke of venereal disease outside of a doctor's office." This family situation— the puritanical, middle-class respectability of his home, the inhibited, resentful father, the domineering, demanding mother—left a deep impression on Hemingway and throws light upon some of his basic attitudes: his revolt against bourgeois respectability, his hostility toward women, the immature sexual behavior of his characters, his incapacity to live or to depict "the life of the couple."

All during his boyhood, he spent his summer vacations on his family's property on a lake in the north of Michigan. Even today, forests cover much of this lovely, wild country, where a few descendants of the original Ojibways still live. Here he hunted and fished, fell in and out of love, and had his first sexual experiences with Indian girls in the forest. It was a paradise for a boy growing up, and later on he would often describe it with nostalgia (as in that superb story "Big Two-Hearted River"). But he soon realized that terror and brutality always lurked beneath the idyllic aspects of nature. Many of his early stories deal with the theme of the "initiation" of a sensitive boy becoming aware of the irrational cruelty of life. Why, when the natural world is so beautiful, should there be so much suffering in it? He never stopped asking that question.

He was a good student at the Oak Park High School (although he ran away from home a couple of times) and was particularly interested in writing for the school paper. After graduation, he did not go to the university. He got a job as reporter on the Kansas City *Star* and began to learn how to write simple, direct, concrete newspaper prose. He stayed with the paper for nearly a year. This and subsequent experiences as a journalist contributed much to the formation of his distinctive style. He never lost his gifts as a reporter.

By now, America had entered World War I and Hemingway wanted to get into it. Rejected by the army because of defective vision, he joined the ambulance corps and was assigned to the Italian front. Soon after his arrival there, on July 8, 1918—a date he would never forget—he was seriously wounded near the village of Fossalta on the Piave. The wound left a psychic scar that never healed, and references to it recur obsessionally in his work. All his heroes, from Jake Barnes to Colonel Cantwell, are "wounded men," wounded both in the flesh and in the spirit. After a long convalescence in a Milan hospital, he was decorated with the *Croce al merito di guerra* and joined the Italian army for the two months before he was demobilized. He arrived home in January 1919, after a war experience of only a few months, a good part of which was spent in the hospital. But these few months left an indelible impression. The spectacle of the absurdity and the senseless misery of war certainly had much to do with his becoming a writer and with the kind of a writer he became.

After the war, sharing the feelings of restlessness and revolt of his generation, he was unable to resume the narrow, middle-class life he had known in Oak Park. Like so many other writers and artists at this time, he was determined to reject the bourgeois, puritanical world of his parents. His experience in Europe had confirmed his vocation as a writer and had made him determined to escape from Oak Park and live abroad. In 1921, after his marriage to Hadley Richardson, he got a job as correspondent for a Canadian newspaper and he and his wife went to Paris, where a large American literary colony had grown up.

Finally, encouraged by literary friends like Gertrude Stein, Ezra Pound, and Ford Madox Ford, he decided to devote all his time to writing. He settled down in a small apartment on the rue Notre-Dame des Champs and worked. He had little money, and no one wanted to publish his stories, which publishers called not "stories" but "sketches" or "vignettes." At first he had a hard time. But he persisted, and finally a Paris avantgarde publishing house run by Robert McAlmon brought out his first work, a very small collection, *Three Stories and Ten Poems*. In 1924, Bill Bird, an American who produced limited editions on a hand press in the cellar of an old house on the Quai d'Anjou (Three Mountains Press), issued *In Our Time,* a slim volume of thirty-two pages. It was composed of brief sketches describing fragmentary incidents of violence that Hemingway had observed during the war and during his career as a reporter. The two works, together with a number of additional stories, were collected to make his first commercially published book, *In Our Time* (1925). It contained the seeds of all that Hemingway was to become and revealed him as the creator of that naked, muscular, antiliterary style that imposed itself as "the style of his time." Philip Toynbee has defined its importance. "In his style, he has succeeded in cutting out the cackle." In fact, as a result of Hemingway, serious writers could never employ a certain kind of literary cackle again.

The matter and the manner of *In Our Time* were developed in Hemingway's first novel, *The Sun Also Rises* (1926). He described so well the feverish Montparnasse of the 1920s and the life there of the international set of expatriate Bohemians who spent their time drinking—drinking such a lot—at the Select or the Dome, dining on the Ile Saint Louis, dancing at low bals musettes behind the Montagne Sainte-Genevieve, falling in love with women like Lady Brett, who wore tight sweaters, sat at the bar with their legs crossed, and threw back their whisky like a man, going to the bullfights in Pamplona and drinking a lot there, too.

Life and art flowed together then and his daily experience, transformed by his craft, nourished the books he was writing. With *The Sun Also Rises* and with *Men Without Women* (a collection of short stories published in 1927) his position as an artist was firmly established and his friend, the poet Archibald MacLeish, could write of him as a "celebrity at twenty-five, a master at thirty." It was good to be alive on the Left Bank in the 1920s. The gods smiled on the handsome, athletic, gifted young man from Oak Park, Illinois. The sun was high in the sky. Evening, it seemed, would never come.

In 1928, Hemingway returned to the United States with the first chapters of a new novel and a new wife, Pauline Pfeiffer, a *Vogue* magazine writer. He took a house at Key West on the tip of Florida, where the deep-sea fishing was good and where he continued working on his novel, *A Farewell to Arms*. It was during that summer his father, worried by bad health and financial difficulties, killed himself. Like the wound at Fossalta, this tragedy preyed on Hemingway's mind over the years and seemed to him to be obscurely related to his own personal destiny.

A Farewell to Arms was published in the autumn of 1929, and the book immediately achieved not only the critical success of his earlier works but a popular success as well. Readers who were shocked by the "amorality" and the "cynicism" of *The Sun Also Rises,* were won over by this story of love and death on the Italian front. A new lyricism appears in the language, a new tenderness in the emotions. The public found it easier to "identify" with Lieutenant Frederic Henry and the English nurse, Catherine Barkley, than with the impotent Jake Barnes or the somewhat hardened Lady Brett.

But this was to be Hemingway's last real success for a long time. The years of the 1930s, of the economic depression, of socially conscious literature, of the proletarian novel, of ideological struggle, were not propitious to the novelist of the lost generation, of the golden and irresponsible 1920s. Hemingway was essentially an esthete who honored the religion of art. But the 1930s had little use for *"l'art pour l'art";* the Marxist critics then in vogue branded it as a heresy of a decadent bourgeois society. Like Ezra Pound or Gertrude Stein or F. Scott Fitzgerald, Hemingway found himself "out of key with his time."

Faced with the double problem of making an adjustment to a society temperamentally alien to him and to a maturity which he was unwilling to accept, Hemingway sought various ways out of his dilemma. All during the 1930s, he flung himself with even greater intensity into the masculine, violent world of hunting and bullfighting. He devoted himself to the composition of books on these subjects, books which exasperated the fashionable Marxist critics since they were provocatively without "social significance." In 1932, he published *Death in the Afternoon,* on which he had been working since the midtwenties. It is a manual of bullfighting, but much else besides—a homage to Spain, a country he loved; a "natural history of death," that violent death which Hemingway considered the most important thing a writer can write about and which revealed itself in its most dramatic forms on the battlefront and in the *corrida;* a series of meditations on the writer's art. He speaks of his profession with gravity: "Prose is architecture and not interior decoration and the baroque is finished." Besides being the best study of the bullring that exists in any language outside of Spanish, it has an exuberant, personal tone that redeems occasional irritating mannerisms of style and the equally irritating pose of the he-man continually vaunting his manhood. With the passing of the years, the "hardboiled" surface became a more and more elaborately contrived façade to hide the sensitivity behind it. For Hemingway, like his heroes, was really hardboiled only on the outside—he was a tender tough guy.

The following year, he went on a long safari in Africa. He writes about it in *The Green Hills of Africa* (1935), an attempt "to write an absolutely true book, to see whether the shape of a country and the pattern of a month's action can, if truly presented, compete with a work of the imagination." The answer, as far as this book is concerned, is definitely no. However, like *Death in the Afternoon,* it has considerable interest as a personal document. (By now, Hemingway had flung his earlier scrupulous objectivity to the winds and was always talking, sometimes even a bit garrulously, about himself.) In a kind of "brief history of American literature," for example, he indicated his preferences among the authors of the United States.

They are Henry James, Stephen Crane, and Mark Twain, especially Mark Twain, since he claims that "All modern American literature came out of a book by Mark Twain called *Huckleberry Finn.*"

No one liked *The Green Hills of Africa* very much; the opinion was that a book on big-game hunting had little to say to Americans at a time when the country was in the midst of the great depression and the unemployed were selling apples in the street. Nor did it appeal to Europeans either, with the outbreak of the Civil War in Spain and the triumph of Naziism in Germany.

Hemingway himself, even though he tried to distract himself with sport and games, with parties and pleasure cruises with "smart" people (he chose his companions at this period largely from the world of café society, claiming to disdain writers and to despise critics), was well aware that something was going wrong. He expressed that malaise in two long short stories (both with African settings), "The Snows of Kilimanjaro" and "The Short Happy Life of Francis Macomber," which rank among his finest achievements. Harry, in "The Snows of Kilimanjaro," is a gifted writer who has never fulfilled his promise. His bitter reflections on the waste of talent, as he lies dying of a gangrenous wound during a safari, indicate something of Hemingway's doubts and misgivings about the direction of his own career. And "The Short Happy Life of Francis Macomber," which dissects the devouring female, Mrs. Macomber, with a cold and brilliant surgical precision, underlines that hostility toward women that persists throughout his work.

With *To Have and Have Not* (1937), Hemingway, evidently disturbed by the growing critical hostility toward him, seems to have decided to write a novel of "social significance." But his heart was not really in it and the results were not happy. This confused account of the life and death of Harry Morgan, a noble-hearted and superlatively virile rum-runner of the Florida Keys, fails to convince the reader on any level. Struc-turally, it represents an attempt to make a novel out of three short stories. And ideologically it does not persuade us that Harry Morgan is basically very different from the gangsters, the boxers, and the other tough guys of Hemingway's earlier work, in spite of his inarticulate declara-tions about human solidarity and the social responsibilities of the individual. One critic asserted that "the social sig-nificance of *To Have or Have Not* is negligible. The dice which Hemingway is rolling are so openly and flagrantly loaded . . . and the social assertions and findings are so naive, fragmentary, and casual that they cannot be offered as a criticism of the established order." Hemingway, of course, was by instinct an aristocrat and an artist and could never really believe in the optimistic doc-trines of human perfectibility that per-meated the New Deal or in the possibility of the salvation of the individual through social reform.

But when the Civil War broke out in Spain, he could, for personal and subjec-tive reasons, support the Loyalists as passionately as his socially conscious friends. He really needed a cause to be-lieve in, a cause that would shield him from the *nada* or at least conceal it from him a little. He had always loved Spain and the Spanish people, and he didn't want them "to be kicked around." He approached the problems of the revolu-tion with all the nonideological humani-tarianism of the American liberals, whose fuzziness of thought, lack of dialectical rigor, and undisciplined senti-mentality so irritated the orthodox Com-munists among the Loyalists. For Hem-ingway (until he went there and finally got to know better) the war in Spain at

first seemed like another romantic, nine-teenth-century revolution, in which the good and evil sides were defined in terms of light and darkness. Gustave Regler, the German novelist who fought in the International Brigade, speaks frequently of Hemingway in his autobiography, *The Owl of Minerva:* "Hemingway always had a natural taste for Kipling's jungle laws . . . A man so unpolitical as he could not understand what was going on in Spain. Everything was black or white for him. For him, we members of the International Brigade had the irresistible scent of death about us, like the bull-fighters, and because of this he was in-vigorated in our company."

Hemingway arrived in Spain in Febru-ary 1937, as a war correspondent, and remained there for about a year, writing articles, doing the script for a docu-mentary film, *The Spanish Earth,* finish-ing a play, *The Fifth Column,* of which the less said the better. The war also provided him with the subject for *For Whom the Bell Tolls,* his longest and most ambitious novel. Published in 1940, when the American public began to be seriously alarmed by the threat of totali-tarianism in Europe, it was hailed as Hemingway's greatest work. It suited the mood of the moment and was well adapted for the color film with Ingrid Bergman and Gary Cooper that was based on it.

It is hard to believe that the taut vignettes of *In Our Time* and the ro-mantic bravura passages of *For Whom the Bell Tolls* were written by the same man. Ever since *Death in the Afternoon,* the famous Hemingway style had been losing its lean, monosyllabic austerity; in many pages of *For Whom the Bell Tolls,* the old laconic restraint gives place to the richest of rhetoric. Sometimes—as when Pilar describes the days and nights of eat-ing and drinking and lovemaking with her bullfighter in Malaga—they enchant us with their lyrical, full-bodied sensuousness; but again—as in the love scenes between Maria and the American volunteer, Robert Jordan—they become somewhat embarrassingly sentimental. Characteristically, Hemingway is at his best when he is trying to convey how things feel or when he is describing scenes of death and physical violence. The slaughter of the Fascists by Pablo and his band, for instance, rises to heights of terror and bears comparison with the Stendhalian description of the retreat of Caporetto in *Farewell to Arms*.

For Whom the Bell Tolls reaffirmed Hemingway's literary position. It also seemed to point to a basic reorientation of his art. The stripped, muscular prose of his beginnings was replaced, as we have said, by richer, more allusive, more consciously "literary" language. The old cynicism and despair seemed to have given away to a positive belief in liberal political and social values and a moving faith in romantic love. But on close examination, it is less "positive" than it might appear at the first reading. The evolution of Robert Jordan—who, at the end, lies dying alone on a hillside, not so much to defend a cause in which he has ceased to believe as to assure the safe escape of the woman he loves—reflects Hemingway's own political disillusionment, the confirmation of his deeply rooted distrust of ideologies. In reality, the novel restates once again, in ambiguous, romantic terms and on a larger, but not necessarily a more impressive scale, one of Hemingway's persistent themes: grace under pressure, victory in defeat.

The love scenes in the book were in part inspired by Hemingway's own sentimental adventures in Spain with the dashing blonde correspondent, Martha Gellhorn, with whom he had fallen in love (in Malcolm Cowley's phrase) "like a big hemlock tree crashing down through the underbrush." As soon as he could obtain a divorce, he married Miss Gellhorn in 1940. She decided that they should spend what turned out to be a very uncomfortable honeymoon in war-torn China as magazine and newspaper correspondents. This union ended in divorce four years later, since Miss Gellhorn was apparently unwilling to sacrifice her professional activity to domesticity. (In his books, Hemingway's heroines are usually depicted as soft, yielding, submissive, very feminine women, happy slaves of the male master, but in his life he seemed to marry one independent career girl after another.)

Fortunately for Hemingway, there were wars to go to—first the Spanish Civil War, then, briefly, China, and then World War II. When hostilities were declared, he was living on his estate, Finca Vigia, a few kilometers outside of Havana. He immediately put his motorboat at the disposition of the American government for submarine detection. In 1943 he flew to Europe as a correspondent for *Collier's*.

"Papa," as he called himself, bearded and boisterous, played his usual swashbuckling role in the invasion, "captured the Ritz" at the time of the liberation of Paris, followed the First Army into the Ardennes. He was in fine form. He roamed through combat areas with a flask of gin on one hip, a flask of vermouth on the other, and was always ready to mix a "dry." The troops, although they usually didn't know exactly who he was, always recognized him as a "Very Important Person" and he enjoyed the acclaim.

In 1945, with a new wife, Mary Welsh, a *Time* magazine correspondent he had met in London, he returned to Finca Vigia and settled down to write "a big book about the war." But it did not go well, and he interrupted work on it to begin *Across the River and into the Trees,* which he started in Cortina d'Ampezzo in 1949 and finished in Venice during the following winter. It was his first novel in ten years, in fact his first book since *For Whom the Bell Tolls*. It was a disconcerting performance for all those who admired Hemingway. To some it seemed that he had written "a travesty of himself." The critic of the *Manchester Guardian* summed it up: "This is a bad book; most interesting, but all wrong."

Its hero, a battle-scarred, "beat-up" American colonel over fifty, serving in the Allied occupation forces in Trieste, falls in love with Renata, a Venetian countess of nineteen, who, naturally, is mad about him. It is *A Farewell to Arms,* thirty years later. It is transparently, often unblushingly autobiographical, and Hemingway, as usual, made little effort to disguise these personal elements. Like Frederic Henry and the author, Colonel Cantwell as a young officer had fought on the Italian front in 1918. Both the colonel and his creator had their "knee cap shot off at Fossalta," both suffer from high blood pressure, both talk in the same way, both have the same passionate prejudices—hatred, for example, of General Patton and of Sinclair Lewis, of whom Hemingway paints an unnecessarily cruel portrait—and the same tastes—a love for Venice, for Torcello, for duck shooting, for good Valpolicella, for "dry" made in proportions of sixteen to one, for pretty and adoring young girls.

But the old magic current flows through the best parts of this curious book. A disappointing novel, it is still a fascinatingly frank personal document in the drama of the aging Hemingway. It tingles through the superb descriptions of Venice (which have all the old genius for the evocation of place) and through the passages on duck hunting in the lagoons. Hemingway had his first brush with death in this region when he was a boy

of nineteen and the entire Veneto had remained charged with memories for him. But he is less happy in creating a character here. Colonel Cantwell is a caricature, a moving, sometimes pathetic caricature, but a caricature all the same. Carlos Baker tells us that the unbelievably beautiful, unbelievably submissive Contessa is a symbol of lost youth. This may well be, but she never emerges as a person, and remains a kind of dream girl, a fantasy of what an older gentleman would like his "last great love" to be like.

In spite of his often-expressed contempt for critics, Hemingway was troubled by the barrage directed against *Across the River and into the Trees.* Using the jargon of the ring that he liked to affect, he realized that "the Old Champ" would have to score a literary knockout the next time if he hoped to keep his title. Two years later, he made his triumphant comeback with *The Old Man and the Sea,* which, from the moment of its first publication in *Life,* was hailed as a masterpiece. The most hostile critic could find little reproach in this exemplary brief novella. Santiago, an old Cuban fisherman, after bitter, frustrating weeks of catching nothing at all, finally captures the biggest fish ever, in the course of an epic battle which lasts three days and three nights, leaving him nearly dead with exhaustion but full of the high exaltation of his victory over a noble adversary. But as he tows his catch back to land, the sharks attack and strip all the flesh from the carcass. Santiago returns with only the naked skeleton—and the glorious memory of the struggle he had won.

That is all. But Hemingway has packed much substance into little space. This book is the quintessence of his art. All the old elements are there. He has gone back to his earlier, simpler style, but it has acquired a new, almost Biblical grandeur. And once again he restates the theme of man's moral victory in the face of material defeat, presented this time in the form of a fishing story which takes place in the waters off Cuba, a setting he knew intimately and describes with unerring mastery. The action, stripped to the barest essentials, is a parable of the resolution of the conflict between man and nature through love among all living creatures. We are back in a grave, archaic world, a world of "men without women" (the only actors in the drama are Santiago, a little boy, and the great fish), the kind of a world in which Hemingway always felt most at home.

Tormented by a gnawing sense of the decline of his creative powers, Hemingway found it more and more difficult to endure that solitude which, as he had so eloquently proclaimed, is necessary for the artist. He needed people about him to assure him that he was still the champion. He needed the now forbidden alcohol, "the giant killer" which gave brief respite from the depression which weighed more and more heavily upon him. He needed to travel from place to place, seeking to escape the inescapable. His health kept failing, for he had never really recovered from an airplane crash while on a safari in Africa in 1953. His once powerful body, of which he was so boyishly proud, whose strength and skill counted so much for him, was showing signs of long abuse. With his ponderous gait and his white beard, he seemed old before his time. And, of course, being Hemingway, it was impossible for him to accept philosophically the loss of physical vitality, the dulling of the sensations that come inevitably with the years.

Restlessly he roved back and forth between two continents. He went from Cuba to Cortina d'Ampezzo, from Paris to Idaho. In 1958–1959, he spent most of the year in Europe, largely in Spain, where he was preparing an article on bullfighting for *Life*. It was published in three parts in September 1960, under the title "Dangerous Summer." Certain passages recall *Death in the Afternoon*, but on the whole it is good journalism and nothing more, marred occasionally by a clumsy coyness and a tendency to boast.

When he returned from Spain, he was tired and irritable, subject to bursts of rage (especially when he had been drinking) and also to frequent bouts of deep depression. He steadily lost weight and his huge frame became gaunt and fragile. He had great difficulty in carrying on a conversation. Words did not come easily anymore. During much of the last year of his life, he was in and out of the Mayo Clinic in Minnesota, where he was being treated for high blood pressure and diabetes and undergoing shock treatments for his worsening nervous depression. In the first week of June 1961, he left the hospital. His weight had gone down to 155 pounds and he was very weak. A friend drove him and his wife back to their chalet in the mountains at Ketchum, Idaho. On the Sunday morning following his return he rose early. His wife was still sleeping. He went downstairs, took his rifle, and ended the life which had become a burden to him.

John Brown, who has worked for many years in the Cultural Affairs section of the U.S. Department of State, is a professor in the Department of English at Wesleyan University.

THE 1954 PRIZE

By KJELL STRÖMBERG

IN A WAY, it is surprising that William Faulkner was honored with a Nobel Prize before Ernest Hemingway. Of all the American novelists who made their mark between the two wars, Hemingway was the first to be widely known and appreciated in Europe. As early as the 1920s, his works had been translated into French, German, and the Scandinavian languages, while Faulkner had to wait until the late 1930s to be translated. The reason was doubtless that Hemingway's language was far more accessible than Faulkner's and that he was much less exclusive in his choice of subjects, which were concerned with the most current topics. However, Faulkner and John Dos Passos were the favorites of European literary circles, while Hemingway and Steinbeck (who was to win the prize later) were looked upon as brilliant reporters rather than true creative novelists.

Competition for the literature prize was not particularly keen in 1954. Some thirty candidates were entered in the fray, including three who were eventually to become laureates—Halldór Laxness from Iceland, the Spanish poet Juan Ramón Jiménez and, for the first time, Albert Camus. There was also a "returnee," Concha Espina, long since honored by a monument in her native town of Santander and nominated anew by an old Prizewinner—Jacinto Benavente, who had won the prize in 1922.

Hemingway had been nominated almost every year since 1947, when the first report on him was written by the aged Academician Per Hallström. Hallström was unable to muster much enthusiasm for a body of work with which he could scarcely have been very familiar, although as a youth he had spent a few years in the United States. He presented Hemingway as the most prominent representative of the "lost generation," those young people who had gone to war for reasons of political idealism and a dream of universal peace which haunted their vast country. In their writing they translated their eventual disillusionment and their sense of loss of country.

Hallström judged this characterization insufficient when applied to Hemingway, because this hearty sportsman, with his senses still fresh and incredibly perceptive, must not have been much given to empty dreams and somber thoughts, but endowed rather with a fierce appetite for everything which life could offer a young man in search of adventure. He remarks that Hemingway's violent realism, his lean style, and his ebullient vitality had already established him as a model for many young Scandinavian writers. He had full confidence in Hemingway for all questions concerned with shooting big game, Spanish bullfighting, the military life, and even the more serious matters of war.

Indeed, it was only the two novels based on his war experiences—*A Farewell to Arms* and *For Whom the Bell Tolls*—that Hallström credited with deeply human interest and truly artistic value; but he nevertheless refused to recognize in Hemingway an artist of the first rank. His insistence on an objectivity sought at all costs, his meticulous portrayal of things seen and heard struck Hallström as leaving nothing to the imagination, without which there can be no poetry.

In a second report in 1953, Hallström seemed to be making an exception for Hemingway's last novel—or rather novella—*The Old Man and the Sea,* which had just been published. He conceded that it was "a work of great power and extraordinary clarity," with gripping action solidly developed within a framework of sky and sea which are extremely well observed, yielding "an incontestable element of beauty." However, neither this report, although favorable enough, nor the brief supplement added to it a year later, goes on to give an unconditional recommendation of Hemingway for the prize.

As it had on occasion in the past, the Academy voted to disregard its reporter. On October 28, Ernest Hemingway was declared the winner of the Nobel Prize for Literature for 1954, "for his powerful mastery of the art of storytelling, most recently displayed in *The Old Man and the Sea,* and for his influence on contemporary style." Doubtless the Nobel judges, in selecting this final work which Hallström had picked out for particular praise, wished it to be considered a gesture of courtesy toward the dean of the Academy, who at that time was nearly ninety years old.

Since the current address of the new laureate, a tireless traveler, was not known to the Academy, the secretary sent two cables—one to Cuba, where Hemingway had lived for the last decade, the other to his agent in Paris. Hemingway was actually at his Cuban finca, resting up after an incredibly coincidental pair of air crashes which had befallen him earlier that year in the Uganda bush. He was just regaining the use of his hands and his left leg, although he was still suffering from serious internal injuries. His strong constitution was soon to restore him to health; and by now he could walk without great difficulty. Nevertheless, he was obliged to obey his physician's strict orders and give up the trip to Stockholm which he had been looking forward to with enthusiasm. The old sea dog came very close to yielding to the blandishments of the young Swedish consul in Havana, Per Aurell, son-in-law of the Academician Sigfrid Schwertz. The consul invited Hemingway to a picnic, which was interrupted by two tropical storms before he had a chance to offer Hemingway, his wife, and the doctor direct transportation to Gothemburg on a new freighter.

"Old Man Hemingway Has Caught the Noblest Fish in the Sea" read the front-page banner headline in the New York *World-Telegram* over its front-page story on the fifth Nobel Prize to be awarded to an American writer. For some reason or other people everywhere spoke of "old Hemingway," although as a matter of record he was only fifty-five at the time. In the *World-Telegram* it was simply a complimentary reference to the title of his latest book. A New York radio announcer suggested that the Swedish Academy had awarded him the prize so soon out of fear that he would end up drowned or dead in an air crash before long. Commentators recalled that, besides his two recent crashes, Hemingway

had taken part in five wars and six revo-
lutions, never failing to throw himself
into the thick of the action, while
Faulkner had stayed quietly on his
Southern Farm. Orville Prescott, literary
critic of *The New York Times,* expressed
the general satisfaction with which the
award was to be welcomed throughout
North America, commenting that this
year there was no doubt that the best
man had won.

The same reaction came from the
British and French press. Several Parisian journalists lightly considered what
the effect might be if the old globe
trotter, famous for calling a spade a
spade, should show up in Academy
circles in Sweden. No one would object,
one Stockholm newspaper remarked, if
Hemingway were to start wrestling with
the Academicians after an assiduous session of *skål* tippling. There were, of
course, those who, although approving
the honor shown to the new American
school as represented by William Faulkner, maintained that it was overly generous to vote a second Nobel to the same
school "for a few differences in syntax."

The American ambassador to Sweden,
John Morse Cabot, accepted the prize
(the highest sum ever awarded until
then) from the Swedish king on behalf of
the absent writer, and he read the acceptance speech which Hemingway had for-
warded from Cuba at the traditional
banquet in the Stockholm Town Hall.

Translated by Dale McAdoo.

Knut Hamsun

1920

"For his monumental work,

Growth of the Soil"

Illustrated by G. LAMBERT

PRESENTATION ADDRESS

By HARALD HJÄRNE

CHAIRMAN OF THE NOBEL COMMITTEE

OF THE SWEDISH ACADEMY

IN ACCORDANCE with the statutes of the Nobel Foundation, the Swedish Academy has awarded the literary Prize for 1920 to the Norwegian novelist Knut Hamsun for his work, *Growth of the Soil*.

It would be superfluous to give a detailed account of a book that in a short time has spread everywhere in its original form or in translation. Through the originality of its plot and style, it has aroused the liveliest interest in many countries and has found favorable reception with the most diverse groups of readers. Only recently a leading and distinctly conservative English reviewer wrote that this book, which had appeared in England only this year, was universally acclaimed as a masterpiece. The reasons for this incontestable success will no doubt hold the attention of literary critics for a long time, but even now, under the impact of first impressions, they deserve to be pointed out at least in their broad features.

In spite of current opinions of our time, those who want to find in literature above all a faithful reproduction of reality, will recognize in *Growth of the Soil* the representation of a life that forms the basis of existence and of the development of societies wherever men live and build. These descriptions are not distorted by any memories of a long, highly civilized past; their immediate effect is due to the evocation of the harsh struggle all active men must in the beginning endure (in varying external conditions, of course) against an indomitable and rebellious nature. It would be difficult to conceive of a more striking contrast with works usually called "classic."

Nonetheless, this work may rightly be called classic, but in a deeper and more profound sense than usual if this epithet is to express something other and more than vague praise. The classic, in the culture we have inherited from antiquity, is less the perfect which calls for imitation than the significant which is taken directly from life and which is rendered in a form of enduring value even for future ages. The insignificant, that which in itself is of no consequence, cannot be comprehended in this notion any more than that which is formally provisional or defective. But apart from that, whatever is precious in human life, although it may appear common, can be placed in the same category as the extraordinary and the brilliant, with a significance and a form of equal value, once it is presented for the first time in its proper light. In this sense it is no exaggeration to maintain that in *Growth of the Soil* Hamsun has given to our times a classic that can be measured against the best we already have. Antiquity does not possess in this respect a monopoly inaccessible to future generations; for life is always new and inexhaustible and as such can always be presented in new forms created by new geniuses.

Hamsun's work is an epic of labor to which the author has given monumental lines. It is not a question of different kinds of labor which divide men within and among themselves; it is a question of the concentrated toil which in its purest form shapes men entirely, which mollifies and brings together divided spirits, which protects and increases their fruits with a regular and uninterrupted progress. The labor of the pioneer and the first farmer with all its difficulties, under the poet's pen, thus takes on the character of a heroic struggle that yields nothing to the grandeur of the manly sacrifice for one's country and companions in arms. Just as the peasant poet Hesiod described the labors of the field, so Hamsun has put in the foreground of his work the ideal laborer who dedicates his whole life and all his powers to clearing the land and to triumphing over the obstacles with which men and the forces of nature confront him. If Hamsun has cast behind him all the weighty memories of civilization, he has by his own work contributed to a precise understanding of the new culture that our era expects to arise from the progress of physical labor as a continuation of ancient civilization.

Hamsun does not present so-called types on his stage. His heroes and heroines are all very much alive, all in quite modest circumstances. Certain among them, and the best, are unimaginative in their goals and thoughts, the principal example being the tireless and silent farmer himself. Others are drifting, troubled, and often even bewildered by egoistic aspirations and follies. They all carry the mark of their Norwegian origin; they are all conditioned in some manner by "the fruits of the earth." It is one of the characteristics of our sister languages that often the same words express very different nuances of meaning by the images they evoke. When we Swedes speak of "the fruits of the earth," we think immediately of something fertile, abundant, succulent, preferably in an agricultural region that has been cultivated for a long time. The thought of Hamsun's book is not oriented in this direction. "The earth" here is the rugged and forbidding fallow soil. Its fruits do not fall from a cornucopia of abundance; they comprise all that can germinate and grow in this ungrateful soil, the good and the bad, the beautiful and the ugly, among men and animals as well as in the forest and the fields. Such are the kinds of fruits Hamsun's work offers for our harvest.

However, we Swedes, or at least many Swedes, do not feel strange in the regions and circumstances described to us here. We rediscover the atmosphere of the North with all that is a part of its natural and social milieu, and with many parallels on both sides of the frontier. Moreover, Hamsun also presents Swedish characters who are drawn to the newly cultivated land, most of them no doubt attracted by the mirage of brilliant economic success, as the cities on the Norwegian coasts appear on the horizon like snares of the great worldly life enticing defenseless hearts from the heavy toil of the land.

These and other quite human projections, far from weakening, reinforce the impression produced by the classic content of the story. They dissipate the apprehension one could feel in seeing the light of the ideal at the expense of truth; they guarantee the sincerity of the design, the truth of the images and the characters. Their common humanity escapes no one. The proof is in the welcome this work has found among peoples of different mentalities, languages, and customs. Furthermore, through the light touch of smiling humor with which the author treats even the saddest things he relates, he has proved his own compassion for human destiny and human nature. But in the story, he never departs from the most complete artistic serenity. The style, stripped of vain ornaments, renders the reality of things with certainty and clarity, and one rediscovers in it, under a personal and powerful form, all the richness of nuance of the writer's mother tongue.

Mr. Knut Hamsun—In facing the rigors of the seasons as well as the fatigues of a long trip particularly arduous at this time in order to come to receive the Prize awarded you, you have given great joy to the Swedish Academy, which will certainly be shared by all the persons present at this ceremony. In the name of the Academy, I have tried as well as possible in the short time accorded me to express at least some of the major reasons for which we appreciate so highly your work which has just been crowned. Thus, in addressing myself now to you personally, I do not wish to repeat what I have said. It remains for me only to congratulate you in the name of the Academy and to express the hope that the memories you will keep of your visit with us will be ties that will link you to us also in the future.

ACCEPTANCE SPEECH

By *KNUT HAMSUN*

What am i to do in the presence of such gracious, such overwhelming generosity? I no longer have my feet planted on the ground, I am walking on air, my head is spinning. It is not easy to be myself right now. I have had honors and riches heaped on me this day. I myself am what I am, but I have been swept off my feet by the tribute that has been paid to my country, by the strains of her national anthem which resounded in this hall a minute ago.

It is as well perhaps that this is not the first time I have been swept off my feet. In the days of my blessed youth there were such occasions; in what young person's life do they not occur? No, the only young people to whom this feeling is strange are those young conservatives who were born old, who do not know the meaning of being carried away. No worse fate can befall a young man or woman than becoming prematurely entrenched in prudence and negation. Heaven knows that there are plenty of opportunities in later life, too, for being carried away. What of it? We remain what we are and, no doubt, it is all very good for us!

However, I must not indulge in homespun wisdom here before so distinguished an assembly, especially as I am to be followed by a representative of science. I will soon sit down again, but this is my great day. I have been singled out by your benevolence, chosen amongst thousands of others, and crowned with laurels! On behalf of my country I thank the Swedish Academy and all Sweden for the honor they have bestowed on me. Personally, I bow my head under the weight of such great distinctions, but I am also proud that your Academy should have judged my shoulders strong enough to bear them.

A distinguished speaker said earlier tonight that I have my own way of writing, and this much I may perhaps claim and no more. I have, however, learned something from everyone and what man is there who has not learned a little from all? I have had much to learn from Sweden's poetry and, more especially, from her lyrics of the last generation. Were I more conversant with literature and its great names, I could go on quoting them *ad infinitum* and acknowledge my debt for the merit you have been generous enough to find in my work. However, coming from a person like me, this would be mere name dropping, shallow sound effects without a single bass note to support them. I am no longer young enough for this; I have not the strength.

No, what I should really like to do right now, in the full blaze of lights, before this illustrious assembly, is to shower every one of you with gifts, with flowers, with offerings of poetry—to be young once more, to ride on the crest of the wave. That is what I should wish to do on this great occasion, this last opportunity for me. I dare not do it, for I would not be able to escape ridicule. Today riches and honors have been lavished on me, but one gift has been lacking, the most important one of all, the only one that matters—the gift of youth. None of us is too old to remember it. It is proper that we who have grown old should take a step back and do so with dignity and grace.

I know not what I should do—I know not what is the right thing to do, but I raise my glass to the youth of Sweden, to young people everywhere, to all that is young in life.

HUNGER

By KNUT HAMSUN

Translated by Robert Bly

PART ONE

ALL OF THIS HAPPENED while I was walking around starving in Christiania—that strange city no one escapes from until it has left its mark on him. . . .

I was lying awake in my attic room; a clock struck six somewhere below; it was fairly light already and people were beginning to move up and down the stairs. Over near the door, where my wall was papered with old issues of the *Morning Times,* I could make out a message from the Chief of Lighthouses, and just to the left of that an advertisement for fresh bread, showing a big, fat loaf: Fabian Olsen's bakery.

As soon as I was wide awake, I took to thinking, as I always did, if I had anything to be cheerful about today. Things had been a bit tight for me lately; one after the other of my possessions had been taken to my "uncle" at the pawnshop; I was becoming more and more nervous and irritable, and several mornings lately I had been so dizzy I had had to stay in bed all day. Occasionally when my luck was good I took in five kroner or so from one of the newspapers for an article.

It was getting lighter, and I concentrated on the advertisements by the door; I could even read the slim, mocking typeface declaring: "Shrouds available, Miss

Andersen, Main Entrance, to the right." That satisfied me for a long time. The clock below had struck eight before I got up and dressed.

I opened the window and looked out. I could see a clothesline and an open field. Behind them there was some debris from a burned-down blacksmith's shop which the workmen were just now cleaning away. Leaning my elbows on the windowsill, I gazed up into the sky. Today would be clear. The fall had come, that cool and delicious time of year when everything changed color and died. Noises were floating up from the streets, tempting me to go out. This empty room whose floor gave a little with every step was like a badly put-together coffin; the room had no real lock, and no stove; I usually slept on my socks so they would be a little drier by morning. The only nice thing in the room was a small red rocking chair in which I sat in the evenings, and dozed and thought about all sorts of things. When the wind was strong, and the street door of the house had been left open, all kinds of weird whines would come through the floor, and out of the walls, and the *Morning Times* by the door would get tears in it as long as a hand.

I stood up and investigated a little bundle I had over in the corner by the bed, looking for something for breakfast, but found nothing and went back again to the window.

I thought, God only knows if there's any sense in my looking for a job any longer! All these refusals, these partial promises, simple noes, hopes built up and knocked down, new tries that ended each time in nothing—these had squashed my courage for good. The last time, I had tried for a job as a bill collector, but arrived too late; I couldn't have got together fifty kroner for a bond anyway. There was always one thing or another in the way. I had even tried to join the Fire Department. A half hundred of us stood there in the entryway, sticking our chests out to give the impression of strength and tremendous audacity. A captain walked around inspecting these applicants, felt their muscles, and asked a question or two. He merely shook his head as he walked past me, and said I was out because of my glasses. I turned up again, later, without the glasses. I stood there with my eyebrows scrunched up, and made my eyes as sharp as knife ends: he walked past me again, and smiled—he had recognized me. The worst of it was that my clothes were beginning to look so bad I couldn't really present myself any longer for a job that required someone respectable.

How steadily my predicament had gotten worse! By now I was so utterly denuded of objects that I didn't even have a comb left, or a book to read when I felt hopeless. I had spent the entire summer sitting in cemeteries or in the public gardens near the castle, writing articles intended for some newspaper: page after page on almost any subject, filled with odd ideas, inspirations, quirks rising from my restless brain. In desperation I would choose the most outré subjects; the pieces would cost me hours and hours of labor, and were never accepted. When a piece was done I plunged immediately into a new one, and therefore wasn't very often crushed by an editor's refusal; I told myself all the time that eventually my luck would turn. And in fact, sometimes when I had luck, and things were going my way, I could get five kroner for one afternoon's work.

I stood up from the window again, went over to the washstand and sprinkled some water on my shiny trousers to make them look blacker and newer. When I had finished that, I put paper and pencil in my pocket as usual and went out. I slipped down the stairs very quietly so as not to attract my landlady's attention; my rent had been due a few days ago and I had nothing to pay her with at the moment.

It was nine. The rattle of wagons and the hum of voices filled the air—growing into a great orchestra of sound into which the noise of people walking and the cracks of the drivers' whips fit perfectly. The traffic noise on all sides cheered me up immediately, and I began to feel more content and at peace. I had much more to do of course than merely to take a morning stroll in the fresh air. What did my lungs care for fresh air? I was powerful as a giant and could stop a wagon with my shoulders. A rare and delicate mood, a feeling of wonderful lightheartedness had taken hold of me. I began examining the people I met or passed, I read the posters on walls, noticed a glance thrown at me from a streetcar, let every trivial occurrence influence me, every tiny detail that crossed my eyes and vanished.

If one only had something to eat, just a little, on such a clear day! The mood of the gay morning overwhelmed me, I became unusually serene, and started to hum for pure joy and for no particular reason. In front of a butcher's shop there was a woman with a basket on her arm, debating about some sausage for dinner;

as I went past, she looked up at me. She had only a single tooth in the lower jaw. In the nervous and excitable state I was in, her face made an instant and revolting impression on me—the long yellow tooth looked like a finger sticking out of her jaw, and as she turned toward me, her eyes were still full of sausage. I lost my appetite instantly, and felt nauseated. When I came to the main market square, I went over to the fountain and drank a little water. I looked up: ten o'clock by the Church of Our Saviour.

I kept on going through streets, rambling on with no purpose in mind at all. I stopped at a corner without needing to, turned and went up small alleys without having anything to do there. I just drifted on, floating in the joyful morning, rolling along without a care among other happy people. The air was clear and bright and my mind was without a shadow.

For the last ten minutes an old man had been limping ahead of me. He had a bundle in one hand, and was using his entire body to move forward, working with all his strength and yet making very little progress. I could hear him puffing from the effort. It occurred to me that I might carry his bundle; but I made no attempt to overtake him. On Grænsen Street I met Hans Pauli, who said hello and hurried by. Why should he be in such a hurry? I certainly didn't plan to ask him for money; in fact I wanted first of all to return to him a blanket I'd borrowed from him a few weeks ago. As soon as I was in better shape I would; the last thing I wanted was to owe a man a blanket; perhaps today, as a matter of fact, I would get an article started on "Crimes of the Future" or "Freedom of the Will," something like that, something salable enough so I could get five kroner at least. . . . Thinking about the article, I suddenly felt a strong desire to work on it immediately, and drain off my mind.

I'd find a good spot in the public gardens and keep on until I had the whole thing done.

However, the old cripple was still making the same wiggly movements ahead of me in the street. Finally it began to irritate me to have this feeble creature in front of me all the time. His journey evidently had no end; maybe he was determined to go to exactly the same place as I and I would have him blocking my view the whole way. In my excited condition I had become convinced that at each crossing he had hesitated, as though waiting to see what direction I would take, and then had taken a stronger hold on his bundle and limped off with all his might to get a head start. I walked on, looking at this tedious creature, and became more and more full of rage at him; it was clear he was destroying my good spirits bit by bit, little by little dragging the pure and magnificent morning down to his own ugliness. He looked like a huge humping insect determined to make a place for himself in the world by force and violence and keep the sidewalk all to himself. By the time we got to the top of the hill, I wanted no more part of it; I stopped in front of a shop window, and waited till he had time to get away; but when I started off again after a few minutes, the man cropped up in front of me again: he must have stopped also. Without thinking, I took three or four quick steps, caught up with him, and slapped him on the shoulder.

He stopped short. We began staring at each other.

"Can you give me a little something for a glass of milk?" he said at last, and let his head fall to the side.

Now there was no turning back! I fumbled in my pockets and said, "Oh, yes, milk. Hmm. Money isn't easy to get these days, and I'm not sure how much you really need it."

"I haven't eaten a thing since yesterday in Drammen," the man said. "I don't have an øre and I still can't find work."

"What do you do?"

"I'm a welt binder."

"A what?"

"Welt binder. I can also make the whole shoe."

"Well, that's different," I said. "Wait here a few minutes, and I'll see if I can't find something for you, a little something at least."

I ran down Pile Street, where I knew of a pawnshop on the second floor; it was one I had never been to either. As I went in the main entrance I quickly slipped off my waistcoat, rolled it up and put it under my arm; then I went up the stairs and knocked on the door. I bowed and threw the waistcoat down on the counter.

"One and a half kroner," said the man.

"Very good," I answered. "If it hadn't begun to be a little too tight for me, I don't know how I could have parted with it."

I took the money and went back. Actually, pawning this waistcoat was a wonderful idea; I would still have money left over for a good fat breakfast, and by evening my piece on "Crimes of the Future" would be in shape. Life began immediately to seem more friendly, and I hurried back to the man to get him off my hands.

"Here you go," I said, giving him one of my coins. "I'm delighted that you came to me first."

The man took the money and began to look me up and down. What was he standing there staring at? I got the sensation that he was inspecting my trousers particularly, and I became irritated at this impertinence. Did this old fool imagine I was really as poor as I looked? Hadn't I just as good as begun my ten-kroner article? On the whole, I had no fears for the future; I had many irons in

the fire. What business was it of this heathen savage if I helped him out on such a marvelous day? The man's stare irritated me, and I decided to give him a little lesson before I let him go. I threw back my shoulders and said, "My dear man, you have gotten into a very bad habit, namely, staring at a man's knees after he gives you money."

His head settled back against the wall, and his mouth fell open. Behind the idiotic forehead something was going on, he had concluded that I was trying to trick him in some way and he handed the money back.

I stamped my foot, swore, and told him to keep it. Did he think I intended to go to all this trouble for nothing? When you came down to it, I probably owed him the money, I just happened to remember an old debt, he was looking at a punctilious man, one honorable right down to his fingernails. In short, the money was his. . . . Nonsense, nothing to thank me for, it was a pleasure. Goodbye.

I walked off. At last I was rid of this painful pest, and could be undisturbed. I went back up Pile Street and stopped in front of a grocery. The window was crammed with food, and I decided to go in and get something to take along.

"Some cheese and a French loaf!" I said, and threw my half krone down on the counter.

"All of this is to go for bread and cheese?" the woman asked in an ironic tone, without looking at me.

"The entire fifty øre," I replied, not at all upset.

I took my bundles, said good morning with the most exquisite politeness to the old fat woman, and started off at full speed toward the castle and the public gardens. I found a bench to myself and began chewing savagely at my lunch. It did me good; it had been a long time since I'd had such a well-balanced meal and I gradually became aware of the same feeling of tired peace which one feels after a long cry. My courage had now returned; it was not enough any longer to write an essay on something so elementary and simple-minded as "Crimes of the Future," which any ass could arrive at, let alone read in history books. I felt ready for a more difficult enterprise, I was in the mood to conquer obstacles and I determined on a consideration in three parts of Philosophical Consciousness. Naturally I'd find a moment to break the neck of some of Kant's sophistries. . . . When I reached to take my writing materials to begin work, I discovered that my pencil was gone—I had forgotten and left it in the pawnshop: my pencil was still in the waistcoat pocket.

God, how eager everything was to go wrong around me! I swore several times, leaped up from the bench, and strolled back and forth on the path. Everything was silent; near the queen's summerhouse two nursemaids were wheeling their baby carriages along; otherwise, not a person was to be seen anywhere. I was profoundly bitter, and strolled up and down in front of my bench like a maniac. How amazingly everything fell to pieces on all sides! An essay in three parts left high and dry for no reason than that there was missing from my pocket a ten-øre pencil! Suppose I went down to Pile Street again and got the pencil back? There would still be time to get a lot done before the mob would come and fill the park. Moreover, there was so much at stake with this investigation of Philosophical Consciousness, perhaps the happiness of many persons. Who could tell? I told myself that the piece could very well be a great help for dozens of young people. Actually, I wouldn't attack Kant after all, I could avoid that, I would just have

to make an invisible detour when I came to the problem of Space and Time; but Renan would have to take care of himself, Renan, that old preacher. . . . In any case, what was essential was an article of so and so many pages; the unpaid room rent and the landlady's long look in the morning when I met her on the stairs bothered me all day and even cropped up in my gay moods when I hadn't another dark thought in my head. This would have to come to an end. I walked rapidly out of the park to get my pencil from the pawnshop.

At the bottom of the hill I overtook and passed two women. As I walked by them, I brushed the arm of one. I looked up; she had a plump, slightly pale face. All at once she blushed and became wonderfully beautiful—I don't know the reason; perhaps from a word she had heard from someone passing, perhaps because of some silent thought inside her. Or was it because I had touched her arm? Her full bosom heaved noticeably several times, and she clenched her hands firmly on her parasol handle. What was she thinking?

I stopped and allowed her to go on ahead; actually at that moment I couldn't have gone farther anyway, the entire series of events seemed to me so curious. I was in an excitable mood, angry with myself for the business with the pencil, and extremely stimulated by all the food just eaten on an empty stomach. Suddenly my thoughts shot off on a lunatic direction, and I felt myself possessed by a strange desire to frighten this woman, to follow her and hurt her in some way or other. I caught up again and walked past, then abruptly turned and looked back at her to study her. I stopped and stared at her face to face, and on the spot a name came to me I'd never heard before, a name with a smooth, nervous sound: Ylayali. When she was very close, I drew myself up straight and said in an impressive voice, "Miss, you are losing your book."

I could hear my heart thump audibly as I said that.

"My book?" she said to her companion. She walked on.

My malice increased and I followed the two. I was conscious all the time that I was following mad whims without being able to do anything about it. My deranged consciousness ran away with me and sent me lunatic inspirations, which I obeyed one after the other. No matter how much I told myself that I was acting idiotically, it did not help; I made the most stupid faces behind the women's backs, and I coughed furiously several times as I went by them. Walking on in this way, very slowly, always a few steps ahead, I could feel her eyes on my back, and I bowed my head involuntarily in shame at persecuting her. Gradually I began to feel a marvelous sense of being far, far away, in another place entirely; I had a sort of vague conviction that it wasn't I who was walking there on the sidewalk and bowing my head. In a few minutes, the women had reached Pascha's Bookstore. I had already stopped at the first window, and as they went by, I stepped out and said once more, "Miss, you are losing your book."

"Book, what book?" she said in a frightened voice. "Whatever sort of book is he talking about?"

She stopped. I gloated cruelly over her confusion; the bewilderment in her eyes fascinated me. Her thought could not grasp my desperate and petty persecution; she has no book at all with her, not even a page of a book, and yet now she looks through her pockets, gazes repeatedly at her hands, turns her head and examines the sidewalk behind her, strains her small and tender brain to its limit to find out what sort of book I am talking about. Her face turns various colors,

shows now one and now another expression, and her breath is audible; even the buttons on her dress seem to stare at me like a row of alarmed eyes.

"Don't bother with him," her friend said, and took her arm. "He's drunk—don't you see how drunk he is!"

Despite my alienation from myself at that moment, and even though I was nothing but a battleground for invisible forces, I was aware of every detail of what was going on around me. A big brown dog ran across the street, toward the trees and the Tivoli; it had a small collar made of Mexican silver. Farther up the street, a window on the first story opened and a girl with her sleeves rolled up leaned out and began polishing the panes on the outside. Nothing escaped my eyes, I was sharp and my brain was very much alive, everything poured in toward me with a staggering distinctness as if a strong light had fallen on everything around me. The women before me had two blue feathers in their hats, and plaid kerchiefs around their necks. It occurred to me that they were sisters.

They turned in and stopped at Cisler's Music Shop, talking. I stopped also. Then they turned around, returned the same way they had come, passed me once more, turned the corner at University Street, and went up to St. Olaf's Place. I was at their heels, as near as I dared, all the time. They turned once, giving me a half-frightened, half-inquisitive look, and I saw no irritation in their manner, nor any wrinkled brows. This patience with my pestering made me ashamed, and I dropped my eyes. I no longer wanted to torture them, I wanted out of sheer gratitude to keep track of them with my eyes, not lose sight of them until they were safely inside some building.

Outside 2 St. Olaf's Place, a large house with four stories, they stopped once more, and then went in. I leaned against the lamppost near the fountain, and listened for their steps on the stair: the steps died away in the third story. I came in from the lamppost and looked up at the front of the house. Then something odd happened. High up, some curtains moved, an instant later the window opened, a head appeared, and two remarkable eyes rested on me. Ylayali! I said half aloud, and I felt myself turning red. Why didn't she call for help? Why didn't she push one of the flowerpots over on my head or send someone down to chase me away? We stood looking into each other's eyes without moving; this lasted a minute; thoughts shot between the window and the street, and not a word was said. She turned away. I felt something wrenched in me, a delicate shock went through my system; I saw a shoulder which slowly swung about, a back that disappeared into the room. This leisurely turning from the window, and the expression of the shoulder as it turned, was a sign to me. My blood recognized this delicate greeting and at that moment I felt marvelously happy inside. Then I turned and went back down the street.

I didn't dare look back to find out if she had come to the window again: the more I wondered about this, the more restless and excited I became. The chances were she was standing there this instant following all of my movements: I couldn't help knowing that I was being examined in this way from behind. I drew myself up as well as I could and walked on. Small jerks began to appear in my legs, my walk became unsteady precisely because I wanted it to be smooth. In order to seem calm and indifferent I swung my arms pointlessly, spit to the side, and looked up at the sky, but it was no good—I felt the watching eyes on my neck every second and a chill ran through my body. Finally I escaped by turning into a side street, from which

I went on down to Pile Street to get my pencil back.

I had no trouble in retrieving it. The man brought me the waistcoat itself and invited me to go through all the pockets. I found a couple of other pawnshop tickets, which I kept, thanking the man for being so obliging. I became more and more taken with him; at that moment it was extremely important for me to make a good impression on this person. I started off toward the door and then turned back to the counter as if I had forgotten something. I felt I owed him an explanation, some sort of reason, and I began to hum in order to attract his attention. Then I took the pencil and held it up in the air.

"It would never have occurred to me," I said, "to go to such trouble for just any pencil; this case is something special: there is a reason. This stump of a pencil may look insignificant, but this pencil is responsible for getting me where I am in the world, it has given me so to speak my position in life. . . ."

I stopped there. The man came all the way over to the counter.

"Is that so?" he said, looking curiously at me.

"With this pencil," I went on straight-faced, "I wrote my great work on the Philosophical Consciousness in three volumes. You have heard of it, I trust?"

It seemed to him that he had heard the name, the title only.

"Yes, that's it! That was mine! So it isn't really surprising if I wanted that tiny stub of a pencil back: it is very precious to me, it is almost a human being to me. In any case, I am tremendously grateful to you for your kindness and I will remember you for it—no, no, I will remember you for it without question: a promise is a promise, that is the sort of man I am, and you certainly have deserved it. Good day."

I strolled to the door, keeping the

posture of a man who can place another easily in an important post. The polite pawnbroker bowed twice to me as I went; I turned once more and said good day.

On the stairs I met a woman carrying a suitcase. She flattened herself against the wall to let me go by since I looked so prepossessing, and I involuntarily reached in my pocket for something to give her. When I found nothing, my pose collapsed, and I passed her with my head bowed. A moment after, I heard her, too, knocking at the pawnbroker's door: the door had a steel grillwork attached to it, and I recognized the reverberations as the knock disturbed it.

The sun was high, the time nearly twelve. The streets were beginning to come alive as the time approached for strolling in the sun. People laughing and nodding flowed up and down Karl Johan Street. I held my elbows near my sides, made myself small, and slipped unobtrusively by some acquaintances who had stationed themselves near the university to admire the passers-by. I strolled up to the Royal Gardens and fell to brooding.

These people I met on the streets, how gaily and lightly they rolled their shining heads and swung through life as if through a ballroom! Not a single eye had grief in it, no shoulders had burdens, in these happy minds there was not a clouded thought, not even a tiny hidden pain. I walked there, alongside these creatures, young myself, hardly leafed out, and I had already forgotten what happiness was! I hugged these thoughts close to me, and found that a terrible injustice had been done to me. Why had these last few months gone so much against me? I could no longer remember my own joyful nature, and I had the strangest troubles coming from all sides. I could not sit on a park bench by myself or put my foot down anywhere without being besieged by tiny and pointless

events, absurd nonsense, which forced itself into my brain and scattered my powers to the four winds. A dog that shot past me, a yellow rose in someone's lapel, could set my thoughts in motion and obsess me for hours. What was the matter with me? Had the hand of the Lord reached out and pointed at me? Well then, why me? Why not just as well at some man in South America? When I pondered these things, it seemed more and more incomprehensible why precisely I should have been chosen as the guinea pig for a whim of God's favor. It was an extremely odd way of going about things, to leap over the whole human race in order to arrive at me; for example, there was Pascha, the rare-book dealer, and Hennechen, the steamship clerk.

I walked along arguing with myself about these things, and could not stop; I came on the weightiest objections against the Lord's arbitrariness in letting me suffer for everyone else's sins. Even after I had found a bench and sat down, this question remained, occupying my mind and keeping me from any other thought. From that day in May when my setbacks had begun, I could see clearly all the landmarks of a gradually increasing weakness: now I had become too feeble to steer or guide myself, so to speak, where I wanted to go; a cloud of tiny vermin had forced its way inside me and eaten me out hollow. And what if God had decided absolutely to finish me? I stood up and walked back and forth in front of my bench.

My entire being was full of incredible pain at that moment; even my arms ached, and I could hardly stand to carry them in the usual way. I felt a distinct discomfort from my recent large meal also; I was stuffed and overstimulated and walked to and fro without looking up; the people who walked around me on both sides slipped by like ghosts. Finally, my seat was taken by two gentlemen who lit their cigars and talked loudly; I became furious and was about to order them off, but turned instead and went over to an entirely different area of the park, where I found a new bench. I sat down.

Thoughts of God began to occupy me again. It seemed to me utterly reprehensible of Him to block my way every time I tried for a job and to ruin my chances when it was only daily bread that I was asking for. I had noticed very clearly that every time I went hungry a little too long it was as though my brains simply ran quietly out of my head and left me empty. My head became light and floating, I could no longer feel its weight on my shoulders, and I had the sense that my eyes were remaining far too open when I looked at anything.

I sat there on the bench and thought about all this, and became more and more bitter against God for His constant persecutions. If He wanted to draw me nearer to Himself and make me better by pushing me hard and laying obstacles in my path, He was going about it the wrong way, I could assure Him of that. Then I looked up to the sky almost in tears from my defiance and I told Him that, once and for all, silently, inside myself.

Fragments of childhood teachings ran through my mind, I heard the music of the Bible in my ears, and I talked softly to myself, letting my head fall sarcastically to the side. Why should I be troubled for what I would eat, or for what I would drink, or for what I would put on this vile bag of worms which is called my earthly body? Had not the Heavenly Father cared for me as for those creatures who had no place to lay their heads, and had not His hand in His graciousness pointed at His insignificant servant? God had poked His finger down into my nerves and gently, almost without thinking, brought a little confusion among those threads. And God had pulled His finger back, and behold—there were filaments and fine rootlike threads on His finger from the threads of my nerves. And there remained an open hole behind His finger which was the finger of God, and a wound in my brain behind the path of His finger. But after God had touched me with the finger of His hand, He let me be and touched me no more and let nothing evil come upon me. He let me depart in peace and He let me depart with the open hole. And nothing evil will come upon me from God who is the Lord through all Eternity. . . .

Phrases of band music were coming on the wind all the way from the Student's Promenade. So it was after two. I took out my papers to try some writing; as I did so, my book of barber coupons fell out of my pocket. I opened the book and counted the pages: there were six left. Thank God! I said without thinking; now I could still be shaved for several weeks and look decent! My mood instantly changed for the better because of this little property which I still had left; I smoothed the coupons out carefully and stowed the book away in my pocket.

However, I was unable to write. After a couple of lines, nothing more wanted to come; my thoughts were elsewhere and I couldn't pull myself up to the effort. Everything around bothered me and distracted me; everything I saw obsessed me. Some flies and gnats were sitting on my paper and this disturbed me; I breathed on them to make them go, then blew harder and harder, but it did no good. The tiny beasts lowered their behinds, made themselves heavy, and struggled against the wind until their thin legs were bent. They were absolutely not going to leave the place. They would always find something to get hold of, bracing their heels against a comma or an unevenness in the paper, and they intended to stay exactly where they were until they themselves decided it was the right time to go.

These minuscule monsters kept me busy a long time; I crossed my legs and settled down leisurely to watch them. Suddenly one or two high notes of a clarinet drifted up to me from the concert and started my thoughts off in a new direction. Depressed at not being able to do my article, I poked the papers in my pocket and leaned backward over the bench. In this instant, my head was so clear that I could follow the most difficult train of thought without any effort. Lying in this position, letting my eyes float down over my chest and legs, I noticed the tiny leaping movement my feet made every time my heart beat. I sat up partway and gazed down at my feet. At that moment a strange and fantastic mood came over me which I had never felt before—a delicate and wonderful shock ran through all of my nerves as though a stream of light had flowed through them. As I stared at my shoes, I felt as if I had met an old friend, or got back some part of me that had been torn off: a feeling of recognition went through me, tears came to my eyes, and I experienced my shoes as a soft whispering sound coming up toward me. "Getting weak!" I said fiercely to myself and I closed my fists and said, "Getting weak." I was furious with myself for these ridiculous sensations, which had overpowered me even though I was fully conscious of them. I spoke harsh and sensible phrases, and I closed my eyes tightly to get rid of the tears. Then I began, as though I had never seen my shoes before, to study their expression, their mimelike movements when I moved my toes, their shape, and the worn-out leather they had; and I discovered that their wrinkles and their white seams gave them an expression, provided them with

a face. Something of my own being had gone over into these shoes, they struck me as being a ghost of my "I," a breathing part of myself. . . .

I sat there and tried to puzzle out these feelings a long time, perhaps an entire hour. A little old man arrived and took up the other end of my bench; as he sat down, he was puffing heavily after his walk, and said: "Ah ya, ya, ya, ya, ya, ya, yaaah!"

The moment I heard his voice, a wind swept through my head, I let shoes remain shoes, and I had the sensation already that the confused state of mind I had just gone through belonged to some time long ago, perhaps a year or two in the past, and was in the process of vanishing entirely from my memory. I settled down to examine the old man.

What was there about him of interest to me? Nothing, not the slightest thing! Only the fact that he was carrying a newspaper, folded, an outdated issue with the classified section showing; evidently something was wrapped in it. I became inquisitive and couldn't take my eyes from that paper; I got the insane idea that this might be a rare issue, perhaps the only one of its kind. My curiosity rose and I began to slide back and forth on my bench. Perhaps it was hiding official papers, dangerous documents stolen from some files. I had the vague impression of the existence of some secret treaty, a plot.

The man sat motionless, thinking. Why didn't he carry his paper like every other man, with the front page showing? What sort of cunning lay behind that? He looked as though he didn't want to let the parcel out of his hands, not for all the money in the world, he didn't even dare trust it to his own pockets. I'd be willing to risk my life that there was something more here than met the eye.

I concentrated. The very fact that it was impossible to penetrate this enigma made me wild with curiosity. I searched my pockets for something to give the man in order to start a conversation with him; I came on my barber coupons but replaced them. Suddenly I decided to be completely shameless; I patted my empty shirt pocket and said, "May I offer you a cigarette?"

No, thank you, the man did not smoke, he had had to quit in order not to make his eyes worse, he was nearly blind. Thank you anyway very much!

How long was it that his eyes had been weak? Was he able to read? Newspapers, for example?

"Not even newspapers, a shame!"

The man turned toward me. Both of his sick eyes had a film, which gave them a glassy appearance; they looked whitish, and made a revolting impression.

"You are not from here?" he asked.

No. Isn't he able even to read the headlines, for example, of that paper he has there?

Just barely. In any case, he could tell right away that I wasn't from here—there was something in my voice that told him. It didn't need to be much: he had very sharp hearing; at night when everyone else was asleep he could hear the people in the next room breathing. . . . "I wanted to ask you, where do you live?"

A lie appeared full-blown in my head. I lied automatically, without looking forward or back, and answered, "On St. Olaf's Place, number 2."

Is that right? The man knew every stone on St. Olaf's Place. There was a fountain there, street lamps, a couple of trees, he remembered it very well. . . .

"What was the number of your apartment?"

I stood up; I wanted to get to the bottom of this, driven wild by my notion about the newspaper. I intended to find out the secret, no matter what it cost.

Well, if you're unable to read even a newspaper, I don't see. . . .

"In number 2, did you say?" the man continued, paying no attention to my impatience. "Once I knew every last person in number 2. Whom do you rent from?"

I found a name quickly in order to get this over—invented one on the spot and tossed it out to bring down my tormentor.

"Happolati," I said.

"Oh, yes, Happolati." The man nodded, and had not missed a single syllable in this difficult name.

I looked at him astonished; he sat there very soberly, with a thoughtful air. I had barely finished pronouncing this stupid name, which had popped into my head, and this man was already at home with it and pretending that he had heard it before. Meanwhile, he laid his parcel down on the bench, and I felt my curiosity become unbearable. I saw clearly that there were two greasy spots on the paper.

"Doesn't your landlord work on a ship?" the man asked; his voice had not a trace of irony in it. "I seem to remember that he worked on a ship."

"On a ship? I don't mean to contradict you, but I wonder if the one you know isn't the brother; this one is J. A. Happolati, a businessman."

I figured this would settle his hash, but he kept on.

"They say he's got quite a head on him," the old man said, pushing forward.

"Oh, he is very sharp," I answered. "A tremendous head for business, he sells everything you could imagine: Russian goosedown and chicken feathers, hides, pulpwood, ink . . ."

"Amazing!" the old man broke out. "Is that so?"—very excited.

I was beginning to be drawn in. The plot ran away with me, and one lie after the other popped into my head. I sat down again, forgot the newspaper and the rare documents, became enthusiastic, and got into the swing of it. The gullibility of the little dwarf made me reckless; I was going to stuff him full of lies, no matter what happened, and drive him like a knight from the field.

I wondered if he had heard about the electric prayer book that Happolati had invented?

"What was that, an electric—"

"With electric letters that can light up in the dark? A fantastically big operation, a million kroner going into it, factories and printing presses working now, mobs of engineers on contract already, I've heard some hundred men."

"I'm not really surprised," the man replied calmly. That was all he said: he believed every word I had spoken and did not fall over with amazement. This disappointed me a bit; I had hoped to see him dumfounded at my inventions.

I pulled up a couple of other desperate lies, went all the way, dropped the detail that Happolati had been prime minister of Persia for nine years.

"You probably do not really realize what it means to be prime minister of Persia?" I asked. It was greater than being king here, more like being a sultan, if he knew what that involved. Happolati, however, had settled down marvelously in the job and had never taken a false step. And I told him about Ylayali, his daughter, an enchanted creature, a princess who owned three hundred slaves and slept on a bed made of yellow roses; she was the most beautiful being I had ever seen, I had never seen any woman in my life, so help me God, that could begin to compare with her!

"So, she must have been pretty, then, eh?" the old man mumbled with an absent air, looking down at the ground.

Pretty? She was magnificent, that sort of magnificence ought to have been prohibited! Her eyes were as soft as silk, and

her arms the color of amber! A simple glance from her was like a kiss from any other woman, and when she spoke my name her voice poured through my veins like wine right into my heart. And why shouldn't she be that beautiful? Who did she think she was, a filing clerk or a receptionist in the Fire Department? She was simply out of a fairy tale, he could take my word for it, she was a masterpiece, divine!

"Yes, I'm sure she was," the man said, a little bewildered.

His composure bored me; I had become excited by the sound of my own voice and spoke in deadly seriousness. The material stolen from secret files, the agreements signed with some foreign power or other, all this I had forgotten entirely; the small flat bundle lay on the bench between us and I hadn't the slightest desire any longer to see what was in it. I was completely taken up with my own stories, strange visions were passing before my eyes, my blood went to my brain, and I was lying as fast as I could.

All at once the man seemed about to leave. He got halfway up and asked, so as not to break it off too abruptly: "This Happolati, if I'm not mistaken, is quite rich now?"

How did this blind and revolting old fool dare to throw about this remarkable name which I had myself created, treating it as though it were just an ordinary name, plastered on the front of every grocery in town? He never stumbled over a single consonant and never omitted a syllable; this name had sunk deep into his brain and put down roots instantly. I became annoyed, and an inner bitterness began to rise in me against this creature whom nothing could disconcert and nothing could make suspicious.

"I wouldn't know," I answered roughly. "I wouldn't know anything about that. Let me tell you, moreover, once and for all that his name is Johan Arendt Happolati, judging from his initials."

"Johan Arendt Happolati," the man repeated, somewhat astonished at my violence. Then he fell silent.

"You should see his wife," I said, raving. "A fatter human being. . . . I suppose you don't think she was really fat?"

"Oh no, I certainly wouldn't deny that, especially—you know—that kind of a man . . ."

The old creature answered meekly and quietly to every one of my outbursts and fumbled for words as if he were afraid to say something wrong and make me angry.

"Goddammit, man, I suppose you think I've been sitting here stuffing you full of lies?" I shouted, completely out of my mind. "I'll bet you never believed there was a man with the name Happolati! Never in my life have I seen such obstinacy and viciousness in an old man! What in the hell has got hold of you anyway? And you have probably been thinking to yourself, on top of all this, that I am actually broke, haven't you, and that this is my best suit, and that I haven't a cigarette case in my pocket at all? The way you have treated me is something I am not used to, I will tell you flatly, and I won't take it, so help me God, neither from you nor from anybody else, and you may as well know that now!"

The man got to his feet. He stood there with his mouth open, completely dumb, and listened to my outburst to the end; then he reached hurriedly for his bundle on the bench and walked away, nearly running down the path, with his little old man's steps.

I sat down on the bench and watched his back go farther and farther away, seeming to fold more and more in on itself. I don't know where the impression came from, but it occurred to me that I had never seen a more dishonest, a more vile back than this one, and I wasn't at all sorry that I had given him what he deserved before he left. . . .

The light began to fail, the sun was sinking, a faint rustling came from the trees nearby, and the nursemaids who were sitting in groups by the climbing bars got ready to push their baby carriages home. I was tranquil and in good spirits. The excited state I had just been in slowly passed away and I returned to normal, became relaxed, and began to feel sleepy. The huge amount of bread I had eaten was no longer bothering me particularly. I leaned back on the bench in a marvelous mood, closed my eyes, and became more and more drowsy; I slipped off and was about to fall into a deep sleep when a park attendant placed his hand on my shoulder and said, "You mustn't sleep sitting here."

"No, no," I said and jumped up. All at once the hideous position I was in drove in on me with all its force. I had to do something, light on something or other! Trying for a job had not worked; my recommendations were old by now and written by people so totally unknown they were virtually worthless anyway; and this series of refusals all through the summer had been a heavy blow to my morale. Nevertheless, my rent was due now, and I had to find a way out. Everything else would have to wait.

I had taken my pencil and paper out again and was sitting mechanically writing 1848 in all the corners. If only one good thought would rush in, then words would come! That had happened before, I had had times when I could write out a long piece with no effort at all, and it would turn out to be first-rate besides.

I wrote 1848 twenty times, wrote it crossways and intersecting and every possible way, waiting for a usable idea to come. A swarm of vague thoughts were batting about in my brain. The mood of the approaching dusk made me despondent and sentimental. Fall was here and had already begun to put everything into a deep sleep—the flies and small creatures had received their first shock; high in trees and down near the earth you could hear the sounds of a laboring life, breathing, restless, and rustling, struggling not to die. The whole community of insects would rouse themselves one more time, poke their yellow heads up out of the moss, lift their legs, put out expeditions, feeling with their long antennae, and then suddenly collapse, roll over, and turn their stomachs to the sky. Every plant had received the mark—the delicate breath of the first frost had passed over it. Grass stems held themselves stiffly up toward the sun, and the fallen leaves slipped across the ground with a sound like that of traveling silkworms. It was the hour of fall, well into the festival of what is not eternal. The roses have taken on a fever, their blood-red leaves have a strange and unnatural flush.

I myself felt like an insect about to go under, attacked by annihilation in this world ready to go to sleep. I jumped up, laboring with profound terrors, and took three or four long steps up the path. No! I cried, and clenched both fists, this has to end! And I sat down again, brought out the pencil and paper in order to grapple with the article. When the rent was right before my eyes, it would never do to give up.

My thoughts slowly started to assemble. I paid attention to them and wrote down with care a couple of well-thought-out pages, a sort of introduction: it could have been a beginning to several things, a travel piece or a political essay, whichever I felt like. The pages led one on, and made a good introduction to either sort of piece.

Next I started looking about for a specific question which I could discuss, a person, a problem I could fasten on. I couldn't come on anything. During this struggle, chaos began to appear again in my thoughts, I could feel my brain literally go click, my head began emptying, and finally it was balancing lightly and without content on my shoulders. I felt this ghastly emptiness inside with my whole body. I seemed to myself hollowed out from head to toe.

"Lord, my God and my Father!" I cried in agony, and I repeated this appeal many times in succession without adding a word.

The wind rustled in the leaves, it was getting ready to rain. I sat there a while yet and stared hopelessly at my papers, finally folded them together and placed them slowly in my pocket. The air had become chilly, and I had no waistcoat now; I turned my collar up to my neck, stuck my hands in my pockets, then stood up and left.

If it only could have gone this time, this one time! My landlady had inquired about the rent with her eyes twice now, and I had had to duck my head and sneak past with an embarrassed greeting. I could not do it again; the next time I met those eyes, I would release my room and make some honest nest for myself. The way it all was going, that time could not be far off.

When I came down to the park gate, I saw the little old troll again whom I had chased away in a rage. The mysterious bundle was lying alongside him on the bench, opened; in it were several sorts of food which he was just eating. I immediately had the impulse to go to him and apologize, ask him to forgive my behavior, but his food put me off. His ancient fingers, which looked like ten folded claws, were clutching the sandwiches in a repulsive way. I felt nauseated and walked past without speaking. He didn't recognize me; his eyes stared at me like dry horns and his face was entirely blank.

I walked on.

I stopped as I always did when I passed any newspaper building, and read the late editions posted outside in order to study the classified section for job openings, and this time I was lucky enough to find one I could apply for; a grocer on Grønland Street wanted someone for a few hours' bookkeeping every day; wages by arrangement. I wrote the man's address down and prayed to God silently for this position—I would accept much less than anybody else for the work, half a krone would be princely or perhaps even less; the price would not be a consideration.

When I got home I found on my table a note from my landlady in which she asked me either to pay my rent in advance or to move as soon as I could. I mustn't be offended at this, it was a request she had to make. With best wishes, Mrs. Gundersen.

I wrote a letter of application to the grocer, whose name was Christie, 31 Grønland Street, sealed the envelope and took it down to the mailbox at the corner. Then I went back up to my room and sat down to think in my rocking chair, as the room grew more and more dark. It was beginning to be difficult to stay up late now.

I woke very early the next morning. When I opened my eyes, it was still half dark, and it was quite a while before I heard the clock in the apartment beneath strike five. I wanted to fall asleep again, but couldn't manage it; I became more and more alert and lay there thinking thousands of things.

All at once, one or two remarkable sentences occurred to me, good for a short story or a sketch, windfalls in language, as good as I had ever come on. I lay saying the words over to myself and decided they were excellent. Soon several other sentences joined the two; instantly I was wide awake, stood up, and took paper and pencil from the table at the foot of my bed. It was like a vein opening, one word followed the other, arranged themselves in right order, created situations; scene piled on scene, actions and conversations welled up in my brain, and a strange sense of pleasure took hold of me. I wrote as if possessed, and filled one page after the other without a moment's pause. Thoughts poured in so abruptly, and kept on coming in such a stream, that I lost a number of them from not being able to write them down fast enough, even though I worked with all my energy. They continued to press themselves on me; I was deep into the subject, and every word I set down came from somewhere else.

The session lasted a wonderfully long time before it ended! I had fifteen, twenty written pages lying on my knees in front of me when I finally stopped and laid the pencil down. Now if those pages were only worth anything, I was saved! I leaped out of bed and dressed. It grew more and more light, and I could halfway make out the Chief of Lighthouses' message down by the door; near the window there was already enough light to write by, if one had to. I started immediately making a clean copy.

A strange mist, with lights and colors in it, rose from these fantasies; startled, I came on one good thing after the other and told myself that it was the best piece I had ever read in my life. I became giddy with contentment, gladness swelled up in me, I felt myself to be magnificent. I weighed the piece in my hand and assessed it on the spot with a rough guess as five kroner. No one would ever haggle about five kroner for this. On the contrary. In view of the quality, one could

KNUT HAMSUN

call it pure thievery to get the piece for
ten. The last thing I had in mind was to
do such a remarkable work free; my
experience was that one did not find
stories of that sort lying about on the
street! I decided definitely on ten kroner.

It grew lighter and lighter in the room:
I glanced down by the door and I could
read without any great difficulty the delicate skeletonlike letters of Miss Andersen's offer of shrouds, Main Entrance, to
the right; the clock had struck seven
some time ago.

I stood up and remained standing in
the center of the room. All in all, Mrs.
Gundersen's notice had come rather con-
veniently. This really wasn't any room
for me; the curtains on the windows were
a very ordinary green, and there weren't
even enough pegs on the walls to hang
your wardrobe on. The sad rocking chair
in the corner was actually a joke of a
chair: if one started laughing at it, one
could die laughing. It was too low for a
grown man, and besides, it was so tight,
one needed a shoehorn to get back out of
it. In short, this room was simply not
furnished in a way appropriate to intellectual effort, and I did not intend to
keep it any longer. I would not keep it
under any circumstances! I had been
silent in this hole and stood it here and
stayed on here too long already.

Borne up by hope and contentment,
thinking all the time of my marvelous
story, which I took out of my pocket
every other minute to look at, I decided
to get it over with right now and move. I
took out my bundle, a red handkerchief
which contained two clean collars and
some crumpled newspaper which I had
carried my bread home in, rolled it all
together with my blanket, and added my
store of white writing paper. Then, just
to make sure, I looked in every corner to
see that I hadn't left anything, and when
nothing turned up, I walked to the window and looked out. The morning was

dark and misty; no one had arrived yet at
the burned-down smithy site and the
clothesline down in the courtyard was
stretched tight from wall to wall,
shrunken by the mist. There was nothing
new, so I turned away from the window,
took the blanket under my arm, bowed to
the Chief of Lighthouses' announcement,
bowed to Miss Andersen's shroud, and
opened the door.

All at once I remembered the landlady; she certainly ought to be notified of
my departure so she might realize that
she was dealing with a self-respecting
person. I wanted to thank her also in
writing for the couple of days I had used
the room beyond my time. The certainty
that I was saved now for a long while
dominated me so entirely that I even
promised to give my landlady five kroner
when I came into them one of these
days: I wanted to prove to her without
possibility of doubt what an honorable
man she had had under her roof.

I left the note behind on the table.

I stopped by the door and turned
around one more time. The delicious
feeling of having come out on top at last
filled me with joy and made me thankful
to God and to the universe and I knelt
down by the bed and thanked God aloud
for His great goodness toward me that
morning. I knew, oh I knew so well, that
the inspiration and holy breath I had just
experienced and written down was a
wonderful working of God in my soul,
an answer to my cry of need of yesterday. It is God! It is God! I cried to
myself, and I was so moved over my own
words I sobbed; now and then I had to
stop and listen a moment to hear if
anyone should be coming up the stairs.
At last I stood up and left; I slipped
noiselessly down all the flights of stairs
and made it to the outer door unseen.

The streets were shiny from the rain
that had fallen in the dawn hours, the
sky hung low and thick over the city,

there was not a ray of sunlight anywhere. What would this day bring? I started as usual in the direction of the City Hall and saw that the clock showed eight-thirty. I had, therefore, a couple of hours to waste; there was no sense in getting to the newspaper office before ten, perhaps eleven; I could wander around till that time, and in the meantime think of some avenue that would lead to breakfast. The best was that I had no fear of going to bed hungry tonight; those times, thank God, were over! That phase was behind me now, a bad dream, from now on it was upward all the way!

But in the meantime my green blanket was becoming a problem; I certainly couldn't make a spectacle of myself carrying something like that around under my arm in broad daylight. What would people think of me? So I walked along trying to think of some place where it would be safe until later. It struck me suddenly that I could walk over to Semb's and have them wrap it. The bundle would instantly look more respectable and there would be no shame any longer in carrying it. I carried it into the store and communicated my errand to one of the clerks.

He looked first at the blanket, then at me; I had the sensation that he shrugged his shoulders, invisibly, with a kind of contempt, as he took the parcel. That wounded me.

"For God's sake, be careful!" I shouted. "Two delicate vases are inside. That package has to get to Smyrna!"

That helped immensely. With every movement of his hands and body the clerk begged my forgiveness for not having sensed that there were expensive objects inside the blanket. When he had finished his wrapping, I thanked him for his help like a man who has often sent valuable objects to Smyrna. He even opened the door for me as I left.

I started wandering around among the people in the main marketplace, and particularly hovered near the women who were selling potted plants. The heavy red roses smoldering in the foggy morning, blood-colored and uninhibited, made me greedy, and tempted me powerfully to steal one—I asked the prices merely so I could come as near them as possible. If I got more money than I needed, I would buy one, no matter what happened afterwards; I could always skimp a little here and there in my daily budget to make up for it.

It was ten, and I walked to the newspaper office. Scissors, who spent his day cutting out news notes from other newspapers, was absently leafing through old issues, the editor had not yet come in. Following Scissors' inquiry, I delivered over my great manuscript to him, made him understand that it was a matter of more than ordinary importance, and impressed firmly on his mind that the editor should receive it personally as soon as he arrived. I would pop in later in the day for his answer myself.

"Very good!" Scissors said, and went back to his paper.

It seemed to me he had taken it a little too calmly, but I said nothing, just nodded casually to him and left.

Now I had a lot of time. If the weather would only clear up! It was really a miserable day, nothing fresh, no wind; the women were using umbrellas just to be safe, and the wool hats of the men looked comical. I made one more trip through the market to see the vegetables and the roses. I felt a hand on my shoulder, and turned: "Queeny" was saying good morning.

"Good morning, yes," I answered in a questioning tone in order to find out what he wanted as quickly as possible. I was not too fond of Queeny.

He looked curiously at the brand-new package under my arm and asked, "What have you there?"

"I bought some cloth at Semb's for a suit," I answered in a casual tone. "I don't know why I should go around so threadbare any longer; one can be too stingy in bodily things too, you know."

He looked at me intently.

"How is it going then?" he said slowly.

"Fine, much better than I had expected."

"Have you found something to do then?"

"Something to do?" I answered and looked mightily surprised. "I am the bookkeeper at the Christie Foodstore."

"Is that so?" he said, and drew back a little. "You have no idea how happy I am about that. Just so friends don't get it all away from you. Goodbye."

A few seconds later, he turned around and came back. He pointed with his stick to my parcel and said, "Let me recommend my tailor for your suit. You'll never, never find a better tailor than Isaksen. Just say I sent you."

Why was he sticking his nose into my business? What was it to him which tailor I used? I got angry. The sight of this aimless, painted-up creature somehow enraged me and I reminded him in a brutal tone of the ten kroner he had borrowed from me. Before he had even replied, I regretted having asked him for it; I felt ashamed and didn't look him in the eyes. At that moment a woman came along, I stepped quickly back to let her go by, and then took the opportunity to slip away.

What should I do with myself, waiting? I couldn't sit in a café with an empty pocketbook, and I couldn't think of any acquaintances I could go visit at this time of day. I headed instinctively for the upper part of town, got rid of some time on the way between the marketplace and Grænsen Street, read the *Afternoon Times* which had just been posted outside the office, made a swing down Karl Johan, turned around again, and walked straight to Our Saviour's Church yard, where I found a quiet bench on the slope near the chapel. I sat there in privacy, dozing in the damp air, and daydreamed, half asleep and chilly. Time passed. Was it absolutely certain that my sketch was a small masterpiece and inspired? God knows it wasn't free of faults here and there! Everything considered, it could very well not be accepted, no, simply not accepted! Maybe it was not entirely free of mediocrity, maybe it was downright bad—how did I know but that at this very moment it wasn't already in the wastebasket? My peace of mind was shaken; I leaped up and rushed out of the cemetery.

Once on Akers Street again, I glanced into a shop window and saw that it was only a few minutes past twelve. This made me despair even more. I had been so sure it was long past noon; there was no sense in visiting the editor before four. I had ominous feelings about the fate of my sketch; the more I thought about it, the more unreasonable it seemed that I could have written anything worthwhile in such a short time, and half asleep beside, and my brain wild and feverish. I had deceived myself, that's all, had been overjoyed all morning for nothing! That's all! . . . I walked with long steps up Ullevaals Street, past the St. Hanshaugen district, came to the edge of town, walked through building sites and farmers' fields and finally found myself on a country road that went on farther than I could see.

I stopped there and decided to turn around. The walk had made me warm, and I walked back slowly and extremely depressed. I met two hayracks, the drivers lying on their backs on top of the loads, singing. Both were bareheaded, with round faces untouched by grief. I thought to myself as I walked along that they were sure to say something, throw out some remark or other, play a practical joke. When I was near enough, one of them shouted, asking me what I had under my arm.

"A blanket," I answered.

"What time is it?" he asked.

"I'm not sure, about three I think."

The two laughed and drove by. As they did, I felt the flick of a whip on one ear and my hat was jerked off. They couldn't let me get by without some sort of prank. Furiously, I reached for my ear, picked my hat up from the ditch, and went on. Farther on, in St. Hanshaugen, I met a man who informed me that it was already past four.

Past four! It was already past four! I pulled up stakes for town and the newspaper office. Perhaps the editor had already been there and left! I walked and ran around everyone, stumbled, bumped against wagons, left all the other pedestrians behind, ran even with the horses, hurried like a madman to get there in time. I twisted in through the outer door, took the stairs in four leaps, and knocked.

No one answered.

He's gone! He's gone! I thought. I tried the door. It was open. I knocked once more and walked in.

The editor was sitting at his desk, his face turned to the window, his pen in hand about to write. When he heard my panting good day, he turned halfway around, glanced at me, shook his head, and said: "I haven't had time yet to read your piece."

I was so overjoyed that he hadn't tossed it out yet that I said, "No, I understand that. There's no hurry about it. A couple of days, maybe, or . . . ?"

"Well, we'll see. In any event, I have your address."

And I forgot to tell him that I no longer had an address.

The audience was over; I stepped back, bowing, and left. Hope blazed up in me again, nothing was lost yet, on the contrary, I could still win, be utterly victorious, for that matter. And my brain instantly fell to imagining a great council in heaven where it had just this moment been decided that I should win, receive ten kroner flat for my story. . . .

If I only had somewhere to stay tonight! I debated the best place to poke myself into, and was so absorbed in this question that I stopped still in the center of the street. I forgot where I was and stood like a solitary buoy in the middle of the ocean with the water flowing and roaring around it. A paperboy held out the evening paper *Viking* to me. "Get it here, sensational!" I looked up and started—I was outside Semb's again.

I quickly turned my back, hid the parcel in front of me, and hurried down Kirke Street worried and ashamed that they might have noticed me from the window. I passed Ingebret's and the theater, and at the ticket office turned down toward the harbor and the fortress. I found another bench and started casting about again.

How in God's name would I find a room tonight? Maybe there was a hole somewhere I could slip into and stay hidden in until morning? My pride would not allow me to go back to the room I had: nothing could ever force me to go back on my word. I pushed that thought away with great indignation and smiled arrogantly to myself about the tiny red rocking chair. By an association of ideas, I suddenly found myself in a large, two-windowed room I had once had on Hægdehaugen Street, I saw a tray on the table full of thick slices of bread and butter. It shifted its features, now it was a piece of beef, a tempting piece, a snow-white napkin, all sorts of bread, a silver fork. The door opened: my landlady came in offering me more tea. . . .

Delusions and dreams! I told myself that if I did eat food now, my head would get upset again, I would have the same feverish brain and ridiculous ideas to deal with. I simply couldn't take food, I wasn't made that way; that was one of my characteristics, a peculiar thing with me.

Perhaps some possibility of a bed would turn up when it was nearer evening. There was no hurry; at the worst, I could always find a place out in the woods; the entire environs of the city were at my disposal and the weather could not be regarded as cold yet.

In front of me, the sea rocked in its heavy drowsiness; ships and fat, broad-nosed barges dug up graves in the lead-colored plain, shiny waves darted out the right and left and kept going, and all the time the smoke poured like feathery quilts out of the smokestacks and the sound of pistons penetrated faintly through the heavy moist air. There was no sun and no wind, the trees behind me were wet, and the bench I sat on was cold and damp. Time passed; I settled down to doze a little; grew sleepy and a bit chilly in my back. Soon after, I felt my eyes begin to close. I let them close . . .

When I woke, it was all dark around me, I jumped up confused and half frozen, grabbed my parcel and started walking. I walked faster and faster to warm up, beat my arms, rubbed my lower legs, which were numb, and came up near the firehouse. It was nine; I had slept several hours.

What should I do now? I had to go somewhere. I stood gaping up at the firehouse, wondering if it would be possible to slip in one of the entrances and go through just the instant when the guard's back was turned. I climbed the stairs intending to engage the guard in conversation; he immediately lifted his ax in present-arms position, waiting to see what I had to say. This ax, lifted with its edge toward me, was like a cold blow

right through my nerves: I became mute with fright before this armed man and involuntarily started to retreat. I didn't say a word, just slipped steadily backward. To save face, I rubbed my hand over my forehead as if I had forgotten something, and sneaked off. When I was standing on the sidewalk again, I felt saved, as if I had just escaped from a tremendous danger. I hurried away.

Cold and hungry, more and more miserable, I pushed on down Karl Johan Street. I started to swear, not caring whether anyone could hear me or not. Near the Senate House, just where the trees begin, a new association of ideas called up a painter I knew, a young man whom I had once saved from a brawl in the amusement park, and whom I later had visited. I snapped my fingers and took off down Tordenskjold Street, found a door with a card on it reading C. Zacharias Bartel, and knocked.

He came to the door himself; he gave off a ghastly reek of beer and tobacco.

"Good evening!" I said.

"Good evening! Is it you? Why in hell have you come so late? It can't be seen really in artificial light. I've added a hay-rack since you saw it last, and changed a few things. You must see it in the daylight, there's no use looking at it now."

"Let me see it now anyway!" I said. Actually, I couldn't think what painting he was standing there talking about.

"Absolutely, totally impossible!" he answered. "The whole thing would look yellow! Also, there's one more thing." He leaned toward me, whispering, "I have a little girl visitor tonight, so we'll have to give it up."

"Oh, yes, well, yes, you're right, there's no question then."

I stepped down, said good night, and left.

So there was no way out of it then but to find some place out in the woods. If only the ground hadn't been so damp! I patted my blanket and felt more and more relieved at the thought of sleeping out. I had spent so much time looking for a room in the city that I was sick and tired of the whole thing. I felt a delicious pleasure in letting it all go, just relaxing and floating along the street without a worry in my head. I walked to the clock at the university, saw that it was after ten, and from there I headed north. I stopped once on Hægdehaugen Street outside a grocery store that had some food displayed in the window. A cat lay there asleep beside a French loaf, just behind it was a bowl of lard and several jars of meal. I stood for a while looking at these groceries, but since I had nothing to buy them with, I turned away and pushed on. I walked very slowly, finally passed Majorstuen, walked on and on, walked for hours, and at last got out to the Bogstad Woods.

I left the road here and sat down to rest. Then I started looking for a likely place, gathered together some ling and juniper boughs and made a bed on top of a little hill where it was moderately dry. I opened my parcel and took out the blanket. I was exhausted from the long walk and lay down immediately. I tried all sorts of positions before I finally got settled down: my ear smarted somewhat, it was slightly swollen from the crack the farm worker had given it and I couldn't lie on it. I took off my shoes and put them under my head with the wrapping paper on top of them.

The darkness brooded around me. Nothing moved. But high above my head rustled endless music, the air, that distant tuneless humming which never fell silent. I listened so long to this eternal feeble sound that it began to get me confused: it was certainly symphonies coming from the orbiting universes above me, stars that were singing a song. . . .

"It's not, more likely the devil!" I said, and laughed aloud to bolster me a little. "It is the night owls of Canaan hooting!"

I got up, lay down again, put on my shoes, tramped around awhile in the dark, and lay down again, fought and battled against rage and terror till far into the morning hours, when I finally fell asleep.

It was broad daylight when I woke, and I had the feeling it was near noon. I put on my shoes, wrapped up my blanket, and started back to town. No sun today either, and I was shivering like a dog. My feet were numb and water began to come out of my eyes as though they couldn't bear the light.

It was three in the afternoon. My hunger began to be painful. I was weak, and walked along throwing up here and there on the sly. I took a swing down to the Steam Kitchen, read the menu and twitched my shoulders in case anyone was watching, as though to say corned meat and pork were not food for me; after that, I walked down by the railroad station.

All at once a curious confusion slipped into my head; I walked on, not wanting to pay any attention to it, but it grew worse and worse; finally I had to sit down on a doorstep. My whole consciousness underwent some change, a tissue in my brain parted. I took a couple of breaths and remained sitting there astonished. I was conscious, I could feel clearly a little pain in my ear from yesterday, and when an acquaintance came by, I knew him immediately and stood up to give him a small nod and bow.

What sort of a new and painful sensation was this, which was being added to the others? Did it come from sleeping on the ground? Or was it because I hadn't had breakfast yet? All in all, there was absolutely no sense in living in this way; and by Holy Christ I did not understand what I had done to deserve this clear persecution either! Suddenly it struck me that I could just as well make a rat of myself right now and take the blanket off to "Uncle's" artesian well. I could pawn it for a krone and get three respectable meals, and keep myself going until I found something else—I would have to get around Hans Pauli later. I was already on my way to the well when I stopped in front of the entrance, shook my head doubtfully, and then turned around.

After I was some distance away, I grew more and more glad that I had won this severe test. The awareness that I was honorable rose to my head, filled me with magnificent conviction that I had character. I was a white beacon tower in the middle of a dirty human ocean full of floating wreckage. To pawn someone else's property for a single meal, to eat and drink oneself into damnation, to look in your own face and call yourself rat and have to drop your eyes—never! Never! I had never really seriously considered it; it had just occurred to me loosely; a man wasn't really responsible for these accidental, floating notions, especially when he had a ghastly headache and had nearly killed himself dragging around a blanket that belonged to another person.

There will certainly be some way to find help in any case when the time comes! For example, the grocer on Grønland Street, had I been pestering him every hour on the hour since I answered his ad? Had I rung his bell too early and too late and been sent away? I hadn't so much as appeared there once for my answer! The effort might not be entirely in vain—maybe luck was with me this time. Luck had a habit of following curious paths. So I went off to Grønland Street.

The last disturbance that had swept through my brain had left me a bit faint, and I walked very slowly, thinking about what I would say to the grocer. He could very well be a good soul. If the whim struck him, he might give me a krone in advance, even, without my asking for it: people like that now and then get wonderful notions in their heads.

I slipped into a doorway and darkened my trouser knees with a little spit so I'd look respectable, stowed my blanket behind a box in one dark corner, strode across the street, and entered the small store.

A man was standing there pasting bags together from old newspapers.

I said that I would like to speak with Mr. Christie.

"That is me," the man answered.

So! My name was such and so, I had taken the liberty of answering his advertisement, and I was wondering if he had been able to use me.

He repeated my name several times and began to laugh. "Well, we'll see now!" he said, and took my letter out of his pocket. "Would you be so good as to note how you deal with figures, my good man? You have dated this letter with the year 1848." And he laughed from deep in his chest.

"Yes, that was a shame," I said, crestfallen, "a moment of absent-mindedness, distraction, I admit it."

"Well, you see I have to have a man who doesn't make mistakes with figures," he said. "I regret it—your handwriting is extremely clear, I liked your letter also, but . . ."

I waited a little while; it was inconceivable that was the man's last word. He went back to making his paper bags.

"Yes, that's embarrassing," I said. "A gruesome embarrassment, but of course it won't happen again, and this slip of the pen surely can't have made me totally unfit to keep books?"

"No, I didn't say that," he answered, "but for the moment it seemed important enough to me so that I decided on another man on the spot."

"So the position is taken then?" I asked.

"Yes."

"Good Lord, then there's nothing more to do about it!"

"No. I'm sorry about it, but . . ."

"Goodbye!" I said.

Now a brutal rage blazed up in me. I took my parcel from the entry, ground my teeth, ran into peaceful pedestrians on the sidewalks and did not ask pardon. When one man stopped and scolded me in a sharp tone for my behavior, I turned around, screamed a solitary meaningless word into his ear, and shook my fist right under his nose. I walked on, frightened by a blind rage I could not control. He called to a policeman. I wanted nothing more at that moment than to have a policeman between my two hands for a minute, so I slowed my pace on purpose to give him time to catch me, but no one came. Was there some particular reason why absolutely every last one of a man's most serious and most sincere endeavors should fail? Why had I written 1848 anyway? What was that damned year to me? Now I was walking around starving so that my intestines were curling up inside me like snakes, and moreover there was no guarantee that food would come to me by the day's end either. And as time went on, I was becoming spiritually and physically more and more hollowed out, I let myself sink to less and less honorable deeds every day. I told blank lies without a blush, cheated poor people out of their rent, and fought against the grossest impulses to make off with someone else's blanket, all without remorse, without bad conscience. Rotten patches were beginning to appear in my insides, black spongy areas that were spreading. And up in heaven God was sitting, keeping an open eye on me, and taking care that my defeat proceed after the correct rules of the art, evenly and slowly, with no break in rhythm. But in the pit of hell the evil devils roamed around bursting with rage because it was taking me so long to commit a mortal sin, an unforgivable sin, one for which God in His righteousness would have to throw me down. . . .

I increased my pace, pushed myself faster and faster, swung suddenly to the left, and strode excitedly and angrily into a light, elegant entry. I did not stop, did not pause a second—yet my consciousness took in the whole decorative arrangement of the vestibule in that half second: every insignificant detail of the doors, molding, floor tiling was utterly clear to me inwardly as I sprang up the stairs. I rang a bell violently on the third floor. Why did I stop precisely on the third floor? And why did I choose this bell, which was farthest from the stair?

A young woman in a gray dress, trimmed with black, opened the door. She looked at me astonished for a little while, then shook her head and said, "No, we don't have anything for you today." And she made a motion to close the door.

Why had I thrown myself in the path of this person? She took me obviously to be a beggar; suddenly I became cool and calm. I took off my hat and made a proper bow; then as if I had not heard her sentence, I said in the politest conceivable voice, "I do beg your pardon, madam, for having rung so loud. I wasn't familiar with your bell. I believe that there is an invalid gentleman here who has advertised for a man to give him outings in a chair?"

She stood still awhile, trying out this fantastic lie on her tongue; she seemed to be undecided about me.

"No," she said finally, "there is no invalid gentleman here."

"Are you sure? An elderly man, two hours' outing each day, half krone an hour?"

"No."

"Then I must ask you for your pardon again," I said. "Possibly it is the second floor. In any case, I merely wanted to recommend for the post a man in whom I have taken an interest. My own family is Wedel-Jarlsberg." Then I bowed once more and withdrew. The young woman turned beet red and in her embarrassment could not move from the spot but stood rooted staring after me as I went down the stairs.

My peace of mind was back, and my brain clear. The woman's words saying she had nothing to give me today had affected me like a cold shower of rain. It had gone so far now that everybody in the world could glance at me and say to himself: There goes a beggar, one of those people who get their food handed to them through a door!

On Møller Street I stopped outside a restaurant and sniffed the marvelous odor of meat cooking inside; I had already put my hand on the doorknob and was ready to drift in when I caught myself in time and walked away. When I got down to the main market square, I looked around for a place to sit but found all the benches taken. I walked around the church on all sides looking for a quiet place to flop down. Naturally! I said bitterly to myself, naturally, what else! I started to walk again. I made a swing past the corner fountain and took a swallow of water, started to walk once more, dragged myself along, one foot after the other, stopped a long while outside every store window, turned to watch every wagon as it rattled past. I felt a sort of shimmering heat inside my head, and the beating in my temples was strange. The water I had drunk did not agree with me, and I walked on, throwing up a little here, a little there, in the gutter. Finally I made it to the Cemetery of Christ. I sat down with my elbows on my knees, my head in my hands: bent over like that, it was better, and I didn't feel the small gnawing in my chest any longer.

A stonecutter was lying on his stomach on top of a huge granite slab nearby, cutting an inscription; he was wearing blue spectacles and reminded me suddenly of an acquaintance whom I had nearly forgotten, a man who worked in a bank; I had met him some time ago in the Oplandske Café.

If I could just get rid of shame once and for all and go to him! Tell him the truth right out, that the situation was becoming desperate for me now, it was getting difficult to stay alive! I could give him my barber coupons. . . . Holy God, my barber coupons! coupons worth up to a krone! I rummaged anxiously for this valuable treasure. When I didn't find it fast enough, I leaped up, searched, sweating with fear, and found them at last at the bottom of my breast pocket, along with other papers, some blank, some written on, all of no value. I counted the six coupons many times forward and backward. I didn't have much use for them—it might be taken as a whim of mine, an eccentricity, that I no longer bothered to shave. I had help to the value of half a krone, a good silver half krone from the Kongsberg mine! The banks closed at six, I could probably find my man at the Oplandske Café around seven or eight.

I sat up and warmed myself for a long time with this thought. Time went by, the chestnut leaves around me moved heavily in the wind, the day was ending. Wasn't it really a little sordid to come sneaking up with six barber coupons to a gentleman who occupied a post in a bank? Maybe he had two barber books in marvelous shape in his pocket, coupons entirely different from mine, clean and crisp ones, very likely. I felt in all my pockets for a couple of things I could give him to boot, but found nothing. Suppose I offered him my tie? I could easily spare that now as long as I just buttoned my coat a little tighter, and I had to do that anyway since I no longer had a waistcoat. I took my tie off—it was the large formal kind and covered half my chest—brushed it off carefully, and wrapped it in a piece of white writing paper together with my barber coupons. Then I left the churchyard and started for the café.

The clock on the city jail said seven. I hovered about the café, poked about along the iron fence, and kept an eye on everyone going in or out. Finally, at about eight I saw him coming, fresh and elegantly dressed, up the hill; he cut across the street toward the café. My heart beat wildly like a little bird in my chest as I caught sight of him, and without even saying hello, I blurted out something.

"A half krone, my friend!" I said, becoming impertinent. "Here—here is fair exchange for it!" and I pushed the little packet into his hand.

"Don't have it!" he said. "Swear to God!" And he turned his coin purse inside out for me. "I was out last night, and I'm broke; believe me, it's absolutely true."

"No, no, I believe you, old boy!" I said and took him at his word. There was in fact no reason for him to lie with so little at stake; it struck me, too, that his blue eyes were a bit moist as he rummaged in his pocket, finding nothing. I took a step back.

"Forgive the whole thing!" I said. "I wasn't in a really big fix anyway."

I was already half a block down the street when he called after me about the packet.

"Keep it, keep it!" I answered. "You are very welcome to it! It is only a couple of small things, doesn't amount to anything—about everything I own in the world." I was moved by my own words, which sounded so pathetic in the early twilight, and I started to cry.

The wind sprang up, the clouds hurried across the sky, and it became cooler and cooler as it got dark. I walked along crying down the entire street to its end, feeling more and more pity for myself, and I repeated again and again several words, a cry from the heart which would always start the tears once more when they were about to stop: "My God and my Lord, I have such tribulation!"

An hour went by in this way, endlessly, slowly, sluggishly. I puttered about on Torv Street for a long time, sat on steps, slipped into doorways when anyone came by, or stood staring blankly into the shops where people were bustling around with merchandise and money; finally I found myself a cozy place behind a pile of lumber between the church and the market tents.

Well, I definitely could not go back to the woods tonight, no matter what happened, I didn't have energy enough for it, it was too far out there. I would get through the night as best I could, where I was—if it got too cold I could always walk a few times around the church. I didn't need to make any elaborate plans for that. So I leaned back and dozed.

The noise around me grew less, the shops were closed. I heard fewer and fewer steps of passers-by; finally all the windows around me were dark. . . .

I opened my eyes and became aware of a shape standing in front of me; the shiny buttons that glittered in my direction made me guess a policeman. I couldn't see the man's face.

"Good evening!" he said.

"Good evening!" I answered, and felt afraid. I stood up somewhat embarrassed. He stood awhile without moving.

"Do you live near here?" he asked.

Without thinking, out of sheer habit, I named my old address, the little attic room I had left.

He stood quiet a moment.

"Have I done anything wrong?" I asked in anxiety.

"Oh no, not at all!" he answered. "But I think it is time for you to go home now, it's cold lying here."

"Yes, it is chilly, I can feel it."

So I said good night and instinctively made my way to my old place. Now if I were only careful I could go up without being heard—there were eight flights of stairs in all, and only the two top ones had creaky steps.

I took my shoes off downstairs and started up. The house was quiet. On the third floor I heard the slow ticktock of a clock, and a child who cried a little; after that, I heard nothing. I found my door, lifted it a bit on its hinges and opened it without using the key, as I often did; I walked in and closed the door silently behind me.

Everything was just as I had left it— the curtains were pulled aside, and the bed was empty. On the table I caught a glint from some paper, probably my note to the landlady. The chances were she hadn't even been up here then since I had left. I ran my hands over the white spot and found to my surprise that it was a letter. A letter? I took it over to the window and studied as well as I could in the dark the scrawl of the address, and at last made out my own name. Aha! I thought, the landlady's reply, warning me not to set foot in the room again, if I had such an idea!

Then I walked slowly, very slowly, out of the room, carrying my shoes in one hand and the letter in the other, my blanket under my arm. I tiptoed and grit my teeth on the creaking steps and made it safely down all the stairs and finally stood in the entryway once more.

I put my shoes on again, taking a good long time tying the laces, sat for a moment motionless when I was done, stared blankly ahead of me, holding the letter in my hands.

Then I stood up and walked away.

A gas lamp was flickering up the street, so I walked right under it, rested my parcel against the lamppost, and opened the letter, doing it all with an exaggerated slowness.

The letter shot through me like a stream of light, and I heard myself give a little cry, a meaningless sound of joy: the letter was from the editor, my piece was accepted, being set in type immediately! "A few minor changes . . . a couple of typographical errors corrected . . . shows real ability . . . will appear tomorrow . . . ten kroner."

I laughed and cried, leaped in the air and ran down the street, stopped and beat my legs, swore wholesale at no one about nothing. And time went by.

The whole night until dawn I went yodeling around the streets, dumfounded with joy, and said over and over: shows real ability, actually a little masterpiece, a stroke of genius. And ten kroner!

PART TWO

A COUPLE OF WEEKS LATER I found myself out of doors one night. I had been sitting in one of the cemeteries again, working on an article for a newspaper; while I was still writing, it got to be 10 p.m., the darkness came, and the gate was about to be locked. I was hungry, terrifically hungry; the ten kroner had unfortunately not gone very far. Now it was two, nearly three, days since I had eaten anything and I felt faint—moving the pencil was almost too much effort. I had the blade part of a pocketknife and a bunch of keys in my pocket, but not a trace of money.

After the cemetery gate was locked, I should have gone straight home, but I felt an instinctive dread of my dark and empty room—an abandoned tinsmith's workshop I had finally gotten permission to stay in for the time being. So I staggered instead on down the street, roamed aimlessly past the city jail, all the way to the harbor and to a bench on the railroad pier, where I sat down.

For a few moments I didn't have a single sad thought. I forgot my troubles and felt peaceful looking at the harbor that lay serene and lovely in the dusk. I had the habit of cheering myself up by reading through the article I had just written, which always seemed to my afflicted brain the very best piece I had done. I pulled my manuscript out of my pocket, held it close up to my eyes, and read through one page after the other. Finally I grew tired and put the papers in my pocket. Everything was still; the sea stretched away like bluish mother-of-pearl, and small birds flew silently past me, going from one place to another. A policeman walked up and down a little way off. Otherwise, not a person could be seen, and the entire harbor was silent.

I counted up my money once more: one half a pocketknife, one key chain, but not an øre. Suddenly I reached into my pocket and pulled the papers up once more. It was an automatic thing to do, an unconscious reflex. I found a white page among them, not written on, and— God knows where I got the idea—I folded it into a cone and closed it carefully so that it looked as though it was full, and then threw it as far as I could out in front of me. The wind carried it a little farther, then it lay there quietly.

Hunger was beginning to attack me now. I sat staring at the white paper cornucopia, which looked as though swollen by shiny silver coins, and I egged myself on to believe that it really did contain something. I sat there inviting myself in a normal voice to guess how much was in it—if I guessed right, the money was mine! I imagined the small exquisite ten-øre coins at the bottom and the fat, fluted krone pieces on top—a whole paper cone full of money! I sat gazing at it with huge eyes and urged myself to go and steal it.

Then I heard the policeman cough— and why did it suddenly occur to me to do the same? I stood up and coughed, repeating the cough three times so he would be sure to hear it. Now, won't he jump for that paper cone when he comes near? I sat rejoicing over this joke, I rubbed my hands in ecstasy and swore magnificently. His nose will stretch when he sees that! After this trick, he'll want to sink into the hottest puddle in hell! I had become intoxicated with starvation, my hunger had made me drunk.

A few minutes later the policeman came along, clicking his iron heels on the stones, keeping watch to all sides. He took his time, he had the whole night before him: he didn't see the paper cone until it was very close. Then he stopped and stared at it. It looked so white and valuable lying there, perhaps a little purse of money, no? A little store of silver? . . . He picked it up. Hmmm! It is light, very light. Maybe an expensive feather, decoration for a hat. . . . He opened it carefully with his large hands and peeked in. I laughed, I laughed and hit my knees, I laughed like a madman. And not a sound came from my mouth, my laughter was feverish and silent, it was intense like a sob. . . .

Then the stones clattered again, and the policeman made a swing back over the pier. I sat there with tears in my eyes, hiccuping from shortness of breath, out of my mind with feverish laughter. I started to talk aloud, told myself the story of the paper cone, mimicked the gestures of the poor policeman, peeked into my empty hand, and repeated again and again: He coughed when he threw it away! He coughed when he threw it away! I joined new phrases to these sentences, made titillating additions, revised the whole story, and brought it to the point: he coughed only once—haugh, haugh!

I exhausted all my variations on these words and it was well on into the evening before my gaiety subsided. A sleepy calm came over me, a lovely fatigue which I couldn't oppose. The darkness was thicker now, a light breeze furrowed the pearl-gray sea. The ships whose masts I could see outlined against the sky looked, with their black bodies, like silent monsters who had raised their bristles and were laying in wait for me. I had no pain, the hunger had smoothed that out. Instead I felt pleasantly empty, untouched by anything around me, glad to be unseen by everybody. I put my legs up on the bench and leaned back—in that position I could feel best the good feeling of isolation. There wasn't a cloud in my mind, not a suggestion of discomfort; I had not a single desire or longing unfulfilled so far as my thoughts could reach. I lay with eyes open in a sense of alienation from myself. I felt wonderfully out of myself.

Not a sound came to disturb me—the soft dark had hidden the whole world from me, and buried me in a wonderful peace—only the desolate voice of stillness sounded monotonously in my ear. And the dark monsters out there wanted to pull me to themselves as soon as night came, and they wanted to take me far far over seas and through strange lands where no human being lives. And they wanted to bring me to Princess Ylayali's castle, where an undreamed-of happiness was waiting for me, greater than any person's! And she herself would be sitting in a blazing room all of whose walls were amethyst, on a throne of yellow roses, and she would reach her hands out to me

when I entered, greet me, and cry "Welcome" as I came near to her and kneeled: "Welcome, O knight, to me and to my land! I have been waiting twenty summers for you, and have called your name every bright summer night, and when you were in grief I wept here, and when you slept I breathed marvelous dreams into your head. . . ." And the beautiful creature took my hand as I rose, and led me on through long corridors where huge crowds of people shouted Hurrah, through sunlit orchards where three hundred young girls were playing and laughing, and into another chamber made all of brilliant emerald. The sun shone into it, choral music floated through galleries and halls toward me, perfumed air moved over me. I held her hand in mine, and felt a mad occult delight shoot through my blood; I put my arms around her and she whispered: "Not here, come farther in!" So we walked into the red chamber all of whose walls were ruby—an overwhelming joy which made me faint. Then I felt her arms around me, she breathed in my face, whispering: "Welcome now, my sweet! Kiss me! Again . . . again. . . ."

From my bench I saw stars in front of my eyes and my thought shot forward into a tornado of light. . . .

I had fallen asleep where I lay, and the policeman was waking me. I sat up, ruthlessly called back to life and misery. My first sensation was a stupid astonishment at finding myself out in the open air, but soon a bitter depression replaced that; I was just on the point of crying with grief over still being alive. It had been raining while I slept, my clothes were soaked through, and I felt a damp chill in my legs. The darkness was thicker, and it took effort to make out clearly the policeman's face in front of me.

"That's right," he said. "Stand up now!"

I stood up instantly: if he had ordered me to lie down again, I would have obeyed also. I felt hopeless and without energy; on top of that, I began almost immediately to feel the hunger again.

"Wait a minute, you idiot," the policeman cried after me. "You're leaving your hat behind! O.K., now go ahead!"

"I knew there was something I—something I'd forgotten," I stammered in true absent-mindedness. "Thanks. Good night."

And I staggered off.

If a man only had a bite to eat! Bread—one of those marvelous loaves of rye bread that a man could chew on as he walked. I walked along, deciding on exactly the kind of rye bread that would be best now. I was unbelievably hungry, longed to be dead and gone, became sentimental and cried. My road of misery would never end! All of a sudden I stopped on the street, stamped on the cobblestones, and swore aloud. What was it he had called me? Idiot? I would show that policeman what it meant to call me an idiot. Then I turned around and ran back down the street. I felt fiery hot with anger. Toward the bottom of the street I stumbled and fell, but hardly noticed it, jumped up again and ran on. By the time I got to the railway station I was so tired that I didn't feel able to keep on all the way to the pier; besides, during the run my anger had subsided. I stopped for breath. What was the difference what a policeman said?—"Yes, but there are some things I won't stand for!" "You're right!" I interrupted myself. "But he didn't know any better!" This excuse calmed me down; I repeated to myself that he didn't know any better. So I turned around a second time.

My God, what weird things you get into! I said angrily to myself—running like a madman on wet streets when it is black as pitch! The pains of hunger were unbearable and never let me alone. I

swallowed spit over and over to take the edge off, and I felt it did some good. I had had very little to eat generally for several weeks, even before this current trouble, and my strength now was falling off noticeably. Whenever I had been lucky and scraped up five kroner by some maneuver or other, the money never managed to last long enough to get me back on my feet before a new famine fell on me. My back and my shoulders bothered me most; the small ache in my chest I could stop for a moment by coughing hard or walking carefully bent over, but my back and shoulders I couldn't do anything with. How could it be that nothing ever turned up for me! Didn't I have the same right to life as anybody else, Pascha, the rare-book seller, for example, or Hennechen, the steamship clerk? And didn't I have shoulders like a giant and two strong arms for work, and hadn't I in fact tried to get a job chopping wood on Møller Street to earn my bread? Was I lazy? Hadn't I applied for jobs, and listened to lectures, and written articles, and read and worked night and day like a madman? And hadn't I lived like a miser, eaten bread and milk when I was rich, bread when I wasn't, and gone hungry when I had nothing? Did I live in a hotel, did I have a suite of rooms on the second floor? I lived in a shack, a loft, in a tinsmith's shop deserted by both God and man since last winter because snow came in. So I had nothing at all to rebuke myself with on that score.

I walked along thinking all this over, and there wasn't even so much as a spark of malice or envy or bitterness in my brain.

Outside a paint store I stopped and looked in the window; I tried to read the labels on a couple of cans, but it was too dark. Angry at myself for this new whim, and upset and irritated that I couldn't find out what the labels said, I banged once on the window and then went on. Farther along I saw a police officer, speeded up, sidled up to him, and without the slightest preamble said, "It's ten o'clock."

"No, it's two," he answered, surprised.

"No, it's ten," I said. "It's ten o'clock." Growling with anger, I went two steps nearer, clenched my fist, and said, "Listen, take my word for it, it's ten o'clock."

He stood meditating this for a bit, looking me over and gazing at me, baffled. Finally he said very softly, "In any case, it's certainly time for you to be going home. Would you like me to walk with you partway?"

This gesture of friendliness disarmed me. I felt tears coming to my eyes, and I quickly said, "No, thank you! I have just been out at a club a little too late. I'm much obliged to you."

He raised his hand and touched his hat as I left. His friendliness had overwhelmed me and I cried because I didn't have a five-kroner piece to give him. I stood looking after him as he slowly wandered on, hit myself on the forehead, and the farther he got away, the louder I sobbed. I cursed myself for my poverty, called myself various names, discovered wounding phrases for myself, priceless and rich finds of abusive terms which I heaped on myself. I kept this up until I was nearly home. When I got to the door, I discovered I had lost my keys.

Yes, naturally, I said bitterly to myself, why not indeed, why shouldn't I have lost them? Here I have my home, in a place that is a stable downstairs and a tinsmith shop upstairs; the door is locked at night, no one here to open it, so why shouldn't I lose my keys? I am wet as a dog, and a little bit hungry, just a tiny bit hungry, and a bit ridiculously tired in the knees—why shouldn't I lose the keys then? As a matter of fact, why shouldn't the whole house move out to Aker just when I came home and wanted to go

in? . . . And I laughed to myself, callous from hunger and exhaustion. I heard the horses stamping in their stables, and I could see my window upstairs, but I could not open the door and I could not get in. Tired and furious, I decided therefore to return to the pier and look for my keys.

The rain had started again, and I could already feel water soaking through on my shoulders. Near the city jail I suddenly had a bright idea: I would ask the police to open the door. I went straight to a patrolman and asked him earnestly to go with me and let me in if he could.

"Yes, if I could, certainly!" But he couldn't, he didn't have any keys. The police keys were not here but in the Detective Bureau.

"What should I do then?"

"What I would do is go to a hotel and get a room."

"But I can't really go to a hotel—I haven't got an øre. I was out tonight, at a club, you understand. . . ."

We stood a little while on the steps of the jail. He thought and considered it all and looked me over. Rain poured down in the street.

"Then go to the Officer on Duty and register as homeless."

As homeless? I had never thought of that. By Christ, that was a good idea! I thanked the policeman on the spot for this excellent thought. "Could I simply go in and say that I am homeless?"

"That's all! . . ."

"Name," asked the Officer on Duty.

"Tangen—Andreas Tangen."

I don't know why I lied. Ideas were flying all about in my head, and my brain gave me more notions than I could put into use; I hit on this curious name in an instant and tossed it out without hesitation. I lied when it wasn't necessary.

"Position?"

Now he was pushing me against the wall. Hmm. I thought first of turning

into a tinsmith, but didn't dare—I had given a name unusual for a tinsmith; besides, I was wearing glasses. I decided to jump in, so I took a step forward and said rapidly and solemnly: "Journalist."

The Officer on Duty gave a little start before he wrote that down, and I stood before the counter impressive as a homeless cabinet minister. He suspected nothing: the officer could understand about my hesitating a bit with my answer. What next, a journalist in the city jail, with no roof over his head!

"With which paper—Mr. Tangen?"

"With the *Morning Times,*" I said. "Unfortunately, I was out tonight, a little too late, I guess. . . ."

"Well, we won't mention that!" he broke in, and went on with a smile: "When young people go out . . . we understand." He rose and bowed politely to me, saying to a policeman, "Show this gentleman up to the reserved section. Good night."

My boldness made a cold chill go over my back, and I clenched my hands as I walked, to stiffen myself a little.

"The gas light will burn for ten minutes," the policeman said from the door.

"And then it goes out?"

"Then it goes out."

I sat on my bed and listened to the key being turned. The bright cell looked friendly; I felt snug and lucky indoors and listened with pleasure to the rain outside. How could I wish for anything better than this cozy cell? My contentment grew—sitting on the bed with my head in my hands and eyes fixed on the gas lamp on the wall, I took to going over the events in my first involvement with the police. This was the first, and I had carried it off! Mr. Tangen, the journalist, I beg your pardon. . . . And then the *Morning Times!* I had really stuck him in the heart with that *Morning Times!* Well, we won't mention that, eh? Sat in evening clothes in an expensive club until 2 a.m., forgot the doorkeys and his billfold (holding several thousand) at home! Show this gentleman up to the reserved section. . . .

The gas suddenly went off, so suddenly it was strange—no dwindling, no flickering. I sat in a deep darkness. I couldn't even see my hand, or the white walls around me, nothing. There was nothing to do but to go to bed. So I undressed.

I still was not sleepy, however, and could not fall asleep. I remained a while looking into the dark—this dense substance of darkness that had no bottom, which I couldn't understand. My thoughts could not grasp such a thing. It seemed to be dark beyond all measurement, and I felt its presence weigh me down. I closed my eyes and took to singing half aloud and rocking myself back and forth on the cot to amuse myself, but it did no good. The dark had captured my brain and gave me not an instant of peace. What if I myself become dissolved into the dark, turned into it? I sat up in bed and struck out with my arms.

My nervous condition had completely taken over, and no amount of struggle against it helped. I sat there, a prey to the weirdest fantasies, gurgling to myself, humming lullabies, sweating in my effort to be calm. I stared out into the dark, and had never in all my life seen such blackness. There was no doubt that what I was faced with here was a special kind of blackness, an extreme element which no one before had ever noticed. The most ridiculous ideas occupied me, and everything frightened me. The tiny hole in the wall by my bed bothered me a great deal—a nail hole I found, a gouge in the wall. I felt of it, blew into it to try to guess its depth. It wasn't just an innocent hole, that was very clear—it was obviously a complicated and secretive hole that I had to be careful of. Dominated entirely by thoughts of this hole, driven out of my mind by curiosity and fear, I finally had to get out of bed and fumble for my knife blade so I could measure its depth and convince myself it didn't go all the way into the next cell.

I got back in bed to try to sleep, but actually I started again to fight against the darkness. The rain outdoors had stopped and I could not hear a sound. For a long time I lay listening for footsteps on the street, and listened hard until I had heard one passer-by, a policeman, to judge by the sound. All at once I snapped my fingers a couple of times and laughed. Hellfire and damnation! I suddenly imagined I had discovered a new word! I sat up in bed, and said: It is not in the language, I have discovered it—*Kuboaa*. It has letters just like a real word, by sweet Jesus, man, you have discovered a word! . . . *Kuboaa* . . . of tremendous linguistic significance.

The word stood out clearly in front of me in the dark.

I sat with wide eyes astonished at my discovery, laughing with joy. Then I fell to whispering: they could very well be spying on me, and I must act so as to keep my invention secret. I had arrived at the joyful insanity hunger was: I was empty and free of pain, and my thoughts no longer had any check. I debated everything silently with myself. My thoughts took amazing leaps as I tried to establish the meaning of my new word. It needn't mean either *God* or the *Tivoli Gardens,* and who had said it had to mean *cattle show?* I clenched my fists hard and repeated again: Who said it had to mean *cattle show?* When I thought it over, it was in fact not even necessary that it mean *padlock* or *sunrise.* In a word like that it was very easy to find meaning. I would just wait and see. In the meantime, I would sleep on it.

I lay back on the cot and chuckled, but said nothing, did not commit myself either for or against. Some time went by

and I remained excited, the new word plagued me incessantly, kept on returning, finally took control of my thoughts entirely and made me sober down. I had formulated my opinion on what the word did not mean, but I had not yet come to a decision on what it *did* mean. "That is a secondary matter!" I said aloud to myself, and grabbed myself by the arm and repeated that it was a secondary matter. The word, thanks to God, has been discovered and that was the main thing. But thoughts pestered me constantly and kept me from falling asleep: nothing seemed to me good enough for this remarkable word. Finally I sat up a second time in bed, took my head between both hands, and said, "No, no, that is exactly what is impossible—letting it mean *emigration* or *tobacco factory!* If it could have meant something like that, I would have made the decision a long time ago and taken the consequences." No, the word was actually intended to mean something spiritual, a feeling, a state of mind—if I could only understand it? And I thought and thought to find something spiritual. It occurred to me that someone was talking, butting into my chat, and I answered angrily: "I beg your pardon? For an idiot, you are all alone in the field! *Yarn?* Go to hell!" Why should I be obligated to let it mean *yarn* when I had a special aversion to its meaning *yarn?* I had discovered the word myself, and I was perfectly within my rights to let it mean whatever I wanted it to, for that matter. So far as I knew, I had not yet committed myself. . . .

But my brain sank deeper and deeper in chaos. At last I leaped out of bed to find the water faucet. I wasn't thirsty, but my head was feverish and I felt an instinctive need for water. When I had drunk, I lay down again on the bed and decided that come hell or high water I would sleep. I closed my eyes and forced myself to be calm. I lay there several minutes without moving a muscle, I started to sweat and felt my blood hurtling through my veins. No, it was fantastic, wonderful that he should look in the paper cone for money! He coughed, you know, only once. Could he be still walking around down there! Sitting on my bench? . . . Bluish mother-of-pearl. . . . Ships. . . .

I opened my eyes. How could I keep them closed when I couldn't sleep! The same darkness was brooding around me, the same fathomless black eternity which my intelligence fought against and could not grasp. What could I compare it to? I made the wildest, most desperate efforts to find a word black enough to suit that darkness, a word so hideously black that it would blacken my mouth when I said it. God in heaven, how black it was! And I started again to think about the harbor, the ships, the dark monsters who lay waiting for me. They wanted to pull me to themselves and hold me fast and sail with me over land and sea, through dark kingdoms no man had ever seen. I felt myself on board ship, drawn on through waters, floating in clouds, going down, down. . . . I gave a hoarse shriek of fear, and hugged the bed; I had been on such a perilous journey, fallen down through the sky like a shot. How good and saved I felt when I grabbed the hard sides of the cot! That is what it is like to die, I said to myself, now I will die! Then I sat up in bed and asked intensely, "Who said that I will die? Haven't I found the word myself, and haven't I the right to decide what it is going to mean?" . . . I heard myself raving, could hear it while I was still talking. My madness was a delirium from faintness and exhaustion, but I still had my wits. Then a thought shot through my brain—I had become insane. Possessed by terror, I got out of bed. I reeled over to the door and tried to open it, threw myself a couple of times against it to force it, knocked my head against the wall, moaned aloud, bit my fingers, cried and swore. . . .

It was all quiet; only my own voice came rolling back from the walls. I had fallen on the floor, not able any longer to lurch around the cell. Lying there, I saw something far up, right in front of my eyes, a grayish rectangle on the wall, a shade of white in it, a touch—it was daylight. Oh, how wonderfully I breathed then! I threw myself flat on the floor and wept with joy over this blessed gleam of light, sobbed with gratitude, kissed the window, and behaved like a madman. And at that moment I knew very well what I was doing. All my despair was suddenly gone, all depression and pain ended, and so far as my thoughts could discover, I did not have then a single frustrated desire. I sat up straight on the floor, folded my hands, and waited patiently for the break of day.

What a night this had been! That no one had heard the noise surprised me. But I was, of course, in the reserved section, high above the prisoners. A homeless cabinet minister, if I may be so bold. Going on in the highest spirits, I turned my eyes toward the window that grew lighter and lighter, I amused myself by imitating a cabinet minister—I called myself Von Tangen, and gave my speech in ministerial style. My fantasizing had not stopped, I was simply much less excited. Leaving the wallet in my residence was an oversight on my part which I sincerely regret! Might I have the honor to show his honor, the cabinet minister, to his bed? Then, in the greatest seriousness, with many ceremonial touches, I went to the cot and lay down.

By now it was light enough so I could recognize some of the outlines of the cell, and a little later I could make out the heavy handle on the door. That entertained me; the monotonous darkness, so maddeningly dense that it kept me from seeing myself, was broken. My blood became more quiet, and soon I felt my eyes close.

I was wakened by a couple of thumps on my door. I leaped to my feet and dressed hurriedly; my clothes were still wet from the night before.

"Report downstairs to the Officer of the Day," said a policeman.

Good Lord, was there still some red tape to go through! I thought, frightened.

I came down into a large room where thirty or forty men were sitting, all homeless. One by one they were called up by the clerk, and one by one given a meal ticket. The Officer of the Day said constantly to the policeman at his side, "Did he get a ticket? Don't forget to give them tickets. They look as if they could use a meal."

I stood looking at these tickets, and wanted one for myself.

"Andreas Tangen, journalist!"

I stepped forward and bowed.

"My dear man, what are *you* doing here?"

I explained the whole situation, gave the same story as the night before, lied through my teeth, lied with great frankness: was out a little too late, I'm afraid, lost my doorkeys. . . .

"I see," he said, and smiled. "So that is it! Did you sleep well?"

"Like a cabinet minister!" I answered. "Like a cabinet minister!"

"I am pleased at that!" he said, standing. "Good morning!"

I turned and left.

A ticket, ticket for me, too! I hadn't eaten for three endless days and nights. A loaf of bread! But no one offered me a ticket and I didn't dare ask for one. That would have caused suspicion instantly. They would have wanted to poke around in my private affairs and find out who I really was—then they would arrest me for giving false information. With my head high, millions in stocks and bonds, and my hands clasped beneath my coat-tails, I departed from the city jail.

The sun was already warm, it was ten, and the traffic on Youngstorvet Street was going full blast. Where should I go now? I slapped my pocket to make sure my manuscript was there—when it was eleven I would go to see the editor. I stood awhile on the steps watching life go by on the street; meanwhile my clothes began to dry off. Hunger came back, gnawing me in the chest, sending sudden shoots and delicate pinpricks that hurt. Did I really have not one friend, not one acquaintance I could go to? I rummaged through my memory for a man worth ten øre and found none. Anyway, it was a lovely day all in all; sun and light poured down around me; the clear heavens flowed like a gentle sea over the Lier Hills off there. . . .

Without realizing it, I was on the way home.

I was truly starving, and along the street I found a sliver of wood to chew on. That helped. Strange I hadn't thought of that before!

The door was open, the boy who worked in the stable said good morning as usual.

"Fine weather!" he said.

"Yes," I answered. That was all I found to say. Could I possibly ask him to lend me a krone? He would certainly do it if he had it. Besides, I had once written a letter for him.

He stood, thinking over something he wanted to say.

"Fine weather it is. Hmmm. I have to pay the landlady today. Could you lend me five kroner, I wonder? Just for a few days? You helped me once before."

"No, Jens, I really can't. Not now. Maybe later, though, later today." And I staggered on up the stairs to my room.

There I threw myself down on the bed

and laughed. What incredible luck that he asked me first! My honor was saved. Five kroner. God help us! You could just as well have asked me for five shares in the Steam Kitchen, or for an estate out in Aker.

The thought of those five kroner started me laughing louder and louder. What a solid type I was! Five kroner! Here's a real man for you! My sense of the ridiculous grew stronger, and I gave in to it: ugh— How this place smells of cooking! Ever since lunch this strong smell of hamburger steak, awful! And I pushed open the window to get this frightful smell out. Waiter, roast beef! Facing the table, this rickety table I had to support with my knees while I was writing, I bowed deeply and asked, "May I inquire if you would like a glass of wine?" "No?" "I am Tangen, the cabinet minister. Unfortunately I've been out a bit too late . . . keys. . . ."

Without any check, my thoughts again took off on their wild course. I was aware all the time that I was talking gibberish, and I didn't speak a single word without hearing and understanding it. I said to myself: Now you are talking gibberish again! And I couldn't help it. It was like being awake while you talk in your sleep. My brain was calm, without aches or any pressure, and my mood was clear and cloudless. I sailed off, and I made no move to stop myself.

Come in! Yes, just come in! You can see, entirely of ruby! Ylayali! Ylayali! The red soft sofa of silk! She is breathing so rapidly! Kiss me, my darling, again, again. Your arms are amber, your mouth is burning. . . . Waiter, I asked for roast beef. . . .

The sun shone in my window, downstairs I could hear the horses chewing their oats. I sat gumming my wood chip, gay, happy as a child. I constantly felt for my manuscript; I never thought con-

sciously of it, but my instinct told me of it, my blood reminded me. Finally I pulled it out.

It had gotten wet, so I spread it out and left it in the sun. Then I started walking up and down my room. How depressing it all was! Small tin shavings lay scattered all over the floor, but there was no chair to sit in, not even a nail in the bare walls. Everything had been taken down to "Uncle" and used up. A few dozen sheets of paper on the table, covered with a heavy layer of dust, were my sole possessions; the old green blanket on the bed was lent to me a couple of months ago by Hans Pauli . . . Hans Pauli! I snapped my fingers. Hans Pauli Pettersen would help me! I tried to remember his address. How could I have forgotten Hans! He would certainly be furious that I hadn't come to him first thing. I grabbed my hat, gathered up my manuscript, and hurried down the stairs.

"Jens," I shouted into the stalls, "I'm positive I'll be able to do something for you this afternoon!"

I saw by the clock at the city jail that it was past eleven, so I decided to go to the newspaper immediately. Outside the editor's door I stopped to make sure my pages were in the right order; I smoothed them out carefully, stuck them back in my pocket, and knocked. I could hear my heart thumping as I walked in.

Scissors was at work as usual. I asked timidly after the editor. No answer. Scissors was sitting with a pair of long shears on the hunt for small bits of news in the country papers.

I repeated my question and stepped nearer.

"The editor is not here yet," Scissors finally said, without looking up.

"When do you expect him?"

"Couldn't say, couldn't say at all."

"How late will the office be open?"

To this I got no answer, and I had to

leave. Scissors had not even glanced at me the whole time; he had heard my voice and recognized me from that. You are in so well here, I thought, that they don't even bother to answer you. Maybe the editor had told him to do that? It was true that ever since he had accepted my famous little article for ten kroner I had flooded him with work, ran to his door nearly every day with unusable pieces he had to read through and return. Maybe he wanted to put an end to it, give me hints to stay away. . . . I started off in the direction of the Homan district, where Pettersen lived.

Hans Pauli Pettersen was a farmer's son, living in the attic of a five-story house, Hans Pauli Pettersen was therefore poor. But if he had a krone, he wouldn't be stingy with it. I would get it as certainly as if I were holding it right now. So I walked along, rejoicing over this krone the whole way, convinced I would soon have it. When I arrived, the street door was locked and I had to ring.

"I would like to see Mr. Pettersen, the student," I said, and started to go in. "I know his room."

"Pettersen?" the girl repeated. "Is he the one who used to live in the attic? He has moved." She didn't know exactly where, but he had asked them to send his letters on to Hermansen on Toldbod Street, and she gave the number.

I walked all the way down to Toldbod Street full of hope and faith to ask for Hans Pauli's address. It was my last chance, I had to reach for it. On the way I passed a new house in front of which a couple of carpenters were planing. From the pile I took a couple of shiny shavings, put one in my mouth, and saved the other in my pocket for later. I walked on. I moaned from hunger. In a baker's window I had seen an incredible immense loaf for ten øre, the largest loaf one could buy for that price. . . .

"I've come to find out where Mr. Pettersen, the student, lives."

"Bernt Ankers Street, number 10, attic." Was I possibly going there? If so, would I be so good as to take along a couple of letters that were here?

I walked up to the main part of the city again, the same road I had taken down, passing the carpenters who were sitting now with their lunch pails between their knees eating good warm food from the Steam Kitchen, passing the bakery window where the loaf was still lying, and finally reached Bernt Ankers Street half dead with exhaustion. The door was open, and I trudged up the heavy stairs to the attic. I took the letters from my pocket so that I could give them to Hans Pauli as soon as I went in, and put him in a good mood with one crack. He would never never refuse his help when I told him my situation, not Hans, never, he had such a big heart, I had always said that about him. . . . On the door I found his card: "H. P. Pettersen. Student of Theology. —Gone home for vacation."

I sat down on the spot, sat on the bare floor, tired beyond belief, exhausted and defeated. I repeated mechanically two or three times: "Gone home!" "Gone home!" Then I lapsed into utter silence. There wasn't a tear in my eyes, I didn't have a thought or a feeling. With eyes wide open I sat staring at the letters without doing a thing. Ten minutes went by, perhaps twenty or more. I sat there in the same place, not moving a finger. This dull stupor was almost like a nap. At last I heard someone coming up the stairs; I stood up and said, "I'm looking for Mr. Pettersen, the student—I have two letters here for him."

"He has gone home," the woman replied. "But he will be back after the holidays. I can take the letters, if you want me to."

"Oh, thank you, that would be a great help," I said. "He will get them then when he comes. They could be important. Good morning."

When I was outside, I stopped and said aloud in the middle of the street with clenched fists: "I will tell you one thing, my dear Lord and God: you are a you-know-what!" Then I nodded furiously and repeated through clenched teeth up toward the clouds: "I swear to God you are a you-know-what!"

I walked several steps and then stopped again. Suddenly changing my whole posture, I folded my hands, twisted my head over to the side a little, and asked in a soft sanctimonious voice: "Have you taken your troubles to him, my child?"

That didn't sound right.

"Capital H," I said. "H as big as a cathedral!" Once more. "Have you called upon Him, my child?" Then I lowered my head and made my voice sorrowful and answered, "No."

That didn't sound right either.

You can't lie, you moron! Yes, you should have said, yes, I have called out to my God and my Father! And then you have to get the right tone in your words, the most soupy, mournful tone you have ever heard. O.K., once more! Ah, that was better. But you have to sigh, sigh, like a horse with colic. That's the idea!

So I walked along giving myself advice, and stamping impatiently when I didn't take it, and scolding myself as a blockhead while astonished passers-by turned around to watch me.

I sucked on my wood shaving without stopping, and staggered on up the street as rapidly as I could. Before I knew it, I was all the way down to the market square by the railway station.

The clock on the Church of Our Saviour showed one-thirty. I stood awhile, thinking. I felt a faint sweat on my face which trickled into my eyes. Would you be interested in a walk down to the pier? I said to myself. I mean, only, of course, if you can spare the time? I bowed to myself, and walked down to the railway station pier.

The ships lay off the piers, the sea was rocking in the sunshine. Everywhere there was busyness, steam whistles shrieking, longshoremen with boxes on their shoulders, cheerful loading songs from the barges. A cake seller was sitting near me, with her brown nose leaning over her merchandise: the tiny board in front of her was wickedly full of cakes, and I turned away with effort. The odor from her merchandise was filling the entire wharf—ugh! open the windows! I turned to the man sitting next to me, and put the case to him forcibly about the disproportionate number of cake sellers around, cake sellers here, there, everywhere—no? Well, surely he had to admit . . . But the dear man smelled trouble and didn't let me finish before he stood up and left. I stood up too, and followed him, determined to point out to him his error.

"Thinking of sanitary considerations alone," I said, and put my hand on his shoulder. . . .

"Pardon me, I am a stranger and I don't know anything about sanitary considerations," he said, and looked at me in fright.

"Well, if you are a stranger, that changes everything. . . . Could I be of any help to you? Show you around? No, sure? That would be a pleasure for me, and it wouldn't cost you a thing. . . ."

He wanted badly to get rid of me, however, and walked hurriedly across the street to the other sidewalk.

I went back to my bench and sat down. I was very nervous and the large street organ that had started playing down the street made it worse. A rapid mechanical music, some fragment of Weber, to which a small girl was singing a mournful song. The sorrowful, flutelike sound of the organ shivered in me, my nerves began to vibrate like a sounding board, and an instant later I slumped backward on the bench, whining and humming with the music. What odd things the feelings stuck to when one was hungry! I felt drawn up by the notes, dissolved in them, I began to flow out into the air, and could see very clearly what I was flowing over, high over mountains, dancing on in waves over brilliant areas. . . .

"One øre!" the little organ grinder's daughter said, and stretched out her tin plate, "only one øre!"

"Yes!" I answered mechanically, and leaped up, rummaging in my pocket. The child, however, thought I was only mocking her, and backed off without saying a word. This speechless humility was too much for me; if she had scolded at me, I would have liked it better. Pain shot through me and I called her to come back. "I don't have a single øre," I said. "But I'll give you something later, in the morning perhaps. What is your name? That is a very nice name, I won't forget that. Till tomorrow then. . . ."

I knew that she hadn't believed me, even though she had not said a word, and I cried out with despair because this tiny waif had refused to believe me. At the end I called her back once more, ripped off my suitcoat, and was about to give her my waistcoat. "I'll make it all good," I said. "Wait just a minute. . . ."

I had no waistcoat!

How could I be looking for it then! It had been weeks since I owned it! What was the matter with me? The astonished girl waited no longer, she carefully drew back and left. And I had to let her go. People gathered around me, laughing aloud, a policeman forced his way in to

me and wanted to know what was going on.

"Nothing," I answered, "nothing at all! I was only trying to give that girl over there my waistcoat . . . for her father. . . . You don't have to stand around laughing about that. All I have to do is go home and put on another."

"No disturbing of the peace!" said the policeman. "So, move along now!" And he pushed me away. "Is this your stuff?" he shouted after me.

"Yes, my God, my newspaper article, papers, important ones! How could I have been so careless?"

I grabbed my manuscript, checked to see that it was in the right order, and walked without pausing or even looking around me to the newspaper office. The clock on Our Saviour's said four.

The office was closed. I slipped silently down the stairs, frightened as a thief, and stood at loose ends outside on the street. What should I do now? I leaned against the building, stared down at the sidewalk, and thought. A safety pin lay glittering by my feet; I bent down and picked it up. What if I took off my coat buttons, how much would I get for them? Maybe there was no sense to it. Buttons were buttons, though on examining them from all sides I saw they were as good as new. In any case, it was well worth trying, I could take my knife blade, slit them off, and cart them away to the pawnbroker. The hope of selling these five buttons cheered me up instantly, and I said: "See, it's all going to come out all right!" My joy overpowered me, and I immediately started cutting the buttons off, one after the other. All that time, I kept up a silent chatter with myself:

"Well, you see, a man becomes a bit pressed for money, just temporary of course. . . . Worn out, you say? You mustn't make reckless statements. Just show me someone who wears out fewer buttons than I do. I wear my coat open all the time, that's the truth; it's become a quirk of mine, a habit. . . . No no, if you don't *want* to. But I must have ten øre for them at the very least. . . . God in heaven, who said you *had* to do it? You can just shut up and leave me alone. . . . All right, all right, go and *get* the police then. I'll wait here while you're looking for a policeman. And I won't steal a thing from you. . . . Yes, good day! Good day! My name actually is Tangen, I've been out a little too late. . . ."

Someone was coming down the stairs. I returned in a second to reality, recognized Scissors, and put the buttons carefully in my pocket. He tried to go by, didn't answer my greeting, suddenly became very occupied in looking at his fingernails. I stopped him and inquired after the editor.

"He is out."

"You are lying!" I said. Then, with an audacity that surprised even myself, I continued: "I have to talk with him; it is urgent. I have some information from the Governor's Mansion."

"Can't you just tell it to me?"

"To you?" I said, and passed a withering eye over him. It helped. He walked straight back up the stairs and unlocked the door. My heart was in my mouth. I clenched my teeth hard to give me courage, knocked, and walked into the editor's private office.

"It's you! Good day!" he said cheerfully. "Sit down."

If he had ordered me out right away, it would have been easier; I felt near crying, and said, "Forgive me for . . ."

"Sit yourself down," he repeated.

So I sat down and explained that I had a piece I felt strongly about seeing in his paper. I had worked on it with tremendous diligence, it had cost me considerable labor.

"I will read it," he said, taking it. "Of course everything you write will cost you labor; the only trouble with your work perhaps is excitability. If you could only be a little more composed! There is too much fever all the time. Anyway, I'll read it." Then he turned again to his desk work.

There I sat. Did I dare ask him for a krone? Explain to him why there was fever all the time? He would be certain to help me; he had done it before.

I stood up. Hmm! The last time I was here he had grumbled about the lack of cash and had finally sent a messenger out to scrape up some for me. Maybe it would be the same thing now. That would be bad. Couldn't I see in the first place that he was working?

"Was there anything else?" he asked.

"No!" I said, and made my voice strong. "When should I stop in again?"

"Oh, whenever it's convenient," he answered. "A couple of days or so."

I couldn't get my application past my lips. The friendliness of this man seemed to me beyond description, and I ought to know how to appreciate it. Better to starve to death. So I left.

Not once, not even when I was outside again and felt the hunger return, did I repent having left the office without asking for that krone. I took the second wood shaving out of my pocket and put it in my mouth. It helped once more. Why hadn't I done that before? Shame on you! I said aloud. Could you actually have thought of asking this man for a krone and embarrassing him a second time? And I grew downright angry with myself for the shamelessness I was almost guilty of. "By God, that was the shabbiest thing I ever heard of!" I said. "Rushing at a man and nearly clawing his eyes out just because you want a krone, you worthless dog! Go on, then, march! Faster! Faster, you clod! I'll teach you!"

I began running so as to punish myself, left street after street behind me, pushed myself on with inward jeers, and screeched silently and furiously at myself whenever I felt like stopping. With the help of these exertions I ended up far along Pile Street. When I finally did stop, almost weeping with anger that I couldn't run any farther, my whole body trembled, and I threw myself down on a house stoop. "Not so fast!" I said. And to torture myself right, I stood up again and forced myself to stand there, laughing at myself, and gloating over my own fatigue. Finally, after a few minutes, I nodded and so gave myself permission to sit down; however, I chose the most uncomfortable spot on the stoop.

Lord, Lord, how wonderful it was to rest! I dried the sweat from my face, and drew in huge clean breaths of air. How I had run! But I didn't regret it, I deserved it. Why had I ever wanted to ask for that krone? There you see the results! So I started talking gently to myself, delivering advice as a mother might do. I became moved, more and more; tired and weak, I started crying—a silent, inner crying, an interior sobbing without a tear.

For a quarter of an hour or more I sat there. People came and went, and no one bothered me. Small children played around me, a tiny bird sang in a tree on the other side of the street.

A policeman came over to me and said, "Why are you sitting here?"

"Why am I sitting here?" I asked. "For fun."

"I've been watching you the last half hour," he said. "You've been sitting here nearly a half hour?"

"About that," I answered. "So what?" I stood up angry and left.

Back at the market, I stopped and looked down at the street. For fun! What sort of an answer was that? From exhaustion, you should have said, and then you should have made your voice all tearful—you are a lunkhead, you will never learn to be a real hypocrite! From exhaustion and fatigue! And you should have sighed like a horse.

When I passed the firehouse I stopped again, possessed by a new whim. I snapped my fingers, gave out a loud laugh that astounded the passers-by, and said, "What you should do is to go out to Pastor Levison's! By God and hell, that is what you shall do. Well, it won't hurt to try. What have you got to lose? Besides, it's such marvelous weather."

I went into Pascha's Bookstore, found his address in a directory, and started out there. "Now this is serious!" I said. "No idiotic tricks! Conscience, you say? No rubbish—you are too poor to have a conscience! You are hungry, hungry, this is a grave matter now, this is urgent! But you have to twist your head to the side and get some music in your voice. You don't want to? All right, then, I won't go a step farther with you, and you can get that straight. Now: you are sorely troubled, you have been battling with the Powers of Darkness, with silent monsters in the darkness, a darkness so immense that one gets the horrors just thinking of it, you hunger and thirst after wine and milk, and receive them not. That is the state that you are in. Now you stand here, not worth a tinker's damn. However, you do believe in grace, thank the Lord for that, you still have not lost your faith! The next thing is to fold your hands together and show you are a real crackerjack at believing in grace! With respect to Mammon, you hate Mammon in all his works and all his ways; with a psalmbook, it is another matter entirely —a couple of kroner, as a token, to remember this." . . . I stopped short and read on the minister's door: "Office Hours: 12–4."

"No nonsense now!" I said. "This has

to be serious! O.K., down with the head, a little more. . . ." I rang at his house door.

"I am looking for the pastor," I said to the girl who answered, though I couldn't make myself put in the name of God, too.

"He is not here," she answered.

Not here! Not here! That demolished my plan, completely destroyed everything I had intended to say. What good had I gotten from this long walk? I stood there.

"Was it something special?" asked the girl.

"No, no!" I answered. "Certainly not! It was just that God has sent us such marvelous weather, and I wanted to walk out and say hello."

I stood there and she stood there. I carefully pushed my chest out so that she would notice the safety pin holding my suitcoat together; I begged her with my eyes to see what I had come for; but she, poor thing, understood nothing at all.

"Yes, wonderful weather. Is the pastor's wife at home, I wonder?"

"She is, but she has arthritis and has to lie on the sofa and can't move around. . . ." Would I perhaps like to leave a message or something?

"No, thank you. I take walks like this now and then, get a little exercise. After lunch the air was so clear."

I started back. What was the sense of chattering any more? Besides, I was beginning to feel a dizziness: no question of it, I was heading for a collapse, a real one. Office Hours: 12–4. I had knocked an hour too late: grace hour is over!

At the main market I sat down on one of the benches near the church. God in heaven, how black it was starting to look around me! I was too tired to cry, my last bit of energy was gone, I just sat there without ideas or plans, sat motionless and starved. My chest burned the most, an evil sort of smarting went on in there all the time. Chewing the shaving

no longer did any good either; my teeth were tired of their fruitless labor, and I let them rest. I gave up. On top of it all, a piece of brownish orange peel I had found on the street and immediately started gnawing on made me nauseated. I was sick; my pulse swelled up bluish on my wrists.

What actually was I waiting for? I had run around the whole day after one krone in order to stay alive a few more hours. What was the difference, really, if what was inevitable happened one day earlier or one day later? If I had been behaving like a reasonable man, I would have gone home and lain down quietly a long time ago, just given up. For an instant my brain was utterly clear. I was going to die; fall had come and everything was ready to hibernate. I had tried every way out, used every possible means I knew of. I hugged that idea with sentimentality and every time I thought hopefully of a possible way out, I whispered, nay-saying: "You fool, you, your whole body has started to die!" What I should do is to write a few letters, get everything ready, and have myself prepared. I would get myself clean, and make my bed; I would lay my head on my pile of writing paper, the purest thing I had left, and I could put the green blanket. . . .

The green blanket! At one stroke I was wide awake, my blood rose to my brain, and my heart gave a leap. I stood up and started walking, I felt full of life again, and I repeated over and over the disjointed words: The green blanket! The green blanket! I walked faster and faster as if it were a question of going back for something, and in a few minutes I was home again in my tinsmith's shop.

Without pausing a moment or weakening in my decision, I walked over to the bed and rolled up Hans Pauli's blanket. If this bright idea doesn't save me, it will be strange! The stupid misgivings that appeared in me I rose infinitely above; I said goodbye to the whole bunch. I was no hero, I was not virtue's fool, I had all my wits. . . .

Then I put the blanket under my arm and went to 5 Steners Street.

I knocked and walked into the large, unfamiliar room for the first time; the bells over the door made a whole flock of desperate clangs above me. A man entered from a side room chewing, his mouth full of food, and took his place behind the counter.

"Could you lend me a half krone on my glasses?" I said. "I'll redeem them in a couple of days, for sure."

"What? But aren't they steel-rimmed?"

"Yes."

"No, I can't do it."

"Well, no, you're probably right. It was really just a joke. But here I've got a blanket which I really haven't any use for any more, and I thought you might be able to take it off my hands."

"Unfortunately I have an entire storeroom full of bedclothes," he answered. When I got it unrolled, he glanced at it and said loudly, "You have to excuse me, I can't possibly use that either!"

"I wanted to show you the worst side first," I said. "It is much better on the other side."

"No, no, that won't make any difference, I don't want it, and you will never get ten øre for it anywhere!"

"I know it isn't worth anything," I said, "but I thought it might go if it were sold with another old blanket at an auction."

"No, no, it won't do."

"Twenty-five øre?" I said.

"Listen, I won't have it, I don't want it on my premises!" So I put the blanket under my arm again and went home. I acted as though nothing had happened, spread the blanket again on the bed, smoothed out the wrinkles as I always did, and tried to erase every trace of my last action. I couldn't possibly have been in my right mind when I decided to try this filthy trick. The more I thought of it, the more irrational it seemed. It must have been a sudden attack of weakness, some failure of energy far inside that had caught me off guard. I hadn't just fallen in the snare with closed eyes either, I had sensed that something was going wrong on the spot, and I had explicitly attempted first with the glasses, and I was so glad that I hadn't been able to commit this sin which would have stained the last hours of my life.

I wandered out again on the street.

I sat down once more on a bench near the Church of Our Saviour, dozed with my head on my chest, limp again after the recent excitement, sick and fatigued from hunger. Time went by.

I managed to sit the hour out; it was a bit lighter outside than inside the house; it struck me also that the pain in my chest was not so wild out of doors. I would get back to my room soon enough anyway.

So I dozed and thought and felt sharp pains. I had found a tiny stone, which I polished and stuck in my mouth to have something to chew on; otherwise I didn't move a muscle, not even my eyes. People came and went. Wagon noise, noise of horses, and chatter filled the air.

Of course I could try the buttons? It wouldn't do any good, naturally, and besides I was really sick. But when I thought of it, wouldn't I actually go almost past "Uncle"—my private "Uncle"—on the way home?

Finally I stood up and slowly walked and staggered along the street. I began to feel a burning above my eyebrows, it was fever coming, and I hurried on as fast as I could. I passed the bakery where the loaf of bread was on display. Now, I said with elaborate decisiveness, we are not stopping here! But suppose I just went in and asked for a piece of bread? That was only an idea, a passing thought. Ugh! I whispered, shaking my head. I walked on looking at myself ironically. I knew very well that it was no use to expect anything free from that shop.

On Repslager Street, two lovers were standing in a doorway whispering; farther down, a girl stuck her head out of the window. I was walking so slowly and thoughtfully that I appeared to have a lot of different things on my mind—so the girl came out of the house.

"How're you doing today, honey? Oh, my God, are you sick? What's wrong with your face?" She hurried back into the house.

I stopped. What *was* wrong with my face? Had I actually started dying? I felt my cheeks: Thin, naturally I was thin: my cheeks were as concave as two bowls—God in heaven! I pushed on.

But then I stopped once more. I must be unbelievably thin. My eyes would soon be all the way through my head. I wonder how I actually look? What in the hell is going on that a man has to turn himself into a living freak out of sheer hunger? I felt rage one more time, its final flaring up, a muscular spasm. "What's wrong with your face, eh?" Here I was walking around with a better head than anyone else in the country, and a pair of fists that could, so help me God, grind a longshoreman into small bits, into powder, and I was becoming a freak from hunger in the middle of the city of Christiania! Was there any sense or reason in that? I had slept in the harness and worked day and night like a minister's mare; I had read till my eyes fell out of their sockets, and starved my hairs out of my head—and in hell's name, what for? Even whores on the street fled so as not to have to look at me. But now that was going to stop—do you hear me— *stop,* and hell take the whole thing! . . .

With steadily increasing rage, I ground my teeth in despair, and with sobs and oaths I went on and roared wildly, paying no attention to the people going by. I started once more to punish my flesh, ran my forehead deliberately against lampposts, drove my fingernails deep into the backs of my hands, bit my tongue madly every time it failed to pronounce clearly and then laughed wildly whenever I caused a fairly good pain.

Yes, but what shall I do? I finally said to myself. Then I stamped on the sidewalk several times, repeating, What shall I do?

A man walking past me said with a smile: "You could go and ask them to lock you up."

I looked after him. It was a well-known lady-killer whom everyone called "The Duke." Not even he understood my condition, a man I knew, whose hand I had shaken. I stopped still. Locked up? Well, I was mad, that was true. I felt insanity in my blood, I felt it rushing through my brain. So that is where I will end? Yes, yes! I started my slow, mournful walk again. That was where my ship would tie up!

Suddenly I stopped short again. But not locked up! I said, not that! And I got almost hoarse with fear. I begged on my own behalf, beseeched the air and the sky not to be locked up. Then I would go to the city jail again, be imprisoned in a dark cell where there wasn't even a glimmer of light. Not that! There were other ways out that I hadn't tried yet. And I would try them; I would be more diligent, spend much more time on it, and go doggedly around from house to house. There was the music seller Cisler, for example. I had not tried him. There was surely some way. . . . I walked on, talking this way until I got myself crying once more from emotion. Only not to be locked up!

Cisler? Was that perhaps a sign to me from higher powers? His name had occurred to me, suddenly, for no reason at all, and he actually lived some distance away: I would look him up anyway, walk slowly and rest once in a while. I knew the store, I had been there often, and bought a little music there in the old days. Should I ask him for a half krone? That might embarrass him, better to ask for a whole krone.

I entered the shop and inquired for the manager; they showed me into his office. There he sat, handsome, dressed in the latest style, looking through some papers.

I stammered, excuse me, and stated my errand. Forced by need to turn to him. . . . Wouldn't be very long before I could pay him back. . . . As soon as I was paid for my article in the paper. . . . If he would do me such a great favor. . . .

Even while I was talking, he turned back to his desk and went on with his work. When I was through, he looked up at me sideways, shook his elegant head, and said, No! No sort of explanation. Not a word.

My knees shook violently and I leaned against the little polished rail. I had to try once more. Why should his particular name have occurred to me when I was standing down there in Vaterland Street? I felt some twinges of pain in my left side, and I started to sweat. Hmm. "I am really very weak," I said. "Unfortunately a little ill; but certainly it would be no more than two or three days before I could pay it back. Would it be too much to ask . . . ?"

"My dear fellow, why are you coming to me?" he said. "To me you are a complete blank, come in off the street. Go to the paper, where they know you."

"But only for tonight!" I said. "The office is closed now and I am extremely hungry already." He shook his head insistently and kept on shaking it even after I had taken hold of the doorknob.

"Goodbye!" I said.

That was no sign from higher powers, I thought, and smiled bitterly; I could give signs from that altitude myself if I had to. I toiled on, one block after the other, now and then resting a minute on a stoop. Just as long as I wasn't locked up! Fright of the cell accompanied me all the time and gave me no peace: every time I saw a policeman ahead, I staggered into a side street to avoid meeting him. Now we will count one hundred steps, I said, and then try our luck again! One of these times it will work.

It was a small yarn shop, a place I had never been in. A man stood behind the counter alone; farther back there was an office with a porcelain name plate on the door, and a long series of full shelves and tables. I waited until the last customer, a young woman with dimples, had left. How happy she looked! I did not try to impress this girl with the safety pin in my coat, but turned away.

"Can I help you?" asked the clerk.

"Is the manager here?" I said.

"He is on a trip in the mountains," he answered. "Was it something special?"

"It's about a few øre for food," I said, trying to smile. "I am hungry and I haven't a single øre."

"Then you are as rich as I am," he said, and began arranging packages of yarn.

"Oh, don't say no—not now!" I said, suddenly cold over my whole body. "Really, I am nearly dead from hunger, it is many days since I've eaten anything at all."

Without a word, or a trace of humor in his actions, he began one by one turning his pockets inside out. Would I take his word for it then?

"Only five øre," I said. "I'll give you ten back for it in a couple of days."

"My dear fellow, what do you want me to do, steal from the till?" he asked in an impatient voice.

"Yes!" I said. "Yes, take five øre from the till!"

"I won't be the one who does that," he said decisively, and then added, "and while we're at it, let me tell you that I think we've had enough of this."

I slumped out, sick with hunger and hot with shame. It is time all this came to an end! This thing was really going on too long. I had held myself straight for so many years, kept upright in such hard times, and now all of a sudden I had sunk to the coarsest sort of begging. This one day had brutalized my mind entirely, shamelessness had spattered me. I had even had the gall to become pathetic and stand weeping in front of the most insignificant shopkeepers. And what good had it done? Wasn't I still without even a piece of bread to stick in my mouth? I had succeeded in making me disgusting to myself. Yes, yes, this thing had to come to an end now! But they were locking the door at home already, and I had to hurry if I didn't want to spend the night in the city jail again. . . .

That deadline gave me strength—sleeping in jail I did not want to do. With my body bent over, hands pressed against my ribs on the left to dull the pain a bit, I flailed on ahead, keeping my eyes fastened to the sidewalk to avoid greetings from any possible acquaintances, and got to the firehouse. Thank God. Our Saviour's clock showed only seven o'clock, I had three hours yet before the door closed. How frightened I had been.

Anyway, not a thing had been left untried, I had done everything I could. Imagine that I hadn't had luck even once the whole day! If I told that to someone, no one would believe it; if I wrote it, everyone would swear it was invented. Not in a single place! Well, well, there was nothing to do then—most of all, don't go and be weepy again. How revolting that was! I can assure you it lowers you considerably in my estimation! If hope was gone, it was gone. I wonder if I couldn't steal a handful of oats from the stable? A flicker of light, an idea—I knew that the stable was locked.

I took it easy and crept at a slow snail's pace. I felt thirsty, luckily for the first time all day. I walked on, looking for a place to get a drink. I was a long way from the market square, and I didn't want to ask at a private house; I could wait of course until I got home—that would take fifteen minutes. Of course it wasn't at all certain I could keep down a mouthful of water either; my stomach was sensitive to everything now—I even felt nauseated from the spit I swallowed as I walked.

The buttons! I hadn't tried with the buttons yet? I stopped stock still, and started smiling. Maybe there was a solution! I was not completely finished! No question, I would get ten øre for them, tomorrow I would lay hands on ten more some place or other, and Thursday I would be paid for my newspaper article! I would see, it would be all right! Imagine forgetting the buttons! I pulled them out of my pocket and looked at them while I walked; my eyes grew dark with joy, I didn't see much of the street I was walking on.

How well I knew that large basement shop, my refuge in the dark evenings, my vampire friend! One by one, all my possessions had vanished down there, the little things I had brought from home, my last book. On the auction days I enjoyed going there to watch, and I rejoiced every time my books seemed to have found a good home. Magelsen, the actor, had my watch, and I was almost proud of that; a diary in which I had written my first little poetic ventures had been bought by an acquaintance, and my overcoat had found shelter in the closet of a photographer's studio. So I had nothing to complain about there.

I held my buttons ready in my hand, and walked in. "Uncle" was sitting at his desk, writing.

"I'm in no hurry," I said, afraid of disturbing him and putting him in a bad mood. My voice sounded so curiously hollow that I hardly recognized it myself, and my heart thumped like a hammer.

He came toward me smiling as he always did, put both his hands palm down on the counter, and looked me straight in the eye without saying anything.

"Well, I have something here, and I wanted to ask you if you had any use for—something that was really in the way at home, you understand, no room for them, some buttons."

"What was that, what was that about buttons?" And he bent his head down nearly to my hand.

Could he give me a few øre for them? . . . As much as he thought right. . . . He was the best judge of that. . . .

"For the buttons?" And "Uncle" stared at me, amazed. "For *these* buttons?"

"Just enough for a cigar or whatever you think right. I was just going by anyway and thought I'd stop in."

The old pawnbroker laughed and went back to his desk without saying a word. I stood there. I hadn't actually hoped for much, and yet I had thought it was possible I would get something. The laugh was a death sentence. I suppose the glasses wouldn't do much good either.

"Naturally I will put my glasses in with them," I said. "That goes without saying." I took them off. "Just ten øre, or if you prefer, five øre?"

"You know very well that I can't lend you anything on your glasses," "Uncle" said. "I've told you that before."

"But I need a stamp," I said dully. "I can't even mail the letter I need to send. A ten- or a five-øre stamp, whatever you think yourself."

"God bless you, be on your way now!" he answered, and shooed me out with his hands.

"All right, that's the way it will have to be!" I said to myself. I put the glasses back on mechanically, picked up the buttons, and left. I said good night and latched the door after me as I always did. You can see, there is nothing more to be done! When I was back up on the sidewalk, I stopped and looked at the buttons once more. "That he wouldn't even take them!" I said. "They are almost new—I don't understand it at all!"

While I was making these observations to myself, a man brushed past me and started down. In passing, he had given me a little shove, we both said excuse me, and I turned around and looked after him.

"Say, is it you?" he said from down on the steps. He came back up and I recognized him. "God help us, you look terrible!" he said. "What were you doing down there?"

"Oh—had some business. You're going down there, I see."

"Yes. What did you bring to him?"

My knees shook, I leaned against the wall for support, and reached out my hand with the buttons, open.

"Holy Christ!" he shouted. "What are you doing? This is going too far."

"Goodbye!" I said, and started to go. I felt a sobbing inside me.

"No, wait a minute!" he said.

What should I wait for? He was on his way to "Uncle" himself, bringing his engagement ring, perhaps, been starving for several days, avoiding his landlady.

"Well, all right," I answered. "If you won't be too . . ."

"Of course not," he said, taking hold

of my arm. "But the truth is, I don't trust you, you are an absolute idiot. You had better come right down here with me."

I knew what he had in mind, and suddenly I felt again a little ache of honor, and I answered: "Can't do it! I have to be in Bernt Ankers Street at eight-thirty, and . . ."

"Eight-thirty, that's fine! Now, it is only eight. Look at this watch, it's right here in my hand—that is what I'm going to take down. So, get in there, you starving old devil! I'll get at least five kroner for you."

And he pushed me in.

PART THREE

A WEEK WENT BY in joy and gladness.

I was over the worst this time again, I had food every day, my spirits rose, and I pushed one iron after the other into the fire. I had three or four essays in the works, which plundered my poor brain of every spark, every idea that occurred to it; my writing seemed to me better than it had ever been. The last article, in which I had put so much stock, for which I had so much hope, had already been returned by the editor. I tore it up immediately, angry and insulted, without even reading it over. I intended, in the future, to try another newspaper also, so as to have several outlets.

In the last resort, if everything failed, I always had the ships to turn to. *The Nun* was lying off the pier ready to sail, and I could probably sign on to go to Archangel or wherever the ship was going at the moment. So there was no lack of possibilities on many sides.

The last crisis had been hard on me: I was beginning to lose a lot of hair, headaches were also a great bother, particularly during the mornings, and my general nervousness stayed on. During the day I sat writing with my hands wrapped in rags simply because they were so sensitive that my own breath on them was painful. When Jens Olai slammed the stable doors downstairs hard, or when a dog came into the yard at the back and started to bark, the sound went right through the marrow of my bones like needles, and I felt the pain everywhere. I was in poor shape.

Day after day I toiled on my articles, taking off barely time enough to gobble down my food before I set to writing again. During those days, both the bed and my little rickety table were swimming in notes and scribbled-over manuscripts that I took turns working on, adding new ideas that occurred to me in the course of the day, crossing out material or freshening up the dead passages with a lively word here or there, and pushing on from sentence to sentence with great labor. Finally one afternoon one of my essays was finished; I put it gaily in my pocket and started off to see my editor, whom I called "the Chief." It was about time I made a move to get more money, I had not many øre left.

The Chief asked me to wait a bit, to sit down, he would be with me in a minute. . . . He went on writing.

I looked around me in the tiny office: busts, lithographs, clippings, and an enormous wastebasket that looked as if it could swallow a man, bones and all. I felt sad, looking at this monstrous maw, this dragon—mouth always open, ready to receive more rejected articles, newly crushed hopes.

"What's today's date?" the Chief suddenly asked from his desk.

"The twenty-eighth," I answered, glad to be of service to him.

"The twenty-eighth." He wrote on. Finally he found envelopes for a couple of letters, tossed some papers in the wastebasket, and looked at me. When he saw that I was still standing by the door, he made a half-serious, half-joking gesture with his hands, pointing at a chair.

I turned partly away so that he wouldn't see, as I unbuttoned my coat, that my waistcoat was missing, and I took my manuscript from my pocket.

"It is just a small sketch of Correggio," I said, "and I'm afraid it's written in the wrong style. . . ."

He took the sheets from my hand and started leafing through them. He turned to face me.

So this is how he looked, close-up, the man whose name I had heard since I was a child and whose paper had had a tremendous influence on me all my life. His hair was curly, and his fine brown eyes a trifle restless; one of his quirks was brushing his nose with his thumb every once in a while. A country preacher could not have looked more full of milk and honey than this formidable writer, whose words had always left long bloody marks wherever they fell. A strange feeling of fear and awe toward this man came over me, I felt tears coming to my eyes, and I involuntarily moved a step closer in order to tell him how much he meant to me for everything he had taught me, and to ask him not to be too hard on me—I was only a poor devil with enough troubles already.

He looked up, putting my manuscript pages slowly together again, and sat there thinking. To help him get rid of me more easily, I reached my hand out and said, "Oh, well, it's probably not usable." I smiled then, to give the impression that it wasn't very serious to me.

"Everything we use has to be popularly written. You know the kind of public we have. But I wonder if you couldn't take this and make it a little more elementary? Or else write about something that people feel more at home with?"

His consideration astounded me. I realized that my article was rejected, and yet I could not have had a more beautiful rejection. So as not to bother him any longer, I said, "Yes, I'm sure I can do that."

I walked to the door. Hmm. He had to forgive me for having wasted his time with this. . . . I bowed and reached for the knob.

"If you need it," he said, "I'd be glad to give you a small advance. You can always work it off."

Since he had just seen that my writing was unsuitable, his offer seemed slightly humiliating and I answered, "No, thanks, I'm all right for a while. But thank you very much. Goodbye!"

"Goodbye!" the Chief answered, and turned back instantly to his work.

He had treated me in any case with a courtesy I didn't deserve, and I was grateful for that: I must learn how to appreciate it. I determined not to come back until I could bring him a piece I was really satisfied with, which would take the Chief by surprise and get him to turn over ten kroner to me without thinking of it. So I walked home and set to work again.

On each of the following evenings, after the street lamps had been lit, usually about eight o'clock, a curious thing would take place.

As I left the building, after the day's labor and troubles, for a little walk in the streets, a woman dressed in black would be standing by a lamppost just outside the door; she would turn to look at me and follow me with her eyes as I walked past. I noticed that she always had the same dress on, and the same heavy veil that hid her face and fell over her breast, and that she carried a small umbrella with an ivory ring in the handle.

It was the third evening now that I had seen her, always in the same spot; as soon as I had passed, she would turn and slowly walk up the street, away from me.

My excitable brain shot out antennae, and I immediately felt sure that her visit had something to do with me. I was about to address her several times, ask her if she was looking for someone, if she needed any help, if I could walk her home, badly dressed as I was, give her some protection in these dark streets; but I had a vague fear of it all costing me something, a glass of wine, a carriage ride, and I was broke; my empty pockets had a depressing effect on me, and I didn't even have the courage to look inquiringly at her as I passed. Hunger was beginning to take hold in me again, I hadn't had any food since last night—of course, that wasn't very long, but I was beginning to weaken noticeably. I simply couldn't starve any more the way I used to. A single day without food now could make me feel dazed, and I made incessant retching efforts as soon as I drank any water. At night I got into bed fully dressed, just as I was during the day, and froze anyway, shivering with cold, and even stiffened while I slept. The old blanket could not keep out the drafts, and I woke every morning with my nose stopped up by the icy air coming in from outdoors.

I wandered around in the streets, trying to figure out how to keep going until I finished my next essay. If I only had a candle, I could try pushing on right through the night. It would only take a couple of hours once I warmed up to it—tomorrow morning I could go see the Chief again.

I walked straight into the Oplandske Café, looking for my young banker friend to scrounge ten øre for a candle. They let me go from room to room without bothering me; I walked past a dozen tables at which chattering customers sat eating and drinking, got to the back of the restaurant, even into the Red Room, without finding my man. Disappointed and irritated, I went back out on the street and drifted off in the direction of the castle.

Wasn't this great, what the hell was going on, why was there never any end to my troubles! Taking long strides, my coat collar turned brutally up to my chin, my fists clenched in my pants pockets, I walked along, cursing my unlucky stars. Not a really carefree hour for seven, eight months, not even sufficient food for a week before poverty brought me to my knees again. And into the bargain I had to go and be honorable right in the middle of my misery—what a laugh, honorable all the way through! God help us all, what a fool I had been. I started recounting to myself how I had once gone around with a bad conscience from taking Hans Pauli's blanket to the pawnshop. I laughed mockingly at my tender scrupulousness, spit contemptuously in the street, and couldn't find words strong enough to describe my idiocy. If that were only now! If this minute I found a schoolgirl's savings on the street or the last øre of some poor widow, I would jump for it and stick it in my pocket, steal it with calm deliberation, and sleep like a top all night. I hadn't suffered so unspeakably for nothing, my patience was finished, I was ready for anything that came along.

I walked around the castle three or four times, decided to start home, took a couple more swings through the park, and walked finally down Karl Johan Street.

It was about eleven. The street was rather dark, people were wandering about all over, silent couples and noisy groups mingled. The great hour had begun, the mating time when the secret exchanges took place and the joyful adventures began. Rustling petticoats, one or two quick sensual laughs, swelling breasts, rapid heavy breathing; down by the Grand Hotel a voice called, "Emma!" The whole street was a warm swamp, with mists rising from it.

I unconsciously checked my pockets

for two kroner. The sexual energy visible in all the gestures of those going by, even in the dim flame of the gas lamps, and the motionless steamy night had all begun to affect me—this air filled with whispers, embraces, hesitant confessions, half-pronounced words, tiny squeals. Even the cats were making love with high-pitched shrieks in the door of Blomqvist's Café. And I didn't have two kroner. What a misery, unheard of, to be this broke! What a disgrace, what a humiliation! I started thinking again about the last mite of some poor widow which I wanted to steal, some schoolboy's cap or handkerchief, some beggar's sack which I would have taken instantly to a rag merchant and drunk up. To console myself, and give myself a little shield, I took to finding every possible fault with the happy people going by me: I shrugged my shoulders in disgust and looked contemptuously after them as they went by, couple after couple. These babyish, aimless, candy-eating students who think they are really being rakish and Continental every time they manage to pat a girl on the breast! These bachelors, bank clerks, butchers, philanderers who don't even draw the line at sailors' wives, or those fat sows from the cattle market who flop down in the nearest doorway for a glass of beer! What Helens! The place beside them still warm from some night watchman or horse hostler of the night before: the throne was always empty, always open, don't hesitate, step right up! . . . I gave a long spit over the sidewalk without bothering about whom it might hit, became furious, full of contempt for these people rubbing against each other and pairing off right before my eyes. I raised my face and felt how blessed I was at being able to keep my path clean.

By the Senate House I met a girl who looked straight at me as we passed.

"Good evening!" I said.

"Good evening!" She stopped.

Hmm. Was she out walking so late? Wasn't it a little dangerous for a young woman to be out on Karl Johan this time of night? No? But hadn't she ever been addressed, molested, I mean hadn't anyone just asked her outright to come home with him?

She looked at me surprised, examined my face to see what I was really saying. Then she suddenly put her hand in under my arm, and said, "All right, let's go then!"

I walked with her. When we were a few steps past the taxi stand, I stopped, freed my arm, and said, "Listen, my dear, I don't have a single øre." And made as if to go my way.

At first she refused to believe me, but after she had felt in all my pockets and found nothing, she got angry, tossed her head, and called me a dried-out stick.

"Good night!" I said.

"Wait a minute," she said. "Aren't those gold rims on your glasses?"

"No."

"All right, go to hell then!"

I walked off.

A few seconds later she came running after me and called to me again.

"You can come home with me anyway," she said.

I felt humiliated by this free offer from a pitiful street whore, and said so. Besides, it was getting late and I had to be somewhere; she really couldn't afford sacrifices of that kind, anyway.

"Now I really *want* you to come."

"But I won't go under these circumstances."

"You're on your way to some other girl," she said.

"No," I answered.

The truth was there wasn't much spring left in me these days. Women had become to me almost like men. Hunger and misery had dried me up. I felt, nevertheless, my embarrassing position in relation to this unusual whore, and I determined to save face.

"What is your name?" I asked. "Marie? So! Now, Marie, listen to me." And I started to explain my behavior. The girl grew more and more astonished. Did she really believe then that I was one of those types who run around the streets at night chasing young girls? Did she really think something that bad about me? Had I ever said anything improper to her up to now? Did people who had evil ideas in mind behave as I did? The fact was I had addressed her and walked a few steps with her just to see how far she would allow it to go. My name, by the way, was such and such, Pastor such and such. Good night! Go and sin no more!

With that I left.

I rubbed my hands, delighted, over my fine story, and talked aloud to myself. What a joy it was to go around doing good deeds! I had maybe given that fallen creature just the shove she needed toward an upright behavior for the rest of her life! And she would be grateful when she thought back on it, maybe even remember me on her deathbed with thanksgiving. Oh, it still paid to be honorable, honorable and righteous! My spirits were high as could be, I felt strong and ready for anything. If I only had a candle, I could finish my article! I walked along, jingling my new doorkey in my hand, hummed, whistled, and debated about how to get a candle. There was nothing else to do, I would have to take my writing stuff downstairs, out under the street lamp. I unlocked the street door and walked up to get my papers.

When I came back down, I locked the street door from the outside and took up my place under the street lamp. Everything was quiet, I heard only the heavy clanking sound of a policeman's footsteps down in Tvær Street, and far away, in the direction of St. Hanshaugen, dogs barking. There was nothing to disturb me, I pulled my coat collar up around my eyes and started thinking as hard as I could. It would be a tremendous help if I were only lucky enough to get the last part of this essay right. I was at a difficult point just now, I needed an imperceptible transition to the next thing, and after that a smooth, gradual finale, a long calm passage which would finally end in a climax as abrupt and shocking as a shot or the sound of a mountain breaking apart. End.

The words would not come. I read the whole piece over from the beginning, read every sentence aloud, and I could not marshal my ideas for this spectacular climax. While I stood there working, who should come but a policeman; he took up a position in the middle of the street a little way off, and ruined my mood completely. What was it to him if I stood here for a moment writing a marvelous climax to an essay for the Chief? God, it was absolutely impossible for me to keep my head above water, no matter what I did! I stood there an hour. The policeman went his way. It got to be too cold for standing still. Discouraged and depressed over this new try come to nothing, I finally opened the street door and went in.

My room was cold, and the darkness so deep I could hardly see the window. I felt my way over to the bed, pulled off my shoes, and set about warming my feet between my hands. At last I lay down to sleep—fully dressed, as I had been doing for a long time.

In the morning I sat up in bed as soon as it was light, and started work on my article again. I sat there without moving until noon; by then I had worked out ten or twenty lines. And I still had not gotten to the finale.

I got up, pulled on my shoes, and

started walking back and forth in the room to warm up. Frost was on the windows; I looked out, it was snowing; in the courtyard a thick blanket of snow was lying on the cobblestones and the pump.

I fussed around in my room, walked mechanically back and forth, scraped on the walls with my fingernails, rested my forehead carefully against the door, tapped on the floor with my forefinger, and listened attentively; I was listening for nothing but I listened quietly and thoughtfully as if I were engaged on a matter of considerable importance. All this time I said aloud, over and over, so even I heard it: But God in heaven, this is insanity! I kept on anyway, just as crazily. After a long while, perhaps a couple of hours, I pulled myself together by force, bit my lips, and took hold as best I could. This had to come to a stop! I found a sliver to chew on and sat down, determined to write some more.

A couple of short sentences came into existence with considerable effort, a few miserable words I tortured into being just to make some headway. Then I stopped, my head was empty, I couldn't do any more. When it was obvious that I couldn't go on, I began staring with eyes wide open at these final words, at this unfinished page, gaped at the curious shaky letters which gazed up at me from the paper like small shaggy beings, and at the end I couldn't understand what was going on, I had no thoughts at all.

Time passed. I heard traffic noise outdoors. Noise from wagons and horses, Jens Olai's voice floated up to me from the stable where he was talking to the horses. I was in a real stupor. I smacked my lips once or twice but undertook nothing else. My chest was giving me pain.

Dusk began to fall, I sank into myself more and more, grew tired and lay back on the bed. To warm my hands a bit, I pushed my fingers through my hair, back and forth, crossways and sideways; small handfuls came loose, tufts came away between my fingers and spread over the pillow. I didn't worry about that, it was as if it were not happening to me; I had plenty of hair anyway. After a while I attempted to rouse myself from this curious drowsiness which had floated into all my limbs like a fog; I sat up, coughed as hard as my chest would allow—and fell back once more. Nothing to do, I was dying with open eyes, helpless, staring up at the ceiling. Finally I put my forefinger in my mouth and started sucking on it. Something started to flicker in my brain, an idea that had gotten free in there, a lunatic notion. Suppose I took a bite? Without a moment's hesitation I shut my eyes and clamped down hard with my teeth.

I leaped up. Finally I was awake. A little blood trickled from the finger, and I licked it off. There wasn't much pain, the wound didn't amount to anything, but I was suddenly myself again. I shook my head, walked to the window, and found a rag for my finger. While I stood puttering about with that, my eyes suddenly filled, I cried softly to myself. The poor bitten thin finger looked so pitiful. My God, I was a long way down.

It got darker—perhaps it would be possible for me to write the finale tonight if I only had a candle. My brain was clear once more. Thoughts came and went as usual, and I wasn't suffering so horribly; hunger wasn't bothering me as much as it did several hours ago, I could certainly hold out till the next day. Maybe I could get a candle on credit if I went to the grocery store and simply explained the situation. I was well known there—in the good days when I still had money I had bought many a loaf in their shop. There was no doubt whatever that

I could get a candle on the strength of my good name. So for the first time in weeks I brushed up my clothes a bit and whisked away the loose hairs on my coat collar as well as I could in the dark. Then I felt my way down the stairs.

When I got out on the street, it occurred to me that perhaps I ought to ask for some bread instead. I became indecisive, stopped and thought for a while. "No, absolutely not!" I finally replied to myself. I was unfortunately not in condition now to tolerate food—it would be the same story as before: visions and "feelings" and crazy ideas. My article would never get finished that way, and it was important I visit the Chief soon before he forgot who I was. Absolutely not! I decided definitely on a candle. I walked into the grocery store.

A woman stood at the counter, making purchases; at my side, a number of small parcels were lying, wrapped in various sorts of paper. The clerk, who recognized me and knew what I usually bought, left the woman for a moment, wrapped a loaf of bread quickly in newspaper, and laid it in front of me.

"No—actually it is a candle I need tonight," I said. I said it very softly and humbly so as not to irritate him and so spoil my chance for the candle.

He hadn't expected that answer; it was the first time I had ever asked for anything besides bread from him.

"All right, you'll have to wait a bit then," he said, and returned to the woman's order.

She received her articles and paid, giving him a five-kroner bill, took the change back from it, and left.

The clerk and I were now alone.

He said, "Oh, yes, it was a candle." He tore open a package of candles and handed one to me.

He looked at me and I looked at him; I couldn't get my request out.

"Oh yes, that's right, you paid," he said suddenly. He said flatly that I had paid: I heard every word. He began pulling up silver coins from the till, krone after krone, shiny, fat coins—he gave me back change for a five-kroner bill, the woman's bill.

"There you are!" he said.

I stood there gaping at the money a second, I was aware that something was wrong somewhere, but I didn't go into it, I thought of nothing at all; I was dazed at the treasure that lay there glittering before my eyes. I gathered the coins up mechanically.

I remained standing by the counter, dumb with amazement, defeated, humiliated; I took a step toward the door and stopped again. I fixed my gaze on a certain point on the wall where a training collar with a small bell hung, and underneath it, a package of shoelaces. I stood gazing at these objects.

The clerk thought I wanted to exchange a few words since I was taking so much time in going, and he said, while tidying up some wrapping paper that was loose on the counter: "It looks as if we're going to have winter now."

"Hmm. Yes," I answered. "It looks as if we're going to have winter now. It looks that way." A second later I added, "Well, it's about time, I think. But it certainly does look that way. Of course it's about time, too."

I heard myself speaking this gibberish but took in each word I spoke as if it were coming from another person.

"Oh, do you think so?" said the clerk.

I put my hand with the money into my pocket, turned the knob, and went out; I heard myself say good night, and the clerk answer.

I was a few steps down the street when the shop door was thrown open and the clerk shouted after me. I turned around without a trace of surprise or a twinge of fear; I simply gathered the coins together in my hand and got ready to give them back.

"For you, you forgot your candle," the clerk said.

"Oh, thank you," I answered calmly. "Many thanks!"

I kept on walking down the street, carrying the candle in my hand.

My first rational thought had to do with the money. I went over to a street lamp and counted it, weighed it in my hand and smiled. In any case, this help was magnificent, incredible, I had been wonderfully helped for a long, long time! I put my hand with the money back in my pocket and walked on.

Outside a basement café in Stor Street I stopped, debating coldly and soberly whether I should risk a small lunch immediately. I heard the clatter of plates and knives inside, and the thump of meat being pounded. The temptation was too great, I walked in.

"One roast beef!" I said.

"One roast beef!" the girl shouted through a little opening in the wall.

I sat down at a small table for one, just inside the door, and prepared to wait. It was a bit dark there, I felt fairly well hidden, and I set myself to think. Once in a while the girl looked over at me with a certain curiosity.

My first really dishonorable act was taken, my first theft, compared to which all my earlier pranks were insignificant; my first tiny, huge fall. . . . So be it! Nothing to do about it. Anyway, I still had freedom of action. I could make it up to the clerk at a later date, when the time was right. I didn't have to keep on being dishonorable, but even so I had never promised I would live any more honorably than anyone else, I hadn't signed any contract. . . .

"Do you think my order will be here soon?"

"Yes, right away." The girl opened the little sliding door and looked into the kitchen.

But suppose the thing came to a head one day? Suppose the clerk were to get suspicious, start to think over the business of the bread and the five kroner the woman got change for? It wasn't impossible it would all come to him one day, maybe the next time I went in. Good God, what a mess! . . . I shrugged my shoulders surreptitiously.

"Here we are!" the waitress said in a friendly way, and set the plate of beef down. "But wouldn't you rather go into the next room? It's awfully dark here."

"No, thank you. Let me stay here," I answered. Her friendliness touched me. I paid for the beef immediately and gave her for a tip whatever coins I got hold of in my pocket; when I did, I closed her hand over them. She smiled, and I said as a joke, my eyes wet: "Keep that to buy an estate with. . . . You're very welcome!"

I started eating; gradually I became more and more ravenous and swallowed whole pieces without chewing them. I tore at the meat like a cannibal.

The waitress came to me again.

"Would you like to have something to drink?" she said. And she leaned over me slightly.

I looked at her; she talked very quietly, almost bashfully. She lowered her eyes.

"I was thinking of a glass of beer, or whatever you'd like . . . on me. . . . No cost. . . . If you would like to. . . ."

"No, thank you very much!" I answered. "Not this time. I'll come back another day."

She went back and sat down behind the counter. I could only see her head. A strange person!

When I was finished, I walked straight to the door. I felt nauseated already. The waitress stood up. I was afraid of getting into the light, frightened of showing myself too clearly to this girl who had no idea of my real poverty, so I said a rapid good night, bowed, and left.

The food began to bother me, my stomach felt upset, and I would not be able to hold the food down very long. I walked along emptying my mouth, in every dark crook I passed, fought against the nausea which was making me hollow all over again, clenched my fists, steeled myself, stamped on the sidewalk, and swallowed again in a rage what was trying to come up—all in vain! I ran at last into a doorway, doubled over, blinded from the tears that sprang from my eyes, and vomited everything.

Now I was bitter; I walked along the street, sobbing. I cursed the cruel gods, whoever they were, who were persecuting me so, sentenced them to hell and eternal damnation and pain for their infamy. There was very little chivalry among the gods, very little chivalry at all, I could tell you that! . . . I went over to a man who was looking into a store window and asked him as fast as I could what in his opinion one ought to feed a man who had been starving for a long time. It was a matter of life and death, I said. The man couldn't keep beef down.

"I've heard that milk is good in those cases, boiled milk," the man answered, utterly astonished. "For whom, if I may ask, are you inquiring?"

"Many thanks!" I said. "Boiled milk is probably a very good idea."

I walked away.

At the first café I came to, I walked in and asked for some boiled milk. I got the milk, drank it down still scorching as it was, swallowed every drop greedily, and walked out. I started home.

Now the curious thing happened again. Outside the street door of my house, leaning against the lamppost and directly in the light, a person was standing whom I could see even from a long way off—it was the woman dressed in black. The same woman who had been

there the previous nights. There was no question about it: for the fourth time running, she had appeared at exactly the same spot. She stood there without moving.

I found this so extraordinary that involuntarily I slowed up. In that instant my brain was working well, even though it was rather excited, and my nerves on edge from the last meal. I walked as usual close to her and past her, got almost to the door, and was about to go inside. Then I stopped. I had an impulse suddenly. Without reasoning with myself at all, I turned around and walked over to the woman, looked into her face and said, "Good evening!"

"Good evening!" she answered.

"Pardon me, but are you looking for someone? I have noticed you here before. Could I be of any help, I wonder? Forgive me for intruding."

Well, she didn't know exactly. . . .

"No one is living inside that door except three or four horses and me—actually the building is a stable and a tinsmith shop. You are probably on a wild-goose chase then, though I'm sorry to say it, if you're looking for someone here."

She turned her face to the side and said, "I'm not looking for anyone, I'm just standing here."

Well, only standing there, but standing there night after night merely on a sort of whim! That was a bit odd—the more I thought about it, the more confused I became. So I decided to be bold. I jingled the coins in my pocket a little and asked her outright to come with me and have a glass of wine somewhere. . . . We'll celebrate the coming of winter, he-he. . . . It wouldn't take long. . . . But perhaps she'd rather not?

No, thank you, she thought she'd better not. She couldn't do it. But would I be so kind as to walk with her a little way. It was rather dark, and it was embarrassing sometimes to walk up Karl Johan Street alone at this time of night.

Delighted.

We started off; she walked at my right side. A peculiar, beautiful feeling came over me. The consciousness of being close to a young girl. I walked along looking at her the whole way. The perfume in her hair, the warmth that poured out from her body, the odor of femininity around her, the sweet breath whenever she turned toward me—it all flowed into me, took control of my senses entirely. I could just make out a plump, slightly pale face behind the veil, and full breasts that pushed out her cape. The thought of all that beauty I sensed was there hidden under the cape and the veil made me feel bewildered, and idiotically happy for no sensible reason. I couldn't hold out any longer, I touched her with my hand, ran my fingers over her shoulder, and smiled like a moron. I heard my heart thumping.

"You're a strange one!" I said.

"Really? Why do you think so?"

"Well, in the first place because you have the curious habit of standing outside a horse barn night after night, with no point in it at all, merely on a sort of whim. . . ."

On the other hand, she could have a purpose of sorts; actually she liked to stay up late, she had always been terribly fond of that. Did I like to go to bed before midnight?

"I? If there is anything in the world I really hate, it is going to bed before twelve o'clock at night!"

Oh, is that so! So that's why, you see, she took a walk like this in the evening when nothing else was going on; she lived up on St. Olaf's Place. . . .

"Ylayali!" I cried.

"Beg your pardon?"

"I merely said Ylayali. . . . Well, well, go on!"

She lived up on St. Olaf's Place, it was

lonesome at times, with her mama who wasn't much good to talk to because she was so deaf. Was there anything odd then in her liking to be out of the house a little?

"No, not at all!" I answered.

"You seem very sure of that." I could hear by her voice that she was smiling.

Didn't she have a sister?

Yes, she had an elder sister. But how did I know that? She had gone to Hamburg.

Recently?

Yes, five weeks ago. Where did I find out that she had a sister?

I didn't find it out at all, I just asked.

We fell silent. A man passed us, carrying a pair of shoes under his arm. Otherwise, the street was empty as far down as we could see. Over by the Tivoli a long string of colored lights was shining. The snow had stopped. The sky was clear.

"Heavens, aren't you freezing without an overcoat?" she suddenly asked, looking at me.

Should I tell her why I didn't have an overcoat? Be open about my situation right now and frighten her away—just as well now as later. Still, it was sweet to walk here beside her and keep her in ignorance a little while. I lied, and answered, "Oh, no, not at all." So as to change the subject, I asked, "Have you seen the little zoo over at the Tivoli?"

"No," she answered. "Is it something worth seeing?"

What if she decided she wanted to go there? In those bright lights, among all the people! She would be shocked, I would scare her out of the place with my frightful clothes, my skinny face which I hadn't washed in two days, she would even find out that I had no waistcoat. . . .

"No, I don't think so," I said. "There's not much there to see." A couple of simple ideas luckily occurred to me then, which I immediately put to use, odds and ends from my looted brain: "One can't expect much of such a small zoo. And looking at animals in cages doesn't interest me in general. They know that we are standing there looking at them—they sense the hundreds of inquisitive looks, and it has an effect on them. What I prefer are animals who aren't aware of being watched, shy creatures fussing about in their lairs, lying with half-closed eyelids, licking their claws, and thinking. Don't you think so?"

Yes, she thought I was right.

"The animals that have all their terror and original wildness are the ones that are valuable. The stealthy silent steps in the dead of night, the sighs from boughs, the eeriness of pinewoods, cries from the passing birds, the wind, smell of blood, thunder in the sky; in short, the spirit of wild nature that is still inside the wild creature. . . ."

But I was afraid all this was boring her, and the sense of my own immense poverty seized me again, and depressed me. If I had only been halfway decently dressed, I could have given her the pleasure of a walk in the Tivoli! I couldn't understand this woman who evidently enjoyed being escorted all the way up Karl Johan by a half-naked beggar. What in God's name was she thinking of? And why was I walking here, playing roles and smiling idiotically at nothing? Did I have any sensible reason, really, to let myself be lured by this little silken wren into such a long walk? Wouldn't this overtax me? Didn't I feel the cold of death slip right into my heart every time the slightest wind hit us? And wasn't insanity already setting up house in my brain, purely from lack of food for months on end? She was actually keeping me from going home and sipping a little milk, one more spoonful of milk which I maybe could keep down. Why didn't she just turn her back and let me go to hell? . . .

I became confused, my despair pushed me over the edge, and I said, "Actually, you shouldn't be walking with me; I am degrading you in the eyes of other people by my clothes alone. That is the truth now; I really mean it."

She was taken aback. She looked up at me swiftly and said nothing. Finally she said, "Good heavens!" She said nothing more.

"What do you mean by that?" I asked.

"Oh, please, don't talk like that. . . . We haven't far to go now." And she walked a little faster.

We got to University Street, and we could see the lights in St. Olaf's Place already. Now she walked more slowly again.

"At the risk of being indiscreet," I said, "may I ask you your name before we part? And won't you just for an instant lift your veil so I can see you? I would be very grateful."

Pause. We walked on. I waited.

"You have seen me before," she answered.

"Ylayali!" I said again.

"You followed me once for half a day and almost home. Were you drunk then?" I could hear again that she was smiling.

"Yes," I said. "Yes, unfortunately I was drunk that time."

"That was very bad of you!"

And I admitted contritely that it was very bad of me.

We were at the fountain now; we stopped and looked up at all the bright windows at 2 St. Olaf's Place.

"You mustn't come with me any farther," she said. "I enjoyed the evening, thank you!"

I lowered my head and didn't dare say anything. I took off my hat and stood bareheaded. Would she consider letting me take her hand?

"Why don't you ask me to go back with you a little way?" she said jokingly.

[181]

But she looked down at the toes of her shoes.

"My God," I said, "yes! If you would let me!"

"Yes, but only a little way."

So we turned around.

I was utterly confused now, I didn't know which end was up; this creature had turned all my expectations upside down. I was delighted, wonderfully glad; I felt as if I were about to collapse from joy. She had expressly wanted to walk back with me, it was her idea, not mine. I walked along, keeping my eyes on her, and became more and more frisky, and she encouraged it, drawing me nearer to her with every word. I forgot for a moment my poverty and misery, my whole horrible situation, I felt the warm blood racing through my body just as in the old days while I was still in one piece physically, and I decided to feel my way further with a little trick.

"Actually, it wasn't you I was following that time," I said. "I was following your sister."

"Was it my sister?" she said, and couldn't have been more amazed. She stopped, looked at me, and waited for me to answer. She was asking in dead earnest.

"Yes," I answered. "Hmm. I mean, I was following the younger of the two women who were walking ahead of me."

"The younger? Aaah!" She laughed all at once, a high, full laugh like a child's. "How sly you are! You said that just to get me to take off my veil. I saw through that. Well, you'll have to turn blue in the face from waiting then . . . as punishment."

We started laughing and joking, we talked without stopping the whole time, I didn't know what I was saying, I was happy. She told me she had seen me one time earlier, a long time ago, in the theater. I was with three friends and had behaved like a lunatic; no question, I had

been drunk that time too, that was naughty.

"Why did you think that?"

"Well, because you laughed all the time."

"So. Yes, yes, I laughed a lot in those days."

"But not now?"

"Oh yes, now too. Being alive is wonderful!"

We were down to Karl Johan.

She said, "This is as far as we go!" So we turned around and walked back up University Street. When we got up to the fountain again, I slowed up, knowing I would not be able to go with her any farther.

"Now you have to turn around," she said, stopping.

"Yes, I have to," I replied.

But a minute later she thought I could certainly come with her to the door. After all, there was nothing wrong with that, was there?

"No," I said.

But as I stood by the door, all my misery drove in on me again. How could a man keep up his courage when he was broken in two like this? Here I stood, before a young woman, dirty, in rags, deformed by hunger, not washed, half naked—enough to make one sink into the earth. I shrank together, unconsciously stooped a little, and said, "Must I never see you again?"

I had no hope of ever getting to meet her again, I was almost longing for a sharp no which would stiffen me up and make me numb.

"You could."

"When?"

"I don't know."

Pause.

"Won't you be kind enough to lift your veil just for a single instant," I said, "so I can see whom I am talking with? Just one minute. I have to see whom I'm talking to."

Pause.

"You can meet me here Tuesday evening," she said. "Would you want to do that?"

"Lord yes, if you'll let me!"

"Eight o'clock."

"Good."

I ran my hand down over her cape, brushing the snow off it just to get a chance to touch her. I felt great pleasure just in being so near her.

"So you mustn't think that I'm a bad girl then," she said. She smiled again.

"No. . . ."

Suddenly, with a resolute motion, she pulled her veil up on her forehead; we stood looking at each other a second. "Ylayali!" I said. She stood on tiptoe, threw her arms around my neck, and kissed me full on the mouth. I could feel her breast rise and fall, she was breathing rapidly.

In an instant she pulled herself away, called good night in a whispering, husky voice, turned and ran up the stairs without another word. . . .

The street door closed.

The next day it snowed still more, a heavy wet snow, great blue flakes that fell and turned to slush. The air was raw and cold.

I woke up rather late, my brain strangely confused by all the excitement of the night before, and my heart drunk from that beautiful meeting. In delight I lay awhile awake, imagining that Ylayali was lying beside me: I reached my arms out, embraced myself, and kissed the air. Finally I got up, went out, and bought a fresh glass of milk, and immediately after, some roast beef. I was no longer hungry—but my nerves were still jangled.

I went off to look for some used clothes. It struck me that I could perhaps buy a used waistcoat very cheaply, something to have on under my coat, anything

would do. I walked up the stairs to the secondhand store and picked up a waistcoat which I started to examine. While I was fooling with that, an acquaintance came by, nodded and called to me. I left the waistcoat lying there and walked down to him. He was an engineer on his way to his office.

"Come along and have a glass of beer," he said. "Only come right now, I don't have much time. . . . Who was that woman you were walking with last night?"

"Suppose I informed you," I said, jealous merely that he thought of her, "that she is my fiancée?"

"Marvelous!" he said.

"Yes, that was all arranged last night."

I had knocked him down with that, he believed me without qualification. I lied through my teeth to get rid of him. We got our beer, drank it, and left.

"Good morning! . . . By the way," he said suddenly, "I owe you, you know, several kroner, and it is a crime that I haven't paid them back long ago. But I will pay them back first thing."

"Good, thank you," I said. But I knew he would never pay me back.

The beer unfortunately went to my head, I became extremely warm. Thoughts of last night's adventure flooded over me, made me almost delirious. What if she didn't come on Tuesday? What if she had started thinking it over and became suspicious! . . . Suspicious about what? . . . My mind suddenly went off on a tangent, and became obsessed with the matter of the money. I felt appalled at myself, deathly afraid. The theft stood out before me in all its details: I saw the little shop, the counter, my emaciated hand as I picked up the money, and I imagined to myself the police procedure as they came to arrest me. Irons on wrists and ankles—no, only on wrists, perhaps only one wrist; then hearing the clerk filling out forms, the sound of his pen scraping, his glance, his terrible glance: Now, Mr. Tangen: the cell, eternal darkness. . . .

Hmm. I clenched my fists hard to give me courage, walked faster, and got to the main market square. Here I sat down.

No pranks now! How in hell could anyone prove that I had stolen anything? Besides, the clerk himself would never dare report the incident even if he suddenly remembered one day how it had all gone—he would not want to be fired. No fuss, no scenes, if you please!

But the coins felt heavy in my pocket and kept me from being calm. I started scrutinizing my feelings and found that I had been without the slightest doubt happier before, while I was walking around suffering in honor. And Ylayali! Hadn't I also dragged her down too, with my sinful hands! O God, God in heaven! Ylayali!

I was drunk as a coot, I leaped up suddenly and started toward the cake seller near the Elephant Apothecary. I could still save myself from dishonor, it was not too late, far from it, I would show the whole world what I was capable of! On the way I got the money ready, got every øre into my fist. I bent over the woman's cake board as if I wanted to buy something and suddenly put the money into her hand. I didn't say a word, I turned and left instantly.

How wonderful it felt to be an honorable man again! My empty pockets no longer weighed me down, it was a delight to me to be broke again. Examining it truly, these coins had actually cost me many a secret groan, I had thought of them again and again with shudders. I was not a hardened and damned soul, my honorable nature had risen against that sordid deed, yes it had. Thanks to God, I had raised myself in my own estimation. "Go thou and do as I have done!" I said, looking out over the crowded marketplace, simply do as I have done. I had

given a paradise of joy to a poor old woman—she didn't know right now if she was coming or going. Her children would not be climbing into bed hungry tonight. . . . I got myself all worked up with these thoughts and was sure my behavior had been really excellent. Thank God, the money was now out of my hands.

Both excited and drunk, I walked along the street, ready to do great deeds. My joy over being able to come pure and honorable to my meeting with Ylayali, and look her straight in the face, ran away with me, being half drunk anyway. I had no more pains, my head was clear and empty, it felt like a head of pure light which balanced there shining on my shoulders. I felt an urge to pull off practical jokes, to do astounding things, turn the town upside down, and roar. All the way along Grænsen Street I acted like a lunatic; I heard a faint ringing in my ears, and in my brain the alcohol was going full blast. Pushed on by foolhardiness, I got the idea of going up to a city messenger—one who had not said a word to me—and telling him my age; then I would take his hands, look him intensely in the face, and leave again without a word of explanation. I could distinguish the nuances in voices of passers-by, and in their laughter; I made note of several small birds hopping in front of me on the street, and fell to studying the expressions on the cobblestones, in which I found all sorts of omens and wonderful signs. While still at work with this, I came to the square by the Senate House.

Abruptly I stopped and stared at the row of carriages for hire. The drivers were walking around talking with each other, the horses stood bent forward against the snow. "Come along!" I said, giving myself a nudge in the ribs. I walked quickly over to the first carriage and climbed in. "Ullevaals Street, number 37!" I shouted. We rolled away.

As we drove along, the driver began to look behind and bent his head to peep into the carriage where I was sitting under the oilskin hood. Had he become suspicious? There was no question but that my miserable clothes were making him have second thoughts.

"I've got to meet this man," I shouted, forestalling his question, and I explained to him urgently that I absolutely had to meet this man.

We stopped outside number 37, I hopped out, ran up the stairs all the way to the third floor, found a bell knob and pulled. The bells inside gave six or seven frightful clangs.

A girl came and unlocked the door; I noticed that she was wearing gold-drop earrings and black cloth buttons on her bodice. She looked at me, frightened.

"I am looking for Kierulf, Joachim Kierulf, he is a wool buyer, if I might add that, not the sort of man you'd ever forget . . ."

The girl shook her head.

"No Kierulf living here," she said.

She stared at me and took hold of the door, ready to close it again. She made no effort to help—she looked actually as if she knew the person I was asking for, if she would only make the effort, the lazy thing. I got angry, turned my back on her, and ran back down the stairs. "He wasn't there!" I cried to the driver.

"He wasn't there?"

"No. Drive to Tomte Street, number 11."

I was in a wild state of mind and communicated something of that to the driver; he was convinced it was a matter of life and death and drove off without a word. He used his whip on the horses.

"What is the man's name?" he asked, turning on his seat.

"Kierulf, the wool buyer, Kierulf."

The driver agreed that no one could make a mistake about this man. Didn't he usually wear a light-colored coat?

"What was that?" I shouted. "Light-colored coat? Are you out of your mind? What do you think I'm looking for, a teacup?" This light-colored coat displeased me and spoiled my image of the man.

"What was the name you said—Kierulf?"

"Yes, that's it," I said. "Is there anything wrong with that? That name is no disgrace."

"Doesn't he have red hair?"

It was very likely that he did have red hair, and as soon as the driver mentioned it, I was certain he was right. I felt grateful to the poor old driver and told him that he had hit the thing right on the nose—the man was exactly as he said he was. As a matter of fact, I said, it would be an extremely rare thing if a man like that did *not* have red hair.

"I've had him in my cab then several times," the driver said. "He had a knobby stick with him too."

This made the man stand out vividly to me, and I said, "Ha, yes, the truth is, no one has *ever* seen this man *without* that knobby stick in his hand! You can be positive of that, absolutely positive."

Yes, there was no question, it was the same man that he had driven before. He recognized him. . . .

We drove so that the horse's shoes threw sparks.

Even in my highly worked-up state, I never lost for a moment my presence of mind. We drove past a policeman, and I took note that his badge was number 69. This figure struck me as gruesomely exact, in an instant it was driven like a sliver into my brain. 69, precisely 69, I would never forget that!

I leaned back in the carriage, a prey to the maddest impulses, crept down under the oilskin hood so that no one would see me moving my mouth, and let myself go, chattering idiotically with myself. Insanity flooded through my brain again

KNUT HAMSUN

and I let it come, fully aware throughout of being under the influence of powers I could not control. I started to laugh, silently and passionately, for no reason whatever, still giddy and drunk from the two glasses of beer I had had. Shortly afterwards, my brilliant excitement started to fade, I became more and more calm. My sore finger felt cold, and I put it between my neck and collar to warm it a little. Finally we came to Tomte Street. The cab stopped.

I climbed out slowly, absent-mindedly, depressed, my head heavy. I walked in through the street door, found a court-yard, which I crossed, then I pushed against a door, which opened. I went through and found myself in a hallway, a sort of anteroom, with two windows. Two chests stood, one on top of the other, in a corner, and against the long wall an old painted settee with a rug spread over the seat. To the right, in the next room, I could hear voices and cries of children, and over me in the second story the sound of someone hammering on an iron plate. I took all this in as soon as I entered.

I walked calmly through the room, to the door in the opposite wall, without hurry or thought of escape, opened it also, and found myself in Vognmands Street. I looked up over the door of the house I had just left, and read: *Food and Lodging for Travelers.*

I had not walked through the house in order to escape from the driver who was waiting for me. I walked very soberly along Vognmands Street with no fear and no sense of having done anything wrong. Kierulf, this wool buyer who had been haunting my brain, this person whom I felt positive existed, whom it was essential I find, was gone from my con-sciousness, whisked away together with other mad notions that came and went in turn. I recalled him now only as a faint sensation, a memory.

I sobered up more and more as I walked, felt fatigued and listless, and pulled my feet along. Snow was still falling in huge wet flakes. Finally I ended up on Grønland Street, near the church, where I sat on a bench to rest awhile. Everyone walking by looked at me in astonishment I was thinking.

My good God, what a situation I am in now! I was so deeply sick and tired of my whole miserable life that it wasn't worth fighting any longer to keep it. Circumstances had won, they had been too harsh. I was completely worn down, just a shadow of my old self. My shoul-ders had a serious slump in them from favoring my one side, and I had gotten the habit of leaning over when I walked in order to spare my chest a little. I had examined my body a couple of days ago one noon up in my room, and I cried the whole time over it. I had worn the same shirt for many weeks now, it was still from old sweat, and it had rubbed the point of my navel raw. A little blood water came out of the wound; even though there was no pain, it was pitiful to have this sore place in the middle of my stomach. There was nothing to do about it, and it wouldn't heal by itself this way; I had washed it, dried it care-fully, and put the same shirt on again. Nothing else to do. . . .

I sat on the bench thinking all this over, feeling sad; I was disgusted at myself; even my hands looked revolting to me. The flabby and shameless expres-sion on the back of my hands pained me, brought me disgust. Looking at my emaciated fingers, I felt a nausea move in me, I hated my whole sagging body, and I shuddered having to carry it, to feel it around me. God, if the whole thing would only end now! I sincerely wanted to die.

Completely defeated, lowered in my own estimation, sullied, I got up me-chanically and started to walk home. O

the way I passed a house on which I saw these words engraved: "Shrouds available, Miss Andersen, Main Entrance, to the right." "Old memories!" I said, remembering my earlier room on Hammersborg Street, the tiny rocking chair, the newsprint wallpaper down by the door, the Chief of Lighthouses' announcement, Fabian Olsen the Baker's freshly baked bread. Yes, I was so much better off in those days than now—one night I had written a piece worth ten kroner, now I couldn't write anything any more. I could not write a single thing now, my head became instantly empty as soon as I tried. It was time to end the whole business now! I kept on walking.

As I got nearer and nearer to the grocery store, I had the vague sense of approaching danger, but I held firm to my resolve: I was going to turn myself in. I walked calmly up the steps, meeting in the door a small girl who had a cup in her hand: I let her go past and closed the door. The clerk and I once more stood face to face alone.

"Well," he said, "it's dreadful weather."

What was he leading up to? Why didn't he just grab me at once? I became angry and said, "I did not come here to chatter about the weather."

The violence of it flabbergasted him. His little grocer-brain misfired; it had never really occurred to him that I had cheated him of five kroner.

"Don't you know that I robbed you?" I said impatiently, breathing heavily, shivering, and all set to use force if he refused to come to the point instantly.

But the poor creature had no idea of anything.

God in heaven, what stupid people one has to live with! I scolded him firmly, explained to him point by point exactly how it had all taken place, acted out for him where I stood and where he stood

when he was giving change, where the money lay, how I had gathered it up in my hand and closed my fist around it— he understood it now, but he still took no action. He turned his head this way and that, listened for footsteps in the next room, put his finger to his lips to get me to talk lower, and at the end said, "That was not a pretty thing to do!"

"No, no, wait a minute!" I cried, feeling a desperate need to contradict him and egg him on. It wasn't really as low and shoddy as he thought with his miserable grocer-brain. I did not *keep* the money, of course, that had never occurred to me. I had wanted no good whatever out of it for myself, my honorable temperament would never have allowed that. . . .

"What did you do with it?"

I gave it away to an old and poor woman, every øre, if he wanted to know; that was the sort of person I was, I never forgot the poor, no matter. . . .

He stood thinking this over a little and became obviously very unsure whether I was an honest man or not. Finally he said, "Don't you think you should have returned the money instead?"

"All right, listen now," I said, arrogantly. "I didn't want to bring any unpleasantness on you, I wanted to spare you. But that is the thanks one gets for being generous. I've been standing here explaining the whole thing to you, and you feel no more shame than a dog, and don't make a single move to settle what is between us. Therefore I am washing my hands of you. You can go to hell. Goodbye!"

I walked out, slamming the door after me.

But when I was home in my room, in my pitiful hole, soaked through from the wet snow, and my knees shivering from the day's exertions, my arrogant mood vanished, and I collapsed again into depression. I regretted my attack on the poor clerk, wept, grabbed hold of my throat to punish myself for my low trick, and made an enormous racket. The clerk had naturally been in terror of losing his job, had not dared to make a fuss over the five kroner the store had lost. And I had taken advantage of his fear, had tortured him with my loud talking, impaled him with every word I had shouted out. The manager himself was probably sitting in the back room about to come out at any moment and see what was going on. No, there was no limit any longer to the disgusting things I was capable of!

But why then hadn't I been locked up? That would have concluded the whole thing. I had as much as reached my wrists out for the handcuffs. I would not have offered the slightest resistance. On the contrary, I would have helped the officer. Oh, God of heaven and of earth, I would give a whole day of my life for one happy second now! My entire life for a mess of pottage! Hear me this once only! . . .

I went to bed in my wet clothes. I had a dim feeling that I would probably die during the night, and I used my last energy to smooth up my bed a little so it would look decent around me in the morning. I folded my hands and chose a good position.

Suddenly I remembered Ylayali. To think that I had forgotten her all night! Some light penetrated very weakly into my consciousness again, a tiny ray of sunlight, making me ecstatically warm. More sunlight flowed in, a gentle delicate silky light, which brushed so sweetly against me. Then the sun grew stronger and stronger, blazing brilliantly on my temples, piercing with heavy and burning heat into my emaciated brain. At the end a mad open fire blazed up before my eyes, a heaven and an earth ignited, men and animals of fire, mountains of fire, devils of fire, a chaos, a wilderness, a universe on fire, a smoking final day.

I saw and heard no more. . . .

The next morning I woke sweating, my whole body damp—my fever had gone up considerably. In the beginning I wasn't clear in my mind what was happening to me, I looked around me astonished, felt my being had somehow entirely changed, did not recognize myself. I felt over my arms and down over my legs, could not get over the fact the window was on one wall and not on the wall exactly opposite, and I heard the stamping of the horses downstairs as if they came from overhead. I was also rather nauseated.

My hair lay on my forehead wet and cold; I sat up on my elbow and looked down at the pillow: wet hair was also lying there in small tufts. My feet had swollen during the night inside my shoes; there was no pain, but I could barely move my toes.

Toward late afternoon, when it was already beginning to be dusk, I got up and started puttering about the room. I tried walking with short, deliberate steps, careful to keep my balance and spare my feet as much as I could. I was not really suffering, and I didn't cry; on the whole I wasn't even sad; I was on the contrary wonderfully at peace—the thought that anything could be any different than it was never once crossed my mind.

Finally I went out.

Only my hunger bothered me, and I felt it despite my nausea. I began to notice a shameless appetite again, a ravenous desire for food inside that grew steadily worse and worse. It gnawed without mercy in my chest, kept up a strange and silent labor in there. It was like a couple of dozen tiny creatures who put their heads over to one side and gnawed awhile, then put their heads over to the other side and gnawed awhile, lay for a moment absolutely still, started again, bored their way in without making noise or hurrying, and left behind them empty areas wherever they went. . . .

I wasn't sick, merely weak, and I started sweating again. I decided to go to the marketplace and rest there, but it was a long, tiresome walk. When I was nearly there, I stopped at the corner of Torvet Street and the marketplace. Sweat ran down in my eyes, clouded my glasses, and made me blind—I stopped to dry myself off a bit. I paid no attention to where I was standing, I didn't worry about it: the noise around me was terrific.

Suddenly I heard a cry, a cold sharp "Look out!" I heard the shout, heard it very well, and I gave a start to the side, took a step as quickly as my feeble legs would allow. A monster of a bread cart shot past me, brushing my coat with its wheel; if I had been a little quicker I would have gotten by scot-free. I could have moved a bit faster, a tiny bit faster, if I had strained myself—but there was nothing to do about it now, one foot hurt, a couple of toes had been crushed. It felt as if they had just curled up, so to speak, inside my shoe.

The driver pulled in the horses with all his might; he turned on his seat and asked in a frightened voice how I was. Oh, it could have been much worse . . . it probably wasn't so bad . . . I didn't think there was anything broken . . . I hoped not. . . .

I limped over to a bench as fast as I could; all the people who had stopped, and were now staring at me, made me self-conscious. It actually wasn't any fatal blow, I had even been lucky, considering that some catastrophe was clearly looking for me. The worst part was that my shoe had been split open; the sole was torn loose from the top. I held my foot up and saw blood in the gap. Well, this was not done intentionally by either of the parties, the driver was certainly not trying to make things worse for me than they were; he looked extremely frightened. Maybe if I had asked him for a little bread from his van I would have gotten it. He would certainly have given me some gladly. May God pay him back only with blessings, wherever he is!

I was bitterly hungry and didn't know what to do with my exorbitant appetite. I writhed about on the bench, and pulled my knees up against my chest as hard as I could. When it was dark, I shuffled over to the city jail—God knows how I got there—and sat down on the edge of the balustrade. I ripped one of my coat pockets out and started chewing on it, not for any purpose particularly, and in a hopeless mood, my eyes staring straight in front of me without seeing. I heard some small children who were playing around me, and I instinctively became alert whenever someone walked past me; otherwise, I was oblivious to the world.

All at once I got the idea of walking down to one of the open-air booths underneath and getting a piece of raw meat. I stood up, crossed the balustrade, over toward the far end of the booths, and walked down the stairs. When I was nearly down to the butcher stalls, I shouted up through the stair arch and motioned angrily backwards as if talking to a dog up there, and then spoke boldly to the first butcher I met.

"Would you be so good as to give me a bone for my dog?" I said. "Just a bone— it doesn't have to have any meat on it, just something he can carry around in his mouth."

I got a bone, a gorgeous little bone with some meat still on it, and put it under my coat. I thanked the man so warmly that he looked at me astonished.

"Nothing to thank me for," he said.

"Oh yes, there is," I said. "This was very good of you."

I walked back up. My heart thumped inside.

I sneaked into a blacksmith's yard, as far in as I could go, and stopped in front of a fallen-down gate in the back. There was not a light visible anywhere, the darkness was sweet and thick all around me; I started chewing on my bone.

It had no taste at all; a nauseating odor of dried blood rose from the bone, and I started throwing up immediately, I couldn't help it. I tried again—if I could only keep it down, it would do some good; the problem was to get it to stay down there. But I vomited again. I grew angry, bit fiercely into the meat, ripped off a small piece, and swallowed it by force. That did no good either—as soon as the small pieces became warm in the stomach, up they came again. I clenched my fists madly, started crying from sheer helplessness, and gnawed like a man possessed. I cried so much that the bone became wet and messy with tears. I vomited, swore, and chewed again, cried as if my heart would break, and threw up again. Then I swore aloud and consigned all the powers of the universe to hell.

Silence. Not a person around, no lights, not a sound. I was in a wild state, I breathed heavily and audibly, and sobbed, gnashing my teeth, every time I had to abandon these bits of meat which might have satisfied my hunger. When nothing helped, no matter how hard I tried, I threw the bone against the gate, maddened by the most impotent hatred. Carried away by rage, I shouted and roared threats up to the sky, shrieked God's name hoarsely and savagely, and curled my fingers like claws. . . . I'll tell you this, you sacred Baal in the sky, you do not exist, and if you do, I'll curse you so that your heaven will start shuddering with hellfire! I'm telling you this, you know I offered myself as your servant, and you rejected me, you pushed me away, and now I turn my back on you for all eternity because you did not know your time of visitation! I'm telling you this, I know that I am going to die, and I mock you anyway, even face to face with death, you Apis in the sky! You have used force against me and you don't realize that force does not work with me. Couldn't you have seen that? Were you asleep when you made my heart and my soul? I am telling you this, all my energy and every drop of blood in me rejoices that I mock you and spit on your grace. From this hour on, I will renounce all your works and all your ways, I will exile my thoughts if they think of you again, and I will rip my lips out if they say your name once more. Now if you do exist, I will tell you my final word in life or in death, I tell you goodbye. And so I am dumb, and I turn my back on you, and I go my way. . . .

Silence.

I was trembling from excitement and exhaustion, and kept on standing in the same spot, whispering oaths and epithets, hiccuping after my long crying spell, fatigued and sluggish after my lunatic outburst of rage. Hell! All I was capable of, even deep in misery, was rhetoric and belles-lettres, it was all talk. I stood there maybe a half hour, hiccuping and whispering and holding on to the gate. Finally I heard voices, a conversation between two men who were coming into the yard. I slunk away from my spot, pulled myself along by holding on to the sides of houses, and came out into the lit streets. While I staggered on down Youngsbakken Street, my brain suddenly started off in a most peculiar direction. It struck me that the old shacks in the corner of the marketplace, the leantos holding miscellaneous stuff, and the ancient stalls with secondhand clothes were really a disgrace to the town. They destroyed the view in the market, ruined the city, ugh, tear the whole mess down! I walked along, turning over in my mind what the cost would likely be to move the Geographical Society Building, whose lovely lines always pleased me whenever I passed it, down there. Probably a moving job of that sort couldn't be done for less than seventy to seventy-two thousand kroner—a nice sum, one might say, a tidy little sum as spending money, to start with anyway. And I nodded my empty head, and agreed that it would be a tidy enough sum for spending money, to start with. My whole body was shivering, and I hiccuped deeply now and then after my long cry.

I had the sensation that there wasn't much life left in me, that I was singing the last verse. It was all one to me; my imminent death didn't bother me in the slightest—on the contrary, I went wandering on through the town, down to the wharfs, farther and farther from my room. For that matter, I could very easily have lain right down in the street and died. My pains were making me more and more callous: I felt a throbbing in my sore foot, I even had the impression the pain was moving up my whole leg; the pain, however, was never really unbearable. I had lived through worse sensations.

I arrived finally at the railway pier. There was no traffic, no noise; once in a while a person could be seen, a longshoreman or a sailor, strolling around with his hands in his pockets. I noticed a lame man who looked sharply at me as we passed. Without pausing a second, I stopped him, raised my hand to my hat, and asked whether *The Nun* had sailed yet. When I had finished saying that, I couldn't stop myself from snapping my fingers once right in his face, and saying, "Yes, by God, *The Nun!*" I had entirely forgotten *The Nun*. The thought of it must have been sleeping somewhere far

inside, I was carrying it around without being aware of it myself.

"Oh hell yes, *The Nun* is gone."

Could he possibly tell me where it had sailed to?

The man thought awhile, standing on his longer leg and holding the shorter one in the air; the shorter one hung there faintly swinging.

"No," he said. "Do you know what it took on here?"

"No," I answered.

But I had already forgotten *The Nun* anyway, and I asked the man how far it was to Holmestrand, measured in good old geographical miles.

"To Holmestrand? I would guess . . ."

"Or to Veblungsnæs?"

"What I was about to say, I would guess to Holmestrand . . ."

"Never mind, suddenly I remember it," I interrupted him again. "You wouldn't be so good as to give me a little smidgen of tobacco, just a tiny bit!"

I got the tobacco, thanked him warmly, and walked off. I didn't make use of the tobacco, just stuck it in my pocket. The man did not take his eyes off me, possibly I had awakened suspicion in some way or other. Pausing or walking, I felt that suspicious stare on me, and I didn't feel like being followed by this character. I turned around and went back to him, looked at him and said, "Welt binder."

Just that: "Welt binder." Nothing else. I looked very sternly at him as I said it, I felt I was giving him a fierce and terrible stare—it was as if I were looking at him from another world. I stood there a moment after I spoke that word. Then I plodded up toward the market square by the railway station again. The man did not utter a sound, he just kept his eyes on me.

"Welt binder?" I stopped suddenly. The truth was exactly as I had sensed it the first instant: I had met this cripple before. Up on Grænsen Street one sunny morning: I had pawned my waistcoat then. It seemed like an eternity since that day.

While I stood thinking about this—I was standing leaning against a house at the corner of Torvet and Havne Street—I suddenly gave a start and felt a longing to creep away on my hands and knees. At last I just stared ahead in dismay, and swallowed my shame, there was nothing to do about it—I was face to face with the Chief. I became shameless and took a step out from the house wall to make sure he would notice me. I did that not to awaken pity but simply to humiliate myself, to put myself in the stocks. I could easily have flopped down in the street also and invited the Chief to walk over me, step on my face. I didn't even say good evening to him.

The Chief seemed to sense that I was trying to make some signal; he slowed up a little, and I said, in order to stop him: "I should have brought something to you, but it is still not finished."

"Oh?" he answered, questioning. "You haven't got it ready yet?"

"No, I haven't got it ready."

But now tears suddenly came into my eyes because of his friendliness, and I coughed and cleared my throat sharply to stiffen myself up. The Chief brushed his nose with his thumb; he stood looking at me.

"Do you have anything to live on meanwhile?" he said.

"No," I answered, "I don't. I haven't eaten anything yet today, but . . ."

"God help us, man, that won't do— you can't walk around starving to death!" he said. And he reached at the same time for his wallet.

Now I began to feel shame, I lurched over to the house wall again, and held on to it. I stood watching the Chief poke about in his wallet, but I said nothing.

He handed me a ten-kroner bill. He didn't make any fuss about it, he just gave me ten kroner. At the same time he repeated that it wouldn't do for me to starve to death.

I stuttered out an objection and did not take the bill right away. "That was shameful of me to . . . This is much too much. . . ."

"Oh, nonsense," he said, and looked at his watch. "I'm waiting for a train, I think I hear it coming now."

I took the money, was paralyzed with joy, and didn't say another word, I didn't even thank him.

"It's not worth being embarrassed about," the Chief said at last. "Besides, you can always write for it, I know that."

Then he left.

When he was a few steps away, I remembered all at once that I had not thanked him for his help. I tried to catch up to him but couldn't go fast enough, my leg didn't work right and I nearly fell on my face several times. He got farther and farther away. I gave up the chase, thought of shouting after him but didn't dare, and when I finally did decide to do it and called once, then twice, he was already too far off, my voice had grown too weak.

I stood there on the sidewalk looking after him, weeping silently. "I never saw such a thing!" I said to myself. "He gave me ten kroner!" I walked back and stood right where he had stood and acted out all his movements. Then I held the bill up to my wet eyes, inspected it on both sides, and started to swear—swore to high heaven that there was absolutely no question about it: I was holding a ten-kroner bill in my hand.

Sometime later—perhaps considerably later, for the city had become very quiet by this time—I found myself standing, strangely enough, outside 11 Tomte Street. This is where I had cheated a cabbie who had driven me once, and where I had walked straight through the house without having been noticed. I collected myself for a moment and wondered about it all, and then walked in through the door for the second time, right into the *Food and Lodging for Travelers*.

Here I inquired about a place to stay and immediately got a room.

Tuesday.

Sunlight, no wind, a wonderfully clear day. The snow was gone; everywhere life and happiness and glad faces, smiles and laughter. The columns of water arched up over the fountains, turned gold from the sunlight and deep blue from the blue sky. . . .

About two in the afternoon I left my room on Tomte Street where I was still living very comfortably on the Chief's ten-kroner note, and went out. I was in the highest spirits and wandered around all afternoon in the busiest streets I could find, looking at people. Even before the clock showed seven in the evening, I made a swing up to St. Olaf's Place and took a furtive look up at the windows of number 2. In one hour I would see her! I walked around in a sweet, delightful anxiety the whole time. What would happen? What would I find to say when she came down the stairs? Good evening? Or should I just smile? I decided to let it go with just a smile. Of course I would bow very deeply also.

I sneaked off again, a little ashamed of being there so early, strolled along Karl Johan Street awhile, keeping my eye on the university clock. When it was eight, I started up University Street. On the way it occurred to me that I would maybe be a minute or two late, and I pushed on as fast as I could. My foot was rather painful, otherwise I was in good spirits.

I took up my position by the fountain and caught my breath. I stood there quite a while looking at the windows in number 2, but she didn't come. Well, I would wait awhile anyway, I was in no hurry; perhaps something was keeping her. I waited some more. Surely I hadn't dreamed the whole thing? The first meeting—had that been all a fantasy the night I was in bed, feverish? I began to cast about wildly and was not absolutely positive either way.

"Hmmm!" came from behind me.

I heard this slight clearing of the throat, and I heard light steps nearby, but I didn't turn around, I kept on staring at the stairway inside the house.

"Good evening!" I heard then.

I was so astounded to see her coming from that direction that I forgot to smile, I didn't even take off my hat right away.

"Have you been waiting long?" she said, breathing a little rapidly after her walk.

"No, not at all, I just came a moment ago," I answered. "But nothing lost if I had. Do you know, I was positive that you would be coming from the other direction?"

"I walked with Mama to some friends' house—Mama is visiting them tonight."

"I see!" I said.

We had started walking now. A policeman stood on the street corner watching us.

"But where are we going then?" she said, stopping.

"Wherever you want to, wherever you'd like to go."

"Oh, having to decide yourself is so boring."

Pause.

Then I said, just to have something to say, "Your windows are dark, I see."

"Yes!" she answered, gaily. "The servant girl is off tonight too. So I am home all alone."

We both stood looking up at the windows of number 2 as if neither of us had ever seen them before.

"Shall we go up to your place then?" I said. "I'll sit quietly by the door, like a mouse, if you want me to. . . ."

But then I shivered and regretted intensely being so bold. What if she became offended and walked away? What if I would never get to see her again? And my miserable clothes! I waited, frightened, for her answer.

"You certainly won't sit down by the door," she said.

We went up.

Out in the corridor, which was dark, she took my hand and led me. I didn't have to be so quiet, she told me, I could certainly talk if I wanted to. We walked in. While she lit a candle—she didn't light a lamp, but a candle—while she lit the candle, she said with a tiny laugh: "You mustn't look at me, ugh, I am ashamed of myself! But I will never do it again."

"What won't you ever do again?"

"I'll never . . . no, such a . . . I'll never kiss you again."

"Oh, really, won't you?" I said, and we both laughed. I reached for her, and she glided to the side, slipped away 'to the other side of the table. We stood looking at each other a little while, the candle standing between us.

Then she started to take off her veil, and her hat, but all the time she kept her playful eyes on me, watching all my movements so I wouldn't be able to catch her. I made one more try, tripped on the carpet, and fell: my sore foot didn't want to work. I got up extremely embarrassed.

"Good Lord, how you are blushing!" she said. "Do you feel as clumsy as all that?"

"Yes."

Then we started again, running around the table.

"Aren't you limping?"

"I'm limping a little, it doesn't amount to anything."

"The last time you had a sore finger, today you have a sore foot. It's awful, the number of troubles you have!"

"Someone ran over me slightly the other day."

"Ran over? So, drunk again? Your living habits are a disgrace, young man!" She scolded me with her forefinger, and looked grave. "Now we'll sit down!" she said. "No, not over there by the door: you are too shy, over here, you there, and I here, like that. . . . Oh, shy people are such a bore! You, for example, you might have put your hand on the back of my chair, you could certainly have thought that up by yourself, couldn't you? Because if I suggest anything of that sort, you immediately turn two huge saucer eyes at me as if to say you don't really believe your ears. Yes, you do, I've seen it several times already, you are doing it now too. But don't try to get me to believe you are modest like that all the time—I know what you are like. You were awfully fresh that day when you were drunk and followed me nearly home, pestering me with your witticisms: 'You are losing your book, miss, really honestly, you are losing your book, miss!' Aa-ha-ha! That was frightful of you!"

I sat fascinated looking at her. My heart beat wildly, blood was racing through my veins. What a marvelous sensation to be sitting in a human house again and to hear a clock tick, and to talk with a spirited young girl instead of with myself!

"Why don't you say anything?"

"Oh, what a sweet creature you are!" I said. "I am sitting here in love with you, right now I am your captive entirely. There is nothing to do about it. You are the strangest person. . . . Sometimes your eyes shine so, I've never seen anything like it, they look like flowers. No?

No, no, maybe not like flowers, but . . . I am head over heels in love with you, and it won't do me a bit of good. What is your name? You really have to tell me now what your name is. . . ."

"Mine, no, what is your name? Good Lord, here I have nearly gone and forgotten it again! All day yesterday I thought to myself that I must ask you. Well, I can't say *all* day yesterday. I certainly did not think about you *all* day."

"Do you know what my name for you was? I called you Ylayali, what do you think of that? A wonderful, flowing sound. . . ."

"Ylayali?"

"Yes."

"Is that a foreign language?"

"Hmmm. No, no."

"Well, it isn't really ugly."

After long negotiations, we told each other our names. She sat down beside me on the sofa and pushed the chair away with her foot. We started chattering again.

"You've had a shave tonight too," she said. "You look on the whole a little better than you did last time, but only just a teeny bit better—I wouldn't want you to think. . . . No, last time you were really awful. On top of it all, you went around with an old rag on your finger. And in that condition you were absolutely determined to take me in for a glass of wine! No, thank you!"

"Then it was because I looked so bad that you refused to go in with me that time?" I said.

"No," she answered, looking down. "No, God help me, that wasn't it! I didn't even think about that at the time."

"Well," I said, "I'm afraid you're sitting here under the mistaken assumption that I can dress and live exactly as I want to, aren't you? But I can't do it, I am poor, very poor."

She looked at me.

"Is that so?" she said.

"Yes, I'm afraid it is."

Pause.

"Good gracious, I am poor myself," she said, with a bold toss of her head.

Every one of her words made me drunk, went straight to my head like sips of wine, despite the fact that she was more or less the usual kind of Christiania girl, with her slang and daring little sallies and snappy talk. Yet she delighted me with the way she had of letting her head fall a little to one side as she listened to me talk. I felt her breath too, so close to my face.

"Do you know?" I said. "You mustn't be angry now . . . when I was in bed last night I arranged my arm just so . . . like that . . . as if you were lying in it. That is the way I went to sleep."

"Really! That was lovely!" Pause. "Of course there had to be a lot of distance between us before you could do something like that, because if there hadn't been . . ."

"You think that otherwise I wouldn't have done it?"

"That's right, I don't think you would have."

"You should prepare for anything from me," I said, "and everything." I drew myself up and put my arm around her waist.

"Oh, should I do that?" was all she said.

It irritated me that she thought I was too timid and respectable. I threw out my chest, took the leap, and closed my hand over hers. She, however, withdrew it very quietly and moved a little way away. That finished off my courage; I felt ashamed and looked over toward the window. My situation was so humble that I had to be careful not to put on airs. It would have been a different matter altogether if I had met her while I still looked like a man, in my prosperous days when I still had a few reserves. I felt dejected and depressed.

"There you see!" she said. "That's a perfect example. A person can bring you down with just a tiny wrinkle in the forehead, demolish you just by moving away a few inches. . . ." She laughed mischievously, her eyes entirely closed, as if she really couldn't bear to be looked at.

"Oh, you little fox!" I burst out. "All right, you'll see then." And I threw my arms firmly around her shoulders. Girl at a distance, beware! So she took me for an inexperienced boy. By the Lord, she would change her tune. . . . No one should say about me that I couldn't keep up in *this* game. By the living Jesus, if all I had to do was to stay with it . . .

As though there were anything in this world I couldn't do!

She sat quietly all this time, with her eyes still closed: neither of us spoke; I pressed her hard against me, crushed her body against my chest, and she did not say a word. I could hear our heartbeats, hers and mine, they sounded like horses stamping.

I kissed her.

I didn't know what I was doing any longer, I said some nonsense that she laughed at, mumbled sweet names at her lips, brushed her cheek, kissed her again and again. I opened a button or two in her bodice and glimpsed her breasts, white, swelling breasts that peeked out like two marvels behind her lace.

"I have to see!" I said, and struggled with several more buttons, trying to make the opening larger. But my efforts were too rough, I couldn't make any headway with the last few buttons near her waist which were tight anyway. "But I have to see . . . a little more. . . ."

She threw her arms around my neck, very slowly and tenderly; from her nostrils that were rosy and trembling I could feel her breath right against my face. With one hand she began to undo the buttons herself, one after the other. She laughed self-consciously, a short laugh, looking up at me several times to see if I noticed how frightened she was. She loosened the ties, unhooked the corset over her breasts, was excited and afraid. And I fumbled with my coarse hands among these buttons and hooks. . . .

In order to divert attention, she ran her left hand over my shoulder and said, "You have so many loose hairs lying here!"

"Yes," I said, and tried to press my mouth in toward one of her breasts. At this moment her clothes were entirely open. All at once she seemed to think better of it, she seemed to feel she had gone too far. She pulled her clothes back together and sat up a little. So as to hide her shyness over the unbuttoned clothes, she started talking again about all the fallen hair which lay on the shoulders of my coat.

"What can have made all that hair fall out?"

"Don't know that."

"You drink too much, of course, and maybe even . . . No, I won't even say it! You should be ashamed of yourself! I would never have thought that of you! To think of you so young and already losing your hair! . . . Now, if you please, I want you to describe how you live—what you really do. I'm sure your habits are frightful! But only the truth now, you understand, no covering up! I'll be able to tell anyway when you are trying to hide something. All right, tell me now!"

Oh, how tired I was! I would have been so glad just to sit there quietly looking at her rather than to embark on such labors. I was no good for anything, I was just a block of wood.

"All right, start now!" she said.

I took the opportunity and I told her everything, telling nothing but the truth. I didn't make anything worse than it was,

I wasn't trying to make her pity me—I even told her about my stealing five kroner one night.

She sat listening to me with open mouth, pale and frightened, her clear eyes deeply troubled. I tried to repair it again, to lift the gloom that had settled in the room. I straightened up and said, "Oh well, that is all over now! No use talking about that any longer, I'm over the hump now, I'm safe. . . ."

But she was still depressed. "Oh, my God!" was all she said, and then she would be quiet. She would wait a minute and then say it again and once more lapse into silence. "Oh, my God!"

I began to joke, took hold of her to tickle her, lifted her to my chest. She had buttoned her dress again, and that annoyed me. Why should she have buttoned her dress again? Was I of less value in her eyes now than if I had earned my fallen hair by leading a corrupt life? Would she have thought more of me if I had been a roué? . . . No nonsense now! All that was required of me was to follow through— And if that was all that was required, I was just the man for it.

I had to start again.

I pulled her over, simply drew her down on the sofa. She struggled, not very much, and looked at me astonished.

"No . . . what is it?" she said.

"What is it?"

"No . . . no, no . . . ?"

"Yes, yes. . . ."

"No, listen!" she cried. Then she added a wounding sentence. "Sometimes I think you are insane."

I felt checked a little suddenly, and I said, "You don't mean that!"

"Yes, you look so strange! And that morning when you were following me— you weren't drunk then?"

"No. But on the other hand I wasn't starving either—I had just eaten."

"That's even worse then."

"Would you prefer me to have been drunk?"

"Yes . . . oh, I am afraid of you! Oh God, can't you just let me go!"

I thought about that. No, I couldn't let her go, I would lose too much that way. No hanky-panky foolishness this time of the night on a sofa! Good Lord, what excuses women can think up at a time like this! As if I didn't know it was all nothing but bashfulness, modesty! I must be firm, then! Come now, be good! No more nonsense!

She struggled rather hard, too hard to be struggling only from modesty. I knocked the candle over accidentally, so it went out. She made desperate opposition, and even gave out a little whimper.

"No, don't! Don't! You can kiss me on my breast if you want to instead. My sweet thing!"

I stopped instantly. She sounded so dismayed, so helpless, that I felt a blow inside. She was offering me a compensation by giving me permission to kiss her breast! How lovely, how lovely and how naïve! I could have fallen on my knees before her.

"You darling!" I said, utterly confused. "I don't understand this. . . . I don't really grasp which game all this is. . . ."

She got up and lit the candle again with shaking hands. I sat there on the sofa, my mind blank. What would happen now? I was very ill at ease.

She glanced at the wall where the clock was, and gave a start.

"Oh dear, the girl will be home soon!" she said. These were the first words she had said since we sat up.

I understood this hint and stood. She reached for her cape as if to put it on, then thought better of it, let it lie, and walked over to the fireplace. She was pale and became more and more nervous. So that it shouldn't look as if she were just showing me out, I said, "Was your father in the army?" and at the same time I got ready to leave.

"Yes, he was. How did you know that?"

"I didn't know it, it just suddenly occurred to me."

"That was strange!"

"Yes, I suppose. When I come into certain places, I can sense things. That's all part of my insanity. . . ."

She looked up quickly but said nothing. I felt my presence was painful to her, and wanted to make my farewell short. I walked to the door. Would she kiss me again now? Or even let me take her hand? I waited.

"Are you going now?" she said, still standing by the fireplace.

I didn't answer. I felt humbled and bewildered and looked at her without saying anything. God, what I had destroyed! It didn't seem to bother her that I was ready to go; she was lost to me once and for all, and I searched for some way to tell her goodbye, some deep, heavy words that would get through to her and maybe impress her a little. Then I behaved exactly opposite to the way I had intended: I acted wounded instead of being proud and cold; disturbed and insulted, I started to chatter on about trivialities. The telling words refused to come, I was carrying on like a numbskull. Everything became drivel and rhetoric again.

Why hadn't she just told me simply and clearly to leave? I asked. Well, well, why not? There was no reason to be so polite. Instead of reminding me that the girl would soon be coming back, she could simply have said this: You must leave now, because I must go over and fetch my mother, and I'd rather not have you escort me down the street. Now, wasn't that what she was thinking? Oh yes, that is what she was thinking any-

way, I understood it right away. It didn't need much to make me understand— simply the way she reached for her cape and then left it where it was had shown me immediately. As I said, I sensed a lot of things. Perhaps that wasn't really so insane as it seemed. . . .

"Oh my God, forgive me for that word! It just popped out!" she cried. But she stood where she' was and still did not come over to me.

I was unrelenting, and went on. I stood there jabbering, all the time with the painful sensation that I was boring her, that not a single one of my words had really penetrated. Nevertheless, I couldn't stop. Actually, in my opinion, a man didn't have to be insane to be sensitive. There were people who could be wounded by trifles and whom a single hard word would kill. I gave her to understand that I was that sort of person. My poverty in fact had actually sharpened some of my faculties and so had increased my sufferings too, that's right, increased my sufferings. Of course that sharpening had its good side as well, it was a help in certain situations. The intelligent poor man of course is a much finer observer than the intelligent rich man. The poor man has to look carefully around him every time he takes a step, he wisely mistrusts every word he hears from others; for him the simplest acts involve obstacles and problems. His senses are sharp, he is a man of feeling, he has experienced painful things, his soul has been burned and scarred. . . .

And I went on a long time about these scars on my soul. But the longer I talked, the more upset she became; finally she blurted out, "Oh my God!" a couple of times in despair, wringing her hands. I could see I was torturing her; I didn't want to torture her, but I kept on doing it anyway. At last I felt most of what needed saying had been said; the look of despair on her face moved me, and I shouted:

"All right, I'm leaving, I'm leaving! Don't you see I already have my hand on the doorknob? Goodbye! I am saying goodbye! You could at least answer me when I say goodbye two times, and am standing here ready to leave. I won't even ask you to let me see you again, because I know that would be painful to you, but I want you to answer me this: Why didn't you let me be? What did I ever do to you? I wasn't really bothering you, was I? And why were you suddenly cold to me as if you didn't know me any more? Now you've taken everything I had left, I'm worse off now than I was before. But so help me God, I'm not insane. You'll realize now if you think about it that there is nothing wrong with me. Come here then and give me your hand! Or let me come over to you! May I do that? I won't do anything bad, I will just kneel in front of you one minute, kneel there on the floor in front of you, just one moment—may I? No, no, all right, I won't do it, I can see you're frightened, I won't, listen, I *won't* do it. But, my God, why are you so terrified? I'm standing still, I'm not moving a muscle. I wanted to kneel on the carpet a moment, right there, on that big red patch by your foot. But you became frightened, I could see instantly in your eyes that you were afraid, so I stood still. I didn't move an inch while I was asking you if I could do it, did I? I was just as motionless then, when I showed you the spot where I wanted to kneel, there on that red rose in the carpet, as I am now. I didn't even point with my finger, I didn't point at all, I let it go so as not to scare you, I just nodded over in that direction, like this! And you understood very well which rose I meant, but you won't allow me to kneel there—you're afraid of me, and you don't dare come near me. I don't understand, though, how you could let

yourself call me insane. That is not true, and you don't believe it yourself any longer, do you? One summer, a long time ago, I did go crazy—I was working too hard and I forgot to eat as I should have. My mind was full of ideas. I forgot day after day—I ought to have remembered to eat, but I constantly forgot. So help me God, it is the truth! May God strike me down right here if I am lying! There, you can see, you are being unjust with me. And I didn't do it from having no money—I had credit, my credit was excellent, at both Ingebret's Grocery and Gravesen's. I often had a lot of money in my pockets, and yet I never bought food —simply because I forgot to. It's really the truth! You don't say anything, you never answer, you never leave your spot at the fireplace, you're just waiting for me to go. . . ."

She came swiftly to me and reached out her hand. I looked very mistrustfully at her. Was she really doing that spontaneously? Or was she doing it just to get rid of me? She put her arms around my neck, there were tears in her eyes. I just stood looking at her. She reached up her lips to me; I couldn't believe her, this was only a sacrifice, a way to get it all over with.

She said something which sounded to me like "I love you anyway!" She said it so softly and inaudibly that perhaps I didn't hear quite right, maybe she didn't say exactly those words, but she threw her arms passionately around my neck, she kept both arms around my neck, even raised herself on tiptoe to be taller and remained on tiptoe a little while.

I was afraid she had forced herself to show me this affection, and all I said was "How beautiful you are now!"

That was all I said. I stepped back, bumped the door with my shoulder, and walked out backwards. And she stayed where she was.

PART FOUR

WINTER HAD COME, a raw wet winter almost without snow, a foggy and dark night that went on forever; for a whole week there would be no break in the fog. The street lamps burned almost all day, and people bumped each other anyway in the fog. The city sounds, the chimes from the church steeples, harness bells on the horses, voices of people, hoof clatter, all came through the thick air sounding muffled and underground. Week after week went by and the weather remained exactly the same.

I still had my room in the Vaterland district.

I became more and more attached to this *Food and Lodging for Travelers;* I was still living there even though I was now broke again. My money had long since been used up, but I continued to come and go in the house as if I had some right to it and belonged there. The landlady had not said a word so far, but my not being able to pay her worried me. Three weeks went by this way.

For several days now I had been writing again, but I wasn't able to do anything that satisfied me any more—I was simply under a cloud, even though I worked and slaved night and day. No matter what I tried, it was no use, my luck was gone.

A room on the second floor, the best guest room in the house, was where I was laboring away. I had been undisturbed up there since that first night when I had had plenty of money and could pay. I kept hoping, of course, the whole time that I would finish one of my articles and then be able to pay my room bill and whatever else I owed. That was why I was working so doggedly. I had one piece in particular I had started on and expected great things from, an allegory about a fire in a bookstore, a profound idea on which I intended to expend all my industry, finish it and bring it to the Chief in order to pay him back. The Chief would discover that this time he had really helped a person of talent; I hadn't the slightest doubt he would come to that conclusion; all I had to do was wait for the inspiration. And why shouldn't the inspiration come over me at any moment? My health was better now; I got a little food every day from the landlady, some bread and butter morning and evening, and my nervous state had almost disappeared. I no longer covered my hands when I wrote and I could look down into the street from my second-story window without becoming dizzy. I was much better in every way, and therefore I was a little surprised that I hadn't already finished my allegory. I didn't understand what the trouble was.

One day I got a glimpse of how weak I had really become, and how sluggish and incompetent my brain was. My landlady came up to my room with a bill which she asked me to look at—there must be something wrong with the addition, she said, her own accounts showed a different figure, but she could not find the error.

I sat down to add it up; my landlady sat facing me and watched. I added up the twenty or so numbers, first down, getting the same figure already there, and then up, and got the same result a second time. I looked at her; she was sitting waiting for my conclusion. As I glanced at her, it struck me that she was pregnant—that was clear to me, even though I hadn't looked at her for more than an instant.

"It's added correctly," I said.

"Would you check the entries then," she answered. "It can't be so much—I'm positive of it."

So I began to check every entry: 2 loaves of bread at 25 øre; 1 lamp glass,

18; soap, 20; butter, 32. . . . No particularly brilliant head was needed to go through these sums, this little uncomplicated grocery bill, and I tried hard to find the error she mentioned, but could not. After I had been grappling with these figures a couple of minutes, I felt them starting to dance around in my brain—I no longer made any distinction between debit and credit. I mixed them all up in one. Finally I came to a grinding halt at the following entry: $3\frac{5}{16}$ pound of cheese @ 16. My brain went click, and I stared dumfounded at the cheese, unable to go on.

"This is awfully squiggly handwriting!" I said in despair. "And right here someone has written, so help me God, five-sixteenths of a cheese. Who ever heard of anything like that—look here, you can see for yourself!"

"Oh yes," the landlady answered, "it's always written that way. That was some caraway cheese. It's right! Five-sixteenths works out the same as five ounces. . . ."

"Yes, yes, I know that!" I broke in, though in fact I couldn't understand a thing any more.

I tried again to get through this little exercise in addition which a couple of months ago I could have done in one minute. I sweated and concentrated with all my might on these enigmatic figures, and blinked my eyes thoughtfully as though I were making a real study of the matter, but I had to give up. Those five ounces of cheese finished me—it was as though something had broken in my brain.

However, to make it look as though I were still working on the bill, I moved my lips and now and then spoke some number aloud, and I moved my finger lower and lower in the column, as if I were making progress and would soon come to a decision. My landlady sat waiting. Finally I said, "I've gone over the whole thing from beginning to end and

there is no mistake here, so far as I can see."

"You don't think so?" answered the woman. "No mistake?" But I saw clearly that she didn't believe me. And it suddenly seemed to me I noticed a faint tone of contempt in her speech, a note of indifference which I had not heard in her voice before. She said that I perhaps wasn't used to sixteenths; she said also that she would have to take the bill to someone more used to such work to get it really checked. She didn't say all of this in a wounding tone, to make me feel ashamed, but in a thoughtful and serious tone. When she got to the door and was about to leave, she said, without turning around, "Excuse me for having interrupted your work!"

She left.

Shortly after, she opened the door once more and walked in again—she must have gone no farther than the stairs before turning around.

"The truth is the truth," she said, "and you mustn't take it wrong, but don't you owe me something on your bill? You came, I think, three weeks ago yesterday? Wasn't that it? Making ends meet with a large family is not easy, so I can't let anyone live here on credit, I'm very sorry. . . ."

I stopped her.

"I'm working on an article, as I mentioned to you before," I said, "and as soon as it is done, I will pay you everything I owe. You don't have to worry about that."

"Yes, but suppose you never finish that article?"

"I will. The right mood may come tomorrow morning, or even tonight yet—it's not at all impossible that the inspiration for it will come this evening, and then my article will be all done in a quarter of an hour at the most. You understand, with my work it's very different than with other people's—I can't just sit down and do so much every day. I have to wait for the right moment. And nobody can tell in what hour or day the inspiration will come! It has its own time."

My landlady left. But her confidence in me was clearly very shaken.

As soon as I was alone, I leaped up and started tearing my hair in despair. No, nothing would do any good for me, there was no salvation! My brain was bankrupt! Had I become completely a moron now since I couldn't even figure out the price of a piece of caraway cheese? But, on the other hand, could I ask myself questions like this if I were entirely witless? And besides all that, didn't I see, as clear as day, while I was struggling with the bill, that my landlady was pregnant? I had no way of knowing that fact, no one had mentioned anything about it, it hadn't occurred to me by association either, I was simply sitting there and saw it, and I understood it immediately, in the very same moments I was battling hopelessly with the sixteenths. How was I to explain that?

I walked to the window and looked out; my window faced on Vognmands Street. Some children were playing below on the cobblestones—poorly dressed children in the middle of a poor street. They were throwing an empty bottle from one to another with shrieks. A moving van rolled slowly by them—it must be an evicted family, since they were not moving at either of the two usual moving dates. That thought occurred to me the instant I looked. On the van there were bedclothes and furniture, worm-eaten bedsteads and dressers, chairs with three legs, painted red, rugs, ironworks, tin pans. A small girl, very young, an ugly child with a runny nose, was sitting on top of the load, holding on tight with her poor blue hands to keep from falling off. She sat on top of a bundle of frightful, stained mattresses

that had been slept on by children, and looked down at the children throwing the empty bottle around. . . .

I stood watching all this and hadn't the slightest difficulty grasping what was going on. While I stood at the window taking this in, I also heard my landlady's hired girl singing in the kitchen, which was not far from my room—I recognized the tune, and I listened to see if she would make a mistake. I said to myself that an idiot could not have done all this, I was, thank God, in my right mind as much as anyone was.

Suddenly I saw two of the children in the street squaring off to fight, two small boys: I recognized one of them as the landlady's son. I opened the window to hear what they were saying to each other, and immediately a flock of children gathered under my window and looked up wistfully. What were they hoping for? For me to throw something down? Dried-out flowers, bones, cigar ends, something or other they could chew on or play with? They looked up at my window with their little pale-blue faces and endlessly sad eyes. Meantime, the two diminutive enemies continued to hurl words at each other. Words like huge, cold-blooded reptiles poured out of their childish lips, frightful nicknames, whore language, sailor's curses which they had probably learned down at the wharf. They were both so taken up that they didn't notice the landlady who came storming out to see what was happening.

"You should see," explained her son. "He got me in the throat—I couldn't even breathe for an hour!" Then turning to the young evildoer who was standing smiling maliciously at him, he suddenly became wild with rage and shouted, "Go to hell, you blockhead, you Egyptian snot! A snotty louse like you grabbing people's throats! By God, I swear to hell I'll . . ."

And the mother, the pregnant wife

who dominated the whole narrow street with her sheer size, said to the ten-year-old, taking hold of his arm to pull him along, "Shh! Hold your trap! Stop your swearing now! You sound as if you'd been brought up in a whorehouse! Shut up now and come in!"

"No, I won't!"

"Yes you will!"

"No, I won't!"

I stood at the window watching the mother's anger rising. This disagreeable scene had a strong effect on me, I couldn't stand it any longer, and I shouted down to the boy to come up here a minute. I shouted to him twice just to interrupt them and stop the wrangle. The last time I shouted very loud, and the mother turned and looked up at me bewildered. An instant later, she regained her control, gave me an insolent look, positively an arrogant look, and turned back to her son with a scolding remark. She talked loud enough so I could hear it, and said, "You should be ashamed of yourself, letting people see what a bad boy you are!"

I stood there taking in all this, and there was nothing, not even a single insignificant detail, that I missed. My attention was as keen as it could be, I breathed in every little thing sensitively, and thoughts occurred to me about each thing as it happened. So it was impossible that anything was wrong with my brain. How could there be anything wrong with it, in view of all this?

Listen now, I'll tell you something, I said all of a sudden, you have been going around long enough worrying about your brains, and troubling yourself about that —now let's have an end to that nonsense! Is it a mark of insanity to notice and observe details as exactly as you do? You almost make me laugh, that's the truth. There is something funny in this whole thing, there really is. Everyone fails once in a while, and they always fail precisely in the most simple problems: that doesn't mean anything, it's just chance. As I've said before, I'm just a hairbreadth away from bursting out laughing at you. About that grocery bill with its piddling five-sixteenths of rat cheese, because that's all it was—how ridiculous, a cheese with caraway seeds in it—as far as this absurd cheese is concerned, the brightest man in the world could easily stumble over that—even the smell of cheese like that is enough to finish a man off. . . . I went on mocking the cheese unmercifully. . . . "No, give me something I can eat!" I said. "Give me, if you please, five-sixteenths of a pound of good creamery butter! That's more like it!"

I laughed feverishly at my own jokes and found them extremely amusing. There was really nothing the matter with me any more, I was in good shape.

My courage rose higher as I walked back and forth in the room talking with myself; I laughed aloud and felt wildly happy. It was as if all I had needed really was this little animated interlude, this moment of clear joy without a trace of sorrow, to get my head in working order again. I sat down at the table and started pushing my allegory forward. And it went very well, better than it had for a long time. The writing didn't go fast, but I felt the little I did do was absolutely first-rate. I worked on for an hour without becoming tired.

I was at an extremely critical point now in my allegory concerning a fire in a bookstore—it struck me strongly that everything that had come before was as nothing compared to this point. I wanted to give shape now to the really deep thought that it was not the books that were burning, it was brains, human brains, and I wanted to create a pure St. Bartholomew's Day out of these burning brains. Suddenly the door was thrown open and the landlady barged in. She walked right to the center of the room, without even pausing on the threshold.

I gave a hoarse cry—it was exactly as if someone had hit me.

"What?" she said. "Did you say something? We have a new guest and we must have this room for him. You can sleep tonight in the family room downstairs— you can have a bed to yourself." And before she had heard my answer she started gathering up my papers on the desk, getting them all mixed up.

My joyful mood was gone, I felt angry and depressed and immediately got up. I let her clear the table and said nothing— I didn't speak a word. She handed all the papers to me.

There was nothing for me to do, I had to leave the room, here was another precious moment spoiled! I met the new guest on the stairway, a young man with large blue anchors tattooed on the backs of his hands. Behind him came a longshoreman with a sailor's chest on his shoulder. The guest was without doubt a seaman, perhaps just a guest for one night; he probably wouldn't occupy my room any longer than that. Maybe I would be lucky again in the morning when the man was gone and get the inspiration back again—all that was lacking now was five minutes' inspiration, and then my allegory on the bookstore fire would be done. Well, there was nothing to do, fate was fate. . . .

I had never been in the family's own part of the house before—it was just a single room where they all lived night and day—husband, wife, the wife's father, and four children. The hired girl lived in the kitchen, where she also slept at night. With considerable aversion I approached the door and knocked. No one answered, though I heard talk inside.

The husband did not say a word as I walked in, did not even answer my greet-ing—he merely glanced at me with indifference, as if he had nothing to do with me. He was sitting playing cards with a man I had seen down at the pier— a dock worker whom people called "Glassy." An infant was lying on the bed gurgling to itself, and on a wooden settee bed an old man, the landlady's father, was sitting bent over, his head lowered over his hands as though his chest or stomach were hurting him. His hair was nearly white, and in his bent-over position he looked like a lizard with its head bent to the side, listening.

"I've come down here because I need a place to sleep tonight, I'm afraid," I said to the husband.

"Did my wife send you?" he asked.

"Yes. A new man has moved into my room."

To this the husband answered nothing—he went on with his card game.

The husband sat like this, day after day, playing cards with anyone who happened to come by; he played for nothing, merely to kill time and have something to keep his hands busy. He did not do a thing otherwise and moved only so much as he had to; his wife, meanwhile, trudged up and down the stairs, ran the house, and saw to it that the rooms were filled. She had connections with various longshoremen and dock workers whom she paid a certain commission for every new customer they brought her, and she often let these dock workers stay overnight besides. Tonight it was "Glassy" who had brought in the new guest.

Two of her children came in, a couple of small girls with thin freckled urchin faces; their clothes were pitiful. Shortly afterward the landlady came in also. I asked her where she wanted to put me tonight, and she answered curtly that I could sleep here along with everyone else or out in the hall on the settee, wherever I preferred. While she talked, she moved around the room, fussing with various things which she took care of, not once looking at me.

I lost my bravado at her answer; I stood by the door and tried to look small, and acted as if I were perfectly content to change my room for another for one night. I carefully put a friendly expression on my face so as not to provoke her and perhaps be thrown out of the house completely. I said, "Oh, this'll be fine!" and then was quiet.

She bustled around in the room still.

"By the way, I'll have to remind you that I simply cannot afford to let people have board and room on credit," she said. "I've told you that before also."

"Yes, you have, but it'll only be a couple of days now before I'll have my article done," I answered. "And then I will be glad to give you an extra five-kroner piece to boot, very happy to do it."

But she quite obviously had no faith in my writing, I could see that. On the other hand, I couldn't let myself be proud and storm out of the house only because of one tiny insult—I knew very well what was waiting for me if I left.

A couple of days went by.

I was sleeping in the family room; the hall had no stove and it was too cold there. I slept at night on the floor. The seaman was still living in my room and did not appear to be moving out soon. One noon the landlady came in and said the seaman had paid her for a whole month in advance; he was going to take a first mate's examination before he shipped out; that was why he was staying in town. As I listened, I understood that my room was gone for good.

I walked out in the hall and sat down. If I were to get any writing done, I would have to do it in the hall, where it was quiet. I was no longer excited by my allegory now—I had a new idea, a really

marvelous plan: I was going to compose a one-act play, *The Sign of the Cross,* set in the Middle Ages. I had already thought out the main character thoroughly, a magnificent, fiery prostitute who had sinned right in the temple, not out of weakness or out of lust but from a sheer hatred of God, sinned right at the foot of the altar, with the altar cloth under her head, simply out of a delicious contempt for eternity.

I became more and more fascinated with this character as the afternoon went on. Finally she stood before me, living; all her characteristics stood out vividly. Her body would be deformed and repulsive; tall, extremely thin, and rather dark—and when she walked, her long legs would gleam through the fabric of her clothing at every step. She would also have large, protruding ears. In brief, she would be nothing much to look at, hardly bearable in that respect. What was wonderful about her was her marvelous lack of shame—the extra measure of deliberate and desperate sinning which she had done. She fascinated me almost too much: my brain was bulging with this rare monstrosity of a person. I wrote for two whole hours at a stretch on my play.

After I had finished ten, or perhaps twelve pages, all of which cost me considerable labor and were interrupted by wasted times when I went off on a tangent and had to tear the results up, I felt tired, almost stiff with cold and exhaustion; I stood up and went out to take a walk. For the last half hour I had been disturbed also by the children crying, so that I couldn't have written more just then anyway. I took a long walk along Drammens Street and was gone until after dark; as I walked along, I thought only of what would happen next in my play. While I was on that walk, I had this experience.

I was standing outside a shoeshop toward the bottom of Karl Johan Street, almost at the railway station market. God knows why I had stopped just outside this particular shoeshop! I was looking in through the window, though without thinking that I needed shoes; my thoughts were far off, in some other part of the world. People talking away walked past me, and nothing they said registered. Then a loud voice said, "Good evening!"

The one saying hello was Queeny.

"Good evening!" I answered in a distant way. I looked at Queeny awhile before I recognized him.

"Well, how goes it?" he asked.

"Fine, fine . . . as usual!"

"Listen," he said, "are you still at Christie's?"

"Christie's?"

"Yes, didn't you say last time that you were keeping the books for the Christie Foodstore?"

"Oh! No, that is finished. It was impossible to work with him—we separated by mutual consent."

"What happened?"

"Oh, I set down a number wrong one day. . . ."

"And he saw it, eh?"

Saw it? Queeny was implying right to my face that I had been cheating. He put in his question quickly; obviously he was very interested. I looked at him, felt deeply insulted, and did not answer.

"Oh well, Lord knows that can happen to anyone!" he said, to comfort me. He still believed that I had been fired for dishonesty.

"What is all this about Lord knows that can happen to anyone?" I asked. "Deliberately making a mistake? Do you really think I could do something as low as that? Me?"

"But, old boy, I thought sure you said . . ."

I threw my head back, turned away from Queeny, and stared down the street. My eyes fell on a red dress which was coming toward us, it was a woman walking with a man. If I hadn't just had this conversation with Queeny, and hadn't been offended by his vulgar suspicion, and made this toss of my head, this red dress would likely have gone by me without my noticing it. And what concern was it of mine anyway? Suppose it was a lady-in-waiting at the court, what was that to me?

Queeny talked on and on, trying to retrieve his error; I didn't listen to him at all, I just stood there the whole time staring at this red dress coming closer. Something moved in my chest, I felt a delicate dart of pain—I whispered to myself without moving my mouth.

"Ylayali!"

Queeny turned around now too, noticed the couple, the woman and the man, raised his hat, and followed them with his eyes. I did not raise my hat, or maybe I did raise my hat. The red dress continued on up Karl Johan Street and disappeared.

"Who was that with her?" Queeny asked.

" 'The Duke,' didn't you see him? His nickname is 'The Duke.' Do you know her?"

"Yes, a little. Don't you know her?"

"No," I answered.

"It seemed to me you tipped your hat very elaborately."

"Oh, did I?"

"So you're not sure, eh?" Queeny said. "That's strange! What's more, you were the only one she looked at the whole time."

"Where did you meet her?" I asked.

"I don't really know her well at all. The thing was, it was one evening last fall. It was late, we were three lambs out on a spree, that sort of thing—we'd just left the Grand and we saw this woman walking alone, by Cammermeyer's Bookstore, so we spoke to her. She answered very coldly at first, but one of our party, a character not afraid of hell or high water, asked her right out if he could walk her to her door to make sure she got home safely, otherwise he wouldn't be able to sleep the whole night. He chattered constantly while they were walking, made up one thing after the other, swore his name was Waldemar Atterdag and that he was a photographer. Finally she herself had to laugh at this cheerful soul who hadn't been put off by her coldness, and it ended with him walking home with her."

"Yes, and what happened then?" I asked, holding my breath.

"What happened? Oh, come now! We don't ask that about a lady."

We were silent a moment, both Queeny and I.

"Well, I'll be, that was 'The Duke'! So that's what he looks like!" he said then, thoughtfully. "But of course if she is out with him I can't answer for her virtue."

I still remained silent. Yes, "The Duke" would obviously make the grade with her! So be it! What did that have to do with me? I said goodbye to her and all her charms: goodbye! I attempted to console myself by imagining the worst possible things about her, I took a positive pleasure in dragging her through the mud. The only thing that annoyed me was my taking off my hat to the couple, if I had really done it. Why should I tip my hat to people like that? She meant nothing to me any more, nothing at all. She wasn't even the slightest bit beautiful to me, she had lost all her beauty, frightful, how ugly she had become! It wasn't out of the question that she had looked only at me—that wouldn't surprise me: she was probably feeling remorse now. But that didn't mean that I had to fall down at her feet, and bow and scrape like a fool, especially when she had clearly lost so much of her good looks lately. "The Duke" could have her then, and good riddance! Perhaps one day I

would simply walk proudly right past her without even glancing in her direction. It wasn't impossible that I might do that even if she were to look straight at me, and what's more even if her dress were absolutely blood red! That could very easily happen! Yes, that would be a triumph! If I knew anything about anything, I would finish my play this very night, and within eight days I would bring that girl to her knees. Charms and all, yes, even with all her charms. . . .

"Goodbye!" I said curtly.

But Queeny pulled me back. He asked, "What do you do with yourself now during the day?"

"Do? I write, naturally. What else should I do? That is where I get my income. At the moment I am working on a great play, *The Sign of the Cross,* with a theme drawn from the Middle Ages."

"Heavens!" said Queeny, without irony. "If that gets produced . . ."

"Don't worry on that score, at all!" I answered. "In about eight days' time, I think you will hear a lot more of me."

With that I left.

When I got home, I went immediately to my landlady and asked her for a lamp. It was very important to me to have this lamp—I didn't intend to go to bed tonight, my play was racing through my head, and I hoped to write a great deal of it before morning. I presented my request in a very humble voice when I noticed that she made an irritated face just seeing me come in the door. I had nearly finished a remarkable play, I said; all that was lacking now were a couple of scenes, and I hinted that one theater or another would very likely perform it almost before it was finished. And if she would do me this great favor, I . . .

But the lady of the house had no lamp. She thought about it, but could not remember there being an extra lamp anywhere. If I wanted to wait until after midnight, maybe I could use the kitchen lamp. But why didn't I just buy a candle!

I didn't reply. I didn't have the ten øre for a candle, and she knew that very well. There I was, naturally, stuck again! The hired girl, in fact, was sitting in the family room now, just sitting there, and wasn't in the kitchen at all, so the kitchen lamp wasn't being used. I thought about all this but said nothing.

The girl suddenly turned to me.

"Didn't I see you leaving the Royal Castle an hour or so ago? You must have been there for dinner!" And she laughed at her joke.

I sat down, took out my manuscript, and was determined to work here anyway, right where I sat. I held the papers on my knees and stared firmly at the floor so as not to be distracted; but it was no good, I couldn't write a word. The landlady's two small daughters came in and started to tease the cat—a strange sick cat with almost no hair at all. When they blew into the cat's eyes, water poured from its eyes down over its nose. The landlord and a couple of other men sat at the table playing *cent et un*. Only the wife was, as usual, industrious; she sat sewing on something. She knew very well that I couldn't write in all this uproar, but she didn't bother about me any longer—she had even smiled when the hired girl asked about my whereabouts at dinnertime. The entire house had become hostile; it was as if it had taken only the single disgrace of my having to give up my room to another man for me to be treated exactly like an intruder. The hired girl, a little brown-eyed sluttish type with bangs and a flat chest, even made fun of me every night as I picked up my bread and butter. She never failed to ask me where I was in the habit of taking dinner, since she never seemed to notice me picking my teeth outside the Grand Café. It was obvious she was aware of my miserable circumstances, and enjoyed letting me know it.

I began to brood about all this suddenly, and I wasn't able to find a single speech for my play. I tried again and again; it was no use. My head started to buzz in a strange way, and I finally gave up. I put my manuscript into my pocket and looked around. The hired girl was sitting opposite me, and I gazed at her small back and her sloping shoulders, still half grown. Why should she attack me? And if I had been at the castle, what then? Could that have harmed her? She had been extremely impertinent lately, laughing at me whenever I happened to stumble on the stair or happened to get caught on a nail so that my coat ripped. And only yesterday she had picked up the first drafts of various scenes which I had thrown away in the corridor, actually had stolen these rejected fragments of my play, and had read them aloud in the family room, making fun of them in everyone's hearing, merely to amuse herself at my expense. I had never annoyed her and had never to my knowledge even asked her for a favor. On the contrary, I made my bed on the floor myself every night so as not to cause her any extra work. She made fun of me also because my hair was falling out. Strands of hair lay floating around in the washbasin every morning, and she made a great deal out of that. My shoes were by now in rather bad shape, especially the one driven over by the bread cart, and she found a few jokes there also. "God have mercy on you and your shoes!" she would say. Or: "Look at that shoe, it's the size of a doghouse!" She was right that my shoes were worn out, but I couldn't buy any others for the moment.

While I was sitting there brooding on this and pondering over the open enmity of the hired girl, the two small daughters started to tease the old man over in his bed. They both were hopping around him, completely absorbed in their entertainment. Each of them had straws which they were sticking into his ears. I looked on awhile and kept out of it. The old man did not move a finger to defend himself; he merely glared at his tormentors with furious eyes every time they poked him, and then shook his head to get free whenever the straws did get inside an ear.

I became more and more bothered by this teasing and could not take my eyes from it. The father looked up from his cards and laughed at the children's tricks; he called the attention of the other players to them also. Why didn't the old man move? Why didn't he throw the children aside with his arms? I took a step toward the bed.

"Let them be! Let them be! He's paralyzed," the landlord shouted.

Afraid of being turned out into the night, really afraid of angering the husband by mixing in this scene, I walked silently back to my old place and showed no emotion. Why should I risk my shelter and my bread and butter by sticking my nose into a family quarrel? No nonsense now for an old coot already half dead! I felt I was as deliciously hard as flint.

The little thieves kept on with their plaguing. It irritated them that the old man wouldn't hold his head still, and they began to jab for his eyes and nostrils also. He stared at them with a bitter expression, but said nothing; he could not move his arms. Suddenly he raised the upper part of his body and spit right into the face of one of the small girls; he lifted himself a second time and spit at the other too, but missed her. The landlord, as I watched, threw his cards down on the table and rushed over to the bed. He was red in the face and cried: "So you have the gall to sit there and spit in the eyes of children, do you, you old pig!"

"But, good God, they were torturing him!" I shouted, out of my mind. I didn't move from where I was; however, I was afraid of being thrown out, and I did not even shout with much force; my whole body shuddered from rage.

The landlord turned toward me.

"Now listen to him! What the hell does this have to do with you? Just keep your trap shut, and do as you're told—that's the best thing for you."

Now the landlady's voice rang out, and the whole house went into an uproar.

"God, if I don't think you are all crazy!" she shrieked. "If you want to stay in here, then you have to be quiet, both of you! Oh no, it's not enough that I have to keep house for bums and hoboes, I have to have people screaming as if they were in a madhouse besides! But I won't have any more of that, and that's final! Shh! Shut up, you kids, and wipe your noses, unless you want me to come and do it. I've never seen such people! Coming in out of the street without even enough money to delouse themselves, and the first thing you know, they are showing off in the middle of the night, fighting with the people who live in the house! I want no more of that, get that straight, and all those who don't belong here can go their own way. I want some peace in my own house, and I'm going to have it!"

I said nothing, I didn't open my mouth. I sat down near the door again and just listened. Everyone started to shout at one time, even the children and the hired girl, who tried to explain how the whole thing started. If I was quiet as a mouse, it would probably blow over— if I said nothing, the chances are it wouldn't go any farther. And what was I supposed to say? Wasn't it winter outdoors, and night on top of it? Was this the time to pound the table and fly off the handle? No idiotic tricks now! So I sat motionless and didn't walk out, even though I had been very nearly ordered out. I stared coldly at the wall, on which there was a colored lithograph of Christ, and kept my mouth obstinately shut during her raving.

"Well, if I'm the one you want to get rid of, that's all right with me," said one of the players.

He stood up. The other players stood up also.

"No, I didn't mean you. Or you two either," the landlady answered. "When I'm ready, I'll make it clear enough whom I mean. If I have to. It'll be clear all right. . . ."

She kept on talking, gave me these jabs at regular intervals and dragged the whole thing out so as to make it more clear to me that I was the one she meant. Silence! I said to myself. Just be quiet! She had not told me to go, not flatly, not in so many words, just no high-flown stuff on my part, no out-of-place pride! Just take it! . . . That colored lithograph showed a Christ with remarkably green hair. His hair was rather like green grass or, more exactly and precisely, heavy mountain grass. Yes, yes, a very sharp observation on my part, really, just like uncut mountain grass. . . . A number of associations suddenly shot through my brain: from the green grass I moved to the Biblical saying about all flesh being like grass that is thrown into the furnace, and from there to the Last Judgment, when everything would be burned up, and then a little detour to the Lisbon earthquake, then I had a vague memory of a Spanish spittoon made of brass and a penholder made of ebony I had seen at Ylayali's house. Oh yes, it was all transitory! Just like grass thrown into a furnace! It all ended with four pine boards and a burial shroud—at Miss Andersen's, Main Entrance, to the right. . .

All of this flew around in my head during those moments of despair when my landlady was just about to chase me out the door.

"He isn't listening!" she shouted. "I am telling you to get out of this house, now you've heard it! I swear to God I think this man is crazy! Now get out, right this minute, and no more gab about it!"

I looked at the door, I didn't want to go, I didn't want to go! A mad idea occurred to me: if there had only been a key in the lock, I would have turned it and locked myself in with the others; and then I couldn't have left the house. I had a dread of going out in the street that was positively hysterical. But the lock in the door had no key; so I stood up; all hope was gone.

My landlord's voice suddenly rang out over his wife's. I stopped, astounded. The man who had just threatened me was now, strangely enough, taking my side. He said, "You can't just throw people out in the street in the middle of the night. There's a law against it."

I didn't know if there were any law or not, I doubted it, but possibly there was. The wife had second thoughts, calmed down rapidly, and said nothing more to me. She even put two pieces of bread and butter in front of me for my evening snack, but I didn't take them—simply out of gratitude to the husband, I didn't take them; I said something about having had something to eat while I was out.

When I finally went into the hall to go to bed, the landlady followed me, paused on the threshold, and while her huge pregnant stomach jutted out toward me, said in a loud voice, "But this is your last night in this house, I want you to understand that."

"Yes, yes!" I answered.

It might be possible for me to find some rent money tomorrow if I put some thought to it. I would manage to get some sort of roof over my head. For the moment I was overjoyed not to have to leave tonight.

I woke about five or six in the morning. It was still dark when I woke, but I got up instantly anyway. I had slept in my clothes because of the cold in the hall, so I had no dressing to do. I took a drink of water, managed to open the door quietly, and left the house at once; I was afraid of meeting the landlady again.

The only things moving on the streets were one or two patrolmen who had been on duty all night; a little later, two men came along extinguishing the gas lanterns. I drifted about aimlessly, walked up to Kirke Street and then started down toward the fortress. Still cold and sleepy, my knees and back tired from my long walk, and extremely hungry, I sat down on a bench and dozed for a while. For three weeks I had lived on nothing but the bread and butter my landlady had given me twice a day; now a day had passed since I had last eaten; the ugly gnawing was beginning inside me once more, and I would have to do something soon. Thinking that thought, I fell asleep again on my bench. . . .

I was awakened by people talking nearby; when my eyes were open, I saw that it was bright day and everyone was up and walking around. I stood up and walked off. The sun blazed over the eastern hills, the sky was white and clear, and in my joy over the beautiful morning after so many dark weeks, I forgot my troubles entirely; I had been worse off before. I beat my chest with my fists and sang a few bars for myself. My voice sounded so rusty, its sound was so weak and pitiful, that I was moved to tears by it. The magnificent day, the clear sky overflowing with light moved me also, and I burst into loud sobs.

"What is the matter?" asked a man.

I didn't reply, just walked faster, hiding my face from people.

I walked down to the wharfs. A large ship flying a Russian flag lay at the pier, unloading coal. I read its name, *Copégoro,* on the prow. I was fascinated for a long time watching what was going on aboard the foreign ship. Although some ballast had already been taken on board, the ship must have been nearly empty, since I could read IX FEET on the depth scale painted on the side, and when the coal heavers walked over the deck with their heavy boots, the whole ship gave out a hollow sound.

The brilliant sunlight, the salt air from the sea, and all the busy and energetic movements gave me energy and cheered me up. All of a sudden it occurred to me that I might knock off a couple of scenes for my play while I was sitting here. I took out my manuscript.

I tried to compose a few lines for one of the monks, some sentences absolutely power-mad and stuffed with narrow-mindedness, but I couldn't do it. So I skipped the monk and worked on a long speech, the speech the judge delivers to the whore who violated the temple; I wrote a half page on this and then had to give up. I couldn't get the right tone in the language. All the workaday life around me, the loading chants, the noise of the winches, the constant rattling of the iron chains, was incompatible with the moody, self-absorbed atmosphere of the Middle Ages, which I wanted to be present in my play like a fog. I shoved my papers together and stood up.

Despite everything, I was really writing well, wonderfully, and I was positive I could accomplish a lot if I only had the right conditions. If I only had some place to go to! I thought and thought, stopped right in the street to think, but could not hit on a single quiet place in the whole city where I could hole up for a little while. There was nothing else to do, I would have to go back to the lodging house in Vaterland which I had just left.

I winced at that, and kept assuring myself that this scheme would never work, but I kept on walking anyway and drew nearer and nearer to the forbidden spot. It was humiliating, certainly, I admitted it myself, degrading in fact, yes, positively degrading; but that didn't help either. Pride was not one of my faults; if I might make such a large generalization, I would say that I was one of the least arrogant creatures that had ever existed to date. I kept on walking.

At the street door I stopped and thought again. Well, well, whatever happened would happen, I would take the risk! But, after all, was this really such an important step as all that? In the first place, I would only be in the house a couple of hours, and second, I would never, as God was my judge, ever take refuge under this roof again. I started across the courtyard. Even while walking over the uneven stones of the courtyard I was still uncertain and nearly turned around. I clenched my teeth. No out-of-place pride now! If worst came to worst, I could always make the excuse that I had stopped in to say goodbye, and then take my leave after a conversation touching on my little debt to the house. I opened the hall door.

I stopped and stood still. Right in front of me, hardly two steps away, the landlord, coatless and hatless, crouched, peeking through the keyhole into the living room. He motioned to me silently to be quiet and peeked through the keyhole again. He was laughing.

"Come over here!" he said in a whisper.

I came on tiptoe.

"Look at that!" he said, laughing with a silent, convulsed laugh. "Take a look! Hee-hee! Look at them on the bed! Can you see old Grandpa? Can you see him?"

On the bed, right under the colored lithograph of Christ, and very close to me, I made out two shapes, the landlady and the new sailor; her legs showed very white against the dark quilt. And on the settee along the other wall was her father, the paralyzed old man, looking on, crouched over his hands, bent over as usual, unable to move. . . .

I turned back to my landlord. He had the greatest difficulty in keeping from laughing out loud. He held his hand over his mouth.

"Can you see Grandpa?" he whispered. "Oh God, can you see him there? Sitting there and watching!" He ducked down again to look in the keyhole.

I walked to the window seat and sat down. The glimpse of the two had brought my train of thought to an end, and my good mood was gone. But why should I care about all this? When the husband himself went along, in fact thought it great entertainment, why should I bother myself with it? As for the old man, well, one just can't worry about every old man. Maybe he couldn't even see, maybe he just sat there sleeping; God knows maybe he was even dead. It wouldn't surprise me at all if he were sitting there stone-dead. So my conscience could be left out of it.

I took out my manuscript again, determined to ignore all such distractions. I had broken off right in the middle of the judge's speech: "God and the Law tell me to do this, my council, my self and my own conscience tell me to do this; therefore . . ." I looked out the window, trying to figure out what his conscience told him to do. I heard a small sound from inside the living room. That sound had nothing to do with me, nothing whatever—the old man was dead anyway, he had probably died this morning about four; and I didn't give a hoot one way or the other about the sound. So then why in hell was I wasting time thinking about it? Be calm!

My self and my own conscience tell me to do this; therefore . . .

But everything was working against me. The husband at the keyhole did not keep still—every now and then I heard his suppressed laughter or saw him shaking; something was happening out on the street too that distracted me. A small boy had been sitting, playing by himself on the far sidewalk; he was playing peacefully, expecting no harm—fastening together some long strips of paper. Suddenly he jumped up swearing; he walked backwards out on the street, keeping his eyes on a grown man with a red beard who was leaning out of a second-story window, spitting down on his head. The child sobbed with anger, and, unable to do more, swore up at the window while the man laughed in his face—five minutes perhaps went by this way. I turned away so as not to see the boy sobbing.

My self and my own conscience tell me to do this; therefore . . .

I simply could not go farther. Finally, I couldn't see sense in any of it—even what I had already written looked useless, in fact the whole idea was ridiculous nonsense. One could not really talk about conscience in the Middle Ages: the inventor of conscience was that old professor of the dance, Shakespeare. My whole story, therefore, was unrealistic and false. Were all the pages worthless? I read them through again and changed my mind: I found wonderful places, long passages that were absolutely first-rate. I was overcome once more by the mad intoxication; I wanted to jump in and get the play done.

I stood up and walked toward the door, ignoring the landlord's angry gestures to me to make less noise. My mind made up, I walked out of the hall, up the stairs to the second floor, and into my old room. The sailor was not occupying it at the moment, that much was certain, and what harm was there in my sitting there a few minutes? I wouldn't touch any of his things, I wouldn't even use his

table, just sit down on the chair near the door and be happy. I unfolded the pages hastily on my knees.

For several minutes the work went on swiftly. Speech after speech popped up in my head perfectly formed and I wrote on without a pause. I filled one sheet after the other, leaped over all obstacles, humming softly in delight over my rich mood. I was almost unconscious of myself. The only sound I heard during all this time was my own joyful humming. I got a new idea too, an excellent one, about a church bell that would suddenly burst out ringing at a certain point in the plot. Everything went marvelously.

Then I heard steps on the stairs. I shivered and almost leaped out of my skin; at that moment I was timorous, wary, afraid of everything, oversensitive from hunger. I listened nervously, held my hand and the pencil motionless, and listened—I couldn't write a single word. The door opened, the pair from the living room walked in.

Even before I had the time to say "Excuse me," the landlady cried, truly astonished, "Well, I'll be damned to hell if he isn't sitting here again!"

"I beg your pardon!" I said, and was about to go on, but stopped.

The landlady threw the door as wide open as it would go, and shrieked, "Now go! If you don't, God help me, I swear I will call the police!"

I stood up.

"I just wanted to say goodbye," I mumbled. "And so I've been waiting here. I haven't touched a thing, I've just been sitting on this chair. . . ."

"It's all right," the sailor said. "What the devil's the difference? Let him go!"

When I got to the bottom of the stairs, I suddenly became raging mad at this gross, swollen-up woman who was following on my heels to get me out as fast as possible, and I stopped an instant, my mouth full to the brim with hideous names I wanted to toss at her. But I reconsidered just in time and held my tongue, purely out of gratitude to the sailor who was coming along behind us and would have to hear it. The landlady followed me step for step, scolding at me all the time, while at the same time my rage grew with every step I took.

As we crossed the courtyard, I walked very slowly, still trying to decide if I should let go against the landlady. At this moment I was possessed by rage, and I thought of frightful acts of bloodshed, a blow that would knock her down dead on the spot, a kick in the stomach. A messenger in uniform passed me in the street door and said good morning; I did not answer. He turned to the landlady behind me and I heard him ask for me, but I didn't turn around.

A few steps beyond the door, the messenger caught up with me, greeted me once more, and stopped me this time. He handed me an envelope. I tore it open, unwillingly and hastily, and a ten-kroner note fell out of the envelope, but no letter, not a word.

I looked at him and asked, "What sort of nonsense is this? Who is the letter from?"

"I don't know, sir," he answered. "But it was a woman who gave it to me."

I stood where I was. The messenger left. Then I put the bill back into the envelope, crumpled the whole thing up in my fist, turned around, walked up to the landlady who was still peeping after me from the door, and threw the paper right in her face. I didn't say a thing, didn't utter a syllable, but I did wait to make sure she opened the crumpled paper before I left. . . .

That is what I would call the proper way to behave! Say nothing, not even write on the envelope, just quietly crumple it up into a big ball and throw it right between your enemy's eyes! There is an example of someone acting with dignity! That's exactly what they deserve, these animals!

When I got to the corner of Tomte Street and the railway station square, the street suddenly began to go around in circles, I could hear a hollow humming in my head, and I slumped over against a house wall. I simply could not walk any farther, couldn't even straighten up from my awkward position. I remained slumped over and felt myself beginning to lose consciousness. This attack of weakness merely strengthened my irrational rage, and raising my foot, I stamped as hard as I could. I also used various tricks trying to come to: clenched my teeth, wrinkled my forehead, rolled my eyes in despair, and it helped a little. My brain grew clearer, I understood that I was close to total collapse. I put my hands against the wall and shoved to push myself away from it. The street was still dancing around. I began to hiccup from fury, and struggled with every bit of energy against my collapse, fought a really stout battle not to fall down. I didn't want to fall, I wanted to die standing. A wholesale grocer's cart came by, and I saw it was filled with potatoes, but out of fury, from sheer obstinacy, I decided that they were not potatoes at all, they were cabbages, and I swore violent oaths that they were cabbages. I heard my own words very well, and I took the oath again and again on this lie, and swore deliberately just to have the delightful satisfaction of committing such clear perjury. I became drunk over this superb sin, I lifted three fingers in the air and swore with trembling lips in the name of the Father, the Son, and the Holy Ghost that they were cabbages.

Some time passed. I let myself sink down on a stoop and dried the sweat from my neck and forehead, fanned myself, and forced myself to calm down. The sun slowly sank, it was late afternoon. I began to brood over my situation again; my hunger was ghastly, and in a few hours it would be night; I had to find a solution while there was still time. My thoughts started circling again about the lodging house I had been evicted from; I absolutely did not want to return there, but I couldn't stop thinking about it. The landlady had been well within her rights, of course, in throwing me out. How could I expect to live in someone's place when I didn't pay! On top of it all, she had given me food now and then—even last night, after I had annoyed her, she had offered me two slices of bread and butter, just out of her goodness, she offered them because she knew that I needed them. So I had no complaints coming, and while I sat there on the stoop, I started asking and begging her forgiveness, silently, for my behavior. I especially regretted bitterly having shown myself ungrateful to her at the end, throwing that envelope in her face. . . .

A ten-kroner note! I gave a whistle. The letter the messenger brought—who had sent it? For the first time I thought about it and understood instantly how it all hung together. I became sick with shame and pain and whispered Ylayali several times in a hoarse voice, shaking my head. Didn't I only yesterday decide to walk proudly past her when I met her and be utterly cold? What I had actually done was to awaken her pity and lure a little alms money from her. No, no, no, there was no end to my degradations! Not once in my relations with her had I ever been able to keep a dignified position—no, I sank every time, sank further, sank to my knees, to my waist, sank over my head in disgrace, and I would never come up again, never! This humiliation was the worst of all! Accepting ten kroner in beggar's alms without being able to throw them back to the giver, scrambling with both hands for coins no matter where they came from, and keeping them, using them for rent money even though one felt disgust inside. . . .

Wasn't there some way to get those ten kroner back? Going to the landlady and asking her to return the money would be useless, but there might be some other solution if I put my mind to it, if I just made a real effort and thought. In this case it wouldn't be enough, God knows, just to think in the ordinary way, I would have to make my whole body help me to look for a way to regain those ten kroner. So I sat down to think, and think hard.

It was probably almost four o'clock, and in a couple of hours I could go to see the Director if I had my play done by that time. I took out the manuscript and resolved firmly that I would finish the last three or four scenes; I meditated and sweated and read everything over from the beginning, but the speeches would not come. No rot now! I said, no hoity-toity stuff here! And I started to write blindly where I had broken off, I simply wrote down everything that occurred to me, just to get the play done in a hurry and get it over with. I tried to assure myself that I was experiencing a new creative mood, I lied to my own face, defrauded myself openly, and wrote on headlong as if I didn't even need to look for the right word. This is good! I've really hit on something here! I kept whispering to myself, just get it all down! But the last speeches I had put down began to seem suspicious to me finally—they were in such stark contrast to the earlier scenes, and there was nothing even remotely medieval about the monk's lines. I snapped my pencil off between my teeth, leaped up, tore my manuscript in two, ripped every page of it in shreds, threw my hat down on the street and jumped on it. "I am a lost man!" I whispered to myself. "Ladies and gentlemen, I am a lost man!" And I repeated that over and over as I went on jumping on my hat.

A policeman was standing a few feet away watching me—he stood right in the middle of the street, looking. When I raised my head, our eyes met—maybe he had been standing there a long time watching me. I picked up my hat, put it on, and walked over to him.

"Do you know what time it is?" I asked.

He waited a little before he hauled out his watch, and all the while he kept his eyes on me.

"Nearly four," he answered.

"Right!" I said. "Nearly four! Absolutely right! You know your job, I've seen that, and I won't forget you."

With that, I walked off. He was too astonished to speak, and stood looking after me with open mouth, still holding the watch in his hand. When I was about up to the Royal Hotel, I turned and looked back: he was still standing in the same position, following me with his eyes.

That's the way to treat these animals! With the most well-bred insolence! That impresses these animals, that puts the fear of God in them. . . . I was unusually pleased with myself and sang a few bars. Giddy with excitement, feeling no pain at all any more, feeling nothing at all unpleasant, I walked on, light as a feather, floated all around the market, curved around by the booths, and sat down on a bench near the Church of Our Saviour.

Did it really matter one way or the other whether I sent the ten kroner back or not? Once I had received it, it was mine, and certainly the house it came from was not hard up. I had to accept it, actually, since it had been expressly sent to me—there would have been no sense in letting the messenger keep it. There would be no point either in sending back a completely different ten-kroner note from the one I received. So there was nothing to do about it.

I tried to become engrossed in all the bustle going on around me and occupy my thoughts with irrelevant details, but it didn't work and I kept coming back to the ten-kroner note. Finally I clenched my fists and got angry. It would wound her, I said, if I sent the money back—why in the world should I do it then? I always had to go around thinking I was too good for everything, shaking my head condescendingly and saying no, thanks. Now you see where that leads: here I am again tossed right out on the street. Even when I had the perfect opportunity to do it, I didn't hold on to my nice warm lodging house—no, I became proud, leaped up at the first word and started to pound the table, gave ten-kroner notes away left and right and walked out. . . . I scolded myself fiercely for having left my rooming house and so having drawn all this trouble upon myself.

For the money, damn the whole thing! The hell with it! I had not asked for that ten-kroner note and in fact I had hardly even held it in my hands—I had given it away immediately, paid off some total strangers I hadn't the faintest desire to see again. That's the sort of man I am, I pay all my debts right down to the last øre. And if I knew Ylayali, she did not regret having sent me the money. Then why was I getting so worked up about it? Actually, the very least she could have done was to send me ten kroner now and then. The poor girl was in love with me, no doubt of that, maybe madly in love with me even. . . . I puffed myself up inside with this thought. There was no doubt—she was in love with me, the poor thing! . . .

It was five. I fell into depression again after my long stretch of nervous excitement, and began to hear the empty humming in my head again. I stared straight ahead, kept my eyes motionless, gazing off toward the Elephant Apothecary. Hunger was raging in me now, and I felt considerable pain. While I sat there staring down the street, a figure began to distinguish itself more and more from the background—finally it came perfectly clear and in focus and I recognized it: the cake seller next to the Elephant Apothecary.

I gave a start, sat up on the bench, and started to think. All this had its own justice, that was the same woman in front of the same table in the same spot! I whistled once or twice and snapped my fingers, then I got up from the bench and started to walk toward the apothecary. No nonsense now! I didn't give a damn if those coins I gave her were from the devil's private stock, or good honest hunks of silver from the Kongsberg mine! Enough is enough, a man can die, you know, from too much pride. . . .

I walked over to the corner, took aim at the woman, and drew up in front of her. I smiled, nodded as though we were friends, and chose my words to give the impression that my return was very much a matter of course.

"Good afternoon!" I said. "Perhaps you don't recognize me this time?"

"No," the woman answered slowly. "I don't think I do." She looked at me.

I smiled still more, as if to say her not recognizing me was one of her rare little jokes. I said, "Don't you remember, I gave you a whole pile of kroner one day? On that occasion I said nothing, as I recall, I don't believe I did—I usually don't in those situations. When one is dealing with honorable people, I have found there is no need really to write everything down and, so to speak, sign a contract for every little thing. Ha-ha.

Yes, I'm the one who handed you the money."

"Well, well, was that you! Yes, now I recognize you again, now that I think of it. . . ."

I didn't want her to start thanking me for the money, so I broke in quickly; my eyes were already roving over her table looking for something to eat. "Yes, and I've come now to get the cakes."

She didn't understand that.

"The cakes," I repeated. "I've come now to get them. In any case, some, the first installment, I won't need them all today."

"You've come to get them?" she asked.

"Yes, of course, I've come to get them, yes!" I answered and laughed loudly as though she should have realized a long time ago that I had come to get them. As I did so, I picked up a piece from the table, a sort of French roll, which I started to eat.

When the woman saw that, she straightened up a little, made an involuntary movement to protect her goods, and said something to the effect that she had not expected me to return and rob her.

"No?" I said. "Oh, you hadn't?" Well, she was really a strange woman! Had anyone ever given her for safekeeping a walletful of money, and then not asked for it back eventually? Well, there, you see! I suppose she thought perhaps that this money was all stolen since I had thrown it down like that? No? She didn't think so? That was good! It was, if I might say so, very nice of her to give me the benefit of the doubt! Ha-ha! She was really a very good person!

"But why did you give me the money then?" The woman was exasperated and shouted that at me.

I explained why I had given her the money, and explained it calmly and precisely: I had a habit of conducting myself in this manner because I believed in humanity. Always, if anyone offers me a contract or an I O U, I shake my head and say, no, thanks. That is the way I am, it's true, so help me God.

But she still didn't understand it.

I had to adopt other means. I spoke in a sharp tone and said I wanted no twaddle. Hadn't anyone ever paid her in advance for goods just as I had? I asked. For example, people of means, people in the consular service for instance? Never? Well, I could not be responsible for the fact that she was unfamiliar with that procedure. It was perfectly ordinary procedure in other countries. Had she ever, by the way, been out of this country? No? Well, there, you see! She really had no right to an opinion in this matter. . . . I picked up several more cakes from her table.

She growled angrily, refused obstinately to turn over to me any merchandise she had on the table, even took one cake out of my hand and put it back in its place on the board. I became angry then, pounded the table, and threatened her with the police. I had tried to be easy with her, I said; if I took everything that belonged to me, I would absolutely clean her out, because what I gave to her that time was a really massive sum of money. But I didn't intend to take even as much as I deserved, I actually would accept half value. And I would never return again, to boot. God help us, that's the last thing I would ever do, seeing what sort of person *she* was.

Finally she picked out a few, naming an incredible price for them, four or five cakes, to which she tacked the highest price she could think of, and told me to take them and go. I went on arguing with her, complained that she had cheated me out of at least a kroner in the calculation and had absolutely robbed me blind with her fantastic prices. "Don't you know that there is a law against cheap tricks of that sort?" I said. "God have mercy on

you. You could get slavery for life for that, you old bat!" She threw me one more cake and told me, almost grinding her teeth, to go.

So I left her.

"God, you'll never see anything to match a crooked cake seller!"

All the time while I was walking through the marketplace eating my cakes, I talked aloud about the woman and her disgusting behavior, repeated what we had said to each other—it seemed to me I had come out far superior in that exchange. I ate the cakes in full view of everyone as I went on talking.

The cakes disappeared one after the other. It didn't seem to matter how many I got down, I remained ferociously hungry. Why didn't they help! I was so greedy for them that I almost gobbled down the last cake of them all, which I had set aside almost from the start for the boy down in Vognmands Street, the small boy whose head the man had spit on. I thought of him all the time, couldn't make myself forget his face when he leaped up, crying and swearing. He had turned and looked toward my window, too, when the man spit on him, as if to find out whether I was laughing at him too. God knows, maybe I wouldn't even find him now! I hurried as fast as I could down to Vognmands Street, passing the spot where I had torn up my play; some bits of paper were still lying there. I managed to avoid the policeman who had been so surprised at my behavior, and at last I arrived at the stoop where the boy had been sitting.

He was not there. There was almost no one on the street. It was getting dark and I couldn't see the boy anywhere. Maybe he had gone in. I put the cake down carefully on the threshold, leaning it up against the door, knocked hard, and ran off down the street. "He'll find it all

right!" I said to myself. "He'll find it first thing when he comes to the door!" And my eyes grew damp over my idiotic joy at the boy finding the cake.

I walked back to the wharf area by the railway station.

I wasn't hungry any more, though the sweet food I had eaten was beginning to give me a stomach ache. Wild ideas popped up again in my head. What if I quietly went over and cut off the mooring ropes on one of the ships? What if I suddenly cried fire? I walked farther out on the pier, found myself a wooden box to sit on, and folded my hands; I could feel my brain moving nearer and nearer to chaos. I did not move this time, did absolutely nothing to prevent it.

I just sat there staring at the *Copégoro,* the ship with the Russian flag. I caught sight of a man at the rail; the red port lantern was shining down on his head. I stood up to speak to him. I had nothing in mind at all with my conversation, I didn't even expect to get an answer. I said, "Are you sailing tonight, Captain?"

"Yes, in a little while," he answered. He spoke Swedish. Probably born then in Finland, I thought.

"Hmm. You wouldn't need a man, would you?" I didn't care at that moment whether I got a no or not, it was all the same to me which answer he gave me. I waited, watching him.

"Oh, no," he answered. "We'd have to have a young man."

"A young man!" I straightened up, whipped off my glasses and put them in my pocket, walked up the gangplank and strode on board.

"I am inexperienced," I said, "but I can do whatever you give me to do. Where does this ship go?"

"We have ballast to Leeds. After that, coal to Cádiz."

"Good!" I said, pushing myself on him. "It makes no difference to me where it's going. I will do my job, and that's all I care for."

He stood awhile looking at me, thinking it over.

"Have you ever worked on a ship before?" he asked.

"No. But as I said, give me a job, and I'll do it. I am used to doing all sorts of work."

He thought it over some more. In my head I already saw myself going along, and I wanted badly to go; I began to be afraid he would chase me back on shore.

"What do you think, Captain?" I asked, finally. "No matter what job it is, I'll do my share. More! If I couldn't do more than my share, I would really be worthless. I can take two watches in a row if I have to. That would do me good, and wouldn't bother me at all."

"All right, all right, we can try it," he said, and smiled a little at my last words. "If it doesn't work out, we can always part company in England."

"Yes, that's right!" I answered, overjoyed. I repeated that we could always part company in England if it didn't work out.

So he gave me a job to do. . . .

When we were out on the fjord, I straightened up, wet from fever and exertion, looked in toward land and said goodbye for now to the city, to Christiania, where the windows of the homes all shone with such brightness.

THE LIFE AND WORKS OF
KNUT HAMSUN

By ROLF NETTUM

WHEN KNUT HAMSUN made his literary debut in 1890 with the first-person novel *Sult* (*Hunger*), he introduced a new epoch in Scandinavian literature. A new type of literary hero entered the stage—the sensitive, impressionable intellectual who was the product of the industrial and scientific expansion of the nineteenth century. Hamsun's hero-poet, who walked the streets of Oslo and almost starved to death, represented a new interest in psychological literature. Through him, subconscious phenomena, vague, irrational feelings, and the most curious fancies and impulses find expression, the partition between the conscious and the subconscious layers of the mind disappears because of the physical anomaly of constant hunger. The perspective throughout is ironic: A morally superior self observes in wonder an alien, inferior self; watching his own subconscious, the hero is alternately impressed and amused by it, yet he must choose to deny it since the inferior self is constantly urging him to compromise in the struggle for survival that underlies his life. In order to hold his own in the life struggle, the protagonist has to retain his moral integrity and cannot avail himself of dishonest means—even though it be a petty thing such as taking a friend's sleeping blanket to the pawnbroker.

The book itself contains no indictment of society. Life is viewed from a different angle. The protagonist battles mighty forces in the universe—later in his writings Hamsun uses the expression "God of life" to describe these forces. Hamsun's hero in *Hunger* stands up in defiance and revolt against "Jehovah, the great Baal," whom he condemns as the invisible god of life and existence. He clenches his fists and decides not to yield to adversity in a test which requires all his spiritual resources. In his own eyes Hamsun's hero is an exceptional human being, a poet whose incessantly productive mind is itself an answer to this challenge. His imagination creates a new reality, one more beautiful at the same time it is more strange than the old. During transports of inspiration he experiences mystical ecstasies lifting him above the real world of shabby rooming houses, suspicious policemen, and his constant need of money. The results of these withdrawals is complete isolation from the outside world—the world of objects—and a feeling of *angst* which quivers underneath this self-concern and consciousness. A fascination with escape develops when he fears that his subconscious will get the best of him and drive him insane, making him drift down toward the harbor: Should he withdraw from the struggle for existence by jumping in, thereby giving up his pride and admitting defeat?

Instead he flees abroad on a foreign ship. It is not easy to condemn him since his spiritual resources throughout the book seem to be inexhaustible. The violent urge to live and the strong fear of death are contingent on each other just as descent from the heights of ecstasy to the depths of despair illustrate the tension that rules his dynamic soul.

The real name of the author of this book that made so significant a break with Norway's socially oriented literature was Knud Pedersen. It was not until Pedersen had come of age that he assumed the pen name Hamsun—a name similar to that of the place he grew up, Hamsund, a village far from Norway's cultural centers. Hamsun's father was a farmer and tailor, living on a small farm in the Gudbransdal valley in central Norway, a district known for its old rural arts and crafts. When Knud was three years old, the family moved to northern Norway, to the island of Hamaröy, situated between Bodö and Narvik.

Northern Norway is a region with impressive natural scenery and startling contrasts between a dark, somber winter and the "eternal day of summer" underneath the blazing light of the midnight sun. The marked rhythm of the seasons made a great impression on the young boy, who lived in a land that was still very much of a fairy-tale land with a motley life, extensive fisheries, and colorful fairs. The old folk beliefs and superstitions and myths were still current, and the Lapps with their unique way of life and their strange dress fed a small boy's imagination. Society here was undeveloped and somewhat feudal, with wealthy landowners and merchants in command. Their unfettered existence and high level of culture fascinated the boy, and in his more socially oriented novels, in which he attacks modern technical civilization, Hamsun constantly recalls and idealizes this romantic milieu of patriarchal relationships. Above all, however, it was nature and animal life that filled Hamsun's childhood with poetry, and his first literary effort was a touching little burial hymn for a dead female reindeer.

At the age of nine Knut Hamsun was wrenched from his idyllic life and placed in the home of an unmarried uncle who needed help in his work as postmaster and farmer. This uncle was strict and had no understanding of children, and the boy suffered from the hard physical labor and harsh punishment. For a human being with Hamsun's exceptionally sensitive makeup the years he spent with his uncle were to have important consequences, and he saw his uncle as the incarnation of all evil powers. His new life also isolated him from other children, and forced him, not unlike the hero of *Hunger,* to live in his own world of imagination. He felt lonely and unsure of himself with other people. These years made him an outsider and he had no intimate contact with parents or brothers and sisters. But the loneliness bore fruit and he experienced happy hours when he could lie in the grass and write with his toes against the sky, or withdraw into a cave in the mountains and listen to a summer shower. The joy of being alone in nature was a constant motif in his writings and solitude helped his alert senses to register every little nuance in the life of nature.

As early as possible he broke out of his isolation and attempted a number of various jobs. He wandered north and made a sort of living as trader and itinerant worker. He stood behind the counter in a rural store, tried his mettle as shoemaker and carpenter's apprentice, was a deputy sheriff, and for a time a school-teacher. His own formal education had not taken him past elementary school, yet he had read as many books as he could find, and his earliest literary impressions were from the Bible, a hymn book, and cheap, romantic novels that ran as serials in the newspapers. The years on the road provided him with much of the marvelous material he used in the vagabond trilogy he published fifty years later.

Hamsun was no more than eighteen years of age when his first book was printed in 1887. Today it can be rated no more than a curiosity, but its title—*Den Gaadefulde (The Mysterious Man)*— was an indication of what was to come. The language and style are clumsy, the psychology is naive, and the book is no more than wish-dreams about social and erotic victories by an adolescent boy. Much better is *Bjørger,* which was published the following year, and foretells the later novel *Hunger.* A disguised auto-biography, the hero experiences the bitterness that life holds, while the central theme of the book was the dream of poetic glory.

Both these books were printed in small towns in northern Norway and attracted no attention at all. Although Hamsun himself was convinced of his own literary ability, many years were to pass before his talent came to fruition. The struggle to make a living was exceedingly hard; during two winters he lived on the very edge of starvation in Oslo, and his novel *Hunger* is based on his experiences at that time. Later, he was a farm laborer and roadworker in southern Norway and also tried, without success, to be a lecturer and a literary man.

He was in the United States for two brief periods (1882–1884 and 1886–1888), just at the time that the stream of migrants from overseas reached its zenith. Here he lived a rootless life, working as an itinerant helper on the prairie in Dakota, as an assistant shopkeeper, and for a time as a secretary to a Norwegian-American Unitarian minister in Minneapolis. He is also supposed to have been a trolley conductor in Chicago, but this period in his life is obscured. He contributed polemical writings to the immigrant press and he tried to become known as a writer within the Scandinavian immigrant milieu. He was most happy when he was lecturing in local clubs, or appearing as a humorous speaker at bazaars and festive get-togethers.

His financial breakthrough came after his return to Scandinavia when he went to Copenhagen, where a few chapters of *Hunger* were published in a magazine in 1888. Encouraged by this success he published *Fra dit moderne Amerikas Aandsliv (The Intellectual Life of Modern America,* 1889), a witty and disrespectful book in which for the first time he gave free rein to his sense of humor as it was nourished by the writings of Mark Twain. In principle, Hamsun assumed a subjective viewpoint, shunned all objectivity, and was consciously partial. The book is of greater interest for studying Hamsun's psyche and his opinions than as a description of the cultural life of the young democracy. Impudent and supercilious, he looks upon himself as a European intellectual aristocrat who can freely criticize the culture of a young country with no real traditions. Here he reveals his antidemocratic leanings; later in his life Hamsun regretted writing this book, considering it a boyish prank.

Following his first success, Hamsun made a great point of keeping alive the notoriety that he had earned. In 1891 he made a lecture tour along the Norway coast from Bergen to Oslo—the manuscripts and notes for these lectures were found only a few years ago—and discussed and criticized the previous generation of Norwegian writers. Sharply and pointedly, Hamsun opposed the school of realism which examined social and ethical problems. He maintained that the predecessors of his generation—not excepting Henrik Ibsen, whose greatness Hamsun was never to acknowledge—had depicted broad, simple, human types instead of individuals. Hamsun wanted art to be "aristocratic," concentrating on unique psychological cases and the highly complicated products of the modern age. Hamsun was a contemporary of Sigmund Freud, although Freud was relatively unknown at this time, and many of the same influences were at work. This was a time when new trends coalesced: impulses from German romanticism, the philosopher von Hartmann's teachings about the subconscious, the pessimism of the woman-hater Schopenhauer, and Nietzsche's preachings about superman. Hamsun's ultimate goal now was to make way for imagination, dreams, and beauty.

It was an event of great local importance when Hamsun terminated his lecture tour in the capital. Ibsen—in the audience and seated in the first row—was the primary target for Hamsun's sarcasm, and Hamsun was accused of personal advertising. As a result, he felt the need of explaining and defending himself, and his next novel, *Mysterier* (*Mysteries,* 1892), may be looked upon as a brief in his own defense. The protagonist is the kind of big bluff that Hamsun had been accused of being, and he feels the same desire to tease the bourgeoisie and turn their dogma inside out. But Hamsun also wanted to demonstrate what kind of individual he valued as a hero: one with a lyrical temperament and a knowledge of the mystical connection between man and nature. In this book Hamsun also examines himself and his potentialities. The hero at last becomes the victim of

his own complicated personality and ends by taking his own life. *Mysteries* is a rich and luxurious tale, as well as chaotic and obscure, with a murky symbolism which gives us insight into Hamsun's psyche and his view of life. A few less significant novels on contemporary themes followed, mainly polemical attacks on artists and politicians—"books of the clenched fist" Hamsun later called them. One of them, *Ny jord* (*New Earth,* 1893), is noteworthy because in it the author defends businessmen against the intellectuals.

Hamsun scored his next success with the novel *Pan* (1894), which brought him fame in Russia and in Germany. The action takes place in northern Norway during a brief and hectic summer suffused in the light of the midnight sun. This short novel contains the finest nature lyricism in Scandinavian literature. Here Hamsun reached his peak as a stylistic innovator. The story is a simple yet tragic love story whose lovers, Glahn and Edvarda, are a classical pair, a modern counterpart to Tristan and Isolde.

In his next love story, *Victoria* (1898), the protagonist is also a lyrical and asocial dreamer, the son of the miller attached to a great manor, and new social considerations play a significant role when he falls in love with Victoria, the daughter of the big landowner. Although bourgeois marriage is not for him, his great passion induces him to write beautiful poetry and we find that Johannes wants Victoria merely to be his inspiration, his muse.

All Hamsun's protagonists are variations on the same type, yet they are depicted with unparalleled freshness and vividness. They love life as manifested in physical love and in nature, and do not live fully unless they are in a state of ecstasy. They are esthetes but take no interest in society, and they remain passive in an oriental manner. Hamsun himself felt a certain attraction toward the oriental way of life and its fatalism in ccntrast to the restless way of life of the West. Around the turn of the century, Hamsun traveled through Russia and the Caucasus to Turkey and documented his trip in a charming travel book called *I Æventyrland* (*In a Fairy-tale Country*, 1903), while impressions gained in Georgia inspired him to write a historical drama, *Dronning Tamara* (*Queen Tamara*, 1903). This latter work was not Hamsun's first attempt as a dramatist, even though he did not have a very high regard for the drama as art.

His trilogy, *Ved Rikets Port* (*By the Gate of the Kingdom*, 1895), *Livets Spill* (*Game of Life*, 1896), and *Aftenrøde* (*Sunset*, 1898), is very uneven. The second play, with its distant, northern Norwegian milieu is very poetic and was a great success at the Moscow Art Theater under the direction of Stanislavsky. The rhythm of this particular play is closely related to the works of Chekhov. The main character in the trilogy was in his youth a promising scientist with very definite, radical opinions. Hamsun makes a firm statement about old age when in the epilogue of the trilogy we meet the hero again as a conservative nonentity, when age has clipped his wings. Hamsun's regard for woman as an enigmatic and capricious being is shown in *Game of Life*, where the mysterious Teresita is shown as an embodiment of blind erotic passion. His last play, *Livet ivold* (*In the Grip of Life*, 1910), contains a disquieting description of a former actress's attempts to hold on for dear life to her waning youth. Hamsun himself could never resign himself to growing old.

Desire for revolt is the theme in Hamsun's great verse-drama, *Munken Vendt* (*The Monk Vendt*, 1904), which strongly shows the influence of Ibsen's *Peer Gynt*. Concurrently with this "clenched fist" drama he issued his only collection of poems, *Det vilde Kor* (*The Wild Chorus*). Hamsun's musical lines signified a renewal of Norwegian lyrics, and many later poets are indebted to him. The collection contains a number of love poems, melodious expressions of chivalrous worship and adoration of woman. Several of these poems remind one of the old ballads, others have a tinge of the exotic. In all of them appears Hamsun's typical hero: a wanderer of changeable moods who gives himself over to the intoxication to be derived from nature and love. One group of poems, "Feberdikt" ("Fever Poems"), points toward expressionism; they were written while the poet had a fever, giving a hallucinatory picture of impressions from the "soul's borderland." There is no dearth of polemical strains, but the high point of the collection is a poem written in homage to the national leader Björnstjerne Björnson, one of the very finest lyrical portraits in Scandinavian art, and the little poem "Skjaergårdsø" ("Island among the Skerries"), a mood piece which ends in a dream about Nirvana.

"There was an aroma of jasmine in a forest of lilacs, and there trembled a joy through someone I know, not for the sake of the jasmines, but on account of everything, a window with a light in it, a memory, life entire. But when he was called away from the forest of lilacs, he had already been paid for this annoyance. And that is the way it is: the mere grace of receiving life is the abundant payment for all of life's annoyances, each and every one." This is the sum total of Hamsun's wanderer, his last words, and they appear in the second volume of a trilogy which the author published under his real name, Knud Pedersen.

The trilogy consists of *Under Høststjernen* (*Under the Autumn Star*, 1907), *En Vandrer Spiller med Sordin* (*A Wanderer Plays on Muted Strings*, 1909), and *Den siste Glede* (*The Last Joy*,

1912). These titles indicate the main theme of the three books, the autumnal sadness that fills the worshiper of life as he stands before the gateway to old age and death. The novels were written in resignation and have an undertone of hard-won composure. Once again the wanderer leaves city life behind and sets out on the open road, hiding his identity as a writer and taking an occasional job here and there as a laborer, letting nature and hard physical work counterbalance his waning life force and his growing spleen. Meanwhile, he seeks a third source of regeneration in reminiscences from his childhood, a time when he had the happy and immediate ability to perceive through his senses. He recalls the genuine religiosity of the mind of a child —when the wild geese were flying on their way to a foreign country he had been taught to bend his head and piously fold his hands. The aging wanderer attempts to revive this meek attitude toward life—but it is not easy. The trilogy ends in a mixture of gratitude for life and sorrow as it slides away from him.

Hamsun's wanderer and worshiper of life has come to the end of the road. It is obvious in *The Last Joy* that this lyrical, self-centered protagonist no longer fascinates the author; from here on he regards his alter ego with a great deal of irony. This did not, however, mean the end of Hamsun as a writer, and he turned about to become more extrovert. His later works show him on a new course as he becomes portrayer and a critic of society. He creates a whole gallery of folk types, a multitude of sharply observed individuals, humorous as well as entertaining, whom he himself regarded with humor and detached irony. The Danish Nobel Prizewinner Henrik Pontoppidan spoke derisively about Hamsun's "flea circus," but often warmth and compassion are behind his words. Hamsun is a superb technician, and with these later books he became one of the most widely read European authors of the interwar period. The milieu depicted bears the impress of the northern Norway of his youth, the characters speak a queer northern Norwegian dialect, and the society is the old patriarchal one he knew so well.

During this period, Hamsun also participated frequently in public debate, attacking Anglo-Saxon materialism, the tourist traffic, and what he regarded as a democratic leveling out of society. In these debates, he takes the side of the old landowners: the patriarchal relationship, involving responsibility and trust, is his ideal, and frugality, industry, and agriculture are the medicines that will cure the vacuity of civilization. Hamsun became a morality preacher.

This new attitude was undoubtedly connected with his own personal experience. In the 1890s he had been briefly married, but the marriage had been dissolved. In 1909 he married again, this time to the young actress Marie Andersen, and they had four children. In a few volumes of reminiscences, his wife, who also became very well known as the author of children's books, has given us an interesting picture of their life together. With this new marriage Hamsun's bohemian, wandering life now came to an end. He became a faithful husband and a kind and thoughtful father, settling as a farmer in the same district in the far north where he had spent his childhood. Later he moved with his family to the estate of Nørholm on the southern coast of Norway and made it into a model farm.

Sværmere (*Dreamers*, 1904) was the beginning of Hamsun's transition to a new novelistic form. This change was not fully developed until the publication of *Rosa* and *Benoni* (both published in 1908), in which the hero is not an intellectual but a vigorous and aggressive man of the people, who by dint of his cunning and business knowledge makes his dream of social power and prestige a reality.

The clash between the dying aristocracy and the new type of society is the main theme of *Børn af Tiden* (*Children of the Age*, 1913) and *Segelfoss By* (*Segelfoss Town*, 1916). Segelfoss is a happy little place until the new era, represented by a Norwegian-American who has returned to the old country to establish a factory, takes over. There are strikes and labor unrest, the old crafts are forgotten and pride in one's work declines, people begin to sell their farms and would rather work behind a counter; lawyers, canned goods, and imported textiles spell the ruin of good taste and frugality. The reader will share Hamsun's sorrow over the decline of what is old only with difficulty, and he will hardly be converted to renouncing the use of canned goods because the exaggerations in Hamsun's satire appeal to laughter rather than to tears.

Hamsun's most famous novel, *Markens Grøde* (*Growth of the Soil*, 1917), the work for which he received the Nobel Prize in 1920, contains thoughts and ideas indicating the author's violent reaction to World War I. It also contains arguments against abortions, a matter which he views in the light of the contempt for human life that was so prevalent during the war years. *Growth of the Soil* remains a work with a very clear point of view, a didactic work whose philosophical basis is loosely related to the writings of the Age of Enlightenment of the eighteenth century. It is an idyll in the vein of pastoral poetry, borne up by great pathos. Indeed, the book has been criticized for being too idyllic: some feel that Isak Sellanraa, the tiller of the soil, gets ahead too easily and too swiftly. But that is the way it ought to be, and the novel gives an idealized picture of the struggles of a backwoods-man who clears the forest and tills the soil.

Isak, the lonesome, giant pioneer, settles all by himself in the wilds and with his own hands builds his farm. He is the very embodiment of Hamsun's old dream about the harmonious man. The book is a poet's dream, yet it has for that reason less of the typical Hamsun in it than any of his other books. Isak is not a complicated person nor a sensitive man, he is healthy and plain. His roots are in the soil. There is in the book, however, one man who is closely related to Hamsun's earlier characters—and to Hamsun himself: Sheriff Geisler, an adventurer and a vagabond. Through him Hamsun lauds the blessings of agriculture and warns the farmer Isak against trying other sources of income. When copper is found on Isak's property, Isak listens to Geisler and refuses to extract it. When Geisler warns against gambling and speculation, it is Hamsun who is speaking to that other self we met earlier in *Hunger*.

In *Growth of the Soil*, Hamsun was settling accounts with the philosophy and view of life that he had entertained when young. Hamsun, the model agriculturist, attempted to live like Isak on his own farm and to combat his tendencies toward romantic loafing.

The novel's popularity and success was partly caused by World War I, a time when people were willing to receive with great alacrity a book that pointed to a reality other than war and destruction.

Several novels of lower quality somewhat disappointed the large readership that he had gained with *Growth of the Soil. Konerne ved Vandposten* (*The Women at the Pump*, 1921) and *Siste Kapitel* (*The Last Chapter*, 1923) expose the emptiness and spiritual barrenness of man, and are biting satires in the vein of Jonathan Swift. But he was once again at his best with his trilogy about the fantasist August: *Landstrykere* (*Vagabonds,* 1927), *August* (1930), and *Men Livet lever* (*The Road Leads On,* 1933). August is Hamsun's finest character portrayal. As a type he is the exact opposite of Isak, unreliable and restless, unable to stay anywhere for any length of time. He is an aimless schemer who starts all kinds of enterprises with no real substance to them, while gaining neither fame nor fortune. But Hamsun is fond of this vital fellow August, and the action-filled trilogy, based again on Hamsun's own experiences wandering in northern Norway about 1880, indicates clearly a conflict within Hamsun's inner self. It also deals with the problem of well-being and happiness in modern society.

Hamsun's last novel, *Ringen sluttet* (*The Ring Is Closed,* 1936), carries on the theme of a man who has resigned from society as a protest against the hustle and competition so prevalent today.

When Norway was invaded by Nazi Germany in April of 1940, Knud Pedersen Hamsun chose to align himself with the occupying power. This action was a terrible disappointment for his admirers, and for many years after he was considered by Norway as a traitor. The renewed interest in his art did not come until the end of the 1950s, when his books *Pan* and *Hunger* were filmed. But still many ask the question, how was it possible for Hamsun to end up this way? Did he—the worshiper of life in all its forms—become a Nazi? The answer must be no. Hamsun admired the patriarchal society, the wealthy and the powerful with their generosity and their fatherly ways. His complete lack of political insight, closely connected with his antisocial, intellectual bent, made him mistake Hitler for a noble fatherly type.

Also, Hamsun had had his biggest literary successes in Germany and was a great admirer of that country. Hamsun never believed in the use of force and he was never an anti-Semite. Yet from his works we see he had respect for the individual, but not a very great feeling of solidarity with the people, the masses. These same people were enraged when he wrote articles in support of Vidkun Quisling, the German collaborator.

In his defense, it should be pointed out that Hamsun was over eighty when the Germans invaded Norway; a cerebral hemorrhage and increasing deafness may have impaired his good judgment. But there were some few favorable aspects to the total picture of Hamsun's political commitments, and he secretly worked to obtain pardon for some young men of the resistance movement who had been sentenced to die. When he was enticed to go to Berlin in 1943, in order to meet Hitler himself, he shocked everyone by upbraiding Hitler for his mistakes and errors—making the dictator extremely angry. Hamsun retained his independence to the end.

When Norway was liberated, Hamsun —then eighty-six years old—was arrested and interned in an old people's home, his property impounded. Here, during his last years, humbled and degraded, he wrote his final book, *På gjengrodde stier* (On Overgrown Paths, 1949). The fact that the book was published during his ninetieth year tells us much about his vitality—this was seventy-two years after his first little work, *The Mysterious Man,* had been printed. The ring was closed, and at the end of his life Hamsun was once again the propertyless bohemian who still could not help marveling at the mystery of life. He died at Nørholm in 1952, almost ninety-three years old.

Translated by Erik J. Friis.

Rolf Nyboe Nettum is Professor of Scandinavian Literature at the University of Oslo in Norway.

THE 1920 PRIZE

By KJELL STRÖMBERG

IN AWARDING the Nobel Prize for Literature in 1920 to Knut Hamsun, the Swedish Academy could be confident of general approval, at least in the Scandinavian countries. Hamsun proved to be a popular laureate.

Two Swedes and two Danes had already received the celebrated award, and although Norway had had only one winner, he was a prestigious one—Björnstjerne Björnson, a supranational poet and an unchallenged master of every literary form. Björnson won his Prize in 1903, when Norway was still joined to Sweden by a mutual king. Since the end of the political union in 1905 and the death of Ibsen in 1906, no Norwegian author had been seriously considered by the literary jury which awards the Nobel Prize. It is not surprising that on the western slope of the Scandinavian peninsula people were beginning to resent this state of affairs, especially since there was no lack of talented, even brilliant, writers among the heirs of Ibsen and Björnson.

In 1920, no fewer than three Norwegians figured among the fifteen candidates: Knut Hamsun, Arne Gaborg, and Hans E. Kinck, and all three had some claim to eminence. Kinck and Gaborg had each been proposed a number of times over the years, and both had been the subjects of detailed reports to the Academy. Hamsun had been proposed

only once, in 1918, a year in which no Prize for Literature had been awarded. In 1920, his candidacy was revived at the last minute by his old friend and warm admirer, Erik Axel Karlfeldt, who was then permanent secretary of the Academy. Karlfeldt himself had been nominated for a prize the year before, but he had refused. It was Karlfeldt who carried out the brisk campaign for Hamsun, assisted by the enthusiastic backing of two other Academicians, Albert Engström and Anders Österling, who were both fascinated by the vagabond Norwegian genius. Karlfeldt easily won his point with little discussion, in spite of a rather negative report from the chairman of the jury, Per Hallström.

Hallström's official report is unequivocally laudatory, particularly in its treatment of Hamsun's early novels—*Hunger, Pan, Mysteries,* and *Victoria.* All of these books bear the marks of the lion's claw, in spite of the undeniable influence of the great Russian writers, especially Dostoevsky. There was less enthusiasm for his philosophical dramas in verse, which Hallström found rather a potpourri of *Peer Gynt* and *Cyrano de Bergerac,* incoherent and rather hard to take. The report recognized without reservation the lofty tenor and extraordinary freshness of inspiration in Hamsun's recent work, *Growth of the Soil.* Hallström concluded

[229]

that if we considered only Hamsun's creative artistic genius, not one of his countrymen could be compared to this brilliant, if sometimes erratic mind. He was above all a disrupting, anarchic force, scarcely the man to bow before that "impulse toward an ideal" which Alfred Nobel invoked when he set up his awards. For this reason the Swedish Academy stressed that the award was being given exclusively "for his monumental work, *Growth of the Soil.*"

It was not only in the Scandinavian countries that people were pleased by the choice of Hamsun. In Germany and the Slavic countries, where his work was known either in the original or in translation, the selection elicited favorable and in some cases enthusiastic comment. "He is the direct heir of the great Norwegian writers, on a par with Ibsen and Björnson," we read in the *Dagens Nyheter,* a leading Swedish newspaper not normally given to ratifying the Academy's choices. The German press was no less enthusiastic, and for good reason. During World War I, Hamsun had been notoriously pro-German. His attitude arose from a kind of badly digested Nietzschean racism, which fortunately left few traces in his books. This passion for *die blonde Bestie,* "the blond beast," was later to lead him to mental aberrations bordering on madness.

In France, the naming of the new laureate was greeted rather coldly. To begin with, he was practically unknown, in spite of the fact that by 1920 his works had been translated into some twenty languages. Here only a few of his early novels were known in translations. In Russia, long before the Revolution, Hamsun could boast of a cult as impressive as Gorki's among young Russian intellectuals.

In both England and North America, where Hamsun was not well known, the leading newspapers merely noted the award without lengthy comment. The reticence of the American press could in part be explained by the critical attitude, almost arrogant in its violence, which he had shown toward "the American way of life" in his early writings after his rough experience as a vagabond in the United States.

At the time of the award, Hamsun was sixty years old. This man of legendary aloofness traveled to Stockholm to receive his award. Although he avoided all contact with the press, he quickly became the hero of the day. He refused to give the address on behalf of all the laureates, which normally is given by the winner of the Prize for Literature at the official banquet following distribution of the Prizes. To everyone's surprise, however, he rose to propose a toast to the youth of all nations of the world in return for the tributes paid him by the students of Stockholm. He was in such fine fettle after the banquet that when he got back to the Grand Hotel he insisted on sharing his Prize with his Swedish friends Karlfeldt and Engström. Angered by their refusal to accept it, he was determined to give his check and diploma to his room steward, but he ended by forgetting them in the elevator, where they were found the next morning.

Translated by Dale McAdoo.

Hermann Hesse

1946

"For his inspired writings which,

while growing in boldness and penetration,

exemplify the classical humanitarian

ideals and high qualities of style"

Illustrated by DIGNIMONT

PRESENTATION ADDRESS

By ANDERS ÖSTERLING

PERMANENT SECRETARY

OF THE SWEDISH ACADEMY

THIS YEAR'S NOBEL PRIZE FOR LITERATURE has been awarded to a writer of German origin who has had wide critical acclaim and who has created his work regardless of public favor. The sixty-nine-year-old Hermann Hesse can look back on a considerable achievement consisting of novels, short stories, and poems, partly available in Swedish translation.

He escaped from political pressure earlier than other German writers and, during World War I, settled in Switzerland, where he acquired citizenship in 1923. It should not be overlooked, however, that his extraction as well as his personal connections had always justified Hesse in considering himself as much Swiss as German. His asylum in a country that was neutral during the war allowed him to continue his important literary work in relative quiet, and at present Hesse, together with Mann, is the best representative of the German cultural heritage in contemporary literature.

With Hesse, more than with most writers, one has to know his personal background to understand the rather surprising components that make up his personality. He comes from a strictly Pietist Swabian family. His father was a well-known church historian, his mother the daughter of a missionary. She was of French descent and was educated in India. It was taken for granted that Hermann would become a minister, and he was sent to the seminary at the cloister of Maulbronn. He ran away, became an apprentice to a watchmaker, and later worked in bookshops in Tübingen and Basle.

The youthful rebellion against the inherited piety that nonetheless always remained in the depth of his being, was repeated in a painful inner crisis, when in 1914, as a mature man and an acknowledged master of regional literature, he went new ways which were far removed from his previous idyllic paths. There are, briefly, two factors that caused this profound change in Hesse's writings.

The first was, of course, the World War. When at its beginning he wanted to speak some words of peace and contemplation to his agitated colleagues and in his pamphlet used Beethoven's motto, *"O Freunde, nicht diese Töne,"* he aroused a storm of protest. He was savagely attacked by the German press and was apparently deeply shocked by this experience. He took it as evidence that the entire civilization of Europe in which he had so long believed was sick and decaying. Redemption had to come from beyond the accepted norms, perhaps from the light of the East, perhaps from the core hidden in anarchic theories of the resolution of good and evil in a higher unity. Sick and doubt-ridden, he sought a cure in the psychoanalysis of Freud, eagerly preached and practiced at that time, which left lasting traces in Hesse's increasingly bold books of this period.

This personal crisis found its magnificent expression in the fantastical novel *Der Steppenwolf* (1927), an inspired account of the split in human nature, the tension between desire and reason in an individual who is outside the social and moral notions of everyday life. In this bizarre fable of a man without a home, hunted like a wolf, plagued by neuroses, Hesse created an incomparable and explosive book, dangerous and fateful perhaps, but at the same time liberating by its mixture of sardonic humor and poetry in the treatment of the theme. Despite the prominence of modern problems Hesse even here preserves a continuity with the best German traditions; the writer whom this extremely suggestive story recalls most is E. T. A. Hoffmann, the master of the *Elixiere des Teufels*.

Hesse's maternal grandfather was the famous Indologist Gundert. Thus even in his childhood the writer felt drawn to Indian wisdom. When as a mature man he traveled to the country of his desire he did not, indeed, solve the riddle of life; but the influence of Buddhism soon entered his thought, an influence by no means restricted to *Siddhartha* (1922), the beautiful story of a young Brahman's search for the meaning of life on earth.

Hesse's work combines so many influences from Buddha and St. Francis to Nietzsche and Dostoevsky that one might suspect that he is primarily an eclectic experimenter with different philosophies. But this opinion would be quite wrong. His sincerity and his seriousness are the foundations of his work and remain in control even in his treatment of the most extravagant subjects.

In his most accomplished novellas we are confronted both directly and indirectly with his personality. His style, always admirable, is as perfect in rebellion and demonic ecstasy as in calm philosophical speculation. The story of the desperate embezzler Klein, who flees to Italy to seek there his last chance, and the marvelously calm description of his late brother Hans in the *Gedenkblätter* (1937) are masterly examples from different fields of his creativity.

In Hesse's more recent work the vast novel *Das Glasperlenspiel* occupies a special position. It is a fantasy about a mysterious intellectual order, on the same heroic and ascetic level as that of the Jesuits, based on the exercise of meditation as a kind of therapy. The novel has structure in which the concept of the game and its role in civilization has surprising parallels with the ingenious study *Homo ludens* by the Dutch scholar Huizinga. Hesse's attitude is ambiguous. In a period of collapse it is a precious task to preserve the cultural tradition. But civilization cannot be permanently kept alive by turning it into a cult for the few. If it is possible to reduce the variety of knowledge to an abstract system of formulas, we have on the one hand proof that civilization rests on an organic system; on the other, this high knowledge cannot be considered permanent. It is as fragile and destructible as the glass pearls themselves, and the child that finds the glittering pearls in the rubble no longer knows their meaning. A philosophical novel of this kind easily runs the risk of being called recondite, but Hesse defended his with a few gentle lines in the motto of the book, ". . . then in certain cases and for irresponsible men it may be that nonexistent things can be described more easily and with less responsibility in words than the existent, and therefore the reverse applies for pious and scholarly historians; for nothing destroys description so much as words, and yet there is nothing more necessary than to place before the eyes of men certain things the existence of which is neither provable nor probable, but which, for this very reason, pious and scholarly men treat to a certain extent as existent in order that they may be led a step further toward their being and their becoming."

If Hesse's reputation as a prose writer varies, there has never been any doubt about his stature as a poet. Since the death of Rilke and George he has been the foremost German poet of our time. He combines exquisite purity of style with moving emotional warmth, and his musical form is unsurpassed in our time. He continues the tradition of Goethe, Eichendorf, and Mörike and renews its poetic magic by a color peculiar to himself. His collection of poems, *Trost der Nacht* (1929), mirrors with unusual clarity not only his inner drama, his healthy and sick hours, and his intense self-examination, but also his devotion to life, his pleasure in painting, and his worship of nature. A later collection, *Neue Gedichte* (1937), is full of autumnal wisdom and melancholy experience, and it shows a heightened sensibility in image, mood, and melody.

In a summary introduction it is impossible to do justice to the many changing qualities which make this writer particularly attractive to us and which have justly given him a faithful following. He is a problematic and a confessional poet with the wealth of the South-German mind, which he expresses in a very individual mixture of freedom and piety. If one over-looked the passionate tendency to protest, the ever-burning fire that makes the dreamer a fighter as soon as the matters at stake are sacred to him, one might call him a romantic poet. In one passage Hesse says that one must never be content with reality, that one should neither adore nor worship it, for this low, always disappointing, and desolate reality cannot be changed except by denying it through proving our superior strength.

Hesse's award is more than the confirmation of his fame. It honors a poetic achievement which presents throughout the image of a good man in his struggle, following his calling with rare faithfulness, who in a tragic epoch succeeded in bearing the arms of true humanism.

Unfortunately, reasons of health have prevented the poet from making the journey to Stockholm. In his stead the envoy of the Swiss Federal Republic will accept the Prize. Your Excellency, I ask you now to receive from the hands of His Majesty the King the Prize awarded by the Swedish Academy to your countryman, Hermann Hesse.

ACCEPTANCE SPEECH

By *HERMANN HESSE*

IN SENDING CORDIAL and respectful greetings to your festive gathering, I should like above all to express my regrets at not being able to be your guest in person, to greet and to thank you. My health has always been delicate, and I have been left a permanent invalid by the afflictions of the years since 1933 that have destroyed my life's work and have again and again burdened me with heavy duties. But my mind has not been broken, and I feel akin to you and to the idea that inspired the Nobel Foundation, the idea that the mind is international and supranational, that it ought to serve not war and annihilation, but peace and reconciliation.

My ideal, however, is not the blurring of national characteristics, such as would lead to an intellectually uniform humanity. On the contrary, may diversity in all shapes and colors live long on this dear earth of ours. What a wonderful thing is the existence of many races, many peoples, many languages, and many varieties of attitude and outlook! If I feel hatred and irreconcilable enmity toward wars, conquests, and annexations, I do so for many reasons, but also because so many organically grown, highly individual, and richly differentiated achievements of human civilization have fallen victim to these dark powers. I hate the great simplifiers, and I love the sense of quality, of inimitable craftsmanship and uniqueness. As your grateful guest and colleague I therefore extend my greetings to Sweden, your country, to her language and civilization, her rich and proud history, and her perseverance in maintaining and shaping her individual nature. I have never been to Sweden, but for decades many a good and kind thing has come to me from your country since that first present which I received from it: it is now forty years ago and it was a Swedish book, a copy of the first edition of *Christ Legends* with a personal dedication by Selma Lagerlöf. In the course of years there has been many a valuable exchange with your country until you have now surprised me with the final great present. Let me express to you my profound gratitude.

DEMIAN

By HERMANN HESSE

Translated by Michael Roloff and Michael Lebeck

Prologue

I cannot tell my story without reaching a long way back. If it were possible I would reach back farther still—into the very first years of my childhood, and beyond them into distant ancestral past.

Novelists when they write novels tend to take an almost godlike attitude toward their subject, pretending to a total comprehension of the story, a man's life, which they can therefore recount as God Himself might, nothing standing between them and the naked truth, the entire story meaningful in every detail. I am as little able to do this as the novelist is, even though my story is more important to me than any novelist's is to him—for this is my story; it is the story of a man, not of an invented, or possible, or idealized, or otherwise absent figure, but of a unique being of flesh and blood. Yet, what a real living human being is made of seems to be less understood today than at any time before, and men—each one of whom represents a unique and valuable experiment on the part of nature— are therefore shot wholesale nowadays. If we were not something more than unique human beings, if each one of us could really be done away with once and for all by a single bullet, storytelling would lose all purpose. But every man is more than just himself; he also represents the unique, the very special and always significant and remarkable point at which the world's phenomena intersect, only once in this way and never again. That is why every man's story is important, eternal, sacred; that is why every man, as long as he lives and fulfills the will of nature, is wondrous, and worthy of every consideration. In each individual the spirit has become flesh, in each man the creation suffers, within each one a redeemer is nailed to the cross.

Few people nowadays know what man is. Many sense this ignorance and die the more easily because of it, the same way that I will die more easily once I have completed this story.

I do not consider myself less ignorant than most people. I have been and still am a seeker, but I have ceased to question stars and books; I have begun to listen to the teachings my blood whispers to me. My story is not a pleasant one; it is neither sweet nor harmonious, as invented stories are; it has the taste of nonsense and chaos, of madness and dreams—like the lives of all men who stop deceiving themselves.

Each man's life represents a road toward himself, an attempt at such a road, the intimation of a path. No man has ever been entirely and completely himself. Yet each one strives to become that—one in an awkward, the other in a

*more intelligent way, each as best he can.
Each man carries the vestiges of his
birth—the slime and eggshells of his
primeval past—with him to the end of
his days. Some never become human,
remaining frog, lizard, ant. Some are
human above the waist, fish below. Each
represents a gamble on the part of nature
in creation of the human. We all share
the same origin, our mothers; all of us
come in at the same door. But each of
us—experiments of the depths—strives
toward his own destiny. We can understand one another; but each of us is able
to interpret himself to himself alone.*

1. Two Realms

I shall begin my story with an experience I had when I was ten and attended
our small town's Latin school.

The sweetness of many things from
that time still stirs and touches me with
melancholy: dark and well-lighted alleys,
houses and towers, chimes and faces,
rooms rich and comfortable, warm and
relaxed, rooms pregnant with secrets.
Everything bears the scent of warm intimacy, servant girls, household remedies,
and dried fruits.

The realms of day and night, two
different worlds coming from two opposite poles, mingled during this time. My
parents' house made up one realm, yet its
boundaries were even narrower, actually
embracing only my parents themselves.
This realm was familiar to me in almost
every way—mother and father, love and
strictness, model behavior, and school. It
was a realm of brilliance, clarity, and
cleanliness, gentle conversations, washed
hands, clean clothes, and good manners.
This was the world in which morning
hymns were sung and Christmas celebrated. Straight lines and paths led into
the future: there were duty and guilt, bad

conscience and confession, forgiveness
and good resolutions, love, reverence,
wisdom and the words of the Bible. If
one wanted an unsullied and orderly life,
one made sure one was in league with
this world.

The other realm, however, overlapping
half our house, was completely different;
it smelled different, spoke a different language, promised and demanded different
things. This second world contained
servant girls and workmen, ghost stories,
rumors of scandal. It was dominated by a
loud mixture of horrendous, intriguing,
frightful, mysterious things, including
slaughterhouses and prisons, drunkards
and screeching fishwives, calving cows,
horses sinking to their death, tales of
robberies, murders, and suicides. All
these wild and cruel, attractive and hideous things surrounded us, could be found
in the next alley, the next house. Policemen and tramps, drunkards who beat
their wives, droves of young girls pouring
out of factories at night, old women who
put the hex on you so that you fell ill,
thieves hiding in the forest, arsonists
nabbed by country police—everywhere
this second vigorous world erupted and
gave off its scent, everywhere, that is,
except in our parents' rooms. And that
was good. It was wonderful that peace
and orderliness, quiet and a good conscience, forgiveness and love, ruled in
this one realm, and it was wonderful that
the rest existed, too, the multitude of
harsh noises, of sullenness and violence,
from which one could still escape with a
leap into one's mother's lap.

It was strange how both realms
bordered on each other, how close together they were! For example, when
Lina, our servant girl, sat with us by the
living-room door at evening prayers and
added her clear voice to the hymn, her
washed hands folded on her smoothed-
down apron, she belonged with father
and mother, to us, to those that dwelled

in light and righteousness. But afterwards, in the kitchen or woodshed, when she told me the story of "the tiny man with no head," or when she argued with neighborhood women in the butchershop, she was someone else, belonged to another world which veiled her with mystery. And that's how it was with everything, most of all with myself. Unquestionably I belonged to the realm of light and righteousness; I was my parents' child. But in whichever direction I turned I perceived the other world, and I lived within that other world as well, though often a stranger to it, and suffering from panic and a bad conscience. There were times when I actually preferred living in the forbidden realm, and frequently, returning to the realm of light—necessary and good as it may have been—seemed almost like returning to something less beautiful, something rather drab and tedious. Sometimes I was absolutely certain that my destiny was to become like mother and father, as clear-sighted and unspoiled, as orderly and superior as they. But this goal seemed far away and to reach it meant attending endless schools, studying, passing tests and examinations, and this way led past and through the other, darker realm. It was not at all impossible that one might remain a part of it and sink into it. There were stories of sons who had gone astray, stories I read with passion. These stories always pictured the homecoming as such a relief and as something so extraordinary that I felt convinced that this alone was the right, the best, the sought-for thing. Still, the part of the story set among the evil and the lost was more appealing by far, and—if I could have admitted it—at times I didn't want the Prodigal Son to repent and be found again. But one didn't dare think this, much less say it out loud. It was only present somehow as a premonition, a possibility at the root of one's consciousness. When I pictured the devil to myself I could easily imagine him on the street below, disguised or undisguised, or at the country fair or in a bar, but never at home with us.

My sisters, too, belonged to the realm of light. It often seemed to me that they had a greater natural affinity to my father and mother; they were better, better mannered, had fewer faults than I. They had their faults, of course; they had their bad moments, but these did not appear to go very deep as they did with me, whose contact with evil often grew so oppressive and painful, and to whom the dark world seemed so much closer. Sisters, like parents, were to be comforted and respected; if I had quarreled with them I always reproached myself afterwards, felt like the instigator, the one who had to ask for forgiveness. For by offending my sisters I offended my parents, all that was good and superior. There were secrets I would far rather have shared with the lowest hoodlum than with my sisters. On good days, when my conscience did not trouble me, it was often delightful to play with them, to be good and decent as they were and to see myself in a noble light. That's what it must have been like to be an angel! It was the highest state one could think of. But how infrequent such days were! Often at play, at some harmless activity, I became so fervent and headstrong that I was too much for my sisters; the quarrels and unhappiness this led to threw me into such a rage that I became horrible, did and said things so awful they seared my heart even as I said them. Then followed harsh hours of gloomy regret and contrition, the painful moment when I begged forgiveness, to be followed again by beams of light, a quiet, thankful, undivided gladness.

I attended the Latin school. The mayor's son and the head forester's son were in my class; both visited me at home at times, and though they were quite unruly, they were both members of the good, the legal world. Yet this did not mean that I had no dealings with some of the neighborhood boys who attended public school and on whom we usually looked down. It is with one of them that I must begin my story.

One half-holiday—I was little more than ten years old—two neighborhood kids and I were roaming about when a much bigger boy, a strong and burly kid from public school, the tailor's son, joined us. His father drank and the whole family had a bad name. I had heard much about Franz Kromer, was afraid of him, didn't at all like that he came up to us. His manners were already those of a man and he imitated the walk and speech of young factory workers. Under his leadership we clambered down the riverbank by the bridge and hid below the first arch. The narrow strip between the vaulted wall of the bridge and the lazily flowing river was covered with nothing but refuse, shards, tangled bundles of rusty wire and other rubbish. Occasionally one could pick up something useful here. Franz Kromer instructed us to comb the area and show him what we found. He would either pocket it or fling it into the river. He put us on the lookout for objects made of lead, brass, and tin, all of which he tucked away—also an old comb made of horn. I felt very uneasy in his presence, not only because I knew that my father would not have approved of my being seen in his company, but because I was simply afraid of Franz himself, though I was glad that he seemed to accept me and treat me like the others. He gave instructions and we obeyed—it seemed like an old habit, even though this was the first time I was with him.

After a while we sat down. Franz spit into the water, and he looked like a man; he spit through a gap between his teeth and hit whatever he aimed at. A conversation started up, and the boys began boasting and heaping praise on themselves for all sorts of schoolboy heroics and tricks they had played. I kept quiet and yet was afraid I'd be noticed, that my silence might particularly incur Kromer's wrath. My two friends had begun to shun me the very moment Franz Kromer had joined us. I was a stranger among them and felt that my manners and clothes presented a kind of challenge. As a Latin school boy, the spoiled son of a well-to-do father, it would be impossible for Franz to like me, and the other two, I felt acutely, would soon disown and desert me.

Finally, out of sheer nervousness, I began telling a story too. I invented a long tale about a robbery in which I filled the role of hero. In a garden near the mill, I said, together with a friend, I had stolen a whole sackful of apples one night, and by no means ordinary apples, but apples of the very best sort. It was the fear of the moment that made me seek refuge in this story—inventing and telling stories came naturally to me. In order not to fall immediately silent again, and perhaps become involved in something worse, I gave a complete display of my narrative powers. One of us, I continued, had had to stand guard while the other climbed the tree and shook out the apples. Moreover, the sack had grown so heavy that we had to open it again, leaving half the apples behind. But half an hour later we had returned and fetched the rest.

When I had finished I waited for approval of some sort. I had warmed to my subject toward the end and been carried away by my own eloquence. The two younger ones kept silent, waiting, but Franz Kromer looked sharply at me out of narrowed eyes and asked threateningly:

"Is that true?"

"Yes," I said.

"Really and truly?"

"Yes, really and truly," I insisted stubbornly while choking inwardly with fear.

"Would you swear to it?"

I became very afraid but at once said yes.

"Then say: By God and the grace of my soul."

"By God and the grace of my soul," I said.

"Well, all right," he said and turned away.

I thought everything was all right now, and was glad when he got up and turned to go home. After we had climbed back up to the bridge, I said hesitantly that I would have to head for home myself.

"You can't be in that much of a hurry." Franz laughed. "We're going in the same direction, aren't we?"

Slowly he ambled on and I didn't dare run off; he was in fact walking in the direction of my house. When we stood in front of it and I saw the front door and the big brass knocker, the sun in the windows and the curtain in my mother's room, I breathed a sigh of relief.

When I quickly opened the door and slipped in, reaching to slam it shut, Franz Kromer edged in behind me. In the cool tiled passageway, lit only by one window facing the courtyard, he stood beside me, held on to me and said softly:

"Don't be in such a rush, you."

I looked at him, terrified. His grip on my arm was like a vise. I wondered what he might have in mind and whether he wanted to hurt me. I tried to decide whether if I screamed now, screamed loud and piercingly, someone could come down from above quickly enough to save me. But I gave up the idea.

"What is it?" I asked. "What do you want?"

"Nothing much. I only wanted to ask you something. The others don't have to hear it."

"Oh, really? I can't think of anything

to say to you. I have to go up, you know."

Softly Franz Kromer asked: "You know who owns the orchard by the mill, don't you?"

"I'm not sure. The miller, I think."

Franz had put his arm around me and now he drew me so close I was forced to look into his face inches away. His eyes were evil, he smiled maliciously; his face was filled with cruelty and a sense of power.

"Well, I can tell you for certain whose orchard that is. I've known for some time that someone had stolen apples there and that the man who owns it said he'd give two marks to anyone who'd tell him who swiped them."

"Oh, my God!" I exclaimed. "You wouldn't do that, would you?"

I felt it would be useless to appeal to his sense of honor. He came from the other world: betrayal was no crime to him. I sensed this acutely. The people from the other world were not like us in these matters.

"Not say anything?" laughed Kromer. "Kid, what do you take me for? Do you think I own a mint? I'm poor, I don't have a wealthy father like you and if I can earn two marks I earn them any way I can. Maybe he'll even give me more."

Suddenly he let go of me. The passageway no longer smelled of peace and safety, the world around me began to crumble. He would give me away to the police! I was a criminal; my father would be informed—perhaps even the police would come. All the dread of chaos threatened me, everything ugly and dangerous was united against me. It meant nothing that I'd filched nothing. I'd sworn I had!

Tears welled up in my eyes. I felt I had to strike a bargain and desperately I groped through all my pockets. Not a single apple, no pocket knife, I had nothing at all. I thought of my watch, an old silver watch that didn't work, that I wore just for the fun of it. It had been my grandmother's. Quickly I took it off.

I said: "Kromer, listen! Don't give me away. It wouldn't be fair if you did. I'll give you my watch as a present, here, take a look. Otherwise I've nothing at all. You can have it, it's made of silver, and the works, well, there's something slightly wrong with them; you have to have it fixed."

He smiled and weighed the watch in his palm. I looked at his hand and felt how brutal and deeply hostile it was to me, how it reached for my life and peace.

"It's made of silver," I said hesitantly.

"I don't give a damn for your silver and your old watch," he said scornfully. "Get it fixed yourself."

"But, Franz!" I exclaimed, trembling with fear that he might run away. "Wait, wait a moment. Why don't you take it? It's really made of silver, honest. And I don't have anything else."

He threw me a cold scornful look.

"Well, you know who I'll go to. Or I could go to the police too. . . . I'm on good terms with the sergeant."

He turned as if to go. I held on to his sleeve. I couldn't allow him to go. I would rather have died than suffer what might happen if he went off like that.

"Franz," I implored, hoarse with excitement, "don't do anything foolish. You're only joking, aren't you?"

"Yes, I'm joking, but it could turn into an expensive joke."

"Just tell me what I'm supposed to do, Franz. I'll do anything you ask."

He looked me up and down with narrowed eyes and laughed again.

"Don't be so stupid," he said with false good humor. "You know as well as I that I'm in a position to earn two marks. I'm not a rich man who can afford to throw them away, but you're rich—you even have a watch. All you have to do is give me two marks; then everything will be all right."

I understood his logic. But two marks! That was as much and as unattainable as ten, as a hundred, as a thousand. I didn't have a pfennig. There was a piggy bank that my mother kept for me. When relatives came to visit they would drop in five- or ten-pfennig pieces. That was all I had. I had no allowance at that time.

"I just don't have any," I said sadly. "I don't have any money at all. But I'll give you everything else I have. I have a Western, tin soldiers, and a compass. Wait, I'll get them for you."

Kromer's mouth merely twisted into a brief sneer. Then he spit on the floor.

Harshly he said: "You can keep your crap. A compass! Don't make me mad! You hear, I'm after money."

"But I don't have any, I never get any, I can't help it."

"All right, then you'll bring me the two marks tomorrow. I'll wait for you after school down near the market place. That's all. You'll see what'll happen if you don't bring it."

"But where am I going to get it if I don't have any?"

"There's plenty of money in your house. That's your business. Tomorrow after school. And I'm telling you: if you don't have it with you . . ." He threw me a withering look, spit once more, and vanished like a shadow.

I couldn't even get upstairs. My life was wrecked. I thought of running away and never coming back, or of drowning myself. However, I couldn't picture any of this very clearly. In the dark, I sat down on the bottom step of our staircase, huddled up within myself, abandoning myself to misery. That's where Lina found me weeping as she came downstairs with the basket to fetch wood.

I begged her not to say a word, then I

went upstairs. To the right of the glass
door hung my father's hat and my
mother's parasol; they gave me a feeling
of home and comfort, and my heart
greeted them thankfully, as the Prodigal
Son might greet the sight and smell of
old familiar rooms. But all of it was lost
to me now, all of it belonged to the clear,
well-lighted world of my father and
mother, and I, guilty and deeply engulfed
in an alien world, was entangled in adventures and sin, threatened by an
enemy,—by dangers, fear, and shame.
The hat and parasol, the old sandstone
floor I was so fond of, the broad picture
above the hall cupboard, the voice of my
elder sister coming to me from the living
room were all more moving, more precious, more delicious than ever before,
but they had ceased to be a refuge and
something I could rely on; they had become an unmistakable reproach. None of
this was mine any more, I could no
longer take part in its quiet cheerfulness.
My feet had become muddied, I could
not even wipe them clean on the mat;
everywhere I went I was followed by a
darkness of which this world of home
knew nothing. How many secrets I had
had, how often I had been afraid—but
all of it had been child's play compared
with what I brought home with me
today. I was haunted by misfortune, it
was reaching out toward me so that not
even my mother could protect me, since
she was not even allowed to know.
Whether my crime was stealing or lying—(hadn't I sworn a false oath by God
and everything that was sacred?)—was
immaterial. My sin was not specifically
this or that but consisted of having
shaken hands with the devil. Why had I
gone along? Why had I obeyed Kromer
—better even than I had ever obeyed my
father? Why had I invented the story,
building myself up with a crime as
though it were a heroic act? The devil

held me in his clutches, the enemy was
behind me.

For the time being I was not so much
afraid of what would happen tomorrow
as of the horrible certainty that my way,
from now on, would lead farther and
farther downhill into darkness. I felt
acutely that new offenses were bound to
grow out of this one offense, that my
presence among my sisters, greeting and
kissing my parents, were a lie, that I was
living a lie concealed deep inside myself.

For a moment, hope and confidence
flickered up inside me as I gazed at my
father's hat. I would tell him everything,
would accept his verdict and his punishment, and would make him into my con-
fessor and savior. It would only be a
penance, the kind I had often done, a
bitterly difficult hour, a ruefully difficult
request for forgiveness.

How sweet and tempting that sounded!
But it was no use. I knew I wouldn't do
it. I knew I now had a secret, a sin which
I would have to expiate alone. Perhaps I
stood at the parting of the ways, perhaps
I would now belong among the wicked
forever, share their secrets, depend on
them, obey them, have to become one of
their kind. I had acted the man and hero,
now I had to bear the consequences.

I was glad when my father took me to
task for my muddy boots. It diverted his
attention by sidestepping the real issue
and placed me in a position to endure
reproaches that I could secretly transfer
to the other, the more serious offense. A
strange new feeling overcame me at this
point, a feeling that stung pleasurably: I
felt superior to my father! Momentarily I
felt a certain loathing for his ignorance.
His upbraiding me for muddy boots
seemed pitiful. "If you only knew"
crossed my mind as I stood there like a
criminal being cross-examined for a
stolen loaf of bread when the actual
crime was murder. It was an odious,

hostile feeling, but it was strong and deeply attractive, and shackled me more than anything else to my secret and my guilt. I thought Kromer might have gone to the police by now and denounced me, that thunderstorms were forming above my head, while all this time they continued to treat me like a little child.

This moment was the most significant and lasting of the whole experience. It was the first rent in the holy image of my father, it was the first fissure in the columns that had upheld my childhood, which every individual must destroy before he can become himself. The inner, the essential line of our fate consists of such invisible experiences. Such fissures and rents grow together again, heal and are forgotten, but in the most secret recesses they continue to live and bleed.

I immediately felt such dread of this new feeling that I could have fallen down before my father and kissed his feet to ask forgiveness. But one cannot apologize for something fundamental, and a child feels and knows this as well and as deeply as any sage.

I felt the need to give some thought to my new situation, to reflect about what I would do tomorrow. But I did not find the time. All evening I was busy getting used to the changed atmosphere in our living room. Wall clock and table, Bible and mirror, bookcase and pictures on the wall were leaving me behind; I was forced to observe with a chill in my heart how my world, my good, happy, carefree life, was becoming a part of the past, was breaking away from me, and I was forced to feel how I was being shackled and held fast with new roots to the outside, to the dark and alien world. For the first time in my life I tasted death, and death tasted bitter, for death is birth, is fear and dread of some terrible renewal.

I was glad when I finally lay in my bed. Just before, as my last torment, I had had to endure evening prayers. We had sung a hymn which was one of my favorites. I felt unable to join in and every note galled me. When my father intoned the blessing—when he finished with "God be with us!"—something broke inside me and I was rejected forever from this intimate circle. God's grace was with all of them, but it was no longer with me. Cold and deeply exhausted, I had left them.

When I had lain in bed awhile, enveloped by its warmth and safety, my fearful heart turned back once more in confusion and hovered anxiously above what was now past. My mother had said good night to me as always. I could still hear her steps resound in the other room; the candle glow still illuminated the chink in the door. Now, I thought, now she'll come back once more, she has sensed something, she will give me a kiss and ask, ask kindly with a promise in her voice, and then I'll weep, then the lump in my throat will melt, then I will throw my arms around her, and then all will be well; I will be saved! And even after the chink in the door had gone dark I continued to listen and was certain that it simply would have to happen.

Then I returned to my difficulties and looked my enemy in the eye. I could see him clearly, one eye screwed up, his mouth twisted into a brutal smile, and while I eyed him, becoming more and more convinced of the inevitable, he grew bigger and uglier and his evil eye lit up with a fiendish glint. He was right next to me until I fell asleep, yet I didn't dream of him nor of what had happened that day. I dreamed instead that my parents, my sisters, and I were drifting in a boat, surrounded by absolute peace and the glow of a holiday. In the middle of the night I woke with the aftertaste of this happiness. I could still see my sisters' white summer dresses shimmer in the sun as I fell out of paradise back into reality, again face to face with the enemy, with his evil eye.

Next morning, when my mother came rushing up shouting that it was late and why was I still in bed, I looked sick. When she asked me whether anything was wrong, I vomited.

This seemed to be something gained. I loved being slightly sick, being allowed to lie in bed all morning, drinking camomile tea, listening to my mother tidy up the other rooms or Lina deal with the butcher in the hallway. Mornings off from school seemed enchanted, like a fairy tale; the sun playing in the room was not the same sun shut out of school when the green shades were lowered. Yet even this gave me no pleasure today; there was something false about it.

If only I could die! But, as often before, I was only slightly unwell and it was of no help, my illness protected me from school but not from Franz Kromer who would be waiting for me at eleven in the market place. And my mother's friendliness, instead of comforting me, was a distressing nuisance. I made a show of having fallen asleep again in order to be left alone to think. But I could see no way out. At eleven I had to be at the market. At ten I quietly got dressed and said that I felt better. The answer, as usual under these circumstances, was: either I went straight back to bed or in the afternoon I would have to be in school. I said I would gladly go to school. I had come up with a plan.

I couldn't meet Kromer penniless. I had to get hold of my piggy bank. I knew it didn't contain enough, by no means enough, yet it was something, and I sensed that something was better than nothing, and that Kromer could at least be appeased.

In stocking feet I crept guiltily into my mother's room and took the piggy bank out of her desk; yet that was not half as bad as what had happened the day before

with Kromer. My heart beat so rapidly I felt I would choke. It did not ease up when I discovered downstairs that the bank was locked. Forcing it was easy, it was merely a matter of tearing the thin tin-plate grid; yet breaking it hurt—only now had I really committed a theft. Until then I had filched lumps of sugar or some fruit; this was more serious stealing, even though it was my own money I stole. I sensed how I was one step nearer Kromer and his world, how bit by bit everything was going downhill with me. I began to feel stubborn; let the devil take the hindmost! There was no turning back now. Nervously I counted the money. In the piggy bank it had sounded like so much more, but there was painfully little lying in my hand: sixty-five pfennigs. I hid the box on the ground floor, held the money clasped in my fist, and stepped out of the house, feeling more different than I had ever felt before when I walked through the gate. I thought I heard someone calling after me from upstairs but I walked away quickly.

There was still a lot of time left. By a very devious route, I sneaked through the little alleys of a changed town, under a cloudy sky such as I had never seen before, past staring houses and people who eyed me with suspicion. Then it occurred to me that a friend from school had once found a thaler in the cattle market. I would gladly have gone down on my knees and prayed that God perform a miracle and let me make a similar find. But I had forfeited the right to pray. And in any case, mending the box would have required a second miracle.

Franz Kromer spotted me from a distance, yet he approached me without haste and seemed to ignore me. When he was close, he motioned authoritatively for me to follow him, and without once turning back he walked calmly down the Strohgasse and across the little footbridge until he stopped in front of a new building at the outskirts. There were no work-men about, the walls were bare, doors and windows were blanks. Kromer took a look around, then walked through the entrance into the house and I followed him. He stepped behind a wall, gave me a signal, and stretched out his hand.

"Have you got it?" he asked coolly.

I drew my clenched fist out of my pocket and emptied my money into his flat outstretched palm. He had counted it even before the last pfennig piece had clinked down.

"That's sixty-five pfennigs," he said and looked at me.

"Yes," I said nervously. "That's all I have. I know it's not enough, but it's all I have."

"I thought you were cleverer than that," he scolded almost mildly. "Among men of honor you've got to do things right. I don't want to take anything away from you that isn't the right sum. You know that. Take your pennies back, there! The other one—you know who—won't try to scale down the price. He pays up."

"But I simply don't have another pfennig. It's all I had in my bank."

"That's your business. But I don't want to make you unhappy. You owe me one mark, thirty-five pfennigs. When can I have them?"

"Oh, you'll get them for sure, Kromer. I just don't know when right now—perhaps I'll have more tomorrow or the day later. You understand, don't you, that I can't breathe a word about this to my father."

"That's not my concern. I'm not out to do you any harm. I could have my money before lunch if I wanted, you know, and I'm poor. You wear expensive clothes and you're better fed than I. But I won't say anything. I can wait a bit. The day after tomorrow I'll whistle for you. You know what my whistle sounds like, don't you?"

He let me hear it. I had heard it before.

"Yes," I said, "I know it."

He left me as though he'd never seen me before. It had been a business trans-action between the two of us, nothing more.

I think Kromer's whistle would frighten me even today if I suddenly heard it again. From now on I was to hear it repeatedly; it seemed to me I heard it all the time. There was not a single place, not a single game, no activity, no thought which this whistle did not penetrate, the whistle that made me his slave, that had become my fate. Frequently I would go into our small flower garden, of which I was so fond on those mild, colorful autumn afternoons, and an odd urge prompted me to play once more the childish games of my earlier years; I was playing, so to speak, the part of someone younger than myself, someone still good and free, innocent and safe. Yet into the midst of this haven—always expected, yet horribly surprising each time—from somewhere Kromer's whistle would erupt, destroying the game, crushing my illusions. Then I would have to leave the garden to follow my tormentor to wicked, ugly places where I would have to give him an account of my pitiful finances and let myself be pressed for payment. The entire episode lasted perhaps several weeks, yet to me they seemed like years, an eternity. Rarely did I have any money, at most a five- or ten-pfennig piece stolen from the kitchen table when Lina had left the shopping basket lying around. Kromer upbraided me each time, becoming more and more contemptuous: I was cheating him, depriving him of what was rightfully his, I was stealing from him, making *him* miserable! Never in my life had I felt so distressed, never had I felt more hopeless, more enslaved.

I had filled the piggy bank with play money and replaced it in my mother's desk. No one asked for it but the possibility that they might never left my thoughts. What frightened me even more than Kromer's brutal whistling was my mother's stepping up to me—wasn't she coming to inquire about the piggy bank?

Because I had met my tormentor many times empty-handed, he began finding other means of torturing and using me. I had to work for him. He had to run various errands for his father; I had to do them for him. Or he would ask me to perform some difficult feat: hop for ten minutes on one leg, pin a scrap of paper on a passer-by's coat. Many nights in my dreams I elaborated on these tortures and lay drenched in a nightmare's sweat.

For a while I actually became sick. I vomited frequently and came down with frequent chills, yet at night I would burn and sweat. My mother sensed that something was wrong and was very considerate, but this only tortured me the more since I could not respond by confiding in her.

One night, after I had gone to bed, she brought me a piece of chocolate. It reminded me of former years when, if I had been a good boy, I would receive such rewards before I fell asleep. Now she stood there and offered me the piece of chocolate. The sight was so painful that I could only shake my head. She asked me what was wrong and stroked my hair. All I could answer was: "No, no! I don't want anything." She placed the chocolate on my night table and left. The next morning, when she wanted to ask me about my behavior of the night before, I pretended to have forgotten the episode completely. Once she brought the doctor, who examined me and prescribed cold baths in the morning.

My condition at that time was a kind of madness. Amid the ordered peace of our house I lived shyly, in agony, like a ghost; I took no part in the life of the others, rarely forgot myself for an hour at a time. To my father, who was often irritated and asked me what was the matter, I was completely cold.

2. Cain

My salvation came from a totally unexpected source, which, at the same time, brought a new element into my life that has affected it to this very day.

A new boy had just been enrolled in our school. He was the son of a well-to-do widow who had come to live in our town; he wore a mourning band on his sleeve. Being several years older than I, he was assigned to a grade above me. Still, I could not avoid noticing him, nor could anyone else. This remarkable student seemed much older than he looked; in fact, he did not strike anyone as a boy at all. In contrast to us, he seemed strange and mature, like a man, or rather like a gentleman. He was not popular, did not take part in our games, still less in the general roughhouse, and only his firm, self-confident tone toward the teachers won the admiration of the students. He was called Max Demian.

One day—as happened now and again—an additional class was assigned to our large classroom for some reason or other. It was Demian's class. We, the younger ones, were having a Scripture lesson; the higher grade had to write an essay. While the story of Cain and Abel was being drummed into us, I kept glancing toward Demian whose face held a peculiar fascination for me, and I observed the intelligent, light, unusually resolute face bent attentively and diligently over his work; he didn't at all look like a student doing an assignment, but rather like a scientist investigating a problem of his own. I couldn't say that he made a favorable impression on me;

on the contrary, I had something against him: he seemed too superior and detached, his manner too provocatively confident, and his eyes gave him an adult expression—which children never like—faintly sad, with flashes of sarcasm. Yet I could not help looking at him, no matter whether I liked or detested him, but if he happened to glance my way I averted my eyes in panic. When I think back on it today, and what he looked like as a student at that time, I can only say that he was in every respect different from all the others, was entirely himself, with a personality all his own which made him noticeable even though he did his best not to be noticed; his manner and bearing was that of a prince disguised among farm boys, taking great pains to appear one of them.

He was walking behind me on the way home from school, and after the others had turned off he caught up with me and said hello. Even his manner of greeting, though he tried to imitate our schoolboy tone, was distinctly adult and polite.

"Shall we walk together for a while?" he asked. I felt flattered and nodded. Then I described to him where I lived.

"Oh, over there?" he said and smiled. "I know the house. There's something odd above the doorway—it interested me at once."

I didn't know offhand what he meant and was astonished that he apparently knew our house better than I did myself. The keystone of the arch above the doorway bore no doubt a kind of coat of arms but it had worn off with time and had frequently been painted over. As far as I knew it had nothing to do with us and our family.

"I don't know anything about it," I said shyly. "It's a bird or something like that and must be quite old. The house is supposed to have been part of the monastery at one point."

"That's quite possible." He nodded. "Take a good look at it sometime! Such things can be quite interesting. I believe it's a sparrow hawk."

We walked on. I felt very self-conscious. Suddenly Demian laughed as though something had struck him as funny.

"Yes, when we had class together," he burst out. "The story of Cain who has that mark on his forehead. Do you like it?"

No, I didn't. It was rare for me to like anything we had to learn. Yet I didn't dare confess it, for I felt I was being addressed by an adult. I said I didn't much mind the story.

Demian slapped me on the back.

"You don't have to put on an act for me. But in fact the story is quite remarkable. It's far more remarkable than most stories we're taught in school. Your teacher didn't go into it at great length. He just mentioned the usual things about God and sin and so forth. But I believe—" He interrupted himself and asked with a smile: "Does this interest you at all?"

"Well, I think," he went on, "one can give this story about Cain quite a different interpretation. Most of the things we're taught I'm sure are quite right and true, but one can view all of them from quite a different angle than the teachers do—and most of the time they then make better sense. For instance, one can't be quite satisfied with this Cain and the mark on his forehead, with the way it's explained to us. Don't you agree? It's perfectly possible for someone to kill his brother with a stone and to panic and repent. But that he's awarded a special decoration for his cowardice, a mark that protects him and puts the fear of God into all the others, that's quite odd, isn't it?"

"Of course," I said with interest: the

idea began to fascinate me. "But what other way of interpreting the story is there?"

He slapped me on the shoulder.

"It's quite simple! The first element of the story, its actual beginning, was the mark. Here was a man with something in his face that frightened the others. They didn't dare lay hands on him; he impressed them, he and his children. We can guess—no, we can be quite certain—that it was not a mark on his forehead like a postmark—life is hardly ever as clear and straightforward as that. It is much more likely that he struck people as faintly sinister, perhaps a little more intellect and boldness in his look than people were used to. This man was powerful: you would approach him only with awe. He had a 'sign.' You could explain this any way you wished. And people always want what is agreeable to them and puts them in the right. They were afraid of Cain's children: they bore a 'sign.' So they did not interpret the sign for what it was—a mark of distinction—but as its opposite. They said: 'Those fellows with the sign, they're a strange lot'—and indeed they were. People with courage and character always seem sinister to the rest. It was a scandal that a breed of fearless and sinister people ran about freely, so they attached a nickname and myth to these people to get even with them, to make up for the many times they had felt afraid—do you get it?"

"Yes--that is—in that case Cain wouldn't have been evil at all? And the whole story in the Bible is actually not authentic?"

"Yes and no. Such age-old stories are always true but they aren't always properly recorded and aren't always given correct interpretations. In short, I mean Cain was a fine fellow and this story was pinned on him only because people were afraid. The story was simply a rumor,

something that people gab about, and it was true in so far as Cain and his children really bore a kind of mark and were different from most people."

I was astounded.

"And do you believe that the business about killing his brother isn't true either?" I asked, entranced.

"Oh, that's certainly true. The strong man slew a weaker one. It's doubtful whether it was really his brother. But it isn't important. Ultimately all men are brothers. So, a strong man slew a weaker one: perhaps it was a truly valiant act, perhaps it wasn't. At any rate, all the other weaker ones were afraid of him from then on, they complained bitterly and if you asked them: 'Why don't you turn around and slay him, too?' they did not reply 'Because we're cowards,' but rather 'You can't, he has a sign. God has marked him.' The fraud must have originated some way like that.—Oh well, I see I'm keeping you. So long then."

He turned into the Altgasse and left me standing there, more baffled than I had ever been in my life. Yet, almost as soon as he had gone, everything he had said seemed incredible. Cain a noble person, Abel a coward! Cain's mark a mark of distinction! It was absurd, it was blasphemous and evil. How did God fit in in that case? Hadn't He accepted the sacrifice of Abel? Didn't He love Abel? No, what Demian had said was completely crazy. And I suspected that he had wanted to make fun of me and make me lose my footing. He was clever all right, and he could talk, but he couldn't put that one over, not on me!

I had never before given as much thought to a biblical story or to any other story. And for a long time I had not forgotten Franz Kromer as completely; for hours, for a whole evening in fact. At home I read the story once more as written in the Bible. It was brief and unambiguous; it was quite mad to look for a special, hidden meaning. At that rate every murderer could declare that he was God's darling! No, what Demian had said was nonsense. What pleased me was the ease and grace with which he was able to say such things, as though everything were self-evident; and then the look in his eyes!

Something was very wrong with me, though; my life was in very great disorder. I had lived in a wholesome and clean world, had been a kind of Abel myself, and now I was stuck deeply in the "other world," had fallen and sunk very low—yet it hadn't basically been my fault! How was I to consider that? And now a memory flashed within me that for a moment almost left me breathless. On that fatal evening when my misery had begun, there had been that matter with my father. There, for a moment, I had seen through him and his world of light and wisdom and had felt nothing but contempt for it. Yes, at that moment I, who was Cain and bore the mark, had imagined that this sign was not a mark of shame and that because of my evil and misfortune I stood higher than my father and the pious, the righteous.

I had not experienced the moment in this form, in clearly expressed thoughts, but all of this had been contained within it; it had been the eruption of emotions, of strange stirrings, that hurt me yet filled me with pride at the same time.

When I considered how strangely Demian had talked about the fearless and the cowardly, what an unusual meaning he had given the mark Cain bore on his forehead, how his eyes, his remarkable adult eyes had lit up, the question flashed through my mind whether Demian himself was not a kind of Cain. Why does he defend Cain unless he feels an affinity with him? Why does he have such a powerful gaze? Why does he speak so contemptuously of the "others," of the timid who actually are the pious, the chosen ones of the Lord?

I could not bring these thoughts to any conclusion. A stone had been dropped into the well, the well was my youthful soul. And for a very long time this matter of Cain, the fratricide, and the "mark" formed the point of departure for all my attempts at comprehension, my doubts and my criticism.

I noticed that Demian exerted equal fascination over the other students. I hadn't told anyone about his version of the story of Cain, but the others seemed to be interested in him, too. At any rate, many rumors were in circulation about the "new boy." If I could only remember them all now, each one would throw some light on him and could be interpreted. I remember first that Demian's mother was reported to be wealthy and also, supposedly, neither she nor her son ever attended church. One story had it that they were Jewish but they might equally well have been secret Mohammedans. Then there was Max Demian's legendary physical prowess. But this could be corroborated: when the strongest boy in Demian's class had taunted him, calling him a coward when he refused to fight back, Demian had humiliated him. Those who were present told that Demian had grasped the boy with one hand by the neck and squeezed until the boy went pale; afterwards, the boy had slunk away and had not been able to use his arm for a whole week. One evening some boys even claimed that he was dead. For a time everything, even the most extravagant assertions were believed. Then everyone seemed to have had their fill of Demian for a while, though not much later gossip again flourished: some boys reported that Demian was intimate with girls and that he "knew everything."

Meanwhile, my business with Kromer

took its inevitable course. I couldn't escape him, for even when he left me alone for days I was still bound to him. He haunted my dreams and what he failed to perpetrate on me in real life, my imagination let him do to me in those dreams in which I was completely his slave. I have always been a great dreamer; in dreams I am more active than in my real life, and these shadows sapped me of health and energy. A recurring nightmare was that Kromer always maltreated me, spit and knelt on me and, what was worse, led me on to commit the most horrible crimes—or, rather, not so much led me on as compelled me through sheer force of persuasion. The worst of these dreams, from which I awoke half-mad, had to do with a murderous assault on my father. Kromer whetted a knife, put it in my hand; we stood behind some trees in an avenue and lay in wait for someone, I did not know whom. Yet when this someone approached and Kromer pinched my arm to let me know that this was the person I was to stab—it was my father. Then I would awake.

Although I still drew a connection between these events and the story of Cain and Abel, I gave little thought to Max Demian. When he first approached me again, it was, oddly enough, also in a dream. For I was still dreaming of being tortured. Yet this time it was Demian who knelt on me. And—this was totally new and left a deep impression on me—everything I had resisted and that had been agony to me when Kromer was my tormentor I suffered gladly at Demian's hands, with a feeling compounded as much of ecstasy as of fear. I had this dream twice. Then Kromer regained his old place.

For years I have been unable to distinguish between what I experienced in these dreams and in real life. In any event, the bad relationship with Kromer continued and by no means came to an end after I had finally paid my debt out of any number of petty thefts. No, for now he knew of these new thefts since he asked each time where I had gotten the money, and I was more in bondage to him than ever. Often he threatened to tell everything to my father but even then my fear was hardly as great as my profound regret at not having done so myself at the very beginning. In the meantime, miserable though I was, I did not regret everything that happened, at least not all the time, and occasionally I even felt that everything had had to happen as it did. I was in the hands of fate and it was useless to try to escape.

Presumably, my parents also were distressed by the state I was in. A strange spirit had taken hold of me, I no longer fitted into our community, once so intimate; yet often a wild longing came over me to return to it as to a lost paradise. My mother in particular treated me more like an invalid than a scoundrel, but my true status within the family I was better able to judge from my sisters' attitude. Theirs was one of extreme indulgence, which made it plain that I was considered a kind of madman, more to be pitied for his condition than blamed, but possessed by the devil nonetheless. They prayed for me with unusual fervor and I was infinitely miserable when I realized the futility of these prayers. Often I felt a burning need for relief, for genuine confession, and yet sensed in advance that I would be unable to tell my mother or father, and explain everything properly. I knew that everything I said would be accepted sympathetically, that they would, yes, even feel sorry for me, but that they would not understand, that the whole thing would be regarded as a momentary aberration, whereas in truth it was my fate.

I realize that some people will not believe that a child of little more than ten years is capable of having such feelings. My story is not intended for them. I am telling it to those who have a better knowledge of man. The adult who has learned to translate a part of his feelings into thoughts notices the absence of these thoughts in a child, and therefore comes to believe that the child lacks these experiences, too. Yet rarely in my life have I felt and suffered as deeply as at that time.

One day it rained. Kromer had ordered me to meet him at the Burgplatz, and there I stood and waited, shuffling among the wet chestnut leaves that were still falling from the black wet trees. I had no money with me but I had managed to put aside two pieces of cake and had brought them along so as to be able to give Kromer something at least. By now I was used to standing in some corner and waiting for him, often for a very long time, and I accepted it the same way one learns to put up with the inevitable.

Kromer showed up finally. He didn't stay long. He poked me in the ribs a few times, laughed, took the cake, even offered me a damp cigarette (which, however, I did not accept), and was friendlier than usual.

"Yes," he said nonchalantly before going away, "before I forget it, you might bring your sister along the next time, the older one, what's her name."

I failed to get his point and made no reply. I only looked at him, surprised.

"Don't you understand? You're to bring your sister."

"No, Kromer, that's impossible. I wouldn't be allowed to and she wouldn't come in any case."

I was prepared for this new ruse or pretext of his. He did this often: demanded something impossible, frightened and humiliated me, then gradually offered some bargain as a way out, and I had to buy myself off with some money or a gift.

This time, however, it was altogether different. My refusal did not seem to make him angry at all.

"Well, anyway," he said in a matter-of-fact tone, "think it over. I'd like to meet your sister. We'll find a way one of these days. You could simply take her along on a walk and then I could join you. I'll give you a whistle tomorrow, then we can talk about it some more."

After he had left, something of the nature of his request suddenly dawned on me. I was still quite ignorant in these matters but I knew from hearsay that boys and girls when they grew older were able to do certain mysterious, repulsive, forbidden things together. And now I was supposed to—it suddenly flashed on me how monstrous his request was! I knew at once that I would never do it. But what would happen then? What revenge would Kromer take on me? I didn't dare think of it. This was the beginning of a new torture for me.

Inconsolable, I walked across the desolate square, hands in my pockets. Further and greater agonies awaited me!

Suddenly a vigorous cheerful voice called me. I was startled and began to flee. Someone ran after me, a hand grasped me gently from behind. It was Max Demian.

"Oh, it's you," I said mistrustfully. "You gave me a terrible shock."

He looked down at me and never had his look been more adult, superior, the look of someone who could see through me. We had not spoken to each other for a long time.

"I feel sorry for you," he said in his polite yet decisive manner. "Listen, you can't let yourself be frightened like that."

"Well, one can't always help it."

"So it seems. But look: if you practically go to pieces in front of someone who hasn't done you any harm, then that someone begins to think. He's surprised, he becomes inquisitive, he thinks you're emarkably high-strung and reaches the onclusion that people are always like hat when they're deathly afraid. Cowrds are constantly afraid, but you're not a coward, are you? Certainly, you're no hero either. There are some things you're afraid of, and some people, too. And that should never be, you should never be afraid of men. You aren't afraid of me? Or are you?"

"Oh, no, not at all."

"Exactly. But there are people you are frightened of?"

"I don't know. . . . Why don't you let me be?"

He kept pace with me—I had quickened my steps with thoughts of escaping—and I felt him glancing at me from the side.

"Let's assume," he began again, "that I don't mean to do you any harm. At any rate, you've no need to be afraid of me. I'd like to try out an experiment on you. It might be fun and you might even learn something from it. Now pay attention!— You see, I sometimes practice an art known as thought reading. There's no black magic about it but if you don't know how it's done it can seem very uncanny. You can shock people with it, too. Now let's give it a try. Well, I like you, or I'm interested in you and would like to discover what goes on inside you. I've already taken the initial step in that direction: I've frightened you—so that you're nervous. There must be things and people that you're afraid of. If you are afraid of someone, the most likely reason is that this someone has something on you. For example, you've done something wrong and the other person knows it—he has a hold on you. You get it? Very clear, isn't it?"

I looked up helplessly at his face, which was as serious and intelligent as ever, and kind. Yet its detached severity lacked tenderness; impartiality or something similar was visible in it. I was

hardly aware of what was happening to me: he stood before me like a magician.

"Have you got it?" he asked once more.

I nodded, unable to speak.

"I told you, reading other people's thoughts seems strange but it's perfectly natural. For instance, I could tell you almost exactly what you thought about me the time I told you the story of Cain and Abel. Well, this isn't the time to talk of that. I also think it possible that you dreamed about me once. But let's put that aside, too. You're bright and most people are stupid. I like talking to a bright fellow now and then, someone I can trust. You don't mind, do you?"

"Of course not. But I don't understand . . ."

"Let's keep to our amusing experiment for the moment. So, we've discovered that boy S is easily frightened—he's afraid of someone—he probably shares a secret with this other person, a secret that makes him feel uneasy. Roughly speaking, does this correspond to the facts?"

As though in a dream, I succumbed to his voice and influence. His voice seemed to come from within myself. And it knew everything. Did it know everything more clearly and better than I did myself?

Demian slapped me firmly on the shoulder.

"So that's what it is. I thought it might be. Now just one more question: do you happen to know the name of the boy who left you back there at the Burgplatz?"

I was terrified. He had touched my secret.

"What boy? There wasn't any boy there, only me."

"Go on." He laughed. "What's his name?"

"Do you mean Franz Kromer?" I whispered.

He gave me a satisfied nod.

"Excellent. You're all right, we'll become friends yet. But first I have to tell you something: this Kromer, or whatever his name is, his face tells me he's a first-rate bastard. What do you think?"

"Yes," I sighed, "he's pretty bad. But he mustn't hear about this. For God's sake. He mustn't find out anything. Do you know him? Does he know you?"

"Relax. He's gone and he doesn't know me—not yet. But I'd like to meet him. He goes to public school, doesn't he?"

"Yes."

"What grade's he in?"

"The fifth. But don't say anything to him. Please."

"Don't worry, nothing will happen to you. I take it you don't want to tell me more about this Kromer?"

"I can't."

He was silent for a while.

"Too bad," he said. "We could have carried the experiment a stage further. But I don't want to get you all upset. However, you realize, don't you, that your fear of him is all wrong? Such fear can destroy us completely. You've got to get rid of it, you've simply got to, if you want to turn into someone decent. You understand that, don't you?"

"Certainly, you're completely right. . . . But it's so complicated. . . . You've no idea . . ."

"You've seen that I know quite a few things about you, far more than you would have imagined.—Do you owe him any money?"

"Yes, that too. But that's not the main thing. I can't tell you, I just can't."

"Wouldn't it help if I gave you as much as you owe him?"

"No, that's not it. And you promise not to tell anyone about it? Not a word?"

"You can trust me, Sinclair. You can tell me your secret some other time."

"Never!" I shouted.

"As you like. All I meant was: perhaps you'll tell me more some other time. Voluntarily, of course. You don't think I would treat you the way Kromer does, do you?"

"Oh, no—but what do you know about that anyhow?"

"Nothing whatever. I've merely thought it over and I'd never do it Kromer's way, you can believe that. Besides, you don't owe me anything."

We did not speak for a long time, and I began to calm down, yet I found Demian's knowledge all the more puzzling.

"I'm going home now," he said and gathered his coat closer around him in the rain. "There's just one more thing I'd like to say to you since we've gotten so far—you ought to get rid of this bastard! If there's no other way of doing it, kill him. It would impress and please me if you did! I'd even lend you a hand."

The story of Cain suddenly recurred to me, and I became afraid again. Everything began to seem so ominous to me that I began to whimper. I was surrounded by too much that I didn't understand.

"All right." Max Demian smiled. "Go on home. We'll find a way, even though killing him would be the simplest. In cases like this, the simplest course is always the best. Your friend Kromer isn't the best friend to have."

I found my way home and it seemed to me that I had been away for a year. Everything looked different. Something like a future, like hope, now separated me from Kromer. I was no longer alone. Only now did I realize how horribly alone I had been with my secret for weeks on end. And at once I remembered a thought I had had several times before: that a confession to my parents would lighten my load but would not entirely relieve me of it. Now I had almost confessed, to another, to a stranger, and the sense of relief was like a fresh breeze.

Nonetheless, my fear was far from conquered and I was prepared for a long series of terrible wrangles with my enemy. That was why it seemed remarkable that matters took such a calm, such a discreet course.

For one day, for two, for a whole week there was no sound of Kromer's whistle near our house. I hardly dared believe it and I constantly lay in wait for the moment when suddenly, when least expected, he would reappear. He seemed to have vanished. Mistrusting my new freedom, I refused to believe in it, that is, until I finally ran into Franz Kromer. When he saw me he flinched, his face twitched, and he turned away so as to avoid meeting me.

It was an unprecedented moment for me! My enemy fleeing from me, my devil afraid of me! A thrill of happy surprise overwhelmed me.

One day I ran into Demian again. He was waiting for me in front of school.

"Hello," I said.

"Good morning, Sinclair. I only wanted to hear how things were going. Kromer isn't bothering you any more, is he?"

"Is that your doing? How did you manage it? I don't understand it at all. He's staying away altogether."

"That's good. If he should turn up again—I don't think he will, but he's quite ruthless—just tell him not to forget Max Demian."

"But what's the connection? Did you pick a fight and beat him up?"

"No, that's not my way of doing things. I merely talked to him as I did to you and was able to make it clear to him that it is to his advantage to leave you alone."

"You didn't pay him any money, I hope."

"No, that's your method."

He evaded all my questions, leaving me with the same uneasy feeling toward him I'd had before: a strange mixture of gratitude and awe, admiration and fear, sympathy and inward resistance.

I decided to seek him out and talk at length about all these matters, as well as about the Cain business.

But it did not happen that way.

Gratitude is not a virtue I believe in, and to me it seems hypocritical to expect it from a child. Thus my total ingratitude toward Max Demian does not astonish me too much. Today I have no doubt whatever that I would have been sick and ruined for life had he not freed me from Kromer's clutches. Even at that time I was conscious that this liberation was the greatest experience of my life—but the liberator himself I deserted as soon as he had performed his miracle.

As I have said, ingratitude does not surprise me. What does startle me, in retrospect, is my lack of curiosity. How was I able to go on living a single day without trying to come nearer to the secret which Demian had revealed to me? How was it I did not want to hear more about Cain, more about Kromer, more about Demian's ability to read other people's thoughts?

It is almost incredible, and yet it was so. I suddenly found myself extricated from a demonic labyrinth. I again saw the world bright and joyful before me and no longer succumbed to fits of suffocating fear. The spell was broken, I was no longer damned and tormented. I was a schoolboy again, and my whole being sought to regain its peaceful equilibrium as quickly as possible, making a particular effort to repel and forget the ugly, threatening things I had come to know. The whole episode of my guilt and fright slipped from my memory with incredible speed and without apparently leaving any scars or deep impressions behind.

However, today I can understand why I strained to forget my savior so quickly. I fled from the valley of sorrow, my horrible bondage to Kromer, with all the strength at the command of my injured soul: back to where I had been happy and content, back to the lost paradise that was opening up again now, back to the light, untroubled world of mother and father, my sisters, the smell of cleanliness, and the piety of Abel.

Already, the day after my short talk with Demian, when I was fully convinced at last of having regained my freedom and no longer feared losing it again, I did what I had wanted to do so often and desperately before—I confessed. I went to my mother, I showed her the damaged piggy bank filled with play money and I told her for how long I had bound myself through my own guilt to an evil tormenter. She did not understand everything but she saw; she saw my changed expression, heard the change in my tone of voice, and felt that I was cured and had been restored to her.

And now began the feast of my re-admittance to the fold, the return of the Prodigal Son. Mother took me to my father, the story was repeated, there were questions and exclamations of surprise, both parents stroked my head and breathed sighs of relief after the long period of oppression. Everything was marvelous, everything happened as the stories I had read said they would, everything resolved itself in wonderful harmony.

I drugged myself on the satisfaction of having regained my peace of mind and the confidence of my parents, I became a most exemplary boy at home, played more than ever with my sisters and during the devotional periods sang all my favorite hymns with the fervor of one who has been saved, who has been converted. It came from my heart, there was nothing false about it.

Still, not everything was back in order. And this is the fact that really accounts for my neglect of Demian. I should have confessed to *him*. The confession would have been less emotional and touching, but it would have been far more fruitful. I had returned to my former, my Edenic world. This was not Demian's world, and he would never have been able to fit into it. He too—though differently from Kromer—was a tempter; he, too, was a link to the second, the evil world with which I no longer wanted to have anything to do. I did not want to sacrifice Abel to glorify Cain, not just now when I had once more become Abel.

Those were the superficial reasons. The inner ones, however, were as follows: I was free of Kromer and the devil's hands but through no power or effort of my own. I had tried to pass through the labyrinth of the world but the way had proved too intricate for me. Now that a friendly hand had extricated me, I retreated, looking neither to the left nor to the right, but went straight to my mother's lap and the security of a pious, sheltered childhood. I turned myself into someone younger, more dependent, more childish than I was. I had to replace my dependence on Kromer with a new one, for I was unable to walk alone. So, in the blindness of my heart, I chose to be dependent on my father and mother, on the old, cherished "world of light," though I knew by now that it was not the only one. If I had not followed this course I would have had to bank on Demian and entrust myself to him. That I did not do so at the time seemed to me to be the result of my justifiable suspicion of his strange ideas; in reality it was entirely because of my fear. For Demian would have been far more exacting than my parents; he would have tried to make me more independent by using persuasion, exhortation, mockery, and sarcasm. I realize today that nothing in the world is more distasteful to a man than to take the path that leads to himself.

Yet six months later I could not resist the temptation and I asked my father during a walk what one was to make of the fact that some people considered Cain a better person than Abel.

He was much taken aback and explained that this was an interpretation entirely lacking in originality, that it had already arisen in Old Testament times and had been taught by a number of sects, one of which were called the "Cainites." But of course this mad doctrine was merely an attempt on the part of the devil to destroy our faith, for, if one believed that Cain was right and Abel in the wrong, then it followed that God had made a mistake; in other words, the God of the Bible was not the right and only one, but a false God. Indeed, the Cainites had taught and preached something of the sort. However, _his heresy had long since disappeared from the face of the earth and he was only surprised that a school friend of mine should have heard anything about it. He warned me most seriously against harboring such ideas.

3. Among Thieves

If I wanted to, I could recall many delicate moments from my childhood: the sense of being protected that my parents gave me, my affectionate nature, simply living a playful, satisfied existence in gentle surroundings. But my interest centers on the steps that I took to reach myself. All the moments of calm, the islands of peace whose magic I felt, I leave behind in the enchanted distance. Nor do I ask to ever set foot there again.

That is why—as long as I dwell on my childhood—I will emphasize the things that entered it from outside, that were new, that impelled me forward or tore me away.

These impulses always came from the "other world" and were accompanied by fear, constraint, and a bad conscience. They were always revolutionary and threatened the calm in which I would gladly have continued to live.

Then came those years in which I was forced to recognize the existence of a drive within me that had to make itself small and hide from the world of light. The slowly awakening sense of my own sexuality overcame me, as it does every person, like an enemy and terrorist, as something forbidden, tempting and sinful. What my curiosity sought, what dreams, lust and fear created—the great secret of puberty—did not fit at all into my sheltered childhood. I behaved like everyone else. I led the double life of a child who is no longer a child. My conscious self lived within the familiar and sanctioned world, it denied the new world that dawned within me. Side by side with this I lived in a world of dreams, drives, and desires of a chthonic nature, across which my conscious self desperately built its fragile bridges, for the childhood world within me was falling apart. Like most parents, mine were no help with the new problems of puberty, to which no reference was ever made. All they did was take endless trouble in supporting my hopeless attempts to deny reality and to continue dwelling in a childhood world that was becoming more and more unreal. I have no idea whether parents can be of help, and I do not blame mine. It was my own affair to come to terms with myself and to find my own way, and like most well-brought-up children, I managed it badly.

Everyone goes through this crisis. For the average person this is the point when the demands of his own life come into the sharpest conflict with his environment, when the way forward has to be sought with the bitterest means at his command. Many people experience the dying and rebirth—which is our fate—only this once during their entire life. Their childhood becomes hollow and gradually collapses, everything they love abandons them and they suddenly feel surrounded by the loneliness and mortal cold of the universe. Very many are caught forever in this impasse, and for the rest of their lives cling painfully to an irrevocable past, the dream of the lost paradise—which is the worst and most ruthless of dreams.

But let me return to my story. The sensations and dream images announcing the end of my childhood are too many to be related in full. The important thing was that the "dark world," the "other world," had reappeared. What Franz Kromer had once been was now part of myself.

Several years had gone by since the episode with Kromer. That dramatic time filled with guilt lay far in the past and seemed like a brief nightmare that had quickly vanished. Franz Kromer had long since gone out of my life, I hardly noticed when I happened to meet him in the street. The other important figure in my little tragedy, Max Demian, was never to go out of my life again entirely. Yet for a long time he merely stood at its distant fringes, visible but out of effective range. Only gradually did he come closer, again radiating strength and influence.

I am trying to see what I can remember of Demian at that time. It is quite possible that I didn't talk to him once for a whole year or even longer. I avoided him and he did not impose himself on me in any way. The few instances that we met, he merely nodded to me. Sometimes it even seemed as though his friendliness was faintly tinged with derision or with ironic reproach—but I may have imagined this. The experience that we had shared and the strange influence he had exerted on me at that time were seemingly forgotten by both of us.

I can conjure up what he looked like and now that I begin to recollect, I can see that he was not so far away from me after all and that I did notice him. I can see him on his way to school, alone or with a group of older students, and I see him strange, lonely, and silent, wandering among them like a separate planet, surrounded by an aura all his own, a law unto himself. No one liked him, no one was on intimate terms with him, except his mother, and this relationship, too, seemed not that of a child but of an adult. When they could, the teachers left him to himself; he was a good student but took no particular trouble to please anyone. Now and again we heard of some word, some sarcastic comment or retort he was rumored to have made to a teacher, and which—as gems of provocation and cutting irony—left little to be desired.

As I close my eyes to recollect I can see his image rise up: where was that? Yes, I have it now: in the little alley before our house. One day I saw him standing there, notebook in hand, sketching. He was drawing the old coat of arms with the bird above our entrance. As I stood at the window behind the curtain and watched him, I was deeply astonished by his perceptive, cool, light-skinned face that was turned toward the coat of arms, the face of a man, of a scientist or artist, superior and purposeful, strangely lucid and calm, and with knowing eyes.

And I can see him on another occasion. It was a few weeks later, also in a street. All of us on our way home from school were standing about a fallen horse. It lay in front of a farmer's cart

still harnessed to the shaft, snorting piti-
fully with dilated nostrils and bleeding
from a hidden wound so the white dust
on one side of the street was stained. As I
turned away nauseous I beheld Demian's
face. He had not thrust himself forward
but was standing farthest back, at ease
and as elegantly dressed as usual. His
eyes seemed fixed on the horse's head
and again showed that deep, quiet, almost fanatical yet dispassionate absorp-
tion. I could not help looking at him for
a time and it was then that I felt a very
remote and peculiar sensation. I saw
Demian's face and I not only noticed
that it was not a boy's face but a man's; I
also felt or saw that it was not entirely
the face of a man either, but had something feminine about it, too. Yet the face
struck me at that moment as neither
masculine nor childlike, neither old nor
young, but somehow a thousand years
old, somehow timeless, bearing the scars
of an entirely different history than we
knew; animals could look like that, or
trees, or planets—none of this did I
know consciously, I did not feel precisely
what I say about it now as an adult, only
something of the kind. Perhaps he was
handsome, perhaps I liked him, perhaps I
also found him repulsive, I could not be
sure of that either. All I saw was that he
was different from us, he was like an
animal or like a spirit or like a picture,
he was different, unimaginably different
from the rest of us.

My memory fails me and I cannot be
sure whether what I have described has
not to some extent been drawn from later
impressions.

Only several years later did I again
come into closer contact with him.
Demian had not been confirmed in
church with his own age group as was
the custom, and this again made him the
object of wild rumors. Boys in school
repeated the old story about his being
Jewish, or more likely a heathen, and

others were convinced that both he and
his mother were atheists or belonged to
some fabulous and disreputable sect. In
connection with this I also remember
having heard him suspected of being his
mother's lover. Most probably he had
been brought up without any religious
instruction whatever, but now this
seemed to be in some way ominous for
his future. At any rate, his mother decided to let him take Confirmation lessons after all, though two years later than
his age group. So it came about that he
went to the same Confirmation class as I
did.

For a time I avoided him entirely. I
wanted no part of him; he was surrounded by too many legends and
secrets, but what bothered me most was a
feeling of being indebted to him that had
not left me since the Kromer affair. I
now had enough trouble with secrets of
my own, for the Confirmation lessons
coincided with my decisive enlightenment
about sex, and despite all good intentions, my interest in religious matters was
greatly diminished. What the pastor discussed lay far away in a very holy but
unreal world of its own; these things
were no doubt quite beautiful and
precious, but they were by no means as
timely and exciting as the new things I
was thinking about.

The more indifferent this condition
made me to the Confirmation lessons, the
more I again became preoccupied with
Max Demian. There seemed to be a bond
between us, a bond that I shall have to
trace as closely as possible. As far as I
can remember, it began early one morning while the light still had to be turned
on in our classroom. Our scripture
teacher, a pastor, had embarked on the
story of Cain and Abel. I was sleepy and
listened with only half an ear. When the
pastor began to hold forth loudly and
urgently about Cain's mark I felt almost
a physical touch, a warning, and looking

up I saw Max Demian's face half turned round toward me from one of the front rows, with a gleaming eye that might express scorn as much as deep thought, you could not be sure. He looked at me for only a moment and suddenly I listened tensely to the pastor's words, heard him speak about Cain and his mark, and deep within me I felt the knowledge that it was not as he was teaching it, that one could look at it differently, that his view was not above criticism.

This one minute re-established the link between me and Demian. And how strange—hardly was I aware of a certain spiritual affinity, when I saw it translated into physical closeness. I had no idea whether he was able to arrange it this way himself or whether it happened only by chance—I still believed firmly in chance at that time—but after a few days Demian suddenly switched seats in Confirmation class and came to sit in front of me (I can still recall it precisely: in the miserable poorhouse air of the overcrowded classroom I loved the scent of fresh soap emanating from his nape) and after a few days he had again changed seats and now sat next to me. There he stayed all winter and spring.

The morning hours had changed completely. They no longer put me to sleep or bored me. I actually looked forward to them. Sometimes both of us listened to the pastor with the utmost concentration and a glance from my neighbor could draw my attention to a remarkable story, an unusual saying. A further glance from him, a special one, could make me critical or doubtful.

Yet all too frequently we paid no attention. Demian was never rude to the teacher or to his fellow students. I never saw him indulge in the usual pranks, not once did I hear him guffaw or gossip during class, and he never incurred a teacher's reprimand. But very quietly, and more with signs and glances than

whispering, he contrived to let me share in his activities, and these sometimes were strange.

For instance, he would tell me which of the students interested him and how he studied them. About some of them he had very precise knowledge. He would tell me before class: "When I signal with my thumb So-and-so will turn round and look at us, or will scratch his neck." During the period, when it had almost completely slipped my mind, Max would suddenly make a significant gesture with his thumb. I would glance quickly at the student indicated and each time I saw him perform the desired movement like a puppet on a string. I begged Max to try this out on the pastor but he refused. Only once, when I came to class unprepared and told him that I hoped the pastor would not call on me that day, he helped me. The pastor looked for a student to recite an assigned catechism passage and his eyes sweeping through the room came to rest on my guilty face. Slowly he approached me, his finger pointing at me, my name beginning to form on his lips—when suddenly he became distracted or uneasy, pulled at his shirt collar, stepped up to Demian, who was looking him directly in the eye and seemed to want to ask him something. But he turned away again, cleared his throat a few times, and then called on someone else.

Even though these tricks amused me, I began to notice gradually that my friend frequently played the same game with me. It would happen on my way to school that I would suddenly feel Demian walking not far behind me and when I turned around he was there in fact.

"Can you actually make someone think what you want him to?" I asked him.

He answered readily in his quiet, factual, and adult manner.

DEMIAN

"No," he said, "I can't do that. You
see, we don't have free will even though
the pastor makes believe we do. A person
can neither think what he wants to nor
can I make him think what I want to.
However, one can study someone very
closely and then one can often know almost exactly what he thinks or feels and
then one can also anticipate what he will
do the next moment. It's simple enough,
only people don't know it. Of course you
need practice. For example, there is a
species of butterfly, a night-moth, in
which the females are much less common
than the males. The moths breed exactly
like all animals, the male fertilizes the
female and the female lays the eggs.
Now, if you take a female night-moth—
many naturalists have tried this experiment—the male moths will visit this
female at night, and they will come from
hours away. From hours away! Just
think! From a distance of several miles
all these males sense the only female in
the region. One looks for an explanation
for this phenomenon but it is not easy.
You must assume that they have a sense
of smell of some sort like a hunting dog
that can pick up and follow a seemingly
imperceptible scent. Do you see? Nature
abounds with such inexplicable things.
But my argument is: if the female moths
were as abundant as the males, the latter
would not have such a highly developed
sense of smell. They've acquired it only
because they had to train themselves to
have it. If a person were to concentrate
all his will power on a certain end, then
he would achieve it. That's all. And that
also answers your question. Examine a
person closely enough and you know
more about him than he does himself."

It was on the tip of my tongue to mention "thought reading" and to remind
him of the scene with Kromer that lay so
far in the past. But this, too, was strange
about our relationship: neither he nor I
ever alluded to the fact that several years

before he had intruded so seriously into
my life. It was as though nothing had
ever been between us or as though each
of us banked on it that the other had forgotten. On one or two occasions it even
happened that we caught sight of Kromer
somewhere in the street. Yet we neither
glanced at each other nor said a word
about him.

"What is all this about the will?" I
asked. "On the one hand, you say our
will isn't free. Then again you say we
only need to concentrate our will firmly
on some end in order to achieve it. It
doesn't make sense. If I'm not master of
my own will, then I'm in no position to
direct it as I please."

He patted me on the back as he always
did when he was pleased with me.

"Good that you ask," he said, laughing. "You should always ask, always
have doubts. But the matter is very simple. If, for example, a night-moth were to
concentrate its will on flying to a star or
on some equally unattainable object, it
wouldn't succeed. Only—it wouldn't
even try in the first place. A moth con-
fines its search to what has sense and
value for it, on what it needs, what is
indispensable to its life. And that's how a
moth achieves the incredible—it develops
a magic sixth sense, which no other creature has. We have a wider scope, greater
variety of choice, and wider interests
than an animal. But we, too, are confined
to a relatively narrow compass which we
cannot break out of. If I imagined that I
wanted under all circumstances to get to
the North Pole, to achieve it I would
have to desire it strongly enough so that
my whole being was ruled by it. Once
that is the case, once you have tried
something that you have been ordered to
do from within yourself, then you'll be
able to accomplish it, then you can harness your will to it like an obedient nag.
But if I were to decide to will that the
pastor should stop wearing his glasses, it

[263]

would be useless. That would be making a game of it. But at that time in the fall when I was resolved to move away from my seat in the front row, it wasn't difficult at all. Suddenly there was someone whose name preceded mine in the alphabet and who had been away sick until then and since someone had to make room for him it was me of course because my will was ready to seize the opportunity at once."

"Yes," I said. "I too felt odd at that time. From the moment that we began to take an interest in each other you moved closer and closer to me. But how did that happen? You did not sit next to me right away, first you sat for a while in the bench in front of me. How did you manage to switch once more?"

"It was like this: I didn't know myself exactly where I wanted to sit but I wanted to shift from my seat in the front row. I only knew that I wanted to sit farther to the back. It was my will to come to sit next to you but I hadn't become conscious of it as yet. At the same time your will accorded with mine and helped me. Only when I found myself sitting in front of you did I realize that my wish was only half fulfilled and that my sole aim was to sit next to you."

"But at that time no one fell ill, no one who had been ill returned, no new student joined the class."

"You're right. But at the time I simply did as I liked and sat down next to you. The boy with whom I changed seats was somewhat surprised but he let me do as I pleased. The pastor, too, once noticed that some sort of change had occurred. Even now something bothers him secretly every time he has to deal with me, for he knows that my name is Demian and that something must be wrong if I, a D, sit way in back in the S's. But that never penetrates his awareness because my will opposes it and because I continuously place obstacles in his path. He keeps noticing that there's something wrong, then he looks at me and tries to puzzle it out. But I have a simple solution to that. Every time his eyes meet mine I stare him down. Very few people can stand that for long. All of them become uneasy. If you want something from someone and you look him firmly in both eyes and he doesn't become ill at ease, give up. You don't have a chance, ever! But that is very rare. I actually know only one person where it doesn't help me."

"Who is that?" I asked quickly.

He looked at me with narrowed eyes, as he did when he became thoughtful. Then he looked away and made no reply. Even though I was terribly curious I could not repeat the question.

I believe he meant his mother. He was said to have a very close relationship with her, yet he never mentioned her name and never took me home with him. I hardly knew what his mother looked like.

Sometimes I attempted to imitate Demian and fix my will with such concentration on something that I was certain to achieve it. There were wishes that seemed urgent enough to me. But nothing happened; it didn't work. I could not bring myself to talk to Demian about it. I wouldn't have been able to confess my wishes to him. And he didn't ask either.

Meantime cracks had begun to appear in my religious faith. Yet my thinking, which was certainly much influenced by Demian, was very different from that of some of my fellow students who boasted complete unbelief. On occasion they would say it was ridiculous, unworthy of a person to believe in God, that stories like the Trinity and Virgin Birth were absurd, shameful. It was a scandal that we were still being fed such nonsense in our time. I did not share these views. Even though I had my doubts about certain points, I knew from my childhood the reality of a devout life, as my parents led it, and I knew also that this was neither unworthy nor hypocritical. On the contrary, I still stood in the deepest awe of the religious. Demian, however, had accustomed me to regard and interpret religious stories and dogma more freely, more individually, even playfully, with more imagination; at any rate, I always subscribed with pleasure to the interpretations he suggested. Some of it—the Cain business, for instance—was, of course, too much for me to stomach. And once during Confirmation class he startled me with an opinion that was possibly even more daring. The teacher had been speaking about Golgotha. The biblical account of the suffering and death of the Savior had made a deep impression on me since my earliest childhood. Sometimes, as a little boy, on Good Friday, for instance, deeply moved by my father's reading of the Passion to us, I would live in this sorrowful yet beautiful, ghostly, pale, yet immensely alive world, in Gethsemane and on Golgotha, and when I heard Bach's *St. Matthew Passion* the dark mighty glow of suffering in this mysterious world filled me with a mystical sense of trembling. Even today I find in this music and in his *Actus Tragicus* the essence of all poetry.

At the end of that class Demian said to me thoughtfully: "There's something I don't like about this story, Sinclair. Why don't you read it once more and give it the acid test? There's something about it that doesn't taste right. I mean the business with the two thieves. The three crosses standing next to each other on the hill are most impressive, to be sure. But now comes this sentimental little treatise about the good thief. At first he was a thorough scoundrel, had committed all those awful things and God knows what else, and now he dissolves in

tears and celebrates such a tearful feast of self-improvement and remorse! What's the sense of repenting if you're two steps from the grave? I ask you. Once again it's nothing but a priest's fairy tale, saccharine and dishonest, touched up with sentimentality and given a highly edifying background. If you had to pick a friend from between the two thieves or decide which of the two you had rather trust, you most certainly wouldn't select that sniveling convert. No, the other fellow, he's a man of character. He doesn't give a hoot for 'conversion,' which to a man in his position can't be anything but a pretty speech. He follows his destiny to its appointed end and does not turn coward and forswear the devil, who has aided and abetted him until then. He has character, and people with character tend to receive the short end of the stick in biblical stories. Perhaps he's even a descendant of Cain. Don't you agree?"

I was dismayed. Until now I had felt completely at home in the story of the Crucifixion. Now I saw for the first time with how little individuality, with how little power of imagination I had listened to it and read it. Still, Demian's new concept seemed vaguely sinister and threatened to topple beliefs on whose continued existence I felt I simply had to insist. No, one could not make light of everything, especially not of the most sacred matters.

As usual he noticed my resistance even before I had said anything.

"I know," he said in a resigned tone of voice, "it's the same old story: don't take these stories seriously! But I have to tell you something: this is one of the very places that reveals the poverty of this religion most distinctly. The point is that this God of both Old and New Testaments is certainly an extraordinary figure but not what he purports to represent. He is all that is good, noble, fatherly, beautiful, elevated, sentimental—true! But the world consists of something else besides. And what is left over is ascribed to the devil, this entire slice of world, this entire half is suppressed and hushed up. In exactly the same way they praise God as the father of all life but simply refuse to say a word about our sexual life on which it's all based, describing it whenever possible as sinful, the work of the devil. I have no objection to worshiping this God Jehovah, far from it. But I mean we ought to consider everything sacred, the entire world, not merely this artificially separated half! Thus alongside the divine service we should also have a service for the devil. I feel that would be right. Otherwise you must create for yourself a God that contains the devil too and in front of which you needn't close your eyes when the most natural things in the world take place."

It was most unusual for him to become almost vehement. But at once he smiled and did not probe any further.

His words, however, touched directly on the whole secret of my adolescence, a secret I carried with me every hour of the day and of which I had not said a word to anyone, ever. What Demian had said about God and the devil, about the official godly and the suppressed devilish one, corresponded exactly to my own thoughts, my own myth, my own conception of the world as being divided into two halves—the light and the dark. The realization that my problem was one that concerned all men, a problem of living and thinking, suddenly swept over me and I was overwhelmed by fear and respect as I suddenly saw and felt how deeply my own personal life and opinions were immersed in the eternal stream of great ideas. Though it offered some confirmation and gratification, the realization was not really a joyful one. It was hard and had a harsh taste because it implied responsibility and no longer be-

ing allowed to be a child; it meant standing on one's own feet.

Revealing a deep secret for the first time in my life, I told my friend of my conception of the "two worlds." He saw immediately that my deepest feelings accorded with his own. But it was not his way to take advantage of something like that. He listened to me more attentively than he had ever before and peered into my eyes so that I was forced to avert mine. For I noticed in his gaze again that strange animal-like look, expressing timelessness and unimaginable age.

"We'll talk more about it some other time," he said forbearingly. "I can see that your thoughts are deeper than you yourself are able to express. But since this is so, you know, don't you, that you've never lived what you are thinking and that isn't good. Only the ideas that we actually live are of any value. You knew all along that your sanctioned world was only half the world and you tried to suppress the second half the same way the priests and teachers do. You won't succeed. No one succeeds in this once he has begun to think."

This went straight to my heart.

"But there are forbidden and ugly things in the world!" I almost shouted. "You can't deny that. And they are forbidden, and we must renounce them. Of course I know that murder and all kinds of vices exist in the world but should I become a criminal just because they exist?"

"We won't be able to find all the answers today," Max soothed me. "Certainly you shouldn't go kill somebody or rape a girl, no! But you haven't reached the point where you can understand the actual meaning of 'permitted' and 'forbidden.' You've only sensed part of the truth. You will feel the other part, too, you can depend on it. For instance, for about a year you have had to struggle with a drive that is stronger than any other and which is considered 'forbidden.' The Greeks and many other peoples, on the other hand, elevated this drive, made it divine and celebrated it in great feasts. What is forbidden, in other words, is not something eternal; it can change. Anyone can sleep with a woman as soon as he's been to a pastor with her and has married her, yet other races do it differently, even nowadays. That is why each of us has to find out for himself what is permitted and what is forbidden —forbidden for him. It's possible for one never to transgress a single law and still be a bastard. And vice versa. Actually it's only a question of convenience. Those who are too lazy and comfortable to think for themselves and be their own judges obey the laws. Others sense their own laws within them; things are forbidden to them that every honorable man will do any day in the year and other things are allowed to them that are generally despised. Each person must stand on his own feet."

Suddenly he seemed to regret having said so much and fell silent. I could already sense what he felt at such moments. Though he delivered his ideas in a pleasant and perfunctory manner, he still could not stand conversation for its own sake, as he once told me. In my case, however, he sensed—besides genuine interest—too much playfulness, too much sheer pleasure in clever gabbing, or something of the sort; in short, a lack of complete commitment.

As I reread the last two words I have just written—complete commitment—a scene leaps to mind, the most impressive I ever experienced with Max Demian in those days when I was still half a child.

Confirmation day was approaching and our lessons had the Last Supper for their topic. This was a matter of importance to the pastor and he took great pains explaining it to us. One could almost taste the solemn mood during those last hours of instruction. And of all times it had to be now that my thoughts were farthest from class, for they were fixed on my friend. While I looked ahead to being confirmed, which was explained to us as a solemn acceptance into the community of the church, I could not help thinking that the value of this religious instruction consisted for me not in what I had learned, but in the proximity and influence of Max Demian. It was not into the church that I was ready to be received but into something entirely different—into an order of thought and personality that must exist somewhere on earth and whose representative or messenger I took to be my friend.

I tried to suppress this idea—I was anxious to involve myself in the Confirmation ceremony with a certain dignity, and this dignity seemed not to agree very well with my new idea. Yet, no matter what I did, the thought was present and gradually it became firmly linked with the approaching ceremony. I was ready to enact it differently from the others, for it was to signify my acceptance into a world of thought as I had come to know it through Demian.

On one of those days it happened that we were having an argument just before class. My friend was tight-lipped and seemed to take no pleasure in my talk, which probably was self-important as well as precocious.

"We talk too much," he said with unwonted seriousness. "Clever talk is absolutely worthless. All you do in the process is lose yourself. And to lose yourself is a sin. One has to be able to crawl completely inside oneself, like a tortoise."

Then we entered the classroom. The lesson began and I made an effort to pay attention. Demian did not distract me.

After a while I began to sense something odd from the side where he sat, an emptiness or coolness or something similar, as though the seat next to me had suddenly become vacant. When the feeling became oppressive I turned to look.

There I saw my friend sitting upright, his shoulders braced back as usual. Nonetheless, he looked completely different and something emanated from him, something surrounded him that was unknown to me. I first thought he had his eyes closed but then saw they were open. Yet they were not focused on anything, it was an unseeing gaze—they seemed transfixed with looking inward or into a great distance. He sat there completely motionless, not even seeming to breathe; his mouth might have been carved from wood or stone. His face was pale, uniformly pale like a stone, and his brown hair was the part of him that seemed closest to being alive. His hands lay before him on the bench, lifeless and still as objects, like stones or fruit, pale, motionless yet not limp, but like good, strong pods sheathing a hidden, vigorous life.

I trembled at the sight. Dead, I thought, almost saying it aloud. My spellbound eyes were fixed on his face, on this pale stone mask, and I felt: this is the real Demian. When he walked beside me or talked to me—that was only half of him, someone who periodically plays a role, adapts himself, who out of sheer complaisance does as the others do. The real Demian, however, looked like this, as primeval, animal, marble, beautiful and cold, dead yet secretly filled with fabulous life. And around him this quiet emptiness, this ether, interstellar space, this lonely death!

Now he has gone completely into himself, I felt, and I trembled. Never had I been so alone. I had no part in him; he was inaccessible; he was more remote from me than if he had been on the most distant island in the world.

I could hardly grasp it that no one besides me noticed him! Everyone should have looked at him, everyone should have trembled! But no one heeded him. He sat there like a statue, and, I thought, proud as an idol! A fly lighted on his forehead and scurried across his nose and lips—not a muscle twitched.

Where was he now? What was he thinking? What did he feel? Was he in heaven or was he in hell?

I was unable to put a question to him. At the end of the period, when I saw him alive and breathing again, as his glance met mine, he was the same as he had been before. Where did he come from? Where had he been? He seemed tired. His face was no longer pale, his hands moved again, but now the brown hair was without luster, as though lifeless.

During the next few days, I began a new exercise in my bedroom. I would sit rigid in a chair, make my eyes rigid too, and stay completely motionless and see how long I could keep it up, and what I would feel. I only felt very tired and my eyelids itched.

Shortly afterwards we were confirmed, an event that calls forth no important memories whatever.

Now everything changed. My childhood world was breaking apart around me. My parents eyed me with a certain embarrassment. My sisters had become strangers to me. A disenchantment falsified and blunted my usual feelings and joys: the garden lacked fragrance, the woods held no attraction for me, the world stood around me like a clearance sale of last year's secondhand goods, insipid, all its charm gone. Books were so much paper, music a grating noise. That is the way leaves fall around a tree in autumn, a tree unaware of the rain running down its sides, of the sun or the frost, and of life gradually retreating inward. The tree does not die. It waits.

It had been decided that I would be

sent away to a boarding school at the end of the vacation; for the first time I would be away from home. Sometimes my mother approached me with particular tenderness, as if already taking leave of me ahead of time, intent on inspiring love, homesickness, the unforgettable in my heart. Demian was away on a trip. I was alone.

4. Beatrice

At the end of the holidays, and without having seen my friend again, I went to St. ———. My parents accompanied me and entrusted me to the care of a boy's boardinghouse run by one of the teachers at the preparatory school. They would have been struck dumb with horror had they known into what world they were letting me wander.

The question remained: was I eventually to become a good son and useful citizen or did my nature point in an altogether different direction? My last attempt to achieve happiness in the shadow of the paternal home had lasted a long time, had on occasion almost succeeded, but had completely failed in the end.

The peculiar emptiness and isolation that I came to feel for the first time after Confirmation (oh, how familiar it was to become afterwards, this desolate, thin air!) passed only very slowly. My leave-taking from home was surprisingly easy, I was almost ashamed that I did not feel more nostalgic. My sisters wept for no reason; my eyes remained dry. I was astonished at myself. I had always been an emotional and essentially good child. Now I had completely changed. I behaved with utter indifference to the world outside and for days on end voices within preoccupied me, inner streams, the forbidden dark streams that roared below the surface. I had grown several inches in the last half year and I walked lanky and half-finished through the world. I had lost any charm I might ever have had and felt that no one could possibly love me the way I was. I certainly had no love for myself. Often I felt a great longing for Max Demian, but no less often I hated him, accusing him of having caused the impoverishment of my life that held me in its sway like a foul disease.

I was neither liked nor respected in my boys' boardinghouse. I was teased to begin with, then avoided and looked upon as a sneak and an unwelcome oddity. I fell in with this role, even exaggerated it, and grumbled myself into a self-isolation that must have appeared to outsiders like permanent and masculine contempt of the world, whereas, in truth, I often secretly succumbed to consuming fits of melancholy and despair. In school I managed to get by on the knowledge accumulated in my previous class—the present one lagged somewhat behind the one I had left—and I began to regard the students in my age group contemptuously as mere children.

It went on like this for a year or more. The first few visits back home left me cold. I was glad when I could leave again.

It was the beginning of November. I had become used to taking short meditative walks during all kinds of weather, walks on which I often enjoyed a kind of rapture tinged with melancholy, scorn of the world and self-hatred. Thus I roamed in the foggy dusk one evening through the town. The broad avenue of a public park stood deserted, beckoning me to enter; the path lay thickly carpeted with fallen leaves which I stirred angrily with my feet. There was a damp, bitter smell, and distant trees, shadowy as ghosts, loomed huge out of the mist.

I stopped irresolute at the far end of the avenue: staring into the dark foliage

I greedily breathed the humid fragrance of decay and dying to which something within me responded with greeting.

Someone stepped out of one of the side paths, his coat billowing as he walked. I was about to continue when a voice called out:

"Hello, Sinclair."

He came up to me. It was Alfons Beck, the oldest boy in our boarding-house. I was always glad to see him, had nothing against him except that he treated me, and all others who were younger, with an element of ironic and avuncular condescension. He was reputed to be strong as a bear and to have the teacher in our house completely under his thumb. He was the hero of many a student rumor.

"Well, what are you doing here?" he called out affably in that tone the bigger boys affected when they occasionally condescended to talk to one of us. "I'll bet anything you're making a poem."

"Wouldn't think of it," I replied brusquely.

He laughed out loud, walked beside me, and made small talk in a way I hadn't been used to for a long time.

"You don't need to be afraid that I wouldn't understand, Sinclair. There's something to walking with autumnal thoughts through the evening fog. One likes to compose poems at a time like that, I know. About moribund nature, of course, and one's lost youth, which resembles it. Heinrich Heine, for example."

"I'm not as sentimental as all that," I defended myself.

"All right, let's drop the subject. But it seems to me that in weather like this a man does the right thing when he looks for a quiet place where he can drink a good glass of wine or something. Will you join me? I happen to be all by myself at the moment. Or would you rather not? I don't want to be the one who leads you astray, mon vieux, that is, in case you

happen to be the kind that keeps to the straight and narrow."

Soon afterwards we were sitting in a small dive at the edge of town, drinking a wine of doubtful quality and clinking the thick glasses. I didn't much like it to begin with, but at least it was something new. Soon, however, unused to the wine, I became very loquacious. It was as though an interior window had opened through which the world sparkled. For how long, for how terribly long hadn't I really talked to anyone? My imagination began to run away with me and eventually I even popped out with the story of Cain and Abel.

Beck listened with evident pleasure—finally here was someone to whom I was able to give something! He patted me on the shoulder, called me one hell of a fellow, and my heart swelled ecstatically at this opportunity to luxuriate in the release of a long pent-up need for talk and communication, for acknowledgment from an older boy. When he called me a damned clever little bastard, the words ran like sweet wine into my soul. The world glowed in new colors, thoughts gushed out of a hundred audacious springs. The fire of enthusiasm flared up within me. We discussed our teachers and fellow students and it seemed to me that we understood each other perfectly. We talked about the Greeks and the pagans in general and Beck very much wanted me to confess to having slept with girls. This was out of my league. I hadn't experienced anything, certainly nothing worth telling. And what I had felt, what I had constructed in imagination, ached within me but had not been loosened or made communicable by the wine. Beck knew much more about girls, so I listened to his exploits without being able to say a word. I heard incredible things. Things I had never thought possible became everyday reality, seemed normal. Alfons Beck, who was eighteen, seemed to be able to draw on a vast body of experience. For instance, he had learned that it was a funny thing about girls, they just wanted to flirt, which was all very well, but not the real thing. For the real thing one could hope for greater success with women. Women were much more reasonable. Mrs. Jaggelt, for example, who owned the stationery store, well, with her one could talk business, and all the things that had happened behind her counter wouldn't fit into a book.

I sat there enchanted and also dumbfounded. Certainly, I could never have loved Mrs. Jaggelt—yet the news was incredible. There seemed to be hidden sources of pleasure, at least for the older boys, of which I had not even dreamed. Something about it didn't sound right, and it tasted less appealing and more ordinary than love, I felt, was supposed to taste—but at least: this was reality, this was life and adventure, and next to me sat someone who had experienced it, to whom it seemed normal.

Once it had reached this height, our conversation began to taper off. I was no longer the damned clever little bastard; I'd shrunk to a mere boy listening to a man. Yet all the same—compared with what my life had been for months—this was delicious, this was paradise. Besides, it was, as I began to realize only gradually, very much prohibited—from our presence in the bar to the subject of our talk. At least for me it smacked of rebellion.

I can remember that night with remarkable clarity. We started on our way home through the damp, past gas lamps dimly lighting the late night: for the first time in my life I was drunk. It was not pleasant. In fact it was most painful, yet it had something, a thrill, a sweetness of rebellious orgy, that was life and spirit. Beck did a good job taking charge of me, even though he cursed me bitterly as a "bloody beginner," and half led, half car-

ried me home. There he succeeded in smuggling me through an open window in the hallway.

The sober reality to which I awoke after a brief deathlike sleep coincided with a painful and senseless depression. I sat up in bed, still wearing my shirt. The rest of my clothes, strewn about on the floor, reeked of tobacco and vomit. Between fits of headache, nausea, and a raging thirst an image came to mind which I had not viewed for a long time: I visualized my parents' house, my home, my father and mother, my sisters, the garden. I could see the familiar bedroom, the school, the market place, could see Demian and the Confirmation classes— everything was wonderful, godly pure, and everything, all of this—as I realized now—had still been mine yesterday, a few hours ago, had waited for me; yet now, at this very hour, everything looked ravaged and damned, was mine no longer, rejected me, regarded me with disgust. Everything dear and intimate, everything my parents had given me as far back as the distant gardens of my childhood, every kiss from my mother, every Christmas, each devout, light-filled Sunday morning at home, each and every flower in the garden—everything had been laid waste, everything had been trampled on *by me!* If the arm of the law had reached out for me now, had bound and gagged me and led me to the gallows as the scum of the earth and a desecrator of the temple, I would not have objected, would have gladly gone, would have considered it just and fair.

So that's what I looked like inside! I who was going about contemptuous of the world! I who was proud in spirit and shared Demian's thoughts! That's what I looked like, a piece of excrement, a filthy swine, drunk and filthy, loathsome and callow, a vile beast brought low by hideous appetites. That's what I looked like, I, who came out of such pure gardens where everything was cleanliness, radiance, and tenderness, I, who had loved the music of Bach and beautiful poetry. With nausea and outrage I could still hear my life, drunk and unruly, sputtering out of me in idiotic laughter, in jerks and fits. There I was.

In spite of everything, I almost reveled in my agonies. I had been blind and insensible and my heart had been silent for so long, had cowered impoverished in a corner, that even this self-accusation, this dread, all these horrible feelings were welcome. At least it was feeling of some kind, at least there were some flames, the heart at least flickered. Confusedly I felt something like liberation amid my misery.

Meanwhile, viewed from the outside, I was going rapidly downhill. My first drunken frenzy was soon followed by others. There was much going to bars and carousing in our school. I was one of the youngest to take part, yet soon enough I was not merely a fledgling whom one grudgingly took along, I had become the ringleader and star, a notorious and daring bar crawler. Once again I belonged entirely to the world of darkness and to the devil, and in this world I had the reputation of being one hell of a fellow.

Nonetheless, I felt wretched. I lived in an orgy of self-destruction and, while my friends regarded me as a leader and as a damned sharp and funny fellow, deep down inside me my soul grieved. I can still remember tears springing to my eyes when I saw children playing in the street on Sunday morning as I emerged from a bar, children with freshly combed hair and dressed in their Sunday best. Those friends who sat with me in the lowest dives among beer puddles and dirty tables I amused with remarks of unprecedented cynicism, often even shocked them; yet in my inmost heart I was in awe of everything I belittled and lay

weeping before my soul, my past, my mother, before God.

There was good reason why I never became one with my companions, why I felt alone among them and was therefore able to suffer so much. I was a barroom hero and cynic to satisfy the taste of the most brutal. I displayed wit and courage in my ideas and remarks about teachers, school, parents, and church. I could also bear to hear the filthiest stories and even ventured an occasional one myself, but I never accompanied my friends when they visited women. I was alone and was filled with intense longing for love, a hopeless longing, while, to judge by my talk, I should have been a hard-boiled sensualist. No one was more easily hurt, no one more bashful than I. And when I happened to see the young well-brought-up girls of the town walking in front of me, pretty and clean, innocent and graceful, they seemed like wonderful pure dreams, a thousand times too good for me. For a time I could not even bring myself to enter Mrs. Jaggelt's stationery store because I blushed looking at her remembering what Alfons Beck had told me.

The more I realized that I was to remain perpetually lonely and different within my new group of friends the less I was able to break away. I really don't know any longer whether boozing and swaggering actually ever gave me any pleasure. Moreover, I never became so used to drinking that I did not always feel embarrassing after-effects. It was all as if I were somehow under a compulsion to do these things. I simply did what I had to do, because I had no idea what to do with myself otherwise. I was afraid of being alone for long, was afraid of the many tender and chaste moods that would overcome me, was afraid of the thoughts of love surging up in me.

What I missed above all else was a friend. There were two or three fellow students whom I could have cared for, but they were in good standing and my vices had long been an open secret. They avoided me. I was regarded by and large as a hopeless rebel whose ground was slipping from under his feet. The teachers were well-informed about me, I had been severely punished several times, my final expulsion seemed merely a matter of time. I realized myself that I had become a poor student, but I wriggled strenuously through one exam after the other, always feeling that it couldn't go on like this much longer.

There are numerous ways in which God can make us lonely and lead us back to ourselves. This was the way He dealt with me at that time. It was like a bad dream. I can see myself: crawling along in my odious and unclean way, across filth and slime, across broken beer glasses and through cynically wasted nights, a spellbound dreamer, restless and racked. There are dreams in which on your way to the princess you become stuck in quagmires, in back alleys full of foul odors and refuse. That was how it was with me. In this unpleasant fashion I was condemned to become lonely, and I raised between myself and my childhood a locked gateway to Eden with its pitilessly resplendent host of guardians. It was a beginning, an awakening of nostalgia for my former self.

Yet I had not become so callous as not to be startled into twinges of fear when my father, alarmed by my tutor's letters, appeared for the first time in St. ——— and confronted me unexpectedly. Later on that winter, when he came a second time, nothing could move me any more, I let him scold and entreat me, let him remind me of my mother. Finally toward the end of the meeting he became quite angry and said if I didn't change he would have me expelled from the school in disgrace and placed in a reformatory. Well, let him! When he went away that time I felt sorry for him; he had accomplished nothing, he had not found a way to me—and at moments I felt that it served him right.

I could not have cared less what became of me. In my odd and unattractive fashion, going to bars and bragging was my way of quarreling with the world— this was my way of protesting. I was ruining myself in the process but at times I understood the situation as follows: if the world had no use for people like me, if it did not have a better place and higher tasks for them, well, in that case, people like me would go to pot, and the loss would be the world's.

Christmas vacation was a joyless affair that year. My mother was deeply startled when she saw me. I had shot up even more and my lean face looked gray and wasted, with slack features and inflamed eyes. The first touch of a mustache and the eyeglasses I had just begun wearing made me look odder still. My sisters shied away and giggled. Everything was most unedifying. Disagreeable and bitter was the talk I had with my father in his study, disagreeable exchanging greetings with a handful of relatives, and particularly unpleasant was Christmas Eve itself. Ever since I had been a little child this had been the great day in our house. The evening was a festivity of love and gratitude, when the bond between child and parents was renewed. This time everything was merely oppressive and embarrassing. As usual my father read aloud the passage about the shepherds in the fields "watching their flocks," as usual my sisters stood radiantly before a table decked with gifts, but father's voice sounded disgruntled, his face looked old and strained, and mother was sad. Everything seemed out of place: the presents and Christmas greetings, Gospel reading and the lit-up tree. The gingerbread smelled sweet; it exuded a host of memories which were even sweeter. The fragrance of the Christmas tree told of a world that no longer existed. I longed for evening and for the holidays to be over.

It went on like this the entire winter. Only a short while back I had been given a stern warning by the teachers' council and been threatened with expulsion. It couldn't go on much longer. Well, I didn't care.

I held a very special grudge against Max Demian, whom I hadn't seen again even once. I had written him twice during my first months in St. ———— but had received no reply; so I had not called on him during the holidays.

In the same park in which I had met Alfons Beck in the fall, a girl came to my attention in early spring as the thorn hedges began to bud. I had taken a walk by myself, my head filled with vile thoughts and worries—for my health had deteriorated—and to make matters worse I was perpetually in financial difficulties, owed friends considerable sums and had thus continually to invent expenditures so as to receive money from home. In a number of stores I had allowed bills to mount for cigars and similar things. Not that this worried me much. If my existence was about to come to a sudden end anyway—if I drowned myself or was sent to the reformatory—a few small extras didn't make much difference. Yet I was forced to live face to face with these unpleasant details: they made me wretched.

On that spring day in the park I saw a young woman who attracted me. She was tall and slender, elegantly dressed, and had an intelligent and boyish face. I liked her at once. She was my type and began to fill my imagination. She probably was not much older than I but seemed far more mature, well-defined, a full-grown woman, but with a touch of exuberance and boyishness in her face, and this was what I liked above all.

I had never managed to approach a girl with whom I had fallen in love, nor

did I manage in this case. But the impression she made on me was deeper than any previous one had been and the infatuation had a profound influence on my life.

Suddenly a new image had risen up before me, a lofty and cherished image. And no need, no urge was as deep or as fervent within me as the craving to worship and admire. I gave her the name Beatrice, for, even though I had not read Dante, I knew about Beatrice from an English painting of which I owned a reproduction. It showed a young pre-Raphaelite woman, long-limbed and slender, with long head and etherealized hands and features. My beautiful young woman did not quite resemble her, even though she, too, revealed that slender and boyish figure which I loved, and something of the ethereal, soulful quality of her face.

Although I never addressed a single word to Beatrice, she exerted a profound influence on me at that time. She raised her image before me, she gave me access to a holy shrine, she transformed me into a worshiper in a temple. From one day to the next I stayed clear of all bars and nocturnal exploits. I could be alone with myself again and enjoyed reading and going for long walks.

My sudden conversion drew a good deal of mockery in its wake. But now I had something I loved and venerated, I had an ideal again, life was rich with intimations of mystery and a feeling of dawn that made me immune to all taunts. I had come home again to myself, even if only as the slave and servant of a cherished image.

I find it difficult to think back to that time without a certain fondness. Once more I was trying most strenuously to construct an intimate "world of light" for myself out of the shambles of a period of devastation; once more I sacrificed everything within me to the aim of banishing darkness and evil from myself. And, furthermore, this present "world of light" was to some extent my own creation; it was no longer an escape, no crawling back to mother and the safety of irresponsibility; it was a new duty, one I had invented and desired on my own, with responsibility and self-control. My sexuality, a torment from which I was in constant flight, was to be transfigured into spirituality and devotion by this holy fire. Everything dark and hateful was to be banished, there were to be no more tortured nights, no excitement before lascivious pictures, no eavesdropping at forbidden doors, no lust. In place of all this I raised my altar to the image of Beatrice, and by consecrating myself to her I consecrated myself to the spirit and to the gods, sacrificing that part of life which I withdrew from the forces of darkness to those of light. My goal was not joy but purity, not happiness but beauty, and spirituality.

This cult of Beatrice completely changed my life. Yesterday a precocious cynic, today I was an acolyte whose aim was to become a saint. I not only avoided the bad life to which I had become accustomed, I sought to transform myself by introducing purity and nobility into every aspect of my life. In this connection I thought of my eating and drinking habits, my language and dress. I began my mornings with cold baths which cost me a great effort at first. My behavior became serious and dignified; I carried myself stiffly and assumed a slow and dignified gait. It may have looked comic to outsiders but to me it was a genuine act of worship.

Of all the new practices in which I sought to express my new conviction, one became truly important to me. I began to paint. The starting point for this was that the reproduction of the English picture I owned did not resemble my Beatrice closely enough. I wanted to try to paint her portrait for myself. With new joy and hopefulness I bought beautiful paper, paints, and brushes and carried them to my room—I had just been given one of my own—and prepared my palette, glass, porcelain dishes and pencils. The delicate tempera colors in the little tubes I had bought delighted me. Among them was a fiery chrome green that, I think, I can still see today as it flashed up for the first time in the small white dish.

I began with great care. Painting the likeness of a face was difficult. I wanted to try myself out first on something else. I painted ornaments, flowers, small imagined landscapes: a tree by a chapel, a Roman bridge with cypress trees. Sometimes I became so completely immersed in this game that I was as happy as a little child with his paint box. Finally I set out on my portrait of Beatrice.

A few attempts failed completely and I discarded them. The more I sought to imagine the face of the girl I had encountered here and there on the street the less successful I was. Finally I gave up the attempt and contented myself with giving in to my imagination and intuition that arose spontaneously from the first strokes, as though out of the paint and brush themselves. It was a dream face that emerged and I was not dissatisfied with it. Yet I persisted and every new sketch was more distinct, approximated more nearly the type I desired, even if it in no way reproduced reality.

I grew more and more accustomed to idly drawing lines with a dreaming paintbrush and to coloring areas for which I had no model in mind, that were the result of playful fumblings of my subconscious. Finally, one day I produced, almost without knowing it, a face to which I responded more strongly than I had to any of the others. It was not the face of that girl—it wasn't supposed to be that any longer. It was something else, something unreal, yet it was no less valuable to me. It looked more like a boy's face than a girl's, the hair was not flaxen like that of my pretty girl, but dark brown with a reddish hue. The chin was strong and determined, the mouth like a red flower. As a whole it was somewhat stiff and masklike but it was impressive and full of a secret life of its own.

As I sat down in front of the completed painting, it had an odd effect on me. It resembled a kind of image of God or a holy mask, half male, half female, ageless, as purposeful as it was dreamy, as rigid as it was secretly alive. This face seemed to have a message for me, it belonged to me, it was asking something of me. It bore a resemblance to someone, yet I did not know whom.

For a time this portrait haunted my thoughts and shared my life. I kept it locked in a drawer so that no one would take it and taunt me with it. But as soon as I was alone in my small room I took it out and communed with it. In the evening I pinned it on the wall facing my bed and gazed on it until I fell asleep and in the morning it was the first thing my eyes opened on.

It was precisely at this time that I again began having many dreams, as I had always had as a child. It felt as though I had not dreamed for years. Now the dreams returned with entirely new images, and time after time the portrait appeared among them, alive and eloquent, friendly or hostile to me, sometimes distorted into a grimace, sometimes infinitely beautiful, harmonious, and noble.

Then one morning, as I awoke from one of these dreams, I suddenly recognized it. It looked at me as though it were fabulously familiar and seemed to call out my name. It seemed to know who I was, like a mother, as if its eyes had been fixed on me since the beginning of time. With a quivering heart I stared at the sheet, the close brown hair, the half-feminine mouth, the pronounced forehead with the strange brightness (it had dried this way of its own accord) and I felt myself coming nearer and nearer to the recognition, the rediscovery, the knowledge.

I leapt out of bed, stepped up to the face, and from inches away looked into its wide-open, greenish, rigid eyes, the right one slightly higher than the left. All at once the right eye twitched, ever so faintly and delicately but unmistakably, and I was able to recognize the picture. . . .

Why had it taken me so long? It was Demian's face.

Later I often compared the portrait with Demian's true features as I remembered them. They were by no means the same even though there was a resemblance. Nonetheless, it was Demian.

Once the early-summer sun slanted oblique and red into a window that faced westward. Dusk was growing in my room. It occurred to me to pin the portrait of Beatrice, or Demian, at the window crossbar and to observe the evening sun shine through it. The outlines of the face became blurred but the red-rimmed eyes, the brightness on the forehead, and the bright red mouth glowed deep and wild from the surface. I sat facing it for a long time, even after the sun had faded, and gradually I began to sense that this was neither Beatrice nor Demian but myself. Not that the picture resembled me—I did not feel that it should—but it was what determined my life, it was my inner self, my fate or my *daemon*. That's what my friend would look like if I were to find one ever again. That's what the woman I would love would look like if ever I were to love one. That's what my life and death would be like, this was the tone and rhythm of my fate.

During those weeks I had begun to read a book that made a more lasting impression on me than anything I had read before. Even later in life I have rarely experienced a book more intensely, except perhaps Nietzsche. It was a volume of Novalis, containing letters and aphorisms of which I understood only a few but which nevertheless held an inexpressible attraction for me. One of the aphorisms occurred to me now and I wrote it under the picture: "Fate and temperament are two words for one and the same concept." That was clear to me now.

I often caught sight of the girl I called Beatrice but I felt no emotion during these encounters, only a gentle harmony, a presentiment: you and I are linked, but not you, only your picture; you are a part of my fate.

My longing for Max Demian overwhelmed me again. I had had no news of him for years. Once I had met him during a vacation. I realized now that I suppressed this brief encounter in my notes and I realized that it was done out of vanity and shame. I have to make up for it.

Thus, during one of my holidays as I strolled through my home town, wearing the blasé, always slightly weary expression of my bar-crawling days, peering into the same old, despised faces of the philistines, I saw my former friend walking toward me. I had hardly seen him when I flinched. At the same moment I could not help thinking of Franz Kromer. If only Demian had really forgotten that episode! It was so unpleasant to be obligated to him. It was actually a silly children's story but an obligation nonetheless. . . .

He appeared to wait: would I greet him? When I did so as casually as possible he stretched out his hand. Yes, that was his grip! As firm, warm yet cool, and virile as ever!

He scrutinized my face and said: "You've grown, Sinclair." He himself seemed quite the same, as old or as young as ever.

He joined me and we took a walk, but talked of only inconsequential matters. It occurred to me that I had written him several times without getting a reply. I hoped that he'd forgotten that too, those stupid letters! He did not mention them.

At that time I had not yet met Beatrice and there was no portrait. I was still in the midst of my drunken period. At the outskirts of town I asked him to join me for a glass of wine and he did so. At once I made a big show of ordering a whole bottle, filled his glass, clinked mine with his, and displayed my great familiarity with student drinking customs by downing the first glass in one swallow.

"You spend a lot of time in bars, do you?" he asked.

"Well, yes," I replied. "What else is there to do? In the end it's more fun than anything else."

"You think? Maybe so. One part of it is of course very fine—the intoxication, the bacchanalian element. But I think most people that frequent bars have lost that entirely. It seems to me that going to bars is something genuinely philistine. Yes, for one night, with burning torches, a real wild drunk! But again and again, one little glass after the other, I wonder whether that's the real thing or not? Can you see Faust sitting night after night stooped over the bar?"

I took a swallow and looked at him with hostility.

"Well, not everybody's Faust," I said curtly.

He looked at me somewhat taken aback.

Then he laughed at me in his old lively and superior fashion. "Well, let's not fight over it! In any case, the life of a drunk is presumably livelier than that of the ordinary well-behaved citizen. And then—I read that once somewhere—the life of a hedonist is the best preparation for becoming a mystic. People like St. Augustine are always the ones that become visionaries. He, too, was first a sensualist and man of the world."

I distrusted him and didn't want him to gain the upper hand under any circumstance. So I said superciliously: "Well, everybody to his own taste. As for me, I've no ambition to become a visionary or anything of the sort."

Demian gave me a brief shrewd look out of half-closed eyes.

"My dear Sinclair," he said slowly, "I didn't intend to tell you anything disagreeable. Besides—neither of us knows why you happen to be drinking wine at this moment. That which is within you and directs your life knows already. It's good to realize that within us there is someone who knows everything, wills everything, does everything better than we ourselves. But excuse me, I must go home."

We exchanged brief good-bys. I stayed on moodily and finished the bottle. When I wanted to leave I discovered that Demian had paid the bill—which put me in an even worse humor.

My thoughts returned to this small incident with Demian. I could not forget him. And the words he said to me in that bar at the edge of town would come to mind, strangely fresh and intact: "It's good to realize that within us there is someone who knows everything."

How I longed for Demian. I had no idea where he was nor how I could reach him. All I knew was that he was presumably studying at some university and that his mother had left town after he completed preparatory school.

I tried to remember whatever I could of Max Demian, reaching back as far as the Kromer episode. How much of what he had said to me over the years returned to mind, was still meaningful today, was appropriate and concerned me! And what he had said on our last and quite disagreeable meeting about a wasted life leading to sainthood suddenly also stood

clearly before me. Wasn't that exactly what had happened to me? Hadn't I lived in drunkenness and squalor, dazed and lost, until just the opposite had come alive in me with a new zest for life, the longing for purity, the yearning for the sacred?

So I continued to pursue these memories. Night had long since come and now rain was falling. In my memories, too, I heard the rain: it was the hour under the chestnut trees when he had probed me about Franz Kromer and guessed my first secrets. One incident after another came back to me, conversations on the way to school, the Confirmation classes, and last of all my first meeting with him. What had we talked about? I couldn't find it at once, but I gave myself time, concentrating intensely. And now even that returned. We had stood before my parents' house after he had told me his version of the story of Cain. Then he had mentioned the old, half-hidden coat of arms situated in the keystone above our entrance. He had said that such things interested him and that one ought to attend to them.

That night I dreamed of Demian and the coat of arms. It kept changing continuously. Demian held it in his hand, often it was diminutive and gray, often powerful and varicolored, but he explained to me that it was always one and the same thing. In the end he obliged me to eat the coat of arms! When I had swallowed it, I felt to my horror that the heraldic bird was coming to life inside me, had begun to swell up and devour me from within. Deathly afraid I started up in bed, awoke.

I was wide awake; it was the middle of the night and I could hear rain pouring into the room. As I got up to close the window I stepped on something that shone bright on the floor. In the morning I discovered that it had been my painting. It lay in a puddle and the paper had warped. I placed it between two sheets of blotting paper inside a heavy book. When I looked at it again the next day it was dry, but had changed. The red mouth had faded and contracted a little. It now looked exactly like Demian's mouth.

I set about painting a fresh picture of the heraldic bird. I could not remember distinctly what it looked like and certain details, as I knew, could not be made out even from close up, because the thing was old and had often been painted over. The bird stood or perched on something, perhaps on a flower or on a basket or a nest, or on a treetop. I couldn't trouble myself over this detail and began with what I could visualize clearly. Out of an indistinct need I at once began to employ loud colors, painting the bird's head a golden yellow. Whenever the mood took me, I worked on the picture, bringing it to completion in several days.

Now it represented a bird of prey with a proud aquiline sparrow hawk's head, half its body stuck in some dark globe out of which it was struggling to free itself as though from a giant egg—all of this against a sky-blue background. As I continued to scrutinize the sheet it looked to me more and more like the many-colored coat of arms that had occurred to me in my dream.

I could not have written Demian even if I had known his address. I decided, however—in the same state of dreamlike presentiment in which I did everything—to send him the painting of the sparrow hawk, even if it would never reach him. I added no message, not even my name, carefully trimmed the edges and wrote my friend's former address on it. Then I mailed it.

I had an exam coming up and had to do more work than usual. The teachers had reinstated me in their favor since I had abruptly changed my previously despicable mode of life. Not that I had become an outstanding student, but now

neither I nor anyone else gave it any further thought that half a year earlier my expulsion had seemed almost certain.

My father's letters regained some of their old tone, without reproaches or threats. Yet I felt no inclination to explain to him or anyone else how the change within me had come about. It was an accident that this transformation coincided with my parents' and teachers' wishes. This change did not bring me into the community of the others, did not make me closer to anyone, but actually made me even lonelier. My reformation seemed to point in the direction of Demian, but even this was a distant fate. *I* did not know myself, for I was too deeply involved. It had begun with Beatrice, but for some time I had been living in such an unreal world with my paintings and my thoughts of Demian that I'd forgotten all about her, too. I could not have uttered a single word about my dreams and expectations, my inner change, to anyone, not even if I had wanted to. But how could I have wanted to?

5. "The Bird Fights Its Way Out of the Egg"

My painted dream bird was on its way searching for my friend. In what seemed the strangest possible manner a reply reached me.

In my classroom, on my desk, after a break between two lessons I found a note tucked in my book. It was folded exactly the same as notes classmates of mine secretly slipped each other during class. I was only surprised to receive such a note at all, for I had never had that sort of relationship with any student. I thought it would turn out to be an invitation to some prank in which I would not participate anyway—I put the note unread in the front of my book. I came on it again only during the lesson.

Playing with the note I unfolded it carelessly and noticed a few words written on it. One glance was sufficient. One word stopped me cold; in panic I read on while cold fear contracted my heart: "The bird fights its way out of the egg. The egg is the world. Who would be born must first destroy a world. The bird flies to God. That God's name is Abraxas."

After reading over these lines a number of times, I sank into a deep reverie. There could be no doubt about it, this was Demian's reply. No one else could know about my painting. He had grasped its meaning and was helping me interpret it. But how did all of this fit together? And—this oppressed me most of all—what did Abraxas signify? I had never heard nor read the word. "That God's name is Abraxas."

The lesson went on without my taking in a word of it. The next began, the last that morning. It was taught by a young assistant, a Dr. Follens, who had just completed his university studies, whom we liked simply because he was young and unpretentious.

Dr. Follens was guiding us through Herodotus—one of the few subjects that held any interest for me. But today not even Herodotus could hold my attention. I opened the book mechanically but did not follow the translation and remained sunk deep in my own thoughts. Besides, I had frequently confirmed what Demian had told me once during our Confirmation classes: you can achieve anything you desire passionately enough. If I happened to be involved with my own thoughts during a lesson I did not have to worry that the teacher would call on me. If I was distracted or listless, then he would suddenly appear beside me. That had already happened to me. But if I

really concentrated, completely wrapped up in a thought of my own, then I was protected. I had also experimented with the trick of staring a person down and had found that it worked. When still with Demian, I had not succeeded in this; now I often felt that a good deal could be accomplished by a sharp glance, and thought.

I was at present nowhere near Herodotus or school. Suddenly the teacher's voice shot like lightning into my consciousness and I awoke terrified. I heard his voice, he practically stood next to me, I even thought he had called my name. But he was not looking at me. I relaxed.

Then I heard his voice again. Loudly it pronounced the word "Abraxas."

In the course of a long explanation, whose beginning I had missed, Dr. Follens went on: "We ought not consider the opinions of those sects and mystical societies as naïve as they appear from the rationalist point of view. Science as we know it today was unknown to antiquity. Instead there existed a preoccupation with philosophical and mystical truths which was highly developed. What grew out of this preoccupation was to some extent merely pedestrian magic and frivolity; perhaps it frequently led to deceptions and crimes, but this magic, too, had noble antecedents in a profound philosophy. As, for instance, the teachings concerning Abraxas which I cited a moment ago. This name occurs in connection with Greek magical formulas and is frequently considered the name of some magician's helper such as certain uncivilized tribes believe in even at present. But it appears that Abraxas has a much deeper significance. We may conceive of the name as that of a godhead whose symbolic task is the uniting of godly and devilish elements."

The learned little man spoke with intelligence and eagerness but no one paid much attention, and as the name Abraxas did not recur, my thoughts turned back to my own affairs.

"Uniting of godly and devilish elements" resounded within me. Here was something for my thoughts to cling to. This idea was familiar to me from conversations with Demian. During the last period of our friendship he had said that we had been given a god to worship who represented only one arbitrarily separated half of the world (it was the official, sanctioned, luminous world), but that we ought to be able to worship the whole world; this meant that we would either have to have a god who was also a devil or institute a cult of the devil alongside the cult of god. And now Abraxas was the god who was both god and devil.

For a time I pursued this thought eagerly but without making any headway. I even pored over a whole libraryful of books seeking a mention of Abraxas. However, my nature had never been disposed to this kind of direct and conscious investigation where at first one finds only truths that are so much dead weight in one's hand.

The figure of Beatrice with which I had occupied myself so intimately and fervently gradually became submerged or, rather, was slowly receding, approaching the horizon more and more, becoming more shadowy and remote, paler. She no longer satisfied the longings of my soul.

In the peculiar self-made isolation in which I existed like a sleepwalker, a new growth began to take shape within me. The longing for life grew—or rather the longing for love. My sexual drive, which I had sublimated for a time in the veneration of Beatrice, demanded new images and objects. But my desires remained unfulfilled and it was more impossible than ever for me to deceive my longings and hope for something from the women with whom my comrades tried their luck. I dreamed vividly again, more in fact by day than at night. Images, pictures, desires arose freely within me, drew me away from the outside world so that I had a more substantial and livelier relationship with the world of my own creation, with these images and dreams and shadows, than with the actual world around me.

A certain dream, or fantasy, that kept recurring gained in meaning for me. The dream, the most important and enduringly significant of my life, went something like this: I was returning to my father's house—above the entrance glowed the heraldic bird, yellow on a blue background; in the house itself my mother was coming toward me—but as I entered and wanted to embrace her, it was not she but a form I had never set eyes on before, tall and strong, resembling Max Demian and the picture I had painted; yet different, for despite its strength it was completely feminine. This form drew me to itself and enveloped me in a deep, tremulous embrace. I felt a mixture of ecstasy and horror—the embrace was at once an act of divine worship and a crime. Too many associations with my mother and friend commingled with this figure embracing me. Its embrace violated all sense of reverence, yet it was bliss. Sometimes I awoke from this dream with a feeling of profound ecstasy, at others in mortal fear and with a racked conscience as though I had committed some terrible crime.

Only gradually and unconsciously did this very intimate image become linked with the hint about the God I was to search for, the hint that had come to me from the outside. The link grew closer and more intimate and I began to sense that I was calling on Abraxas particularly in this dreamed presentiment. Delight and horror, man and woman commingled, the holiest and most shocking were intertwined, deep guilt flashing through most delicate innocence: that was the appearance of my love-dream image and Abraxas, too. Love had ceased to be the dark animalistic drive I had experienced at first with fright, nor was it any longer the devout transfiguration I had offered to Beatrice. It was both, and yet much more. It was the image of an angel and Satan, man and woman in one flesh, man and beast, the highest good and the worst evil. It seemed that I was destined to live in this fashion, this seemed my preordained fate. I yearned for it but feared it at the same time. It was ever-present, hovering constantly above me.

The following spring I was to leave the preparatory school and enter a university. I was still undecided, however, as to where and what I was to study. I had grown a thin mustache, I was a full-grown man, and yet I was completely helpless and without a goal in life. Only one thing was certain: the voice within me, the dream image. I felt the duty to follow this voice blindly wherever it might lead me. But it was difficult and each day I rebelled against it anew. Perhaps I was mad, as I thought at moments; perhaps I was not like other men? But I was able to do the same things the others did; with a little effort and industry I could read Plato, was able to solve problems in trigonometry or follow a chemical analysis. There was only one thing I could not do: wrest the dark secret goal from myself and keep it before me as others did who knew exactly what they wanted to be—professors, lawyers, doctors, artists, however long this would take them and whatever difficulties and advantages this decision would bear in its wake. This I could not do. Perhaps I would become something similar, but how was I to know? Perhaps I would have to continue my search for years on end and would not become anything, and would not reach a goal. Perhaps I would reach this goal but it would turn out to be an evil, dangerous, horrible one?

I wanted only to try to live in accord with the promptings which came from my true self. Why was that so very difficult?

I made frequent attempts to paint the mighty love apparition of my dream. I never succeeded. If I had I would have sent the painting to Demian. Where he was I had no idea. I only knew that we were linked. When would we meet again?

The tranquillity of the weeks and months of my Beatrice period had long since passed. At that time I felt I had reached a safe harbor, an island of peace. But as always, as soon as I had become accustomed to my condition, as soon as a dream had given me hope, it wilted and became useless. It was futile to sorrow after the loss. I now lived within a fire of unsatisfied longing, of tense expectancy that often drove me completely wild. I often saw the beloved apparition of my dream with a clarity greater than life, more distinct than my own hand, spoke with it, wept before it, cursed it. I called it mother and knelt down in front of it in tears. I called it my beloved and had a premonition of its ripe all-fulfilling kiss. I called it devil and whore, vampire and murderer. It enticed me to the gentlest love-dreams and to devastating shame-lessness, nothing was too good and precious, nothing was too wicked and low for it.

I experienced the whole of that winter as one unending inner turbulence, which I find difficult to describe. I had long since become used to my loneliness—that did not oppress me: I lived with Demian, the sparrow hawk, with the mighty apparition of my dream that was both my fate and my beloved. This was enough to sustain me, for everything pointed toward vastness and space—it all pointed toward Abraxas. But none of these dreams, none of these thoughts obeyed me, none were at my beck and call, I could color none of them as I pleased. They came and took me, I was ruled by them, was their vessel.

However, I was well armed against the outside world. I was no longer afraid of people; even my fellow students had come to know this and treated me with a secret respect that often brought a smile to my lips. If I wanted to I could see through most of them and startled them occasionally. Only I rarely or never tried. I was always preoccupied with myself. And I longed desperately to really live for once, to give something of myself to the world, to enter into a relationship and battle with it. Sometimes when I ran through the streets in the evening, unable to return before midnight because I was so restless, I felt that now at this very moment I would have to meet my beloved—as she walked past me at the next street corner, called to me from the nearest window. At other times all of this seemed unbearably painful and I was prepared to commit suicide.

Just then I found a strange refuge— "by chance," as they say—though I believe there is no such thing. If you need something desperately and find it, this is not an accident; your own craving and compulsion leads you to it.

Twice or three times during my walks I had heard organ music coming from a small church at the edge of town. I had not stopped to listen. The next time I passed this church I heard the music again and recognized Bach. I went to the door, found it locked, and because the street was almost deserted I sat down on a curbstone next to the church, turned up my coat collar, and listened. It was not a big organ but it had good tone. It was being played with a strange, highly personal expression of purpose and tenacity that gave the impression of prayer. I felt that the organist knew the treasures hidden in the music, that he was wooing, hammering at the gate, wrestling for this treasure as for his life. My knowledge of music is technically very limited but from childhood on I have had an intuitive grasp, have sensed music as something self-evident within me.

The organist also played something more modern—it could have been Max Reger. The church was almost completely dark, only a very thin beam of light penetrated the window closest to me. I waited until the music ceased and then paced back and forth until I saw the organist leave the church. He was still young, though older than I, square shouldered and squat, and he moved off rapidly with vigorous yet seemingly reluctant strides.

From then on I occasionally sat outside the church or paced up and down before it during the evening hours. Once I even found the door open and sat for half an hour in a pew, shivering against the cold, yet happy as long as the organist played in the loft. I not only distinguished his personality in the music he played—every piece he performed also had affinity with the next, a secret connection. Everything he played was full of faith, surrender, and devotion. Yet not devout after the fashion of churchgoers and pastors, devout the way pilgrims and mendicants were in the Middle Ages, devout with that unconditional surrender to a universal feeling that transcends all confessions. He also played music composed prior to Bach, and the old Italians. And all this music said the same thing, all of it expressed what was in the musician's soul: longing, a most intimate atonement with the world and a violent wrenching loose, a burning hearkening to one's own dark soul, an intoxicating surrender and deep curiosity about the miraculous.

Once when I shadowed the organist

after he left the church, I saw him enter a small tavern on the edge of town. I could not resist following him in. For the first time I could see him clearly. He sat at a table in the far corner of the small room. He wore a black felt hat. A jug of wine stood before him. His face looked as I suspected it would. He was ugly and a little wild, inquisitive and pigheaded, capricious and determined, yet his mouth had a soft childlike quality. All his masculinity and strength were concentrated in eyes and forehead, while the lower part of the face was sensitive and immature, uncontrolled and somehow very soft. The irresolute, boyish chin appeared to contradict the forehead and eyes—which I liked, those dark-brown eyes, full of pride and hostility.

I sat down opposite him without saying a word. We were the only two guests in the tavern. He gave me a look as though he wanted to shoo me away. But I did not budge, and stared back unmoved until he grumbled morosely: "What on earth are you staring at? Is there something you want?"

"No, I don't want anything from you," I said. "You've given me a great deal already."

He knitted his brows.

"So, you're a music lover. I find it nauseating to be crazy about music."

I did not let him intimidate me.

"I have listened to you often, back there in the church," I said. "But I don't want to trouble you. I thought I might find something, something special; I really don't know what. But don't pay any attention to me. I can listen to you in church."

"But I always lock it."

"Not very long ago you forgot and I sat inside. Usually I stand outside or sit on the curb."

"Really? Next time you can come inside, it's warmer. All you have to do is knock at the door. But you have to bang hard and not while I'm playing. Go ahead now—what did you want to tell me? You're quite young yet, probably a student of some sort. Are you a musician?"

"No. I like listening to music, but only the kind you play, completely unreserved music, the kind that makes you feel that a man is shaking heaven and hell. I believe I love that kind of music because it is amoral. Everything else is so moral that I'm looking for something that isn't. Morality has always seemed to me insufferable. I can't express it very well.— Do you know that there must be a god who is both god and devil at one and the same time? There is supposed to have been one once. I heard about it."

The musician pushed his wide hat back a little and shook the hair out of his eyes, all the while peering at me. He lowered his face across the table.

Softly and expectantly he asked: "What's the name of the god you mentioned?"

"Unfortunately I know next to nothing about him, actually only his name. He is called Abraxas."

The musician blinked suspiciously around him as though someone might be eavesdropping. Then he moved closer to me and said in a whisper: "That's what I thought. Who are you?"

"A student at the prep school."

"How did you happen to hear about Abraxas?"

"By accident."

He struck the table so that wine spilled out of his glass. "By accident! Don't talk *shit,* young fellow! One doesn't hear about Abraxas by accident, and don't you forget it. I will tell you more about him. I know a little."

He fell silent and moved his chair back. When I looked at him full of expectation, he made a face.

"Not here. Some other time. There, take these."

He reached in his coat, which he had not taken off, and drew out a few roasted chestnuts and threw them to me.

I said nothing, took them, ate and felt content.

"All right," he whispered after a moment. "Where did you find out about—him?"

I did not hesitate to tell him.

"I was alone and desperate at one time," I began. "Then I remembered a friend I had had several years back who I felt knew much more than I did. I had painted something, a bird struggling out of the globe. I sent him this painting. After a time I found a piece of paper with the following words written on it: 'The bird fights its way out of the egg. The egg is the world. Who would be born must first destroy a world. The bird flies to God. That God's name is Abraxas.'"

He made no reply. We shelled our chestnuts and drank our wine.

"Another glass?" he asked.

"No, thanks. I don't like drinking."

He laughed, a little disappointed.

"As you like. It's different with me. I'll stay but you can run along if you want."

When I joined him the next time, after he had played the organ, he was not very communicative. He led me down an alley and through an old and impressive house and up to a large, somewhat dark and neglected room. Except for a piano, nothing in it gave a hint of his being a musician—but a large bookcase and a desk gave the room an almost scholarly air.

"How many books you have!" I exclaimed.

"Part of them are from my father's library—in whose house I live. Yes, young man, I'm living with my parents but I can't introduce you to them. My acquaintances aren't regarded very favorably in this house. I'm the black sheep. My father is fabulously respectable and an important pastor and preacher in this town. And I, so that you know the score at once, am his talented and promising son who has gone astray and, to some extent, even mad. I was a theology student but shortly before my state exams I left this very respectable department; that is, not entirely, not in so far as it concerns my private studies, for I'm still most interested to see what kinds of gods people have devised for themselves. Otherwise, I'm a musician at present and it looks as though I will receive a small post as an organist somewhere. Then I'll be back in the employ of the church again."

As much as the feeble light from the small table lamp permitted, I glanced along the spines of the books and noticed Greek, Latin, and Hebrew titles. Meanwhile my acquaintance had lain down on the floor and was busying himself with something.

"Come," he called after a moment, "we want to practice a bit of philosophy. That means: keep your mouth shut, lie on your stomach, and meditate."

He struck a match and lit paper and wood in the fireplace in front of which he sprawled. The flames leapt high, he stirred and fed them with the greatest care. I lay down beside him on the worn-out carpet. For about an hour we lay on our stomachs silent before the shimmering wood, watching the flames shoot up and roar, sink down and double over, flicker and twitch, and in the end brood quietly on sunken embers.

"Fire worship was by no means the most foolish thing ever invented," he murmured to himself at one point. Otherwise neither of us said a word. I stared fixedly into the flames, lost myself in dreams and stillness, recognized figures in the smoke and pictures in the ashes. Once I was startled. My companion threw a piece of resin into the embers: a slim flame shot up and I recognized the bird with the yellow sparrow hawk's head. In the dying embers, red and gold threads ran together into nets, letters of the alphabet appeared, memories of faces, animals, plants, worms, and snakes. As I emerged from my reveries I looked at my companion, his chin resting on his fists, staring fanatically into the ashes with complete surrender.

"I have to go now," I said softly.

"Go ahead then. Good-by."

He did not get up. The lamp had gone out: I groped my way through the dark rooms and hallways of the bewitched old house. Once outside, I stopped and looked up along its façade. Every window was dark. A small brass plate on the front door gleamed in the light from a street lamp. On it I read the words: "Pistorius, pastor primarius."

Not until I was at home and sat in my little room after supper did it occur to me that I had not heard anything about either Abraxas or Pistorius—we'd exchanged hardly a dozen words. But I was very satisfied with my visit. And for our next meeting he had promised to play an exquisite piece of old music, an organ passacaglia by Buxtehude.

Without my being entirely aware of it, the organist Pistorius had given me my first lesson when we were sprawled on the floor before the fire in his depressing hermit's room. Staring into the blaze had been a tonic for me, confirming tendencies that I had always had but never cultivated. Gradually some of them were becoming comprehensible to me.

Even as a young boy I had been in the habit of gazing at bizarre natural phenomena, not so much observing them as surrendering to their magic, their confused, deep language. Long gnarled tree roots, colored veins in rocks, patches of oil floating on water, light-refracting flaws in glass—all these things had held great magic for me at one time: water

and fire particularly, smoke, clouds, and dust, but most of all the swirling specks of color that swam before my eyes the minute I closed them. I began to remember all this in the days after my visit to Pistorius, for I noticed that a certain strength and joy, an intensification of my self-awareness that I had felt since that evening, I owed exclusively to this prolonged staring into the fire. It was remarkably comforting and rewarding.

To the few experiences which helped me along the way toward my life's true goal I added this new one: the observation of such configurations. The surrender to Nature's irrational, strangely confused formations produces in us a feeling of inner harmony with the force responsible for these phenomena. We soon fall prey to the temptation of thinking of them as being our own moods, our own creations, and see the boundaries separating us from Nature begin to quiver and dissolve. We become acquainted with that state of mind in which we are unable to decide whether the images on our retina are the result of impressions coming from without or from within. Nowhere as in this exercise can we discover so easily and simply to what extent we are creative, to what extent our soul partakes of the constant creation of the world. For it is the same indivisible divinity that is active through us and in Nature, and if the outside world were to be destroyed, a single one of us would be capable of rebuilding it: mountain and stream, tree and leaf, root and flower, yes, every natural form is latent within us, originates in the soul whose essence is eternity, whose essence we cannot know but which most often intimates itself to us as the power to love and create.

Not until many years later did I find these observations of mine confirmed, in a book by Leonardo da Vinci, who describes at one point how good, how intensely interesting it is to look at a wall many people have spit on. Confronted with each stain on the wet wall, he must have felt the same as Pistorius and I felt before the fire.

The next time we were together, the organist gave me an explanation: "We always define the limits of our personality too narrowly. In general, we count as part of our personality only that which we can recognize as being an individual trait or as diverging from the norm. But we consist of everything the world consists of, each of us, and just as our body contains the genealogical table of evolution as far back as the fish and even much further, so we bear everything in our soul that once was alive in the soul of men. Every god and devil that ever existed, be it among the Greeks, Chinese, or Zulus, are within us, exist as latent possibilities, as wishes, as alternatives. If the human race were to vanish from the face of the earth save for one halfway talented child that had received no education, this child would rediscover the entire course of evolution, it would be capable of producing everything once more, gods and demons, paradises, commandments, the Old and New Testament."

"Yes, fine," I replied. "But what is the value of the individual in that case? Why do we continue striving if everything has been completed within us?"

"Stop!" exclaimed Pistorius. "There's an immense difference between simply carrying the world within us and being aware of it. A madman can spout ideas that remind you of Plato, and a pious little seminary student rethinks deep mythological correspondences found among the Gnostics or in Zoroaster. But he isn't aware of them. He is a tree or stone, at best an animal, as long as he is not conscious. But as soon as the first spark of recognition dawns within him he is a human being. You wouldn't consider all the bipeds you pass on the street human beings simply because they walk upright and carry their young in their bellies nine months! It is obvious how many of them are fish or sheep, worms or angels, how many are ants, how many are bees! Well, each one of them contains the possibility of becoming human, but only by having an intimation of these possibilities, partially even by learning to make himself conscious of them; only in this respect are these possibilities his."

This was the general drift of our conversations. They rarely confronted me with anything completely new, anything altogether astonishing. But everything, even the most ordinary matters, resembled gentle persistent hammer blows on the same spot within me; all of them helped me to form myself, all of them helped to peel off layers of skin, to break eggshells, and after each blow I lifted my head a little higher, a little more freely, until my yellow bird pushed its beautiful raptor's head out of the shattered shell of the terrestrial globe.

Frequently we also told each other our dreams. Pistorius knew how to interpret them. An example of this comes to mind just now. I dreamed I was able to fly, but in such a way that I seemed catapulted into the air and lost all control. The feeling of flying exhilarated me, but exhilaration turned to fear when I saw myself driven higher and higher, becoming more and more powerless. At that instant I made the saving discovery that I could regulate the rise or fall of my flight by holding or releasing my breath.

Pistorius' comment was: "The impetus that makes you fly is our great human possession. Everybody has it. It is the feeling of being linked with the roots of power, but one soon becomes afraid of this feeling. It's damned dangerous! That is why most people shed their wings and prefer to walk and obey the law. But not you. You go on flying. And look! You discover that you gradually begin to master your flight, that to the great general force that tears you upward there is added a delicate, small force of your own, an organ, a steering mechanism. How marvelous! Lacking that, you would be drawn up to the heights, powerless—which is what happens to madmen. They possess deeper intimations than people who remain earthbound, but they have no key and no steering mechanism and roar off into infinity. But you, Sinclair, you are going about it the right way. How? You probably don't know yourself. You are doing it with a new organ, with something that regulates your breathing. And now you will realize how little 'individuality' your soul has in its deepest reaches. For it does not invent this regulator! It is not new! You've borrowed it: it has existed for thousands of years. It is the organ with which fish regulate their equilibrium—the air bladder. And in fact among the fish there are still a few strange primeval genera where the air bladder functions as a kind of lung and can be used on occasion as a breathing mechanism. In other words, exactly like the lung which you in your dream use as a flying bladder."

He even brought out a zoology book and showed me the names and illustrations of these anachronistic fish. And with a peculiar shudder I felt that an organ from an earlier period of evolution was still alive within me.

6.   Jacob Wrestling

It is impossible to recount briefly all that Pistorius the eccentric musician told me about Abraxas. Most important was that what I learned from him represented a further step on the road toward myself. At that time, I was an unusual young man of eighteen, precocious in a hundred

ways, in a hundred others immature and helpless. When I compared myself with other boys my age I often felt proud and conceited but just as often humiliated and depressed. Frequently I considered myself a genius, and just as frequently, crazy. I did not succeed in participating in the life of boys my age, was often consumed by self-reproach and worries: I was helplessly separated from them, I was debarred from life.

Pistorius, who was himself a full-grown eccentric, taught me to maintain my courage and self-respect. By always finding something of value in what I said, in my dreams, my fantasies and thoughts, by never making light of them, always giving them serious consideration, he became my model.

"You told me," he said, "that you love music because it is *amoral*. That's all right with me. But in that case you can't allow yourself to be a moralist either. You can't compare yourself with others: if Nature has made you a bat you shouldn't try to be an ostrich. You consider yourself odd at times, you accuse yourself of taking a road different from most people. You have to unlearn that. Gaze into the fire, into the clouds, and as soon as the inner voices begin to speak, surrender to them, don't ask first whether it's permitted or would please your teachers or father, or some god. You will ruin yourself if you do that. That way you will become earthbound, a vegetable. Sinclair, our god's name is Abraxas and he is God and Satan and he contains both the luminous and the dark world. Abraxas does not take exception to any of your thoughts, any of your dreams. Never forget that. But he will leave you once you've become blameless and normal. Then he will leave you and look for a different vessel in which to brew his thoughts."

Among all my dreams the dark dream of love was the most faithful. How often

I dreamed that I stepped beneath the heraldic bird into our house, wanted to draw my mother to me and instead held the great, half-male, half-maternal woman in my arms, of whom I was afraid but who also attracted me violently. And I could never confess this dream to my friend. I kept it to myself even after I had told him everything else. It was my corner, my secret, my refuge.

When I felt bad I asked Pistorius to play Buxtehude's passacaglia. Then I would sit in the dusk-filled church completely involved in this unusually intimate, self-absorbed music, music that seemed to listen to itself, that comforted me each time, prepared me more and more to heed my own inner voices.

At times we stayed even after the music had ceased: we watched the weak light filter through the high, sharply arched windows and lose itself in the church.

"It sounds odd," said Pistorius, "that I was a theology student once and almost became a pastor. But I only committed a mistake of form. My task and goal still is to be a priest. Yet I was satisfied too soon and offered myself to Jehovah before I knew about Abraxas. Oh, yes, each and every religion is beautiful; religion is soul, no matter whether you take part in Christian communion or make a pilgrimage to Mecca."

"But in that case," I intervened, "you actually could have become a pastor."

"No, Sinclair. I would have had to lie. Our religion is practiced as though it were something else, something totally ineffectual. If worst came to worst I might become a Catholic, but a Protestant pastor—no! The few genuine believers—I do know a few—prefer the literal interpretation. I would not be able to tell them, for example, that Christ is not a person for me but a hero, a myth, an extraordinary shadow image in which humanity has painted itself on the wall of eternity. And the others, that come to church to hear a few clever phrases, to fulfill an obligation, not to miss anything, and so forth, what should I have said to them? Convert them? Is that what you mean? But I have no desire to. A priest does not want to convert, he merely wants to live among believers, among his own kind. He wants to be the instrument and expression for the feeling from which we create our gods."

He interrupted himself. Then continued: "My friend, our new religion, for which we have chosen the name Abraxas, is beautiful. It is the best we have. But it is still a fledgling. Its wings haven't grown yet. A lonely religion isn't right either. There has to be a community, there must be a cult and intoxicants, feasts and mysteries . . ."

He sank into a reverie and became lost within himself.

"Can't one perform mysteries all by oneself or among a very small group?" I asked hesitantly.

"Yes, one can." He nodded. "I've been performing them for a long time by myself. I have cults of my own for which I would be sentenced to years in prison if anyone should ever find out about them. Still, I know that it's not the right thing either."

Suddenly he slapped me on the shoulder so that I started up. "Boy," he said intensely, "you, too, have mysteries of your own. I know that you must have dreams that you don't tell me. I don't want to know them. But I can tell you: live those dreams, play with them, build altars to them. It is not yet the ideal but it points in the right direction. Whether you and I and a few others will renew the world someday remains to be seen. But within ourselves we must renew it each day, otherwise we just aren't serious. Don't forget that! You are eighteen years old, Sinclair, you don't go running to prostitutes. You must have dreams of love, you must have desires. Perhaps you're made in such a way that you are afraid of them. Don't be. They are the best things you have. You can believe me. I lost a great deal when I was your age by violating those dreams of love. One shouldn't do that. When you know something about Abraxas, you cannot do this any longer. You aren't allowed to be afraid of anything, you can't consider prohibited anything that the soul desires."

Startled, I countered: "But you can't do everything that comes to your mind! You can't kill someone because you detest him."

He moved closer to me.

"Under certain circumstances, even that. Yet it is a mistake most of the time. I don't mean that you should simply do everything that pops into your head. No. But you shouldn't harm and drive away those ideas that make good sense by exorcising them or moralizing about them. Instead of crucifying yourself or someone else you can drink wine from a chalice and contemplate the mystery of the sacrifice. Even without such procedures you can treat your drives and so-called temptations with respect and love. Then they will reveal their meaning—and they all do have meaning. If you happen to think of something truly mad or sinful again, if you want to kill someone or want to commit some enormity, Sinclair, think at that moment that it is Abraxas fantasizing within you! The person whom you would like to do away with is of course never Mr. X but merely a disguise. If you hate a person, you hate something in him that is part of yourself. What isn't part of ourselves doesn't disturb us."

Never before had Pistorius said anything to me that had touched me as deeply as this. I could not reply. But what had affected me most and in the strangest way was the similarity of this exhortation to Demian's words, which I had been carrying around with me for years. They did not know each other, yet both of them had told me the same thing.

"The things we see," Pistorius said softly, "are the same things that are within us. There is no reality except the one contained within us. That is why so many people live such an unreal life. They take the images outside them for reality and never allow the world within to assert itself. You can be happy that way. But once you know the other interpretation you no longer have the choice of following the crowd. Sinclair, the majority's path is an easy one, ours is difficult."

A few days later, after I had twice waited in vain, I met him late at night as he came seemingly blown around a corner by the cold night wind, stumbling all over himself, dead drunk. I felt no wish to call him. He went past me without seeing me, staring in front of himself with bewildered eyes shining, as though he followed something darkly calling out of the unknown. I followed him the length of one street; he drifted along as though pulled by an invisible string, with a fanatic gait, yet loose, like a ghost. Sadly I returned home to my unfulfilled dreams.

So that is how he renews the world within himself! it occurred to me. At the same moment I felt that was a low, moralizing thought. What did I know of his dreams? Perhaps he walked a more certain path in his intoxication than I within my dream.

I had noticed a few times during the breaks between classes that a fellow student I had never paid any previous attention to seemed to seek me out. He was a delicate, weak-looking boy with thin red-blond hair, and the look in his eyes and

is behavior seemed unusual. One evening when I was coming home he was
lying in wait for me in the alley. He let
me walk past, then followed me and
stopped when I did before the front door.

"Is there something you want from
me?" I asked him.

"I would only like to talk with you
once," he said shyly. "Be so kind as to
walk with me for a moment."

I followed him, sensing that he was
excited and full of expectation. His hands
trembled.

"Are you a spiritualist?" he asked
suddenly.

"No, Knauer," I said laughing. "Not in
the least. What makes you think I am?"

"But then you must be a theosophist?"

"Neither."

"Oh, don't be so reticent! I can feel
there's something special about you.
There's a look in your eyes . . . I'm
positive you communicate with spirits.
I'm not asking out of idle curiosity, Sinclair. No, I am a seeker myself, you
know, and I'm so very alone."

"Go ahead, tell me about it," I encouraged him. "I don't know much about
spirits. I live in my dreams—that's what
you sense. Other people live in dreams,
but not in their own. That's the difference."

"Yes, maybe that's the way it is," he
whispered. "It doesn't matter what kinds
of dreams they are in which you live.—
Have you heard about white magic?"

I had to say no.

"That is when you learn self-control.
You can become immortal and bewitch
people. Have you ever practiced any
exercises?"

After I had inquired what these "exercises" were he became very secretive;
that is, until I turned to go back. Then he
told me everything.

"For instance, when I want to fall
asleep or want to concentrate on something I do one of these exercises. I think
of something, a word for example, or a
name or a geometrical form. Then I
think this form into myself as hard as I
can. I try to imagine it until I can
actually feel it inside my head. Then I
think it in the throat, and so forth, until I
am completely filled by it. Then I'm as
firm as though I had turned to stone and
nothing can distract me any more."

I had a vague idea of what he meant.
Yet I felt certain that there was something else troubling him, he was so
strangely excited and restless. I tried to
make it easy for him to speak, and it was
not long before he expressed his real
concern.

"You're continent, too, aren't you?" he
asked reluctantly.

"What do you mean, sexually?"

"Yes. I've been continent for two years
—ever since I found out about the exercises. I had been depraved until then, you
know what I mean.—So you've never
been with a woman?"

"No," I said. "I never found the right
one."

"But if you did find a woman that you
felt was the right one, would you sleep
with Her?"

"Yes, naturally—if she had no objections," I said a little derisively.

"Oh, you're on the wrong path altogether! You can train your inner powers
only if you're completely continent. I've
been—for two whole years. Two years
and a little more than a month! It's so
difficult! Sometimes I think I can't stand
it much longer."

"Listen, Knauer, I don't believe that
continence is all that important."

"I know," he objected. "That's what
they all say. But I didn't expect you to
say the same thing. If you want to take
the higher, the spiritual road you have to
remain absolutely pure."

"Well, be pure then! But I don't

understand why someone is supposed to be more pure than another person if he suppresses his sexual urges. Or are you capable of eliminating sex from all your thoughts and dreams?"

He looked at me despairingly.

"No, that's just the point. My God, but I have to. I have dreams at night that I couldn't even tell myself. Horrible dreams."

I remembered what Pistorius had told me. But much as I agreed with his ideas I could not pass them on. I was incapable of giving advice that did not derive from my own experience and which I myself did not have the strength to follow. I fell silent and felt humiliated at being unable to give advice to someone who was seeking it from me.

"I've tried everything!" moaned Knauer beside me. "I've done everything there is to do. Cold water, snow, physical exercise and running, but nothing helps. Each night I awake from dreams that I'm not even allowed to think about—and the horrible part is that in the process I'm gradually forgetting everything spiritual I ever learned. I hardly ever succeed any more in concentrating or in making myself fall asleep. Often I lie awake the whole night. It can't go on much longer like this. If I can't win the struggle, if in the end I give in and become impure again, I'll be more wicked than all the others who never put up a fight. You understand that, don't you?"

I nodded but was unable to make any comment. He began to bore me and I was startled that his evident need and despair made no deeper impression on me. My only feeling was: I can't help you.

"So you don't know anything?" he finally asked sadly and exhausted. "Nothing at all? But there must be a way. How do you do it?"

"I can't tell you anything, Knauer. We can't help anybody else. No one helped

me either. You have to come to terms with yourself and then you must do what your inmost heart desires. There is no other way. If you can't find it yourself you'll find no spirits either."

The little fellow looked at me, disappointed and suddenly bereft of speech. Then his eyes flashed with hatred, he grimaced and shrieked: "Ah, you're a fine saint! You're depraved yourself, I know. You pretend to be wise but secretly you cling to the same filth the rest of us do! You're a pig, a pig, like me. All of us are pigs!"

I went off and left him standing there. He followed me two or three steps, then turned around and ran away. I felt nauseated with pity and disgust and the feeling did not leave me until I had surrounded myself with several paintings back in my room and surrendered to my own dreams. Instantly the dream returned, of the house entrance and the coat of arms, of the mother and the strange woman, and I could see her features so distinctly that I began painting her picture that same evening.

When the painting was completed after several days' work, sketched out in dreamlike fifteen-minute spurts, I pinned it on the wall, moved the study lamp in front of it, and stood before it as though before a ghost with which I had had to struggle to the end. It was a face similar to the earlier one—a few features even resembled me. One eye was noticeably higher than the other and the gaze went over and beyond me, self-absorbed and rigid, full of fate.

I stood before it and began to freeze inside from the exertion. I questioned the painting, berated it, made love to it, prayed to it; I called it mother, called it whore and slut, called it my beloved, called it Abraxas. Words said by Pistorius—or Demian?—occurred to me between my imprecations. I could not remember who had said them but I felt I could hear them again. They were words about Jacob's wrestling with the angel of God and his "I will not let thee go except thou bless me."

The painted face in the lamplight changed with each exhortation—became light and luminous, dark and brooding, closed pale eyelids over dead eyes, opened them again and flashed lightning glances. It was woman, man, girl, a little child, an animal, it dissolved into a tiny patch of color, grew large and distinct again. Finally, following a strong impulse, I closed my eyes and now saw the picture within me, stronger and mightier than before. I wanted to kneel down before it but it was so much a part of me that I could not separate it from myself, as though it had been transformed into my own ego.

Then I heard a dark, heavy roaring as if just before a spring storm and I trembled with an indescribable new feeling of fearful experience. Stars flashed up before me and died away: memories as far back as my earliest forgotten childhood, yes, even as far back as my pre-existence at earlier stages of evolution, thronged past me. But these memories that seemed to repeat every secret of my life to me did not stop with the past and the present. They went beyond it, mirroring the future, tore me away from the present into new forms of life whose images shone blindingly clear—not one could I clearly remember later on.

During the night I awoke from deep sleep: still dressed I lay diagonally across the bed. I lit the lamp, felt that I had to recollect something important but could not remember anything about the previous hour. Gradually I began to have an inkling. I looked for the painting—it was no longer on the wall, nor on the table either. Then I thought I could dimly remember that I had burned it. Or had this been in my dream that I burned it in the palm of my hand and swallowed the ashes?

A great restlessness overcame me. I put on a hat and walked out of the house through the alley as though compelled, ran through innumerable streets and squares as though driven by a frenzy, listened briefly in front of my friend's dark church, searched, searched with extreme urgency—without knowing what. I walked through a quarter with brothels where I could still see here and there a lighted window. Farther on I reached an area of newly built houses, with piles of bricks everywhere partially covered with gray snow. I remembered—as I drifted under the sway of some strange compulsion like a sleepwalker through the streets —the new building back in my home town to which my tormentor Kromer had taken me for my first payment. A similar building stood before me now in the gray night, its dark entrance yawning at me. It drew me inside: wanting to escape I stumbled over sand and rubbish. The power that drove me was stronger: I was forced to enter.

Across boards and bricks I stumbled into a dreary room that smelled moist and cold from fresh cement. There was a pile of sand, a light-gray patch, otherwise it was dark.

Then a horrified voice called out: "My God, Sinclair, where did you come from?"

Beside me a figure rose up out of the darkness, a small lean fellow, like a ghost, and even in my terror I recognized my fellow student Knauer.

"How did you happen to come here?" he asked, mad with excitement. "How were you able to find me?"

I didn't understand.

"I wasn't looking for you," I said, benumbed. Each word meant a great effort and came only haltingly, through dead lips.

He stared at me.

"Weren't looking for me?"

"No. Something drew me. Did you call me? You must have called me. What are you doing here anyway? It's night."

He clasped me convulsively with his thin arms.

"Yes, night. Morning will soon be here. Can you forgive me?"

"Forgive you what?"

"Oh, I was so awful."

Only now I remembered our conversation. Had that been only four, five days ago? A whole lifetime seemed to have passed since then. But suddenly I knew everything. Not only what had transpired between us but also why I had come here and what Knauer had wanted to do out here.

"You wanted to commit suicide, Knauer?"

He trembled with cold and fear.

"Yes, I wanted to. I don't know whether I would have been able to. I wanted to wait until morning."

I drew him into the open. The first horizontal rays of daylight glimmered cold and listless in the gray dawn.

For a while I led the boy by the arm. I heard myself say: "Now go home and don't say a word to anyone! You were on the wrong path. We aren't pigs as you seem to think, but human beings. We create gods and struggle with them, and they bless us."

We walked on and parted company without saying another word. When I reached the house, it was already daylight.

The best things I gained from my remaining weeks in St. ——— were the hours spent with Pistorius at the organ or in front of his fire. We were studying a Greek text about Abraxas and he read me extracts from a translation of the Vedas and taught me how to speak the sacred "om." Yet these occult matters were not what nourished me inwardly. What invigorated me was the progress I had made in discovering myself, the increasing confidence in my own dreams, thoughts, and intimations, and the growing knowledge of the power I possessed within me.

Pistorius and I understood each other in every possible way. All I had to do was think of him and I could be certain that he—or a message from him—would come. I could ask him anything, as I had asked Demian, without his having to be present in the flesh: all I had to do was visualize him and direct my questions at him in the form of intensive thought. Then all psychic effort expended on the question would return to me in kind, as an answer. Only it was not the person of Pistorius nor that of Max Demian that I conjured up and addressed, but the picture I had dreamed and painted, the half-male, half-female dream image of my *daemon*. This being was now no longer confined to my dreams, no longer merely depicted on paper, but lived within me as an ideal and intensification of my self.

The relationship which the would-be suicide Knauer formed with me was peculiar, occasionally even funny. Ever since the night in which I had been sent to him, he clung to me like a faithful servant or a dog, made every effort to forge his life with mine, and obeyed me blindly. He came to me with the most astonishing questions and requests, wanted to see spirits, learn the cabala, and would not believe me when I assured him that I was totally ignorant in all these matters. He thought nothing was beyond my powers. Yet it was strange that he would often come to me with his puzzling and stupid questions when I was faced with a puzzle of my own to which his fanciful notions and requests frequently provided a catchword and the mpetus for a solution. Often he was a bother and I would dismiss him peremptorily; yet I sensed that he, too, had been sent to me, that from him, too, came back whatever I gave him, in double measure; he, too, was a leader for me—or at least a guidepost. The occult books and writings he brought me and in which he sought his salvation taught me more than I realized at the time.

Later Knauer slipped unnoticed out of my life. We never came into conflict with each other; there was no reason to. Unlike Pistorius, with whom I was still to share a strange experience toward the end of my days in St. ———.

On one or on several occasions in the course of their lives, even the most harmless people do not altogether escape coming into conflict with the fine virtues of piety and gratitude. Sooner or later each of us must take the step that separates him from his father, from his mentors; each of us must have some cruelly lonely experience—even if most people cannot take much of this and soon crawl back. I myself had not parted from my parents and their world, the "luminous" world, in a violent struggle, but had gradually and almost imperceptibly become estranged. I was sad that it had to be this way and it made for many unpleasant hours during my visits back home; but it did not affect me deeply, it was bearable.

But where we have given of our love and respect not from habit but of our own free will, where we have been disciples and friends out of our inmost hearts, it is a bitter and horrible moment when we suddenly recognize that the current within us wants to pull us away from what is dearest to us. Then every thought that rejects the friend and mentor turns in our own hearts like a poisoned barb, then each blow struck in defense flies back into one's own face, the words "disloyalty" and "ingratitude" strike the person who feels he was morally sound like catcalls and stigma, and the frightened heart flees timidly back to the charmed valleys of childhood virtues, unable to believe that this break, too, must be made, this bond also broken.

With time my inner feelings had slowly turned against acknowledging Pistorius so unreservedly as a master. My friendship with him, his counsel, the comfort he had brought me, his proximity had been a vital experience during the most important months of my adolescence. God had spoken to me through him. From his lips my dreams had returned clarified and interpreted. He had given me faith in myself. And now I became conscious of gradually beginning to resist him. There was too much didacticism in what he said, and I felt that he understood only a part of me completely.

No quarrel or scene occurred between us, no break and not even a settling of accounts. I uttered only a single—actually harmless—phrase, yet it was in that moment that an illusion was shattered.

A vague presentiment of such an occurrence had oppressed me for some time; it became a distinct feeling one Sunday morning in his study. We were lying before the fire while he was holding forth about mysteries and forms of religion, which he was studying, and whose potentialities for the future preoccupied him. All this seemed to me odd and eclectic and not of vital importance; there was something vaguely pedagogical about it; it sounded like tedious research among the ruins of former worlds. And all at once I felt a repugnance for his whole manner, for this cult of mythologies, this game of mosaics he was playing with secondhand modes of belief.

"Pistorius," I said suddenly in a fit of malice that both surprised and frightened me. "You ought to tell me one of your dreams again sometime, a real dream, one that you've had at night. What you're telling me there is all so—so damned *antiquarian*."

He had never heard me speak like that before and at the same moment I realized with a flash of shame and horror that the arrow I had shot at him, that had pierced his heart, had come from his own armory: I was now flinging back at him reproaches that on occasion he had directed against himself half in irony.

He fell silent at once. I looked at him with dread in my heart and saw him turning terribly pale.

After a long pregnant pause he placed fresh wood on the fire and said in a quiet voice: "You're right, Sinclair, you're a clever boy. I'll spare you the antiquarian stuff from now on." He spoke very calmly but it was obvious he was hurt. What had I done?

I wanted to say something encouraging to him, implore his forgiveness, assure him of my love and my deep gratitude. Touching words came to mind—but I could not utter them. I just lay there gazing into the fire and kept silent. He, too, kept silent and so we lay while the fire dwindled, and with each dying flame I felt something beautiful, intimate irrevocably burn low and become evanescent.

"I'm afraid you've misunderstood me," I said finally with a very forced and clipped voice. The stupid, meaningless words fell mechanically from my lips as if I were reading from a magazine serial.

"I quite understand," Pistorius said softly. "You're right." I waited. Then he went on slowly: "Inasmuch as one person can be right *against* another."

No, no! I'm wrong, a voice screamed inside me—but I could not say anything. I knew that with my few words I had put my finger on his essential weakness, his affliction and wound. I had touched the

spot where he most mistrusted himself. His ideal *was* "antiquarian," he was seeking in the past, he was a romantic. And suddenly I realized deeply within me what Pistorius had been and given to me was precisely what he could not be and give to himself. He had led me along a path that would transcend and leave even him, the leader, behind.

God knows how one happens to say something like that. I had not meant it all that maliciously, had had no idea of the havoc I would create. I had uttered something the implications of which I had been unaware of at the moment of speaking. I had succumbed to a weak rather witty but malicious impulse and it had become fate. I had committed a trivial and careless act of brutality which he regarded as a judgment.

How much I wished then that he become enraged, defend himself, and berate me! He did nothing of the kind—I had to do all of that myself. He would have smiled if he could have, and the fact that he found it impossible was the surest proof of how deeply I had wounded him.

By accepting this blow so quietly, from me, his impudent and ungrateful pupil, by keeping silent and admitting that I had been right, by acknowledging my words as his fate, he made me detest myself and increased my indiscretion even more. When I had hit out I had thought I would strike a tough, well-armed man—he turned out to be a quiet, passive, defenseless creature who surrendered without protest.

For a long time we stayed in front of the dying fire, in which each glowing shape, each writhing twig reminded me of our rich hours and increased the guilty awareness of my indebtedness to Pistorius. Finally I could bear it no longer. I got up and left. I stood a long time in front of the door to his room, a long time on the dark stairway, and even longer outside his house waiting to hear if he would follow me. Then I turned to go and walked for hours through the town, its suburbs, parks and woods, until evening. During that walk I felt for the first time the mark of Cain on my forehead.

Only gradually was I able to think clearly about what had occurred. At first my thoughts were full of self-reproach, intent on defending Pistorius. But all of them turned into the opposite of my intention. A thousand times I was ready to regret and take back my rash statement—yet it had been the truth. Only now I managed to understand Pistorius completely and succeeded in constructing his whole dream before me. This dream had been to be a priest, to proclaim the new religion, to introduce new forms of exaltation, of love, of worship, to erect new symbols. But this was not his strength and it was not his function. He lingered too fondly in the past, his knowledge of this past was too precise, he knew too much about Egypt and India, Mithras and Abraxas. His love was shackled to images the earth had seen before, and yet, in his inmost heart, he realized that the New had to be truly new and different, that it had to spring from fresh soil and could not be drawn from museums and libraries. His function was perhaps to lead me to themselves as he had led me. To provide them with the unprecedented, the new gods, was not in him.

At this point a sharp realization burned within me: each man has his "function" but none which he can choose himself, define, or perform as he pleases. It was wrong to desire new gods, completely wrong to want to provide the world with something. An enlightened man had but one duty—to seek the way to himself, to reach inner certainty, to grope his way forward, no matter where it led. The realization shook me profoundly, it was the fruit of this experience. I had often speculated with images

of the future, dreamed of roles that I might be assigned, perhaps as poet or prophet or painter, or something similar.

All that was futile. I did not exist to write poems, to preach or to paint, neither I nor anyone else. All of that was incidental. Each man had only one genuine vocation—to find the way to himself. He might end up as poet or madman, as prophet or criminal—that was not his affair, ultimately it was of no concern. His task was to discover his own destiny—not an arbitrary one—and live it out wholly and resolutely within himself. Everything else was only a would-be existence, an attempt at evasion, a flight back to the ideals of the masses, conformity and fear of one's own inwardness. The new vision rose up before me, glimpsed a hundred times, possibly even expressed before but now experienced for the first time by me. I was an experiment on the part of Nature, a gamble within the unknown, perhaps for a new purpose, perhaps for nothing, and my only task was to allow this game on the part of primeval depths to take its course, to feel its will within me and make it wholly mine. That or nothing!

I had already felt much loneliness, now there was a deeper loneliness still which was inescapable.

I made no attempt at reconciliation with Pistorius. We remained friends but the relationship changed. Yet this was something we touched on only once; actually it was Pistorius alone who did. He said:

"You know that I have the desire to become a priest. Most of all I wanted to become the priest of the new religion of which you and I have had so many intimations. That role will never be mine—I realize that and even without wholly admitting it to myself have known it for some time. So I will perform other priestly duties instead, perhaps at the organ, perhaps some other way. But I must always have things around me that I feel are beautiful and sacred, organ music and mysteries, symbols and myths. I need and cannot forgo them. That is my weakness. Sometimes, Sinclair, I know that I should not have such wishes, that they are a weakness and luxury. It would be more magnanimous and just if I put myself unreservedly at the disposal of fate. But I can't do that, I am incapable of it. Perhaps you will be able to do it one day. It is difficult, it is the only truly difficult thing there is. I have often dreamed of doing so, but I can't; the idea fills me with dread: I am not capable of standing so naked and alone. I, too, am a poor weak creature who needs warmth and food and occasionally the comfort of human companionship. Someone who seeks nothing but his own fate no longer has any companions, he stands quite alone and has only cold universal space around him. That is Jesus in the Garden of Gethsemane, you know. There have been martyrs who gladly let themselves be nailed to the cross, but even these were no heroes, were not liberated, for even they wanted something that they had become fond of and accustomed to—they had models, they had ideals. But the man who only seeks his destiny has neither models nor ideals, has nothing dear and consoling! And actually this is the path one should follow. People like you and me are quite lonely really but we still have each other, we have the secret satisfaction of being different, of rebelling, of desiring the unusual. But you must shed that, too, if you want to go all the way to the end. You cannot allow yourself to become a revolutionary, an example, a martyr. It is beyond imagining—"

Yes, it was beyond imagining. But it could be dreamed, anticipated, sensed. A few times I had a foretaste of it—in an hour of absolute stillness. Then I would gaze into myself and confront the image of my fate. Its eyes would be full of wisdom, full of madness, they would radiate love or deep malice, it was all the same. You were not allowed to choose or desire any one of them. You were only allowed to desire *yourself*, only your fate. Up to this point, Pistorius had been my guide.

In those days I walked about as though I were blind. I felt frenzies—each step was a new danger. I saw nothing in front of me except the unfathomable darkness into which all paths I had taken until now had led and vanished. And within me I saw the image of the master, who resembled Demian, and in whose eyes my fate stood written.

I wrote on a piece of paper: "A leader has left me. I am enveloped in darkness. I cannot take another step alone. Help me."

I wanted to mail it to Demian, but didn't. Each time I wanted to, it looked foolish and senseless. But I knew my little prayer by heart and often recited it to myself. It was with me every hour of the day. I had begun to understand it.

My schooldays were over. I was to take a trip during my vacation—my father's idea—and then enter a university. But I did not know what I would major in. I had been granted my wish; one semester of philosophy. Any other subject would have done as well.

7.   Eva

Once during my vacation I visited the house where years before Demian had lived with his mother. I saw an old woman strolling in the garden and, speaking with her, learned that it was her house. I inquired after the Demian family. She remembered them very well but could not tell me where they lived at present. Sensing my interest she took me into the house, brought out a leather

album and showed me a photo of
Demian's mother. I could hardly remember what she looked like, but now as I
saw the small likeness my heart stood
still: it was my dream image! That was
she, the tall, almost masculine woman
who resembled her son, with maternal
traits, severity, passion; beautiful and
alluring, beautiful and unapproachable,
daemon and mother, fate and beloved.
There was no mistaking her!

To discover in this fashion that my
dream image existed struck me as a
miracle. So there was a woman who
looked like that, who bore the features of
my destiny! And to be Demian's mother.
Where was she?

Shortly afterwards I embarked on my
trip. What a strange journey it was! I
traveled restlessly from place to place,
following every impulse, always searching for this woman. There were days
when everyone I met reminded me of
her, echoed her, seemed to resemble her,
drew me through the streets of unfamiliar cities, through railroad stations and
into trains, as in an intricate dream.
There were other days when I realized
the futility of my search. Then I would
idly sit somewhere in a park or in some
hotel garden, in a waiting room, trying to
make the picture come alive within me.
But it had become shy and elusive. I
found it impossible to fall asleep. Only
while traveling on the train could I catch
an occasional brief nap. Once, in Zurich,
a woman approached me, an impudent
pretty creature. I took hardly any notice
of her and walked past as though she
didn't exist. I would rather have died on
the spot than have paid attention to another woman, even for an hour.

I felt my fate drawing me on, I felt the
moment of my fulfillment coming near
and I was sick with impatience at not
being able to do anything. Once in a railroad station, in Innsbruck I think, I
caught sight of a woman who reminded

me of her—in a train just pulling away. I
was miserable for days. And suddenly the
form reappeared in a dream one night. I
awoke humiliated and dejected by the
futility of my hunt and I took the next
train home.

A few weeks later I enrolled at the
university of H. I found everything disappointing. The lectures on the history of
philosophy were just as uninspired and
stereotyped as the activities of most of
the students. Everything seemed to run
according to an old pattern, everyone
was doing the same thing, and the exaggerated gaiety on the boyish faces looked
depressingly empty and ready-made. But
at least I was free, I had the whole day to
myself, lived quietly and peacefully in an
old house near the town wall, and on my
table lay a few volumes of Nietzsche. I
lived with him, sensed the loneliness of
his soul, perceived the fate that had pro-
pelled him on inexorably; I suffered with
him, and rejoiced that there had been one
man who had followed his destiny so
relentlessly.

Late one evening I was sauntering
through town. An autumn wind was
blowing and I could hear the fraternities
frolic in the taverns. Clouds of tobacco
smoke drifted out open windows with a
profusion of song, loud, rhythmic yet
uninspired, lifelessly uniform.

I stood at a street corner and listened:
out of two bars the methodically re-
hearsed gaiety of youth rang out against
the night. False communion everywhere,
everywhere shedding the responsibility of
fate, flight to the herd for warmth.

Two men slowly walked past behind
me. I caught a few words of their conversation.

"Isn't it just like the young men's
house in a kraal?" said one of them.
"Everything fits down to the tattooing
which is in vogue again. Look, that's
young Europe."

The voice sounded strangely and ad-

monishingly familiar. I followed the two
of them down the dark lane. One of them
was a Japanese, small and elegant. Under
a street lamp I saw his yellow face light
up in a smile.

The other was now speaking again.

"I imagine it's just as bad where you
come from, in Japan. People that don't
follow the herd are rare everywhere.
There are some here too."

I felt a mixture of alarm and joy at
each word. I knew the speaker. It was
Demian. I followed him and the Japanese
through the wind-swept streets; listening
to their conversation I relished the sound
of Demian's voice. It still had its familiar
ring; the same old beautiful certainty and
calm had all their old power over me.
Now all was well. I had found him.

At the end of a street in the suburbs
the Japanese took his leave and unlocked
his house door. Demian retraced his
steps, I had stopped and was waiting for
him in the middle of the street. I became
very agitated as I saw him approach,
upright, with elastic step, in a brown
rubber raincoat. He came closer without
changing his pace until he stopped a few
steps in front of me. Then he removed
his hat and revealed his old light-skinned
face with the decisive mouth and the
peculiar brightness on his broad forehead.

"Demian," I called out.

He stretched out his hand.

"So, it's you, Sinclair! I was expecting
you."

"Did you know I was here?"

"I didn't exactly know it but I definitely wished you were. I didn't catch
sight of you until this evening. You've
been following us for quite some time."

"Did you recognize me at once?"

"Of course. You've changed somewhat. But you have the sign."

"The sign. What kind of sign?"

"We used to call it the mark of Cain
earlier on—if you can still remember. It's

our sign. You've always had it, that's
why I became your friend. But now it
has become more distinct."

"I wasn't aware of that. Or actually,
yes, once I painted a picture of you,
Demian, and was astonished that it also
resembled myself. Was that the sign?"

"That was it. It's good that you're
here. My mother will be pleased, too."

Suddenly I was frightened.

"Your mother? Is she here, too? But
she doesn't know me."

"But she knows about you. She will
recognize you even without my saying
who you are. We've been in the dark
about you for a long time."

"I often wanted to write you, but it
was no use. I've known for some time
that I would find you soon. I waited for
it each day."

He thrust his arm under mine and
walked along with me. An aura of calm
surrounded him which affected me, too.
Soon we were talking as we used to talk
in the past. Our thoughts went back to
our time in school, the Confirmation
classes and also to that last unhappy
meeting during my vacation. Only our
earliest and closest bond, the Franz
Kromer episode, was never mentioned.

Suddenly we found ourselves in the
midst of a strange conversation touching
on many ominous topics. Picking up
where Demian left off in his conversation
with the Japanese, we had discussed the
life most of the students led, then came
to something else, something that seemed
to lie far afield. Yet in Demian's words
an intimate connection became evident.

He spoke about the spirit of Europe
and the signs of the times. Everywhere,
he said, we could observe the reign of the
herd instinct, nowhere freedom and love.
All this false communion—from the
fraternities to the choral societies and the
nations themselves—was an inevitable
development, was a community born of

fear and dread, out of embarrassment, but inwardly rotten, outworn, close to collapsing.

"Genuine communion," said Demian, "is a beautiful thing. But what we see flourishing everywhere is nothing of the kind. The real spirit will come from the knowledge that separate individuals have of one another and for a time it will transform the world. The community spirit at present is only a manifestation of the herd instinct. Men fly into each other's arms because they are afraid of each other—the owners are for themselves, the workers for themselves, the scholars for themselves! And why are they afraid? You are only afriad if you are not in harmony with yourself. People are afraid because they have never owned up to themselves. A whole society composed of men afraid of the unknown within them! They all sense that the rules they live by are no longer valid, that they live according to archaic laws—neither their religion nor their morality is in any way suited to the needs of the present. For a hundred years or more Europe has done nothing but study and build factories! They know exactly how many ounces of powder it takes to kill a man but they don't know how to pray to God, they don't even know how to be happy for a single contented hour. Just take a look at a student dive! Or a resort where the rich congregate. It's hopeless. Dear Sinclair, nothing good can come of all of this. These people who huddle together in fear are filled with dread and malice, no one trusts the other. They hanker after ideals that are ideals no longer but they will hound the man to death who sets up a new one. I can feel the approaching conflict. It's coming, believe me, and soon. Of course it will not 'improve' the world. Whether the workers kill the manufacturers or whether Germany makes war on Russia will merely mean a

change of ownership. But it won't have been entirely in vain. It will reveal the bankruptcy of present-day ideals, there will be a sweeping away of Stone Age gods. The world, as it is now, wants to die, wants to perish—and it will."

"And what will happen to us during this conflict?"

"To us? Oh, perhaps we'll perish in it. Our kind can be shot, too. Only we aren't done away with as easily as all that. Around what remains of us, around those of us who survive, the will of the future will gather. The will of humanity, which our Europe has shouted down for a time with its frenzy of technology, will come to the fore again. And then it will become clear that the will of humanity is nowhere—and never was—identical with the will of present-day societies, states and peoples, clubs and churches. No, what Nature wants of man stands indelibly written in the individual, in you, in me. It stood written in Jesus, it stood written in Nietzsche. These tendencies— which are the only important ones and which, of course, can assume different forms every day—will have room to breathe once the present societies have collapsed."

It was late when we stopped in front of a garden by the river.

"This is where we live," said Demian. "You must come visit us soon. We've been waiting for you."

Elated I walked the long way home through a night which had now turned chill. Here and there students were reeling noisily to their quarters. I had often marked the contrast between their almost ludicrous gaiety and my lonely existence, sometimes with scorn, sometimes with a feeling of deprivation. But never until today had I felt with as much calm and secret strength how little it mattered to me, how remote and dead this world was for me. I remembered civil servants in my home town, worthy old gentlemen who clung to the memories of their drunken university days as to keepsakes from paradise and fashioned a cult of their "vanished" student years as poets or other romantics fashion their childhood. It was the same everywhere! Everywhere they looked for "freedom" and "luck" in the past, out of sheer dread of their present responsibilities and future course. They drank and caroused for a few years and then they slunk away to become serious-minded gentlemen in the service of the state. Yes, our society was rotten, and these student stupidities were not so stupid, not so bad as a hundred other things.

By the time I reached my distant house and was preparing for bed, all these thoughts had vanished and my entire being clung expectantly to the great promise that this day had brought me. As soon as I wished, even tomorrow, I was to see Demian's mother. Let the students have their drunken orgies and tattoo their faces; the rotten world could await its destruction—for all I cared. I was waiting for one thing—to see my fate step forth in a new guise.

I slept deeply until late in the morning. The new day dawned for me like a solemn feast, the kind I had not experienced since childhood. I was full of a great restlessness, yet without fear of any kind. I felt that an important day had begun for me and I saw and experienced the changed world around me, expectant, meaningful, and solemn; even the gentle autumn rain had its beauty and a calm and festive air full of happy, sacred music. For the first time the outer world was perfectly attuned to the world within; it was a joy to be alive. No house, no shop window, no face disturbed me, everything was as it should be, without any of the flat, humdrum look of the everyday; everything was a part of

Nature, expectant and ready to face its destiny with reverence. That was how the world had appeared to me in the mornings when I was a small boy, on the great feast days, at Christmas or Easter. I had forgotten that the world could still be so lovely. I had grown accustomed to living within myself. I was resigned to the knowledge that I had lost all appreciation of the outside world, that the loss of its bright colors was an inseparable part of the loss of my childhood, and that, in a certain sense, one had to pay for freedom and maturity of the soul with the renunciation of this cherished aura. But now, overjoyed, I saw that all this had only been buried or clouded over and that it was still possible—even if you had become liberated and had renounced your childhood happiness—to see the world shine and to savor the delicious thrill of the child's vision.

The moment came when I found my way back to the garden at the edge of town where I had taken leave of Demian the night before. Hidden behind tall, wet trees stood a little house, bright and livable. Tall plants flowered behind plate glass; behind glistening windows dark walls shone with pictures and rows of books. The front door led straight into a small, warm hallway. A silent old maid, dressed in black with a white apron, showed me in and took my coat.

She left me alone in the hallway. I looked around and at once was swept into the middle of my dream. High up on the dark wood-paneled wall, above a door, hung a familiar painting, my bird with the golden-yellow sparrow hawk's head, clambering out of the terrestrial shell. Deeply moved, I stood there motionless—I felt joy and pain as though at this moment everything I had ever done and experienced returned to me in the form of a reply and fulfillment. In a flash I saw hosts of images throng past my mind's eye: my parents' house with the old coat of arms above the doorway, the boy Demian sketching the emblem, myself as a boy under the fearful spell of my enemy Kromer, myself as an adolescent in my room at school painting my dream bird at a quiet table, the soul caught in the intricacies of its own threads—and everything, everything to this present moment resounded once more within me, was affirmed by me, answered, sanctioned.

With tears in my eyes I stared at my picture and read within myself. Then I lowered my eyes: beneath the painting of the bird in the open door stood a tall woman in a dark dress. It was she.

I was unable to utter a word. With a face that resembled her son's, timeless, ageless, and full of inner strength, the beautiful woman smiled with dignity. Her gaze was fulfillment, her greeting a homecoming. Silently I stretched my hands out to her. She took both of them in her firm, warm hands.

"You are Sinclair. I recognized you at once. Welcome!"

Her voice was deep and warm. I drank it up like sweet wine. And now I looked up and into her quiet face, the black unfathomable eyes, at her fresh, ripe lips, the clear, regal brow that bore the sign.

"How glad I am," I said and kissed her hands. "I believe I have been on my way my whole life—and now I have come home."

She smiled like a mother.

"One never reaches home," she said. "But where paths that have affinity for each other intersect the whole world looks like home, for a time."

She was expressing what I had felt on my way to her. Her voice and her words resembled her son's and yet were quite different. Everything was riper, warmer, more self-evident. But just as Max had never given anyone the impression of being a boy, so his mother did not appear at all like a woman who had a full-grown son, so young and sweet were her face and hair, so taut and smooth her golden skin, so fresh her mouth. More regal even than in my dreams she stood before me.

This, then, was the new guise in which my fate revealed itself to me, no longer stern, no longer setting me apart, but fresh and joyful! I made no resolutions, took no vows—I had attained a goal, a high point on the road: from there the next stage of the journey appeared unhampered and marvelous, leading toward promised lands. Whatever might happen to me now, I was filled with ecstasy: that this woman existed in the world, that I could drink in her voice and breathe her presence. No matter whether she would become my mother, my beloved or a goddess—if she could just be here! if only my path would be close to hers!

She pointed up to my painting.

"You never made Max happier than with this picture," she said thoughtfully. "And me, too. We were waiting for you and when the painting came we knew that you were on your way. When you were a little boy, Sinclair, my son one day came home from school and said to me: there is a boy in school, he has the sign on his brow, he has to become my friend. That was you. You have not had an easy time but we had confidence in you. You met Max again during one of your vacations. You must have been about sixteen at the time. Max told me about it—"

I interrupted: "He told you about that? That was the most miserable period of my life!"

"Yes, Max said to me: Sinclair has the most difficult part coming now. He's making one more attempt to take refuge among the others. He's even begun going to bars. But he won't succeed. His sign is obscured but it sears him secretly. Wasn't it like that?"

"Yes, exactly. Then I found Beatrice and I finally found a master again. His name was Pistorius. Only then did it become clear to me why my boyhood had been so closely bound up with Max and why I could not free myself from him. Dear mother, at that time I often thought that I should have to take my life. Is the way as difficult as this for everybody?"

She stroked my hair. The touch felt as light as a breeze.

"It is always difficult to be born. You know the chick does not find it easy to break his way out of the shell. Think back and ask yourself: Was the way all that difficult? Was it only difficult? Wasn't it beautiful, too? Can you think of a more beautiful and easier way?"

I shook my head.

"It was difficult," I said as though I were asleep, "it was hard until the dream came."

She nodded and pierced me with a glance.

"Yes, you must find your dream, then the way becomes easy. But there is no dream that lasts forever, each dream is followed by another, and one should not cling to any particular one."

I was startled and frightened. Was that a warning, a defensive gesture, so soon? But it didn't matter: I was prepared to let her guide me and not to inquire into goals.

"I do not know," I said, "how long my dream is supposed to last. I wish it could be forever. My fate has received me under the picture of the bird like a lover and like a beloved. I belong to my fate and to no one else."

"As long as the dream is your fate you should remain faithful to it," she confirmed in a serious tone of voice.

I was overcome by sadness and a longing to die in this enchanted hour. I felt tears—what an infinity since I had last wept—well up irresistibly in my eyes and overwhelm me. I turned abruptly away from her, stepped to the window, and stared blindly into the distance.

I heard her voice behind me, calm and yet brimful with tenderness as a beaker with wine.

"Sinclair, you are a child! Your fate loves you. One day it will be entirely yours—just as you dream it—if you remain constant to it."

I had gained control of myself and turned toward her again. She gave me her hand.

"I have a few friends," she said with a smile, "a few very close friends who call me Frau Eva. You shall be one of them if you wish."

She led me to the door, opened it, and pointed into the garden. "You'll find Max out there."

I stood dazed and shaken under the tall trees, not knowing whether I was more awake or more in a dream than ever. The rain dripped gently from the branches. Slowly I walked out into the garden that extended some way along the river. Finally I found Demian. He was standing in an open summer house, stripped to the waist, punching a suspended sandbag.

I stopped, astonished. Demian looked strikingly handsome with his broad chest, and firm, manly features; the raised arms with taut muscles were strong and capable, the movements sprang playfully and smoothly from hips, shoulders, and wrists.

"Demian," I called out. "What are you doing there?"

He laughed happily.

"Practicing. I've promised the Japanese a boxing match, the little fellow is as agile as a cat and, of course, just as sly, but he won't be able to beat me. There's a very slight humiliation for which I have to pay him back."

He put on his shirt and coat.

"You've seen my mother?" he asked.

"Yes, Demian, what a wonderful mother you have! Frau Eva! The name fits her perfectly. She *is* like a universal mother."

For a moment he looked thoughtfully into my face.

"So you know her name already? You can be proud of yourself. You are the first person she has told it to during the first meeting."

From this day on I went in and out of the house like a son or brother—but also as someone in love. As soon as I opened the gate, as soon as I caught sight of the tall trees in the garden, I felt happy and rich. Outside was reality: streets and houses, people and institutions, libraries and lecture halls—but here inside was love; here lived the legend and the dream. And yet we lived in no way cut off from the outside world; in our thoughts and conversations we often lived in the midst of it, only on an entirely different plane. We were not separated from the majority of men by a boundary but simply by another mode of vision. Our task was to represent an island in the world, a prototype perhaps, or at least a prospect of a different way of life. I, who had been isolated for so long, learned about the companionship which is possible between people who have tasted complete loneliness. I never again hankered after the tables of the fortunate and the feasts of the blessed. Never again did envy or nostalgia overcome me when I witnessed the collective pleasures of others. And gradually I was initiated into the secret of those who wear the sign in their faces.

We who wore the sign might justly be considered "odd" by the world; yes, even crazy, and dangerous. We were *aware* or in the process of becoming aware and our striving was directed toward achieving a more and more complete state of awareness while the striving of the others was a quest aimed at binding their opinions, ideals, duties, their lives and fortunes more and more closely to those of the herd. There, too, was striving, there, too, were power and greatness. But whereas we, who were marked, believed that we represented the will of Nature to something new, to the individualism of the future, the others sought to perpetuate the status quo. Humanity—which they loved as we did—was for them something complete that must be maintained and protected. For us, humanity was a distant goal toward which all men were moving, whose image no one knew, whose laws were nowhere written down.

Apart from Frau Eva, Max, and myself, various other seekers were more or less closely attached to the circle. Quite a few had set out on very individual paths, had set themselves quite unusual goals, and clung to specific ideas and duties. They included astrologers and cabalists, also a disciple of Count Tolstoi, and all kinds of delicate, shy, and vulnerable creatures, followers of new sects, devotees of Indian asceticism, vegetarians, and so forth. We actually had no mental bonds in common save the respect which each one accorded the ideals of the other. Those with whom we felt a close kinship were concerned with mankind's past search for gods and ideals—their studies often reminded me of Pistorius. They brought books with them, translated aloud texts in ancient languages, showed us illustrations of ancient symbols and rites and taught us to see how humanity's entire store of ideals so far consisted of dreams that had emanated from the unconscious, of dreams in which humanity groped after its intimations of future potentialities. Thus we became acquainted with the wonderful thousand-headed tangle of gods from prehistory to the dawn of the Christian conversion. We heard the creeds of solitary holy men, of the transformations religions undergo in their migrations from one people to another. Thus, from everything we collected in this manner, we gained a critical understanding of our time and of contemporary Europe: with prodigious efforts mighty new weapons had been created for mankind but the end was flagrant, deep desolation of the spirit. Europe had conquered the whole world only to lose her own soul.

Our circle also included believers, adherents of certain hopes and healing faiths. There were Buddhists who sought to convert Europe, a disciple of Tolstoi who preached nonresistance to evil, as well as other sects. We in the inner circle listened but accepted none of these teachings as anything but metaphors. We, who bore the mark, felt no anxiety about the shape the future was to take. All of these faiths and teachings seemed to us already dead and useless. The only duty and destiny we acknowledged was that each one of us should become so completely himself, so utterly faithful to the active seed which Nature planted within him, that in living out its growth he could be surprised by nothing unknown to come.

Although we might not have been able to express it, we all felt distinctly that a new birth amid the collapse of this present world was imminent, already discernible. Demian often said to me: "What will come is beyond imagining. The soul of Europe is a beast that has lain fettered for an infinitely long time. And when it's free, its first movements won't be the gentlest. But the means are unimportant if only the real needs of the soul—which has for so long been repeatedly stunted and anesthetized—come to light. Then our day will come, then we will be needed. Not as leaders and lawgivers—we won't be there to see the new laws—but rather as those who are willing, as men who are ready to go forth and stand prepared wherever fate may

need them. Look, all men are prepared to accomplish the incredible if their ideals are threatened. But no one is ready when a new ideal, a new and perhaps dangerous and ominous impulse, makes itself felt. The few who will be ready at that time and who will go forth—will be us. That is why we are marked—as Cain was—to arouse fear and hatred and drive men out of a confining idyl into more dangerous reaches. All men who have had an effect on the course of human history, all of them without exception, were capable and effective only because they were ready to accept the inevitable. It is true of Moses and Buddha, of Napoleon and Bismarck. What particular movement one serves and what pole one is directed from are matters outside one's own choice. If Bismarck had understood the Social Democrats and compromised with them he would have merely been shrewd but no man of destiny. The same applies to Napoleon, Caesar, Loyola, all men of that species in fact. Always, you must think of these things in evolutionary, in historical terms! When the upheavals of the earth's surface flung the creatures of the sea onto the land and the land creatures into the sea, the specimens of the various orders that were ready to follow their destiny were the ones that accomplished the new and unprecedented; by making new biological adjustments they were able to save their species from destruction. We do not know whether these were the same specimens that had previously distinguished themselves among their fellows as conservative, upholders of the status quo, or rather as eccentrics, revolutionaries; but we do know they were ready, and could therefore lead their species into new phases of evolution. That is why we want to be *ready*."

Frau Eva was often present during these conversations yet she did not participate in quite the same manner. She was a listener, full of trust and understanding, an echo for each one of us who explained his thoughts. It seemed as though all thinking emanated from her and in the end went back to her. My happiness consisted in sitting near her, hearing her voice occasionally and sharing the rich, soulful atmosphere surrounding her.

She was immediately aware of any change, any unhappiness or new development within me. It even seemed to me that my dreams at night were inspired by her. I would often recount them to her and she found them comprehensible and natural; there was no unusual turn in them that she could not follow. For a time my dreams repeated patterns of our daytime conversations. I dreamed that the whole world was in turmoil and that by myself, or with Demian, I was tensely waiting for the great moment. The face of fate remained obscured but somehow bore the features of Frau Eva: to be chosen or spurned by her, that was fate.

Sometimes she would say with a smile: "Your dream is incomplete, Sinclair. You've left out the best part." And then I would remember the part I had left out and not understand how I could have forgotten it.

At times I was dissatisfied with myself and tortured with desire: I believed I could no longer bear to have her near me without taking her in my arms. She sensed this, too, at once. Once when I had stayed away for several days and returned bewildered she took me aside and said: "You must not give way to desires which you don't believe in. I know what you desire. You should, however, either be capable of renouncing these desires or feel wholly justified in having them. Once you are able to make your request in such a way that you will be quite certain of its fulfillment, then the fulfillment will come. But at present you alternate between desire and renunciation and are afraid all the time. All that must be overcome. Let me tell you a story."

And she told me about a youth who had fallen in love with a planet. He stood by the sea, stretched out his arms and prayed to the planet, dreamed of it, and directed all his thoughts to it. But he knew, or felt he knew, that a star cannot be embraced by a human being. He considered it to be his fate to love a heavenly body without any hope of fulfillment and out of this insight he constructed an entire philosophy of renunciation and silent, faithful suffering that would improve and purify him. Yet all his dreams reached the planet. Once he stood again on the high cliff at night by the sea and gazed at the planet and burned with love for it. And at the height of his longing he leaped into the emptiness toward the planet, but at the instant of leaping "it's impossible" flashed once more through his mind. There he lay on the shore, shattered. He had not understood how to love. If at the instant of leaping he had had the strength of faith in the fulfillment of his love he would have soared into the heights and been united with the star.

"Love must not entreat," she added, "or demand. Love must have the strength to become certain within itself. Then it ceases merely to be attracted and begins to attract. Sinclair, your love is attracted to me. Once it begins to attract me, I will come. I will not make a gift of myself, I must be won."

Another time she told me a different story, concerning a lover whose love was unrequited. He withdrew completely within himself, believing his love would consume him. The world became lost to him, he no longer noticed blue sky and green woods, he no longer heard the brook murmur; his ears had turned deaf to the notes of the harp: nothing mattered any more; he had become poor and wretched. Yet his love increased and he would rather have died or been ruined than renounce possessing this beautiful woman. Then he felt that his passion had consumed everything else within him and become so strong, so magnetic that the beautiful woman must follow. She came to him and he stood with outstretched arms ready to draw her to him. As she stood before him she was completely transformed and with awe he felt and saw that he had won back all he had previously lost. She stood before him and surrendered herself to him and sky, forest, and brook all came toward him in new and resplendent colors, belonged to him, and spoke to him in his own language. And instead of merely winning a woman he embraced the entire world and every star in heaven glowed within him and sparkled with joy in his soul. He had loved and had found himself. But most people love to lose themselves.

My love for Frau Eva seemed to fill my whole life. But every day it manifested itself differently. Sometimes I felt certain that it was not she as a person whom I was attracted to and yearned for with all my being, but that she existed only as a metaphor of my inner self, a metaphor whose sole purpose was to lead me more deeply into myself. Things she said often sounded like replies from my subconscious to questions that tormented me. There were other moments when I sat beside her and burned with sensual desire and kissed objects she had touched. And little by little, sensual and spiritual love, reality and symbol began to overlap. Then it would happen that as I thought about her in my room at home in tranquil intimacy I felt her hand in mine and her lips touching my lips. Or I would be at her house, would look into her face and hear her voice, yet not know whether she was real or a dream. I began

to sense how one can possess a love constantly and eternally. I would have an insight while reading a book—and this would feel the same as Eva's kiss. She caressed my hair and smiled at me affectionately and this felt like taking a step forward within myself. Everything significant and full of fate for me adopted her form. She could transform herself into any of my thoughts and each of my thoughts could be transformed into her.

I had been apprehensive about the Christmas vacation—to be spent at my parents' house—because I thought it would be agony to be away from Frau Eva for two whole weeks. But it did not turn out like that. It was wonderful to be at home and yet be able to think of her. When I arrived back in H. I waited two more days before going to see her, so as to savor this security, this being independent of her physical presence. I had dreams, too, in which my union with her was consummated in new symbolic acts. She was an ocean into which I streamed. She was a star and I another on my way to her, circling round each other. I told her this dream when I first visited her again.

"The dream is beautiful," she said quietly. "Make it come true."

There came a day in early spring that I have never forgotten. I entered the hallway, a window was open and a stream of air let in the heavy fragrance of the hyacinths. As no one was about, I went upstairs to Max Demian's study. I tapped lightly on the door and, as was my custom, went in without waiting for a reply.

The room was dark, all the curtains were drawn. The door to the small adjoining room stood open. There Max had set up a chemical laboratory. That's where the only light came from. I thought no one was in and drew back one of the curtains.

Then I saw Max slumped on a stool by the curtained window, looking oddly changed, and it flashed through me: You've seen this before! His arms hung limp, hands in his lap, his head bent slightly forward, and his eyes, though open, were unseeing and dead; in one of his pupils as in a piece of glass a thin, harsh ray of light snapped the iris open and shut, open and shut. The wan face was absorbed in itself and without expression, except for its immense rigidity; he resembled an age-old animal mask at the portal of a temple. He did not seem to breathe.

Overcome by dread I quietly left the room and walked downstairs. In the hallway I met Frau Eva, pale and seemingly tired, which I had never known her to be before. Just then a shadow passed over the window, the white glare of the sun suddenly fled.

"I was in Max's room," I whispered rapidly. "Has something happened? He's either asleep or lost within himself, I don't know which; I saw him look like that once before."

"You didn't wake him, did you?" she quickly asked.

"No. He didn't hear me. I left the room immediately. Tell me, what is the matter with him?"

She swept the back of her hand once across her brow.

"Don't worry, Sinclair, nothing will happen to him. He has withdrawn. It will soon pass."

She stood up and went out into the garden—although it was beginning to rain. I felt that she did not want me to accompany her and so I walked up and down the hallway, inhaled the bewildering scent of the hyacinths, stared at my bird picture above the doorway, and breathed the stifling atmosphere that filled the house that morning. What was it? What had happened?

Frau Eva returned before long. Raindrops clung to her black hair. She sat down in her armchair. She seemed weary. I stepped up to her, bent over her head, and kissed the rain out of her hair. Her eyes were bright and calm but the raindrops tasted like tears.

"Should I go and see how he is?" I asked in a whisper.

She smiled weakly.

"Don't be a little boy, Sinclair!" she admonished me, loudly as though trying to break a spell within herself. "Get along now and come back later. I can't talk to you now."

I half walked, half ran from the house and the town, toward the mountains. The fine rain slanted into my face, low clouds swept by as though weighed down with fear. Near the ground there was hardly a breath of air but in the higher altitudes a storm seemed to rage. Several times the lurid sun broke briefly through harsh rifts in the steel-gray clouds.

Then a loose, yellow cloud swept across the sky, collided with the other, gray bank of cloud. In a few seconds the wind had fashioned a shape out of this yellow and blue-gray mass, a gigantic bird that tore itself free of the steel-blue chaos and flew off into the sky with a great beating of wings. Then the storm became audible and rain rattled down mixed with hail. A brief, incredible, terrifying roar of thunder cracked across the rain-lashed landscape and immediately afterwards a gleam of sunshine burst through. On the nearby mountains the pale snow shone livid and unreal above the brown forest.

When, hours later, I returned wet and wind-blown, Demian himself opened the door.

He took me up to his room. A gas jet was burning in his laboratory and papers were strewn about the floor. He had evidently been working.

"Sit down," he invited, "you must be exhausted, it was horrible weather. One can see that you really were outside. There'll be tea in a moment."

"Something is the matter today," I began hesitantly. "It can't only be a thunderstorm."

He looked at me inquiringly.

"Did you see something?"

"Yes. I saw a picture in the clouds, quite clearly for a moment."

"What kind of picture?"

"It was a bird."

"The sparrow hawk? Your dream bird?"

"Yes, it was my sparrow hawk. It was yellow and gigantic and it flew off into the blue-black clouds."

Demian heaved a great sigh.

There was a knock on the door. The old servant brought in the tea.

"Help yourself, Sinclair, please. I don't believe you saw the bird just by chance."

"By chance? Does one get to see such things by chance?"

"Quite right. No, one doesn't. The bird has a significance. Do you know what?"

"No. I only feel that it signifies some shattering event, a move on the part of destiny. I believe that it concerns all of us."

He was pacing excitedly back and forth.

"A move on the part of destiny!" he shouted. "I dreamed the same kind of thing last night and my mother had a presentiment yesterday which conveyed the same message. I dreamed I was climbing up a ladder placed against a tree trunk or tower. When I reached the top I saw the whole landscape ablaze—a vast plain with innumerable towns and villages. I can't tell you the whole dream yet, everything is still somewhat confused."

"Do you feel that the dream concerns you personally?"

"Of course. No one dreams anything that doesn't 'concern him personally.' But it doesn't concern me only, you're right. I differentiate quite sharply between dreams that reveal movements within my own soul and the other, far rarer dreams in which the fate of all mankind suggests itself. I have rarely had such dreams and never before one of which I could say that it was a prophecy which was fulfilled. The interpretations are too uncertain. But I know for sure that I have dreamed something that doesn't concern me alone. For this dream links up with others, previous dreams I have had, to which it is a sequel. These are the dreams, Sinclair, which fill me with the forebodings I've spoken of to you. We both know that the world is quite rotten but that wouldn't be any reason to predict its imminent collapse or something of the kind. But for several years I have had dreams from which I conclude, or which make me feel, that the collapse of an old world is indeed imminent. At first these were weak and remote intimations but they have become increasingly stronger and more distinct. I still know nothing except that *something* is going to happen on a vast scale, something dreadful in which I myself will be involved. Sinclair, we will take part in this event that we have discussed so often. The world wants to renew itself. There's a smell of death in the air. Nothing can be born without first dying. But it is far more terrible than I had thought."

I stared at him aghast.

"Can't you tell me the rest of your dream?" I asked shyly.

He shook his head.

"No."

The door opened to let in Frau Eva.

"You're not feeling sad, I hope."

She looked refreshed, all trace of fatigue had vanished. Demian smiled at her and she came up to us as a mother approaches frightened children.

"No, we are not sad, mother. We've merely tried to puzzle out these new omens. But it's no use anyway. Whatever happens will suddenly be here; then we shall learn soon enough what we need to know."

But I felt dispirited, and when I took my leave and walked alone through the hallway, the stale scent of the hyacinths seemed cadaverous. A shadow had fallen over us.

8. The End Begins

I had persuaded my parents to allow me the summer semester in H. My friends and I now spent almost all our time in the garden by the river instead of the house. The Japanese, who had been duly beaten in the boxing match, had departed; the disciple of Tolstoi had gone, too. Demian kept a horse and went for long rides day after day. I was frequently alone with his mother.

There were times when I was simply astonished how peaceful my life had become. I had so long been accustomed to being alone, to leading a life of self-denial, to battling strenuously with my agonizing difficulties, that these months in H. seemed to me altogether like a magic dream island on which I was allowed to lead a comfortable, enchanted existence among beautiful and agreeable surroundings. I had a presentiment that this was a foretaste of that new and higher community which we speculated about so much. Yet at any moment this happiness could produce in me the deepest melancholy, for I knew very well that it could not last. It was not my lot to breathe fullness and comfort, I needed the spur of tormented haste. I felt that one day I would waken from these beloved images of beauty and stand, alone again, in the cold world where there was nothing for me but solitude and struggle —neither peace nor relaxation, no easy living together.

At those moments I would nestle with redoubled affection close to Frau Eva, glad that my fate still bore these beautiful calm features.

The summer weeks passed quickly and uneventfully, the semester was nearly over and it would soon be time for me to leave. I dared not think of it, but clung to each beautiful day as the butterfly clings to his honeyed flower. This had been my happy time, life's first fulfillment, my acceptance into this intimate, elect circle —what was to follow? I would battle through again, suffer the old longings, dream dreams, be alone.

One day foreboding came over me with such force that my love for Frau Eva suddenly flared up painful within me. My God, how soon I must leave here, see her no more, no longer hear her dear assured steps throughout the house, no longer find her flowers on my table! And what had I achieved? I had dreamed, had luxuriated in dreams and contentment, instead of winning her, instead of struggling to clasp her forever to myself! Everything she had told me about genuine love came back to me, a hundred delicate admonitions, as many gentle enticements, promises perhaps— what had I made of them? Nothing. Absolutely nothing!

I went to the center of my room and stood still, endeavoring to concentrate the whole of my consciousness on Frau Eva, summoning all the strength in my soul to let her feel my love and draw her to me. She must come, she must long for my embrace, my kiss must tremble insatiably on her ripe lips.

I stood and concentrated every energy until I could feel cold creeping up my fingers and toes. I felt strength radiating from me. For a few moments I felt something contract within me, something bright and cool which felt like a crystal in my heart—I knew it was my ego. The chill crept up to my chest.

Relaxed from this terrible tension I felt that something was about to happen. I was mortally exhausted but I was ready to behold Eva step into the room, radiant and ecstatic.

The clattering of hooves could be heard approaching along the street. It sounded near and metallic, then suddenly stopped. I leaped to the window and saw Demian dismounting below. I ran down.

"What is it, Demian?"

He paid no attention to my words. He was very pale and sweat poured down his cheeks. He tied the bridle of his steaming horse to the garden fence and took my arm and walked down the street with me.

"Have you heard about it?"

I had heard nothing.

Demian squeezed my arm and turned his face toward me, with a strangely somber yet sympathetic look in his eyes.

"Yes, it's starting. You've heard about the difficulties with Russia."

"What? Is it war?"

He spoke very softly although no one was anywhere near us.

"It hasn't been declared yet. But there will be war. You can take my word for that. I didn't want to worry you but I have seen omens on three different occasions since that time. So it won't be the end of the world, no earthquake, no revolution, but war. You'll see what a sensation that will be! People will love it. Even now they can hardly wait for the killing to begin—their lives are that dull! But you will see, Sinclair, that this is only the beginning. Perhaps it will be a very big war, a war on a gigantic scale. But that, too, will only be the beginning. The new world has begun and the new world will be terrible for those clinging to the old. What will you do?"

I was dumfounded, it all sounded so strange, so improbable.

"I don't know—and you?"

He shrugged his shoulders.

"I'll be called up as soon as the mobili-zation order comes through. I'm a lieutenant."

"You, a lieutenant! I had no idea."

"Yes, that was one of the ways I compromised. You know I dislike calling attention to myself so much I almost always went to the other extreme, just to give a correct impression. I believe I'll be on the front in a week."

"My God."

"Now don't get sentimental. Of course it's not going to be any fun ordering men to fire on living beings, but that will be incidental. Each of us will be caught up in the great chain of events. You, too, you'll be drafted, for sure."

"And what about your mother, Demian?"

Only now my thoughts turned back to what had happened a quarter of an hour before. How the world had changed in the meantime! I had summoned all my strength to conjure up the sweetest of images and now fate looked at me suddenly with a threatening and horrible mask.

"My mother? We don't have to worry about her. She is safe, safer than anyone else in the world today. Do you love her that much?"

"Didn't you know?"

He laughed lightly, relieved.

"Of course I knew. No one has called my mother Frau Eva who hasn't been in love with her. You either called me or her today."

"Yes, I called her."

"She felt it. She sent me away all of a sudden, saying I would have to go see you. I had just told her the news about Russia."

We turned around and exchanged a few words more. Demian untied his horse and mounted.

Only upstairs in my room did I realize how much Demian's news, and still more the previous strain, had exhausted me. But Frau Eva had heard me! My houghts had reached her heart. She would have come herself—if . . . How urious all this was, and, fundamentally, ow beautiful! And now there was to be war. What we had talked about so often vas to begin. Demian had known so much about it ahead of time. How trange that the stream of the world was not to bypass us any more, that it now vent straight through our hearts, and hat now or very soon the moment would ome when the world would need us, vhen it would seek to transform itself. Demian was right, one could not be entimental about that. The only remark- ble thing was that I was to share the ery personal matter of my fate with so many others, with the whole world in act. Well, so be it!

I was prepared. When I walked hrough town in the evening every street orner was buzzing, everywhere the word as *war*.

I went to Frau Eva's. We ate supper in he summer house. I was the only guest. No one said a word about the war. Only ater on, shortly before I was to leave, Frau Eva said: "Dear Sinclair, you called me today. You know why I didn't come myself. But don't forget: you know the all now and whenever you need some- ne who bears the sign, you can appeal o me."

She rose to her feet and preceded me nto the garden twilight. Tall and regal he strode between the silent trees.

I am coming to the end of my story. Everything went very rapidly from then n. Soon there was war, and Demian, trangely unfamiliar in his uniform, left s. I accompanied his mother home. It as not long before I, too, took my leave f her. She kissed me on the mouth and asped me for a moment to her breast. Her great eyes burned close and firmly nto mine.

All men seemed to have become brothers—overnight. They talked of "the fatherland" and of "honor," but what lay behind it was their own fate whose un- veiled face they had now all beheld for one brief moment. Young men left their barracks, were packed into trains, and on many faces I saw a sign—not ours—but a beautiful, dignified sign nonetheless that meant love and death. I, too, was embraced by people whom I had never seen before and I understood this gesture and responded to it. Intoxication made them do it, not a hankering after their destiny. But this intoxication was sacred, for it was the result of their all having thrown that brief and terribly disquieting glance into the eyes of their fate.

It was nearly winter when I was sent to the front. Despite the excitement of being under fire for the first time, in the beginning everything disappointed me. At one time I had given much thought to why men were so very rarely capable of living for an ideal. Now I saw that many, no, all men were capable of dying for one. Yet it could not be a personal, a freely chosen ideal; it had to be one mutually accepted.

As time went on though I realized I had underestimated these men. However much mutual service and danger made a uniform mass of them, I still saw many approach the will of fate with great dig- nity. Many, very many, not only during the attack but at every moment of the day, wore in their eyes the remote, reso- lute, somewhat possessed look which knows nothing of aims and signified complete surrender to the incredible. Whatever they might think or believe, they were ready, they could be used, they were the clay of which the future could be shaped. The more singlemindedly the world concentrated on war and heroism, on honor and other old ideals, the more remote and improbable any whisper of genuine humanity sounded—that was all just surface, in the same way that the question of the war's external and political objectives remained superficial. Deep down, underneath, something was taking shape. Something akin to a new humanity. For I could see many men—and many died beside me—who had begun to feel acutely that hatred and rage, slaughter and annihilation, were not bound up with these objectives. No, these objectives and aims were completely fortuitous. The most primitive, even the wildest feelings were not directed at the enemy; their bloody task was merely an irradiation of the soul, of the soul divided within itself, which filled them with the lust to rage and kill, annihilate and die so that they might be born anew.

One night in early spring I stood guard in front of a farm that we had occupied. A listless wind was blowing fitfully; across the Flemish sky cloud armies rode on high, somewhere behind them the suggestion of a moon. I had been uneasy the entire day—something was worrying me deeply. Now on my dark guard post I fervently recalled the images of my life and thought of Frau Eva and of Demian. I stood braced against a poplar tree staring into the drifting clouds whose mysteriously writhing patches of light soon metamorphosed into huge series of swirling images. From the strange weakness of my pulse, the insensitiveness of my skin to wind and rain, and my intense state of consciousness I could sense that a master was near me.

A huge city could be seen in the clouds out of which millions of people streamed in a host over vast landscapes. Into their midst stepped a mighty, godlike figure, as huge as a mountain range, with sparkling stars in her hair, bearing the features of Frau Eva. The ranks of the people were swallowed up into her as into a giant cave and vanished from sight. The goddess cowered on the ground, the mark luminous on her forehead. A dream seemed to hold sway over her: she closed her eyes and her countenance became twisted with pain. Suddenly she cried out and from her forehead sprang stars, many thousands of shining stars that leaped in marvelous arches and semicircles across the black sky.

One of these stars shot straight toward me with a clear ringing sound and it seemed to seek me out. Then it burst asunder with a roar into a thousand sparks, tore me aloft and smashed me back to the ground again, the world shattered above me with a thunderous roar.

They found me near the poplar tree covered with earth and with many wounds.

I lay in a cellar, guns roared above me. I lay in a wagon and jolted across the empty fields. Mostly I was asleep or unconscious. But the more deeply I slept the more strongly I felt that something was drawing me on, that I was following a force that had mastery over me.

I lay in a stable, on straw. It was dark and someone had stepped on my hand. But something inside me wanted to keep going and I was drawn on more forcefully than ever. Again I lay in a wagon and later on a stretcher or ladder. More strongly than ever I felt myself being summoned somewhere, felt nothing but this urge that I must finally get there.

Then I reached my goal. It was night and I was fully conscious. I had just felt the urge pulling mightily within me: now I was in a long hall, bedded down on the floor. I felt I had reached the destination which had summoned me. I turned my head: close to my mattress lay another, someone on it bent forward and looked at me. He had the sign on his forehead. It was Max Demian.

I was unable to speak and he could not or did not want to either. He just looked

at me. The light from a bulb strung on the wall above him played down on his face. He smiled.

He gazed into my eyes for what seemed an endless time. Slowly he brought his face closer to mine: we almost touched.

"Sinclair," he said in a whisper.

I told him with a glance that I heard. He smiled again, almost as with pity. "Little fellow," he said, smiling.

His lips lay very close to mine. Quietly he continued to speak. "Can you remember Franz Kromer?" he asked.

I blinked at him and smiled, too.

"Little Sinclair, listen: I will have to go away. Perhaps you'll need me again sometime, against Kromer or something. If you call me then I won't come crudely, on horseback or by train. You'll have to listen within yourself, then you will notice that I am within you. Do you understand? And something else. Frau Eva said that if ever you were in a bad way I was to give you a kiss from her that she sends by me. . . . Close your eyes, Sinclair!"

I closed my eyes in obedience. I felt a light kiss on my lips where there was always a little fresh blood which never would go away. And then I fell asleep.

Next morning someone woke me: I had to have my wounds dressed. When I was finally wide awake I turned quickly to the mattress next to mine. On it lay a stranger I'd never seen before.

Dressing the wound hurt. Everything that has happened to me since has hurt. But sometimes when I find the key and climb deep into myself where the images of fate lie aslumber in the dark mirror, I need only bend over that dark mirror to behold my own image, now completely resembling him, my brother, my master.

KLINGSOR'S LAST SUMMER

By HERMANN HESSE

Translated by Richard and Clara Winston

Preface

The painter Klingsor spent the last summer of his life, at the age of forty-two, in those southerly regions in the vicinity of Pampambio, Kareno, and Laguno which he had loved in earlier years and often visited. There his last paintings were done, those free paraphrases on the forms of the world of phenomena, those strange, glowing, and yet dreamily tranquil pictures with their twisted trees and plantlike houses which connoisseurs prefer to the works of his "classical" period. At the time his palette had been reduced to a few, extremely vivid colors: cadmium yellow and red, Veronese green, emerald, cobalt, cobalt-violet, French vermilion, and crimson lake.

In late fall the news of Klingsor's death shocked his friends. Many of his letters had contained forebodings or death wishes. This may have nourished the rumor that he had taken his own life. Other rumors, such as always gather around a controversial name, have as little substance as that one. Many asserted that Klingsor had been mentally ill during his last months, and a somewhat myopic art critic attempted to explain the startling and ecstatic quality of his last paintings on the grounds of this alleged madness! That is all nonsense. There is somewhat more foundation to the story —which has been embroidered with a wealth of anecdotes—of Klingsor's heavy drinking. He certainly had this tendency, and no one spoke of it more frankly than Klingsor himself. At certain times in his life, and therefore during his last months also, it was more than a case of frequent drinking bouts. He would also deliberately drown his pain and his sometimes almost unbearable melancholy in wine. Li Po, that author of the profoundest drinking songs, was his favorite, and in his cups he often called himself Li Po and one of his friends Tu Fu.

His works live. And among the small circle of his intimates the legend of his life and of that last summer lives on no less forcefully.

Klingsor

A passionate summer of swift-moving life had begun. The hot days, long as they were, flared up and away like burning streamers. The brief sultry moonlit nights were followed by brief sultry rainy nights. Swift as dreams crowded with images, the glittering weeks moved feverishly on.

Just back home after a night walk, Klingsor stood on the narrow stone balcony of his studio. Below him, dizzyingly precipitate, the old terrace gardens dropped away, a densely shadowed tangle of treetops, palms, cedars, chestnuts, judas trees, red beech, and eucalyptus, intertwined with climbing plants, lianas, wisterias. Above the blackness of the trees the large glossy leaves of the summer magnolias gleamed pallidly, the huge snow-white blossoms half-shut among them, large as human heads, pale as moon and ivory. From the massed leafage, penetrating and rousing, a tartly sweet smell of lemons drifted toward him. From some indefinite distance languorous music winged its way to him, perhaps a guitar, perhaps a piano; there was no saying. A peacock suddenly cried from a yard, twice, three times, piercing the sylvan night with the short, angry, wooden tone of its tormented voice, as if the pain of the whole animal world were sounding shrilly, coarsely from the depths. Starlight flowed through the wooded valley. High and deserted, a white chapel, enchanted and old, peered out of the endless forest. In the distance lake, mountains, and sky flowed together.

Klingsor stood on the balcony, coatless, his bare forearms leaning on the iron railing, and with a touch of sullenness, his eyes hot, read the script of the stars against the pale sky and the gentle lucency on the black, lumpy cloud masses of the trees. The peacock reminded him. Yes, it was night again, late, and he ought to go to sleep now, absolutely and at all costs. Perhaps, if he could really sleep for several nights in succession, sleep soundly for six or eight hours, he would be able to recover, his eyes would be obedient and patient again, his heart calmer and his temples without pain. But then this summer would be over, this crazy, flickering summer dream, and along with it a thousand undrunk glasses would be spilled, a thousand unseen loving looks shattered, a thousand irrecoverable pictures extinguished unseen!

He laid his forehead and his aching eyes against the cool iron railing. That refreshed him for a moment. In a year perhaps, or sooner, these eyes would be blind and the fires in his heart extinct. No, no human being could endure his flaming life for long. Not even he could, not even Klingsor, who had ten lives. Nobody could go on for a long time having all his candles burning day and night, all his volcanoes flaming. Nobody could be ablaze day and night, working feverishly for many hours every day, spending many hours every night in feverish thoughts, forever enjoying, forever creating, forever with all his senses and nerves wide awake and alert, like a palace behind whose every window music rings out day after day, while night after night a thousand candles twinkle. It would come to an end. A great deal of strength had already been squandered, much eyesight consumed, much life bled away.

Suddenly he laughed and stretched. He remembered that he had often before felt like this, often before thought these thoughts, had these fears. In all the good, fruitful, and ardent periods of his life, even in his youth, he had lived like this, had burned his candle at both ends, with a half jubilant, half mournful feeling of wild extravagance, of burning himself up, with a desperate greed to empty the cup to the dregs, and with a deep, hidden dread of the end. Often before he had lived like this, often drained the cup, often burned with high, darting flames. Sometimes these spells had ended gently, in something like a deep, unconscious hibernation. Sometimes the letdown had been terrible, senseless devastation, intolerable pain, doctors, sad renunciations, victory of weakness. And, granted, each time the end of such a period of intensity had been progressively worse, blacker, more shattering. However, he had always survived these lows and after weeks or months, after agony or stupefaction, the

esurrection had come, new fire, new
ruption of the underground volcanoes,
ew and more passionate works, new,
littering frenzy. That was how it had
een, and the times of torment and sub-
dence, the agonizing intervals, had been
orgotten and had vanished. It was good
hat way. This time, too, it would go as it
ad often gone.

Smiling, he thought of Gina, whom he
ad seen this evening, around whom his
houghts had revolved affectionately all
he long walk home through the night.
How beautiful this girl was, and how
warm in her still inexperienced and
amorous ardor. Playfully and tenderly he
murmured under his breath, as if he were
again whispering into her ear: "Gina!
Gina! Cara Gina! Carina Gina! Bella
Gina!"

He stepped back into the room and
urned the light on again. From a small,
haphazard heap of books he took a volume of poems. A poem had come to his
mind, a fragment of a poem which
seemed to him inexpressibly lovely. He
searched for a long time before he found
:

Do not leave me to my sorrow now,
Beloved, do not leave me to the night.
Oh, you who are my match, who are
    my candle,
You who are my sun, who are my light.

With deep enjoyment he sipped the
dark wine of these words. How lovely,
how tender and magical it was: Oh, you
who are my candle. And: You who are
my sun.

Smiling, he paced back and forth in
front of the tall windows, reciting the
verses, calling them out to the distant
Gina: "Oh, you who are my light!" His
voice darkened with tenderness.

Then he opened the portfolio he had
carried with him all evening after his
long day of work. He opened the sketch-
book, looked at the last pages, the ones
he had done yesterday and today. There
was the cone-shaped mountain with the
deep shadows of cliffs; he had rendered it
so it looked very like a crazy masked
face. The mountain seemed to be screaming, splitting open from pain. There was
the small stone fountain, a semicircle on
the mountain slope, the masonry arch
filled with black shadows, a flowering
pomegranate tree blazing above it. It was
all there for him alone to read, a cipher
for himself, hasty, greedy notation of the
instant, swiftly snatched recollection of
every moment in which nature and his
heart sounded newly and loudly in con-
cord. And now came the larger colored
sketches, white sheets with luminous
areas of watercolor: the red villa in the
woods, with a fiery glow like a ruby on
green velvet, and the iron bridge at
Castiglia, red against the blue-green
mountain, the violet dam beside it and
the pink road. Further: the chimney of
the brickworks, red rocket against light,
cool tree-green, blue signpost, brilliant
violet sky with the thick cloud like rolled
steel. This sheet was good; it could stay.
Things had gone less well with the wagon
road to the stable; the reddish brown
against the steely sky was right, it spoke
and sounded, but the picture was only
half finished. The sun had shone on the
paper and made his eyes ache maddeningly. For a long while afterwards he had
bathed his face in a brook. Well, the
brown-red against the malignant metallic
blue was there; that was good, was not
the smallest nuance, not the slightest vi-
bration wrong or off. Without Indian red
he couldn't have brought that off. There,
in this field, lay the secrets. The forms of
nature, their top and bottom, their thick
and thin, could be shifted around; you
could discard all the commonplace
means for imitating nature. You could
falsify colors too, of course; you could
intensify, lower, translate them in a hun-

dred different ways. But if you wanted to use color to create a fictional nature, what mattered was that the few colors stood exactly, with the utmost exactitude, in the same relationships, in the same tensions to one another as they did in nature. Here you remained dependent, here you remained a naturalist, even though you took orange instead of gray and carmine instead of black.

So then, another day had been squandered and the yield was meager. The study of the factory chimney and the jotting in red and blue and perhaps the sketch of the fountain. If it were a cloudy day tomorrow he would go to Carabbina; there was that portico where the women came to do their laundry. Perhaps it would rain again tomorrow; then he would stay home and begin working on the picture of the brook in oils. And now to bed. It was past one o'clock again.

In the bedroom he pulled off his shirt, slapped water over his shoulders so that it dripped down on the red tile floor, jumped into the high bed, and put out the light. Pale Monte Salute looked in through the window. A thousand times Klingsor had traced its forms from his bed. An owl cried from the wooded gorge, deep and hollow, like sleep, like forgetfulness.

He closed his eyes and thought of Gina, and of the portico with the washtubs. God in heaven, so many thousands of things were waiting, so many thousands of cups stood ready poured. Not a thing on earth that he should not have painted. Not a woman in the world whom he should not have loved. Why did time exist? Why always this idiotic succession of one thing after another, and not a roaring, surfeiting simultaneity? Why was he now lying alone in bed again, like a widower, like an old man? You could enjoy, could create, all through this short life; and yet at best

you were always merely singing one song after another. The whole full symphony with all its hundred voices and instruments never sounded all at once.

Long ago, at the age of twelve, he had been Klingsor with the ten lives. The boys played a game of robbers, and each of the robbers had ten lives. Each time you were tagged by your opponent or touched by his thrown javelin, you lost one life. But the game went on as long as you had six, three, even one single life left. Only when you lost the tenth were you out. But he, Klingsor, had made it a matter of pride to win through without losing any of his ten lives and would consider himself disgraced if he came out with nine or with seven. That was how he had been as a boy, in that incredible period when nothing in the world was impossible, nothing in the world was difficult, when everybody loved Klingsor, when Klingsor commanded everyone, when everything belonged to Klingsor. And that was how he had gone on always living with ten lives. And although the surfeit, the full roaring symphony, could never be attained—still his song had not been single-voiced and impoverished. He had always had a few more strings to his bow than others, a few more irons in the fire, a few more coins in his purse, a few more horses on his cart. Thank God!

How full and vibrant the dark stillness of the garden was, like the breathing of a sleeping woman. How the peacock screeched. How the fire burned in his breast, how his heart pounded and cried and suffered and rejoiced and bled. It had been a good summer after all up here in Castagnetta. He lived gloriously in his noble old ruin, looked gloriously out on the caterpillar backs of the innumerable chestnut groves below. It was lovely to descend eagerly now and then from this noble old world of woods and castles and look at the gay colorful toys down below and paint them in their good gay gaudiness: the factory, the railroad, the blue streetcars, the advertising column by the dock, the strutting peacocks, women, priests, automobiles. And how lovely and tormenting and incomprehensible was this feeling in his breast, this love and flickering craving for every bright ribbon and rag of life, this wild sweet compulsion to see and to shape, and yet secretly at the same time, under thin lids, the deep-felt knowledge of the childishness and vanity of all he did.

Fevered, the brief summer night melted away. Vapor rose from the green depths of the valley, sap simmered in a hundred thousand trees, a hundred thousand dreams swelled up in Klingsor's light slumber, his soul strode through his life's hall of mirrors where all images were multiplied and each time met one another with new faces and new meanings and entered into new associations, as though a firmament were being shaken in a dice cup.

One dream image among the many delighted and greatly stirred him. He lay in a forest and had a woman with red hair across his lap, and a black-haired woman leaned against his shoulder and another knelt beside him, holding his hand and kissing his fingers, and everywhere, all around, were women and girls, some still children, with long thin legs, some nubile, some mature and with the signs of knowledge and of fatigue in their restive faces, and all loved him and all wanted to be loved by him. Then war and fury erupted among the women, the red one thrust a raging hand into the black one's hair and pulled her to the ground and was herself dragged down, and all fell upon one another, each one screaming, each tearing, each biting, each hurting, each suffering pain. Laughter, cries of fury and howls of anguish rang out intertwined and tangled, blood flowed everywhere, nails dug bloodily into fat flesh.

With a feeling of sorrow and depression Klingsor awoke for a few minutes. His eyes, wide open, stared at the bright gap in the wall. The faces of the embattled women still lingered, and he recognized and named many of them: Nina, Hermine, Elizabeth, Gina, Edith, Berta, and in a hoarse voice, still caught up in the dream, he said: "Children, stop it! You're lying you know, you're deceiving me, you know; it's not each other you should be tearing to pieces but me, me!"

Louis

Louis the Cruel had dropped out of the blue. Suddenly he was there, Klingsor's old friend, the traveler, the unpredictable wanderer who lived in railroad cars and whose studio was his knapsack. Good times dripped out of the blue on these days, good winds came. They painted together, on the Mount of Olives and in Cartago.

"I wonder whether all this painting business has any real value," Louis said on the Mount of Olives, lying naked in the grass, his back red from the sun. "You know we only paint for lack of anything better to do, my friend. If you always had the girl you like best on your lap at the moment and your favorite soup in your plate, you wouldn't bother with this senseless childish game. Nature has ten thousand colors and we've taken it into our heads to reduce the spectrum to twenty. That's what painting is. We're never satisfied and on top of everything else we have to help the critics earn their livings. On the other hand, a good Marseilles bouillabaisse, caro mio, and a simple lukewarm Burgundy along with it, and afterwards a piccata Milanese, pears and Gorgonzola for dessert, and Turkish coffee—those are realities, dear sir, those are values! How badly people eat in your Palestine here! Ah, I wish I were in a cherry tree and the cherries were growing into my mouth and just above me on the ladder stood the sun-tanned, spirited girl we met this morning. Klingsor, give up painting! I'm inviting you to a good meal in Laguno. It's getting to be about time."

"Do you mean it?" Klingsor asked, screwing up his eyes.

"I mean it. Only first I have to hurry over to the station. You see, to be truthful, I've telegraphed a woman friend that I am dying. She may arrive by the eleven o'clock train."

Laughing, Klingsor tore the unfinished study off his easel.

"You're right, my boy. Let us go to Laguno! Put on your shirt, Luigi. There's great innocence to the morals here, but unfortunately you cannot go into town naked."

They went into town, they went to the station; a beautiful woman arrived; they ate well in a restaurant and Klingsor, who had forgotten during his months in the country, was astonished that all these things still existed, these dear, cheerful things: trout, smoked ham, asparagus, Chablis, Valais Dôle, Benedictine.

After the meal all three of them took the cable railway up through the steep city, passing right between the houses, by windows and hanging gardens. It was very pretty. They stayed in their seats and rode down again, and up and down still again. The world was strangely beautiful and rare, highly colorful, somewhat dubious, somewhat improbable, but lovely. But Klingsor was a bit embarrassed; he put on an air of indifference, for he did not want to fall in love with Luigi's beautiful friend. They dropped in at a café, they walked in the park, deserted in the afternoon heat, they lay down by the water under the huge trees. They saw a great deal that deserved to be painted: red houses like gems set in deep green, snakewood trees and smoke trees seared blue and brown.

"You have painted delightful and jolly things, Luigi," Klingsor said, "things I'm very fond of: flagpoles, clowns, circuses. But to me, the most precious of all is a spot on your picture of the carousel after dark. You know, high up in the night, far above the violet tent and far from all the lights is a cool, small flag, pale pink, so beautiful, so cool, so lonely, so horribly lonely! It's like a poem by Li Po or Paul Verlaine. All the sorrow and all the resignation of the world is in that small, silly pink flag, and all good laughter at sorrow and resignation. Your life is justified for having painted that little flag. I count it one of your major achievements, that flag."

"Yes, I know how you like it."

"You like it yourself. Look, if you hadn't painted a few such things, all the good food and wine and women and coffee would do you little good, you'd be a poor devil. But as it is you're a rich devil and a hell of a good fellow whom people are fond of. You know, Luigi, I often think as you do: that all our art is merely a substitute, a painful substitute bought ten times too dearly for missed life, missed animality, missed love. But it really isn't so. It's altogether different. If we regard the things of the mind as merely paltry substitutes for missing sensuality, we're overestimating the things of the senses. Sensuality isn't worth a hair more than spirituality, and it's the same the other way around. It's all one, everything is equally good. Whether you embrace a woman or make a poem, it's the same. So long as the main thing is there, the love, the burning, the emotion, it doesn't matter whether you are a monk on Mount Athos or a man about town in Paris."

Louis looked slowly across at him, his eyes mocking. "My boy, you're gettin' too fancy for me."

They roamed the vicinity with their beautiful companion. Both of them were good at seeing; that they could do. Within the circuit of a few towns and villages they saw Rome, Japan, the South Seas, and rubbed out the illusions again with sportive fingers. Their whims kindled stars in the sky and extinguished them again. Through the lush nights they sent their globes of light rising. The world was a soap bubble, opera, joyous nonsense.

Louis the Bird flew on his bicycle through the hilly landscape, went here and there while Klingsor painted. Klingsor threw away a good many days; then again he would sit resolutely outside and work. Louis did not want to work. Louis left all of a sudden, together with his woman friend; he sent a postcard from far away. Suddenly he was back, when Klingsor had already given him up for lost. He stood at the door in straw hat and open shirt as if he had never been away. Once again Klingsor drained the drink of friendship from the sweetest cup of his youth. He had many friends, many loved him; he had given much to many, opened his impulsive heart to many. But this summer only two of his friends heard the old cry of his heart fall from his lips: the painter Louis and the writer Hermann, called Tu Fu.

Many a day Louis sat in the field on his painting stool, in the shade of the pear tree, in the shade of the plum tree, and did not paint. He sat and thought, kept paper clipped to the easel and wrote, wrote a great deal, wrote many letters. Are people who write so many letters happy? He wrote strenuously, Louis the Nonchalant; for hours at a time his eyes clung devotedly to the paper. Much that he concealed churned within him. Klingsor loved him for that.

Klingsor behaved differently. He could not keep silent. He could not conceal what lay in his heart. He let his intimates know the secret pangs of his life. Often he suffered from anxiety, from melancholia; often he lay bound and gagged in the dungeon of darkness. Sometimes shadows from his earlier life fell upon his days, casting them in gloom. Then it did him good to see Luigi's face. Then, sometimes, he would vent his feelings to him.

But Louis did not like to see these weaknesses. They pained him, they demanded sympathy. Klingsor made it a practice to reveal his heart to his friend, and realized too late that in so doing he was losing him.

Again Louis began to talk of departure. Klingsor knew that he would be able to hold him only for a few days, for three, perhaps five. Then suddenly Louis would show him his packed suitcases and leave, and not be back for a long time. How short life was, how irrevocable everything was. Louis was the only one of his friends who fully understood his art, whose own art was close to his and equal to it. Now he had spoiled things with this only friend, had chilled him and put him out of sorts, merely out of stupid infirmity and slackness, merely out of the childish and unseemly impulse to spare himself trouble, to keep no secrets, to throw aside dignity. How silly, how boyish that had been. Thus Klingsor berated himself—too late.

On the last day they tramped together through the golden valleys. Louis was in excellent humor; departure was the spring of life to his migratory bird's heart. Klingsor fell in with his mood. Once again they had found the old, easy, playful and mocking tone, and this time they did not let it slip. In the evening they sat in the tavern garden. They had fish baked specially for them, had rice with mushrooms to go with it, and poured maraschino over peaches.

"Where are you bound for tomorrow?" Klingsor asked.

"I don't know."

"Are you going to join that beautiful woman?"

"Yes. Perhaps. Who can tell? Don't ask too many questions. Now, at the end, let's have another good white wine. I'm in favor of a Neuchâtel."

They drank. Suddenly Louis exclaimed: "It's a good thing I'm leaving, old seal. Sometimes, when I sit beside you like this, like now, for instance, something utterly silly occurs to me. It occurs to me that here and now the only two painters our good country can boast of are sitting together, and then I have a horrible feeling in my knees, as if the two of us were cast in bronze and standing hand in hand on a monument, you know, like Goethe and Schiller. After all, it's not their fault that they're condemned to stand there forever holding each other's bronze hands and that they gradually come to seem so odious and such a damned nuisance to us. Maybe they were perfectly decent fellows—years ago I read a play by Schiller that was pretty good. And yet this is what's happened to him now, he's become a monument and has to stand beside his Siamese twin and you see their collected works standing on shelves and hear them analyzed in the schools. It's gruesome. Imagine a professor a hundred years from now preaching to his students: Klingsor, born in 1877, and his contemporary Louis, nicknamed The Glutton, innovators in painting, liberation from the naturalism of color, when we examine this pair of artists closely we find three clearly distinguishable periods! I'd rather throw myself under a locomotive right here and now!"

"It would make more sense to throw the professors under it."

"There aren't any locomotives that big. Our technology is so small-scale."

Stars were already rising. Suddenly Louis clinked glasses with his friend.

"All right, one more toast and let's drink it down. Then I'll mount my wheel and goodbye. Let's not have any long partings. Cheers, Klingsor!"

They touched glasses and drank. In the garden Louis mounted his bicycle, swung his hat, was gone. Night, stars. Louis was in China. Louis was a legend.

Klingsor smiled sadly. How he loved this migratory bird! For a long time he stood on the gravel in the tavern garden, gazing down the empty street.

The Day at Kareno

Together with his friends from Barengo and with Agosto and Ersilia, Klingsor set out on the walk to Kareno. Early in the morning they descended among the strongly scented spireas, the bedewed spiderwebs quivering on the margins of the woods, down through the steep, warm forest into the valley of Pampambio where beside the yellow road bright yellow houses slept, bent forward and half dead, stunned by the summer days. By the dried-up stream bed the white metallic willows hung heavy wings over golden meadows. A colorful troupe, the friends bowled down the rosy road through the misty green of the valley: the men white and yellow in linens and silks, the women white and pink, Ersilia's Veronese green parasol sparkling like a jewel in a magic ring.

"It's a pity, Klingsor," the doctor remarked plaintively in his kindly voice. "Your wonderful watercolors will all be white in ten years. These colors you like so well have no lasting qualities."

"Yes," Klingsor said, "and what is worse, Doctor: your fine brown hair will all be gray in ten years, and a little while later all our good gay bones will be lying in some hole in the ground, including, alas, your beautiful and healthy bones, Ersilia. My friends, let's not start becomng sensible so late in life. Hermann, how does Li Po put it?"

Hermann the Poet stood still and intoned:

Life passes like a flash of lightning
Whose blaze barely lasts long enough
    to see.
While the earth and the sky stand still
    forever
How swiftly changing time flies across
    man's face.
O you who sit over your full cup and
    do not drink,
Tell me whom you are still waiting
    for?

"No," Klingsor said, "I mean the other poem, the rhymed one, about the hair that was still dark at morning. . . ."

Hermann promptly recited:

Only this morning your hair gleamed
    silken and black,
Evening has already sprinkled it with
    snow.
If you would not suffer as on the rack
Hold out your cup and summon the
    moon for your drink-fellow.

Klingsor laughed heartily in his somewhat hoarse voice.

"Good old Li Po! He had inklings; he knew all sorts of things. We know all sorts of things too—he is our wise old brother. This giddy day would please him. It's just the kind of day lovely for dying Li Po's death at evening, in the boat on the quiet river. You'll see, everything is going to be wonderful today."

"What kind of death was it that Li Po died on the river?" Martha, the artist, asked.

But Ersilia interrupted in her dear, deep voice: "Stop it now. I'll begin detesting anybody who says another word about death and dying. Finisca adesso, brutto Klingsor!"

Laughing, Klingsor came over to her. "How right you are, bambina! If I say

another word about dying you can poke your parasol into both my eyes. But seriously, 'tis a glorious day, my dears. A bird is singing today, a bird out of a fairy tale—I heard it once before this morning. A wind is blowing today, a wind out of a fairy tale, the child of heaven who wakens the sleeping princesses and blows reason clear out of people's heads. A flower is blossoming today, a flower out of a fairy tale, it's blue and blooms only once in a lifetime and whoever plucks it wins bliss."

"Did all that mean anything?" Ersilia asked the doctor.

Klingsor heard her.

"What it all meant is: this day will never come again and anyone who fails to eat and drink and taste and smell it will never have it offered to him again in all eternity. The sun will never shine as it does today; it is in a constellation in the sky, a conjunction with Jupiter, with me, with Agosto and Ersilia and all of us, a conjunction that will never come again, not in a thousand years. And therefore I want to walk on your left side for a while, because that brings luck, and carry your emerald parasol—under its light my head will look like an opal. But you must play your part and sing a song, one of your best."

He took Ersilia's arm. His sharp features dipped softly into the blue-green shade of the parasol. He had fallen in love with it; its blatant, sweet color delighted him.

Ersilia began to sing:

Il mio papà non vuole,
Ch'io spos' un bersaglier—

Voices joined in; singing, they walked on to the forest and into the forest, until the climb became too steep. The path led sharply upward like a ladder through the fern, scaling the great mountain.

"What a marvelous straight line this song takes!" Klingsor praised it. "Papa is against the lovers, just as he always is. They take a knife that cuts well and stab Papa to death. He's gone. They do it at night, nobody sees them but the moon, who doesn't betray them, and the stars, who are mute, and God, who's going to forgive them after all. How beautiful and sincere that is. A poet of the present day would be stoned for writing such a thing."

They climbed the narrow mountain path in the sun-splashed shadows of the chestnuts. When Klingsor looked up he saw before his face the slender calves of Martha, the artist, showing pink through her transparent stockings. If he looked back, the green of the parasol arched above Ersilia's curly black hair. Underneath she was silken violet, the only dark patch among all these figures.

At a blue and orange farmhouse fallen summer apples lay in the meadow, cool and sour. They tasted them. Martha spoke enthusiastically about an outing on the Seine, in Paris, before the war. Ah yes, Paris, and the bliss of those days.

"That will never come again. Never again."

"Nor ought it to," the painter exclaimed vehemently, shaking his sparrowhawk's head fiercely. "Nothing ought to come again. Why should it? What childish wishes! The war has glossed over everything in the past, turning it all into a paradise, even the most idiotic things, the things we could well do without. Very well, it was lovely in Paris and lovely in Rome and lovely in Arles. But is it any less lovely today, right here? Paradise isn't Paris and peacetime, Paradise is here. It lives up there on the mountain and in an hour we'll be in the midst of it and will be the thieves to whom it was said: This day you will be with me in Paradise."

They broke out of the mottled shade of the woods path onto the broad open highway that soared, bright and hot, in great spirals to the summit. Klingsor, his eyes shielded by his dark-green glasses, walked last in line, and often fell behind to watch the others moving and see the colored combinations they formed. He had deliberately taken nothing with him for working, not even his small notebook; and nevertheless he stood still a hundred times, stirred by pictures. His gaunt figure stood alone, showing white against the reddish gravel of the road, at the edge of a grove of acacias. Summer breathed hotly upon the mountain. Light poured vertically down. Color steamed multifold out of the depths. Above the nearest mountains, their greens and reds harmonizing with white villages, bluish ridges peered; and beyond, paler and bluer, more and more ridges. Very far away and unreal rose the snow-capped crystalline peaks. Above the acacias and chestnut trees the mighty rocky wall and humpbacked summit of Monte Salute emerged, reddish and light purple. But the people were more beautiful than all the rest. Like flowers they stood in the light beneath the greenery. The emerald parasol glowed like a giant scarab, Ersilia's black hair beneath it, the white slender painter Martha with her rosy face, and all the others. Klingsor drank them in with a thirsty eye, but his thoughts were with Gina. He would not be able to see her for another week. She was sitting in an office in the city, working away at the typewriter; he seldom managed to see her, and never alone. And he loved her, her more than all the others, though she knew nothing about him, did not understand him, regarded him as a strange rare bird, a famous foreign painter. How strange that was, that his longings should cling to her alone, that no other love satisfied him. It was not like him to go far out of his way for a woman. But he did for Gina, in order to be beside her for an hour, to hold her small slender fingers, to thrust his shoe beneath hers, to imprint a quick kiss on the nape of her neck. He thought about that, a droll puzzle to himself. Was this already the turning point? Old age already coming on? Was it only that, the December–May impulse of the man of forty for the girl of twenty?

They had reached the ridge, and beyond, a new world flung itself at their eyes: Monte Gennaro, high and unreal, piled up out of endless steep, sharp pyramids and cones, the sun aslant behind it, each plateau glistening enamel floating on deep violet shadows. Between it and themselves the vast areas of shimmering air, and lost in infinite depths the narrow blue arm of the lake, resting amid the green flames of the forest.

There was a tiny village on the summit: a smallish manor house, four or five other houses, of stone, painted blue and pink, a chapel, a fountain, cherry trees. The company paused by the fountain in the sunlight. Klingsor walked on, through an arched gateway into a shadowy farmyard. Three bluish buildings stood tall in it, with only a few small windows, grass and gravel between them, a goat, nettles. A child ran away from him; he coaxed her to come back, took chocolate from his pocket. The child stopped; he caught her, caressed her, and pressed the chocolate upon her. She was shy and lovely, a dark-brown girl with the alarmed black eyes of a small animal, slender bare legs, brown and gleaming. "Where do you live?" he asked her. She ran to the nearest open door in one of the clifflike houses. From a dark stone room like a primeval cave a woman stepped, the child's mother; she too accepted chocolate. Above dirty clothing the brown throat rose, a firm-muscled, broad face, sun-tanned and beautiful, a broad full mouth, large eyes, crude sweet charm. Those large Asiatic features quietly bespoke sexuality and motherhood. He leaned seductively toward her;

smiling, she held him off, drawing the child between them. He walked on, resolved to return. He wanted to paint this woman, or be her lover, if only for an hour. She was everything: mother, child, mistress, animal, madonna.

Slowly, he returned to the group, his heart full of dreams. On the wall of the estate, whose house seemed empty and locked, crude old cannonballs had been affixed. A whimsical stairway led through shrubbery to a grove and hill with a monument atop it. There, baroque and solitary, stood a bust: Wallenstein costume, curls, tapering wavy beard. Ghosts and phantasms shimmered around the mountain in the glaring midday light. Strange things lurked; the world was tuned to another, remote key. Klingsor drank at the fountain. A swallowtail butterfly flew close and sucked at the sprinkled drops on the limestone rim of the fountain.

The mountain road led along the ridge under chestnuts and walnuts, in sun and shade. At a bend there was a wayside chapel, old and yellow, faded old pictures in the niche, a saint's head, angelically sweet and childlike, a patch of her red and brown garment, the rest crumbled away. Klingsor loved old pictures, especially when they came his way unlooked for; he loved such frescoes; he loved the way these beautiful works returned to dust and the earth.

More trees, vines, dazzling hot road. Another turn: there was their destination, suddenly, unexpectedly: a dark arched gateway, a large tall church of red stone, crashing with self-assurance against the sky, a plaza full of sunlight, dust and peace, grass parched to redness, crackling underfoot, noonday light reflected by glaring walls, a column, a figure atop it, invisible in the blaze of sunlight, a stone balustrade around the broad plaza poised over an infinity of blue. Beyond, the village of Kareno, ancient, narrow, densely dark, Saracen, gloomy stone caves under faded brown brick, lanes oppressively narrow as in a dream and full of darkness, small squares suddenly shrieking aloud in white sunlight, Africa and Nagasaki, above the forest, below the blue abyss, higher still the white, plump, saturated clouds.

"It's funny how much time we need before we know our way around in the world just a little," Klingsor said. "Once when I was going to Africa, years ago, I passed by this place in an express train, three or five or six miles away, and knew nothing about it. From Africa I went on to Asia, and at the time it was terribly necessary that I do so. But everything I found there I am finding here today: primeval forest, heat, beautiful alien people without nerves, sunlight, temples. It takes so long to learn to visit three continents in a single day. Here they are. Welcome, India! Welcome, Africa! Welcome, Japan!"

The friends knew a young lady who lived up here, and Klingsor was greatly looking forward to meeting the unknown woman. He called her the Queen of the Mountains; that was the title of a mysterious Oriental story in the books of his boyhood.

Expectantly, the caravan penetrated the blue-shaded gorge of the lanes. Not a person, not a sound, not a chicken, not a dog. But in the semishade of a window embrasure Klingsor saw a silent figure standing, a lovely girl, black-eyed, red kerchief around her black hair. Her gaze, lying in wait to capture the stranger, struck his. For the span of a long breath they looked fully, gravely into each other's eyes, two alien worlds momentarily close. Then both smiled briefly, the heartfelt eternal greeting of the sexes, the old, sweet, devouring enmity, and with a step around the corner of the house the stranger had fled away and been placed in the girl's hope chest, a picture among

many pictures, a dream among many dreams. The small thorn pricked Klingsor's never-satiated heart; for a moment he hesitated and thought to turn back. Agosto called him; Ersilia began to sing; a shadowy wall vanished and a small, brilliant square with two yellow palazzi lay still and dazzling in the enchanted noon: narrow stone balconies, closed shutters, a glorious stage for the first act of an opera.

"Arrival in Damascus," the doctor called out. "Where does Fatima live, the pearl among women?"

The answer came, surprisingly, from the smaller palazzo. Out of the cool blackness behind the half-closed balcony door a strange tone sounded, then another, and the same repeated ten times, then the octave ten times—a piano was being tuned, a melodious piano in the middle of Damascus.

This must be it; this was where she lived. But the house seemed to lack an entrance; there was only the yellow wall with two balconies, and above them a bit of painting in the stucco of the gable: blue and red flowers and a parrot. There should have been a painted door here and if you knocked three times and pronounced Open Sesame the painted door would fly open and the wanderer be greeted by aromatic fragrances, with the Queen of the Mountain seated on a high dais, behind veils, slave girls cowering on the steps at her feet and the painted parrot flying screeching to her mistress's shoulder.

They found a tiny door in a side street. A loud bell, a devilish mechanism, clanged angrily. A small staircase, narrow as a ladder, led upward. Impossible to imagine how the piano had ever been brought into this house. Through the window? Through the roof?

A large black dog came rushing, a small blond lion after him. A burst of noise; the stairs rattled; in the background the piano sang the same tone eleven times. Sweetly soft light poured out of a room coated with a pinkish whitewash. Doors slammed. Where was the parrot?

Suddenly the Queen of the Mountains stood there, a slender lissome flower, body straight and pliant, all in red, burning flames, image of youth. Before Klingsor's eyes a hundred beloved pictures scattered away and the new picture radiantly took their place. He knew at once that he would paint her, not realistically, but the ray within her that had struck him, the poem, the tart lovely tone: youth, Redness, Blondness, Amazon. He would look at her for an hour, perhaps several hours. He would see her walking, sitting, laughing, perhaps dancing, perhaps hear her singing. The day was crowned; the day had been given its meaning. Anything else that might come was pure gift, superfluity. It was always this way: an experience never came alone. Its birds always flew ahead, there were always harbingers and omens: the Asiatic maternal animal look in that doorway, the black-haired village beauty in the window, and now this.

For a second the feeling darted through him: "If only I were ten years younger, ten brief years, this girl could have me, capture me, wind me around her finger. Now, you are too young, little red queen, too young for the old wizard Klingsor! He will admire you, will get to know you by heart; but he will make no pilgrimage to you, climb no ladder to you, commit no murder for you, and sing no serenades outside your pretty balcony. No, unfortunately he will do none of these things, not the old painter Klingsor, the old ram. He will not love you, he will not cast his eyes at you as he cast his eyes at the Asiatic, at the black-haired girl in the window, who is perhaps not a day younger than you are. He is not too old for her, only for you, Queen of the Mountain, red flower on the hill. For you, wild pink, he is too old. For you the love that Klingsor has to give away between a day full of work and a night full of red wine is not enough. All the better, then, my eye will drink you down, slender rocket, and know you when you have long since faded within me."

Through stone-floored rooms separated by doorless arches they entered a hall where fantastic baroque plaster figures pranced above tall doors and all around ran a dark frieze of painted dolphins, white horses, and pink Cupids floating in a densely populated mythical sea. There were a few chairs and parts of the disassembled grand piano on the floor, nothing else in the large room. But two alluring doors led to two small balconies above the sun-struck operatic plaza, and diagonally across the balconies of the neighboring palazzo thrust out, they too wreathed with paintings. There a fat red cardinal floated like a goldfish in the sun.

They stayed. In the big hall provisions were unpacked, a table set. Wine was brought, rare white wine from the north, the key to hosts of memories. The piano tuner had decamped; the dismantled piano held its peace. Thoughtfully, Klingsor stared at the exposed bowels of glittering strings; then he softly closed the lid. His eyes ached, but the summer day sang in his heart, the Saracen mother sang, blue and soaring the dream of Kareno sang. He ate and clinked his glass with others; he talked gaily in a high voice; and behind it all the apparatus of his workshop operated. His eyes enveloped the wild pink, the field poppy, like water round a fish. A diligent chronicler sat in his brain and carefully wrote down forms, rhythms, movements as if inscribing brazen columns of figures.

Talk and laughter filled the empty room. The doctor's kindly, prudent laugh sounded, Ersilia's low and friendly,

Agosto's strong and subterranean, Martha's birdlike. The poet talked sensibly, Klingsor jokingly. Watching closely, a little shy, the red queen went among her guests, dolphins and horses, sped here and there, stood by the piano, crouched on a cushion, cut bread, poured wine with an inexperienced girlish hand. Joyousness resounded in the cool hall; eyes glistened dark and blue; outside the high balcony doors the dazzling noon stared down, on guard.

The clear, splendid wine flowed into the glasses, delicious contrast to the simple cold meal. The red glow flowed clear from the queen's dress through the high room; alert and clear, the eyes of all the men followed it. She vanished, returned, and had tied on a green sash. She vanished, returned, and had donned a blue kerchief.

After eating, tired and satiated, they set out gaily for the woods, lay down in grass and moss. Parasols gleamed, faces glowed under straw hats, the sun glittered and burned. The Queen of the Mountains lay redly in the green grass, her fine throat rising white from the flame, her high shoe intensely colored and alive on her slender foot. Klingsor, close by her, read her, studied her, filled himself with her, just as he had as a boy read the magical story of the Queen of the Mountains and filled himself with it. They rested, dozed, chattered, flicked at ants, thought they heard snakes. Prickly chestnut shells clung to the women's hair. They thought of absent friends who had missed this hour—there were not many. They wished Louis the Cruel were here, Klingsor's friend, the painter of carousels and circuses. His antic spirit hovered above the group, close by.

The afternoon passed like a year in paradise. There was a great deal of laughter when they parted from the Queen. Klingsor took everything with him in his heart: the Queen, the woods, the palazzo and the dolphin room, the two dogs, the parrot.

Descending the mountain among his friends, there gradually came over him that exuberant mood that he had only on rare days when he had voluntarily let his work go. Hand in hand with Ersilia, with Hermann, with Martha, he danced down the sunlit road, starting songs, taking childlike pleasure in jokes and puns, surrendering to laughter. He ran ahead of the others and lay in ambush to frighten them.

Quickly as they walked, the sun sank more quickly. By the time they reached Palazzetto it had dropped behind the mountain, and in the valley below, it was already evening. They had missed the way and descended too low; they were hungry and tired and had to abandon their plans for the evening: a stroll through the fields to Barengo, a fish dinner in the lakeside village's restaurant.

"My dears," Klingsor said, sitting down on a wall by the wayside, "our plans were all very fine, and I would certainly be grateful for a good dinner among the fishermen or in Monte d'Oro. But we cannot make it that far, or at least I cannot. I'm tired and I'm hungry. I'm not taking another step beyond the nearest grotto, which certainly isn't far. There we can get bread and wine. That's enough. Who's coming?"

They all came. They found the grotto: on a narrow terrace cut into the forested hill stood stone benches and tables under the darkness of trees. From the wine cellar in the cavern the innkeeper brought cool wine. There was bread on the tables. Now they sat eating in silence, glad to be sitting down at last. Beyond the tall tree trunks the day faded out; the blue mountain turned black, the red road white. Down below, on the nocturnal road, they could hear a car, and a dog barking. Here and there stars appeared in the sky, and in the landscape below lights winked on; there was no telling the two apart.

Klingsor sat happily resting, looking out into the night, slowly checking his hunger with black bread, quietly draining the bluish cups of wine. Satiated, he began to talk again and to sing; he rocked to the beat of the songs, played with the women, sniffed the fragrance of their hair. The wine seemed good to him. Practiced seducer, he easily talked down the proposals that they go on their way. He drank wine, poured wine, sent for more wine. Slowly, out of the bluish earthenware cups, symbol of transitoriness, bright spells arose, magic transforming the world, coloring the stars and lights.

They sat in a swing hovering high above the abyss of world and night, birds in a golden cage, homeless, weightless, across from the stars. They sang, these birds, sang exotic songs; out of ecstatic hearts they cast fantasies into the night, into the sky, into the woods, into the enchanted universe. Answers came from stars and moon, from trees and mountains. Goethe sat there and his alter ego Hafis; torrid Egypt and grave Greece rose up; Mozart smiled; Hugo Wolf played the piano in the delirious night.

There was a crash of noise, a blaze of light; below them, straight through the heart of the earth, with a hundred dazzling lighted windows, a railroad train streaked into the mountain and into the night. In the sky above, the bells of an invisible church rang. With a skulking air the half moon rose above the table, glanced at its reflection in the dark wine, marked a woman's mouth and eye off from the darkness, mounted higher, sang to the stars. The spirit of Louis the Cruel sat hunched, solitary, on a bench, writing letters.

Klingsor, King of the Night, tall crown in his hair, leaning back on his throne of stone, directed the dance of the world, set the beat, called forth the moon, willed that the railroad train vanish. At once it was gone, as a constellation plummets over the margin of the sky. Where was the Queen of the Mountains? Was that not a piano sounding in the woods? Was not the mistrustful little lion barking far off? Had she not been wearing a blue kerchief a moment ago? Hello, old world, see to it that you don't collapse! Come here, woods! Go there, black mountain! Keep to the beat! Stars, how blue and red you are, as in the folk song: "Your red eyes and your blue mouth!"

Painting was lovely; painting was a dear, lovely game for well-behaved children. But it was something else, grander and more momentous, to direct the movements of the stars, to project the beat of your own blood, the circlets of color from your own retina, into the world, to send the vibrations of your own soul thrumming out with the wind of the night. Away with you, black mountains! Become a cloud, fly to Persia, rain on Uganda! Come here, spirit of Shakespeare, sing us your drunken fool's song of the rain that raineth every day!

Klingsor kissed a woman's small hand, leaned against a woman's sweetly rising and falling breast. A foot under the table played with his. He did not know whose hand or whose foot; he felt tenderness all around him, gratefully felt old magic renewed. He was still young, it was still far from the end, he was still capable of radiation and allure; they still loved him, the good anxious little females, they still counted on him.

He soared higher. In a low, chanting voice he began to tell a tale, a tremendous epic, the story of a love affair, or rather it was really a trip to the South Seas where in the company of Gauguin and Crusoe he discovered Parrot Island and founded the Free State of the Blessed Isles. How the thousands of parrots had sparkled in the twilight, how their blue tails had glittered, mirrored in the green bay! Their cries, and the hundred-voiced shrieks of the big monkeys, had greeted him like thunder—him, Klingsor, when he proclaimed his Free State. He had called upon the white cockatoo to form a cabinet, and with the sulky rhinoceros bird he had drunk palm wine from heavy coconut cups. O moon of the past, moon of the blissful nights, moon above the pile dwelling among the reeds! The shy brown princess bore the name of Kül Kalüa; slender and long-limbed she strode through the banana forest, gleaming like honey under the succulent roof of the giant leaves, doe-eyed, cat-backed, feline tension in springy ankle and sinewy leg. Kül Kalüa, child, archaic ardor and childish innocence of the sacred southeast; for a thousand nights you lay upon Klingsor's heart and every night was new, each was sweeter, each tenderer than all the others. O festival of the Earth Spirit when the virgins of the Parrot Islands dance before the god!

Over the islands, over Crusoe and Klingsor, over the tale and the listeners, the white-starred night arched, the mountain swelled like gently breathing belly and breasts under the trees and houses and the feet of men; the racing moon danced feverishly over the firmament, pursued by the stars in wild and silent choreography. Strings of stars lined up, the glittering wire of a cable railway to Paradise. Primeval forest darkened maternally, primordial mud wafted the scent of decay and generation, serpents and crocodiles crawled, the stream of forms poured on without bounds or banks.

"I'm going to paint again after all," Klingsor said. "I'll start again tomorrow. But no more of these houses and people and trees. I'll paint crocodiles and starfish, dragons and purple snakes, and everything that is changing, filled with

longing to become man, full of longing to become stars, full of birth, full of decay, full of God and death."

In the midst of his almost whispered words, in the midst of the wild drunken hour, Ersilia's voice sounded low and clear. Quietly she sang the song of *bel mazzo di fiori* under her breath. Tranquillity poured from her song; Klingsor heard it as if it came from some distant floating island across seas of time and solitude. He turned his empty wine cup over, filled it no more. He listened. A child sang. A mother sang. What was he—an errant and reprobate fellow bathed in the mire of the world, a scoundrel and profligate, or was he a silly small child?

"Ersilia," he said with reverence, "you are our lucky star."

Up the mountain through the steep dark woods, clinging to branches and roots, they sought their homeward path, reached the margin of the woods, boarded a field like pirates on a ship. The narrow path through the cornfield breathed night and homecoming, moon glancing against the shiny leaves of corn, rows of grapevines slanting away. Now Klingsor sang, softly, in his somewhat hoarse voice, sang many murmuring songs, German and Malay, with and without words. Singing low he poured out all that had accumulated within him, as a brown wall at evening radiates the stored daylight.

Here one of the friends took his leave, another there, vanishing along narrow paths in the shadow of the grapes. Each left, each went by himself, heading home, alone under the sky. A woman kissed Klingsor good night; burning, her mouth sipped at his. They rolled away, they melted away, all of them. When Klingsor, alone, climbed the stairs to his dwelling, he was still singing. He sang the praises of God and himself; he praised Li

Po and the good wine of Pampambio. Like an idol, he rested upon clouds of affirmation.

"Inwardly," he sang, "I am like a ball of gold, like the dome of a cathedral; people kneel in it, people pray, gold gleams from the wall, the Saviour bleeds in an old painting, the heart of Mary bleeds. We bleed too, we others, we errant souls, we stars and comets; seven and fourteen swords pierce our blessed chests. I love you, blond and dark women, I love all, even the philistines; you are all poor devils like myself, all poor children and misbegotten demigods like drunken Klingsor. Beloved life, I greet you! I greet you, beloved death!"

Klingsor to Edith

Dear star in the summer sky,

How well and truly you have written to me, and how painfully your love calls to me, like eternal song, like eternal reproach. For you are on a good course when you confess to me, when you confess to yourself, every stirring of the heart. But do not call any emotion petty, any emotion unworthy. Every one is good, very good, even hatred, even envy, even jealousy, even cruelty. All we live on are our poor, lovely, glorious feelings, and each one we wrong is a star we have extinguished.

I don't know whether I love Gina. I doubt it very much. I would not make any sacrifices for her. I do not know whether I can love at all. I can desire and can seek myself in others; I can listen for an echo, demand a mirror, seek pleasure, and all that can look like love.

Both of us, you and I, are wandering in the same maze, in the maze of our feelings, which have been scanted in this sorry world, for which reason we take revenge on this evil world, each in his own fashion. But let us, each of us, let the other's dreams remain, because we know how sweet and red the wine of dreams tastes.

Clarity about their feelings and about the "importance" and consequences of their actions is something that only good, self-assured people have, those who believe in life and take no step that they will not be able to approve tomorrow and the day after as well. I am not lucky enough to be one of them, and I feel and act like a man who does not believe in tomorrow and regards every day as his last.

Dear Sylph, I am unlucky in my efforts to express my thoughts. Expressed thoughts are always so dead. Let us allow them to live! I feel deeply and gratefully that you understand me, that something in you is akin to me. I don't know under what heading that should be placed in the book of life, whether our feelings are love, sex, gratitude, or sympathy, whether they are maternal or childish. Often I look at every woman like a cunning old libertine, and often like a little boy. Often the chastest woman tempts me most, and often the lushest. Everything I am permitted to love is beautiful, holy, infinitely good. But why, how long, to what degree I may love—that I cannot judge.

I do not love you alone, as you well know, nor do I love Gina alone. Tomorrow and the day after tomorrow I shall love other women, paint other pictures. But I shall not regret any love I have ever felt, and any wise or foolish act that I have committed for those loves' sakes. Perhaps I love you because you are like me. I love others because they are so different from me.

It is late in the night; the moon stands over Salute. How life smiles, how death smiles!

Throw this silly letter into the fire, and throw into the fire

Your Klingsor

The Music of Doom

The last day of July had come, Klingsor's favorite month; Li Po's grand festival had faded, had not been repeated. Sunflowers in the garden brashly raised their gold to the blue. Together with his faithful Tu Fu, Klingsor tramped through a region that he loved: the parched outskirts of a town, dusty roads beneath high rows of trees, red and orange little houses facing the sandy shore, trucks and quays, long violet walls, colorful poor folk. In the evening he sat in the dust at the edge of the town and painted the colored tents and wagons of an itinerant carnival; he crouched by the side of the road on scruffy, parched greensward, beguiled by the strong colors of the tents. He clung fast to the faded lilac of a tent tassel, to the jolly greens and reds of the clumsy trailer homes, to the blue-and-white framing poles. Fiercely, he wallowed in cadmium, savagely in cool sweet cobalt, drew melting lines of crimson lake through the yellow and green sky. Another hour, no, less, then he would knock off, night would come, and tomorrow August would be starting, August the burning fever month which mixes so much fear of death and timorousness into its ardent cup. The scythe was sharpened, the day declined; death laughed, concealed among the parching leaves. Ring high and blast your trumpet, cadmium! Boast loudly, lush crimson lake. Laugh glaringly, lemon yellow! Come here, you deep-blue mountain in the distance. Come to my heart, you matt dusty green trees. How tired you are, how you let your pious branches droop submissively. I drink to you, lovely things of the world! I give you semblance of duration and immortality, I who am the most transitory, the most believing, the saddest of all, who suffer from the fear of death more than all of you. July is burned out, soon August will be burned out; suddenly the great ghost chills us from the yellowed leaves in the dew-wet morning. Suddenly November sweeps across the woods. Suddenly the great ghost laughs, suddenly the chill settles around our hearts, suddenly the dear pink flesh falls from our bones, the jackal howls in the desert, the vulture hoarsely sings his accursed song. An accursed newspaper in the city publishes my picture, and under it the words: "Outstanding painter, expressionist, great colorist, died on the sixteenth of this month."

Full of hatred he ripped a furrow of Paris blue under the green gypsy wagon. Full of bitterness, he broke the chrome-yellow edge of the curbstones. Full of deep despair, he dashed vermilion in an empty spot, annihilating the challenging white; bleeding, he fought for continuance. He screamed in bright green and Neapolitan yellow to inexorable God. Groaning, he threw more blue into the dreary dusty green; imploringly, he kindled deeper lights in the evening sky. The little palette full of pure unmixed colors, intensely luminous, was his comfort, his tower, his arsenal, his prayer book, his cannon. From it he fired upon wicked death. Purple was denial of death, vermilion was mockery of decay. His arsenal was good; his brave troop stood lined up brilliantly, the rapid rounds from his cannon flashed. But it was no use, all shooting was in vain; and yet shooting was good, was happiness and consolation, was still living, still triumphing.

Tu Fu had left to visit a friend who had his magic citadel over there between the factory and the wharf. Now he returned, bringing with him the Armenian astrologer.

Klingsor, finished with the painting, drew a deep breath of relief when he saw the two faces close by, the good fair hair of Tu Fu and the black beard with white teeth in the smiling face of the magus. With them came the shadow also, the long dark shadow with receding eyes in deep sockets. Welcome, you too, Shadow, fine fellow!

"Do you know what day today is?" Klingsor asked his friend.

"The last day of July, I know."

"I cast a horoscope today," the Armenian said, "and I saw that this evening is going to bring me something. Saturn stands strangely, Mars neutral, Jupiter is dominant. Li Po, aren't you a Leo?"

"I was born on July the second."

"I thought so. Your stars stand confusedly, Friend; only you yourself can interpret them. Fertility surrounds you like a cloud about to burst. Your stars stand oddly, Klingsor; I'm sure you can't help feeling it."

Klingsor packed up his gear. The world he had painted was faded, the green and yellow sky extinguished, the bright blue flag drowned, the lovely yellow slain and withered. He was hungry and thirsty; his throat felt full of dust.

"Friends," he said cordially, "let us spend this evening together. We shall no longer be together again, all four of us; I am not reading that in the stars, but I find it written in my heart. My July moon is over; its last hours glow darkly; in the depths the Great Mother calls. Never has the world been so beautiful, never have I painted so beautiful a picture. Heat lightning flashes; the music of doom has begun. Let us sing along with it, the sweet forbidding music. Let us stay together and drink wine and eat bread."

Beside the carousel, whose tent had just been taken down in preparation for the evening (for it was there as a sunshade), a few tables stood under the trees. A lame waitress was going back and forth; there was a small tavern in the shade. Here they sat at the plank table; bread was brought, and wine poured into the earthenware vessels. Lights glowed into life under the trees. A short distance away the carousel's hurdy-gurdy began to jingle, loosing its shrill music into the evening.

"I mean to drain three hundred cups tonight!" Li Po cried, and toasted the Shadow. "Greetings, Shadow, steadfast tin soldier! Greetings, friends! Greetings, electric lights, arc lamps and sparkling merry-go-round spangles! Oh, if only Louis were here, the fugitive bird! Perhaps he's already flown on ahead of us to heaven. Or perhaps he'll come back tomorrow, the old jackal, and no longer find us and laugh and plant arc lamps and flagpoles upon our grave."

Quietly, the astrologer went and returned with fresh wine, his white teeth smiling gladly in his red mouth.

"Melancholia," he said with a glance at Klingsor, "is a thing we should not carry around. It's so easy—it's the work of an hour, a single intensive hour with clenched teeth, and then one is through with melancholia forever."

Klingsor looked closely at his mouth, at the bright, straight teeth that had once upon a time, in some fervid hour, crunched melancholia and bitten it to death. Could he too do what the astrologer had succeeded in doing? O sweet brief glance into distant gardens: life without dread, life without melancholia! But he knew these gardens were unattainable for him. He knew his destiny was different, Saturn lowered differently upon him, God wanted him to play different tunes upon his strings.

"Each has his stars," Klingsor said slowly. "Each has his faith. I believe in only one thing: in doom. We are driving in a carriage on the edge of an abyss, and the horses have already shied. We are immersed in doom, all of us; we must die, we must be born again. The great turning point has come for us. It is the same everywhere: the great war, the great change in art, the great collapse in the governments of the West. For us in old Europe everything we had that was good and our own has already died. Our fine-feathered Reason has become madness, our money is paper, our machines can do nothing but shoot and explode, our art is suicide. We are going under, friends; that is our destiny. Music in the Tsing Tse key has begun."

The Armenian poured wine.

"As you like," he said. "One can say yes and one can say no; that is only a child's game. Doom is something that does not exist. For doom or resurgence to exist there must be a top and a bottom. But there is no top or bottom; these exist only in man's brain, which is the home of illusion. All paradoxes are illusions: white and black are illusion, death and life are illusion, good and evil are illusion. It is the work of an hour, a single fervent hour with clenched teeth, and one has overcome the kingdom of illusions."

Klingsor listened to his good voice.

"I am speaking of us," he retorted. "I am speaking of Europe, our old Europe that for two thousand years thought itself the world's brain. It is going under. Do you think, Magus, that I don't know you? You are a messenger from the East, a messenger to me also, perhaps a spy, perhaps a warlord in disguise. You are here because the end is beginning, because the scent of doom is in your nostrils. But we are glad to go under, you know, we die gladly, we do not defend ourselves."

"You may also say: we are glad to be born," the Asiatic said, laughing. "To you it seems doom, perhaps to me it seems birth. Both are illusion. The man who believes in the earth as a fixed disk under heaven also sees and believes in sunrise and sunset, in dawn and doom—and all, almost all men believe in that fixed disk! The stars themselves know nothing of rising and setting."

"Have not the stars set, are not the stars doomed too?" Tu Fu cried.

"For us, for our eyes."

He filled the cups; it was always he who undertook to pour, attentively, smilingly. He went away with the empty pitcher to bring more wine. The carousel music blared.

"Let's go over there, it's so lovely," Tu Fu pleaded, and they went over to the carousel, stood by the painted barrier, watched the carousel turn its giddy circles in the piercing glitter of spangles and mirrors. They saw a hundred children with eyes greedily fixed on the brilliance. For a moment Klingsor felt, with deep amusement, the primitiveness and African quality of this whirling machine, this mechanical music, these garish pictures and colors, mirrors and insane ornamental columns. Everything bespoke medicine men and shamans, magic and age-old pied-piperism, and all that wild weird sparkle was at bottom nothing but the darting glitter of the tin lure that the pike thinks is a minnow.

Every child must ride the carousel. Tu Fu gave money to the children; the Shadow beckoned to all the children to come nearer. They clustered around their benefactor, clung to him, begged, thanked. There was a pretty blond girl of twelve who asked repeatedly; she rode on every round. In the glitter of the lights her short skirt blew up around her boyish legs. One child cried. Boys fought. The cymbals clanged sharply along with the organ, poured fire into the beat, opium into the wine. For a long while the four stood amid the tumult.

Then they returned to their quiet table

under the trees. The Armenian filled the cups with wine, stirred up doom, smiled brightly.

"Let us empty three hundred cups today," Klingsor sang. His sun-bleached hair glowed yellow, his laughter boomed. Melancholia knelt, a giant, upon his twitching heart. He held up his glass in a toast, he hailed doom, hailed the desire for death, the Tsing Tse key. The carousel music surged and roared. But inside his heart, dread lurked. The heart did not want to die. The heart hated death.

Suddenly more music assaulted the night, shrill, intemperate, from the tavern. In the nook beside the chimney piece, whose shelf was lined with neatly arranged wine bottles, a player-piano blazed, machine-gun fire, wild, hectoring, impetuous. Sorrow cried from discordant strings, steam-roller rhythm flattened groaning dissonances. There was a crowd here too, light, noise, young men and girls dancing, the lame waitress too, and Tu Fu. He danced with the blond little girl. Klingsor watched. Lightly, sweetly, her short summer dress whirled around the pretty skinny legs. Tu Fu's face smiled amiably, filled with love. The others sat at the chimney piece; they had come in from the garden, were close to the source of the music, in the very midst of it. Klingsor saw tones, heard colors. The magus took one and another bottle from the shelf, opened them, poured. His smile never wavered on his brown intelligent face. The music thumped fearfully in the low-ceilinged hall. Slowly the Armenian opened a breach in the row of old bottles on the mantle, like a temple robber removing, chalice by chalice, the precious utensils from an altar.

"You are a great artist," the astrologer whispered to Klingsor as he filled his cup. "You are one of the greatest artists of this age. You are quite entitled to call yourself Li Po. But, Li Po, you are a poor, harried, tormented, and anxiety-ridden man. You have struck up the music of doom; you sit singing in your burning house, which you yourself have set afire, and you do not feel happy about it, Li Po, even if you empty three hundred cups every day and drink with the moon. You are not happy about it, you are very sorry about it, singer of doom. Won't you stop? Don't you want to live? Don't you want to continue?"

Klingsor drank and whispered back in his somewhat hoarse voice: "Can a man change fate? Is there freedom of the will? Can you, astrologer, guide my stars differently?"

"I cannot guide them, only interpret them. Only you yourself can guide. There is freedom of the will. It is the wisdom of the Magi."

"Why should I practice the wisdom of the Magi when I can practice art? Isn't art just as good?"

"Everythng is good. Nothing is good. The wisdom of the Magi abolishes illusions. It abolishes that worst of illusions which we call 'time.' "

"Doesn't art do that also?"

"It tries to. Is your painted July, which you have there in your portfolio, enough for you? Have you abolished time? Are you without fear of the autumn, of the winter?"

Klingsor sighed and fell silent. Silently, he drank. Silently, the magus filled his cup. Hectically, the unleashed mechanical piano rumbled. Angelically, Tu Fu's face floated among the dancers. July was over.

Klingsor toyed with the empty bottles on the table, arranging them in a circle.

"These are our cannon," he exclaimed. "With these cannon we shoot time to pieces, death to pieces, misery to pieces. I have also shot at death with paints, with fiery green and explosive vermilion and sweet scarlet lake. Often I have hit him on the head; I have driven white and blue into his eye. I have often sent him scurrying. I shall meet him often again, overcome him, outwit him. Look at the Armenian; he is opening another old bottle and the imprisoned sun of past summers shoots into our blood. The Armenian, too, helps us shoot at death; the Armenian, too, knows no other weapon against death."

The magus broke bread and ate.

"I need no weapon against death because there is no death. There is only one thing: dread of death. That can be cured; there is a weapon to use against that. It is a matter of an hour to overcome that dread. But Li Po does not want to. For Li loves death; he loves his dread of death, his melancholy, his misery. Only his dread has taught him all that he can do and all we love him for."

Mockingly, he raised his cup to Klingsor's; his teeth flashed, his face grew more and more jovial. Sorrow seemed alien to him. No one answered. Klingsor shot his wine cannon against death. Death loomed at the open doors of the tavern, which was swollen with people, wine, and dance music. Death loomed at the doors, softly shook the black acacia, lurked darkly in the garden. Everything outside was full of death, filled with death; only here in the crowded hall they still fought on, fought gloriously and bravely against the black besieger who whimpered at the windows.

Mockingly, the magus looked across the table; mockingly, he filled the cups. Klingsor had already broken many cups; the magus had given him new ones. The Armenian had also drunk a great many, but he sat as erect as Klingsor.

"Let us drink, Li," he said in low-voiced mockery. "You love death, you know, you want to be doomed, you are glad to die the death. Didn't you say so, or have I deceived myself—or have you after all deceived me and yourself? Let us drink, Li, let us be doomed."

Rage bubbled up in Klingsor. He stood up, stood erect and tall, the old sparrow hawk with his chiseled face, spat into the wine, hurled his full cup on the floor. The red wine splashed out into the hall; his friends paled, strangers laughed.

But smiling silently the magus fetched a new cup, smilingly filled it, smilingly offered it to Li Po. Then Li smiled, he too smiled. A smile flickered like moonlight over his distorted face.

"Friends," he cried out, "let this foreigner talk! The old fox knows a great deal; he has come out of a deep and hidden den. He knows a great deal, but he does not understand us. He is too old to understand children. He is too wise to understand fools. We who are about to die know more about death than he. We are men, not stars. See my hand, holding a small blue cup of wine! This hand, this brown hand, can do many things. It has painted with many brushes, has wrested fresh segments of the world from the darkness and placed them before men's eyes. This brown hand has stroked many women under the chin and seduced many girls. Many have kissed it, tears have fallen on it, Tu Fu has written a poem to it. This dear hand, friends, will soon be full of earth and maggots; none of you would touch it then. Very well, that is the reason I love it. I love my hand, I love my eyes, I love my soft white belly; I love them with regret and with scorn and with great tenderness because they must all wither and decay so soon. Shadow, dark friend, old tin soldier on Andersen's grave, you too will meet the same fate, dear fellow. Drink with me: Three cheers for our limbs and guts! Long may they live!"

They drank the toast. The Shadow smiled darkly from his deep eye sockets—and suddenly something passed through the hall like a wind, like a spirit. Abruptly the music stopped, the dancers vanished, as if swallowed by the night, and half the lights went out. Klingsor looked at the black doors. Outside stood death. He saw death standing there. He smelled him. Like raindrops in the leaves by the highroad, that was how death smelled.

Then Li Po pushed the cup away, knocked back the chair, and walked slowly out of the hall into the dark garden and on, in the darkness, heat lightning flashing over his head, alone. His heart lay heavy in his breast like the stone upon a grave.

Evening in August

Klingsor had spent the afternoon at Manuzzo and Veglia, painting in sun and wind. In the gathering twilight he had crossed over Veglia, very tired, to a small, sleeping village. He succeeded in routing out a gray-haired innkeeper's wife; she brought him wine. He sat down on the stump of a walnut tree outside the door, unpacked his knapsack, found a piece of cheese and a few plums still left, and had his supper. The old woman sat by, stooped and toothless, and with wrinkled throat working and quiescent old eyes spoke of the life of her hamlet and her family, of the war and the rising prices, and of the state of the fields, of wine and milk and what they cost, of dead grandchildren and emigrant sons. All the constellations and seasons of the farm woman's life lay spread out before Klingsor, clearly, pleasingly, coarsely in their sparse beauty, full of gladnesses and concerns, full of anxiety and life. Klingsor ate, drank, rested, listened, asked about children and livestock, priest and bishop, amiably praised the wretched wine, offered a last plum to her, shook hands, wished her a happy night, and leaning on his stick, laden with his knapsack, climbed slowly up the mountain through the thin woods to his bed for the night.

It was that glorious hour, with the daylight still glowing everywhere but the moon already gleaming and the first bats dipping in the green, shimmering air. One edge of woods stood dissolving in the last light, bright chestnut trunks against black shadows. A yellow cottage softly radiated the daylight it had absorbed, glowing gently like a topaz. The small paths, pink and violet, led through meadows, vineyards, and woods. Here and there an acacia twig had already yellowed. The western sky hung golden and green above the velvet blue mountains.

Oh, to be able to work now, in this last enchanted quarter hour of the ripe summer's day which would never come again! How inexpressibly beautiful everything was now, how peaceful, good, and giving, as if filled with God.

Klingsor sat down in the cool grass, mechanically reached for his pencil, then smilingly let his hand drop again. He was dead tired. He fingered the dry grass, the dry crumbly earth. How much longer, and then this wonderful game was over! How much longer, and then hand and mouth and eyes would be full of earth! A few days ago Tu Fu had sent him a poem. He remembered it now and spoke it slowly under his breath:

> Leaf after leaf descends
> From my life's tree.
> O world's magnificence
> How you fill me,
> How you fill and satiate,
> How you inebriate.
> What burns today
> Is soon decay.
> Soon the wind keens
> Over my brown grave.
> The mother leans
> Over the child's face.
> Let me see her eyes again,

My star is in her eyes.
Nothing else need remain,
All that dies gladly dies.
Only the eternal Mother stays
From whom we came,
Lightly her finger plays,
Inscribes in air: our name.

Well, it was good that it was so. How many of his ten lives did Klingsor have left? Three? Two? It was still more than one, still more than one respectable, ordinary, everyday, commonplace life. And how much he had seen, how much paper and canvas he had covered, how many hearts he had stirred in love and hate, in art and life, how much vexation and fresh wind he had brought into the world. He had loved many women, destroyed many traditions and sanctuaries, dared many new things. He had emptied many full cups, breathed in many days and starry nights, grown tanned under many suns, swum in many waters. Now he sat here, in Italy or India or China; the summer wind puffed whimsically at the crowns of the chestnuts, the world was good, was perfect. It did not matter whether he painted another hundred pictures or ten, or whether he lived another twenty summers or one. He was tired, tired. All that dies gladly dies. Dear, good Tu Fu!

It was time to go home. He would totter into the room, be received by the breeze through the balcony door. He would strike a light and unpack. The heart of the woods with all that chrome yellow and chinese blue might be good; it would make a picture some day. Get going then, it was time.

Nevertheless, he stayed where he was, the wind in his hair, sitting in his flapping, paint-stained linen jacket, a smile and a grief in his twilight heart. Softly, slackly, the wind blew, softly, silently, the bats dipped against the fading sky. All that dies gladly dies. Only the eternal Mother stays.

He might sleep here, at least for an hour. It was warm, after all. He pillowed his head on his knapsack and looked up into the sky. How beautiful the world is, how it satiates.

Footsteps sounded, descending the mountain, walking strongly on loose wooden soles. Between the fern and the broom a figure appeared, a woman; it was already so dark that he could not make out the colors of her dress. She approached closer, with sound, even steps. Klingsor jumped up and called out good evening. She started a little, and paused for a moment. He looked into her face. He knew her but could not remember where he had seen her. She was pretty and dark; her fine, firm teeth flashed. "Well, well!" he exclaimed, holding out his hand to her. He sensed that something linked him with this woman, some small recollection. "Don't we know each other?"

"Madonna! Why, you're the painter from Castagnetta. Do you still remember me?"

Yes, now he knew. She was a peasant woman from the Taverne valley. Once upon a time, in the shadowy and confused past of this summer, he had painted near her house for a few hours, had taken water from her well, had napped for an hour in the shade of the fig tree, and at the end received a glass of wine and a kiss from her.

"You never came back," she complained. "And you promised so that you would."

There was wantonness and provocation in her deep voice. Klingsor revived.

"Ecco, so much the better that you've come to me now. What luck I have, just now, when I'm so lonely and sad."

"Sad? Don't try to fool me, signore, you're a joker, a woman can't believe a word you say. I must go on now."

"Oh, then I'll keep you company."

"This isn't the way you go, and there's no need either. What could happen to me?"

"Not to you, but to me. How easy it would be for some man to come along and strike your fancy and go with you and kiss your sweet mouth and your throat and your beautiful breast, someone else besides me. No, that can't be allowed."

He had ringed her nape with his hand and would not let her go. "My little star. Sweetheart. My sweet little plum. Bite me, or I'll eat you."

He kissed her on her strong, open mouth. Laughing, she bent back; between resisting and protesting she yielded, kissed him back, shook her head, laughed, tried to free herself. He held her tightly, his mouth on hers, his hand on her breast. Her hair smelled like summer, like hay, broom, fern, brambles. Taking a deep breath, for a moment he bent his head back and saw, small and white in the faded sky, the first star rising. The woman spoke no more; her face had become grave. She sighed, placed her hand on his and pressed it more firmly against her breast. He stooped gently, pressed his arm into the unresisting hollows of her knees, and bedded her down in the grass.

"Do you like me?" she asked like a little girl. "Povera me!"

They drank the cup. Wind brushed over their hair and carried their breath with it.

Before they parted he looked in his knapsack and his coat pockets to see if he had anything to give her. He found a small silver case, still half full of cigarette tobacco. He emptied it and gave it to her.

"No, not a present, certainly not!" he assured her. "Only a memento, so you won't forget me."

"I won't forget you," she said. And, "Will you come again?"

He became sad. Slowly he kissed her on both eyes. "I'll come again," he said.

For a while he stood motionless, listening to her wooden clogs clacking downhill, over the meadow at the bottom, through the woods, clacking on earth, on rock, on leaves, on roots. Now she was gone. The woods stood black against the night, the wind brushed warmly over the invisible earth. Something, perhaps a mushroom, perhaps a withered fern, smelled acridly of autumn.

Klingsor could not make up his mind to go home. What was the point of climbing the mountain now, of going into the room with all the pictures? He stretched out in the grass and looked at the stars. At last he slept, and slept until late in the night the cry of an animal or a gust of wind or the coolness of the dew roused him. Then he climbed up to Castagnetta, found his house, his door, his room. Letters lay there, and flowers; friends had dropped by.

Tired as he was, he obeyed the tenacious old habit of every night, unpacking all his things and looking at the day's sketches by lamplight. That one of the depths of the woods was good; the plants and rocks in the light-flecked shade gleamed cool and precious like a treasure chamber. It had been a happy thought to have worked only with chrome yellow, orange, and blue and left out the chrome green. For a long while he studied the sheet.

But what for? What were all these sheets smeared with color for? Why all the toil, all the sweat, all the brief, drunken lust of creativity? Was there redemption? Was there tranquillity? Was there peace?

As soon as he had undressed he sank

exhausted into bed, put out the light and sought sleep, softly humming Tu Fu's verses to himself:

> Soon the wind keens
> Over my brown grave.

Klingsor Writes to Louis the Cruel

Caro Luigi, it is long since I have heard your voice.

Do you still live in the light? Is the vulture already gnawing your bones?

Have you ever used a darning needle to poke at a stopped clock? I did so once, and suddenly the devil got into the works and rattled off all the time that had passed; the hands raced each other around the face, whirling madly away with an uncanny noise, prestissimo, until suddenly everything snapped and the clock gave up the ghost. It is just like that right now with us here: the sun and moon are running amok across the sky, the days flying by, time running away with me as if pouring out of a hole in a bag. I hope the end will come suddenly and this drunken world will cease instead of dropping back again into a respectable tempo.

All through the days I have been too busy to be able to think of anything (how funny that sounds, by the way, when I say such a so-called "phrase" aloud to myself: "to be able to think of anything"). But in the evenings I often miss you. Usually I sit in the forest at one of the many *caves* drinking the popular red wine, which for the most part is of very poor quality but still helps to make life bearable and brings on sleep. Several times I have actually fallen asleep at the table in the grotto, thus proving to the grinning natives that my neurasthenia really cannot be all that bad. Sometimes friends and girls are with me and I prac-

tice my fingers on the Plasticine of female limbs and chatter about hats and heels and art. Sometimes we're lucky enough to hit a good temperature; then we shout and laugh all night long and people are glad that Klingsor is such a jolly old fellow. There is a very pretty woman here who asks after you every time I see her, with passionate interest.

The art we both practice still depends, as a professor would say, too much upon the object (how nice it would be to paint a picture puzzle). We are still—though in a somewhat free handwriting and a way that's upsetting enough to the bourgeois—painting the things of "reality": people, trees, country fairs, railroads, landscapes. In that respect we're still obeying a convention. The bourgeois calls those things "real" which are seen and described pretty much the same way by everybody, or at least by many people. As soon as this summer is over, I have in mind to paint nothing but fantasies for a while, especially dreams. Some of it will be the way you like it, zany and surprising, something like Collofino the Rabbit Hunter's tales of Cologne Cathedral. Even though I feel that the ground under my feet has somewhat thinned out and even though on the whole I have little craving for more years and more accomplishments, still I'd like to send a few more violent rockets into the maw of this universe. A collector recently wrote me that he was delighted to observe that I was experiencing a second youth in my latest works. There's something to that. It seems to me I've only begun to really paint this year. But what I'm experiencing is not so much a springtime as an explosion. Amazing how much dynamite there's still left in me. But dynamite is hard to burn in one of those ranges that make the most of every stick of wood.

Dear Louis, I'm often amused that we

two old libertines are at bottom so touchingly shamefaced and would rather throw our wine glasses at each other's heads than show anything of our feelings. May it remain so, old hedgehog!

Lately we had a grand party on bread and wine at that grotto near Barengo. Our singing echoed gloriously in the tall woods at midnight, the old Roman songs. We need so little for happiness when we grow older and begin freezing down at the feet: eight to ten hours' work a day, a bottle of Piedmontese, a half pound of bread, a cigar, a few girls, and of course warmth and good weather. That we have; the sun is doing its duty splendidly. My head is as tanned as a mummy's.

Some days I have the feeling that my life and work are just beginning, but sometimes it seems to me I've slaved away for eighty years and can soon lay claim to peace and rest. Everybody reaches an end some day, my Louis, and so will I, so will you. God knows what I'm writing you; it's plain that I'm not feeling well. Probably hypochondria; my eyes hurt a great deal, and sometimes a treatise that I read years ago on detachment of the retina preys on my mind.

When I look down from my balcony door, at the view you know, I realize that we have to go on working hard for a good while yet. The world is inexpressibly beautiful and various; it clangs up to me day and night through this high green door, screaming and demanding, and I run out again and again and snatch a piece of it for myself, a tiny piece. The dry summer has done great things to the greenery hereabouts; I never would have thought that I would have to resort to English red and burnt sienna again. And then the whole autumn is waiting, stubble fields, wine harvest, corn harvest, crimson forests. I'll go through all that once more, day after day, and do a few hundred more studies. But then, I feel it,

I shall be turning inward and once again, as I did for a while as a young fellow, paint entirely from memory and imagination, make poems and spin dreams. That also needs to be done.

A great Parisian painter whom a young artist asked for advice once said: "Young man, if you want to be a painter, don't forget that above all it's necessary to eat well. Second, digestion is important; make sure your bowels move regularly. And third, always keep a pretty little mistress." One would think I'd learned these rules and would scarcely ever break them. But this year, it's a curse, even in these simple matters things won't go right for me any more. I eat little and badly, often nothing but bread for whole days on end; I sometimes have stomach trouble (the most useless affliction to have, let me tell you!) and I don't have the right little mistress, but keep busy with four or five women and am just as exhausted as I am hungry. Something is wrong in the clockworks. Ever since I probed it with the needle it's been running again, but fast as the devil, and making such a damnable unfamiliar rattle as it does. How simple life is when health is good. You've never received such a long letter from me before, except perhaps at the time we were arguing about the palette. I'm going to stop; it's nearly five o'clock and the lovely light is beginning. Warm greetings from

Your
Klingsor

Postscript:

I recalled that you liked a little painting of mine, the most Chinese one I've done, with the cottage, the red path, the Veronese-green jagged trees and the distant toy town in the background. I cannot send it to you now because I don't know where you are. But it is yours—I want you to know that just in case.

Klingsor Sends His Friend
Tu Fu a Poem

(DONE IN THE DAYS HE WAS
WORKING ON HIS SELF-PORTRAIT)

Drunk, I sit at night in the wind-whipped
woods.
Autumn has gnawed at the singing
branches;
Murmuring, the tavern keeper runs to the
cellar
To fill my empty bottle of wine.

Tomorrow, tomorrow pale death will
hack
My red flesh with his ringing scythe.
I have long known that the fierce foe
Lies lurking, lies in wait for me.

To mock him I sing half the night
through,
Babble drunken song to the weary
woods;
To laugh at his menace I sing,
To scoff at his warnings I drink.

Wandering long, I have done and
suffered much,
Now at evening I sit, drink, and wait
Fearfully till the flashing scythe
Parts my head from my leaping heart.

The Self-Portrait

In the first days of September, after
many weeks of an unusually dry spell of
torrid sun, there were a few days of rain.
During this time Klingsor, in the high-
windowed salon of his palazzo in Castagnetta, painted his self-portrait, which
now hangs in Frankfurt.

This frightening, yet so magically
beautiful painting, the last of his works
to be entirely finished, came at the end of
that summer's labors, at the end of an
incredibly fervid, tempestuous period of
work, and was its crowning glory. It has
caused much comment that everyone
who knew Klingsor recognizes him immediately and infallibly in this picture,
although no portrait was ever so remote
from a naturalistic likeness.

Like all of Klingsor's later works, this
self-portrait can also be regarded from a
wide variety of viewpoints. To some,
especially those who did not know the
painter personally, the picture is above
all a symphony of colors, a marvelously
harmonized tapestry that in spite of its
brilliant hues gives a sense of tranquillity
and nobility. Others see in it a last bold
and even desperate attempt to win freedom from the object. The face is painted
like a landscape, the hair reminiscent of
leaves and the bark of trees, the eye
sockets like clefts in rock. They say that
this painting is reminiscent of nature
only as some mountain ridges remind us
of human faces, some branches of trees
remind us of hands and legs—all very
remotely, merely symbolically. But there
are many who, on the contrary, see only
the object in this work, only Klingsor's
face, analyzed and interpreted by the
artist himself with unsparing psychological insight—an enormous confession, a
ruthless, crying, moving, terrifying
peccavi. Still others, and these included
some of his bitterest opponents, see in
this portrait merely a product of and the
evidence for Klingsor's alleged madness.
They compare the head in the picture
with the naturalistic original, with photographs, and detect in the distortions and
exaggerations of the shapes negroid, de-
generate, atavistic, animal features. Some
of these critics dwell on the idolatrous
and fantastic aspects of this picture; they
see in it a kind of monomaniac self-
adoration, a blasphemous self-glorifica-
tion, a kind of religious megalomania.
All such interpretations are possible, and
many more.

During the days he was painting this

portrait Klingsor did not go out, except to drink wine at night. He ate only bread and fruit that the housekeeper brought him, went about unshaven, and with his tanned brow and deep-sunken eyes truly looked alarming. He painted seated and from memory; only now and then, and almost always during pauses in the work, would he go to the large, old-fashioned mirror on the north wall, its frame painted with climbing roses. Standing before the mirror he would stretch his head forward, open his eyes wide, and make faces.

He saw many, many faces behind the Klingsor face in the big mirror, between those silly twining roses, and he painted many faces into his picture: sweet and wondering children's faces, young manhood's brow and temples, full of dreams and ardor, scoffing drinker's eyes, lips of a thirsting, persecuted, suffering, seeking libertine, of an *enfant perdu*. But he built up the head majestically and brutally, made it into a jungle idol, a jealous, self-infatuated Jehovah, a totem to whom first-born babes and virgins might be sacrificed. Those were a few of his faces. Another was the face of the doomed and decaying man who accepted his fate: moss grew on his skull, the old teeth stood askew, cracks ran through the white skin, and scales and mold grew in the cracks. These are the features that some friends particularly love the painting for. They say: this is man, ecce homo, here is the weary, greedy, wild, childlike, and sophisticated man of our late age, dying European man who wants to die, overstrung by every longing, sick from every vice, enraptured by knowledge of his doom, ready for any kind of progress, ripe for any kind of retrogression, submitting to fate and pain like the drug addict to his poison, lonely, hollowed-out, age-old, at once Faust and Karamazov, beast and sage, wholly exposed, wholly without ambition, wholly

naked, filled with childish dread of death and filled with weary readiness to die.

And still more remotely, still deeper behind all these faces, slept remoter, deeper, older faces, prehuman, animal, vegetable, stony, as if the last man on earth in the moment before death were recalling once again with the speed of dream all the forms of past ages when the universe was young.

In those madly intense days Klingsor lived like an ecstatic. Nights, he loaded himself with wine, and then would stand, candle in his hand, before the old mirror, study his face in the glass, the woefully grinning face of the habitual drinker. One night he had a girl with him on the couch in the studio, and while he pressed her naked body against his he stared with reddened eyes over her shoulder into the mirror, saw beside her unbound hair his distorted face, full of lust and full of abhorrence of lust. He told her to come back next day, but she had become frightened and did not return.

He slept little at night. Often he awoke from dreadful dreams, his face sweaty, in savage temper and weary of life. But soon he would jump up and stare into the mirror, reading the desolate landscape of those distraught features, examining it gloomily, hatefully, or smilingly, as if gloating over its devastation. He had a dream in which he saw himself being tortured; nails were driven into his eyes, his nostrils pulled apart with hooks. And on the cover of a book that lay to hand he made a charcoal drawing of this tortured face, with the nails in the eyes. We found the strange drawing after his death. Another time, attacked by a bout of facial neuralgia, he hung writhing over the back of a chair, laughing and screaming with pain, but still holding his distorted face to the glass of the mirror, studying the twitches, ridiculing the tears.

And it was not only his face, or his

thousand faces, that he painted into this picture, not only his eyes and lips, the pained ravine of his mouth, the cleft cliffs of his forehead, his rootlike hands, his twitching fingers, the mockery of reason, the death in his eyes. In his idiosyncratic, overcrowded, concise, and jagged brush script he painted his life along with it, his love, his faith, his despair. He painted a band of naked women along with it, driven by in the raging wind like birds, slaughtered victims for the idol Klingsor, and he painted a youth with a suicide's face, also temples and woods, an old bearded god, mighty and stupid, a woman's breast split open by a dagger, butterflies with faces on their wings, and at the back of the picture, on the brink of chaos, Death, a gray ghost driving a spear small as a needle into the brain of Klingsor.

When he had painted for hours, restlessness drove him to his feet. Uneasily, unsteadily, he paced his rooms, the doors slamming behind him, pulled bottles from the cupboard, pulled books from the shelves, rugs from the tables, lay on the floor reading, leaned out of the windows, breathing deeply, rummaged for old drawings and photographs and piled floors and tables and beds and chairs in all the rooms with papers, pictures, books, letters. Everything blew about sadly when the rain-filled wind entered the windows. Among old things he found the picture of himself as a child, a photograph taken at the age of four; he was dressed in a white summer suit and under his light blond, almost white hair a sweetly defiant boy's face looked out. He found the pictures of his parents and photographs of old sweethearts of his youth. Everything occupied, excited, tensed, and tormented him, pulled him back and forth. He snatched up everything, threw the things away again, until his arm twitched once more and he bent

over his wooden panel and went on painting. Deeper and deeper he drew the furrows through the clefts of his portrait, broadened the temple of his life, more and more forcefully addressed the eternity of all existences, louder and louder bemoaned his transitoriness, gave sweeter touches to his smiling likeness, more scornfully mocked his condemnation to decay. Then he sprang to his feet again, a hunted stag, and tramped the prisoner's walk through his rooms. Gladness flashed through him, and the deep delight of creation, like a drenching joyous rainstorm, until pain threw him to the floor again and smashed the shards of his life and his art into his face. He prayed before his picture and spat at it. He was insane, as every creator is insane. But with the infallible prudence of a sleepwalker, in the insanity of creativity he did everything that furthered his work. He sensed with a deep faith that in this cruel struggle with his self-portrait more than the fate and the final accounting of an individual was involved, that he was doing something human, universal, necessary. He felt that he was once again confronting a task, a destiny, and that all the preceding anxiety and his efforts to escape and all the tumult and frenzy had been merely dread of his task and attempts to escape it. Now there was neither dread nor escape, nothing but pushing on, cut and slash, victory and defeat. He conquered and was defeated, he suffered and laughed and fought his way through, killed and died, gave birth and was born.

A French painter paid a call on him. The housekeeper led the visitor into the disorder and filth of an overcrowded room. Klingsor came out of the studio, paint on his sleeves, paint on his face, gray, unshaven. He loped with long strides across the room. The stranger brought him regards from Paris and

Geneva, expressed his deep respect. Klingsor walked back and forth, seemed not to be listening. Abashed, the guest fell silent and began to take his leave. Then Klingsor went up to him, placed his paint-stained hand on his shoulder, and looked deep into his eyes. "Thank you," he said slowly, with effort. "Thank you, dear friend. I'm working, I can't talk. People always talk too much. Don't be angry, and give my friends my regards.

Tell them I love them." And he vanished again into the other room.

At the end of that scourged day he placed the finished painting in the unused empty kitchen and locked the door. He never showed it to anyone. Then he took Veronal and slept through a whole day and night. Then he washed, shaved, put on clean clothes, rode into town, and bought fruit and cigarettes to give to Gina.

A CHILD'S HEART

By HERMANN HESSE

Translated by Richard and Clara Winston

Sometimes we act, go in and out, do this and that, and everything is easy, casual, and unforced; seemingly it could all be done differently. And sometimes, other times, nothing could be done differently, nothing is unforced and easy, and every breath we take is controlled by some outside power and heavy with fate.

What we call the good deeds of our lives, the ones we find easy to tell about, are almost all of that first, "easy" kind, and we easily forget them. Other acts, which we find hard to talk about, we never forget; they seem to be more ours than the others, and they cast long shadows over all the days of our lives.

Our father's house stood tall and bright on a sunlit street. You entered it through a high gate and at once found yourself embraced by coolness, dusk, and stony moist air. A high dark hall silently received you; the red sandstone squares of the flooring led at a slight incline to the stairs, which lay far at the rear, in semidarkness. Many thousands of times I entered through that high gate, and never did I pay attention to gate and hallway, stone flooring and stairs. For these were always merely a passage into another world, "our" world. The hall smelled of stone; it was dusky and high. At the rear of it, the stairs led up out of the dim coolness into light and bright coziness. But the hall and the somber duskiness always came first. There was something of Father about it, something of dignity and power, something of punishment and guilty conscience. A thousand times I passed through, laughing. But sometimes I stepped inside and at once felt crushed and reduced, afraid, and I hurried to the liberating stairs.

One day when I was eleven years old I came home from school. It was one of those days when fate lurks in the corners, when something can easily happen. On such days every failing and disturbance in our own souls seems to be reflected in our surroundings, distorting them. Uneasiness and anxiety grip our hearts, and we seek and find their presumed cause outside us. We see the world as ill arranged and are met by obstacles everywhere.

That was how it was on that day. From early morning on, I was dogged by a sense of guilty conscience. Who knows what its source was—perhaps dreams of the night. For I had done nothing particularly bad. That morning my father's face had worn a suffering and reproachful expression. The breakfast milk had been lukewarm and insipid. Although I had not run into any trouble at school, everything had once more felt dreary, lifeless, and discouraging; everything had combined to form that already familiar feeling of helplessness and despair which tells us that time is endless, that eternally and forever we shall be small and powerless and remain under the rule of this stupid, stinking school, for years and years, and that this whole life is senseless and loathsome.

I had also been vexed by my best friend on that day. Lately I had struck up a friendship with Oskar Weber, the son of a locomotive engineer, without really knowing what drew me to him. He had recently boasted that his father earned seven marks a day, and I had answered at random that my father earned fourteen. He had let that impress him without argument, and that had been the beginning of the thing. Before the week was out I formed a league with Weber. We set up a joint savings account to be used later to buy a pistol. The pistol was displayed in a hardware shop's window, a massive weapon with two blued steel barrels. And Weber had calculated that we only had to save hard for a while and we would be able to buy it. Money was easy to come by; he was often given ten pfennig for errands, or picked up a tip here and there, and sometimes you found money on the street, or things worth money, like horseshoes, pieces of lead, and other things that could be easily sold. Moreover, he promptly contributed a ten-pfennig piece for our savings, and that convinced me and made our whole plan seem both feasible and hopeful.

As I entered the hall of our house that noon and in the cool, cellarlike air felt dark admonishments of a thousand bothersome and hateful things and systems wafting into my face, my thoughts were preoccupied with Oskar Weber. I felt that I did not love him, although I rather liked his good-natured face, which reminded me of a washerwoman's. What attracted me to him was not himself but something else—I might say, his class. It was something that he shared with al-

most all boys of his type and origins: a kind of cheeky facility with life, a thick skin that protected him from danger and humiliation, a familiarity with the small, practical affairs of life, with money, stores and workshops, with goods and prices, with kitchens and laundries and things of that sort. Boys like Weber, who seemed impervious to the blows dealt out in school, who were kindred to and friendly with hired hands, draymen, and factory girls, stood differently and more securely in the world than I did. They knew how much their fathers earned in a day and undoubtedly knew many other things about which I was wholly inexperienced. They laughed at expressions and jokes that I did not understand. Altogether, they could laugh in a way that was closed to me, in a filthy and coarse but undeniably grownup and "manly" way. It did not help that I was smarter than they and knew more in school. It did not help that I was better dressed, combed, and washed. On the contrary, these very differences were to their credit. It seemed to me that boys like Weber could enter without trouble into the "world," as it appeared to me in a nimbus of strangeness and glamour, while the "world" was so utterly closed to me that I would have to conquer each of its gates by a wearisome, endless process of growing older, sitting in school, examinations, and upbringing. It was only natural that such boys also found horseshoes, money, and pieces of lead in the street, that they were paid for errands, received all sorts of gifts in shops, and thrived in every possible way.

I felt obscurely that my friendship with Weber and his savings was nothing but a wild longing for that "world." There was nothing lovable about Weber but his great secret, by virtue of which he stood closer to adults than I did and lived in a more naked, less veiled, more robust world than I did with my dreams and wishes. And I sensed beforehand that he would disappoint me, that I would not be able to wrest from him his secret and the magic key to life.

He had just left me and I knew he was now on his way home, thickset and smug, whistling and cheerful, troubled by no longings, no forebodings. When he met the housemaids and factory girls and saw them leading their mysterious, perhaps wonderful, perhaps criminal life, it was no mystery to him, no vast secret, no danger; it was nothing wild and exciting, but as natural, familiar, and homelike as water is to a duck. That was how it was. And I, for my part, would always stand outside, alone and uncertain, full of intimations but without certainty.

Altogether, on that day life once again tasted hopelessly pallid. The day had some of the quality of a Monday, although it was a Saturday. It smelled of Monday, three times as long and three times as dreary as the other days. Life was damned and disgusting, horrid and full of falsehood. The grownups acted as if the world were perfect and as if they themselves were demigods, we children nothing but scum. These teachers . . . ! I felt striving and ambition within myself; I made sincere and passionate efforts to be good, whether in learning the Greek irregular verbs or in keeping my clothes clean. I struggled to achieve obedience to my parents or silent stoicism before all pain and humiliation. Again and again I rose up, ardent and devout, prepared to dedicate myself to God and to tread the ideal, pure, noble path toward the heights, to practice virtue, to suffer evil silently, to help others. And alas, again and again it remained only a beginning, an attempt, a brief fluttering flight! Again and again, after a few days, even after a few hours, something happened that should not have been allowed, something wretched, depressing, and shaming. Again and again,

in the midst of the noblest and staunchest decisions and vows, I fell abruptly, inescapably, into sin and wickedness, into ordinary bad habits. Why was it this way? Why could I recognize so clearly the beauty and rightness of good intentions, could feel them so deeply within my heart, when all of life (including the adults) reeked everlastingly of ordinariness and everything was so arranged that shabbiness and vulgarity triumphed? How could it be that in the morning, on my knees at my bedside, or at night before lighted candles, I could pledge myself to goodness and the light, could appeal to God and renounce all sin forever and ever—only to commit, perhaps but a few hours later, the most wretched betrayals of this same solemn oath and sincerest resolution, if only by chiming in with tempting laughter, or by lending an ear to a stupid schoolboy joke? Why was that so? Was it different for others? Had heroes, the Romans and Greeks, the knights, the first Christians—had all these others been different from myself, better, more perfect, without bad impulses, equipped with some organ that I lacked, which prevented them from forever falling back from heaven into everyday life, from the sublime into inadequacy and wretchedness? Was original sin unknown to heroes and saints? Was holiness and nobility possible only for a few rare, elect souls? But why, if I were not one of the elect, why was this impulse toward beauty and nobility innate in me? Why did I have this wild, painful longing for purity, goodness, and virtue? Was I being made mock of? Could it possibly be, in God's world, that a person, a boy, would simultaneously have all the sublime and all the evil impulses within himself and be forced to suffer and despair, to cut an unhappy and ridiculous figure, for the amusement of God as he looked on? Could that be so? Rather, wasn't—yes, wasn't the whole world a joke of the devil that ought to be spewed out? If that were so, then was not God a monster, insane, a stupid, horrible prankster? . . . And even as I had this thought, with a faint savor of voluptuous delight in rebellion, my fearful heart punished me for the blasphemy by pounding furiously!

How clearly I see, after thirty years, that stairwell with the tall opaque windows giving on the wall of the house next door and casting so little light, with the white-scoured pine steps and risers and the smooth wooden banister polished from my innumerable sliding descents. Distant as my childhood is, and incomprehensible and fabulous though it seems to me on the whole, I still sharply remember all the suffering and doubts I felt at the time, in the midst of happiness. All those reelings existed in the child's heart, where they have been ever since: doubt of my own worth, vacillation between self-esteem and discouragement, between idealistic contempt for the world and ordinary sensuality. And just as I did then, I later continued to regard these aspects of my nature sometimes as a miserable morbidity, sometimes as a distinction. At times I believed that God wished to lead me on this painful path to a special isolation and deepening of my nature, at other times I took it all as nothing but the signs of shabby weakness of character, of a neurosis such as thousands of people bear wearisomely through their lives.

If I were to reduce all my feelings and their painful conflicts to a single name, I can think of no other word but: dread. It was dread, dread and uncertainty, that I felt in all those hours of shattered childhood felicity: dread of punishment, dread of my own conscience, dread of stirrings in my soul which I considered forbidden and criminal.

At that hour I have been speaking of, this sense of dread once again struck me as I drew nearer to the glass door at the top of the stairs, where the light grew brighter and brighter. The feeling began with a tightness in my stomach that rose to my throat and there became a choking or gagging sensation. Along with this at such moments, and now also, I felt a painful sense of embarrassment, a distrust of all observers, an urge to be alone and to hide.

With this repulsive feeling, truly the feeling of a criminal, I entered the hall and then the living room. I sensed that the devil was afoot today, that something was going to happen. I sensed it as the barometer senses a change in the pressure of the air, with utterly helpless passivity. Ah, here it was again, the inexpressible horror. The demon was skulking through the house. Original sin gnawed at my heart. Vast and invisible, a ghost stood behind every wall, a father and judge.

As yet I knew nothing. It was all mere foreboding, a gnawing, anticipatory uneasiness. In such situations it was often best to fall ill, to throw up and go to bed. Then the dangerous time sometimes passed harmlessly; Mother or Sister came in, I would be given tea and felt surrounded by loving solicitude. I could cry or sleep, and afterwards waken sound and cheerful in a wholly transformed, relaxed, and bright world.

My mother was not in the living room, and only the maid was in the kitchen. I decided to go up to Father's study at the top of a narrow flight of stairs. Although I was also afraid of him, it was sometimes good to turn to him whom I had to ask forgiveness for so many things. With Mother it was easier and simpler to find comfort; but Father's comfort was more valuable. It meant peace with the judging conscience, reconciliation and a new covenant with the good powers. After nasty scenes, interrogations, confessions, and punishments I had often emerged good and pure from Father's room, punished and reproved, to be sure, but full of fresh resolutions, strengthened by the pact with power against the evil enemy. I decided to visit Father and tell him that I was feeling ill.

And so I climbed the short flight of stairs that led to the study. These stairs, with their own special wallpaper smell and the dry sound of the light, hollow wooden treads, were infinitely more fraught with significance and fatefulness than even the entrance hall. Many important causes had led me up these steps; a hundred times I had dragged dread and a tormented conscience up them, or defiance and wild anger, and quite often I had returned down them with absolution and new security. In the dwelling below, mother and child were at home; the atmosphere was mild there. Up here power and spirit dwelt; up here were the courthouse and temple and the "realm of the father."

Rather timidly, as always, I pressed down the old-fashioned latch and opened the door halfway. The smell of the paternal study flowed toward me, the familiar smell of books and ink, attenuated by blue air from half-open windows, by white, clean curtains, a faint dash of cologne water, and an apple on the desk. But the room was empty.

With a sensation half of disappointment and half of relief, I entered. I checked my thumping footsteps, walked on tiptoe, as we often had to up here when Father was napping or had a headache. And as soon as I became aware of how quietly I was moving, my heart began to pound and I again felt, intensified, the anxious pressure in my stomach and my throat. I moved on, skulking and frightened, took a step and another step, and already I had ceased to be a harmless visitor and petitioner and had become an intruder. More than once I had secretly crept into Father's two rooms during his

absence, had explored his secret realm, and twice I had filched something from it.

The memory of these thefts came at once and filled me, and I knew at once that disaster was upon me. Now something was going to happen, now I was doing something forbidden and evil. I had no thought of flight! Rather, I did think of it, thought fervently and longingly of running away, down the stairs and into my own room or into the garden —but I knew that I was not going to, that I could not. How I wished that my father might stir in the adjacent room and come in and break the terrible spell that held me in its grip. If only he would come! If only he could come, scolding for all I cared, but come before it was too late!

I coughed to announce my presence, and when there was no answer I called softly: "Papa!" All remained still; the many books on the walls gave no answer. A pane of the casement window moved in the wind, casting a glint of sunlight on the floor. No one redeemed me, and inside myself I had no freedom to do anything but the demon's bidding. A feeling of criminality contracted my stomach and made my fingertips cold; my heart fluttered with dread. As yet I had no idea what I would do. I knew only that it would be something naughty.

Now I was at the desk. I picked up a book and read a title in English which I did not understand. I hated English—my father always spoke it with Mother when we children were not supposed to understand, and also when they were quarreling. In a bowl lay all sorts of small objects, toothpicks, pen points, tacks. I took two of the pen points and pocketed them. God knows why; I did not need them, had no lack of pens. I did it only to obey the compulsion that was almost choking me, the compulsion to do something bad, to harm myself, to load myself with guilt. I leafed through my father's papers, saw a letter he had begun, read the words, "We and the children are very well, thank God," and the Latin letters of his handwriting looked at me like so many eyes.

Then I stole softly into the bedroom. There stood Father's iron army bed, his brown house slippers under it, a handkerchief on the night table. I inhaled the paternal air in the cool, bright room, and the image of my father rose plainly before my eyes, while reverence and rebellion contested in my overladen heart. For moments I hated him, remembering with spite and malice how he sometimes, on headache days, lay still and flat on his low cot, stretched out at great length, a wet towel on his forehead, sometimes sighing. Certainly I had an inkling that he too, for all his power, had no easy life; that he, of whom I stood in such awe, also experienced timidity and doubts of himself. In a moment my strange hatred evaporated and was followed by pity and sentiment. But in the meanwhile I had opened one of the drawers of his chest. There his linens lay in neat layers, and a bottle of cologne water, which he was fond of. I wanted to sniff it, but the bottle was still unopened and firmly capped; I put it back. Next to it I found a small round box of lozenges which had a licorice taste. I popped a few of them into my mouth. A sense of disappointment overcame me, and at the same time I was glad not to have found and taken anything more.

Already renouncing and preparing to leave, I playfully pulled at one more drawer, my heart somewhat lightened, so that I could promise myself to replace the two stolen pen points. Perhaps a return to grace was possible. Perhaps all could be made good again and I would be saved. God's hand above me might be stronger than all temptation. . . .

I peeped into the crack of the barely opened drawer. Oh, if only socks or shirts or old newspapers had been in it. But there was the temptation, and instantly the tension and the spell of fear returned; my hands trembled and my heart pounded madly. I was looking into a wicker basket, of Indian or some other exotic origin, and there I saw something surprising, alluring: a whole round of pale, sugar-coated dried figs!

I picked it up. It was wonderfully heavy. Then I took two or three figs, put one into my mouth, the others in my pocket. All my fear and excitement had in the end not been in vain. I could no longer leave here feeling redeemed and assuaged; so at least I did not want to leave empty-handed. I took another two or three figs from the ring, which was scarcely lightened, and then a few more, and when my pockets were filled and more than half the round had disappeared, I arranged the remaining figs more loosely on the somewhat sticky rope so that fewer seemed to be missing. Then, in sudden panic, I banged the drawer shut and ran away, through both rooms, down the small staircase and into my room, where I stood still, leaning against my little desk, my knees weak and my lungs gasping for breath.

Soon afterwards our dinner bell rang. With my head empty, filled with depression and disgust, I stuffed the figs into my bookshelf, hiding them behind books, and went to table. At the dining-room door I noticed that my hands were sticky. I washed them in the kitchen. In the dining room I found everyone already at table. I quickly said Good day, Father said grace, and I bent over my soup. I was not hungry; every spoonful was hard to swallow. And beside me sat my sisters, my parents opposite me, all of them bright and cheerful and honorable. I alone, the only criminal, sat wretchedly among them, alone and unworthy, fearing every friendly look, the taste of the figs still in my mouth. Had I closed the bedroom door upstairs? And the drawer?

Now the misery was upon me. I would have let my hand be chopped off if that could have restored my figs to the drawer. I decided to throw the figs away, to take them to school and give them away. If only I were rid of them, if only I never had to see them again!

"You're not looking well today," my father said across the table. I stared at my plate, feeling his eyes on my face. Now he would see it. He saw everything, always. Why was he torturing me beforehand? He might as well lead me away right then and there and beat me to death for all I cared.

"Is something the matter with you?" I heard his voice again. I lied; I said I had a headache.

"You must lie down for a little after eating," he said. "How many more hours of school do you have this afternoon?"

"Only gym."

"Well, gym will do you no harm. But eat something; force yourself a little. It will pass."

I squinted across the table. My mother said nothing, but I knew that she was looking at me. I ate my soup, fought with the meat and vegetables, poured myself two glasses of water. Nothing more happened. I was left alone. When my father spoke the closing grace at the end of the meal, "Lord, we thank thee, for thou art kindly and thy goodness lasteth eternally," something severed me from the bright, holy, confident words and from all who sat at table with me. My folding my hands was a lie, my pious posture a blasphemy.

When I stood up, Mother brushed her hand over my hair and let her palm rest on my forehead for a moment to see whether it was hot. How bitter all that was!

In my room I stood before the bookshelf. The morning had not deceived me; all the signs had been correct. This had become a day of misfortune, the worst I had ever experienced; no human being could endure anything worse. If anything worse ever came upon a person, he would have to take his life. Poison was the best way, or hanging. It was better anyhow to be dead than alive. Everything was so wrong and ugly. I stood there thinking these thoughts, and abstractedly reached out for one of the hidden figs and ate it, and then several more, without really knowing that I was doing it.

I noticed our savings bank, standing on the shelf beneath the books. It was a cigar box that I had nailed closed. With my penknife I had nicked out a crude slit in the lid for the coins. The slit was crudely cut; splinters of wood bristled from it. Even that I could not do properly. I had playmates who could do that sort of thing laboriously and patiently and properly, so that it looked like a cabinetmaker's work. But I always botched such things; I was in a hurry and never finished anything neatly. I was like that with my woodworking, like that with my handwriting and my drawing, like that with my butterfly collection and everything. I was hopeless. And now I stood here and had stolen again, worse than ever before. I still had the pen points in my pocket. What for? Why had I taken them—been compelled to take them? Why did I have to do something I did not want to do at all?

A single coin rattled in the cigar box, Oskar Weber's ten-pfennig piece. Since then nothing had been added. This savings-bank business was another one of my typical undertakings! Everything came to nothing, everything went wrong; whatever I began bogged down at the start. The devil take this idiotic savings bank! I wanted to have nothing more to do with it.

This period between lunch and the afternoon session of school was always wretched and hard to get through on days like today. On good days, on peaceful, sensible, pleasant days, these two hours were lovely and longed for. Then I would either read an Indian book in my room or run back to the schoolyard immediately after eating. There I would always find a few enterprising classmates and we would play, shouting and running and getting hot, until the ringing of the bell called us back to a completely forgotten "reality." But on days like today I did not want to play with anyone, and how could I silence the devil in my heart? I saw what was coming—not yet, not today, but soon, perhaps the next time. One day my fate would descend fully upon me. All that was lacking was a trifle, a mere trifle more of dread and suffering and perplexity, and then it would overflow, then all would end in horror. One day, on just such a day as today, I would be wholly drowned in evil; in defiance and rage and because of the senseless unbearableness of this life I would do something ghastly and decisive, something ghastly but liberating which would forever make an end of the dread and torment. I did not know what it would be; but fantasies and preliminary obsessions about it had more than once run confusingly through my head, notions of crimes with which I would take revenge upon the world and at the same time abandon and destroy myself. Sometimes I thought I would set fire to our house. I saw monstrous flames beating their wings into the night, consuming houses and streets; the whole city would flare gigantically against the black sky. Or at other times the crime was revenge against my father, murder, a cruel killing. But I would then behave like that criminal, that one real criminal, whom I had once seen being led through the streets of our town. It was a burglar who had been caught and was being led to court, handcuffed, a stiff bowler askew on his head, a policeman in front of him

and behind him. This man who was being driven through the streets and through a huge crowd who shouted a thousand curses, nasty jokes, and malignant wishes at him, this man in no way resembled those timorous wretches I sometimes saw being accompanied across the street by a patrolman. Most of them were only poor journeymen who had been caught begging. But this man was no journeyman and did not look foolish, timid, and weepy, nor was he taking refuge in a sheepish stupid grin, such as I had also seen. This man was a real criminal and wore his somewhat crushed hat boldly on a defiant and unbowed head. He was pale and smiling with quiet contempt; alongside such a man the populace reviling him became a rabble. At the time I myself had shouted with the rest, "They've caught him, he ought to be hanged!" But then I saw his upright, proud posture, the way he held his fettered hands in front of him, and the way he wore that bowler hat like a fantastic crown on his head, and the way he smiled—and I fell silent. But I too would smile like this criminal and hold my head stiffly when they led me into court and to the scaffold and when all the people around me crowded forward and shouted insults—I would say neither yes nor no but would simply hold my tongue and despise them.

And when I had been executed and was dead and came before the eternal Judge in heaven, I would by no means bow down and submit. Oh no, not though all the choirs of angels were gathered around him and he radiated pure holiness and dignity. Let him damn me, let him have me boiled in pitch! I would not apologize and not humble myself, would not beg his forgiveness, would not repent! If he asked me: "Did you do such and such?" I would cry out, "Yes, I did it, and more, and I was right to have done it and if I can I will do it again and

again. I killed, I set fire to houses, because I enjoyed it and because I wanted
to mock and anger you. Because I hate
you and I spit at your feet, God. You
have plagued me and hurt me, you have
made laws nobody can keep, you have
set grownups to make life a hell for us
boys."

Whenever I was able to imagine this
scene with sufficient vividness, so that I
felt I would really act and speak along
these lines, I felt for moments gloomily
good. But then came doubts. Would I not
weaken, would I not quail, would I not
give in after all? Or if I carried through
as I was determined to do—would not
God find a way out, some superior de-
ception such as the grownups and the
powerful always contrived, producing
one more trump card at the last moment,
shaming me after all, not taking me seriously, humiliating me under the damnable mask of kindliness? Ah yes, of
course it would end like that.

My fantasies eddied back and forth, let
me win one time, let God win another
time, raised me up to a dauntless criminal and dragged me down again to a
child and a weakling.

I stood at the window looking down at
the small back yard of the house next
door, where poles for staging were leaning against the wall and a few beds of
vegetables were sprouting green in a tiny
garden. Suddenly, in the afternoon stillness, I heard the clang of bells intruding
firmly and somberly upon my visions:
one clear, stern stroke for the hour, and
then another. It was two o'clock, and I
started out of my anxious daydreams and
back to reality. Now our gym hour was
beginning, and even if I had rushed off to
the gymnasium on magic wings I would
still have been late. More bad luck! Day
after tomorrow I would be called up,
scolded, punished. I might as well not go
at all; there was no way to rectify things
now. Perhaps if I had a very good, very

subtle and believable excuse—but at the
moment none occurred to me, brilliantly
though our teachers had educated me in
lying. Right now I was incapable of lying, inventing, constructing a story. It
was better to stay away from school
entirely. What did it matter if a small sin
were added to the great one!

But the striking of the hour had roused
me and numbed my fantasies. I felt suddenly very weak. My room glared at me
with intense reality; desk, pictures, bed,
books, were all charged with austere con-
creteness, all a summons from the world
in which I had to live and which today
had once more shown itself hostile and
dangerous. Hadn't it? Had I not missed
my gym class? And had I not stolen,
wretchedly stolen, and weren't those
damnable figs lying on the bookshelf,
those I had not already devoured, that is?
What did I care now about the criminal,
God, and the Last Judgment! That would
all come along in its own good time—but
now, right at the moment, it was far
away and was silly nonsense, nothing
more. I had stolen and any moment the
crime might be discovered. Perhaps it already had been, perhaps my father upstairs had already opened that drawer
and was confronting my crime, offended
and angered, considering the best way to
bring me to trial. He might even be on
his way down to my room already, and if
I did not flee immediately, in another
minute I would have his grave, bespec-
tacled face before me. For of course he
knew at once that I was the thief. There
were no criminals in our house aside
from me; my sisters never did anything
bad. God knows why. But then why did
my father have to keep such fig rings
hidden in his chest of drawers?

I had already left my room and made
off through the back door and the garden. The meadows and gardens lay in
bright sunlight. Sulphur butterflies flew
across the path. Everything looked

[356]

threatening now, far worse than this morning. Oh, how well I knew this feeling, and yet I thought I had never felt it so painfully before. It was as if everything were looking at me with such matter-of-factness and such untroubled conscience, the town and the church tower, the fields and the path, the flowering grass and the butterflies, and as if everything pretty and pleasurable, everything that usually gave me delight, were now alien and under an evil spell. I was familiar with that, I knew the savor of it, when I ran along through the familiar neighborhood with pangs of conscience. Now the rarest butterfly could flutter across the meadow and alight at my feet—it was nothing, gave no pleasure, did not tempt me, did not comfort me. Now the loveliest cherry tree could offer me its fullest branch—it had no value, there was no joy in it. Now there was nothing to do but flee, from Father, from punishment, from myself, from my conscience, to flee on and on until, inexorably and inescapably, everything that had to come would come anyhow.

I trotted along restlessly, I trudged uphill toward the woods and down from Oak Hill to the mill, across the footbridge and uphill again on the other side, and on through the woods. Here we had had our last Indian camp. Here, last year, when Father was away traveling, our mother had celebrated Easter with us children, hiding the eggs for us in the shrubbery and the moss. During the summer holidays I had once built a castle here with my cousins; it was still partly standing. Everywhere were vestiges of former times, everywhere mirrors out of which a child looked at me who was different from the child I was today. Had I been all those others? So gay, so contented, so grateful, so comradely, so affectionate toward Mother, so untouched by anxiety, so incomprehensibly happy? Had that been me? And how

could I have become what I now was, so utterly different, so wicked, so full of dread, so distraught? Everything was the same as always, the woods and the river, the fern and the flowers, the castle and the anthill, and yet everything was poisoned, shattered. Was there no way back to happiness and innocence? Would what had been never be again? Would I ever again laugh like that, play with my sisters like that, hunt for Easter eggs like that?

I ran and ran, my forehead sweaty, and behind me my guilt ran and with it, huge and fearsome, ran the shadow of my father in hot pursuit.

Lanes ran past me; the margins of the woods dropped away. I came to a halt on top of a hill, cut away from the path, threw myself into the grass, my heart pounding; that might be from running uphill, might stop if I rested. Below me I saw the town and the river, saw the gym where the class was now over and the boys were dashing off in all directions. I saw the long roof of our house. There was my father's bedroom and the drawer from which the figs were missing. There was my small room. There, when I returned, judgment would strike me. But suppose I did not return?

I knew I would. I always went back, every time. That was how it always ended. It was impossible to get away, impossible to flee to Africa or Berlin. I was small, had no money, and nobody would help me. Oh yes, if all children would unite and help one another! They were many; there were more children than parents. But not all children were thieves and criminals. Few were like me. Perhaps I was the only one. But no, I knew that such cases as mine were commoner than that—an uncle of mine had also stolen as a child and had done many bad things which I knew about from eavesdropping on my parents' conversation. That was how I learned everything worth knowing, secretly, by overhearing.

But none of that helped me in the least, and even if that same uncle were here now, he would not help me. He had long since grown up; he was a pastor and would side with the grownups and leave me to my fate. They were all like that. Toward us children they were all somehow liars and swindlers; they played a part, pretended to be different from what they were. Perhaps not Mother, or she less than others.

But suppose I didn't go back home? After all, something could happen to me; I could break my neck or drown or fall under the train. Then everything would be different. Then they would carry me home and everyone would be quiet and frightened and crying; they would all feel sorry for me and nothing would ever be said about the figs.

I knew quite well that it was possible for a person to take his own life. I also thought that some day I would probably do it, later, when everything turned out altogether bad. It would have been good to be sick, but not just with a cough. Really deathly ill, the way I had been the time I had scarlet fever.

Meanwhile it was long past gym class, and also long past the time I was expected home for coffee. Perhaps they were calling and looking for me now, in my room, in the garden and yard, in the basement. But if Father had already discovered the theft, there would be no more searching, for then he would know why I was gone.

I could not go on just lying here. Fate was not forgetting me; it was right at my heels. I began running again. I passed a bench along one of the paths. Another memory was attached to that, a memory that had once been lovely and now burned like fire. My father had given me a penknife. We had gone walking together, in good spirits and at peace, and he had sat down on this bench while I

went into the bushes to cut myself a long hazel switch. And then, in my excitement, I broke the blade of the new knife close to the shaft, and came back to him horrified. At first I wanted to conceal it, but he promptly asked me about the knife. I was terribly unhappy, because of the knife and because I expected a scolding. But then my father had only smiled, touched my shoulder lightly, and said: "What a pity, poor boy." How I had loved him then; how I had inwardly begged his forgiveness for so many things. And now, thinking of my father's expression at that time, of his voice and his sympathy—what a monster I was for having so often saddened and lied to a father like that, and today stolen from him!

When I reached the town again, near the upper bridge and far from our house, twilight was already falling. Lights were already lit in the shop windows. A boy came running out of a shop, stopped abruptly, and called my name. It was Oskar Weber. The last person I wanted to see. Still, I learned from him that the teacher had not noticed my absence from gym class. But where had I been?

"Oh, nowhere," I said. "I wasn't feeling well."

I was taciturn and unfriendly, and after a while, which seemed to me outrageously long, he realized that I wanted to be rid of him. Then he turned nasty.

"Let me alone," I said coldly. "I can go home by myself."

"Really?" he snapped. "I can just as well walk by myself as you, dumbbell! I'm not your poodle, if you want to know. But first what about our savings bank? I put a tenner in it and you haven't put in anything."

"You can have your tenner back today if you're worried about it. I wish I never had to see you again. Do you think I'd take anything from you!"

"You were glad enough to take it not so long ago," he sneered, though he still left open a crack for reconciliation.

But I was hot and angry. All my accumulated fear and helplessness erupted in sheer rage. Weber had nothing to complain about! I was in the right; I had a clear conscience toward him. And I needed someone to make me feel proud and in the right by contrast. All the chaos and bleakness inside me poured furiously into this channel. I did what I ordinarily was careful not to: I put on the gentleman's son, indicated that it was no loss to me to give up friendship with a street urchin. I told him there would be no more of his eating berries in our garden and playing with my toys. I felt myself coming to life again in red-hot fury. I had an enemy, one who was to blame, one I could come to grips with. All my vital impulses gathered together into this releasing, welcome, liberating fury, into fierce delight in hating the foe who this time was not within myself, who stood facing me, staring at me with eyes at first alarmed, then angry, whose voice I heard, whose recriminations I despised, whose abusive language I could top.

Side by side, in a swelling altercation, we walked down the darkening street. Here and there someone glanced out of a door at us. And all the rage and contempt I felt toward myself poured out upon the unfortunate Weber. When he began to threaten that he would tell on me to the gym teacher, I felt rapturous. He was putting himself in the wrong, showing meanness, strengthening me.

When we began fighting in the street, a few people stood still and watched us. We hit each other in stomach and face and kicked each other. For those few moments I had forgotten everything. I was in the right, was not a criminal; the thrill of combat seized me, and although Weber was the stronger, I was more agile,

smarter, faster, and more furious. We grew hot and swung fiercely. When he desperately grabbed and tore my shirt collar, I felt with ecstasy the stream of cold air pouring over my burning skin.

And while we punched, kicked, tore, wrestled, and choked, we did not for a moment stop berating, insulting, and annihilating each other in words, words that grew steadily hotter, more foolish and malicious, more inventive and fantastic. And I was his superior in that, too; I was more malicious and inventive. If he said *louse,* I said *rat.* If he said *bastard,* I shouted *devil.* Both of us were bleeding without feeling a thing, and at the same time our curses and abuse mounted; we threatened each other with the gallows, wished we had knives to drive in each other's ribs and twist; each defiled the other's name, descent, and father.

That was the first and only time I fought such a fight to the end in the full fever of battle, with all the blows, all the cruelties, all the vituperation. I had often watched fights and listened with shuddering pleasure to the vulgar swearwords. Now I myself was shouting them as if I had been accustomed to them from the time I was small and had often practiced using them. Tears ran from my eyes and blood over my mouth. But the world was glorious; it had meaning; it was good to live, good to hit out, good to bleed and make another bleed.

In memory I could never afterward recall how this fight ended. At some point it was over; at some point I stood alone in the quiet darkness, recognized street corners and houses, was close to our own house. Slowly, the intoxication subsided; slowly the thunder and roar of wings ceased, and reality penetrated bit by bit to my senses, first of all to my eyes. There was the fountain. The bridge. Blood on my hand, torn clothes, stockings that had slipped down, pain in my knee, pain in my eye, cap gone—everything came to me gradually, became reality, registered. Suddenly I was exhausted. I felt my legs and arms trembling, groped for the wall of a building.

And there was our house. Thank God! All I knew in this world right now was that there was refuge, peace, light, shelter. With a sigh of relief I pushed back the high gate.

Then, with the smell of stone and damp coolness, recollection suddenly poured over me, multiplied a hundredfold. Oh God! That was the smell of sternness, of law, of responsibility. Of Father and God. I had stolen. I was not a wounded hero returning home from the fray. I was not a poor child finding his way home to be bedded down by his mother with warmth and sympathy. I was a thief, a criminal. Up those stairs was no refuge, bed, and sleep for me, no food and tender care, no comfort and forgetfulness. What awaited me was guilt and judgment.

That evening, in the dusky hallway and stairwell, whose many steps I climbed with an effort, I think I breathed in for the first time in my life the cold of empty space, solitude, fate. I saw no way out, I had no plans, not even fear, nothing but that cold, harsh feeling: "It must be so." Clinging to the banister, I drew myself up the stairs. At the glass door I felt tempted to sit down on the step for one moment, to catch my breath. I did not do it; there was no point. I had to go in. As I opened the door, it suddenly occurred to me to wonder how late it was.

I entered the dining room. There they sat around the table and had just finished eating; a plate of apples was still on the table. It was nearly eight o'clock. I had never come home so late without permission, never been absent for supper.

"Thank God, here you are!" my mother exclaimed. I saw that she had been anxious about me. She ran toward me, then stopped in alarm when she saw my face and my dirtied, torn clothing. I said nothing and looked at no one, but I distinctly felt Father and Mother communicating with one another by looks. My father controlled himself; but although he said nothing I felt how angry he was. Mother took care of me. My face and hands were washed, bandages plastered on my cuts; then I was given supper. Sympathy and solicitude surrounded me. I sat quietly, deeply ashamed, feeling the warmth and enjoying it with a guilty conscience. Then I was sent to bed. I shook hands with Father without looking at him.

After I was in bed, Mother came in to me once more. She took my clothes from the chair and put others there for me, since tomorrow was Sunday. Then she began cautiously asking questions, and I had to tell her about my fight. She thought it bad but did not scold and seemed a little astonished that I was so depressed and timid about it. Then she left.

Now, I thought, she is convinced that everything is all right. I had quarreled and fought and been bloodied, but by tomorrow that would all be forgotten. She did not know about the other thing, the thing that mattered. She had been disturbed, but affectionate and unconstrained. This meant that Father, too, probably knew nothing yet.

And now a terrible sense of disappointment overcame me. I realized that from the moment I had entered the house I had been filled with one intense, consuming desire. I had thought, wished, longed for nothing but that the thunderstorm would crash down upon me at once, that the judgment would descend, that the terror would become a reality and my frightful fear of it cease. I was prepared for anything, could have withstood anything. I wanted to be punished, beaten, locked up. I wanted Father to make me go hungry. I wanted him to curse and reject me. If only the dread and the suspense would end!

Instead, here I lay, had enjoyed love and care, was being gently spared and not called to account for my sin, and had to go on waiting and fearing still longer. They had forgiven me my torn clothes, my long absence, missing my supper, because I was tired and bleeding and they felt sorry for me, but above all because they had no inkling of the other thing, because they knew only of my naughtiness and nothing of my depravity. It would go doubly hard for me when it came to light. Perhaps, as they had once threatened in the past, they would send me to a reformatory where I would have only stale, hard bread to eat and in all the time not taken up by lessons would have to saw wood and clean shoes, and where there were dormitories with monitors who would beat me with a cane and wake me at four o'clock in the morning with cold water. Or else would they turn me over to the police?

But at any rate, no matter what happened, a waiting period was facing me again. I would have to suffer the dread for still longer, carry my secret with me still longer, tremble at every look and footstep in the house, and be unable to look anyone in the eye.

Or was it possible after all that my theft would not even be noticed? That everything would remain as it was? That I had inflicted all this anxiety and torment on myself for nothing. Oh, if that were to happen, if that inexpressible wonder were possible, then I would begin a wholly new life, would thank God and show myself worthy of such goodness by living with utter purity and stainlessness from this moment on! What I had tried so often before and always failed at

would now be possible; now my resolution and my will were strong enough, now after this misery, this hell of torment. My whole being seized upon this wishful thought and clung to it. Comfort rained down from heaven; a blue and sunny future opened up before me. In the midst of these fantasies I finally fell asleep and slept untroubled all through the good night.

Next morning was Sunday, and while still lying in bed I felt, like the taste of a fruit, the peculiar, curiously mixed, but on the whole so precious Sunday feeling I had known ever since I began going to school. Sunday morning was a good thing: sleeping late, no school, prospect of a good dinner, no smell of teachers and ink, plenty of time to myself. That was the main thing. Other, alien, less pleasant notes sounded also, but they were weaker: churchgoing or Sunday school, family walk, having to be careful of my fine clothes. That somewhat spoiled the pure, good, precious taste and smell of Sunday—just as two desserts eaten at the same time, say a pudding and a sauce that went with it, did not quite fit together, or as sometimes candy or cookies bought in small shops had a faint, annoying overtone of cheese or kerosene. You ate them and they were good, but they were not perfect and radiant; there was something about them you had to overlook. Sunday was usually something like that, especially when I had to go to church or Sunday school, which fortunately was not always the case. If I did, the free day acquired an added taste of duty and boredom. And although walks with the whole family could often be very fine, usually something happened. There was a quarrel with my sisters, or I walked too fast or too slow, or I smeared resin on my clothes. Most of the time there was a catch to it.

All right, I could put up with that. I felt good. A vast amount of time had

passed since yesterday. I had not forgotten my crime; I remembered it first
thing in the morning; but now it was so
long ago that the terrors had receded far
away and become unreal. Yesterday I
had atoned for my guilt, even though it
was only by the pangs of conscience. I
had suffered through a wretched, horrible
day. Now I was once more inclined to
trustfulness and innocence and no longer
worried very much. The agony was not
entirely dissipated; a note of threat and
uneasiness still sounded inside my head,
but it was much like the minor duties
and bothers that marred the loveliness of
Sunday.

At breakfast we were all cheerful. I
was given the choice between church and
Sunday school. As always, I preferred
church. There at least I was let alone and
my thoughts could wander. Moreover, the
high, solemn chamber with its colored
windows often seemed beautiful and up-
lifting, and when I squinted my eyes and
peered down the long, dusty nave to the
organ I often saw wonderful pictures.
The organ pipes towering out of the
gloom frequently seemed like a radiant
city of a hundred towers. Moreover,
when attendance was sparse I had often
managed to lose myself in a book of
stories for the entire hour.

On this day I did not take a book
along. Nor did it even occur to me to try
some evasion as I had done in the past.
That much was left of last night; I remembered my vows to be good and
reconciled to God, my parents, and the
world. Even my anger against Oskar
Weber had entirely dissipated. If he had
turned up, I would have received him in
the friendliest spirit.

The service began. I sang the choral
verses with the others; the hymn was
"Shepherd of thy sheep," which we had
learned by heart in school. Once again I
noticed how the verses of a song seemed
so entirely different in singing, especially

when sung in the slow, limping fashion
of church, from the way it was in reading
or reciting from memory. In reading, the
verses were a whole, they had meaning
and consisted of phrases. In singing they
consisted only of words, there were no
phrases at all, no meaning emerged, but
on the other hand the single, long-drawn-
out words had a curiously strong, independent life of their own. Frequently
mere syllables, meaningless in themselves, took forms of their own and
soared off by themselves. For example, as
we sang the lines, "Shepherd of thy sheep
who knowest naught of sleep, them that
stumble darkly, thou wilt guide and
keep," they seemed without coherence
and meaning. I did not think of a shepherd or of sheep; I thought of nothing at
all. Yet that was by no means boring.
Single words, especially "sle-eep," became so strangely full and lovely, rocked
me so softly, and the "stum-ble"
sounded so mysterious and weighty, reminded me of "stomach" and of dark,
strongly emotional, half-understood
things that I had inside my body. And
along with all that, the music of the
organ.

And then came the pastor and the
sermon, which was always so incomprehensibly long, and the strange state of
listening in which for a long time I heard
only the sound of the speaking voice
floating in the air like a bell, then took in
single words sharply and distinctly, along
with their meaning, and tried to follow
what was being said as long as I could. If
only I had been permitted to sit in the
choir instead of among all the men in the
gallery. In the choir, where I had sat at
church concerts, you sank deeply into
heavy, isolated chairs, each of them a
small, firm building, and overhead you
had a strangely attractive, complex, net-
like vault, and high up on the wall the
Sermon on the Mount was painted in soft
colors, and the blue and red garment of

the Saviour against the pale blue sky was so delicate and such a pleasure to look at.

Sometimes the wood of the pew creaked. I disliked it intensely because it was coated with a dreary yellow varnish which you always stuck to slightly. Sometimes a fly buzzed off into one of the windows, which had blue and red flowers and green stars painted at their tops, where they curved into a pointed arch. And then the sermon was suddenly over and I leaned forward to see the pastor disappearing into his narrow, dark tube of a stairway. Everyone sang again, with relief and very loudly, and then people stood up and poured out of the church. I tossed the coin I had been given into the collection plate, whose tinny sound went so ill with all the solemnity, and let the stream of people carry me to the doors and out into the open.

Now came the finest part of Sunday: the two hours between church and Sunday dinner. I had done my duty, and now after sitting so long I was eager for movement, for games or walks, or for a book. At any rate, I was completely free until dinner, when there usually was something good to eat. Contentedly, I sauntered home, filled with amiable thoughts and purposes. The world was all right; it was livable. Peacefully, I trotted through the hallway and up the stairs.

The sun was shining in my room. I looked to my box of caterpillars, which I had neglected yesterday, found a few new cocoons, watered the plants.

Then the door opened.

I paid no attention at first. After a minute the silence began to seem strange. I turned around. There stood my father. He was pale and looked tormented. My welcome stuck in my throat. I saw that he knew. He had come. The trial was beginning. Nothing had turned out well, nothing was atoned for, nothing for-gotten. The sun paled and the Sunday morning collapsed.

Thunderstruck, I stared at Father. I hated him. Why had he not come yester-day? Now I was not girded for this, had no resources, not even repentance and a sense of guilt. And why did he have to keep figs upstairs in his chest of drawers?

He went over to my bookcase, reached behind the books, and took out several figs. There were few left. As he did so, he looked at me with mute inquiry. I could not say anything. Anguish and defiance choked me.

"What's the matter?" I finally brought out.

"Where did you get these figs?" he asked me in that low, controlled voice I so bitterly hated.

I began talking at once. Lying. I said I had bought the figs at a confectioner's, that there had been a whole ring of them. Where did the money come from? From a savings box I had together with a friend. We'd pooled the small coins we were given every so often. Incidentally— here was the box. I produced the box with the slit. Now there was only a ten-pfennig piece left in it because we had bought the figs yesterday.

My father listened with a quiet, com-posed expression. Not for a moment did I believe he felt as calm as he looked.

"How much did the figs cost?" he asked in that soft voice.

"One mark sixty."

"And where did you buy them?"

"At the confectioner's."

"Which one?"

"Haager's."

There was a pause. I was still holding the money box in my freezing fingers. My whole body was cold and shivering.

And now he asked, with a note of menace in his voice: "Is that true?"

Again I talked rapidly. Yes, of course it was true, and my friend Weber had gone into the store, I had only tagged along with him. The money was mainly Weber's, only a little of it came from me.

"Take your cap," my father said. "We'll go over to Haager's together. He'll certainly remember selling you the figs."

I tried to smile. Now the cold had penetrated as far as my heart and stomach. I led the way, picking up my blue cap in the hall. Father opened the glass door. He too had taken his hat.

"Just a moment," I said. "I have to go."

He nodded. I went to the bathroom, locked the door, and was alone, safe for another moment. If only I could die now!

I stayed a minute, stayed two. It was no use. You didn't die. You had to face everything. I unlocked the door and we descended the stairs together.

As we were going out the front door, a happy thought struck me. I said quickly: "But today is Sunday and Haager's isn't open."

That hope lasted just two seconds. My father said calmly: "Then we'll go to his house. Come."

We walked. I straightened my cap, thrust one hand into my pocket, and tried to walk along beside him as though nothing in particular were happening. Although I knew that everybody could see I was a criminal who had just been caught, I tried by a thousand devices to conceal the fact. I struggled to breathe easily and innocently. Nobody needed to see how my whole chest was constricted. I tried to put on a candid expression, to pretend naturalness and security. I pulled up one of my stockings, though it did not need pulling, and smiled, knowing that this smile looked frightfully stupid and forced. The devil was inside me, in my throat and innards, and he was choking me.

We passed the restaurant, passed the

blacksmith, passed the hansom-cab stand, passed the railroad bridge. This was where I had fought with Weber last night. Didn't the cut above my eye still hurt? Oh God! Oh God!

Docilely, I walked on, keeping my composure by terrible efforts. We started down Main Street. How amiable and harmless this street had seemed only yesterday. Must not think. On, on!

We were very close to Haager's house. During those few minutes I had several hundred times lived through in advance the scene that awaited me. Now we were there. Now it was coming.

But it was impossible to endure. I stood still.

"Well? What's the matter?" Father asked.

"I'm not going in," I muttered.

He looked down at me. He had known from the start, of course. Why had he pretended all this and gone to so much trouble. There was no point to it.

"Then you didn't buy the figs at Haager's?" he asked.

I shook my head.

"I see," he said with seeming calm. "Then we might as well go back home."

He behaved decently. He spared me on the street, in front of people. There were many people out walking; someone greeted my father every minute. What playacting! What stupid, senseless torment! I could not be grateful to him for sparing me.

He knew everything, of course! And he let me dance, let me perform my useless capers the way you let a captive mouse dance in its wire trap before you drown it. If only he had hit me over the head with his cane right at the start, without asking me any questions at all! I would have preferred that to the calm and righteousness with which he caught me in my idiotic net of lies and slowly strangled me. Maybe it was better to have a coarse father than such a refined and just one. When the kind of father I read about in stories gave his children a terrible beating in rage or drunkenness, then the father was in the wrong, and although the blows hurt, the child could shrug his shoulders inwardly and despise him. With my father, that wouldn't do. He was too refined, too good, never in the wrong. He always made me feel small and wretched.

With clenched teeth I preceded him into the house and returned to my room. He was still quiet and cool, or rather pretending to be so, for in reality he was very angry, as I clearly felt. Now he began to talk in his usual way.

"I would like to know what the purpose of this farce is? Can't you tell me that? I knew at once that your whole pretty story was a lie. So why were you trying to make a fool of me? You don't seriously think me so stupid as to believe you?"

I continued to clench my teeth. I swallowed. If only he would stop. As if I myself had any idea why I had told him the story! As if I myself had any idea why I could not confess my crime and ask for forgiveness. As if I even had any idea why I had stolen those wretched figs. Had I wanted to? Had I done it on reflection and with reasons, knowing what I was doing? Wasn't I sorry I had done it? Wasn't I suffering because of it more than he?

He waited, his face nervous, tense with the effort of patience. For just a moment, in my unconscious, I fully understood the situation, but I could not have put it into words as I can today. It was this: I had stolen because I had gone into Father's room in need of comfort and because to my disappointment I had found it empty. I had not wanted to steal. When I found Father not there I

had only wanted to spy, to poke among his things, to penetrate his secrets, to find out something about him. That was it. Then the figs lay there and I stole them. And I immediately regretted the act and all day yesterday I had suffered torment and despair, had wanted to die, had condemned myself, had conceived new, good resolutions. But today—today everything was different. I had tasted the repentance and all the rest to the full; I was less emotional now and felt inexplicable but enormous resistances toward my father and toward everything he expected and demanded of me.

If I had been able to tell him that, he would have understood me. But even children, though they are far ahead of adults in cleverness, are perplexed and alone when they confront fate.

Stiff with defiance and determined anguish, I kept silent, let him talk, and watched with pain and a strange gloating delight the way everything went wrong and turned worse and worse, how he suffered and was disappointed, how he appealed in vain to all my better instincts.

When he asked, "Did you steal the figs?" I could only nod. I could not bring myself to do more than nod feebly when he wanted to know whether I was sorry. How could this big, intelligent man ask such foolish questions! As if I would not have been sorry! As if he could not see how the whole affair hurt me, how it twisted my heart. As if at this point I could have taken any pleasure in my act and in those wretched figs!

Perhaps for the first time in my life I felt, almost to the verge of understanding and consciousness, how utterly two well-intentioned human beings can torment each other, and how in such a case all talk, all attempts at wisdom, all reason merely adds another dose of poison, creates new tortures, new wounds, new errors. How was that possible? But it was possible, it was happening. It was absurd, it was crazy, it was ridiculous and desperate—but it was so.

Enough of this story. It ended with my being locked up in the attic all Sunday afternoon. This harsh punishment lost a part of its terrors for reasons that were my secret. For in that dark, unused attic there was a box, covered with dust, half full of old books, some of which were by no means intended for children. I made light for reading by pushing aside one of the roof tiles.

Shortly before I went to bed that sad Sunday night my father cajoled me into talking with him briefly, and that made peace between us. When I lay in bed I had the certainty that he had completely forgiven me—more completely than I had forgiven him.

THE LIFE AND WORKS OF
HERMANN HESSE

By *THEODORE ZIOLKOWSKY*

In 1919, only weeks after the holocaust of World War I had ended, an anonymous pamphlet entitled *Zarathustras Wiederkehr* (Zarathustra's Return) was published in Switzerland. In a dithyrambic language reminiscent of Nietzsche's prophet, the author exhorted the youth of Germany to turn away from the values of the past, to set out in search of its own identity, to listen to "the bird" of its voice within. "If your bird sings and speaks," the essay concluded, "then follow it into every temptation and even into the remotest and coldest solitude and into darkest destiny!" Thoughtful readers noted a similarity of ideas and imagery between this essay and an exciting novel that had appeared that same year. For in *Demian* (1917) an unknown writer who identified himself as Emil Sinclair described his search for identity and values in similar terms, comparing himself to a bird breaking out of the confining shell of conventional society. The pamphlet and novel were widely read; the novel won a distinguished prize; the question of their authorship was debated in the journals and literary circles.

Most readers were astonished to learn, months later, that Hermann Hesse had written both works. For the forty-two-year-old author, generally regarded as a rather conventional chronicler of the Germany of Kaiser Wilhelm, had suddenly aroused a new generation to a sense of freedom and responsibility. He urged members of this generation to liberate themselves from the very past that he had portrayed in his earlier works and to reject accepted codes of behavior in favor of a new responsibility to themselves. Long before his authorship was disclosed, Hesse had vanished from public view. Like Zarathustra returning to his lonely heights, Hesse sought out the Swiss village of Montagnola, nestled against the mountain above Lugano, where he was to remain until his death on August 9, 1962. Here, behind a sign requesting "No Visitors Please," he lived the life of an outsider who has put aside fashionable goals for the sake of personal values.

What sort of works do we expect from this mountain recluse? Realistic panoramas with an epic cast of characters? Works of social intrigue with sophisticated plots? Certainly not. We look, rather, for introspective fictions that pay little heed to timely issues and deal, instead, with supratemporal concerns, as remote from the turmoil of twentieth-century society as Montagnola is from the teeming urban centers of Europe. We listen for the quiet monologues of a man preoccupied with his inner life, Zarathustra hearkening to the voice of his bird. From the heights of Montagnola Hesse gazed back into the mythic Indic past of *Siddhartha* (1922) and the waning Middle Ages of *Narziss und Goldmund* (*Narcissus and Goldmund,* 1930). With the detachment of the outsider he cast an ironic eye on the disenchanted intellectual of the twenties in *Steppenwolf* (1927), and here he undertook the timeless *Morgenlandfahrt* (*Journey to the East,* 1932). In Montagnola, finally, we breathe the air of the futuristic world of *Das Glasperlenspiel* (*The Glass Bead Game,* 1943). Yet in this parade of figures from past, present, and future we see nothing but images of the author, who peers into the mirror of his imagination, seeking ever new reflections of himself.

Born on July 2, 1877, Hesse spent most of his childhood in the idyllic Black Forest town of Calw, where his father directed a Pietist publishing house. It was expected that he would follow the path that was traditional in the family and become a minister or missionary, but by the time he was twelve the gentle family, as his father wrote, was "too nervous, too weak" to handle the strong-willed prodigy at home. He was packed off to school, where he studied so assiduously that he was among the privileged few who passed the dreaded state examinations in 1891 to win one of the coveted places in the school at Maulbronn, which prepared students for the theological seminary at Tübingen. In less than a year, however, Hesse underwent what we would now call an identity crisis and ran away from school. For a time he was sent from one institution to another, including a home for weak-minded children, and even to an exorciser. Eventually, his bewildered parents were persuaded that formal education was simply irrevelant for their son. For a year he

worked as an apprentice in a machine shop in Calw and collected many of the impressions that went into his subsequent stories about simple, working people in small-town Germany. By 1895, the desire to be independent prompted Hesse to leave home and move to the nearby university town of Tübingen, where he worked in a bookshop for four years while he began to write.

Hesse's first literary efforts were self-consciously esthetic in the fashion of the 1890s: precious verse and misty *poèmes en prose* in which he sought to portray "the dream land of my creative days and hours, which lay mysteriously somewhere between time and space"—an almost psychedelic avoidance of a harsh reality that he was unwilling to accept. In 1899, Hesse left this parauniversity life and moved to Basel. Rejecting the highly derivative and escapist romanticism of his earliest works, he tried "to conquer for myself a piece of world and reality." In *Hermann Lauscher* (1901) he looked objectively and even ironically at the years of his literary *bohème.* But it was only with his next novel, *Peter Camenzind* (1904), that Hesse finally achieved the sturdier realism that brought him his first wide recognition as a writer as well as financial independence. In this story of a Swiss peasant boy who gains fame as a writer and succumbs for a time to the lure of the metropolis and the glitter of its literary salons, Hesse retraced the dreams and experiences of his own past. Ultimately the boy renounces what he recognizes to be the empty freedom of estheticism and returns to his village in the Alps for a life of modest service and responsibility.

Repeatedly one notes in Hesse the tendency for life to imitate art. At first, convinced by his own rhetoric, Hesse seemed to believe that he was Camenzind. In 1904, he married and settled down in a remodeled peasant house on the German shore of Lake Constance, where for eight years he turned out stories and poems after the formula of melancholy realism perfected in volumes with such titles as *Diesseits* (In This World, 1907), *Nachbarn* (*Neighbors,* 1909), and *Unterwegs* (*On the Road,* 1911). In *Unterm Rad* (*Beneath the Wheel,* 1906) he employed the popular form of the schoolboy novel in order to portray his own turmoil as a boy in school and to show how easily he himself, like his hero Hans Giebenrath, might have ended in suicide. Similarly, the novel *Gertrude* (1910) differs little from the many works of the period that represented the dilemma of the artist who is unable to achieve happiness in life: in Hesse's novel the hero is a crippled musician whose spiritual affliction is symbolized by his physical disability.

But Hesse had not looked ahead to the doubts that might have plagued the sophisticated Camenzind after several years among the cows and peasants. He had become a successful writer whose services were much in demand—as a reviewer, as an editor, as an anthologist. He wrote on fashionable topics for the best magazines and catered to the intellectual tastes of the day. But even the wine of success smacked of gall, for Hesse began to feel that he was vegetating in "the land of the Philistines" that he despised. Instead of coming to terms with himself, he tried as so often in the past to run away—to Italy, to Germany, to Austria, and through Switzerland. In 1911, finally, his flight led him all the way to Indonesia.

The Orient had long figured prominently in the geography of Hesse's imagination. He had grown up in a home with deep attachments to India: his parents as well as his maternal grandfather had been missionaries there. As a spiritual climate, India was as familiar to Hesse as the Pietist Germany of his youth. "We come to the South and East full of longing, driven by a dark and grateful premonition of home, and we find here a paradise." But his vision of the oriental paradise had not reckoned with the serpent of his own European soul. "We ourselves are different: we are alien here and without any rights of citizenship. We lost our paradise long ago, and the new one that we wish to build is not to be found along the equator and on the warm seas of the East. It lies within us and in our own northern future."

Hesse's reflections on his trip to the East contain the first clear indication of his awareness that any true freedom must be an inner one, and not merely external flight. But he was not yet willing to pursue the consequences of his insight to their necessary conclusion. Shortly after his return he moved his family to Bern, attempting again to avoid inner confrontation by external mobility. His last two important works of the prewar period mirror his dilemma. The novel *Rosshalde* (1914) examines the problem of freedom and responsibility from the standpoint of the painter Veraguth, who reaches the sobering conclusion that a happy marriage is impossible for an artist wholly dedicated to his work. At the same time, the cycle of stories about the lovable vagabond *Knulp* (1915) showed that absolute freedom involves a sense of guilt. Knulp is a man wholly without social attachments: a hippie ahead of time, he regards it as his function to bring "a little nostalgia for freedom" into the lives of ordinary men who are chained down by duty. Yet Knulp's enjoyment of his own freedom is tempered by the melancholy conclusion that he has failed to do anything worthwhile for society.

It was the experience of psychoanalysis in 1916 and 1917 that finally forced Hesse to confront himself: he learned that the freedom he sought was to be found in his own mind rather than in desperate flights through Europe and Asia. The immediate cause for his analysis was a nervous breakdown in 1916. As a pronounced pacifist, dismayed by the outbreak of the war, he alienated many of his former friends and readers through articles that he wrote. He was widely criticized for his alleged lack of loyalty. This brought on a mood of depression that was only partially alleviated by his selfless wartime work with various relief agencies in Switzerland.

Then in 1916 his father died; one of his three sons fell seriously ill for more than a year; and his wife succumbed to a nervous affliction that required her confinement in a mental institution. Almost overnight Hesse's marriage and family collapsed along with his entire literary career. He did not even have the consolation of his art: when asked to prepare an edition of his selected works, he concluded sadly that "there was nothing there to select." Since his trip to India had exhausted his last hope that spiritual relief could be found in flight, he had only one recourse left: to turn inward, finally, to the problems of his own consciousness.

In various essays and letters Hesse has stressed that much of psychoanalysis was already familiar to him from the works of the great writers. Now, in 1916 and 1917, his sessions with Josef B. Lang—a disciple of Jung who shows up in *Demian* under the name Pistorius— helped him to systematize his insights and to come to terms with himself. Hesse learned that the disturbances he attributed to the outside world were related to the perturbations of his own soul. The war, for instance, was not only raging on the battlefield; it seethed in the hearts of an entire generation. *Demian,* written in six weeks of creative fury in 1917, was an attempt to account for the war as the outward manifestation of a great inner revolution taking place within a generation disenchanted with conventional beliefs and answers. To this extent it belongs along with such works as Thomas Mann's *The Magic Mountain* (1924) and Hermann Broch's *The Sleepwalkers* (1931–1932) as a profound fictional analysis of the mood that produced World War I.

Because he did not want this wholly different book to be burdened by the reputation he had won with his largely bland prewar works, Hesse published his novel two years later under the pseudonym of its hero, Emil Sinclair. Catching the spirit of the times so perfectly, it was an instantaneous success among young Germans. In his introduction to the first American edition of *Demian,* Thomas Mann spoke of its "electrifying influence" and compared it, as a document of its generation, to Goethe's *The Sorrows of Young Werther,* which appeared in 1774. If the work were clearly enough "dated" by realistic depiction of external circumstances, it would be simply another late Victorian novel with little appeal for the present. But Hesse has internalized his fiction, producing a mythic pattern of action that is as applicable today as it was fifty years ago. Because *Demian* amounts to a timeless paradigm of alienated youth rebelling against the values of its parents, it has been taken up in the 1970s by a new generation of American youth.

At the same time, *Demian* is an intensely autobiographical work, for Hesse's own vacillations between the confining Pietism of his childhood and his longing for freedom are introduced through the "Two Realms" of which Sinclair becomes aware in the first chapter. The "light" world that he experiences in his father's house represents the claim of love, order, and responsibility. But the ten-year-old Sinclair is aware also of a "dark" world—a world of sex, violence, and uninhibited freedom—that is denied by his parents and toward which the boy feels himself attracted. For he senses, with the first stirrings of puberty, that this "dark" world, rejected so disdainfully by his family, is no less a natural part of life than the "light" world that they have contrived to satisfy their Christian ethics. The novel turns out to be the story of Sinclair's search for a new deity to supersede the Christian God: "a God that contains the devil too and in front of which you needn't close your eyes when the most natural things in the world take place." This search, initiated by Demian, leads Sinclair from one teacher to another until, transcending them all, he discovers a new source of sustaining values within himself.

In this intensely religious book—its obsession with comparative religion reflects a characteristic vogue of the 1920s —Christianity is reduced, or elevated, to a level with the other major religions of the world. "Each and every religion is beautiful," Pistorius tells Sinclair. "Religion is soul, no matter whether you take part in Christian communion or make a pilgrimage to Mecca." And the development of Sinclair amounts to an elaborate allegory of man who moves from the paradise of childhood through the fall into sin and into a redemption in a realm that transcends conventional Christian assumptions regarding good and evil. This triadic rhythm from innocence through despair to a higher awareness, which Hesse later outlined in his essay "Ein Stückchen Theologie" ("A Bit of Theology," 1932), turns out to be the pattern of development for all of Hesse's fictional heroes.

It is only within this religious framework that we recognize the plausibility of Demian's function as a mediator set between Sinclair's initial fall and his final "redemption." The novel, as the subtitle indicates, is actually "The Story of Emil Sinclair's Youth." Why, then, is it named after Demian? The external facts of plot are of very little help here. But if we consider his figure more carefully, we note a group of characteristics that constitute a remarkable yet unmistakable pattern. His most salient physical feature is the "brightness" that illuminates his forehead. Through self-control and an uncanny skill in the psychological manipulation of others he accomplishes various deeds that astonish the other boys. We are told of disputations in which Demian surprises his teachers with his questions and responses. When he talks to Sinclair, he tends to express himself in parables adapted freely from the Bible. He is driven by his faith in the coming of a new spiritual kingdom. And toward the end of the book Demian has assembled around his person a circle of admirers, all of whom are striving for the spiritual kingdom that he foretells.

It seems clear, in view of these characteristics and the generally religious structure of the book, that we are dealing with a fictional transfiguration of Jesus— albeit a wholly ironic one.

By the time Hesse's identity as the author of Demian had become public knowledge, he had left his family behind and retreated to Montagnola. Here, in 1919, he wrote the novellas Klein und Wagner and Klingsors letzter Sommer (Klingsor's Last Summer), as well as two important essays on Dostoevsky (cited by T. S. Eliot in his notes to The Waste Land) in which he expanded more systematically the ideas underlying Demian: he sketched the downfall of European Man with his conventional Judaeo-Christian, Graeco-Roman values under the impact of "Russian Man," who accepts all aspects of life as equally valid. At the same time, Hesse began writing *Siddhartha* in an attempt to show how the individual, who in *Demian* had liberated himself from the past, can succeed in coming to terms with himself.

Siddhartha, the son of a Brahman, has been brought up as a faithful observer of his father's religion. At eighteen, deciding that he cannot find fulfillment in conventional Hinduism, he sets out in search of a more austere discipline. Three years of asceticism among the Samanas bring him to the realization that extreme and exclusive devotion to the spirit is cutting him off from the world of nature and thus leading him even further from the harmony that he seeks. So in a complete reversal he leaves the realm of spirit and crosses the river to the realm of the senses, where he becomes a prosperous businessman and enjoys the favors of the courtesan Kamala.

At forty, however, he perceives that a life of the senses has brought him no closer to tranquillity than the life of the spirit. Abandoning Kamala and his earthly possessions, he spends twenty more years on the river that lies between the realms of spirit and nature. Here, listening to the whispering of the waters in the company of a wise old sage, he learns the ultimate secret of total surrender to the All and finally achieves absolute harmony of being. "From that hour Siddhartha ceased to fight against his destiny. There shone in his face the serenity of knowledge, of one who is no longer confronted with conflict of desires, who has found salvation, who is in harmony with the stream of events, with the stream of life, full of sympathy and compassion, surrendering himself to the stream, belonging to the unity of all things."

Siddhartha is perhaps Hesse's most satisfying novel esthetically—a tour de force of language and structure. But like *Demian* it is a painfully humorless work,

the product of a troubled religious spirit who has rejected the values of his society and turned into himself to find peace through meditation. During the 1920s, however, Hesse came to realize that he could not survive by meditation alone. Circumstances—notably financial and medical—forced him back into contact with the world that, contrary to his original hopes, had not in fact been restructured by a great revolution of values, but that was continuing along in the same old paths as before. Hesse's response was now more mature. "I don't share a single one of the ideals of our age," he confessed. But instead of raging indignantly at society, he determined to preserve his sanity through humor. The élitist contempt of society that governed *Demian* gave way to the tolerant irony that enchanted Thomas Mann and André Gide. Siddhartha's escapist flight into meditation is replaced by a renewed faith in the essential dignity of man. This new attitude shows up fictionally in *Der Steppenwolf* (*Steppenwolf*, 1927).

Harry Haller, the first-person narrator of the novel, is introduced as a forty-eight-year-old intellectual who holds the society of the 1920s in such contempt that he has promised himself the luxury of suicide at fifty in order to escape a world that is not worthy of him. Haller is so profoundly convinced of his own rectitude and moral superiority to those who surround him that he has been reduced to an existence of fussy fuming. "Were those things that we called 'Culture,' that we called 'Spirit,' that we called 'Soul' and 'beautiful' and 'sacred'—were those things merely a specter, already long dead and still considered genuine and alive only by a few fools like me?" In the course of a carnival season, Haller is suddenly exposed to aspects of reality from which he has hitherto shielded himself: jazz, prostitutes, homosexuals, drug culture. But rather than withdrawing into a select community of kindred souls or retreating into solitary meditation, Haller learns how to survive in the world by laughing at it and by recognizing in its very triviality the "Golden Trace" that gives life its meaning.

Steppenwolf repelled many readers in the 1920s who failed to see that the book is not a glorification of sexual license, drug addiction, and jazz, but a highly ironic search for the eternal in the transitory, the divine in the mundane, the immortals in the jazz era. These readers were reconciled by Hesse's next work, *Narcissus and Goldmund,* published in 1930, which embodies the old conflict between freedom and responsibility in two different heroes of fifteenth-century Europe. Narcissus the priest personifies pure spirit sealed off from the world by the walls of his monastery; while Goldmund, Golden Mouth, Chrysostomus, the monk who runs away from the monastery to seek life, women, and ultimately art, represents the world of nature and the senses.

The story begins in Mariabronn, where Narcissus helps Goldmund to discover that he is not cut out for the life of a celibate. Narcissus disappears from the scene during the central part of the book, while Goldmund brawls his way through the world in a series of picaresque adventures—making love to countless women, becoming a gifted woodcarver, and witnessing war, murder, pillage, and rape. At the end, reappearing to rescue Goldmund from prison and execution, the priest leads him back to the monastery, where the restless artist soon dies. Goldmund has become a physical wreck with features etched by the trials of the world whereas Narcissus, closed off hermetically in his monastic realm, has remained untouched by time. But Goldmund emerges triumphant since, as an artist, he has found the means of overcoming time, for his art, he tells his friend, represents "the overcoming of transitoriness." The very security of his existence has cut Narcissus off from those things that give life its meaning. But since Goldmund dies before he can complete his artistic masterpiece, he cannot transmit his vision to the world. The artist thus gains an intuitive cognition denied to the intellectual, but is prevented from revealing it in its ultimate form.

The dilemma of ineffability with which *Narcissus and Goldmund* ends becomes the central theme in *The Journey to the East,* published in 1932. Even the title is ironic because the narrator, H. H., never succeeds in telling us about his journey. In the period after "the Great War" H. H. had joined the League of Eastern Wayfarers in order to participate in a great pilgrimage to the East. (Hesse is referring, of course, both to his own voyage to Indonesia and to the cult of oriental mysticism that became fashionable in the 1920s.) But early in the journey the servant Leo disappeared, and this seemingly trivial incident produced such dissension in the ranks that all members deserted one by one. When H. H. attempts, ten years later, to write the history of the League, he discovers that he remembers nothing but superficial details: its spirit has escaped him completely. What if the Order had not disintegrated around him? What if he himself had unwittingly deserted the League? He succeeds in finding Leo, whose harmonious existence contrasts sharply with his own wretchedness: Leo assures H. H. that the Order is still intact, and he leads him to its archives so that H. H. can finish his history. But in the archives H. H. learns that the humble servant Leo is in reality the Superior of the Order, that he incorporates its ideal of selfless service. The narrator himself had been so much obsessed with his own individuality that he had neglected the first rule of the Order—service to others—and had thus become apostate. Once he realizes his error, he is punished by the ironic smile of the assembled members and is then readmitted to their ranks.

To lend form to his parable of the artist's dilemma and the difficulties of communication, Hesse has cast it in the framework of a Gothic romance of the eighteenth century—the historical period in which he was spiritually most at home. At the same time, the whole narrative is a cunningly contrived symbolic autobiography. All the places mentioned, many of the incidents, and most of the characters (introduced under sobriquets) are taken directly from the author's own life. The first twelve years in Montagnola were marked by few outward events. In 1923, Hesse had become a Swiss citizen; in 1924, he was married briefly for a second time. After 1924, he came down from his mountain for an occasional lecture, for regular spa cures, and for winters in Zurich. But this outward calm masked the most fruitful period of his creative life. Apart from the novels, he wrote many of his finest poems, essays, and stories in these years. He edited numerous volumes—from medieval Latin tales to German romantic poetry—and reviewed scores of books for leading journals. He took up painting and produced illustrated manuscripts of the modern fairy-tales that he wrote. This time of happiness and productivity was culminated, finally, by his third marriage in 1931 to Ninon Ausländer.

If *The Journey to the East* symbolically reflects these serene years, then *The Glass Bead Game,* published in 1943, records Hesse's reaction to the more somber events of the thirties. Begun in 1931 as a hymn to the esthetic kingdom of the spirit, Hesse's late masterpiece became, by the time of its publication, a repudiation of disengagement in favor of personal commitment.

Set in a future society some four hundred years hence, most of the action takes place in a glorified government-supported research institute for world culture called Castalia. Here, in a purified atmosphere unsullied by material concerns, a community of students and scholars devotes itself to the cultivation of a symbolic institution known as the Glass Bead Game—"a *unio mystica* of all disparate elements of the *Universitas Litterarum.*" Unlike Hesse's earlier heroes, Joseph Knecht develops his talents in a life virtually unmarked by conflict or rebellion. Singled out in his childhood for his great musical and scholarly abilities, he rises smoothly through the hierarchy of the Order until, in his forties, he becomes the Magister Ludi, the chief functionary of the pedagogical province whose values he accepts as his own.

But during his eight years as Magister Ludi, Knecht begins to notice certain inconsistencies within the Order that he represents. In his best friend, the musician Tegularius, he witnesses the ravages of a brilliant mind that devolves with such insistent narcissism upon itself and its own narrow specialty that it becomes useless as a functioning member of the Order. In addition, the Castalian realm of Culture and Mind has gradually isolated itself so completely from the realms of Church and State that it now regards itself as an end in itself: pure intellect arrogantly refusing to be humanized by religious spirit or to put itself in the service of society.

When Knecht finally brings these matters to the attention of the directing Board of Educators, he discovers that the institution is so deeply committed to preserving its traditions that it is unwilling to change. "The imaginative power and farsightedness of your historic-political observations was acknowledged; but none of your specific conjectures, or shall we say prophecies, was fully approved.

. . . We cannot grant that the Castalian ideal, the ideal of high culture under the aegis of disciplined meditation, has any powers to shape history, any vital influence upon world political conditions." At this point it becomes clear that what began as the portrayal of a utopian ideal has become, in fact, a systematic critique of any institution devoted to knowledge cultivated in isolation from society.

Joseph Knecht, unlike the earlier heroes, does not seek to "restructure" the institution violently. Instead, he chooses to carry out a quiet act of commitment, in the faith that the institution will be moved by his example. Resigning his office, Knecht leaves Castalia and goes out into the world to tutor Tito, the son of a former classmate: eschewing the grand gesture, he contents himself with a simple human relationship, which leads to his death. For shortly after he has assumed his new duties, Knecht is challenged by his pupil to a swim at dawn. Unwilling at this point to lose the confidence of his pupil, Knecht plunges into the icy lake and drowns. He does so, as Hesse later explained, "because he cannot disappoint this boy who is so difficult to win over."

This attitude emerged from Hesse's own experiences in the face of the political events of the thirties. Hesse protested against Nazism just as courageously as he had argued for pacifism during World War I. Unable for reasons of health—notably sciatica and increasingly poor eyesight—to participate in organized relief activities, he sheltered scores of refugees in Montagnola and aided others to escape from Hitler's Germany.

The Glass Bead Game was Hesse's last major work. He kept writing steadily for the next fifteen years—poems, essays, autobiographical reflections, circular letters to his friends, and hundreds of letters to readers all over the world. And during these years he collected many awards in addition to the Nobel Prize. All indications suggest that in the immediate postwar period it was Hesse's pacifism, his humanism, and his sense of human dignity that appealed to a world trying to reestablish values that had been corrupted or obscured by inhuman forces. In addition, his literary traditionalism constituted an important bridge to the cultural past that had been so grievously neglected in the war years.

However, it is not the author of *The Glass Bead Game* who has enjoyed such a spectacular popularity among American youth in the sixties. Other factors, startlingly similar to those in effect after World War I, have led young readers once again to the escapist Hesse of *Siddhartha* and the revolutionary Hesse of *Demian*. A conspicuous religious impulse has turned many young people, in their search for values, away from conventional Judaeo-Christianity and toward a variety of exotic, largely oriental forms of worship. Many of these same seekers, in their desire to "do their own thing" and their willingness to let others do the same, have attained an ethical position that goes well beyond good and evil. And these attitudes have alienated them from a generation of parents who still cling to the Manichaean distinctions of the fifties and who are motivated by traditional values.

Theodore Ziolkowsky, Professor of Modern Languages at Princeton University, has written several articles and books on Hesse.

THE 1946 PRIZE

By KJELL STRÖMBERG

In the period just before World War II, the list of candidates proposed for the Nobel Prize for Literature varied little from year to year. The same names would be repeated annually, until finally they disappeared as death overtook many authors who had not been selected by the committee. With rare exceptions, the winners had spent a good number of years in the anteroom. Apparently the four-year suspension in the awards because of the war resulted in something of a renewal of the literary and academic circles which are privileged to nominate candidates. From 1946 on, when peace brought resumption of the awards, new candidates sprang up in numbers to enter the lists at the side of the old guard. Among the new candidates we find five who were later to win—two from France (André Gide and François Mauriac), two from England (T. S. Eliot, for the second successive year, and Sir Winston Churchill), and one from Russia (Boris Pasternak).

It was, however, an "old timer," Hermann Hesse, a candidate who had been under consideration for the last fifteen years, who received the 1946 Nobel Prize. Hesse, a naturalized Swiss, was born in Germany in 1877 and was thus two years younger than Thomas Mann (Nobel Prize, 1929). Hesse and Mann were often linked together as representatives and eloquent champions of that Western humanism so brutally savaged between the two wars, especially by the new masters of their native land. Hesse had always been more or less obscured by the shadow of Mann, but it is worth noting that Thomas Mann himself never missed a chance to praise his younger colleague's work. Mann had been the first to propose him as a candidate. Outside the field of Germanic specialists he was virtually unknown abroad before winning the Nobel Prize. In his first report on Hesse's career, in 1931, Per Hallström, permanent secretary of the Swedish Academy, defended forcefully, in the face of German criticism, his thesis that Hesse was basically not a novelist and philosopher but a lyric poet who was wholly occupied with his personal problems. Hesse, he declared, showed his true originality in his long novels, published in the 1920s, on the theme of the profound crisis of conscience which was destroying the Western world in the wake of the general bloodletting of the war.

In spite of his own frank admiration of Hesse, Hallström was not convinced that these disturbing books, which depict the human soul as prey to so many temptations and destructive forces, really represent the literary and spiritual tendencies which the late Alfred Nobel wished to encourage by his prize—"unless the inventor of dynamite had wanted to glorify an instinct for evil by blindly causing human thought to explode." In short, in all good conscience he could not unreservedly recommend Thomas Mann's candidate for "the great Swedish world prize for literary achievement." (In an article in the *Neue Zürcher Zeitung* honoring Hesse on his sixtieth birthday, Mann had publicly called for the award to be made to his old friend and companion in exile, the "unjustly unknown" author of *Steppenwolf*.)

On several occasions, Hallström plunged again into Hesse's lengthy books and reported on them to his committee. In the end, it was through his lyric poetry that Hesse finally made his impression on his Swedish judges. In Österling's opinion, shared by several other Academy specialists in the field, his later poetry was everything that was most perfect in German in our day. Impelled as it was by the desire to reward pure poetry flourishing in a hostile climate, the Academy could scarcely find a better occasion and a more worthy object. Such was the conclusion of this searching examination. After weighing everything in the critical balance, poetry and prose alike, the academicians agreed to give the prize for 1946 to Hesse "for his inspired writings, which, while growing in boldness and penetration, exemplify the classic humanitarian ideals and high qualities of style."

Hesse's health had long been delicate, and he lay gravely ill in the sanatorium at Tessin above Lake Lugano when the unexpected news of the award came to him. He was unable to travel to Stockholm to receive the prize, so it was entrusted to Henri Vallotton, the Swiss Minister to Sweden, who delivered Hesse's acceptance speech.

Translated by Dale McAdoo.